Maxim Jakubowski is a London-based novelist and editor. He was born in the UK and educated in France. Following a career in book publishing, he opened the world-famous Murder One bookshop in London. He now writes full-time. He has edited over twenty bestselling erotic anthologies and books on erotic photography, as well as many acclaimed crime collections. His novels include *It's You That I Want to Kiss, Because She Thought She Loved Me* and *On Tenderness Express*, all three recently collected and reprinted in the USA as *Skin in Darkness*. Other books include *Life in the World of Women, The State of Montana, Kiss Me Sadly, Confessions of a Romantic Pornographer, I Was Waiting For You* and, recently, *Ekaterina and the Night*. In 2006 he published *American Casanova*, a major erotic novel which he edited and on which fifteen of the top erotic writers in the world collaborated, and his collected erotic short stories as *Fools For Lust*. He compiles two annual acclaimed series for the Mammoth list: *Best New Erotica* and *Best British Crime*. He is a winner of the Anthony and the Karel Awards, a frequent TV and radio broadcaster, a past crime columnist for the *Guardian* newspaper and Literary Director of London's Crime Scene Festival.

THE NEW MAMMOTH BOOK OF
PULP FICTION

EDITED BY MAXIM JAKUBOWSKI

RUNNING PRESS
PHILADELPHIA · LONDON

Constable & Robinson Ltd.
55–56 Russell Square
London WC1B 4HP
www.constablerobinson.com

Some material from this book first published in the UK
as *The Mammoth Book of Pulp Fiction*, 1996

This revised edition published in the UK by Robinson,
an imprint of Constable & Robinson Ltd., 2014

A copy of the British Library Cataloguing in Publication
Data is available from the British Library

UK ISBN: 978-1-47211-112-8 (paperback)
UK ISBN: 978-1-4721-1180-7 (e-book)

1 3 5 7 9 10 8 6 4 2

First published in the United States in 2014 by Running Press Book Publishers,
A Member of the Perseus Books Group

Books published by Running Press are available at special discounts for bulk purchases in the
United States by corporations, institutions, and other organizations. For more information,
please contact the Special Markets Department at the Perseus Books Group, 2300 Chestnut
Street, Suite 200, Philadelphia, PA 19103, or call (800) 810-4145, ext. 5000, or e-mail
special.markets@perseusbooks.com.

US ISBN: 978-0-7624-5221-7
US Library of Congress Control Number: 2013949486

9 8 7 6 5 4 3 2 1
Digit on the right indicates the number of this printing

Running Press Book Publishers
2300 Chestnut Street
Philadelphia, PA 19103-4371

Visit us on the web!
www.runningpress.com

Printed and bound by CPI Group (UK) Ltd, Croydon, CR0 YY

Contents

ACKNOWLEDGEMENTS

Introduction and collection © 1996, 2014 by Maxim Jakubowski.

THE DIAMOND WAGER by Samuel Dashiell, © 1929 by Samuel Dashiell. First appeared in *Detective Fiction Weekly*. Copyright not renewed.

FLIGHT TO NOWHERE by Charles Williams, © 1955 by Charles Williams. First appeared in *Manhunt*. Reproduced by permission of Abner Stein. Appeared in *The Mammoth Book of Pulp Fiction* edited by Maxim Jakubowksi (Robinson, 1996).

THE TASTING MACHINE by Paul Cain, © 1949 by Peter Ruric. First appeared in *Gourmet* as by Peter Ruric.

FINDERS KILLERS! by John D. MacDonald, © 1953 by John D. MacDonald. First appeared in *Detective Story Magazine*. Reproduced by permission of Vanessa Holt Ltd. Appeared in *The Mammoth Book of Pulp Fiction* edited by Maxim Jakubowksi (Robinson, 1996).

THE MURDERING KIND! by Robert Turner © 1953, Robert Turner. First appeared in *Detective Tales*.

CIGARETTE GIRL by James M. Cain, © 1952 by Flying Eagle Publications, Inc. First published in *Manhunt*. Reprinted by permission of Harold Ober Associates. Appeared in *The Mammoth Book of Pulp Fiction* edited by Maxim Jakubowksi (Robinson, 1996).

THE GETAWAY by Gil Brewer, © 1976 by Gil Brewer. First appeared in *Mystery*. Reproduced by permission of A. M. Heath & Co. Ltd. Appeared in *The Mammoth Book of Pulp Fiction* edited by Maxim Jakubowksi (Robinson, 1996).

PREVIEW OF MURDER by Robert Leslie Bellem, © 1949 by Robert Leslie Bellem. First appeared in *Thrilling Detective Magazine*. Appeared in *The Mammoth Book of Pulp Fiction* edited by Maxim Jakubowksi (Robinson, 1996).

FOREVER AFTER by Jim Thompson, © 1960 by Jim Thompson. First appeared in *Shock*. Reproduced by permission of Vanessa Holt Ltd. Appeared in *The Mammoth Book of Pulp Fiction* edited by Maxim Jakubowksi (Robinson, 1996).

THE BLOODY TIDE by Day Keene, © 1950 by Day Keene. First appeared in *Black Mask Magazine*. Reproduced by permission of Al James on behalf of the Estate of Day Keene. Appeared in *The Mammoth Book of Pulp Fiction* edited by Maxim Jakubowksi (Robinson, 1996).

DEATH COMES GIFT-WRAPPED by William P. McGivern, © 1950 by William P. McGivern. First appeared in *Black Mask Magazine*. Reproduced by permission of Maureen Daly McGivern on behalf of the Estate of William P. McGivern. Appeared in *The Mammoth Book of Pulp Fiction* edited by Maxim Jakubowksi (Robinson, 1996).

THE GIRL BEHIND THE HEDGE by Mickey Spillane, © 1954 by Mickey Spillane. First appeared in *Manhunt*. Reproduced by permission of the author. Appeared in *The Mammoth Book of Pulp Fiction* edited by Maxim Jakubowksi (Robinson, 1996).

ONE ESCORT - MISSING OR DEAD by Roger Torrey, ©1940 by Roger Torrey. First appeared in *Detective Aces*.

DON'T BURN YOUR CORPSES BEHIND YOU by William Rough, © 1954. First appeared in *Detective Story Magazine*.

A CANDLE FOR THE BAG LADY by Lawrence Block, © 1968 by Lawrence Block. First appeared in *Alfred Hitchcock's Mystery Magazine*. Reproduced by permission of the author. Appeared in *The Mammoth Book of Pulp Fiction* edited by Maxim Jakubowksi (Robinson, 1996).

BLACK PUDDING by David Goodis, © 1954 by David Goodis. First appeared in *Manhunt*. Reproduced by permission of A. M. Heath & Co. Ltd. Appeared in *The Mammoth Book of Pulp Fiction* edited by Maxim Jakubowksi (Robinson, 1996).

A MATTER OF PRINCIPAL by Max Allan Collins, © 1989 by Max Allan Collins. First appeared in *Stalkers*. Reproduced by permission of the author. Appeared in *The Mammoth Book of Pulp Fiction* edited by Maxim Jakubowksi (Robinson, 1996).

CITIZEN'S ARREST by Charles Willeford, © 1966 by Charles Willeford. First appeared in *Alfred Hitchcock's Mystery Magazine*. Reproduced by permission of Abner Stein. Appeared in *The Mammoth Book of Pulp Fiction* edited by Maxim Jakubowksi (Robinson, 1996).

SLEEPING DOG by Ross Macdonald, © 1965 by Ross Macdonald. First appeared in *Argosy*. Reproduced by permission of David Higham Associates. Appeared in *The Mammoth Book of Pulp Fiction* edited by Maxim Jakubowksi (Robinson, 1996).

THE WENCH IS DEAD by Fredric Brown, © 1953 by Fredric Brown. First appeared in *Manhunt*. Reproduced by permission of A. M. Heath & Co. Ltd. Appeared in *The Mammoth Book of Pulp Fiction* edited by Maxim Jakubowksi (Robinson, 1996).

SO DARK FOR APRIL by Howard Browne, © 1953 by Howard Browne. First appeared in *Manhunt*. Reproduced by permission of the author. Appeared in *The Mammoth Book of Pulp Fiction* edited by Maxim Jakubowksi (Robinson, 1996).

WE ARE ALL DEAD by Bruno Fischer, © 1955 by Bruno Fischer. First appeared in *Manhunt*. Reproduced by permission of Ruth Fischer on behalf of the Estate of Bruno Fischer. Appeared in *The Mammoth Book of Pulp Fiction* edited by Maxim Jakubowksi (Robinson, 1996).

DEATH IS A VAMPIRE by Robert Bloch, © 1944 by Robert Bloch. First appeared in *Thrilling Mystery Magazine*. Reproduced by permission of A. M. Heath & Co. Ltd. Appeared in *The Mammoth Book of Pulp Fiction* edited by Maxim Jakubowksi (Robinson, 1996).

THE BLUE STEEL SQUIRREL by Frank R. Read, © 1946 by Frank R. Read. First appeared in *Detective Story Magazine*.

A REAL NICE GUY by William F. Nolan, © 1980 by William F. Nolan. First appeared in *Mike Shayne Mystery Magazine*. Reproduced by permission of the author. Appeared in *The Mammoth Book of Pulp Fiction* edited by Maxim Jakubowksi (Robinson, 1996).

STACKED DECK by Bill Pronzini, © 1987 by Bill Pronzini. First appeared in *New Black Mask Magazine*. Reproduced by permission of the author. Appeared in *The Mammoth Book of Pulp Fiction* edited by Maxim Jakubowksi (Robinson, 1996).

SO YOUNG, SO FAIR, SO DEAD by John Lutz, © 1973 by John Lutz. First appeared in *Mike Shayne Mystery Magazine*. Reproduced by permission of the author. Appeared in *The Mammoth Book of Pulp Fiction* edited by Maxim Jakubowksi (Robinson, 1996).

EFFECTIVE MEDICINE by B. Traven, © 1954 by B. Traven. First appeared in *Manhunt*. Reproduced by permission of A. M. Heath & Co. Ltd. Appeared in *The Mammoth Book of Pulp Fiction* edited by Maxim Jakubowksi (Robinson, 1996).

NICELY FRAMED, READY TO HANG! by Dan Gordon, © 1952 by Dan Gordon. First appeared in *Detective Tales*.

THE SECOND COMING by Joe Gores, © 1966 by Joe Gores. First appeared in *Adam's Best Fiction*. Reproduced by permission of the author. Appeared in *The Mammoth Book of Pulp Fiction* edited by Maxim Jakubowksi (Robinson, 1996).

PALE HANDS I LOATHED by William Campbell Gault, ©1947. First appeared in *Detective Story Magazine*.

THE DARK GODDESS by Schuyler G. Edsall, © 1955 by Schuyler G. Edsall. First appeared in *Mystery Detective*.

ORDO by Donald E. Westlake, © 1977 by Donald E. Westlake. First appeared in *Enough*. Reproduced by permission of James Hale Literary Agency. Appeared in *The Mammoth Book of Pulp Fiction* edited by Maxim Jakubowksi (Robinson, 1996).

All efforts have been made to contact the respective copyright holders. In some cases, it has not proven possible to ascertain the whereabouts of authors, agents or estates. They are welcome to write to us c/o the book's publishers.

I owe a particular vote of thanks to various authors and editors who provided invaluable assistance in tracing copyright holders and living relatives, and recommended particular stories. A bow of the fedora, then, to Max Allan Collins, Ed Gorman, Martin H. Greenberg, Gary Lovisi, William F. Nolan and Bill Pronzini.

INTRODUCTION

Maxim Jakubowski

There is no such thing as pulp fiction.

Sweeping assertion, hey?

And, I suppose, a perfect touch of controversy to open a volume which I hope you will find full of surprise, action, shocks galore, sound and fury, pages bursting with all the exhilarating speed and bumps of a rollercoaster ride.

Which is what all the best storytelling provides.

So long live pulp fiction!

First, let's bury the myth that pulp fiction is a lower form of art, the reverse side of literature as we know it. Until pyrotechnic film director Quentin Tarantino spectacularly hijacked the expression, most ignorant observers and accredited denizens of the literary establishment relegated pulp writing to a dubious cupboard where we parked the guilty pleasures we were too ashamed to display in public. Pulp was equated with rubbish. Crap of the basest nature. How arrogant of them to dismiss thus what, for many, was a perfect form of entertainment!

What we have come to call, to know as, pulp writing came about from the magazines where much of its early gems first appeared: the colourful publications, so often afflicted with endearing but terrible names, which cheapskate publishers insisted on printing on the cheapest available form of paper, pulp paper; sadly this is another reason for the aura that now surrounds them, as so few have survived the onslaught of time and decay, and the rare remaining examples have become increasingly collectable, albeit all too often in crumbling form on the shelves.

Many of the names have gone down in legend: *Black Mask*, *Amazing*, *Astounding*, *Spicy Stories*, *Ace-High*, *Detective Magazine*, *Dare-Devil Aces*, *Thrills of the Jungle*, *High Seas Adventures*, *Fighting Aces*, *Secret Service Operator 5*, etc . . . to the nth degree. There were literally hundreds of such often live-by-night magazines with wildly exotic and frequently misleading names from their initial appearance at the beginning of the 1920s in America. And I would not pretend that everything they published was made of gold. Far from it. We are talking commercial fiction, mostly catering to the lowest common denominator. But then do our modern paperbacks have loftier ambitions and a superior hit-rate, quality-wise?

But what makes them stand out is the fact that the pulps had one golden rule which unsung editors insisted upon and good and bad writers alike religiously followed: adherence to the art of storytelling. Every story in the pulps had a beginning and an end, sharply etched economical characterization, action, emotions, plenty going on. The mission was to keep the reader hooked, to transport him into a more interesting world of fantasy and make-believe, spiriting him away from the drab horizons of everyday life (remember, there was no television in those very early days, or CDs or other modern leisure addictions).

This compact with the consumer might appear self-evident, and was indeed very much a continuation of the Victorian penny dreadfuls and novels written by instalments in newspapers and magazines by the likes of Conan Doyle, Charles Dickens and so many other overlooked pioneer scribes just a few decades earlier, but it is a tradition that has sadly since been lost to the trappings of Literature with a capital L and pretension. We now have partly forgotten the pleasures of old-time radio but at least the pulp magazines have left us with millions of words of splendid, lurid, cheap and exciting writing. And not only does this inheritance still afford much pleasure but it can also be said to have influenced many commercial writers practising their art long after the literal disappearance of the pulp magazines due to wartime paper shortages. The spirit of pulp continued unabated after the war and ended in the pages of the paperback books that took over the literacy baton in England and America. The 1950s were in fact a further golden age for pulp writing, with the exploding paperback market opening opportunities by the dozen as imprints mushroomed and thrived, providing fertile ground for the remaining pulp survivors and newer generations of popular writers, many of whom, particularly in the fields of mystery and science-fiction writing, would go on to better things and, eventually, to the respectability of the hardcover book. Many of these authors were also busy contributing to the renaissance of popular genre magazines now in digest format, with tales that often echoed or prefigured their novels, and are represented in this selection.

This anthology restricts itself to crime and mystery stories in the pulp tradition. Strictly speaking, of course, the pulp magazines ventured further afield, encompassing science fiction, fantasy, horror, spy tales, aviation yarns, spicy stories (that would not make even a maiden blush today), jungle capers, westerns and a pleasing variety of superheroes like The Shadow, Doc Savage, the Spider and other masked and unmasked crusaders. But tales of noir streets, gorgeous molls and shady villains fighting ambiguous sleuths and dubious heroes are the archetypes that represent pulp writing at its best.

There are very few popular fiction magazines left alive today and those there are tend to prefer a more refined type of tale, but still pulp fiction survives in the writings of many authors. Because pulp fiction is a state of mind, a mission to entertain, and literature would be so much poorer without it, its zest, its speed and rhythm, its unashamed verve and straightforward approach to storytelling.

However long the present anthology might be, I regret it couldn't be ten times longer. The pulp magazines and writers and their successors are still unknown territory and the brave researcher with time on his hands could, I am confident, mine so much more from these yellowing pages and honour even more forgotten writers and give them their five minutes in the sun. As it is there are so many writers it wasn't possible to include here, for reasons of space or availability of rights. In no particular order: Ed McBain (as Evan Hunter and Richard Marsten), Raymond Chandler, Cornell Woolrich, Andrew Vachss, Loren D. Estleman, Carroll John Daly, Brett Halliday, Raoul Whitfield, Mark Timlin, Richard Prather, Leigh Brackett, Erle Stanley Gardner (pre Perry Mason), James Ellroy, Clark Howard, Max Brand. In addition, rising paper costs prevented me from making this volume even heavier, as I had to withdraw material by Ed Gorman, James Reasoner, Ed Lacy, Frank Gruber, Loren D. Estleman, Derek Raymond, Robert Edmond Alter, Frederick C. Davis and Jonathan Craig – so look out for these names elsewhere. They are certainly worth a detour. But the list could be endless. Check them all out. Thrills absolutely guaranteed.

The stories selected span seven decades of popular writing, from Dashiell Hammett to current masters like Donald E. Westlake and Lawrence Block. In between you will find the great names of yesteryear and familiar bylines from the paperback world. Enjoy the forbidden thrills. And when you have turned over the final page, I just know you will repeat after me: pulp fiction will never die.

Almost 18 years after the initial publication of *The Mammoth Book of Pulp Fiction*, we return with a revised edition and truly the appeal of pulp fiction has not diminished one iota in the intervening years. Readers and fans are still endlessly fascinated by these hardboiled stories of times past, tough guys and pliant femmes fatales and the tradition vigorously continues in movies and the books of more contemporary writers who carry the flame onwards against all the tides of fashion.

Pulp fiction remains the stuff of dreams and still captures the sense of wonder in our collective imagination and, in the process, supplies first-class entertainment and thrills.

Eight stories from the initial volume have been deleted to make place for nine tales, many of which make their first appearance in book form since their initial publication in long-forgotten if legendary magazines. Most are by authors who are now long forgotten but measure up honourably to all the big names of noir and pulp and are well worth rediscovering.

In addition, we take great pride in presenting what we believe is a lost story by Dashiell Hammett. 'The Diamond Wager' was recently unearthed by hardy internet detectives and doesn't appear in any of Hammett's bibliographies, but we are convinced it was written by the great man of pulp himself under the somewhat transparent pseudonym of Samuel Dashiell (his birth certificate was actually bylined Samuel Dashiell Hammett). Further it has been established that between 1926 and 1927 he did work for Samuel's Jewelers of San Francisco, just a couple of years before the story appeared in *Detective Fiction Weekly*! Strong evidence indeed.

Long live pulp!

Maxim Jakubowski, 2013

THE DIAMOND WAGER

Dashiell Hammett, writing as

Samuel Dashiell

I always knew West was eccentric. Ever since the days of our youth, in various universities – for we seemed destined to follow each other about the globe – I had known Alexander West to be a person of the most bizarre, though not unattractive, personality. At Heidelberg, where he renounced water as a beverage; at Pisa, where he affected a one-piece garment for months; at the Sorbonne, where he consorted with the most notorious characters, boasting an acquaintance with Le Grand Raoul, an unspeakable ruffian of La Villette.

And in later life, when we met in Constantinople, where West was American minister, I found that his idiosyncrasies were common topics in the diplomatic corps. In the then Turkish capital I naturally dined with West at the Legation, and except for his pointed beard and Prussian mustache, being somewhat more gray, I found him the same tall, courtly figure, with a keen brown eye and the hands of generations, an aristocrat. But his eccentricities were then of more refined fantasy. No more baths in snow, no more beer orgies, no more Libyan negroes opening the door, no more strange diets. At the Legation, West specialized in rugs and gems. He had a museum in carpets. He had even abandoned his old practice of having the valet call him every morning at eight o'clock with a gramophone record.

I left the Legation thinking West had reformed. "Rugs and precious stones," I reflected; "that's such a banal combination for West." Although I did recall that he had told me he was doing something strange with a boat on the Bosphorus; but I neglected to inquire about the details. It was something in connection with work, as he had said, "Everybody has a pleasure boat; I have a work boat, where I can be alone." But that is all I retained concerning this freak of his mind.

It was some years later, however, when West had retired from diplomacy, that he turned up in my Paris apartment, a little grayer, straight and keen as usual, but with his beard a trifle less pointed – and, let's say, a trifle less distinguished-looking. He looked more the successful businessman than the traditional diplomat. It was a cold, blustery night, so I bade West sit down by my fire and tell me of his adventures; for I knew he had not been idle since leaving Constantinople.

"No, I am not doing anything," he answered, after a pause, in reply to my question as to his present activities. "Just resting and laughing to myself over a little prank I played on a friend."

"Oho!" I declared; "so you're going in for pranks now." He laughed heartily. I could hardly see West as a practical joker. That was one thing out of his line. As he held his long, thin hands together, I noticed an exceptionally fine diamond ring on his left hand. It was of an unusual luster, deep-set in gold, flush with the cutting. His quick eye caught me looking at this ornament. As I recall, West had never affected jewelry of any kind.

"Oh, yes, you are wondering about this," he said, gazing into the crystal. "Fine yellow diamond; not so rare, but unusual, set in gold, which they are not wearing any longer. A little present." He repeated blandly, after a pause, "A little present for stealing."

"For stealing?" I inquired, astonished. I could hardly believe West would steal. He would not play practical jokes, and he would not steal.

"Yes," he drawled, leaning back away from the fire. "I had to steal about four million francs – that is, four million francs' worth of jewels." He noted the effect on me, and went on in a matter-of-fact way: "Yes, I stole it, stole it all. Got the police all upset; got stories in the newspapers. They referred to me as a super-thief, a master criminal, a malefactor, a crook, and an organized gang. But I proved my case. I lifted four million from a Paris jeweler, walked around town with it, gave my victim an uncomfortable night, and walked in his store the next day between rows of wise gentlemen, gave him back his paltry four million, and collected my bet, which is this ring you see here."

West paused and chuckled softly to himself, still apparently getting the utmost out of this late escapade in burglary. Of course, I remembered only recently seeing in the newspapers how some clever gentleman cracksman had succeeded in a fantastic robbery in the Rue de la Paix, Paris, but I had not read the details.

I was genuinely curious. This was, indeed, West in his true character. But to go in for deliberate and probably dangerous burglary was something which I considered required a little friendly counsel on my part. West anticipated my difficulty in broaching the subject.

"Don't worry, old man. I pinched the stuff from a good friend of ours, really a pal, so if I had been caught it would have been fixed up, except I would have lost my bet."

He looked at the yellow diamond.

"But don't you realize what would have happened if you had been caught?" I asked. "Prank or not, your name would have been aired in the newspapers – a former American minister guilty of grand larceny; an arrest; a day or so in jail; sensation; talk; ruinous gossip!"

He only laughed the more. He held up an arresting hand. "Please don't call me an amateur. I did the most professional job that the Rue de la Paix has seen in years."

I believe he was really proud of this burglary.

West gazed reflectively into the fire. "But I wouldn't do it again – not for a dozen rings." He watched the firelight dance in the pure crystal of the stone on his finger. "Poor old Berthier, he was wild! He came to see me the night I lifted the diamonds, four million francs' worth, mind you, and they were in my pocket at the time. He asked me to accompany him to the store and go over the scene. "He said perhaps I might prove cleverer than detectives, whom he was satisfied were a lot of idiots. I told him I would come over the next day, because, according to the terms of our wager, I was to keep the jewels for more than twenty-four hours. I returned the next day, and handed them to him in his upstairs office. The poor wretch that I took them from was downstairs busy reconstructing the 'crime' with those astute gentlemen, the detectives, and I've no doubt that they would eventually have caught me, for you don't get away with robbery in France. They catch you in the end. Fortunately I made the terms of my wager to fit the conditions."

West leaned back and blinked satisfyingly at the ceiling, tapping his finger tips together. "Poor old Berthier," he mused. "He was wild."

As soon as West had mentioned that his victim was a mutual friend, I had thought of Berthier. Moreover, Berthier's was one of those establishments in which a four-million-franc purchase or a theft of the same size might not seem so unusual. West interrupted my thoughts concerning Berthier.

"I made Berthier promise that he would not dismiss any employee. That also was in the terms of our wager, because I dealt directly with Armand, the head salesman and a trusted employee. It was Armand who delivered the stones." West leaned nearer, his brown eyes squinting at me as if in defense of any reprehension I might impute to him. "You see, I did it, not so much as a wager, but to teach Berthier a lesson. Berthier is responsible for his store, he is the principal shareholder, the administration is his own, it was he and it was his negligence in not rigidly enforcing more elementary principles of safety that made the theft possible." He turned the yellow diamond around on his finger. "This thing is nothing, compared to the value of the lesson he learned."

West stroked his stubby beard. He chuckled. "It did cost me some of my beard. A hotel suite, an old trunk, a real Russian prince, a fake Egyptian prince, a would-be princess, a first-class reservation to Egypt, a convenient bathroom, running water and soapsuds. Poor old Armand, who brought the gems – he and his armed assistants – they must have almost fainted when, after waiting probably a good half-hour, all they found in exchange for a four-million-franc necklace was a cheap bearskin coat, a broad-brimmed hat, and some old clothes."

I must admit that I was growing curious. It was about a week ago when I had seen this sensational story in the newspapers. I knew West had come to tell me about it, as he had so often related to me his various escapades, and I was getting restive. Moreover, I knew Berthier well, and I could readily imagine the state of his mind on the day of the missing diamonds.

I had a bottle of 1848 cognac brought up, and we both settled down to the inner warmth of this most friendly of elixirs.

II

"You see," West began, with this habitual phrase of his, "I had always been a good customer of Berthier's. I have bought trinkets from Berthier's both in New York and Paris since I was a boy. And in getting around as I did in various diplomatic posts, I naturally sent Berthier many wealthy clients. I got him the work on two very important crown-jewel commissions; I sent him princes and magnates; and of course he always wanted to make me a present, knowing well that the idea of a commission was out of question.

"One day not long ago I was in Berthier's with a friend who was buying some sapphires and platinum and a lot of that atrocious modern jewelry for his new wife.

"Berthier offered me this yellow diamond then as a present, for I had always admired it, but never felt quite able to buy it, and knowing at the same time that even if I did buy it he would have marked the price so low as to be embarrassing.

"However, we compromised by dining together that night in Ciro's; and there he pointed out to me the various personalities of that international crowd who wear genuine stones. 'I can't understand,' Berthier said, after a comprehensive observation of the clientele, 'how all these women are not robbed even more regularly than they are. Even we jewelers, with all our protective systems, are not safe from burglary.'

"Berthier then went on to tell me of some miserable wretch who, only the day before, had smashed a show window down the street and filched several big stones. 'A messy job,' he commented, and he informed me that the police soon apprehended this window burglar.

"He continued, with smug assurance: 'It's pretty hard for a street burglar to get away with anything these days. It's the other kind,' he added, 'the plausible kind, the apparently rich customer, the clever, ingenious stranger, with whom we cannot cope.'"

When West mentioned this "clever, ingenious stranger," I had a mental picture of him stepping into just such a rôle for his robber of Berthier's; but I made no comment, and let him go on with his story.

"You see, I had always contended the same thing. I had always held that jewelers and bankers show only primitive intelligence in arranging their protective schemes, dealing always with the hypothetical street robbery, the second-story man, the gun runner, while they invariably go on for years unprotected against these plausible gentlemen who, in the long run, are the worst offenders. They get millions where the common thief gets thousands.

"I might have been a bit vexed at Berthier's cocksureness," West continued by way of explanation, "but you see, I am a shareholder in a bank that was once beautifully swindled, so I let Berthier have it straight from the shoulder.

" 'You fellows deserve to be robbed,' I said to Berthier. 'You fall for such obvious gags.'

"Berthier protested. I asked him about the little job they put over on the Paris house of Kerstner Freres. He shrugged his shoulders. It seems that a nice gentleman who said he was a Swiss," West explained, "wanted to match an emerald pendant that he had, in order to make up a set of earrings. Kerstners' had difficulty in matching the emerald which the nice Swiss gentleman had ordered them to purchase at any price.

"After a search Kerstners' found the stone and bought it at an exorbitant price. They had simply bought the same emerald. Of course, the gentleman only made a mere hundred thousand francs, a simple trick that has been worked over and over again in various forms.

"When I related this story, Berthier retorted with some scorn to the effect that no sensible house would fall for such an old dodge as that. I then asked Berthier about that absurd robbery that happened only a year ago at Latour's, which is a very 'sensible' house and incidentally Berthier's chief competitor."

West asked me if I knew about this robbery. I assured him I did, inasmuch as all Paris had laughed, for the joke was certainly on the prefect of police. On the new prefect's first day in office some ingenious thief had contrived to have a whole tray of diamond rings sent under guard to the prefect, from which he was to choose one for an engagement present for his recently announced fiancée.

The thief impersonated a clerk right in the prefect's inner waiting room, and, surrounded by police, he took the tray into the prefect's office, excused himself for blundering into the wrong room, slipped the tray under his coat, walked back to the waiting room, and after assuring the jeweler's representatives that they wouldn't have to wait long, he disappeared. Fortunately, the thief was arrested the following day in Lyons.

West laughed heartily as he talked over the unique details of this robbery. I poured out some cognac. "Well, my genteel burglar," I pursued, "that doesn't yet explain how you yourself turned thief and lifted four millions."

"Very simple," West replied. "Berthier was almost impertinent in his self-assurance that no one could rob Berthier's. 'Not even the most fashionably dressed gentleman nor the most plausible prince could trick Berthier's,' he asserted with some vigor. Then he assured me, as if it were a great secret, 'Berthier never delivers jewels against a check until the bank reports the funds.'

"'There are always loopholes,' I rejoined, but Berthier argued stupidly that it was impossible. His boastful attitude annoyed me.

"I looked him straight in the eye. 'I'll bet you, if I were a burglar, I could clean your place out.' Berthier laughed in that jerky, nervous way of his. 'I'd pay you to rob me,' he said. 'You needn't; but I'll do it anyway,' I told him.

"Berthier thought a bit. 'I'll bet you that yellow diamond that you couldn't steal so much as a baby's bracelet from Berthier's.' 'I'll bet you I can steal a million,' I said.

" 'It's a go,' said Berthier, shaking my hand. 'The yellow diamond is yours if you steal anything and get away with it.'

"'Perhaps three or four million,' I said.

"'It's a bet, steal anything you want,' Berthier agreed.

"'I'll teach you smart Rue de la Paix jewelers a lesson,' I informed him.

"Accordingly, over our coffee, we arranged the terms of our wager, and I suppose Berthier promptly forgot about it."

West sipped his cognac thoughtfully before restoring the glass to the mantel, and then went on:

"The robbery was so easy to plan, yet I must admit that it had many complications. I had always said that the plausible gentleman was the loophole, so I looked up my old friend Prince Meyeroff, who is always buying and selling and exchanging jewels. It's a mania with him. I had exchanged a few odd gems with him in Constantinople, as he considered me a fellow connoisseur.

"I found him in Paris, and soon talked him into the mood to buy a necklace. In fact, he had disposed of some old family pieces, and was actually meditating an expensive gift for his favorite niece.

"I explained to the prince that I had a little deal on, and asked him to let me act as his buyer. I had special reasons. Moreover, he was one of my closest friends back in St. Petersburg. Meyeroff said he would allow me a credit up to eight hundred thousand francs for something very suitable for this young woman who was marrying into the old French nobility.

"I told the prince to go to Berthier's and choose a necklace, approximating his price, but to underbid on it. I would then go in and buy it at the price contemplated.

"I figured this would give them just the amount of confidence in me that would be required to carry off a bigger affair that I was thinking of.

"Meanwhile I bethought myself of a disguise. I let my beard grow somewhat to the sides and cut off the point. I affected a broad-brimmed, low-crowned hat, and a half-length bearskin coat. I then braced up my trousers almost to my ankles. Some days later – in fact, it was just over a week ago – I went to Berthier's, after I ascertained that Berthier himself was in London. I informed them I wanted to buy a gift or two in diamonds, and it was not many minutes before I had shown the clerks that money was no object with me.

"They brought me out a most bewitching array of necklaces, tiaras, collars, bracelets, rings. A king's ransom lay before my eyes. Of course, I fell in love with a beautiful flat stone necklace of Indian diamonds with an enormous square pendant. I fondled it, held it up, almost wept over it, but decided, alas that I could not buy it. Four million francs, the salesman, Armand, had said. I shook my head sadly. Too expensive for me. But how I loved it!

"I finally decided that a smaller one would be very nice. It was the one with a gorgeous emerald pendant, *en cabochon*, which Prince Meyeroff had seen and described to me. I asked the price.

"Armand demurred. 'You have chosen the same one that a

great connoisseur has admired. Prince Meyeroff wanted it, but it was a question of price.'

" 'How much?' I asked.

" 'Eight hundred thousand francs.'

"Of course, I was buying for the prince, so with a great flourish of opulence I arranged to buy the smaller necklace, though I continued flirting with that handsome Indian string. I assumed the name of Hazim, gave my home town as Cairo, and my present address a prominent hotel in the Rue de Rivoli.

"I ordered a different clasp put on the necklace, and departed for my bank, declaring I was expecting a draft from Egypt. I then went to my apartment, sent to the hotel an old trunk full of cast-off clothes, from which I carefully removed the labels. My beard was proving most disciplined, rounding my face out nicely. Picture yourself the flat hat, the bulgy fur coat, my trousers pulled up toward the ankles!

III

"I returned to Berthier's next day and bought the necklace for Meyeroff. I paid them out of a bag, eight hundred thousand francs, and received a receipt made out to Mr Hazim of Cairo and the Rue de Rivoli. I again looked longingly at the Indian necklace. I casually mentioned what a delight it would be for my daughter who was engaged to an Egyptian prince.

" 'I must get her something,' I told Berthier's man. He tried all his arts on me. Four million was not too much for an Egyptian princess, and in Egypt, where they wear stones. He emphasized the last phrase. I hesitated, but went out with my little necklace, saying I'd see later.

"I had a hired automobile of enormous proportions waiting outside, which must at least have impressed the doorman at Berthier's, whom I had passed many times in the past, but who failed to recognize me in this changed get-up. You see, Egyptians don't understand this northern climate, and are inclined to dress oddly.

"I then went to my hotel and made plans for stealing that four-million-franc necklace. In the hotel I was regarded as a bit of an eccentric, so no one bothered me. I had two rooms and a bath. Flush against the wall of my salon, toward the bath,

I placed a small square table. I own a beautifully inlaid Louis XVI glove box which, curiously, opens both at the top and at the ends. The ends hinge onto the bottom and are secured by little gadgets at the side, stuck in the plush lining. It makes an admirable jewel case, especially for necklaces; and, moreover, it was just the thing I needed for my robbery. I placed this box on the little table with the end flush against the wall.

"It looked simple. With a hole in the wall fitting the end of the glove box, I could easily contrive to pull down the shutterlike end and draw the contents through the wall into the bathroom.

"Being a building of modern construction, it would not require much work to punch a hole through the plaster and terracotta with a drill-bit. I decided on that plan, for the robbery was to take place precisely at three o'clock the following afternoon and in my own rooms.

"That afternoon I decided to buy the Indian necklace. I passed by Berthier's and allowed myself to be tempted by the salesman Armand. 'I can't really pay so much for a wedding gift,' I said, 'but the prince is very rich.' I told Armand that naturally I felt a certain pride about the gift I should give my daughter under such special circumstances.

"Armand held up the gorgeous necklace, letting the lights play on the great square pendant. 'Anyway, sir, the princess will always have the guarantee of the value of the stones. That is true of any diamond purchased at Berthier's.'

"And with that thought, I yielded. I asked for the telephone, saying I must call my bank and arrange for the transfer of funds. That also was simple. I had previously arranged with Judd, my valet, to be in a hotel off the Grands Boulevards, and pretend he was a banker if I should telephone him and ask him to transfer money from my various holdings."

West interrupted his narrative, gulping down the remainder of the cognac. The wrinkles about his eyes narrowed in a burst of merriment.

"It was really cute," he continued. "I telephoned from Berthier's own office, asking for this hotel number on the Elysee exchange. Naturally no one remembers all the bank telephone numbers in Paris, and when Judd answered the telephone his deferential tones might have been those of an accredited banker.

" 'Four million tomorrow,' I said, 'and I'll leave the transfer to your judgment. I want the money in thousands in a sack. I'll come with Judd, so you won't need to worry about holding a messenger to accompany me. I am only going as far as Berthier's. It's a wedding gift for my daughter.'

"Judd must have thought me crazy, although it would take a lot to surprise him.

"Armand listened to the conversation. Two other clerks heard it, and later I was bowed out to the street, where my enormous hired car awaited. My next job was to get a tentative reservation on the *Latunia*, which was leaving Genoa for Alexandria the following day. Prince Hazim, I called myself at the steamship office. This was for Berthier's benefit, in case they should check up on my sailing. Then I went to work.

"I went to the hotel and drew out a square on the wall, tracing it thinly around the end of the box. I slept that night in the hotel. In the morning I arose at nine o'clock, paid my bill, and told the hotel clerk I was leaving that evening for Genoa.

"I called at Berthier's still wearing the same bearskin coat and flat hat, and assured myself that the necklace was in order. Armand showed it to me in a handsome blue morocco case, which made me a bit apprehensive. He was profoundly courteous.

"I objected to the blue box, but added that it would do for a container later on, as I had an antique case to transport both the necklaces I was taking with me. I told him of my hasty change of plans. Urgent business, I said, in Egypt.

"Armand was sympathetic. I promised to return at three o'clock with the money. I went to the hotel and ordered lunch and locked the doors. I had sent Judd away after he had brought me some tools. It was but the work of fifteen minutes to cut my square hole through the plaster. I wore out about a dozen drills, however, getting through that brittle terracotta tile.

"At one o'clock, when the lunch came up, I had the hole neatly through to the bathroom. I covered it with a towel on that side, and in the salon I backed a chair against it over which I threw an old dressing gown.

"I quickly disposed of the waiter, locked the door, and replaced the table at the wall. Taking out the necklace I had bought for Prince Meyeroff, I laid it doubled in the glove box. It was a caged rainbow, lying on the rose-colored plush lining. The box I stuck flush with the square aperture.

"I had provided myself with a stiff piece of wire something like an elongated buttonhook. A warped piece of mother-of-pearl inlay provided a perfect catch with which to pull down the end of box.

"I tried the invention from the bathroom. I had overlooked one thing. I forgot that when the hole was stopped up by the box it would be dark. Thanks to my cigarette lighter, I could see to pull down the hinged end and draw out the jewels. I tried it. The hook brought down the end without a sound. I could see the stones glowing in the flickering light of the briquet. I began fishing with the hook, and the necklace with its rounded emerald slid out as if by magic.

"I fancied they might make a grating sound in the other room, so I padded the hole with a napkin. I'll cough out loud, or sing, or whistle, I said to myself. Then I thought of the bath water. I turned on the tap full force; the water ran furiously. I walked into the salon, swinging the prince's necklace in my hand; the water was making a terrific uproar. Satisfied as to this strategy, I turned off the water.

"But what to do to disguise the box at the close-fitting square hole still bothered me. My time was getting short. I must do some important telephoning to Berthier's. I must try the outer door from the bedroom into the hall. I must have my travel cap ready and my long traveling coat across the foot of the bed. I must let down my trousers to the customary length. I must get ready my shaving brush.

"It was five minutes to three. They were expecting me at Berthier's with four million francs. Armand was probably at this moment rubbing his hands, observing with satisfaction that suave face of his in the mirrors.

"Still there was that telltale, ill-fitting edge of the hole about the box. I discovered the prince's necklace was still hanging from my hand. It gave me quite a surprise. I realized this was a ticklish business, this robbing of the most ancient house in the Rue de la Paix. I laid the necklace in the box, closing the end. The hole was ugly, although the bits of paint and plaster had been well cleaned up from the floor.

"I had a stroke of genius. My flat black hat! I would lay it on its crown in front of the hole, with a big silk muffler carelessly thrown against it, shutting off any view of the trap. I tried that plan, placing the box near the side of the hat. It looked like any casual litter of objects. My old trunk was on the other side of the table to be sacrificed with its old clothes as necessary stage properties.

"I then tried the camouflage. I picked up the box, walked to the center of the room. The hat and muffler concealed the hole. I then walked to the table and replaced the box, this time casually alongside the hat, deftly putting the end in the hole. The hat moved only a few inches and the muffler hung over the brim, perfectly hiding and shadowing the trap, though most of box was clearly visible. It looked perfectly natural. I then placed the box farther out, moved the hat against the hole, and the trap was arranged.

"Now to try my experiment in human credulity. I telephoned Berthier's. Armand came immediately. 'Hazim,' I said. 'I wish to ask you a favor.' Armand recognized my voice, and inquired if I were carrying myself well. 'My dear friend,' I began in English, 'I have found that the Genoa train leaves at five o'clock, and I am in a dreadful rush and am not half packed. I have the money here in my hotel. Could you conceivably bring me the necklace and collect the money here? I would help me tremendously.'

"I also suggested that Armand bring someone with him for safety's sake, as four million in notes, which had to be expedited through two branch banks, was not an affair to treat lightly. Someone might know about it. I knew Berthier's would certainly have Armand guarded, with one or perhaps two assistants.

"Armand was audibly distressed, and asked me to wait. It seemed like an hour before the response came. 'Yes, Mr Hazim, we shall be pleased to deliver the necklace on receipt of the funds. I shall come with a man from our regular service and will have the statement ready to sign.'

"I urged him to hurry, and said I would be glad to turn over the money, as the presence of such an amount in my rooms made me nervous.

"That was exactly three fifteen. I quickly arranged the chairs so two or three would have to sit well away from the table. I opened the trunk as if I were packing. I telephoned the clerk to be sure to send my visitors to the salon door of my suite.

"My cap and long coat were ready in the bedroom. The door into the hall was almost closed, but not latched, so I would not have to turn the knob. I quickly removed my coat and vest, and laid them on a chair in the bedroom, ready to spring into. I wore a shirt with a soft collar attached. I removed my ready-tied cravat and hung it over a towel rack and turned my collar inside very carelessly as if for shaving purposes.

"In the bowl I prepared some shaving lather, and when that was all ready I was all set for making off with the prince's necklace and that other one – if it came.

"I'll admit I was nervous. I was considering the whole plot as a rather absurd enterprise, and all I could think of was the probably alert eyes and ears of the two or more suspicious employees on the glove box.

IV

"They arrived at twenty-five minutes to four. There were only two of them. I hastily lathered the edges of my spreading beard, and called out sharply for them to enter. The boy showed in Armand and a dapper individual who was evidently a house detective of Berthier's. Armand was all solicitude. I shook hands with him with two dry fingers, holding a towel with the other hand, as I had wished to make it apparent that I was deep in a shaving operation.

" 'Just edging off my beard a little.'

"The two men were quite complacent.

" 'And the necklace?' I asked eagerly.

"Armand drew the case from inside his coat and opened it before my eyes. We all moved toward the window. I was effusive in my admiration of the gems. I fluttered about much like the old fool that I probably am, and finally urged them to sit down.

"I then brought the glove box and showed the prince's necklace to both of them, and continued raving about both necklaces.

"We compared the two. The Indian was, of course, even more magnificent by contrast. The detective laid the smaller necklace back in the box, while I asked Armand to lay the big one over it in the box into which I was going to pack some cotton. My glove box was smaller and therefore easier and safer to carry,

I said. I held the box open while Armand laid the necklace gingerly inside. I was careful to avoid getting soap on the box, so I replaced it gently on the table near the hat, getting the end squarely against the hole. It seemed I had plenty of time.

"I even lingered over the box and wiped off a wayward fleck of soap-suds. The trap was set. I could not believe that the rest would be so easy, and I had to make an effort to conceal my nervousness.

"The two men sat near each other. I explained that as soon as I could clear the soap off my face I would get the sack of money and transact the business. I took Armand's blue box from Berthier's and threw it in the top tray of the trunk. They appeared to be the most unsuspecting creatures. They took proffered cigarettes and lighted up, whereupon I went directly into the bathroom, still carrying my towel. I dropped that towel. My briquet was there on the washstand. I hummed lightly as I turned on the hot water in the tub. It spouted out in a steaming, gushing stream. Quickly I held the lighted briquet at the hole, caught the gleam of the warped mother-of-pearl, and pulled at it with the wire.

"It brought the end down noiselessly on the folded napkin in the hole. The jewels blazed like fire. My hand shook as I made one savage jab at the pile with the long hook and felt the ineffable resistance of the two necklaces being pulled out together. I was afraid I might have to hook one at a time, but I caught just the right loops, and they came forward almost noiselessly along the napkin to where my left hand waited.

"I touched the first stone. It was the big necklace, the smaller one being underneath. My heart leaped as I saw the big pendant on one side of the heap not far from the *cabochon* emerald. I laid down the wire and drew them out deftly with my fingers, the gems piling richly in my spread-out left hand, until the glittering pile was free. I thrust them with one movement of my clutching fingers deep into the left pocket of my trousers. The water was churning in my ears like a cascade.

"I shut off the tap and purposely knocked the soap into the tub to make a noise, and walked into the bedroom, grabbing my cravat off the rack as I went. That was a glorious moment. The bedroom was dark. The door was unlatched. The diamonds were in my pocket. The way was clear.

"I pulled up my shirt collar, stuck on the cravat, and fixed it neatly as I reached the chair where my coat and vest lay. I plunged into them, buttoned the vest with one hand, and reached for my long coat and cap with the other. In a second I was slipping noiselessly through the door into the hall, my cap on my head, my coat over my arm.

"I had to restrain myself from running down that hall. I was in flight. It was a great thrill, to be moving away, each second taking me farther away from the enemy in that salon. Even if they are investigating at this moment, I thought, I should escape easily.

"I was gliding down those six flights of steps gleefully, released from the most tense moments I have ever gone through, when suddenly a horrible thought assailed me. What if Berthier's had posted a detective at the hotel door. I could see my plans crashing ignominiously. I stopped and reflected. The hotel has two entrances; therefore the third person, if he is there, must be in the lobby and therefore not far from the elevator and stairway.

"I thought fast, and it was a good thing I did. I was then on the second floor. I called the floor boy, turning around quickly as if mounting instead of descending.

"'Will you go to the lobby and ask if there is a man from Berthier's waiting? If he is there, will you tell him to come up to apartment 615 immediately?'

"I stressed the last word and, slipping a tip into the boy's hand, started up toward the third floor. With the boy gone, I turned toward the second floor, walked quickly down to the far end, where I knew the service stairway of the hotel was located. As I plunged into this door I saw the boy and a stout individual rushing up the steps toward the third floor. I sped down this stairway, braving possible suspicion of the employees. I came out in a kind of pantry, much to the surprise of a young waiter, and I commenced a tirade against the hotel's service that must have burned his ears. I simulated fierce indignation.

"'Where is that good-for-nothing trunkman?' I demanded. 'I'm leaving for Genoa at five, and my trunk is still unmoved.' Meanwhile I glared at him as if making up my mind whether I would kill him or let him live.

"'The trunkmen are through there,' said the waiter, pointing to a door. I rushed through.

"Inside this basement I called out: 'Where in hell is the porter of this hotel?'

"An excited trunkman left his work. I repeated fiercely the instructions about my trunk, and then asked how to get out of this foul place. I spotted an elevator and a small stairway, and without another word was up these steps and out in a side street off the Rue de Rivoli.

"I fancied the whole hotel was swarming with excited people by this time, and I jumped into a cruising taxi-cab.

"'Trocadero,' I ordered, and in one heavenly jolt I fell back into the seat while the driver sped on, up the Seine embankment to a section of quiet and reposeful streets.

"I breathed the free air. I realized what a fool I was; then I experienced a feeling of triumph, as I felt the lump of gems in my pocket. I got out and walked slowly to my apartment, went to the bath and trimmed my beard to the thinnest point, shaving my cheeks clean. I put on a high-crown hat, a long fur-lined coat, took a stick, and sauntered out, myself once more, Mr West, the retired diplomat, who would never think of getting mixed up in such an unsightly brawl as was now going on between the hotel and the respected and venerable institution known as Berthier's."

West shrugged his shoulders.

"That's all. Berthier was right. It was not so easy to rob a Rue de la Paix jeweler, especially of four million francs' worth of diamonds. I had returned to my apartment, and was hardly through my dinner when the telephone rang.

"'This is Berthier,' came the excited voice. He told me of this awful Hazim person. He asked if he might see me.

"That night Berthier sat in my library and expounded a dozen theories. 'It's a gang, a clever gang, but we'll catch them,' he said. 'One of them duped our man in the hotel lobby by calling him upstairs.'

"'But if you catch the men, will you catch your four millions?' I asked, fingering the pile of stones in my pocket.

"'No,' he moaned. 'A necklace is so easy to dispose of, stone by stone. It's probably already divided up among that bunch of criminals.'

"I really felt flattered, but not so much than as when I read the newspapers the next day. It was amusing. I have them all in my scrapbook now."

"How did you confess?" I asked West.

"Simple, indeed, but only with the utmost reluctance. I found the police were completely off the trail. At six o'clock the next afternoon I went to Berthier's, rather certain that I would be recognized. I walked past the doorman into the store, where Armand hardly noticed me. He was occupied with some wise men. I heard him saying: 'He was not so tall, as he was heavily built, thick body, large feet, and square head, with a shapeless mass of whiskers. He was from some Balkan extraction, hardly what you'd call a gentleman.'

"I asked to see Berthier, who was still overwrought and irritable.

"'Hello, West,' he said to me. 'You're just the man I want. Please come down and talk with these detectives. You must help me.'

"'Nothing doing,' I said. 'Your man Armand has just been very offensive.'

"Berthier stared at me in amazement.

"'Armand!' he repeated. 'Armand has been offensive!'

"'He called me a Balkan, said I had big feet, and that I had a square head, and that I was hardly what one would call a gentleman.'

"Berthier's eyes popped out like saucers.

"'It's unthinkable,' he said. 'He must have been describing the crook we're after.'

"I could see that Berthier took this robbery seriously.

"'I thought you never fell for those old gags,' I said.

"'Old gags!' he retorted, his voice rising. 'Hardly a gag, that!'

"'Old as the hills!' I assured him. 'The basis of most of the so-called magic one sees on the stage.' I paused.

'And what will you do with these nice people when you catch them?'

"'Ten years in jail, at least,' he growled.

"'I looked at my watch. The twenty-four hours were well over. Berthier had talked himself out of adjectives concerning this gang of thieves; he could only sit and clench his fists and bite his lips.

"'Four millions,' he muttered. 'It could have been avoided. That man Armand—'

"I took my cue. 'That man Berthier,' I said crisply, accusingly, 'should run his establishment better. Besides, my wager concerned you, and not Armand—'

"Berthier looked up sharply, his brain struggling with some dark clew. I mechanically put my hand in my trousers pocket and very slowly drew out a long iridescent string of crystallized carbon ending in a great square pendant.

"Berthier's jaw dropped. He leaned forward. His hand raised and slowly dropped to his side.

" 'You!' he whispered. 'You, West!'

"I thought he would collapse. I laid the necklace on his desk, a hand on his shoulder. He found his voice.

" 'Was it you who got those necklaces?'

" 'No, it was I who stole that necklace, and I who win the wager. Please hand over the yellow diamond.'

"I think it took Berthier ten minutes to regain his composure. He didn't know whether to curse me or to embrace me. I told him the whole story, beginning with our dinner at Ciro's. The proof of it was that the necklace was there on the desk.

"And I am sure Armand thinks I am insane. He was there when Berthier gave me this ring, this fine yellow diamond."

West settled back in his chair, holding his glass in the same hand that wore the gem.

"Not so bad, eh?" he asked.

I admitted that it was bit complicated. I was curious about one point, and that was his makeup. He explained: "You see, the broad low-crowned hat reduces one inch from my height; the wide whiskers, instead of the pointed beard, another inch; the bulgy coat, another inch; the trousers, high at the shoes, another inch. That's four inches off my stature with an increase of girth of about one-sixth of my height – an altogether different figure. A visit to a pharmacy changed my complexion from that of a Nordic to a Semitic."

"And the hotel?" I asked.

"Very simple. I had Berthier go round and pay the damages for plugging that hole. He'll do anything I say now."

I regarded West in the waning firelight.

He was supremely content.

"You must have hated to give up those Indian gems after what you went through to get them?"

West smiled.

Samuel Dashiell

"That was the hardest of all. It was like giving away something that was mine, mine by right of conquest. And I'll tell you another thing – if they had not belonged to a friend, I would have kept them."

And knowing West as I do, I am sure he spoke the truth.

FLIGHT TO NOWHERE

Charles Williams

1

It was incredible. There were no signs of violence or even sickness aboard the ship, and the Gulf itself had been calm for weeks. Her sails were set and drawing gently in the faint airs of sunset, her tiller lashed, and she was gliding along on a southeasterly course which would have taken her into the Yucatan Channel. Her dinghy was still there, atop the cabin, and everything was shipshape and in order except that there was not a soul on board.

She was well provisioned, and she had water. The two bunks were made and the cabin swept. Dungarees and foul weather gear hung about the bulkheads, and in one of the bunks was the halter of a woman's two-piece bathing suit. And, subtly underlying the bilge and salt-water smells, there still clung to the deserted cabin just the faintest suspicion of perfume. It would have gone unnoticed except that it was so completely out of place.

The table was not laid, but there were two mugs on it, and one of them was still full of coffee. When the hard-bitten old mate in charge of the boarding party walked over and put his hand against the coffee pot sitting on one burner of the primus stove it was slightly warm. There had been somebody here less than an hour ago.

He went over to the small table where the charts were and opened what he took to be the log book, flipping hurriedly through to the last page on which anything was written. He studied it for a moment, and then shook his head. In forty years at sea he had never encountered a log entry quite like it.

"... *the blue, and that last, haunting flash of silver, gesturing as it died. It was beckoning. Toward the rapture. The rapture* ..."

Before he closed the book he took something from between the pages and stared at it. It was a single long strand of ash-blonde hair. He shook his head again.

Putting the book under his arm, he picked up the small satchel which had been lying in the other bunk and jerked his head for the two seamen to follow him back on deck.

A few yards away in the red sunset the master of the American tanker *Joseph H. Hallock* waited on her bridge for the mate to come aboard.

Freya, of San Juan, P.R., it said under her stern, and the master of the tanker studied her curiously while he waited for the mate. She was a long way from home. He wondered what she was doing this far to the westward, in the Gulf of Mexico, and why a small boat from Spanish Puerto Rico should have been named after a Norse goddess.

The mate came up on the bridge carrying the big ledger and the satchel. "Sick?" the captain asked. "Or dead?"

"Gone," the mate said, with the air of a man who has been talking to ghosts without believing in them. "Just gone. Like that.

"Two of 'em, as near as I can figure it," he went on, sketching it tersely. "A man and a woman, though there wasn't much in the way of women's clothes except half a bathing suit. One or both of 'em was there not over an hour ago."

"Well, as soon as you get that line on her we'd better go back and see," the captain said. "Anything in the log?"

"Gibberish," the older man replied. He passed over the book, and then the satchel. "Cap, you ought to be thankful you've got an honest mate," he said, nodding toward the little bag. "Just guessing, I'd say there's about fifty thousand dollars in there."

The captain pursed his lips in a silent whistle as he opened the bag to stare briefly at the bundles of American currency. He looked outward at the *Freya*, where the men were making the towline fast, and frowned thoughtfully. Then he opened the big journal at the page the mate indicated and read the last entry.

He frowned again.

The rapture ...

When there was no longer any light at all and they had given up the search for any possible survivors and resumed their course, the captain counted the money in the presence of two of the ship's officers and locked it in the safe. It came to eighty-three thousand dollars. Then he sat down alone in his office and opened the journal again . . .

2

It was a hot, Gulf Coast morning in early June. The barge was moored out on the T-head of the old Parker Mill dock near the west end of the waterway. Carter had gone to New Orleans to bid on a salvage job and I was living on board alone. I was checking over some diving gear when a car rolled out of the end of the shed and stopped beside mine. It was a couple of tons of shining Cadillac, and there was a girl in it.

She got out and closed the door and walked over to the edge of the pier with the unhurried smoothness of poured honey.

"Good morning," she said. "You're Mr Manning, I hope?"

I straightened. "That's right," I said, wondering what she wanted.

She smiled. "I'd like to talk to you. Could I come aboard?"

I glanced at the spike heels and then at the ladder leaning against the pier, and shook my head. "I'll come up."

I did, and the minute I was up there facing her I was struck by the size of her. She was a cathedral of a girl. In the high heels she must have been close to six feet. I'm six-two, and I could barely see over the top of the smooth ash-blonde head.

Her hair was gathered in a roll very low on the back of her neck and she was wearing a short-sleeved summery dress the color of cinnamon which intensified the fairness of her skin and did her no harm at all in the other departments.

Her face was wide at the cheekbones in a way that was suggestively Scandinavian, and her complexion matched it perfectly. She had the smoothest skin I'd ever seen. The mouth was a little wide, too, and full lipped. It wasn't a classic face at all, but still lovely to look at and perhaps a little sexy. Her eyes were large and gray, and they said she was nice.

It was hot in the sun, and quite still, and I was a little uncomfortable, aware I'd probably been staring at her. "What can I do for you?" I asked.

"Perhaps I'd better introduce myself," she said. "I'm Mrs Wayne. Shannon Wayne. I wanted to talk to you about a job."

"What kind of job?" I asked.

"Recovering a shotgun that was lost out of a boat."

"Where?" I asked.

"In a lake, about a hundred miles north of here—"

I shook my head. "It would cost you more than it's worth."

"But – " she protested, the gray eyes deadly serious. "You wouldn't have to take a diving suit and air pump and all that stuff. I thought perhaps you had one of those aqualung outfits."

"We do," I said. "In fact, I've got one of my own. But it would still be cheaper to buy a new shotgun."

"No," she said. "Perhaps I'd better explain. It's quite an expensive one. A single-barreled trap gun with a lot of engraving and a custom stock. I think it cost around seven hundred dollars."

I whistled. "How'd a gun like that ever fall in a lake?"

"My husband was going out to the duck blind one morning and it accidentally fell out of the skiff."

I looked at her for a moment, not saying anything. There was something odd about it. What kind of fool would be silly enough to take a $700 trap gun into a duck blind? And even if he had money enough to buy them by the dozen, a single-barreled gun was a poor thing to hunt ducks with.

"How deep is the water?" I asked.

"Ten or twelve feet, I think."

"Well, look. I'll tell you how to get your gun back. Any neighborhood kid can do it, for five dollars. Get a pair of goggles, or a diving mask. You can buy them at any dime store. Go out and anchor your skiff where the gun went overboard and send the kid down to look for it. Take a piece of fishline to haul it up with when he locates it."

"It's not quite that simple," she said. "You see, it's about three hundred yards from the houseboat to where the duck blind is, and we're not sure where it fell out."

"Why?" I asked.

"It was early in the morning, and still dark."

"Didn't he hear it?"

"No. I think he said there was quite a wind blowing."

It made a little sense. "All right," I said. "I'll find it for you. When do we start?"

"Right now," she said. "Unless you have another job."

"No. I'm not doing anything."

She smiled again. "That's fine. We'll go in my car, if it's all right with you. Will your equipment fit in back?"

"Sure," I said.

I got my gear and changed into some sports clothes. She handed me the car keys and I put everything in the trunk.

As soon as we were out the gate she fumbled in her bag for a cigarette. I lit one for her, and another for myself. She drove well in traffic, but seemed to do an unnecessary amount of winding around to get out on the right highway. She kept checking the rear-view mirror, too, but I didn't pay much attention to that. I did it myself when I was driving. You never knew when some meathead might try to climb over your bumper.

When we were out on the highway at last she settled a little in the seat and unleashed a few more horses. We rolled smoothly along at 60. It was a fine machine, a 1954 hardtop convertible. I looked around the inside of it. She had beautiful legs. I looked back at the road.

"Bill Manning, isn't it?" she asked. "That wouldn't be William Stacey Manning, by any chance?"

I looked around quickly. "How did you know?" Then I remembered. "Oh. You read that wheeze about me in the paper?"

It had appeared a few days ago, one of those interesting-character-about-the-waterfront sort of things. It had started with the fact that I'd won a couple of star class races out at the yacht club; that I'd deck-handed a couple of times on that run down to Bermuda and was a sailing nut; that I'd gone to M.I.T. for three years before the war. It was a good thing I hadn't said anything about the four or five stories I'd sold. I'd have been Somerset Maugham, with flippers.

Then an odd thought struck me. I hadn't used my middle name during that interview. In fact, I hadn't used it since I'd left New England.

She nodded. "Yes. I read it. And I was sure you must be the same Manning who'd written those sea stories. Why haven't you done any more?"

"I wasn't a very successful writer," I said.

She was looking ahead at the road. "Are you married?"

"I was," I said. "Divorced. Three years ago."

"Oh," she said. "I'm sorry. I mean, I didn't intend to pry—"

"It's all right," I said. I didn't want to talk about it.

It was just a mess but it was over and finished. A lot of it had been my fault, and knowing it didn't help much. Catherine and I hadn't agreed about my job, my interests in boating or writing – or anything. She'd wanted me to play office politics and golf. We finally divided everything and quit.

I had learned diving and salvage work in the Navy during the war, and after the wreckage settled I drifted back into it, moving around morosely from job to job and going farther south all the time. If you were going to dive you might as well do it in warm water. It was that aimless.

She looked at me and said, "I gathered you've had lots of experience with boats?"

I nodded. "I was brought up around them. My father sailed, and belonged to a yacht club. I was sailing a dinghy by the time I started to school. After the war I did quite a bit of ocean yacht racing, as a crew member. And a friend and I cruised the Caribbean in an old yawl for about eight months in 1946."

"I see," she said thoughtfully. "Do you know navigation?"

"Yes," I said. "Though I'm probably pretty rusty at it. I haven't used it for a long time."

I had an odd impression she was pumping me, for some reason. It didn't make much sense. Why all this interest in boats? I couldn't see what blue-water sailing and celestial navigation had to do with finding a shotgun lost overboard in some piddling lake.

3

She never did say anything about herself, I noticed, and I didn't ask. She always kept working the conversation around to me, and inside an hour she had most of the story without ever seeming actually to be nosy.

We went through another small town stacked along the highway in the hot sun. A few miles beyond the town she turned off the pavement onto a dirt road going up over a hill between some cotton fields. We passed a few dilapidated farmhouses at first, but then they began to thin out. It was desolate country, mostly sand and scrub pine, and we met no one else at all. After about four miles we turned off this onto a private road which was only a pair of ruts running off through the trees. I got out to open the gate. There was a sign nailed to it which read: *Posted. Keep Out.* I gathered it was a private gun club her husband belonged to, but she didn't say. Another car had been through recently, probably within the last day or two, breaking the crust in the ruts.

We went on for about a mile and then the road ended abruptly. She stopped. "Here we are," she said.

It was a beautiful place, and almost ringingly silent the minute the car stopped. The houseboat was moored to a pier in the shade of big moss-draped trees at the water's edge, and beyond it I could see the flat surface of the lake burning like a mirror in the sun.

She unlocked the trunk and I took my gear out. "I have a key to the houseboat," she said. "You can change in there."

She led the way, disturbingly out of place in this wilderness with her smooth blonde head and smart grooming, the slim spikes of her heels tapping against the planks. I noticed the pier ran on around the end of the scow at right angles and out into the lake.

"I'll take the gear on out there," I said. "I'd like to have a look at it."

She came with me. We rounded the corner of the houseboat and I could see the whole arm of the lake. This section of the pier ran out into it about thirty feet, with two skiffs tied up at the end. The lake was about a hundred yards wide, glassy and shining in the sun between its walls of trees, and some two hundred yards ahead it turned around a point.

"The duck blind is just around that point, on the left," she said.

I looked at it appraisingly. "And he doesn't have any idea at all where the gun fell out?"

She shook her head. "No. It could have been anywhere between here and the point."

It still sounded a little odd, but I merely shrugged. "All right. We might as well get started. I'd like you to come along to guide me from the surface. You'd better change into something. Those skiffs are dirty and wet."

"I think I've got an old swimsuit in the houseboat. I could change into that."

"All right," I said. We went back around to the gangplank and walked aboard. She unlocked the door. It was a comfortably furnished five-room affair. She pointed out a room and I went in to change. She disappeared into another room. She was a cool one, with too damned much confidence in herself, coming out to this remote place with a man she didn't even know.

Cool wasn't the word for it. I could see that a few minutes later when she came out on the dock while I was getting the skiff ready. She could make your breath catch in your throat. The bathing suit was black, and she didn't have a vestige of a tan; the clear, smooth blondeness of her hit you almost physically. There was something regal about her – like a goddess. I looked down uncomfortably and went on bailing. She was completely unconcerned, and her eyes held only that same open friendliness.

I fitted the oarlocks and held the boat while she got in and sat down amidships. Setting the aqualung and mask in the stern, I shoved off.

We couldn't have been over seventy-five yards off the pier when I found the gun. If I'd been looking ahead instead of staring so intently at the bottom I'd have seen it even sooner. It was slanting into the mud, barrel down, with the stock up in plain sight. I pulled it out, kicked to the surface and swam to the skiff.

Her eyes went wide and she smiled when she saw the gun. "That was fast, wasn't it?" she said.

I set it in the bottom of the boat, stripped off the diving gear, and heaved that in, too. "Nothing to it," I said. "It was sticking up in plain sight."

She watched me quietly as I pulled myself in over the stern. I picked up the gun. It was a beautiful trap model with ventilated sighting ramp and a lot of engraving. I broke it, swishing it back and forth to get the mud out of the barrel and from under the ramp. Then I held it up and looked at it. She was still watching me.

The barrel could conceivably have stayed free of rust for a long time, stuck in the mud like that where there was little or no oxygen, but the wood was something else. It should have been waterlogged. It wasn't. Water still stood up on it in drops, the way it does on a freshly waxed car. It hadn't been in the water 24 hours.

I thought of that other set of car tracks, and wondered how bored and how cheap you could get.

4

She pulled us back to the pier. I made the skiff fast and followed her silently back to the car, carrying the diving gear and the gun. The trunk was still open. I put the stuff in, slammed the lid, and gave her the key.

Why not, I thought savagely. If this was good clean fun in her crowd, what did I have to kick about? Maybe the commercial approach made the whole thing a little greasy, and maybe she could have been a little less cynical about waving that wedding ring in your face while she beat you over the head with the stuff that stuck out of her bathing suit in every direction, but still it was nothing to blow your top about, was it? I didn't have to tear her head off.

"You're awfully quiet," she said, the gray eyes faintly puzzled.

This was the goddess again. She was cute.

"Am I?" I asked.

We walked back to the pier and went into the living room of the houseboat. She stopped in front of the fireplace and stood facing me a little awkwardly, as if I still puzzled her.

She smiled tentatively. "You really found it quickly, didn't you?"

"Yes," I said. I was standing right in front of her. Our eyes met. "If you'd gone further up the lake before you threw it in it might have taken a little longer."

She gasped.

I was angry and I stuck my neck out another foot.

"Things must be pretty tough when a woman with your looks has to go this far into left field—"

It rocked me, and my eyes stung; a solid hundred and fifty pounds of flaming, outraged girl was leaning on the other end of the arm. I turned around, leaving her standing there, and walked into the bedroom before she decided to pull my head off and hand it to me. She was big enough, and angry enough.

I dressed and was reaching for a cigarette when I suddenly heard footsteps outside on the pier. I held still and listened. They couldn't be hers. She was barefoot. It was a man. Or men, I thought. It sounded as if there were two of them. They came aboard and into the living room, the scraping of their shoes loud and distinct in the hush. I stiffened, hardly breathing now.

Detectives? Wayne himself? Suddenly I remembered the way she'd doubled all over town getting out on the highway and how she'd kept watching the rear-view mirror. I cursed her bitterly and silently. This was wonderful. This was all I lacked – getting myself shot, or named co-respondent in a divorce suit. And for nothing, except having my face slapped around under my ear.

I looked swiftly around the room. There was no way out. The window was too small. I eased across the carpet until I was against the door, listening.

"All right, Mrs Macaulay," a man's voice said. "Where is he?"

Mrs Macaulay? But that was what he'd said.

"What do you want now?" Her voice was a scared whisper. "Can't you ever understand that I don't know where he is? He's gone. He left me. I don't know where he went. I haven't heard from him—"

"We've heard that before. You've made two trips out here in 24 hours. Is Macaulay here?"

"He's not up here, and I don't know where he is—"

Her voice cut off with a gasp, and then I heard the slap. It came again. And then again. She apparently tried to hold on, but she began to break after the third one and the sob which was wrung from her wasn't a cry of pain but of utter hopelessness. I gave it up then, too, and came out.

There were two of them. The one to my left lounged on an armchair, lighting a cigarette as I charged into the room. I saw him only out of the corners of my eyes because it was the other one I wanted. He was turned the other way. He had her down on the sofa and off balance with a knee pressed into her thighs while he held her left wrist and the front of her bathing suit with one hand and hit her with the other. He wasn't as tall as she was, but he was big across the shoulders.

I caught the arm just as he drew it back again. He let her go.

Even taken by surprise that way, he was falling into a crouch and bringing his left up as he stepped back. But I was already swinging, and it was too sudden and unexpected for even a pug to get covered in time. He went down and stayed down.

I started for him again, but something made me jerk my eyes around to the other one. Maybe it was just a flicker of movement. It couldn't have been any more than that, but now instead of a cigarette lighter in his hand there was a gun.

He gestured casually with the muzzle of it for me to move back and stay there. I moved.

I was ten feet from him. He was safe enough, and knew it. I watched him, still angry but beginning to get control of myself now. I didn't have the faintest idea what I'd walked into, except that it looked dangerous. I couldn't place them. They weren't police. And they obviously weren't private detectives hired by her husband, because it was her husband they were looking for. Somebody named Macaulay, and she'd told me her name was Wayne. It was a total blank.

The one I'd hit was getting up. Pug was written all over him. He moved in on me clearing his head, cat-like, ready. He was a good six inches shorter than I was, but he had cocky shoulders and big arms, and I could see the bright, eager malice with which he sized me up. He was a tough little man who was going to cut a bigger one down to size.

"Drop it," the lounging one said.

"Let me take him." The plea was harsh and urgent.

The other shook his head indifferently. He was long, loose-limbed, and casual, dressed in a tweed jacket and flannels. I couldn't tab him. He might have been a college miler or a minor poet, except for the cool and unruffled deadliness in the eyes. He had something about him which told me he knew his business.

"All right," the pug said reluctantly. He looked hungrily at me, and then at the girl. "You want me to ask her some more?"

I waited, feeling the hot tension in the room. It was going to be rough if he started asking her some more. I wasn't any hero, and didn't want to be one, but it wasn't the sort of thing you could watch for very long without losing your head, and with Tweed Jacket you probably never lost it more than once.

Tweed Jacket's eyes flicked from me to the girl and he shook his head again. "Waste of time," he said. "He'd scarcely be here, not with her boyfriend. Check the rooms, though; look at the ashtrays. You know his cigarettes."

The pug went out, bumping me off balance with a hard shoulder as he went past. I said nothing. He turned his face a little and we looked at each other. I remembered the obscene brutality of the way he was holding and hitting her, and the yearning in the stare was mutual.

There was silence in the room except for Shannon Wayne's stirring on the sofa. She sat up, her face puffed and inflamed; her eyes wet with involuntary tears. She clutched the torn strap of her bathing suit, fumblingly, watching Tweed Jacket with fear in her eyes. Tweed Jacket ignored us. The pug came back.

"Nothing. Nobody here for a long time, from the looks of it."

He looked at me hopefully. "How about Big Boy? Let's ask him."

"Forget it. Stick to business."

There was no longer any doubt as to who was boss, but the pug wanted me so badly he tried once more. "This is a quiet place to ask, and he might know Macaulay."

Tweed Jacket waved him toward the door. "No," he said. His eyes flicked over the girl's figure again coolly. "It's Mrs Macaulay he's interested in." They left.

In the dead silence I could hear their footsteps retreating along the pier, and in a moment the car started. I breathed deeply. Tweed Jacket's manner covered a very professional sort of deadliness, and it could easily have gone the other way. Only the profit motive was lacking. He simply didn't believe Macaulay was here.

I turned. She was still holding the front of the bathing suit. "Thank you," she said, without any emotion whatever, and looked away from me. "I'm sorry you had to become involved. As soon as I can change, I'll drive you back to town."

5

It wasn't until ten, that night, that I said goodbye to Shannon Macaulay. We'd driven back to town and stopped at a cocktail lounge. She'd cleared up some of the questions that had been hanging in my mind. She did know where her husband was.

He had been an insurance executive for a marine underwriters outfit in New York. He wasn't in trouble with his firm or the police. I could check that by calling them, she said. The Tweed Jacket, whose name was Barclay, represented some syndicate who were looking for her husband. Why? She evaded that one. I wasn't satisfied with that, but I went along.

And where did I come in? Easy. The phony dive act was necessary because Shannon had to sound me out. See what kind of a guy I was. Check my experience against that article she'd read about me.

They needed more than a diver. Specifically, they wanted me to buy and outfit a boat and take them off the Yucatan coast to recover something from a sunken plane. Then I was to land them secretly in Central America. That explained her questions about my navigational experiences in the Gulf and the Caribbean. What was in it for me? She'd said, "The boat is yours. Plus five thousand dollars."

I'd whistled softly. There was nothing cheap about this deal. I could see myself cruising the world in the *Ballerina*. She was a beautiful auxiliary sloop. I'd wanted her even before she'd been put up for sale. With the *Ballerina* and five thousand bucks I could live the kind of life I always wanted. I could work and play as I pleased. Manning of the *Ballerina*.

That about clinched it. That and Shannon Macaulay. She'd been awfully good about my misunderstanding of her motives that afternoon and grateful for what I'd done.

Look, I asked myself, what was with Shannon Macaulay? I didn't know anything about her. Except that she was married. And her husband was on the lam from a bunch of mobsters. So she was tall. So she was nice-looking. So something said sexy when you looked at her body and her face, and sweet when you looked at her eyes. I *had* seen women before, hadn't I? I must have. They couldn't be something entirely new to a man 33 years old, who'd been married once for four years. So relax.

I tried to relax walking back to the pier, but it wasn't easy. I couldn't figure the Macaulay guy. What was he mixed up with? Why was he so sure he could spot the plane? How did he figure he could shake this mob with something as easy to spot as this big beautiful blonde wife of his? I knew landing them secretly in a foreign country wasn't legal. And I didn't like the possibilities of tangling with Tweed Jacket and his buddy again, but those were risks I'd have to take.

Relax? Hell, I'd wanted to drive her home, but I knew how stupid that was the minute I'd said it. She gave me her number and told me to watch what I said, to make it sound like a lovers' meeting in case Tweed Jacket was tapped in. We'd arrange to meet once more to give me the money I'd need. Just before she drove away, she'd thanked me, saying, "You've got to help me, Bill, I can't let him down."

6

It was about 10:30 when I walked up to the shack at the pier.

Old Christiansen, the watchman, came out. "Fellow was here to see you, Mr Manning," he said. "He's still out there."

"Thanks," I answered, not paying much attention. "Goodnight." It was late for anybody to be coming around about a job. I entered the long shed running out on the pier. It was velvety black inside, and hot. Up ahead I could see the faint illumination which came from the opened doors at the other end. There was a small light above them on the outside.

I started over toward the ladder to the barge and then remembered that old Chris had said somebody was waiting out here to see me. I looked around, puzzled. My own car was sitting there beside the shed doors, but there was no other. Well, maybe he'd gone. But Chris would have seen him. The gate was the only way out.

I saw it then – the glowing end of a cigarette in the shadows inside my car.

The door swung open and he got out. It was the pug. There was enough light to see the hard, beat-up, fight-hungry face. He lazily crushed out his cigarette against the paint on the side of my car.

"Been waiting for you, Big Boy," he said.

"All right, friend," I said. "I've heard the one about the good little man. A lot of good little men are in the hospital. Hadn't you better run along?"

Then, suddenly, I saw him holding and hitting her again and I was glad he'd come. Rage pushed up in my chest. I went for him.

He was a pro, all right, and he was fast. He hit me three times before I touched him. None of the punches hurt very much, but they sobered me a little. He'd cut me to pieces this way. He'd close my eyes and then take his own sweet time chopping me down to a bloody pulp. My wild swings were just his meat; they'd only pull me off balance so he could jab me.

His left probed for my face again. I raised my hands, and the right slammed into my body. He danced back. "Duck soup," he said contemptuously.

He put the left out again. I caught the wrist in my hand, locked it, and yanked him toward me. This was unorthodox. He sucked air when my right came slamming into his belly. I set a hundred and ninety-five pounds on the arch of his foot, and ground my heel.

He tried to get a knee into me. I pushed him back with another right in his stomach. He dropped automatically into his crouch, weaving and trying to suck me out of position. He'd been hurt, but the hard grin was still there and his eyes were wicked. All he had to do was get me to play his way.

He was six or eight feet in front of the pier, with his back toward it. I went along with him, lunging at him with a right. It connected.

He shot backward, trying to get his feet under him. His heels struck the big 12-by-12 stringer running along the edge of the pier and he fell outward into the darkness, cartwheeling. I heard a sound like a dropped canteloupe and jumped to the edge to look down. The deck of the barge lay in deep shadow. I couldn't see anything. I heard a splash. He had landed on the after deck and then slid off into the water.

I went after him, wild with the necessity to hurry. But the minutes it took me to break out the big underwater light and a diving mask made the difference. The ebbing tide had carried him under the pilings supporting the pier and by the time I got to him he was dead. He was caught there, his skull crushed by the fall on the deck. His eyes were open staring at me. I fought the sickness. If I gagged, I'd drown.

7

The next thing I was conscious of was hanging to the wooden ladder on the side of the barge, being sick. I'd left him there. The police could get him out; I didn't want to touch him. I climbed up to the deck and collapsed, exhausted. I was winded, soaked and the cut places on my face were stinging with salt. My right hand was hurt and swollen.

I had to get out to the watchman's shanty and call the police. But then the whole thing caught up with me. This wasn't an accident I had to report. I'd killed him in a fight. I'd hit him and knocked him off the pier, and now he was dead. It wasn't murder, probably, but they'd have a name for it – and a sentence.

Well, there was no help for it. I started wearily to get up, and then stopped. The police were only part of it. *What about Barclay?* And the others I didn't even know? This was one of their boys.

Suddenly, I wasn't thinking of the police any more, or of Barclay's hoodlums, but of Shannon Macaulay. And the *Ballerina*. Of course, the whole thing was off now. Even if I didn't get sent to prison, with those mobsters after me and convinced I had some connection with Macaulay I was no longer of any use to her.

No, the hell with reporting it. Sure, I regretted the whole thing. But I was damned if I was going to ruin everything just because some vicious little egomaniac couldn't leave well enough alone. Leave him down there. Say nothing about it – I stopped.

How? Christiansen knew he was in here. I was all marked up. In a few days, in this warm water, the body would come to the surface, with the back of his head caved in and bruises all over his face. I didn't have a chance in the world. He'd merely come in here to see me, and had never come out. That would be a tough one for the police to solve.

Of all the places in the world, it had to happen on a pier to which there was only one entrance and where everybody was checked in and out by a watchman – No. Wait. Not checked in and out. Just questioned as they came in. No books, no passes. And the watchman only waved them by as they went out.

It collapsed. It didn't mean anything at all, because *nobody* had gone out. Christiansen would never have any trouble remembering that when the police came checking.

There *had* to be a way out of it. I looked across the dark waterway. Everything was quiet along the other side; there was nothing except an empty warehouse, a deserted dock. Nobody had seen it. Barclay probably didn't even know the pug had come out here. He'd done it on his own because he couldn't rest until he'd humiliated a bigger man who'd knocked him down. There was nothing whatever to connect me with it except the simple but inescapable fact he'd driven in here to see me and had never driven out again— I stopped. *Driven?* No. I hadn't seen any car. But how did I know there wasn't one out there? The shed was dark. I got a flashlight and checked. There it was in the corner of the shed. All I had to do was drive it out past the watchman, and the pug had left here alive. It was as simple as that.

Out at the gate the light was overhead, and the interior of the car would be in partial shadow. The watchman's shack would be on the right. I could hunch down in the seat until I was about the pug's size. All the watchman ever did was glance up from his magazine and wave. He wouldn't see my face; nor remember afterward that he hadn't. It was the same car, wasn't it? The man had driven in, and after a while he had driven out.

Wait. I'd still have to get back inside without Christiansen's seeing me. But that was easy too. It must be nearly eleven now. Chris went off duty at midnight. All I had to do was wait until after twelve and come back in on the next man's shift. He wouldn't know where I was supposed to be, or care.

I walked over to the car, flashed the light in, and saw there were no keys. I leaned wearily against the door. I knew where the keys were, didn't I? It would take only a minute. Revulsion swept me.

But I knew it had to be done. I dove down, emptied his pockets, and came up to surface again. I hadn't looked at his face. It took me a few minutes to clear the gear I'd used. Then I tried to fix up my face with hot water applications. After that I changed into dry clothes that were similar in color to the ones he'd been wearing. I dried his keys and started his car.

I hunched down in the seat and drove up to the gate slowly. Chris was in the shack, pouring coffee out of a thermos. He looked over casually, waved a hand, and turned back to his coffee.

I drove the car uptown – away from the waterfront, parked it on a quiet street, and threw the key far into a vacant lot. I was free of him now, the poor little punk. *Why* couldn't he have stayed away?

8

At twelve-thirty I stepped into an all-night drugstore and called a cab. I hoped the driver couldn't see my face.

We passed the last street and were approaching the gate.

He braked to a stop in front of the shanty. The 12-to-8 watchman was looking out the window. "Manning," I called out, keeping my face in shadow. He lifted a hand.

"All right, Mr Manning."

The cab started to move ahead, then stopped. Somebody was calling out from the shack. "Mr Manning! Just a minute –"

I looked around. The watchman was coming out. "I almost forgot to tell you. A woman called about ten minutes ago –"

I wasn't listening. I stared at the window of the shack. Old Chris was looking out, a puzzled frown on his face.

The other watchman was still talking. "– Chris was just about to walk out and tell you. He said you was on the barge."

I couldn't move, or speak. Chris was standing beside him now, looking in at me. "Son of a gun, Mr Manning. I didn't see you go out."

I fought to get my tongue broken loose from the roof of my mouth. "Why – I –" It was impossible to think. "Why, I came out a while ago. Remember? When my friend left. We drove out to have a couple of beers. It must have been a little before twelve—"

"You was in that car?" He peered at me dubiously. "I looked right at it, too, and didn't even see you. I must be getting absent-minded. I was about to walk all the way out there to the barge and tell you that woman called—"

He broke off suddenly, concerned. "Why, Mr Manning. What's wrong with your face?"

I was rattled now, but I tried not to show it to these two old men who meant well, but who would remember everything they saw later on.

"Oh," I mumbled, feeling my face as if I were surprised at the fact of having one. "I – uh – I was getting something out of the storeroom and fell."

"Well, that's too bad," he answered solicitously. "But you ought to put something on them cut places. Might get infected. You never know. I think it's the climate around here, the muggy air, sort of—"

"Yes," I said. "Yes. Thanks."

I got rid of the cabbie, who'd be the third guy to answer any questions asked by the police – or Barclay's bunch of killers.

I tried to think. How much chance did I have now? In a few days he'd float up, somewhere along the waterfront, and the police would start looking. One of the first things they'd do would be to question all the guards along the piers.

Float up? That was it. He couldn't float up. I had to stop it. I looked downward again, and shuddered. Could I go back into that place once more? *Once?* It would take at least a half dozen dives to do it, to make him fast with wire to the bottom of one of those pilings. Too much precious time and breath were wasted in going down and coming up.

There was just one more thing, I thought, and then we had it all. Carter would be back from New Orleans sometime this morning, here aboard the barge, and I wouldn't be able even to look.

I fought with panic. I still had a chance, I told myself. They might never connect me with it. After all, there was no identification on him now that I'd shoved the wallet into the muck. They wouldn't have a picture of him, except possibly one taken as he looked when he came up. Chris might not have had a good look at him when he came in the gate.

But I wouldn't know. That was the terrible part of it. I'd never have any idea at all what was happening until the hour they came after me.

I had to get out of here. I was thinking swiftly now. Quit, and tell Carter I was going to New York. Sell my car, buy a bus ticket, get off the bus somewhere up the line, and come back. Buy the boat, under another name, of course. In three days I could have it ready for sea. We'd be gone before they even came looking for me. If they did.

It didn't occur to me until afterward that never once in all of it did I ever consider the possibility of not buying the boat and not taking Shannon Macaulay.

Suddenly, I had to see her. For the first time in a self-sufficient life I was all at once terribly alone, and I didn't know why, but I had to see her.

That reminded me. The watchman had said that a woman had called. I was still holding in my hand the slip of paper he had given me. It was a telephone number, the same one she had given me in the bar. Maybe something had happened to her. I ran toward the car.

Calling from the watchman's shack would be quicker, but I didn't want the audience. I slowed going through the gate, and the graveyard watchman lifted a hand and nodded. I noted bitterly that old Chris had gone home at last.

I pulled up at the nearest bar and called her. She answered, finally, her voice tense. We put on the lovers' rendezvous tone to take care of possible listeners. She arranged to meet me at the cocktail joint we'd drunk at earlier in the day.

I was sitting in the car in front of it when she pulled up and parked her Caddy. If she were being followed I didn't want to go inside where they might get a look at my marked-up face. I eased alongside. She saw me, and slipped out on the street side and got in. It had taken only seconds.

I shot ahead, watching the mirror. There were cars behind us, but there was no way to tell. There are always cars behind you. I was conscious of the gleam of the blonde head beside me, and a faint fragrance of perfume.

She noticed my face and gasped. *Tell her?* What kind of fool would tell anybody? I had known her less than twenty-four hours; I knew practically nothing about her; I knew she had gotten me into this mess; yet I would have trusted her with anything. I told her. I brushed off her sympathetic offerings, but I didn't find them unpleasant.

I had been watching the mirror carefully. By this time we were well out on the beach highway and traffic had thinned out considerably. There were three cars behind us. One of them stopped. I shot ahead fast, dropping the other two well behind me. As they disappeared momentarily behind some dunes, I slowed abruptly and swung away from the beach. We were some 50 yards from the road, well out of range of passing highlights. I shut the headlights before we stopped rolling.

She started to light a cigarette. "Not yet," I said. Both cars went by, their tail-lights slowly receding down the road.

I lit her cigarette.

"All right, listen," I said. I told her what I was going to do. "There's only one catch to it," I finished. "You'll have to give me the money for that boat with no guarantee you'll ever hear from me again. The word of a man you've known for one day isn't much of a receipt."

"It's good enough for me," she said quietly. "If I hadn't trusted you I would never have opened the subject in the first place. How much shall I make the check?"

"Fifteen thousand," I said. "The boat is going to be at least ten, and there's a lot of stuff to buy. When we get aboard I'll give you an itemized statement and return what's left."

"All right," she said.

"Pick a name," I said. "How about Burton? Harold E. Burton."

She wrote out the check. I held it until it dried, and put it in my wallet. "Now. What's your address?"

"106 Fontaine Drive."

"All right," I said, talking fast. "I should be back here early the third day. This is Tuesday now, so that'll be Thursday morning. The minute the purchase of the boat goes through and I'm aboard I'll mail you an anniversary greeting in a plain envelope, just one of those dime-store cards. I don't see how they could get at your mail, but there's no use taking chances. Other than that I won't get in touch with you. I'll be down there at the boat yard all the time. It's in another part of the city, and I won't come into town at all. I've only been around Sanport for about six months, but still there are a few people I know and I might bump into one of them. I'll already have everything bought and with me except the stores, and I'll order them through a ship chandler's runner—"

"But," she interrupted, "how are we going to arrange getting him aboard?"

"I'm coming to that," I said. "After you get the card, you can get in touch with me, from a pay phone. It's Michaelson's Boat Yard; the name of the sloop is *Ballerina*. I'm just hoping I can get her. She was still for sale last night. But if something happens and she's already sold by the time I get back, I'll make that card a birth announcement instead of an anniversary greeting, and give you the name of the one I actually do buy. All straight?"

"Yes," she said. She turned a little and I could see the blur of her face and the pale gleam of the blonde head. "I like the whole plan, and I like the way your mind works." She paused for a moment, and then added quietly. "You'll never know how glad I am I ran into you. I don't feel so helpless now. Or alone."

I was conscious of the same thing, but probably in a different way than she'd meant it. There was something wonderful about being with her. For a moment the whole mess was gone from my mind.

"You were good on the phone, too," she said. "Thanks for understanding."

In other words, *keep your distance, Buster.* I wondered why she thought she had to warn me. We both knew it was only an act, didn't we? Maybe I was always too aware of her, and she could sense it. "All right. Now," I said curtly. "That leaves the problem of getting him aboard. I'll have to work on that. He's in the house, isn't he?"

"Yes," she said, surprised. "How did you know?"

"Guessing, mostly. You said they'd searched it while you were gone. They wouldn't have had to tear it up much, looking for a grown man. So maybe he told you they had."

"You're very alert. He heard them and told me."

"Why is he hiding there? And how?"

She leaned forward a little and continued. "I've been wanting to get to this. Here's the whole story, briefly.

"About three weeks ago my husband spotted them on the street and knew they'd caught up with us again. He had a plan for getting to Central America and losing them completely, for the last time. It was about completed. It involved a man who'd been a close friend of my husband's in college. He lives in Honduras and is a wealthy plantation-owner with considerable political influence. He's also a rather passionate flying fan. He's always buying planes in the States and having them flown down to him, and my husband was to take this one to him. It would get him out of the country without any trail they could follow, you see? He'd merely take off without filing a flight plan, and disappear. It would be illegal, but as I say this friend of his had political connections.

"However, he had to go alone. It was a light plane and its cruising radius with the maximum amount of fuel was still a little short, so he'd added an extra tank. I was to come later, making sure I wasn't followed. I was to do it over the Memorial Day weekend, and it involved about five different zigzagging commercial flights with the reservations made considerably ahead of time. On a long holiday like that they'd be sold out, you see? Anyone trying to follow me might catch a no-show at one or even two of the airports, but not all of them.

"Two days before I was to leave, my husband came back. He crashed off the Yucatan coast, but got into a life raft and was picked up by a Sanport fishing boat. They docked at night and he got home unseen.

"But now they've found out where we live, and they have the place surrounded. Barclay rented the house right across the street, and they watch me all the time, waiting for me to lead them to him—"

"And they don't know he's inside?"

"I don't think so. You see, they searched it the first time while he was actually gone. They made it look like burglary."

"But didn't you say they'd searched it again today? Yesterday, I mean?"

She nodded. "He's in a sealed-off portion of the attic, and the only way into it is through the ceiling of a second-floor closet. He stays up there nearly all the time. All the time when I'm out of the house. I think they're pretty sure he's gone, but they know if they keep watching me I'll lead them to him sooner or later. I hadn't realized until what happened up at the lake that they might try beating me up. That scares me, because frankly I don't know how much of it I could take."

That angered me and made me realize how much more there was to this girl than her looks. No whining, no heroics – she simply said she didn't know how much of it she could take and went right on with what she had to do. The next time that pug looked at me, I'd look back.

She went on. "And as to what's in the plane, it's money. About eighty thousand dollars. All he has left. He can't take much more, Bill. That plane crash did something to him – and being brought back to Sanport after he thought he had gotten away. And losing the money on top of it, so he couldn't even run any more."

"But you just wrote a check for fifteen thousand—"

"I know. Naturally, he left me some so I could follow him. I sold my jewelry, and borrowed on the car."

I began to catch on then. She was merely handing me the last chance they'd ever have. This girl was a plunger, and when she said she trusted you she trusted you all over.

"Well, wait," I said. "I can probably find a cheaper boat—"

She shook her head. "I don't want to go to sea in a cheap boat. And we'll recover the money from the plane, anyway."

"Do you realize the jam you'll be in if I turn out to be a phony?"

"That was the general idea, Bill, when I said I wanted time to make up my mind about you. Remember?"

"I remember," I said. "Do you mind if I get a little personal? I've been feeling sorry for Macaulay because he was up against a rough proposition alone. I'd like to amend that; I don't know of anybody who's less alone."

She didn't answer for a moment, and I wondered if I'd gotten it off as lightly as I intended. After all, this was an awkward situation for her, and she'd already shown me the road signs once.

It was almost too fast for me then. She slid toward me on the seat, murmuring, "Bill . . . *Bill!*" her face lifted to mine and her arms slipping up around my neck, and then I was overboard in a sea of Shannon Macaulay. Yet even as I swam into that sea, my mind was trying to tell me it was an act and that the reason she was saying my name over and over was to keep me from having my head blown off. And that's what it was.

A voice said, "All right, Jack. Break it up and turn around."

I turned. A light burst in my face, and another voice I recognized as Barclay's said, "You people are oversexed, aren't you?"

Two thoughts caught up with me at once. The first was that they hadn't heard us and didn't suspect anything. Her reaction time had been so fast they'd caught us kissing, just as you'd have expected of two people in a parked car along the beach. That was good.

But it was the second one that pulled the ground from under me. They had that light right in my face, and they'd be blind if they didn't see the marks that pug had left on it.

I had never been more right. "Hmmmmm," Barclay said softly. "So that's where he went."

"Who?" I asked, just stalling for time. I had to think of something. "What are you talking about?"

"Don't be stupid. The guy you hit, up at the lake."

If I denied it they wouldn't believe me anyway, and when he didn't show up they'd go out there and ask the watchmen. They'd know then I'd done something to him. There was a better way: talk like a loud-mouthed fool, and admit it. It didn't have much chance, but at least it had more than the other.

"If that's who you mean," I said. "He did. I guess you haven't seen *his* face. Keep him out of my hair or he's going to be bent worse than that the next time you get him back."

"Where is he now?"

"How would I know?" I said. "Was he supposed to tell me his plans?"

"Skip it, wise guy," he said. "And get out of town. We're too busy to be chasing around after your love instincts. Get out of the car."

I didn't want to, but I got out. I heard her shaky indrawn breath as I closed the door. "*No. No. No –* "

It was a good, cold-blooded, professional job. Nobody said anything. Nobody became excited. I never did even know for sure how many there were besides Barclay. I swung at the first dark shape I saw, because I had to do something; the blackjack sliced down across the muscles of my upper arm and it became a dangling, inert sausage stuffed with pain.

They gave me a good working over. The last thing I heard was Shannon's screams.

When I came to, she was there on her knees beside me, helping. My arm was numb and I felt sick, but she rested there until the pain subsided.

9

Driving back to town, neither of us said anything about the way she'd put on the kissing act to keep my head from being blown up.

Finally, I asked, "What did Macaulay do to them?"

She hesitated.

"It's all right," I said. "If it's none of my business—"

"No," she said slowly, staring ahead at the headlights probing the edge of the surf. "It isn't that. It's just that I don't know the whole story myself."

"Didn't he tell you?"

"Most of it. But not all. He says I'll be safer if I never know. It happened about three months ago. He had to go to the coast on business, for about a week, he said. But three days later he called me late one night, from San Antonio, Texas. I could tell he was under a bad strain. He said for me to pack some bags, and leave right away for Denver. He didn't explain; he just said he was in trouble and for me to get out of New York fast.

"He met me in Denver. It was something that happened at a party he went to, in some suburb of Los Angeles. He didn't want to talk about it, but he finally admitted a man had been killed, and he had seen it."

"But," I said, "All he has to do is go to the police. They'll protect him. He's a material witness."

"It's not that simple," she said. "One of the people involved is a police captain."

"Oh," I said.

It sounded too easy and too pat, but on the other hand there wasn't any doubt she was telling the truth. But what about Macaulay himself?

"How long have you been married?" I asked.

"Eight years."

"And he's been with that marine insurance firm all the time?"

"Yes," she said. "He's been with them ever since he came out of law school, back in the thirties, except for three years in the service during the war."

I shook my head. There was nothing in that. We came into the almost deserted town. I stopped beside her car and got out with her. She put out her hand. "Thanks," she said. "It'll be bad, waiting for that card."

There was nobody on the street. I was still holding her hand, hating to see her leave. But all I said was, "Don't go out of the house at night while I'm gone. If you have to come downtown, do it during rush hours when there are lots of people on the streets."

"I'll be all right," she said.

"If you see a car behind you on the way home, don't worry about it. It'll be mine. That's all." I followed her out. It was an upper-bracket suburb out near the country club. She pulled into a drive and stopped under a carport beside a two-storied Mediterranean house with a tile roof and ironwork balconies. I stared at the house across the street. The windows were all dark. But they were in there, watching her as she got out of the car and fumbled in her bag for the key. She waved a white-gloved hand, and went inside.

I went on, looking the place over. It was the second house from the corner. I turned at the intersection and drove slowly down the side street. There was an alley behind the house. A car was parked diagonally across the street from the mouth of it in the shadows under the trees, and as I went past I saw a man's elbow move slightly in the window. They had it covered front and back. There'd be one at the other end of the alley.

All I had to do was get Macaulay out of there alive. And by that time they'd be after me too.

I made my plans quickly. I drove back to the barge, packed my stuff, cleaned my face up as well as I could. It was morning when I started into town. I thought about the guy under the pier and then tried to dismiss him from my mind. Shannon helped. I couldn't push her out of the picture at all – nor could I forget Macaulay. His story didn't jell. I knew something about that tricky coastline off Central America. He'd have to be a superb navigator to find that spot again.

I sold my Oldsmobile for half of what it was worth and bought a bus ticket to New York. Before I got on the bus; I sent a telegram to Carter explaining that I had to see sick relatives in New York and that he'd have to get a new diver. It was the least I could do.

I fell asleep the minute I hit the seat.

10

We came into New Orleans at ten-fifteen p.m. Through passengers going east were scheduled to change buses, with a layover of forty minutes. I got my bag, ducked out a side door, and caught a cab. I registered as James R. Madigan at a little hotel and went to work on the marks on my face. Another few hours and they'd hardly be noticed.

They might find out I'd left the bus, and they might even trail me to this hotel and eventually start looking for somebody named Madigan, but there the whole thing would end. Harold E. Burton was only a check for $15,000, and the last place they'd ever expect me to go would be back to Sanport.

I studied the rest of it. There'd be the station wagon I had to buy to get back to Sanport with all the gear. I'd store it in a garage after we sailed. After a year or so they'd probably sell it for the storage charges, and if anybody ever bothered to look into it all he'd find would be that it had been left there by a man named Burton who'd sailed for Boston in a small boat and never been heard of again. People had been lost at sea before, especially sailing alone.

After I'd landed them on the Central American coast, I'd return to Florida and could lose myself among the thousands who made a living along the edge of the sea in one way or another, gradually building up a whole new identity. I burned my identification. I fell asleep thinking of Shannon.

It was a little after eight when I awoke. I shaved hurriedly, noting my face was almost back to normal now, and dressed in a clean white linen suit.

A little later, I put in a long-distance call to Sanport, to the yacht broker. I told him I was interested in the *Ballerina*. He said it was available at eleven thousand dollars. I arranged to meet him at Michaelson's yard in Sanport at nine the next morning.

When the banks opened I went into the first one I came to, endorsed the check for deposit, and opened an account, asking them to clear it with the Sanport bank by wire. They said they should have an answer on it by a little after noon.

The used car lots were next. Part of my mind had been occupied with the problem of getting Macaulay out of that house, and now I was starting to see at least part of the answer.

I didn't want a station wagon; I wanted a black panel truck. I found one in the next lot. After trying it out, I told the salesman I'd come back later and let him know. I couldn't buy it until the check cleared.

The wire came back from the Sanport bank a little after one. I cashed a check for three thousand, picked up the truck, and drove over to a nautical supply store. It took nearly two hours to get everything I needed here, chronometer, sextant, azimuth tables, nautical almanacs, charts, and so on, right down to a pair of 7 x 50 glasses and a marine radio receiver. That left the diving gear. Of course there was still the aqualung in the back of her car, but the coast of Yucatan was too far to come back for spare equipment if anything went wrong. I bought another, and some extra cylinders which I had filled. At five o'clock the truck was full of gear, and nothing remained but to check out of the hotel and start back.

No, there was one thing more. I went into a dime store and bought an anniversary greeting card.

I drove all night.

At dawn, I hit the outskirts of Sanport where Michaelson's Boat Yard was located. I parked the car and went into a diner for breakfast. When the workmen started to drift into the yard, I walked in and got a look at the *Ballerina*. She was a beauty.

The yacht broker showed up and we closed the deal for $10,500. I checked the work list with the foreman and arranged for a shakedown cruise the following morning. She was in such good shape that he guaranteed she'd be ready for me that same afternoon. Looking her over, I agreed.

Just then the telephone rang. The girl at the desk said, "Just a minute, please." She looked inquiringly at the super. "A Mr Burton − ?"

"Here," I said. "Thank you."

"Burton speaking," I said.

"Can you talk all right from there?" she asked softly.

I couldn't, so I got her number, walked down to a pay booth and dialed, fumbling in my eagerness. She answered immediately.

"Bill! I'm so glad to hear you—"

It struck me suddenly she didn't have to act now, as she had the other night, because there was no chance anybody could be listening. Then I shrugged it off. Of course she was glad. She was in a bad jam, and she'd had two days of just waiting, biting her nails.

"I didn't do wrong, did I?" she went on hurriedly. "But I just couldn't stand it any longer. The suspense was driving me crazy."

"No," I said. "I'm glad you didn't wait for the card. I was worried about you, too. Has anything happened?"

"No. They're still watching me, but I've been home nearly all the time. But tell me about you. And when can we start?"

"Here's the story," I said, and I told her. We set the sailing date for Saturday night.

And then she asked the big question.

"Have you thought of anything yet? I mean for getting Francis aboard?"

"Yes," I said. "I've got an idea. But something else has occurred to me."

"What's that, Bill?"

"Sneaking him aboard isn't the big job. Getting you here is going to be the tough one."

"Why?"

"They're not sure where he is. But they're covering you every minute."

I went on, talking fast, checking with her about the layout of the house and the streets in the neighborhood.

Finally, I said, "All right. That's about all I needed to know. I think we can pull it off, but I want to work on it a little more. And I've still got to figure out a way to get you."

"And your diving equipment," she said. "It's still in the back of the car."

"I know," I said. "I was just coming to that. There won't be time to fool with it, either, when I come to get you, no matter what kind of plan we work out. Anyway, put that aqualung in a cardboard carton and tie it. Pack what clothes and toilet articles you can get into another carton, and put both of them in the trunk of your car. Around noon tomorrow call Broussard & Sons, the ship chandlers, and ask if they'll deliver a couple of packages to the *Ballerina*, along with the stores. They will, of course. But don't take them to Broussard's yourself.

"Take the car to the Cadillac agency for a supposed repair. As soon as you get inside on the service floor, call a parcel delivery service to come after the cartons. Whoever's following you will be outside and won't see the things come out of your car. If he did they'd be hot on the trail in nothing flat to see where they went. All straight?"

"Yes. Now, when will I call you again?"

"Saturday afternoon about five, unless something happens and you have to get in touch with me sooner."

It took the rest of the morning to check the gear on the sloop and make out a stores list. Broussard's runner came down in the afternoon and picked it up. The yard closed at five. I drove the truck inside and parked it. The night watchman was another problem; as fast as I solved one I had two more to take its place. I had to get them aboard without his seeing them.

I studied the layout of the yard. The driveway came in through the gate where the office and the shops were located, and went straight back to the pier running out at the end of the spit. The *Ballerina*, of course, would be out on the pier after I brought her back in from the shakedown. If I backed the truck up to the pier and left the lights on he wouldn't be able to see them come out the rear doors.

I cleaned the cabin of the boat that night and got a good night's sleep.

The *Ballerina* checked out beautifully the next morning and the yardwork was done. I paid the bill and spent the afternoon checking and stowing all the gear aboard her. Later, I bought a paper, but there was nothing about his body's being found.

With nothing to do, I began thinking of her again. I still hadn't figured a way of getting her aboard. Finally I hit on an idea. If it worked, this time tomorrow we'd be at sea.

11

The stores came down in a truck at a little after nine. I looked quickly for the two cartons, took them aboard, and started checking stores with the driver. When he had it all on the end of the pier I wrote out a check and started carrying it aboard.

I was still at it at eleven o'clock when two strange men came into the yard. They were dressed in seersucker suits and panama hats, and were smoking cigars. They started around the yard, talking to each of the workmen for a minute or two.

Then they were coming toward me. I was just picking up a coil of line; I straightened, watching them. I'd never seen them before as far as I could tell. They showed me a photograph, questioned me briefly, and left.

They worked fast. It couldn't possibly have been more than a few hours since they'd found him, and already they had a picture. Not *a* picture, I thought. Probably dozens of them, being carried all over the waterfront. And it was a photograph of him as he was alive, not swollen and unrecognizable in death.

Anybody but a fool would have known it, I thought. The pug would have a criminal record, and when they have records they have pictures. Maybe they had identified him from his fingerprints. But that made no difference now. The thing was that Christiansen would recognize him instantly.

I shook it off. They'd still be looking for Manning, who had gone to New York. And we'd be gone from here in another twelve hours. I was still tense and uneasy. It was Saturday afternoon, and it grew worse as the afternoon wore along.

It was exactly five o'clock when the telephone rang inside the booth at the gate.

"Bill," she said softly, "I'm getting really scared now. Are we all ready?"

"We're all ready," I said. "Listen. I've got to get Macaulay first. They're not sure where he is, and if it works right they won't even know he's gone. They won't suspect anything's happening. But when you disappear, everything's going to hit the fan."

"I understand," she said.

I went on, "Tell him to dress in dark clothes and wear soft-soled shoes. He's to come out the back door at around 9:10. That'll give him plenty of time to get his eyes accustomed to the darkness and make sure there's nobody in the alley itself. I don't think there will be, because they're too smart to be loitering where somebody might see them and call the police. They're watching the ends of it, sitting in cars. I'll come down Brandon Way and stop at the mouth of the alley at exactly 9:20—"

"But, Bill, you can't stop there. He'll know what you're doing. He'll kill you."

"He'll be busy," I said. "I've got a diversion for him, and I think it'll work. Now, the truck will be between him and the mouth of the alley. Tell Macaulay to come fast the minute the truck stops. And if anything goes wrong he's to *keep coming toward the truck*. If he breaks and goes back he hasn't got a chance. Tell him when he reaches it to stand a little behind the door and just put his hand up on the frame of the window, near the corner. He's not to get in or open the door, until the truck starts moving. If he even puts his weight on the running board while it's stopped, that guy may hear it. Got all that?"

"Yes," she said. "Then what?"

"You're next. Have you ever been to a drive-in movie?"

"Yes. Several times."

"All right. As soon as he leaves the house at 9:10 you lock all the doors. Be standing right by the phone at 9:20. If you hear any commotion or gunshots, call the cops and hide, fast. A prowl car will get there before they can get to you. But if you don't hear anything, you'll know he got away. Leave the house at 9:30. Some of them will follow you, of course. Go to the Starlite drive-in, out near the beach on Centennial Avenue. Centennial runs north and south. Approach from the north, and try to time it so you get there at ten minutes before ten. If you look you'll see a black panel truck parked somewhere in the last block before you get to the entrance. That'll be me. Drive on in.

"Now, all this is important. Be sure you get it right. This is Saturday night, so it'll be pretty full. But you know how they're laid out, fan-wise, spreading out from the screen, and there are always a few parking places along the edge because the angle's poor out there. Enter one of the rows and drive across to the exit, slowly, looking for a good spot. But there aren't any. So you wind up clear over at the end. Sit there twenty minutes, and then back out. You've decided you don't like that, and there must be something better further back. So drop back a row and go back to the entrance side again. Park there for five or ten minutes, and then get out and walk down to the ladies' room in the building where the projector is. Kill about five minutes and then come back to the car. The minute you get in, back out and drive toward the exit. Before you get to it, pull into one of the parking places along the edge, and step out, on the right-hand side. Don't scream when a hand grabs your arm. It'll be mine."

"Won't they still be following me?"

"Not any more," I said. "By the time you come back from the ladies' room I'll know who he is."

"You think he'll get out of his car too?"

"Yes. It's like this. There'll probably be two cars trailing you. When they see you go into a drive-in theatre one man will follow you in to be sure it's not a dodge for you to transfer to some other car. And the other bunch will stay outside near the exit to pick you up coming out, because there's a hellish jam of cars fighting for the exit when the movie breaks up and they could lose you if they both went inside. There's just one thing more. If an intermission comes along, sit tight where you are. You've got to make those two moves and that trip to the powder room while the picture's running and not many people are wandering around. It's darker then too; nobody has his lights on."

"Yes, but how are you going to stop him from following me the second time? Bill, they're dangerous."

"It's all right," I said. "He won't even see me. When he gets out to follow you on foot I'll fix his ignition wires. By the time he tumbles to the fact his car's not going to start, you'll already be down at the other end of the row and in my truck. When the picture's over, we just drive out, along with everybody else."

"All right. But you'll be careful, won't you?"

"Why?" I asked. I couldn't help it.

"Couldn't we put it this way – if anything happens to you we wouldn't get away."

"We'll call it that."

"Yes," she said. Then she added, "That, at the very least."

She hung up.

12

I sweated it out. It was eight-fifty when I reached the neighborhood and cruised slowly to time it right. I was betting a lot on just a flashlight and a black panel truck. The thing was to give him just a little time to look it over, so I wouldn't spring it on him too suddenly. He'd be able to see what I was doing, and as I passed under the street light at the intersection of Fontaine Drive he'd see the black sides of the truck. My headlights would cover the Louisiana license plate. At 9:18 I eased away from the curb.

Switching on the flashlight, I held it in my left hand and shot the beam into dark places under the trees and back among the hedges as I came slowly down the street. After I crossed Fontaine I could see him. He was in the same place, facing this way. I flashed the light into another hedge.

I had to calculate the angles fast now. I was well out in the center of the street, watching the mouth of the alley on his side. He was parked just beyond it. I stopped with my window opposite his, and at the same time I threw the light against the side of his car but not quite in his face.

"You seen anything of a stray kid?" I asked, as casually as I could with that dryness in my mouth. "Boy, about four, carrying a pup—"

It worked.

I could feel the breath ooze out of me as a tough voice growled from just above the light. "Nah. I haven't seen any kid."

"Okay. Thanks," I said. I felt along the edge of the window frame in the opposite door. *Hurry. For the love of God, hurry.*

My fingertips brushed across a hand. I inhaled again.

I let the truck roll slowly ahead three or four feet, and said, "If you see a kid like that, call the station, will you? We'd thank you for it."

I moved the light away from him. He wouldn't be able to see anything for twenty or thirty seconds, and Macaulay was on the far side of the truck, walking along with me. But he had to be in it before we hit the street below Fontaine, under the light. I slipped the clutch and hit the accelerator a couple of times, shooting the flashlight beam along the sidewalk. The door opened soundlessly, and he was sitting beside me. He closed it gently.

There was no outcry behind us. I wanted to step on the gas. Not yet, I thought. Easy. I still hadn't seen him at all. He was only a dark shadow beside me as we rolled on toward the intersection. Then a cigarette lighter flared.

I jerked my face around, whispering fiercely. "*Put that—*"

"It's all right," a smooth voice said. "Just turn at the corner and go around the block."

I saw a lean face, and tweed, and the gun held carelessly in his lap. It was Barclay.

We turned. I was numb all over and there was nothing else to do.

"Park at the mouth of the alley, and do it quietly," Barclay said.

"Mrs Macaulay?" I asked mechanically.

"She's in the house."

"Is she all right?"

"Yes."

I swung around the next corner, and we were on Fontaine, under the big, peaceful trees. "Then you finally killed him, didn't you?"

"Oh. Yes," he replied, almost as if talking to himself. "Too bad."

There was no point in asking what he meant. I was too far behind now to catch up in a week. We parked at the mouth of the alley. Across the street I could see the red tip of a cigarette in the other car. Bitterness welled up in me. I'd fooled them, hadn't I?

Barclay opened the door on his side. "Go in. We'll be leaving soon."

"Leave?"

"Sail. *Ballerina* sleeps four, right?"

He stepped aside in the darkness and followed closely behind me. My mind turned the parts of it over and over with no more comprehension than a washing-machine tumbling clothes. Sail? Four of us? Macaulay was already dead, that was what they'd wanted, wasn't it?

It was – unless she had been lying all the time. I tried to shove the thought out of my mind. It came back. How would they have known I was coming by in the truck unless she had told them?

Maybe I could have got away from him in the alley, but I didn't even try. The whole thing had fallen in on me, and I didn't have anywhere to go. I wanted to see her, anyway. She had lied about it, or she hadn't lied about it. I had to know.

I had wanted to see Macaulay and when I finally saw him he was a corpse on the floor of his living room. He'd been dressed according to the instructions I'd given Shannon. She was there, shocked and speechless, barely able to keep herself together when Barclay escorted me in. Two of his friends were there, too. He gave his instructions tersely.

"Very well. We're finished here," he said. "Who has the keys to her car?"

"Here." The big blond guy fished them from his pocket.

"Give them to Carl," Barclay directed crisply. "You'll go with us in the truck."

He shifted his gaze to the other man. "Take the Cadillac downtown and park it. Meet us on the southeast corner of Second and Lindsay. We'll be going east, in a black panel truck, Manning driving. Get in the front seat with him. When we go in the gate at the boat yard Manning will tell the watchman you've come along to drive the truck back to a garage. If Manning tries any tricks, don't shoot him; kill the watchman. As soon as we're all aboard the boat, take the truck to some all-night storage garage and leave it, under the name of Harold E. Burton, and pay six months' storage charges in advance. Then pick up the Cadillac, drive it to the airport, and leave it. Take a plane to New York, and tell them we should be in Tampa in three weeks to a month. Tell them about Macaulay, but that we have her and it's under control. You got that?"

"Check," Carl said. He took the keys and went out.

I could see a little of it now. They were hanging it on her quite neatly. The police already wanted me, and they'd be after her now too, for killing Macaulay. I didn't know what Barclay wanted with her, but he had her from every angle. There was nowhere we could run.

13

We boarded the *Ballerina* the way Barclay scheduled it and he used my loading plan perfectly. The watchman never suspected a thing. Carl drove the truck off the pier and that was it. I could have jumped over the side and possibly escaped, but he knew I wouldn't. I had nowhere to go, with the police looking for me, and I couldn't leave her. The big one helped her down into the cockpit.

On deck, Barclay said, "Let's sail."

"Where?" I asked.

"I'll give you a course when we're outside. Now, step on it."

"I'll have to light the running lights first. Is that all right with you?"

"Certainly."

"I just wanted to be sure I had your permission."

He sighed in the darkness. "This is no game, Manning. You and Mrs Macaulay are in a bad spot. What happens to her depends on the way the two of you cooperate. Now, get this sloop away before the watchman hears us and comes snooping."

Getting the watchman killed would accomplish nothing. "All right," I said. We moved slowly away from the pier, out toward the channel, going seaward. There was no other traffic.

Barclay sat down across from me in the cockpit, smoking. "Very neat," he congratulated himself above the noise of the engine.

"I suppose so," I said. "If killing people is your idea of neatness."

"Macaulay? We couldn't help it."

"Of course," I said coldly. "It was an accident."

"No. Not an accident. Call it calculated risk." He paused for a moment, the cigarette glowing, and then he went on. "And speaking of that, here's where you fit in. You're also a calculated risk. I can handle small boats well enough to take this sloop across the Gulf, but I couldn't find the place we're looking for. We need you. We won't kill you unless we have to. Score yourself a point.

"But before you start anything, imagine a bullet-shattered knee, with gangrene, and only aspirin tablets or iodine to treat it. And figure what we could do to Mrs Macaulay if you don't play ball.

"One of us will be watching you every minute. Do as you're told, and there'll be no trouble. Is it all clear, Manning?"

"Yes," I said. "Except you keep telling me this is no game, so there must be some point to it. Would you mind telling me where you think you're going, and what you're after?"

"Certainly. We're looking for an airplane."

"You mean the one Macaulay crashed in? You're going to try to find it after you've killed the one person on earth who knew where it is?"

"She knows," he said calmly. "Why do you think we brought her?"

"Look," I said. "He was alone in it when it crashed. How could she possibly know?"

"He told her."

"You'll never find it in a million years."

"We will. He knew where it was, and was certain he could go back to it, or he wouldn't have hired you. So it has to be near some definite location, a reef or something. And if he knew, he could tell her. She's already given me the general location. It's to the westward of Scorpion Reef. You know the spot?"

"It's on the chart," I said curtly. "Listen, Barclay. You're stupid as hell. Even if you found the plane, that money's not recoverable. I didn't tell her, because the main thing they wanted was to get away from your bunch, but that currency's pulp by now. It's been submerged for weeks—"

"Money?" he asked. There was faint surprise in his voice.

"Don't be cute. You're not looking for that plane just to recover the ham sandwich he probably had with him."

"She told you there was money on the plane? Is that it?"

"Of course that's it. What else? They were trying to get to some place in Central America so they could quit running from you and your gorillas—"

"I wondered what she told you."

"What do you mean?"

"You're nuts, Manning. We're not looking for any money. We're after something he stole from us."

"I don't believe it."

"It's not important what you believe. But what makes you so sure, when you'd never met him and knew nothing about him at all?"

"I know her. She wouldn't lie about it."

He chuckled. "Wouldn't she?"

The *Ballerina* began lifting slowly on the long groundswell running in through the mouth of the jetties. I searched the darkness ahead and could see the seabuoy winking on and off. I wondered why Barclay had tried to get off a cock-and-bull story like that. He was in control; why bother to lie?

"I found their bag, the one she sent aboard."

I looked around. It was the voice of George Barfield, down below.

"Any chart in it?" Barclay asked.

"No." Barfield came out carrying something in one hand and sat down beside Barclay. "The satchel was in it, all right. About eighty thousand, roughly. But no chart, none at all."

"*What?*" It exploded from me.

"What's the matter with Don Quixote?" Barfield asked. "Somebody goose him?"

"Could be he just got the point," Barclay murmured. "She told him that money was in the plane."

"Oh," Barfield said. "Well, I wanted to see everything before I died, and now I have. A man over thirty who still believes women."

I felt sick. "Shut up, you punk." I said. "Put that bag down and throw a flashlight on it. There's one on the starboard bunk."

"I've got it here." Barfield put the bag down, flipped on the light and I looked at bundle after bundle of twenties, fifties, and hundreds.

I sold my jewelry and borrowed what I could on the car. It's the last chance we'll ever have. I don't know why they're trying to kill him; it was something that happened at a party—

"All right," I said. "Turn it off, Barfield."

"You're supposed to say, 'turn it off, you punk.' "

"Shut up," I said.

"How long would it take you to learn enough navigation, Joey?"

"Too long," Barclay answered. "Leave him alone."

"I was pretty good at math." Barfield said. "Want me to try it? I could get sick of this guy."

"Stop it," Barclay ordered curtly. "Even if we could find the place alone, we still need a diver."

"Anybody with an aqualung."

"George," Barclay said softly.

"All right. All right."

"What's in the plane?" I asked.

"Diamonds," Barclay answered. "Lots of diamonds."

"Whose?"

"Ours."

"And she knows about it?"

"Yes."

I wanted to hear it all. "And they weren't trying to get to Central America?"

"Yes, they were, at first. But Macaulay couldn't take her in the plane because he had to take a diver."

I was a chump. A sucker. I'd believed her. Even when I'd had intelligence enough to realize the story sounded fishy I'd still believed it. She wouldn't lie. Oh, no, of course not. Hell, how stupid could you get? She couldn't go in the plane because he'd had to add a fuel tank to stretch out its cruising radius. I was their last chance to escape; she had trusted me with all the money they had left – she must have been laughing herself sick all the time. I even imagined her telling her husband about it. *Dear, this poor sap will believe anything.*

And because I'd believed it I had killed that poor vicious little gunman and now the police would be looking for me as long as I lived. Only I wasn't going to be living very long. I was scheduled for extinction when I found Macaulay's plane and brought up what they wanted.

So was she. And wasn't that too bad? I wondered if she realized just what her chances were of selling Barclay and that big thug a sob-story of some kind. As soon as she told them where to look for that plane she was through. There should have been some satisfaction in knowing her double-crossing had got her killed as well as me, but when I looked for it it wasn't there.

So I was going back to feeling sorry for her? I was like hell. The dirty, lying, double-crossing – I stopped, puzzled. If she knew what was in the plane and where it was, why hadn't they grabbed her off long ago? Why had they kept trying to sweat Macaulay out of hiding so they could take him alive and make him tell, when they could have picked her up any time they pleased?

What the hell, was I still trying to find a way out for her? Of course they hadn't wanted her as long as there was a chance she would lead them to Macaulay. Her information about the plane would be second-hand, and they'd only taken her as second choice after Macaulay was dead. She was all they had left.

Well, I thought, they didn't have much.

14

Barclay had me set a course for west of Scorpion Reef. Barfield watched me plot it in the chartroom.

I gave Barclay the corrected course, and he let her fall off another point.

"Now," he said, "ever handle a sailboat, George?"

"No," Barfield replied, across from me. "But if your nipple-headed friend can do it, anybody can."

"Well, you won't have to," Barclay said. "Manning and I will split the watches. You'll be on deck when he has it and I'm asleep. Mrs Macaulay can have the forward part of the cabin; you, I, and Manning can sleep in the two bunks in the after part. And Manning won't go down there when one of us is asleep.

"It's after twelve now," he went on. "Get some sleep, George. Manning can stretch out here in the cockpit and I'll take the first watch, until six. When Manning relieves me, you'll have to come on deck."

I sat down, as near Barclay as I dared, and lit a cigarette. "It would be tragic," I said, "if he blew his stack and killed me before I found your lousy plane for you and the two of you could take turns at it."

"Why should we kill you?"

"Save it," I said. "I knew all along you wouldn't. Just give me a letter of recommendation. You know, something like: 'This will introduce Mr Manning, the only living witness to the fact that we killed Macaulay and that his widow is innocent—'"

"Not necessarily," he said. "You can't go to the police. You're wanted for murder yourself."

He knew I'd have everything to lose and nothing to gain. But if I were dead and lying somewhere in two hundred fathoms of water there was no chance at all. And .45 cartridges were cheap.

I moved a little nearer, watching his face. It was calm and imperturbable in the faint glow from the binnacle. I could almost reach him.

The eyes were suddenly full of a mocking humor. "Here," he said. He handed the .45 automatic to me butt first. "Is this what you want?"

For a fraction of a second I was too startled to do anything. Then I recovered myself and grabbed it out of his hand.

"You really wanted it?" he asked solicitously.

"Come about," I said. "Take her back to the seabuoy."

"What an actor!" His voice was amused.

"You don't think I'd kill you?"

"No."

"So it's not loaded?" Completely deflated, I pulled the slide back. I stared. It *was* loaded.

"You won't pull the trigger," he said, "for several reasons. You can't go back to Sanport, because of the police. You couldn't shoot a man in cold blood. You aren't the type—"

"Go on," I said.

"The third reason is that Barfield is down there in the cabin with another gun, with Mrs Macaulay. If you try anything, she gets it."

"I don't give a damn what happens to Mrs Macaulay," I said.

He smiled. "You think you don't, but that would change with the first scream. You don't have the stomach for that either."

"I'm the original gutless wonder. Is that it?"

"No. You're just weak in a couple of spots where you can't be in a business like this. I've sized you up since that afternoon at the lake."

"Then you knew what she was up to? That's the reason you shoved off and left us?"

"Naturally. Also the reason we roughed you up without really hurting you, that night on the beach. We wanted you to hurry and get this boat for them so we could find where Macaulay was hiding. It worked, except that he forced us to kill him. That's that, and now I'll take my gun back."

Sweat broke out on my face. I had only to squeeze the trigger, ever so gently, and there would be only one of them. He watched me coolly, mockingly.

My finger tightened. I didn't care what happened to her, did I? I cursed her silently, bitterly, hating her for being alive, for being here.

"George," Barclay said quietly.

I went limp. I handed the gun to him, feeling sick and weak all over.

"What is it?" Barfield's voice asked from the companionway.

"Nothing," Barclay said.

I lit a cigarette. My hands shook.

He had wanted me to realize the futility of jumping one of them to get his gun as long as she was where the other could get her. I detested her. Maybe I even actively hated her. She and her lying had ruined everything for me, I was sick with contempt when I thought of her, and yet he'd known he could tie my hands completely by threatening her with violence. I was "weak" all right.

"The hell with Mrs Macaulay," I said. "What did Macaulay do?"

"He stole three-quarters of a million dollars' worth of diamonds from us. Since you were in the salvage business," he went on, "you must have known the *Shetland Queen*."

I looked up suddenly. "Sure. I remember her."

She had gone down in about ten fathoms, off Campeche Bank last fall, and the underwriters had let a contractor salvage as much of the cargo as wasn't ruined. They had saved some machinery and several thousand cases of whiskey that somehow hadn't been smashed. The crew had been saved.

"So that's the first time your diamonds were dunked," I said. "But where does Macaulay fit in?"

I began to get the connection. Salvage – underwriters; the part about his being in the marine insurance business was true.

"They were aboard the *Shetland Queen*," continued Barclay. "But they didn't appear on the cargo manifest or any of the Customs lists. They were in some cases of tinned cocoa which were going to a small importing firm in New Orleans. A cheap way to ship diamonds but tough to explain if something happens to the ship, as in this case. The cocoa was insured, for two or three hundred dollars. We would have looked stupid trying to collect three-quarters of a million dollars from the underwriters when we'd paid a premium on a valuation of three hundred dollars. We couldn't explain that to Customs either.

"Benson & Teen had paid off all claims, including ours, and were salvaging what they could, but they weren't going to waste time bringing up a few dollars' worth of tinned cocoa. They paid, and wrote it off. We made a few feelers. Since they were working inside the ship anyway, why not bring up our cocoa and let us drop our claim? They brushed us. We let it drop, before they got suspicious. We had to wait until they were finished and then do our own salvaging.

"But then some – uh – competitors of ours got wise and also tried to buy the cocoa from Benson & Teen. This was a little too much for Macaulay, who was in charge of the operation. He sent a confidential agent down to the salvage operations to look into this chocolate business on the quiet. This guy asked to have the cocoa brought up and, since he was acting for Benson & Teen through Macaulay, they brought it up. He found out what made it so valuable, devalued it, and phoned Macaulay.

"They had two problems. The first was getting the stones into the States without paying duty or answering any embarrassing questions as to where they had come from. The second was to keep us from getting them. We had two men in the Mexican port keeping an eye on the cargo that was brought in. Macaulay solved both problems at once. He'd been a bomber pilot in the Second World War, and held a pilot's license. He came down to the Gulf Coast, chartered a big amphibian, and came after his agent and the stones. They were to meet in a laguna some ten or fifteen miles east of the Mexican port. They did, but our men were there too. They'd followed Macaulay's man and lost him in the jungle, but saw the plane coming in and got there just as the man was climbing aboard. They recognized Macaulay and opened fire, killing the other man, but Macaulay got away in the plane."

"With your stupid diamonds," I said.

He nodded. "We thought so. Macaulay didn't go back to New York, knowing what he was up against now. His wife disappeared also. The firm said he had suffered a heart attack and resigned. He'd told them, earlier, that he had to go to the coast because of illness in the family. We almost caught up to him two or three times. He never tried to sell any of the diamonds. We figured that, just about the time we ran him down in Sanport. He hadn't sold them because he didn't have them.

"He escaped us in Sanport, taking off in a plane with a man carrying an aqualung diving outfit. Macaulay, by the way, couldn't swim. When we learned about the diver, we knew what had happened. The metal box with the diamonds had fallen into the water when Macaulay's friend was killed.

"We stuck close to Mrs Macaulay, knowing she'd soon lead us to him. But just about that time we suspected he was back in Sanport because of a little story in the paper. About five days after Macaulay took off, a fishing boat docked with a man it had picked up in a rubber liferaft on the Campeche Bank. He told them he was a pilot for some Mexican company and had crashed while going from Tampico to Progreso alone in a seaplane. He took off the minute the fishing boat docked."

"I get it now," I said. "As soon as she got in touch with me you knew the castaway was Macaulay. And you realized he had crashed out there somewhere, but that he knew exactly where the plane was and could find it again, or he wouldn't have been trying to hire a diver."

Barclay nodded. "Correct. We also suspected he was in the house, but taking him alive wasn't going to be easy. He was armed and panicky."

"The thing that puzzles me," I said, "is that you and your meatheaded thugs never did put the arm on her to find out where the plane was. You're convinced now she knows where it is, but you let her come and go there for a week or more right under your noses."

"We weren't certain she knew *then*."

"But you are now. Why?"

He lit a cigarette. Sanport's lights were fading on the horizon.

"It's simple," he explained. "I wrote Macaulay a letter two days ago advising him to tell her."

I shook my head. "Say that again. You wrote him a letter – where?"

"To his house. Even if he weren't there she would get it to him."

"And he'd be sure to tell her, just because you suggested it? Why?"

He smiled again. "Sure, he was an insurance man, wasn't he? I just pointed out that there was always the chance something might happen to him and he ought to protect her."

"By telling her where the plane was?" I asked incredulously. "So he could guarantee her being put through the wringer by you—"

He shook his head gently. "You still don't see Macaulay's point of view. He knew she'd be questioned. But suppose she *didn't* know where the plane was?"

I saw the bastard's logic. "Good God—"

"Right. Life insurance. He was leaving her the only thing that could stop the interrogation."

I saw then what Macaulay must have gone through in those last few hours. He had to tell her.

I leaned my elbows on my knees and looked at him. "*You dirty son—*"

I stopped. I'd forgotten him. She'd been telling the truth.

Barclay had sent that letter to Macaulay only two days ago. I had to talk to her.

Barclay let me, too. He knew he was tying me tighter to Shannon and that I'd be easier to handle that way, so he called Barfield up. Barfield liked his sleep a lot more than he liked me. I could see his face burning as I went below.

She was lying on the starboard bunk with her face in her arms.

15

"Shannon," I said.

"What, Bill?" Her voice was muffled.

"How long have you known what these gorillas are after?"

She turned slowly and looked up with listless gray eyes.

"Since three this afternoon," she said.

I felt weak with relief or joy, or both of them. I'd been right. All the bitterness was gone and I wanted to take her in my arms. Instead I lit a cigarette. "I want to apologize," I said.

She shook her head. "Don't. I sold you out, Bill."

"No," I whispered. "You didn't know. I thought you had lied, but you hadn't. It doesn't matter that he was lying to you."

"Don't make it any worse, Bill. I had six hours to call you, and you could have got away. I tried to, but I couldn't. I thought I owed him that, in spite of what he did. Maybe I was wrong, but I think I'd still do it the same way. I don't know how to explain—"

"You don't have to," I said. "You were telling the truth all the time. That's all that matters."

She stared up at me. "Why does it?"

"I don't know," I said.

I wanted to shout it out to her, or sing it, but I kept my face blank and lit a cigarette for myself.

"I'm sorry about it," I said gently.

She didn't answer for a moment. Then she said, "It's all right. He didn't have a chance, anyway. I think they knew he was in the house, and anything we tried would have failed."

"Why hadn't he ever told you?" I asked.

"Ashamed, I think. He wasn't really a criminal, Bill. There

was just too much of it, and it was too easy, and no one would ever know."

"It's too bad," I said. "It's a dirty shame."

She turned her face a little, and her eyes met mine squarely. "You know I must have suspected it, don't you? Nobody could be stupid enough not to guess there must be more to it than he told me. I did suspect it. I can't deny it. I was cheating when I told you what he told me, because I was afraid it wasn't the truth, or not all the truth. But what could I do? Tell you I thought my husband was lying? Did I owe you more than I did him? Doesn't eight years of time mean anything, or the fact he had never lied to me before, or that he'd always been wonderful to me? I'd do it again. You'll just have to think what you will."

"You know what I think? I'll tell you about it some day."

"Wait, Bill," she whispered. "You don't know all of it yet. When you do, you'll think I'm a fool. He was going to leave me. He wasn't on his way to Honduras when he crashed. He was going to destroy the plane and disappear somewhere on the Florida coast."

I got it then. "And you'd have gone on to Honduras, thinking he would be there? And when he wasn't, you'd have been certain he was dead? Down somewhere in the Gulf, or in the jungle?"

"Yes," she said. Then she smiled a little bitterly. "But I wasn't the one he wanted to convince. If Barclay and his men had managed to follow me down there, they'd give him up as dead too."

"But running out on you? Deserting you, leaving you stranded in a foreign country?"

"Not quite stranded, if you mean money," she said. "You see, it wasn't in the plane. I thought it was, but it was in a bag of his I was supposed to bring down with me. None of it's clear-cut, Bill. He was leaving me, and he had to double-cross his friend who bought the plane, but he wanted me to have the money."

Conscience money, I thought.

Suddenly she was crying silently. "Does it make much sense to you that I still didn't call and tell you, after that?"

"Does it have to?" I asked.

She put both hands alongside her face and said slowly, around the tightness in her throat, "I don't know how to explain it.

When he told me that, I knew I would leave him, but I couldn't run out on him until he was safe."

I tried to see Macaulay, and failed again. How could he inspire that kind of loyalty on one hand and be capable of the things he had done, on the other? I said nothing about it because it might not have occurred to her and it would only hurt her, but he had killed that diver, or intended to until the airplane crash saved him the trouble. The way he had it planned, there couldn't be any second person who knew he was still alive. He'd probably killed him as soon as the poor devil brought up the box in that Mexican laguna. And he would have killed me, in some way.

Then I thought of something else. "Do you really know where that plane is?" I asked.

She nodded. "Yes. He told me very carefully. And I memorized everything he said."

I wondered. She thought she did. Barclay was convinced she did. But apparently I was the only one aboard who had any idea of the immensity of the Gulf of Mexico and the smallness of an airplane. If you didn't know within a few hundred yards you could drag for a thousand years and never find it.

Not that I cared if they found their stupid diamonds or not. It was something else. If they didn't, Barclay would think she was stalling. " — suppose she *didn't* know," he'd said softly. The implication was sickening.

"He didn't show you on a chart?" I asked. "Or make a drawing?"

"No," she said. "But it's near a shoal about fifty miles north-north-east of Scorpion Reef. It's around a half-mile long, running north and south. The plane sank two miles due east of it."

"Was there white water, or did he just see the shoal from the air before he crashed?"

"He didn't say."

That wasn't good. You had to assume too many things. You had to assume that Macaulay had known where he was himself and that the water was shallow enough at that spot to cause surf, so we could find it. If he'd merely seen a difference in the coloration of the water from above, we didn't have a chance. Then you had to have faith in his ability to estimate his bearing and distance from the shoal in the wild scramble to launch the rubber raft.

I tried to reassure myself. He could navigate, or he wouldn't have tried to fly the Gulf in the first place. He gave the location in reference to Scorpion Reef, so he must have sighted Scorpion. Fifty miles was only a few minutes in a plane, so he couldn't have gone far wrong in that distance. And there had to be visible white water. He'd been intending to go back to it in a boat, hadn't he? He must have known what he was doing.

Then something else struck me. "Wait," I said. "Barclay told me to set a course to the *west* of Scorpion Reef. Are you sure you said east?"

"Yes. He must have misunderstood. I said north-northeast."

"Just a minute," I said. I went out into the after part of the cabin and leaned over the chart. With the parallel rulers I laid down a line 33 degrees from Scorpion Reef, picked fifty miles off the edge of the chart with the dividers, and set them on the line. I stared. There was no shoal there.

Beyond, another 20 or 25 miles, lay the Northern Shelves, a wide area of shoaling water and one notation that three fathoms had been reported in 1907. Could he have meant that? But if he had, we didn't have a chance. Not a chance in the world.

In the first place, if he couldn't fix his estimated position within twenty-five miles that short a time after having sighted Scorpion Reef his navigation was so sloppy you had to throw it all out. There went your first assumption, the one you *had* to have even to start: that Macaulay had known where he was himself. And in the second place, that whole area was shoal. God knew how many places you might find white water at dead low tide with a heavy sea running. Trying to find an airplane with no more than that to go on was so absurd it was fantastic.

Fumbling a little with nervousness, I swung the rulers around and ran out a line NNW from Scorpion Reef. Barclay said she had told him that direction. I looked at it and shook my head. That was out over the hundred-fathom curve. Nothing there at all. And if he'd been headed for the Florida coast he wouldn't have been over there in the first place.

I thought swiftly. We'd never find that plane. To anybody even remotely acquainted with salvage work the whole thing was farcical except there was nothing funny about it here, under the circumstances. They were going to think she was stalling. She'd already contradicted herself once, or Barclay had misunderstood her.

Three-quarters of a million dollars was the prize. Brutality was their profession. I thought of it and felt chilly along the back.

16

I was still looking at the chart when the idea began to come to me. I looked at my watch. It was just a little less than two hours since we'd cleared the seabuoy. Guessing our speed at five knots would put us ten miles down that line. Growing excited now, I marked the estimated position and spanned the distance to the beach westward of us with the dividers. I measured it off against the edge of the chart. It was a little less than nine miles.

Hope surged up in me. We could do it. There was still enough glow in the sky over Sanport to guide us, and if there weren't all we had to do was keep the sea behind us and go downwind. The water was warm. You could stay in it all day without losing too much body heat.

I hurried back through the curtain and told her my idea.

She was scared. She couldn't swim very well, but when I told her there wasn't a chance in the world of finding that plane and that they'd kill us anyway, she agreed.

I told her to play sick, grab the belt as she got past Barfield, and go overboard holding it while I handled Barclay.

She nodded. "Thank you for everything," she said softly. She thought we were going to drown.

I put my hand against her cheek. "We'll make it," I said. Just touching her brought back that intense longing to take her in my arms. I stood up abruptly and went back on deck. It was very dark. Barfield growled something and went below. I sat down in the cockpit, on Barclay's right and as near him as I dared.

"Nice talk?" he asked.

"Very nice," I answered.

"She really didn't know what he was doing, did she?"

"No."

"Could be," he said.

My eyes were becoming accustomed to the darkness now. I looked astern and could still see the faint glow over the city.

Involuntarily, I shuddered. There was a lot of dark water between here and the shore.

"Did she tell you where the plane was?" Barclay asked.

"Yes," I said. I repeated what she had said, and asked, "Where did you get the impression it was west of Scorpion Reef?"

"That's what she said," Barclay answered. "She said NNW."

"She was suffering from shock," I said coldly. "I believe she had just seen her husband butchered in cold blood. And, anyway, it's a cinch he wouldn't have been to the westward of Scorpion Reef if he'd been heading for the Florida coast."

"Maybe," he said. "We'll see about it after breakfast. Get some sleep and don't try anything stupid."

I started to say something, but at that moment I heard voices in the cabin. She had started up.

"Where do you think you're going?" Barfield's voice growled.

"I – feel nauseated," she said. I could barely hear her. " – fresh air –"

"Hey, Joey," Barfield called out. "All right to let her up?"

I waited, holding my breath.

"No," Barclay said. "Find her a pail."

If she hadn't passed him we had no chance at all, but it was now or never. I swung. My fist crashed into the blurred whiteness of Barclay's face, and at the same time I yelled, "*Run!*"

Barclay fell back, clawing in his pocket for the gun. She came up through the hatch, moving fast, with Barfield shouting behind her. I could see her for a brief second, standing erect on the deck at the forward end of the cockpit with the bulky life-preserver clutched to her breast. Then she was lunging and falling outward, splashing somewhere in the darkness. I grabbed Barclay's jacket and pushed him into Barfield as he came lunging up. I slid over the rail, and water closed over me. Even as I was going down I tried to keep myself oriented.

The *Ballerina* was off course now, all of its angles gone. I started to swim back, hoping to spot her blonde head or the white of the life belt, but the whitecaps were confusing.

When the sloop was some 75 yards away, I lifted my head and called out, not too loudly, "Shannon. Shannon!" There was no answer. I wondered if I had gone beyond her. I began to be afraid, and called out again.

This time I heard her. "Here," she said. "Over this—" The

voice cut off, and I knew she had gone under. She was off to the left, downwind. I turned.

Another sea broke over me. Then I was floundering in the trough. The blonde head broke surface right beside me. "Thank God," I said silently, and grabbed her dress. She clasped her arms tightly about my neck and tried to pull herself up. We went under. I felt suddenly cold in water that was warm as tea. She had *both* arms about me.

Our heads came out. I shook water from my face. "Shannon! Where's the lifebelt?"

She sputtered and fought for breath. "It – I—" she said, and gasped again. "I lost it."

17

It was the bright sunlight streaming into the cabin that brought me out of it slowly. And then the wonderful nightmare of the night in the water came back to me. The lifebelt was gone, and she knew we couldn't make it. Yet she'd ignored Barclay's hailing from the *Ballerina* as he tried to locate us in the darkness. She'd been wonderful. Scared, but she'd followed my directions fully. Stripped for buoyancy, we tried the hopeless push toward Sanport, orienting on the stars.

It was dawn and we hadn't covered a third of the way, when I choked up enough breath to tell her.

"I couldn't tell you before," I said. "Even – if he had run out on you. But doesn't matter now. Have to tell you. I love you. You've never been out of my mind since you walked out on the edge of that pier—"

She didn't say anything. She brought her arms up very slowly and put them about my neck. We went under, our lips together, arms tight about each other. It was like falling endlessly through a warm, rosy cloud. I seemed to realize, very dimly, that it was water we were sinking through and that if we didn't stop it and swim up we'd drown right there, but apparently there was nothing I could do about it. I didn't want to turn her loose long enough to swim up. We went on falling, through warmth and ecstasy and colors.

We'd broken surface again, and then I'd seen the masts of the sloop. They were still looking for us. Suddenly I realized she'd let go, voluntarily. I'd gotten to her, even as I realized that the sloop was bearing down on us. Barclay'd made good use of those 7 x 50 binoculars. I remember Barfield's whistling as he dragged her aboard. Then I'd blacked out.

It was four in the afternoon when Barfield shook me awake. The husky guy hated my guts all right, but evidently Barclay had told him to lay off. He told me to make some sandwiches and coffee, wake Shannon, and get up on deck. It was while she was dressing and I was preparing the food that the idea came to me. If we could shake these two, all problems were solved. Why go back? Here was the *Ballerina*, the girl I knew I wanted, and eighty thousand dollars. We could change our names, get married in one of those little Caribbean ports. We'd change the name of the boat and its Port of Registry. We'd stay away from the big ports, cruise the world, and they'd never find us.

The dream faded abruptly. My two friends upstairs were calling from on deck. You couldn't dream them away.

I had five days, maybe a week. They had to slip up sometime – I hoped.

Shannon helped me bring the food.

Barclay was at the tiller, and Barfield lounged on the port side, his legs outstretched. He drew them in, and grinned. "Going for a swim, honey?" he asked.

She glanced briefly at him as if he were something that had crawled out of a ditch after a rain, and sat down on the starboard side holding the plate of sandwiches in her lap.

He looked to me. "Take the helm."

He took a sandwich, glanced at me and then at Shannon. "We're about fifty miles from land. Don't try any more swimming stunts and forget about the dinghy. I've thrown away the oars. We'll pistol whip you, Blondie, if either of you tries anything again.

"Now let's get down to business. Tell us exactly what your husband said about that plane crash."

Shannon stared at him, contemptuously.

"All right. It was late in the afternoon, he said, near sunset, when he picked up Scorpion Reef. He was heading for the Florida coast somewhere above Fort Myers. A few minutes later his starboard engine caught fire. He couldn't put it out, and knew he was going to crash. He had noticed a reef or shoal below him just a minute or two before, and tried to get to the downwind side of it, where the sea wouldn't be so rough, but he couldn't make it. He crashed on the east side of it, about two miles off, and the plane sank almost immediately. He just had time to climb out on a wing and throw the raft in the water. As you probably know, he couldn't swim at all."

"Why didn't he try to get the diamonds off with him?"

"He had stowed the box in a locker so it wouldn't go flying around in rough weather. The locker was aft, already under water."

"What about the diver?"

That hurt her. She hesitated, sickness in her eyes. "He said the man didn't have his belt fastened, and was killed in the crash."

Barclay lashed it at her suddenly, "Why was he so sure of his exact bearing from that reef? He didn't have time to take a compass reading before the plane went down, and he didn't have a compass on the raft."

She was quite calm. "It was late afternoon, I said. The sun was setting. The plane, the very northern end of the surf on the shoal, and the sun were all in one straight line."

She looked around suddenly at me. "I remember now, you asked me that, didn't you, Bill? Whether he could see surf from the raft. And I'd forgotten."

I nodded. It would make a difference, all right; but you still had to find the reef. It was hopeless.

Barclay lit a cigarette. "Okay. Now, what was the position?"

"Fifty miles north-northeast of Scorpion Reef."

He stared coldly. "You said westward last night."

"I'm sure I didn't," she replied.

"Make up your mind – fast."

"It's north-northeast."

"We'll see," he said crisply. "George, get that chart, the parallel rulers, and dividers."

Barfield brought them up and the two of them studied the chart. Shannon regarded them as if they were lice. Barclay's face was thoughtful. "North-northeast—"

I knew what he would find, and waited, tensely.

He picked the distance off and set the dividers along the line. Then he turned his head and stared bleakly at Shannon Macaulay.

"Come again?"

"You asked me what he told me," she said indifferently. "I have just repeated it, word for word. What else would you like me to do?"

"Tell the truth, for once."

"I am telling the truth."

He sighed. "The chartmaker was lying. The nearest sounding shown here is 45 fathoms." He paused and nodded to Barfield. "George."

I was too wild to be scared. "Listen, Barclay. This whole thing is going to come unzipped. If he hurts her, it's you I'm coming for, and you're going to have to use that gun to stop me. If you think you can find that reef without my help, go ahead."

It hung poised, ready to go either way. "Don't be a damned fool," I went on. "If she were going to lie, would she give you a stupid position like that? Maybe there is a shoal there, or somewhere within fifteen miles or so. All that area hasn't been sounded. Macaulay could have been off in his reckoning. The only thing to do is go there and see, and you'll never get there unless I take you. You name it. Now."

He saw I was right.

Barfield lounged on the seat with a cup of coffee in his hand. "The hero," he said. "We've got a real, live hero aboard, Joey."

The breeze held steady out of the northeast, day after day, and the miles ran behind us. I'd bought time for us, but I hadn't bought much, and every day's run was bringing us nearer the showdown. I knew what would happen when we got down there and couldn't find any shoal. Something had to happen before then; we had to get a break. But they didn't drop a stitch. When one was asleep the other was watching me, never letting me get too near. And there was always Shannon Macaulay. They had me tied, and they knew it. It was unique, a masterpiece in its own way; we were at sea in a 36-foot sloop, so all four of us had to be sitting right on top of the explosion if it came. I couldn't hide her or get her out of the way.

It was noon, the fourth day out of Sanport. I was working out our position on the chart when an idea began to nudge me. We wouldn't pass near enough to Scorpion Reef to sight it, so they had to take my word as to where we were. Barclay knew approximately, of course, because he checked the compass headings against each day's position, but he had to accept my figures for the distance run.

I was thinking. It might work.

Twenty or twenty-five miles beyond the point where Macaulay was supposed to have crashed lay the beginnings of the Northern Shelves. If there were a shoal or reef in a hundred miles it would be out there. The chances were a thousand to one that it was somewhere in that vast shallow area that he had actually gone into the drink, even though they were about a hundred billion to one against our ever finding where. So if I put us out there when they thought we were on the location she had given them—

We might find a shoal. And any shoal would do.

I set the little cross down 15 miles to the westward and a little north of our actual position and tore up my work sheet. Take ten miles out tomorrow noon and I'd have it made without exciting Barclay's suspicions. It was Wednesday. I told him we'd make it by Friday.

I didn't say anything to Shannon. The object of the whole thing was to get her off the boat, and if she knew why I wanted her off she wouldn't go. She'd have some foolish idea about not letting me face it alone, and I'd never convince her that alone was the only way I had a chance.

Barclay apparently suspected nothing as he checked positions with me the next day. In fact he seemed satisfied with the efforts I had been taking all that day. We kept looking for white water, listening for the sound of surf breaking; but no signs of shoal appeared.

Barclay had become more quiet, cold, and unapproachable as Friday wore on and we saw nothing.

Barfield's face was ugly as he watched Shannon now, and several times I saw him glance questioningly at Barclay. We were all in the cockpit. I had the tiller.

"Listen," I said harshly. "Both of you. Try to get it through your heads. We're not looking for the corner of Third and Main. There are no street signs out here. We're in the general area. But Macaulay could have been out ten miles in his reckoning. My figures could be from two to five miles out in any direction. Error adds up."

He was listening, his face expressionless.

I went on. I had to make them see. "When Macaulay crashed, there was a heavy sea running. There's not much now but a light groundswell. There could have been surf piled up that day high enough to see it five miles away, and now you might think it was just a tide-rip. We've got to criss-cross the whole area, back and forth. It may take two days, or even longer."

He looked coldly at me. "Don't take too long."

Dawn came, the sea was empty and blue as far as the eye could see.

Barclay took the glasses and stood up, scanning the horizon all the way around. Then he said, "Make some coffee, George."

Barfield grunted and went below. In a few minutes Barclay followed him. I could hear the low sound of their voices in the cabin. She sat across from me in the cockpit, her face stamped with weariness. When she saw me looking at her she tried to smile.

I turned and hurried back to her. "Go forward," I said. "Lie down on deck, against the forward side of the cabin. Stay there. If anything happens to me, you can raise the jib alone. Just the jib. Keep running before the wind in a straight line and you'll hit the coast of Mexico or Texas—"

"No," she whispered fiercely.

I peeled her arms loose and pushed her. "*Hurry!*" She started to say something more, looked at my face, and turned, running forward. She stepped up from the cockpit and went along the starboard side of the cabin, stumbling once and almost falling.

I had to hurry. They'd be coming up any minute. I slipped forward and stood on the deck, looking down the hatch.

"*Surf!*" I yelled. "Surf, ho!"

Barclay came up fast, his head turning toward the direction of my arm. I hit him hard and he went sprawling over the side. I was falling too, on top of Barfield as he emerged from the hatch. He bulled his way up on deck, crashing us both down on the deck. A big fist beat at my face, as I groped for his throat. He got his gun out of his hip pocket. I chopped his hand hard enough, and it slid out of his hand along the grating.

He hit me on the temple and my head slammed back against the planks. He was coming to his knees, groping behind him for the gun. I tried to push myself up, and then beyond him I saw her. She ran along the deck and dropped into the cockpit.

She picked up the gun and was swinging it at his head. He should have fallen, but it had no more effect on him than a dropped chocolate eclair. He heaved upward, lashing out behind him with one big arm. She fell, and her head struck the coaming at the forward end of the cockpit. I came to my feet and lunged at him and we fell over and beyond her onto the edge of the deck just as the sloop rolled again and we slid over the side into the water.

I came out into sunlight and sparkling blue, and sobbed for air. Seconds went by, and I knew he wasn't coming up. He'd had the breath knocked out of him when we hit the deck, just before we slid overboard, and he'd drowned down there. I looked around again. There was no trace of Barclay.

I could hear the boat's engine behind me, fainter now, and I turned to see which way it was circling. I stared. It wasn't turning. It was two hundred yards away, going straight ahead for Yucatan with nobody at the helm. I didn't see her anywhere. She'd been knocked out when she fell. And I had lashed the tiller.

I reached down mechanically and started taking off my dungarees and slippers.

Even when you don't have anywhere to go, you keep swimming. I swam toward the boat, disappearing now, and toward the coast of Yucatan a hundred and twenty miles away. The sun was on my left. It climbed higher.

I didn't panic, but I had to be careful about letting the loneliness and immensity of it get hold of me or thinking too much about how near we had been to winning at last. I wondered if she had been killed, or badly hurt, and saw in a moment that wasn't safe either. I concentrated on swimming. One stroke, and then another stroke. Don't think. Don't think about anything.

It could have been an hour, or two hours. I looked off to the right and saw the mast. It was at least a mile away and wouldn't see me, but I gave a sob of relief that almost strangled me because it meant she was all right. She'd only been knocked out. She'd probably never find me, but she could make it.

But the time I'd spent showing Shannon navigational and boat-handling points paid off. She had no idea where I'd gone overboard, but she was cutting the whole area into a big grid, searching.

Each time the groundswell lifted me, I kicked myself as high as I could and waved. Those binoculars paid off. I could see the boat headed toward me, and I knew that Goddess had her ancestral Viking fates working for us at last.

19

We didn't have to do much talking about the way we felt. About all I could say for the next few days was "You Swede, you big, lovely, magnificent Swede." She seemed equally happy. I tried to brush aside the cloud that haunted her. Her last months with Macaulay; the strain of the chase had cut into her more deeply than I realized. I repeated the plans I had for changing the name of the boat and its port of registry; for cruising the small ports where we'd be safe from any pursuit for the eighty thousand dollars which would take care of us both for a long time. She smiled agreement each time, but her eyes gave her away. Several times she awoke at night shivering and I knew it wasn't the tropical breezes. Something continued to haunt her, to keep her from the full paradise that should have been ours.

Time stood still for us. I spent the next few days painting the name, *Freya*, and San Juan as our port of registry on the stern. My living Freya – she liked that better than Swede – helped. She was a natural at anything you taught her. She learned to use the aqualung and we spent hours at it, diving down to look at the myriad wonders of marine life. She became fascinated with it as if it were another world.

And then it happened. We were far off the Northern Shelves working toward the Yucatan straits. The chart told me we were right on the hundred-fathom curve. It was a very hot sunny day and Shannon suggested we go in for a swim. She was beautiful as she adjusted her mask and dived over the side. I fixed my mask and went under the hull to see if we'd begun to collect any marine growth. It was cool and pleasant, and I paused to watch the silvery flow of hair about her head as she swam beneath me.

A few minutes later I noticed a small shovel-nosed shark off to one side and below. I swam down to watch him. It was quite small and not dangerous. When I looked for Shannon she was gone. I swam to the surface but she was nowhere in sight. I began to be uneasy. But maybe she had gone back aboard for some reason. I was turning to look behind me again when a flash of silver caught the corners of my eyes at the edge of the mask. I froze with horror. She was at least a hundred feet below me, going straight down.

Why had she done it? It had been an accident. It must have been. She was deliriously happy with me. She had no reason for throwing her life away. The pressure must have twisted her sense of direction. She'd been confused, and I'd been too far away to help.

No! She'd known exactly what she was doing. There had been hints. She'd known the violence and the terror of being hunted and had said there's no escape. That's why she'd looked at me as if I were an innocent child when I ranted about those little ports. She knew we'd never get away with it.

Alone, I found myself sighting again for 23.50 north, 88.45 west, the spot where she'd gone down. Macaulay could be right. It could be possible to find a pinpoint in the Gulf. There was the exact spot! See, where that seagull is on that driftwood. Looking down into the water I could see a silvery shape.

It was beckoning up at me. I heard her voice say, "Come with me, we'll live in rapture."

Something heavy was on my shoulders. I felt straps across my chest. I was wearing the aqualung.

I screamed.

I can still close my eyes and see the whole thing – the blue, and that last, haunting flash of silver, gesturing as it died. It was beckoning. Toward the rapture. The rapture . . .

20

It was after 2 a.m. when the master of the *Joseph H. Hallock* closed the journal. The poor devil, he thought. The poor, tortured devil. Four o'clock – and we raised the sloop a little after five.

Changing the name of the sloop didn't alter the identity of any kind of seagoing craft. There were papers. And more papers. It was as futile as writing your own name on a borrowed passport. Manning should have known, too, that it took about ten pounds of paperwork and red tape to dock at any foreign port – including fishing villages. They all had port authorities, and they all demanded consular clearances and bills of health from the last port of call; registry certificate, Customs lists, crew lists, and so on, ad infinitum, and in the case of pleasure craft they probably required passports and visas for everybody aboard. Manning should have known they didn't have a prayer of a chance.

He was in his bunk puzzling over it. Suddenly he sat upright. "I'll be damned," he said softly. "I'll just be damned. It would be perfect."

It was sunset again, two days later. The tanker was waddling, full-bellied, up the coast of Florida just south of Fowey Rocks. She was well inshore from the main axis of the Stream, since they had made arrangements by radio to have a Coast Guard boat meet them off Miami and take the *Freya* off their hands. Or at least that was the master's excuse to Mr Davidson, the mate.

When you resolved the contradiction and acknowledged that Manning couldn't possibly have believed any of that moonlit dream about escape to the tropics in a boat, he mused, what did you have left? You had left the twin facts that Manning was a writer, and that he was trying to save himself and that girl he was so much in love with.

They had nowhere to go, the girl had said. Nowhere to go, that is, as long as they were being sought by a gang of criminals and also by the police. But if they weren't being actively sought by anyone, they could come back to their own country, where they would attract less attention than anywhere else on earth. And they would no longer be sought if everyone believed them dead.

But I don't know any of this, he thought. I'm only theorizing. I don't really want to know, absolutely and finally, because I'd be obligated to report it. They hadn't committed any real crime, unless it was a crime to defend oneself, and he hoped they got away with it.

Then he saw what he had been watching for, astern and slightly inshore from the *Freya*. It could be driftwood, or it could be a head, or two heads. He peered aft in the gathering twilight, and almost raised the glasses.

No, he thought reluctantly; if I *know* I have to report it. But nobody is interested in the unverified vaporings of a sentimental old man.

They would make it ashore without any trouble, with the lifebelts. And they probably had enough money to buy some clothes to replace their bathing suits. Not that they would be likely to attract any attention in Florida, however, if they went around in their bathing attire for years.

But they were drifting back rapidly. Would he have to lift the glasses to satisfy himself? The objects separated momentarily for an instant before they merged again as one. And one of them had been definitely lighter in color than the other. The master sighed.

"Bon voyage," he said softly. He turned and went into the chartroom with the glasses still swinging from his neck.

THE TASTING MACHINE

Paul Cain

In fine weather, of which there was a spate that summer, it was the whim of M. Etienne de Rocoque to emerge from his restaurant in East Sixty-first Street at exactly six-thirteen of an evening and stroll west to Fifth Avenue, south to Sixtieth, east to Park Avenue, north to Sixty-first, and so back to the restaurant and home. It had been discovered by long and diligent experiment that the time he now habitually chose for these somewhat circumscribed excursions was the approximate sixteen minutes between the last home-hurrying stragglers of the commercial day and the first diversion-bent explorers of the night: the streets were comparatively deserted.

He was invariably accompanied by Bubu, a Nubian dwarf, who trotted about two paces behind and a little to the left of his master carrying a narghile from which the latter drew long, deeply pleasurable puffs of green Surinam tobacco, dispensed them in great green clouds upon the silky evening air. They were – Etienne globular and enormous in polka-dotted seersucker and Persian slippers, wielding a vast palmetto fan, Bubu tiny and tatterdemalion in a ragged cloth-of-gold jerkin, his eager little ape-face glistening like an eggplant – a striking and somehow heartwarming pair.

Etienne's immensity had confounded medical science, most especially biochemistry, for a long time. Early in life he had worn his liver and certain other gastrically essential equipment down to tenuous and entirely decorative nubbins, had at the time we now observe him subsisted on thin cornmeal gruel and distilled water for upwards of eleven years, but he still tipped the scale at three hundred and three pounds in his shantung shorts. This anomaly had led at least one Harvard professor, nameless here, who had devoted most of his mature life to protein research, shrilly to cry "No!" and fling himself backwards into the Charles River.

On the evening with which this tale is most intimately concerned, a wisteria cab drew close to the curb as Etienne and Bubu were waiting for the light to change at Madison Avenue, a man wearing a curly, obviously false beard thrust his head out and went "His-s-st!" Etienne, after a brief glance, continued across the street, west; he *never* spoke to strangers.

As they crossed Park Avenue on the homeward lap, the wisteria cab again stopped directly in front of them with a thin shriek of brakes, and the man again popped his head out of the window hoarsely to whisper, "His-s-st! I must speag to you!" His accent was deep Balkan Peninsula, darkly belying his blond beard and what Etienne now, on second inspection, saw to be an even blonder wig. For answer, he exhaled a thick cloud of green smoke which momentarily obscured the entire cab and when it had cleared away, they were alone. Bubu giggled soundlessly; they went home.

There, doffing his slippers and wilted seersucker, Etienne enjoyed a tepid shower, then wandered in monstrous nakedness to a front window of his living quarters above the restaurant, peeped; as he had more than half suspected, the cab was across the street. He snapped his fingers. Bubu, slicing a pomegranate in the kitchen, two floors below and in the rear of the house, though mute, was gifted with preternaturally acute hearing, jumped at the first snap and galloped up the stairs.

"Go" – Etienne indicated the cab – "Go and bid the bearded stranger enter."

Bubu grimaced up at him in stunned wonder for a moment and, after a simple handspring, clattered down the stair. Gertrude, the myna bird, who had been indulging in unaccustomed silence since Etienne's return, now, after a deep sigh, sang out, "Man the pumps, men – we're heading into a sou'wester." There was often a certain incongruity in Gertrude's pronouncements, in that while her words and usually her sentiments were most uncouth, her diction was perfect – perhaps a little too much so.

Etienne watched Bubu scuttle across the street and make signs to the stranger, then crossed to sit on a wide divan; in a matter of moments the stair creaked – a touch ominously, he thought – Gertrude gave with a thick and obscene guffaw, and Bubu, bowing to the floor, waved the bearded man into the room.

He was a young man, thin of shank and broad of shoulder – a tall young man with a kind of steely beauty about him. He wore a simple black sack suit, black sneakers, a plain white shirt, and a arrow black four-in-hand tie, carried a large squarish object in Christmas paper: a bit of an anachronism because it was the middle of July. Etienne inclined his head towards a nearby chair, and the young man gratefully sank into it, put the obviously heavy package on the floor between them.

"I am moz happy you decide to speag wiz me now," he gurgled, "elz I'ave to bozzer you day after day until you do."

Etienne nodded almost imperceptibly. "You may as well remove your whiskers," he suggested, "and your wig." He picked up the big palmetto fan, fanned. "It is very warm."

"Ett eez eendeed," said the young man. "Zank you, zank you!" And whipping off his blondness he shoved it into his pocket, disclosing a long tanned Greco face, also bearded, but blue-black, a cap of shiny blue-black hair.

"The accent, too, is obviously a strain," Etienne went on after a moment. "It is entertaining at first but would wear on me terribly in a little time. Shall we dispense with it?"

"Very well, sir," the young man said in perfect English, a touch stiffly.

"And now" – Etienne's roving, faintly amused eyes had come to rest upon the gaudily sealed and beribboned package – "and now, what, in an exceedingly banal but blessedly short phrase, have we here?"

"Ah! . . ." The young man leaned slowly forward until his long nose almost touched a kind of conical projection protruding from the top of the package; his dusky gaze was fixed upon the small still life – a pear, a pipe, a mandolin – that Braque himself had tattooed upon Etienne's left chest these many years ago. "Ah, Monsieur de Rocoque," he intoned breathlessly, "we have here the answer to all your problems, all your prayers – the dearest wish of your heart . . . We have here," his nose grazed the conical projection, "the Tasting Machine . . ."

Etienne's, it must be stated somewhat parenthetically here,

is not a restaurant in the ordinary sense. No one can buy a meal there – a *plat*, a sweet, nor even a glass of wine. Etienne de Rocoque, de Cuisine Transcendantale, is infinitely beyond being a restaurateur and has so been for many years. His is a clientele conspicuous for its far-flung sparseness, an even hundred pampered stomachs scattered about the earth. But once each month or so he plans and cooks and serves one dinner, or one luncheon, or, perhaps, even a breakfast, and to that boon are invited two or three – five on a really festive occasion and *never* more than seven – of the fortunate few who grace his guest list.

From Montreux comes, mayhap, the Duc d'Ange, Montfiore Toeplitz from Madrid, Ling Hang Lo from Chungking, The Hon. Jezebel Gapeingham, O.B.E. from Bath. And Etienne, in this time, redolent of steam and sweat and spices, lopes about his kitchen plucking gastronomic pearls, one after another, out of his pots and pans and ovens to set before these favored four and finally, wilting with joy, presides at table – to taste, alas, only their pleasure.

There is his cross. It is not so much that he cannot share these viands, these fabled wines with them – the pain of that is dulled by years – but that his whole life is limited now, designed for, geared to, actually *dependent* upon their appreciation of his work, their grunts and groans and low-pitched moans of ecstasy. Here is the crux of the matter, then – whisper it softly, softly – even the most superlatively attuned palate sickens of wonder, in time . . . There is his cross . . .

Etienne had paled. This, a phenomenon of whiteness which, even when he was fully clothed, had been known to affect the beholder with a kind of nameless terror, was now, in his huge nudity, little short of stupefying. The young man drew back, closed his eyes. Bubu ran to hide his head in a corner; Gertrude hummed a bar of "Throw out the Life-line," delicately belched. Then Etienne's blood surged to his veins again and he pinkened back to life.

"What do *you* know, dark youth," he demanded in a thunderous whisper, "of *my* problems, *my* prayers, *my* heart's dearest wish?"

"That which I do not know I have divined," said the young man quietly, opening his eyes. "Such is the frailty of flesh that you have come now, finally, to founder in perfection."

Etienne pondered this at length. Here, in a simple and felicitous turn of phrase, this extraordinary fellow had named his malady. Perfection . . .

"And how," he slowly lowered his stare to the package, "and what has this contraption to do with me?"

"Everything."

"And how did you come by it?"

"I invented it."

The young man had leaned forward to tear off almost savagely the ribbons, the bright paper; a glossily dark gray box resembling a small phonograph was revealed, its simplicity marred only by four jointed metal arms on one side, folded now, at the extremities of which were deftly welded a knife, a fork, a spoon, and a kind of two-pronged hook. There was a small round aperture in the same side, and the conical projection on top, which now turned out to be a plexiglass tube containing a single hair-thin filament.

"I invented it," the young man repeated, then breathed devoutly, "for you."

Bubu had turned from the corner, and Gertrude swooped to light upon his shoulder; together they approached to examine the gift with timid skepticism. It is typical of Etienne that he did not laugh, nor smile, nor anything, but accepted the validity of the machine as easily as he would have accepted the color of an Oncidium orchid – not so much from naïvete as from a kind of congenital innocence of cynicism.

And now, although the young man had pressed no buttons, turned no knobs, Etienne momently became aware that the machine was working. There was a deep but gentle whirring sound and slowly, very slowly, one of the metal arms – the one with the fork – was unfolding, reaching out and – *snick*! – it had suddenly speared the largest, ripest, and most luscious grape from a cluster on a nearby salver. Quickly it carried this dripping, glittering morsel to the aperture and popped it in; the filament glowed, ever so faintly and then – Etienne felt his whole soul shudder slightly with gratification – the machine sighed . . .

Softly, languidly, it heaved a tiny sigh of satisfaction.

"Observe that, having chosen the best grape on the bunch, it spurns the rest," the young man murmured. "It, too, is designed only for perfection . . ."

But now the two-pronged hook was reaching towards the salver, seized, with the speed of light, a magnificently unblemished tangerine. The knife went snicker-snee and peeled it in a twinkling. It, too, disappeared into the aperture, and the machine moaned gently, slaveringly smacked its internal lips.

Bubu clapped his heavily bejeweled hands tinklingly in small Nubian delight. Gertrude whistled shrilly, warbled "Damn my eyes – but that's a pretty sight!" Etienne rose. The young man stirred, smiled up at him.

"No longer," he crooned, "shall you be subject to the idiosyncrasies of your patrons' moods, Monsieur: quirks of digestion, ravages of time, and repletion upon the taste buds and the gastric system. No longer need your spirit cringe beneath the human equation with all its foibles and fallibilities . . ." He rose. "The Machine is infallible. Its taste is exquisite. And" – his lips curved for a split second to something almost frighteningly like a sneer – "it will never wear out . . ."

They stood there. The thin suggestion of a sneer had swiftly gone from the young man's mouth, and he was smiling almost tenderly. Gertrude chortled, screeched, "Damn my bloody eyes!" and flew back to her perch. The cuckoo clock on the floor below distantly caroled seven.

"This is it" – Etienne groped for adequate words – "this, indubitably, is beyond adequate words . . . But how did you know? And what, dark youth, is your name?"

"I divine . . ." The young man extracted a square of cobalt linen from his sleeve and gently blew his nose. "And my name is Vincent."

"If you have divined this" – Etienne had squatted to examine more closely the wondrous mechanism; it was silent now, its filament cold, its arms demurely folded – "then, Vincent, you have divined that, though penniless, I am vastly rich in jewels and doo-dads and sundry tokens that admirers of my art have left for me."

The young man nodded, his face expressionless.

Etienne rose again and stroked his jowls. "My treasure chests and coffers bulge and overflow with diamonds, rubies, square-cut emeralds. Ask what you will."

The young man slowly shook his head.

"But," Etienne fell back apace, "I cannot accept this miracle as a gift!"

The young man stopped shaking his head; his voice was barely audible: "I had thought, rather, of a trade, Monsieur."

Etienne beamed. "A trade! Excellent! Then name it!"

The young pan's eyes were fixed upon the small still life that Braque had wrought.

"I had thought, Monsieur," he said, "of Mercedes . . ."

There was a moment of fraught silence. Then Bubu hid his face in his hands, sank to the floor, and frightfully, soundlessly sobbed; Gertrude screamed raucously, "Man the lifeboats, men! Stand by to abandon ship!" Etienne? Etienne was as one turned to stone; his lips framed the word, but no sound came forth.

The young man whispered, "Mercedes," smiled, then stooped to pluck a single grape from the salver and consume it.

"Mercedes . . ."

In the immediately ensuing three and one-half seconds, an aeon of time, a universe of space, a billion thoughts crowded through Etienne's brain, simmered away to these:

How did this young upstart know of Mercedes – and what? Mercedes, whose skin was as the petals of the moonflower, whose hair was Thracian silk, whose mouth was carven, yielding coral. Mercedes, whom he, Etienne de Rocoque, had, after wading through veritable seas of blood, snatched from the harem of a mighty caliph at the age of three and reared in luxury these fifteen years, inviolate from the world. Mercedes, who even now he could hear splashing happily in her perfumed bath. Never had she set her perfect foot beyond his door – yet this unspeakable poltroon had mouthed her name! How? *How?*

And then he saw that Bubu, feigning still to sob, had crawled behind the villainous youth and now was winking up at his master invitingly. All he need do is push – and push he did; Vincent, taken entirely unawares, stumbled back with one of the unintelligible oaths favored by knaves and varlets, turned a highly unlikely double somersault, and smacked his skull smartly against the newel post.

"Quickly," bellowed Etienne, "into the freezer with him!" And moving with well-nigh incredible speed, he snatched up the youth's limp upper body, Bubu grabbed his feet, and they clattered down the stairs.

Gertrude slowly raised one pink and wrinkled talon to scratch her ear. "Glory be to God," she muttered. She sat thinking for a time in silence, jumped when she heard the door of the freezer slam two floors below. Then, conscious of something moving in the room, she turned, looked down; the Tasting Machine, by some means of locomotion known only to God and its inventor, had crept across to just beneath her perch, its fork was poised, *whish-t-t* through the air at the exact moment Gertrude took wing, snipped out one of her tail feathers.

She alighted on the topmost branch of the rubber plant and, breathing heavily, watched it in frightened fascination.

"Glory be to God," she muttered. "Glory be to God . . ."

In Etienne's kitchen and pantries adjacent thereto, there were seven refrigerators. There was one, to begin little, with a capacity of a shade under one hundred and two cubic inches, limited to caviar and the eleven, perfect daisies which he affected as a centerpiece at his rare dinners. There was one for ices, sherbets, mousses, and star sapphires (he had a theory that sapphires are at their best at 16.6 degrees Centigrade and always kept his at that temperature), one for certain cheeses, one for fish, one for fruit, and one for miscellaneous. And there was the Crucifreeze . . .

This formidable compartment, the largest and coldest of the lot, was the masterpiece of L. Shiver & Sons. Hung there in rigid, frost-glazed putrefaction a brace of woodcock that Etienne himself had shot in the late summer of 1924. Hung there a collection of meat and game to slaver the mouths of the gods: goose and grouse, bear and bull, moose and manatee, teal and terrapin. Hung there, now, between a haunch of venison and a neatly halved wild boar: Vincent.

The temperature in the Crucifreeze averaged thirty-two degrees *below* zero, and even in the moment they were within, hanging Vincent up by his heels, Etienne's nakedness turned a pale and rather interesting azure. They hurried out, and he closed and double-locked the door. Bubu scurried around in small, tight circles in sheer excitement, and Etienne, sitting himself down tailor fashion on the meat block, fell to examining the objects that had fallen from Vincent's pockets when they turned him upside down.

There was a business card:

VINCENT VINCENT INC.
"You name it – We invent it."
Purple Building
808 Lexington Avenue RH 4-6509

There were four sonnets "To Mercedes", a package of Home run cigarettes, a nickel, three dimes, and an Egyptian penny. There were two keys tied together with sulphur-yellow ribbon: one was to Etienne's back door, the other was to Mercedes' apartment, which comprised the second floor of the house.

Etienne goggled down at these in agape amazement. It must be understood that no man but Etienne and Bubu (who didn't count, because he was a eunuch) had looked upon Mercedes' beauty – and lived – since he had abducted her, at the tender age of three, from the seraglio of Yussuf Ben in Khur. True, he allowed her to fly her kite from the roof in pleasant weather, but she was always heavily veiled and . . .

The kite! He leaped from the meat block and dashed up the back stairs, snatched up a vast towel in passing, wrapped it around his middle, and emerged on the roof. There it was, two hundred yards or so to the north, northeast – the Purple Building! What simpler than for Mercedes to choose a day when the wind was right to communicate, kitewise, with Vincent Vincent, if she so chose? He staggered back and would have fallen if Bubu, who had followed close behind, had not supported him, and for the third time that evening Etienne paled.

"Perfidy," he piteously wailed, "thy name is woman!" Leaning on Bubu's shoulder, he reeled back down the stairs.

It must here be made of record, somewhat painful record, that Etienne, king among chefs, was a veritable emperor among lovers. The words he whispered into Mercedes' shell-like ears were pure poetry; each morning, noon, and night his impassioned wooing discovered some new expression to delight her heart, bauble to adorn her white perfection, *outré* and exquisite confection to tempt her tongue. Except, and now we come to the painful part, except for one little thing.

When, in the carefree years of his extreme youth's extremity, Etienne had by dint of Gargantuan eating and drinking bouts destroyed his digestion, he had also, in spectacular excesses of amorous dalliance, played frightful havoc with his glandular organization. And so, perforce – it must be faced – his well-nigh perfect lovemaking was only well-nigh perfect.

At Mercedes' door he dismissed Bubu with a heartrending smile, unlocked the door with Vincent's key, and crossed the tiny cuneus foyer to the bedchamber. Mercedes was still in her bath. He stood a moment listening to her laughter, listening to her sweet voice lifted in a childish song, then crossed to the eastern window. It commanded a perfect view of the Purple Building. In the bottom drawer of a commode he found a *Bluejacket's Manual of Semaphore Signaling*, a pair of binoculars, tracing paper that bore the outline of two keys. The evidence was complete and irrefutable. But one thing more he must discover – had the keys been used?

He sat down on a vermilion taffeta tuffet and considered ways and means of Mercedes' execution. Shooting, stabbing, blunt instruments were emphatically out of the question. To mar the wondrously wrought ivory of that beloved body! Etienne shuddered, gulped in pain. Poison, perhaps, something swift and pleasant to the taste. And then she came into the doorway, fresh from her bath, still with the tinkling song upon her lips, and he looked upon her beauty and knew that he could never murder her.

"Darling," she said, and her voice was a golden bell, "I am of delight to see you." She crossed to him and stooped and kissed his forehead. Her mouth was like warm silk.

"Have I been good to you?" he asked, a little tremulously.

"You have been to me an angel," she said simply. "You are the kindest and best man in all the world, and with all my heart I love you."

"Have I ever denied you anything?" The Braque still life beneath his left nipple quivered slightly. "Had you not but to wish for Richebourg '04, or spun-glass slippers, or" – he bobbed his head at her bed in the opposite corner – "a platinum-mounted trundle bed?"

"You have denied me nothing. You are my bounteous and most munificent lord and master." Her eyes had fallen on the damning evidence which he had spread out on the tuffet. "And now, because of mistaken jealousy, I am about to die."

"Mistaken!" It was a broken cry from a breaking heart. "Mistaken?"

She sat down beside him, tenderly fondled his toes. "Mistaken, my love. It all began so innocently, Etienne, almost in jest, this gentle nightmare."

"Jest!"

She nodded. Her enormous eyes flooded with tears for a moment. She dried them with a tiny kerchief, snuffled delicately, went on:

"One day, less than a month agone, my kite, caught in a capricious downdraft, disappeared into an open window of the building there, and when I drew it down, someone had written upon it; these were the words: 'Veiled enchantress of the roof, I am a poor inventor dry of inspiration and close to perishing. Let me look but once upon your face before I go. I ask no more!'

"What harm, thought I," she continued, "what harm in granting this poor devil his dying wish, and so, only for an instant, mind you, I lowered my veil. That, I thought, was an end of it."

"What harm," Etienne echoed hollowly. "What harm!"

"But no!" Mercedes rose, paced to the door and back in obvious agitation. Dear Allah, thought Etienne, what loveliness. "No," she said, sinking down beside him, "a few days later my kite once more – what Fates and Furies direct these things? – swooped to that window, and this time he wrote, 'A plot's afoot against your master, Etienne de Rocoque, and we must join in a counterplot to foil it!' "

"A plot!" Etienne half rose, sank back.

"Aye. And dangling from my kite were these." She indicated the binoculars, manual, tracing paper. "Through infinite trial and error, I learned to communicate with him by semaphore from the window there. He swore that if I breathed a word to you about this dark conspiracy against you, all was lost. He told me his name, learned mine."

"The plot then, what of that?" Etienne cried. "Who was involved?"

Mercedes shook her head. "I begin now to believe that it was only a figment, a tissue of lies," she said. "Because," she lowered her eyes, and her whole delightful body flushed a fragile pink, "a week ago he sent me a sonnet."

"By wigwag?"

She nodded.

"The keys, then," he demanded gently, "what of the keys?"

"That was before," she murmured. "He said that he must have some means of gaining entrance to the house, to – these were his words – 'Nip the fiendish designs upon de Rocoque in the bud, just as they are about to flower.' "

Etienne sighed. "My child, my sumptuous child," he patted her hand, "you have been taken in."

"I know it now!" She leaped to her feet and danced a little dance. "I know it now, my own true love, my king, my benefactor. But I did it all for you! Can you forgive?"

"The keys," Etienne's voice was barely audible, "he never used the keys?"

"Never." Her innocence was a sword, a shield, a banner. "Never!"

Etienne was smiling, went on in a shaky whisper: "And the Tasting Machine. What of that?"

She stopped in mid-pirouette and gazed at him in puzzlement. "The what?"

"This varlet Vincent followed me home a little while ago. He had a machine that he said he had invented especially for me, and when I asked its price, he said – Etienne's voice broke a touch – "its price was you."

Her petaled face darkened; a half-hue with anger, curved to a kind of agony. She caught her breath. "The knave," she muttered in a small spasm of loathing. "The unspeakable blackguard! What have you done with him?"

Etienne rose. "I have put him away," he said, "in a place where he may dwell for a little while upon the bitter lees of vanity and youthful presumption. For only a little while, my sweet. Then I shall burden him with gold and jewels and send him on his way."

"And the Machine?"

"It is an interesting novelty. At some time after nine I am expecting guests, the first in several months. It may amuse them." He crossed to the door.

"I want to see it!" She ran to him, clapping her hands in childish joy. "I *must* see it!"

"Later," he said, and he stooped to kiss her nose. "Later, my one . . .

Then he went out through the tiny foyer, closed and locked the door.

When Etienne came to the front room of his own apartment on the third floor, the day was duskening, there was the small drum of distant thunder. He turned on the lights, and saw, to his startled amazement, that Gertrude had fainted, was hanging upside down from a branch of the rubber plant. Swiftly and gently he disengaged her clenched talons and, hurrying into the bathroom, waved a phial of smelling salts beneath her beak. After a time she opened one eye.

"What is it, my saffron beauty?" he purred solicitously.

She opened her other eye and regarded him dully, expressionlessly. She said no word. He released her and she fluttered out, through the corridor and down the back stairs. Etienne frowned, shrugged, fell to dressing. As was his wont when expecting guests, he wore a belted smock, pantaloons of stiffly starched white duck, a tall and extravagantly flared chef's cap. His chest glittered with jeweled medals – only a small part of his collection, but enough to cover an area of one square cubit.

After a last more or less resigned glance at his reflection in the mirror, he went back to the front room and, picking up the entirely quiescent Tasting Machine, carried it down to the Salle à Manger, placed it on one end of the table, and went on to the kitchen. Bubu was peeling a mangosteen; Gertrude was nowhere to be seen. Etienne peeked into an oven, uncovered a steaming pot and sniffed, gave its contents a reflective stir.

"Where *is* that absurd bird?" he finally demanded.

Bubu turned a fast back somersault, gestured towards the garden.

"She swooned," Etienne continued, "swooned dead away. It's probably the heat."

He went then to the big slate upon which, only as a reminder, he sometimes chalked his menus, scrawled:

Anguilles au Gris, Vert, et Rouge
Anchois Robespierre
Oeufs de Rocs en Gelée
Veloute d'Eperlans Central Park

Agulhacreola au Sauce Nacre
Sylphides à la Crème de Lion Mann
Endive Belge au Goo
Grives, Becfigues, et Béguinettes
et Merles de Corse Bubu

Bubu, avidly watching, swelled with pride. Etienne must indeed be in a magnificent mood thus to honor him in naming a brand new dish. Etienne cocked his head and grinned at Bubu's glee, scrawled on:

Hamburger 61st Street
Coots avec Leeks Navets Farcis Bleu
Ballotines de Oison Mercedes

He stopped and was thoughtful, went to an open window that gave upon the garden. The sky was writhing with thunder clouds and, by an abrupt flash of lightning, he saw Gertrude in the magnolia tree abstractedly tearing a large white blossom into bits. He whistled, but she only glanced fleetingly, fleetingly, in his direction, then lifted her head and bayed mournfully at the darkling, tumultuous sky. It was an eerie sound.

"Bright-feathered imbecile," he muttered tenderly. "She'll get soaking wet in another minute."

A few drops of rain pattered on the sill. He whistled once more, crossed back to the slate, and added:

Salade de Concombres, Ambergris
et Choux Jaune
Jambon à la Prague
Sous la Cendre Teak
Fraises Réve de Bébé Blaque
Péche Attila
Bavaroise Gertrude

He was thoughtful again, crossed to the smallest of the refrigerators, and gently removed the eleven perfect daisies which would serve as an epergne. Opening the refrigerator, he thought of Vincent. It would not do to leave that brash youth too long in the Crucifreeze. Perhaps another half-hour of chilled meditation upon his sins would suffice, then Etienne would free him, pay him handsomely for the Tasting Machine, and send him packing. It was well for Vincent – he smiled wryly – that he was not a vindictive man.

There was a bowl of caviar in the small refrigerator, the luminous, absinthe-greenish kind. It had been flown from Baku the previous day. It occurred to Etienne that it might be as well to test the Machine once more before his guests arrived. He took the bowl into the dining room and placed it on the table; almost immediately the Machine began to hum, whirr softly, ever so softly. The spoon arm slowly unfolded, reached out and – snup! – engulfed a great mouthful, snatched it to the aperture, popped it in. The filament began to glow, and then, sibilantly, sensually, unmistakably, the Machine chortled with pleasure.

Etienne heaved a great and beatific snortle. It worked, and perfectly. He carried the bowl back into the kitchen and put it in the small refrigerator. The Machine's voice followed him for a moment with thin whines of anguish. That was as well, he decided. Let it be ravenous for the feast to come.

He listened then. He could hear Bubu in the cellar – clink and stumble, rumble, plink – as he chose wines to accompany dinner; he could hear the rain outside, a tenuous shuffle of thunder, Gertrude wetly baying at the sky; he could hear the distant surf of tires on Park Avenue.

And then he heard another sound – a slam, a click, a closed door. He wondered for a little while where it came from, then abruptly dropped his spoon and closed a pot, hurried to the Salle. The door was closed, locked.

He pounded on it lightly, then more heavily, then hard. A horrid sweat grew suddenly upon his flesh.

"Mercedes!" he shouted. "Are you there?"

There was no answer and no sound. He smiled a pea-green smile and tried to pull himself together. His nerves . . . Obviously an errant breeze had sprung. He need simply find the key . . . and . . .

The key, the only key, was inside, and this was a heavy, practically impregnable door. Ah, well, a locksmith . . .

"Bubu," he called, but Bubu was in the cellar, and thunder quenched his voice. Thinking of keys, how could he have thought that Mercedes could be here? He himself had locked *her* door.

But wait! If she had traced the keys, and Vincent had made duplicates, then she, too, might . . .

From beyond the door there came – or did he only imagine it? – a faint, far hum, a tremulous, low-pitched moan of – what *was* it like, anticipation?

Etienne whirled, rushed up the stairs. Mercedes' door was open. He shouted for her, shrieked her name. A crash of thunder worried away to silence. Dashing back down the stairs he fell, described a spinning parabola, and landed on his head. There was darkness . . .

He must have been unconscious for a full minute, perhaps more. When he sat up and ruefully rubbed his skull, it seemed that it was spring. Birds were singing, and a gentle fountain somewhere gently played. Then he knew it was the rain, a roaring cloudburst. And over it there was a great, expanding sigh of ecstasy that shook the house.

Etienne remembered then, and clawed his way along the corridor, weakly beat upon the door, and sobbed, "*Mercedes!*" And she answered him.

"Etienne!" she cried, and her sweet, tinkling voice was strained and harsh, like coarse silk tearing. "Etienne – I lied! I—"

And then her words were drowned in such a cataclysmic rhapsody of rapturous squeals and groans and slobbering slurr-ups of delight as to stun the ear and stop the heart. "*Vincent!*" she screamed at last, above this storm of gustatory joy, "Vincent, my love!"

And then her voice was stilled.

Bubu stood, his arms full of dusty bottles, staring down at his master in ajar-jawed astonishment. The rain had slacked, and in the garden Gertrude aped a nightingale, split the satin of her throat with melancholy song. And now the sounds beyond the door subsided slowly to a kind of satiated coda, a roundelay of little grunts and chucklings.

Etienne stumbled to his feet and stared unseeingly at Bubu. Then a little, very little life illumed his eyes.

"Fetch me the ax," he said.

Mercedes' robe was neatly folded on a chair, her spun-glass slippers glittered together on the floor. The Tasting Machine was silent, somnolent, its filament glowing with a blinding white-hot fever. Etienne took it gently into his arms and carried it to the cellar, held it poised for a moment above an open hundred-gallon cask of Thracian wine, then let it go. It came up thrice, and at the last time Etienne fancied – was it his overwrought imagination? – that it called out wispily for help, then choked and strangled, sank, and was entirely gone.

Back in the kitchen he opened an ironwood cabinet and removed a case of thin, brilliantly glistening knives, fell to sharpening them. Bubu was polishing glasses; Gertrude flew in through the open window, perched above the range, and preened her wet, bedraggled feathers.

"Pieces of eight," she squawked. "Pieces of eight!"

The cuckoo clock on the floor above distantly caroled.

Etienne wondered, was it eight or nine? Or did it matter? He went to the slate, gazed at it reflectively for a little time, then slowly erased *Hamburger 61st Street* and scrawled in its place: *Brochettes de Foie Vincent.*

The front doorbell chimed.

"Please answer it," he said to Bubu. "Sir Osbert Fawning and the Dowager Lady Swathe are often early."

FINDERS KILLERS!

John D. MacDonald

1

We waited for him to run, because that was the final proof of guilt that we needed. We had him bottled up in a Chicago apartment. Our boys drove the cabs, delivered the milk, cleaned the street in front and in general covered him like a big tent. I don't know exactly how we gave it away. But we did. We threw it to him.

You can say we were careless. That's in the same league with Monday morning quarterbacking. Our excuse was that we didn't know he was tipped. He walked into the apartment house and never came out again. Three hours later when we took the wire and tape off the fat woman across the hall from where he had lived, we learned how he'd used that cold, dark, drizzly evening to good advantage.

She was a tall woman, and fat. We knew he wore size 10B shoes. Hers were 9A. He tapped at her door. He hit her so hard that she still remembers hearing the tapping, but she can't remember opening the door. Figuring the rest was easy. He merely undressed and wrapped his own clothes around his middle, tying them in place. Then he got into her clothes. He took her raincape and a big floppy hat. Maybe he'd taken the precaution of shaving himself closely. Maybe not. It was a dark night.

He walked out. Aragon, holding the night glasses on the apartment door, didn't spot him. The boys in the cellar played back the recording of him going to bed. It was a sensitive pickup. I heard the shoes drop, the springs creak, the sleepy yawn.

And that was the way Torran walked out on us – walked out with two hundred and forty thousand dollars in brand new treasury notes in five-hundred dollar denominations – all in serial sequence, most of it still in the mint wrappers. In addition he had an estimated twenty-five thousand in smaller bills, all used stuff. He had a lot of the bonds, too. Negotiable stuff. Very hot. Even if they'd just dumped out the bank guards without the holes in the backs of their heads, the bonds would have been hot.

They had carried the guards across the Connecticut line before dumping them out. Torran and Holser. We knew that much. We didn't have to worry about Holser. Some kids on a picnic found Holser a hundred feet from the highway. The thigh had gone bad under the dirty bandage. There was a hole in the back of his head. The slug matched the ones taken from the two guards.

There is not the slightest point in going over the history of how we located Torran. It was dull work. It took seven months. Then we had him bottled. We still couldn't be certain that there wasn't a third party involved. So we watched him. I was the one who advised against moving in and grabbing him. "Wait a little," I said. "He'll either run some more, or he'll have company." Either way, I thought, we couldn't lose.

I'd been with it for seven months. By painstaking spade work I'd uncovered the initial lead that eventually led to him. I was a hero. So Torran slipped away. So I was a bum.

It took three days to prove we hadn't the faintest idea whether he'd left town, and if so, how, and in what direction.

Broughton called me in.

His eyebrows look like white caterpillars. He looks like a deacon in the neighborhood church. He's the Broughton who went into that New Orleans hotel room in '37. He expected one man to be in there. There was a slip. There were four of them. When it was over, Broughton was still standing up. The lead he was carrying didn't pull him down until he got back out into the hall. *That* Broughton!

"Sit down, Gandy," he said.

I sat. No excuses. They never go.

"Washington is disturbed, Gandy," he said.

"As well they might be, Mr Broughton."

"I've watched you carefully, Gandy. You've got a lot of presence. You speak well and you think clearly. But you're too ambitious. You expect too much, too fast."

"And?"

"And I could butter you up to keep you aboard. During your four years with us, you've done well. But now you're marked. You saw what the papers did to us. That was unfortunate. Now you're not Agent Gandy any more in Washington. You're Russ Gandy, the one who lost Torran."

"So I lost him. So I'll find him again."

"That's what I'm trying to tell you. You're being reassigned to duty with the School."

"Why are you telling me this?"

He looked at me and the blue eyes went hard and then softened. "I was pretty ambitious for a while, Gandy. Until the afternoon I had Barrows trapped and he walked away from it."

"I see," I said. I stood up. I was too mad to stay sitting. "Suppose I go find him anyway?"

"Not as an employee of the Bureau. A private citizen has no standing."

"Do I have your permission to dictate a resignation to your secretary?"

He shrugged. "Go ahead. Make it effective as of now."

With my hand on the doorknob I turned and said, "Thanks."

He looked as though he had already forgotten me. "Oh . . . that's all right, Gandy. Just remember that this talk was off the record."

"Of course."

After I dictated the resignation and signed it, I went and cleaned out my desk. In four years I'd cleaned out a lot of desks. This was different. There was no new desk waiting.

My file on Torran belonged to the Bureau. I flipped through it. I knew it by heart. I took out two pictures – not the best two – but good enough, folded them and stuffed them in my pocket. They'd been taken with a telephoto lens from the window across the way where Aragon was holed up.

I left the office without kissing anyone goodbye. The check would be sent to my bank marked for deposit. Four hundred and twenty something. The last check.

*   *   *

I went back to the crummy room I'd rented and in which I'd spent only sleeping time. On four years of salary and expenses, when all you think about night and day is a job of work, you save dough. I looked at the bankbook. Twenty-nine hundred in the savings account. Four thousand in the checking account.

I'd left the little badge and the Bureau weapon and the identification card with Broughton. I sat on the bed and cried without making a sound. Like a kid. He'd been too right. I was ambitious. And they'd taken away my toys.

What the hell was Torran to me now? I took out the pictures. I looked at them. One was an enlargement of the face. Aragon had caught him just as he came out into the sunlight. Torran. A bad boy. No punk. Thirty-four, approximately. Eight of those thirty-four years had been spent in prison. Auburn, Atlanta, Ossining. Armed robbery. Extortion. Now it was a big one. Bank robbery, kidnapping and murder.

The joker was that he looked like a nice guy. Big mouth, slightly crooked nose. Laugh wrinkles around the eyes. The old prison pictures were no good because he'd been out for five years. In the picture he looked like he was on the verge of smiling. Or laughing – at me. How do you figure a guy like that? You can't blame society. Good family, good education. So he was just a wrongo. One of those guys who work twice as hard as anyone else while they try to make it the "easy" way.

Now he had made a big strike. But keeping it was a horse of a new shade.

I looked at the pictures and called him everything in the book. I went out and had a steak; then bought a bottle, brought it home and killed it. It came close to killing me. When I woke up after fifteen hours of sleep it was nine in the morning.

Torran's pictures were on the floor. I picked them up and cursed him some more. It was easier to hate him than to hate myself. Before the war I was an accountant. One year at a desk telling myself I'd get used to it sooner or later. Then five years of war to prove to me that I couldn't settle down. I took the exams and made the Bureau.

After four years it had begun to look to me as though pretty soon I'd be telling J. Edgar to move over and make room for new blood. I liked the chase and I liked to catch them. But you try to be too smart – you try to move too fast. Boom.

I wanted to catch Torran. I wanted to catch him so very bad I could taste it.

But what can one man do? Now the Bureau would be going after him twice as hard. Good sense would have said to drop it. I went in and looked at myself in the mirror. I didn't look so sensible. In fact, I thought I looked a little bit like some of the boys I'd caught during the last four years. Long hard face with heavy bones. Lids that cover maybe too much of the eyes at the outer corners. Big stubborn cleft chin. Hair that's mine, but looks as though it were made from the end of the tail of a handy horse. Beard stubble. I shaved it off. My hand shook. I stopped now and then to drink more water. I got so full of water I wondered when I'd start to make sloshing noises.

After three cups of coffee at the corner café, I could think again. What Broughton had said about private citizens stuck in my head.

My local contacts weren't too bad. By late afternoon it was fixed. In three days I'd have my license as a private investigator in the State of Illinois. License and a permit to carry a gun. So I got in the car and went to Boston. Once you start to do something, you can keep on even though you know it isn't smart.

I left Chicago on Monday at six p.m. I went through Toledo, Cleveland, Buffalo, Syracuse and Albany. I was in Boston at eight o'clock on Tuesday. I went to bed, got up at eight in the morning and located the house in Newton Center where May Marie Sipsol lived with her aunt. It was her bearer bonds that Torran had taken along with the cash. It was just her bad luck that her daddy died exactly when he did.

She was a blonde with a skin like milk in a blue glass – a trembly uncertain mouth, and eyes so close together they threatened to overlap. She wanted none of me. She was a timid eighteen. She spoke of the authorities and what they were doing and she said she couldn't pay me. I said I didn't want pay. I said I wanted a percentage on recovery. I said ten would be enough. The bonds totaled a ten thousand face. Eleven thousand for Russ.

We were alone in a room with Italian antique furniture. It smelled like dust. When I realized that she meant what she said, I took her by the shoulders and shook her until her eyes didn't focus. Her aunt came in and bellowed at me. I pushed the aunt out of the room and locked the door. May Marie whimpered. I shook her again and she wanted to kiss me. Her breath was bad.

Pretty soon she decided that this was a "great love" and that I was a very dramatic type and it was all pretty much like out of a Raymond Chandler movie. By the time the cops the aunt had called started beating on the door, I had our little contract all signed and tucked into the back of my wallet – the wallet with the little holes where the gold badge had been pinned.

She gave the cops and her aunt undiluted hell. She raged like an anemic tigress. I held my breath and kissed her again and left with my contract.

I was back to Chicago on Thursday afternoon. I picked up my documents, bought a .357 Magnum, phoned the office and found out from my only friend there that – in cautious doubletalk – Torran was still at large.

On Friday morning I got up and went to work. I went on the basis that he had left town. Assuming that, I knew he was too smart to use any common carrier. He had no car. So he had stolen a car. Most cars not stolen for repaint and resale are recovered. He wouldn't drive it too far. Not Torran. He'd want to get well out of town. An hour out, or maybe two. I went to headquarters and my pretty new documents gave me the in I needed. Torran had left the apartment house at eight o'clock on a Thursday evening. I copied down a list of the cars stolen after eight and before ten. I was informed that my ex-coworkers had been in. That was all right with me.

One, and the one I liked the best, I almost missed, because it wasn't reported until nearly midnight. The people had gone to a movie eight blocks from where we had Torran bottled up. Their car, a black Pontiac sedan, 1947 model, had been left in the parking lot near the theater. They'd gone into the theater at twenty after eight. That made sense. Torran was smart enough to pick a car that had just been parked, and he'd have had time to get there and watch the lot entrance. He wouldn't want a flashy car.

There was a blue check after the entry. I looked it up in the recovery register. Recovered in Beloit, Wisconsin, on Friday – reported to the Chicago police at one in the afternoon. They had informed the owner and he had said he'd go up and get it Saturday.

None of the others looked as promising.

Friday noon I was in Beloit. When I made inquiries about the car, the local cops gave me a bored look and said that it had already been checked by the Bureau.

After I smiled enough, they let me know the facts. It was on the main drag in a meter zone. It had been tagged for all night parking, then tagged again for overtime in a meter Friday morning. Then they checked against stolen car numbers and towed it in and told Chicago. The answer to my big question was disappointing. Were there any cars stolen from here Thursday night – any time between ten and two? Sorry, no. No missing persons – with car and all? Nope.

A sour lead, and I couldn't tell if I was right. I went back to Chicago and checked out of my room. I waited until night before leaving. Then I left from the parking lot street at eight-thirty. I was Torran, wearing women's clothes. My feet hurt. I was in a stolen car. I wanted to shed the clothes.

I took Route 20 out through Elgin. I stayed well within the speed limits, as no doubt Torran had done. I pretended it was raining. I looked for a chance to change my clothes. I'd need some sort of shelter from the rain, or else have to do it in the car. The longer I kept my own clothes wrapped around me, the more wrinkled and conspicuous they'd get. The ideal spot would be one where I could change and also ditch the women's clothes.

That's a tough assignment on a rainy night in a heavily populated section. I didn't have much hope of it working out. He could have pulled off in any number of places after leaving Starks. At Rockford I turned right on Route 51. I crossed from South Beloit over into Beloit and parked as near as I could to where the car had been found. It was twenty-five after ten. Allow Torran ten minutes to change and he would have gotten in just before quarter to eleven at the latest.

I lit a cigarette and sat in the car for a few minutes trying to think. I went for a walk. Three blocks away was a bus station. Every night a southbound bus left for Rockford, La Salle, Bloomington, Decatur and Vandalia at eleven-fifteen. I liked that one. The hunted animal doubles back on its tracks.

I found the driver having coffee. I asked him if he'd taken the bus on that run the previous Thursday week. He took a tattered mimeographed schedule out of his inside pocket, studied it and said that he had. I asked him if he remembered any specific people on that trip and he gave me a look of complete disgust. "I drive one hell of a lot of buses," he said. I showed him the picture of Torran. It rang no bell.

He warmed up a bit for a five-dollar tip. I sat beside him with my coffee. "Now think back. Did *anything* happen that was unusual that night? It was raining. Remember? Anything at all that might have puzzled you?"

He started to shake his head slowly and then stopped shaking it. He looked into space for a moment. "Now wait a minute. I don't know if this is anything or not. I make my Bloomington stop. Below there, some place just outside Heyworth, a car goes by me doing maybe ninety. Up ahead it slows down to a creep and I got to pass it. Zoom, it goes by me again. Looks like a girl driving. She slows up again and I got to pass her. Then she scoots by again and I don't ever catch up to her again. The third time she goes by she leans on the horn like she was saying hello to somebody. You know – shave and a haircut, two bits."

"Could she have been looking for somebody on the bus?"

"That's what I was thinking."

"Anybody get off at Decatur?"

"Three or four, I think."

"Nothing funny about them, about any one of them?"

"Now, you know, I just remembered. One of them had a ticket to Vandalia, but she got off at Decatur."

"She?"

"Yeah. Big heavy woman with no baggage."

"And a big hat?"

"Damn if that isn't right! One hell of a big hat!"

I added another five to what he already had. I thanked him and went to the ticket office and got a timetable of that late run. It's roughly a hundred and forty miles from Beloit due south to Bloomington. Even with two stops the bus made it in under three hours, getting to Bloomington at ten after two in the morning.

I was in Bloomington at ten minutes of two. A bored man with gray pouches under his eyes lounged behind the ticket grille.

"Were you on a week ago Thursday at this time?"

He yawned. "I'm on every night, friend. In the daytime I try to sleep. The neighborhood is full of kids. I'm learning to hate children."

"Would you remember if someone, it might have been a girl, just missed the southbound bus from Beloit to Vandalia?"

"If you'd come around a year from now, friend, I'd still remember the lady. You don't see much of that material in bus stations. She came plunging in here five minutes after number seventy had pulled out."

"Nice?"

"About five eight. She stood right where you're standing. Hair like harvest wheat – with rain beads caught in it. Moon-pool eyes, pal, and a funny, tough, scratchy little voice, like a tired phonograph needle. She asked me if the bus had left and I said yes and away she went. It was like she pulled me along on a string. I went right to the door. She got into a big gray sedan and went away from here so fast that the tires yelped."

"What make?"

"Oh, the car? Who knows? Big and new. Cad, Buick, Packard. Take any car. Say, that's pretty good! Take any car."

"A dark-eyed blonde. Hair cut short?"

"Nope. Nice and long. The kind to run barefoot through."

"Age?"

"Twenty-two, three, four."

"Clothes?"

"Brother, I was too busy taking them off to take a look at them. Something green, I think. But it could have been blue."

At Decatur I found that I was too close to falling asleep at the wheel, so I checked in at a hotel. In the morning I bought a road atlas and took it into the sandwich shop with me to read while having breakfast. I looked at the map with the idea of trying to outguess them – rather than guess the way they would.

Obviously Torran had phoned from some place along his escape route and told the girl his plan. I had them spotted at Decatur in the rain in her car with Torran still in his disguise and with dawn not too many hours away. Either they were going to make a long run for it together, or she was going to take him to some hideout. If he had called from Beloit – which seemed the most probable, then I could draw a circle two hundred miles in radius around Bloomington and safely assume that she had roared over to Bloomington from some place within that circle.

It didn't look as though she could have made it from St Louis. If she had to get ready for a trip, Springfield might be a logical starting point. Yet, if it were Springfield, why not let Torran ride all the way to Decatur? If it were Peoria, she should have been in Bloomington in plenty of time. Galesburg seemed just about right. If she'd been in Chicago, then why hadn't he gone to see her before he began to suspect that he was being covered?

At any rate, Torran was going to be too smart to make any two-hundred mile run in a big car at that time of night. There are two many town cops who like to wake themselves up in the small hours by hauling down big cars on the road. Torran had gotten into Decatur by bus at just about three in the morning. He hadn't seen the blonde in a long time. He needed to change back to his own clothes. Everything pointed to their holing up close to Decatur. A tourist court was indicated. I was in for some routine legwork.

2

I hit twelve places before lunch. Each place I hit drained some of the confidence out of me. The second place after lunch was called the Sunset Rest Courts and it was three miles out of town on Route 36 heading east.

The woman was very brisk and friendly. "Yes, we had a girl and her mother register a week ago Thursday – I should say Friday morning at three-fifteen. The girl woke me up. We had a light burning that night because we had a vacancy. She said she had planned on driving all night but her mother was taken sick. Nothing serious."

"A blond girl?"

"Yes. Quite pretty. I showed her the vacant room and she seemed satisfied. Here's the register card."

I looked at it. Mrs Walter B. Richardson and Anne Richardson, of Moline. Make of car – Buick. License – Illinois 6c424. All in angular backhand script – finishing school script. I wrote down the license number, fairly certain that they had taken advantage of the dark night to put down the wrong number.

"Are you from the police? Is something wrong? We've never had any trouble here. We try to run a—"

"You're in no trouble. I'm just looking for someone. This

won't even get on the records. Do you know which way they went?"

"Well, Mrs Richardson must have recovered in a terrific hurry. They left here a little after seven. They went out of here so fast that I actually dressed and went over to see if they'd taken anything from the room. I can see the road from my bed. They went up the highway, heading east, and then turned up there at the fork and went south on Route One Twenty-one."

"Did they have any reason to believe that you might have seen which way they went?"

"No. I'm a very light sleeper. I was about to get up anyway. As I say, I just happened to see them turn south."

"Could I take a look at the room?"

"If you want to. There've been quite a few people in it during the week."

"Then maybe there's no point in it. Who cleaned it after they left?"

"I did."

"Did you find anything of interest that was left behind?"

"N-n-no, not really."

"What did you find that puzzled you?"

"A razor blade in the bathroom waste-basket. Lots of women use razor blades, of course. But this one had stiff black stubble on it, and caked shaving cream of some sort. I just thought it seemed odd. No one was in there but the two women between the times I cleaned the bathroom."

I left and drove slowly down 121. It was definitely a secondary road. The shoulder was narrow and the brush was high in the shallow ditch. In the patches where the brush was thickest I went about eight miles an hour.

After about two miles I saw something in the brush. I got out and took a look. An old white rag caught on the base of some weeds. The second time I saw something, it was jackpot. A brown wool dress, ripped down the back and under the arms. Big shoes with the leather stiff from dampness, the stitches pulled by strain. Heavy stockings, a rain cape and a big floppy hat. The works had been rolled into a tight bundle and fastened with a woman's belt. After I was certain of what I had found, I bundled it back up and got ready to toss it farther into the brush. A truck went by, a farm truck, and the driver looked curiously at me. I locked the bundle in the back end of my car with my luggage.

I sat behind the wheel and studied the maps. Either the gray Buick was hot or it wasn't. If it was, I could be in trouble. If it wasn't, then the smartest thing for the two of them to do would be to make a lot of road time. I was willing to accept south as the direction. His first run had been to the north. South looked good.

But the south is pretty roomy. Again I had to try to think like Torran. Unless the girl had brought clothes for him, which wasn't likely, he'd be anxious to pick up a wardrobe. The best wardrobes come from the big cities. The big cities, more often than not, are inclined to have the most alert boys in the cop line. His picture would be widely plastered around. I sat and thought and scratched my head. I just didn't have enough. With Torran alone I could chance guessing his next move. You study a man's life long enough and you can detect the pattern of his thoughts. But Miss X added a new factor. I could guess his decisions but I could not guess either hers or their combined decisions.

So I went to Beloit for the second time. I arrived late Saturday night. Sunday morning I went to the phone company offices, presented my credentials, asked for information about any long-distance calls which had been made from the bus station ten days ago. After some stalling, the chief operator on duty dug into the records and came up with three long-distance calls made from the bus station between ten-thirty and eleven-fifteen. The one to Cleveland I didn't consider. Nor the one to Evansville, Indiana. The one I liked was made at five after eleven to a place called Britcher City, a town of fifteen thousand midway between Urbana and Danville on US 150 east and a bit south of Bloomington. The call was to anyone at Britcher City 3888.

I hadn't checked out of my hotel room. I found a place that would grease my car, change the oil. I took an hour nap and had a quick sandwich before leaving Beloit at noon. It was a hundred-and-ninety-mile trip to Britcher City. I drove by the city limit sign at five minutes of four. I found a square red-brick hotel called the Westan Arms and got a room. I used a pay phone in the lobby to call 3888.

I heard it ring three times at the other end and then a voice said, "Good afternoon. Westan Arms Hotel." I nearly dropped the receiver. "Sorry," I said, "wrong number." I hung up. Sometimes it happens that way.

I went to the desk. The gray-haired woman desk clerk said, "Yes, Mr Gandy?"

The boyish grin was the right one to use. "I've got a problem, ma'am."

"I hope we can help you."

"I believe a young lady left here recently. I don't know what name she was registered under. She may have checked out ten days ago. Blonde tall girl with dark eyes."

"Oh, her!" the woman said with surprising coldness. "Friend of yours?"

"It's very important to me to locate her."

"Well, we don't know much about her, to tell the truth, even though she did live here for two months. Her name is Marta Sharry. Is that the one?"

"I don't know. I'd have to see her handwriting to make certain. Would that be too much trouble?"

She shrugged and turned around to a file behind the counter. She hunted for three or four minutes, then pulled out a card. The angular backhand was familiar.

"That's her writing. Did she leave a forwarding address?"

"No, she didn't. I thought there was something funny about her. No mail and no phone calls, until that last one – all the time she was here. We wondered if she was hiding from somebody."

"Did she act as though she were hiding?"

"No. She used to take liquor to her room and drink it alone. She used to sleep every day until one or two in the afternoon. Along about five o'clock *he* would come for her and she'd go out with him."

It was time for the boyish grin again. "Who is he?"

She smiled a bit wryly. "Every city has its Joe Talley, I suppose. He runs something that is supposed to be a private club. I don't know why the police don't close it. Heaven knows all that goes on there. He'd bring her back here at three and four in the morning. We don't like that sort of guest, but she was quiet and she always paid her bills. I'll bet you Joe Talley knows where she went."

"Did she have a gray Buick?"

The elderly woman sniffed. "Not when she came here, she

didn't. Very remarkable. Joe Talley blossoms out in a new car and suddenly she has his old one, with different plates."

"Where did she garage it?"

"Down at the corner. Landerson's Service."

I pushed the register card back to her. Miss Marta Sharry, New York City. Not much information there. "Where is Talley's place?"

"On Christian Street. Go down Main and turn left on Christian three blocks from here. It's eight blocks out on the left and it looks boarded up, but it isn't. There's an iron deer in the yard. You'll see the sign on the gate. The Talley Ho." She lowered her voice and looked around. "They *gamble* there," she said.

I thanked her with as much enthusiasm as I could manage. I went to the place where she'd kept the car. It was open. A pimply boy was on duty. Just remembering the blonde seemed to up his blood pressure. He had big wet eyes and they glowed.

I made like I was a friend of hers. The license *was* 6c424. That surprised me a bit.

Again I was shot with luck. He smirked and said, "I guess that fancy name, that Marta Sharry, was kind-of a stage name, huh?"

"Oh, she told you her right name?"

He had the decency to blush. "No. She had the registration in one of them little plastic things on the key chain. I took it out once because I wanted to see how old she was. The name on it was something like Anne Richards."

"Anne Richardson?"

"Yeah. That's it."

"Good thing Joe Talley didn't catch you spying on her, eh?"

He licked his lips. His eyes shifted away from me. "I wasn't doing nothing," he said sullenly.

"Did she come and get the car when she left town?"

"She phoned, and I drove it over to her. I helped load her bags in the back. She give me five bucks."

"She seem nervous?"

"No. Kind of excited. Joe Talley came along. He sat beside her in the front seat and I walked back here. I saw her come by ten minutes later and he wasn't with her then."

"What time was that?"

"Sometime before midnight."

★   ★   ★

From there I went to the Talley Ho. There didn't seem to be anyone around. It was a big three-story Victorian frame house, with a cupola, a bunch of scroll saw work and an iron deer standing next to a chipped bird bath in the shaggy lawn under the shade of big elms.

I went back to the hotel and slept until ten. When I went back to the Talley Ho I found the narrow side street lined with parked cars. There was a guard at the gate.

"This is a private club, mister."

"So I've heard. I'm a stranger in town. I thought maybe I could join."

"Maybe you can and maybe you can't. Write us a letter and we'll let you know."

"Couldn't I talk to the manager?"

"No. Sorry. I got my orders. Nobody gets in unless they got a card."

"That's a hell of a note. Miss Sharry wrote me and told me that Joe Talley would treat me right if I ever came through here."

He turned the flashlight on my face again. "You know her?"

"No. I just made up the name."

"No need to get fresh, stranger."

"Hell, I like standing out here. Don't you?"

"Wait a minute," he said. "Anybody comes along I'll be right back, tell 'em. What's your name?"

"Gandy. Russ Gandy."

He was gone five minutes. He came back with a taller man. At their request I came inside the gate. I stood while they put the flash on me again.

"What's your business, Gandy?"

"I'll talk to Talley, if you'll get him out here."

"He's out of town. I'm in charge."

"What's your name?"

"Brankis."

"Come over here a minute, Brankis. This is personal."

We went over by the deer. I tapped a cigarette on its cast-iron muzzle and lit it. "It's like this, Brankis. I ran into you-know-who in Chicago. He told me he had Anne Richardson staked out here. At the Westan Arms. I phoned her couple weeks ago. She told me that a guy named Joe Talley is all right, and—"

"Anne Richardson? Who the hell is she?"

"Don't be cute, Brankis. She's Torran's girl." I purposely made it a little loud.

"Dammit, lower your voice!"

I laughed at him. "Then the name means something to you?"

"How do you figure with Torran?" he said in a half-whisper. "Nobody's ever been hotter than he is. So why should he pop to you?"

"Maybe you can call me an associate, Brankis."

"What kind of a word is that? Associate, yet. Joe isn't going to like any link-up between him and Torran through that girl. She's all mouth."

"Like any lush. Now can I come in and play? I just want to kill some time."

"No, friend. Anybody coming in gets Joe's okay and I told you Joe is out of town."

"That's too bad. I got some merchandise for him."

"Merchandise? What kind of merchandise?"

"Brankis, you must be a real small wheel in this outfit. Annie knows more than you do. She told me Joe Talley is always in the market for this kind of merchandise."

It was too dark to see his face. I waited, hoping it would work. When he spoke he piled the words on too fast to cover up the period of silence. "Oh, that stuff."

"Yes, I got it down at the hotel. Want to come look it over and set a price?"

"Sure. I'll come take a look." He couldn't admit Joe had been leaving him out in the cold, and he had to see the merchandise to know just how far out he'd been left.

We went to the gate and he said, "George, I'll be back in a while. You have any problems, ask Mac what to do."

We went out and got in my car. I stopped for the first cross street and glanced at him, seeing his face for the first time, liking the youngness, the weakness, the loose viciousness of his mouth. I started up, took out my cigarettes and, as I offered him one, I managed to drop the whole pack at his feet. He bent over instinctively to pick them up. As he got into the right position I hit the brakes hard. His head dented the glove compartment door and he sighed once and flowed down onto the floor, like some thick, slow-running liquid.

I parked in shadows and looked him over. All he carried was a sap in black woven leather with a coil spring handle. I bent over him, folded his hat double to cushion the blow and hit him hard behind the ear, flush on the mastoid bone. I took his pulse. It was slow and steady.

I headed toward Danville, found a dirt road that turned left. The sign said the towns of Pilot and Collision were up that road. How does a town get to be called Collision?

The sky had cleared and the moon made a good light. The road was a little soft in spots. Farmhouse lights were off. The road made a right-angle turn to the left and another to the right. When I saw a break in a fence, I got out and checked the ditch. It was shallow and dry. The pasture seemed firm enough. I put the car in low and drove across toward a dark clump of trees. I parked and hauled him out and used my tow rope to tie him to a tree. I wrapped him up so that all he could do would be roll his eyes and wag his tongue. He was limp, sagging in the rope. I sat and smoked and waited for him to come around.

After a long time he sighed. Then he groaned. I knew he could see my cigarette end, glowing in the darkness.

"Whassa marra?" he asked. "Whassa idea?"

I didn't answer him. He was silent for a long time. He said, "What do you want?" Panic crouched behind the level tone.

I watched him and let him sweat. To him, I was just a dark shadow sitting on the front fender of the car.

"What are you going to do to me?" he asked. His voice shook.

A farm dog howled at the moon far away. A sleepy rooster crowed in a half-hearted way. Down the line a diesel hooted at a crossing.

"It was all Joe's idea," he said. "I'm not in on it. He met her in the hotel. She got tight out at the place. She hinted about Torran. Just little hints. So Joe pried it all out of her. She told him how she was waiting for word from Torran when he got ready to make his run for it. She didn't know where or when Torran was going to run. She had five thousand he'd given her in Chicago right after the job, when they split up. She was to buy a car and get it registered under her own name." He stopped talking and waited for me to say something.

He started again, his voice pitched higher than before. "Joe started thinking about all that cash. All that money, and he worked the girl up to where she was thinking of crossing Torran, because Torran had been pretty rough with her. The more he thought about getting his hands on that dough, the better he liked the idea. He talked it over with me. The idea was to get Torran to run with the girl to right where Joe wanted him to run. It had to be done delicate because if Torran felt maybe the girl was steering him some special place, he'd smell a cross."

Again he waited and again I said nothing.

"What are you going to do to me? I'm telling you everything I know." It was half wail and half whine. "Joe fixed her up with the car and figured that because of the dough in serial sequence and the bearer bonds, Torran would want to get out of the country to where maybe he could buy a banana citizenship and get a better percentage than trying to fence the stuff here where it's too hot to touch. And if Joe got the dough here he'd be in the same trouble. Mexico has an easy border to cross, even with them looking for you. So Joe figured help him get into Mexico through the girl, and take it away from him down there.

"Joe goes to Mexico a lot because if you spend too much here, the tax boys get curious. He's got a house down there he rents by the year. In Cuernavaca. As soon as the girl got the word from Torran she told Joe and he flew down to set it up. If Torran goes to Canada or flies out of the country some other place, Joe is licked. The girl was supposed to get away from Torran for a couple minutes and wire me so I could phone Joe. The wire hasn't come yet."

I flipped a cigarette away, stood up, walked over to him. I said casually, "If I kill you, Brankis, you can't phone Joe and tell him about this, can you?"

"Now wait a minute!" he said in a voice like a woman's.

"Or maybe I'll tip Joe Talley that you opened up like a book."

"A deal, mister," he said breathlessly. "I keep my mouth shut and so do you. Honest."

"And I get word on that wire the minute you get it."

"Yeah. Sure!"

I untied him and slapped him around and took him back and left him. I went right to Western Union. A bored night man looked at my credentials without interest, sneered at a twenty-dollar bribe and told me the only ones to see telegrams were the persons to whom said telegrams were addressed. There was no time to arrange a tap on the Talley Ho phone. I added two more twenties. He ignored me. I added two more. One hundred dollars.

He yawned and picked up the money. "It was marked deliver," he said, "and I sent it out twenty minutes before you came in. It was from National City, California, and it read: *Plan to take cruise to Acapulco starting tomorrow*. It was signed *Betty*."

He pocketed my money and shuffled back and sat down and picked up a magazine.

3

Thirty-one hours later I was sitting by a window on the port side of the Mexico City–Acapulco plane as it lifted off the runway at seven in the morning. There was a wad of traveler's checks in my pocket and a bad taste in my mouth. I had wasted too much time getting the *turista* permit, making travel connections.

We climbed through the sunlit air of the great plateau, lifted over the brow of the mountains near Tres Cumbres and started the long, downhill slant to Acapulco on the Pacific. It was hard to figure just how quickly Torran and the girl would get there. My phone calls to California had established that there was no scheduled cruise to Acapulco at the date the wire had indicated.

Probably Torran had made arrangements to have a boat pick him off the lower California coast and smuggle him down to Acapulco. The odds were against his tarrying in Mexico long. Extradition was too simple. The same method of travel would take him down the Central American coastline to some country where an official would listen joyfully to the loud sound of American dollars.

One thing I could be certain of. Joe Talley would be there. And I would know Joe Talley. I'd memorized a recent picture of him – a beefy blond with a rosebud mouth and slate eyes. I knew Torran's face as well as I knew my own.

Traffic wasn't heavy as it was the off season for Acapulco, the summer-rate season. The air was bumpy. A large family across the way was airsick, every one of them. We flew to Cuernavaca, over the gay roofs of Taxco. Brown slowly disappeared from the landscape below us and it began to turn to a deep jungle green.

At nine o'clock we lifted for the last low range of hills and came down to the coast. The Pacific was intensely blue, the surf line blazing white. The hotels were perched on the cliffs that encircled the harbor. The wide boulevard ran along the water's edge.

There are hunches. All kinds. This was one of those. I looked at the city as we came in for the landing. I looked at it and I didn't feel anything and then all of a sudden I felt confident and good. I felt that whatever was going to happen, it would happen right down there.

We made a bumpy landing and as soon as we were down I knew why Acapulco was not at the peak of its season. The heat was like when a barber wraps your face in a steaming towel. It was heat that bored a hole in you and let all the strength run out. It was heat that kept your eyes stinging from the sweat running into the corners.

I stood in the shadow of the wing as they untied the baggage and handed it down. I took my bag and walked across the runway, and it was so hot the soles of my feet began to burn. I took the sedan which had HOTEL DE LAS AMERICAS on the front of it, remembering that it had been recommended to me in Mexico City. No one else was going to that hotel. The airsick family piled into a shabbier sedan labeled HOTEL PAPAGAYO.

The hotel was something right out of the imagination of an assistant to a Hollywood producer. High on the cliff, with cabañas, shops, pools, outdoor cocktail lounges, outdoor dining room and dance floor. I registered, took a cabaña, took a shower and put on the Acapulco clothes I'd bought in Mexico City. Protective coloration. I wanted to look like an American tourist. The shirt had a pattern of tropical parrots. The shorts were lime yellow. The sandals had straps that hurt me across the instep. I topped it off with a white mesh cap with a ballplayer's bill, oval slanting sunglasses.

I told my troubles to the desk clerk. "I'm trying to find a friend here in town. I don't know what hotel he's at. How would I go about it?"

"An American, sir?"

"Yes."

He gave me a list of the six most likely hotels. The flaw was that Joe Talley might not be using his own name. But there was no real reason for him not to do so. His name would mean nothing to Torran. Torran was big time. Talley was a small town crook. And just before lunch I found him. He was at the Papagayo. It was one of those breaks you get. I was just getting out of the taxi in front of the place when I saw him coming across the road from the beach. He had a dark pretty girl with him. Both of them seemed a little unsteady on their feet. They passed right in front of the cab and went into the hotel grounds. Joe was speaking Spanish to the girl. She was giggling. I don't know how good the Spanish was. It sounded good and she seemed to be enjoying it. The black hair on the girl wasn't a dye job. Of that I was certain.

There were enough people around so that I could follow them into the grounds. I shoved money at the cab driver. I got such a wide grin I knew it was too much. I went in. The cabañas were on either side of long walks behind the hotel. Tropical foliage was lush around them. I kept them in sight. They turned into the last but one on the central walk and I saw Talley unlock the door.

I strolled around. I went by to the end of the walk, came back, and when I was sure I wasn't observed, I ducked into the thick brush beside their cabaña. The windows were open. Through the screen I heard the buzz of a fan, the clink of bottleneck on glass, the girl's thin giggle. They kept talking Spanish to each other. They stopped talking after a while. I didn't risk raising my eyes above the sill until I heard the roar of a shower. Then I looked in.

It was Talley who was taking the shower. I could see the girl. She had changed into a white dress. She went over to the bureau and started making up her face. I walked away from there. I had vaguely planned to have Talley lead me to Torran and Anne. If Joe Talley could take Torran, it was all to the good. If he couldn't, he'd knock Torran off balance long enough for me to take him. But Talley was playing. He was like a guy with nothing on his mind. It bothered me. He ought to be pretty well tightened up. Just the thought of coming up against Torran ought to keep him nibbling on his hands. Something had gone wrong in my guessing.

An hour later the girl came out of the cabaña alone. She had a big bright red purse slung over her shoulder. I tossed a mental coin and decided to stay with Joe Talley. So I intercepted her where I could keep Talley's cabaña in sight.

"Do you speak any English?" I asked her.

She gave me a long cold look, then wrinkled her nose in a very charming little smile. "A leedle."

"Can I buy you a drink?"

"Dreenk? No, *gracias*. Other time, maybee."

A nice old lady schoolteacher walked by, glanced at the girl and gave me a sour look. I tried to make a date with the girl, but she walked on.

I shrugged and found a bench where I could see Talley's cabaña. The long hours went by. I was hungry and thirsty and out of cigarettes. I cursed Talley, Torran, Anne Richardson, Mexico and the three hundred and seventy thousand dollars.

When Anne Richardson came by me, it caught me by surprise. I was waiting for Talley to come out. It shook me to see her and know that it could be the one. I went over the ticket agent's description. Hair like harvest wheat, he had said. Moon-pool eyes, whatever those are. The funny, tough, scratchy little voice would be the payoff.

I had to make a quick revision of all my guesses. It was like coming in on the third act, not knowing your lines or what has happened so far. I moved in behind her as she headed down the walk. She wore an aqua cotton two-piece dress with a bare midriff. She walked on high cork soles, and she was tall enough not to need them, and her walk was something to remember and speculate about and bring back to mind on long cold winter nights. A man like Torran should pick inconspicuous women. She was as noticeable as a feather bed in a phone booth.

She went to Joe Talley's cabaña, tried the door and went in. My play was to walk slowly by and see if I could duck into the shrubs again. This time they'd be speaking English, at least. But before I could get by, the door banged open and she came out again, blanched to the color of roquefort, sucking at the air through parted lips. I took a quick step back, caught her wrist and spun her around.

"Let go, let *go*!" she panted, fighting me. The voice was small, scratchy.

"Get back in there, Anne!" I said, pushing her toward the door. Her ankle turned because of the high cork soles and I caught her before she fell. My using her name took a lot of the scrap out of her. Her eyes were wide and hot as she looked at me. Moon-pool eyes, to that ticket agent, are the ones so dark that you can't see where the irises leaves off and the pupils begin.

"Who are you?"

I shoved her again, reached around her to the door and pushed it open, pulled her in. She turned her back to me and I spun her around and caught her hand just as she yanked the small automatic out of her white purse. I tore the gun out of her hand and it hurt her fingers and she yelled with the pain. But I heard it as though it came from a long distance.

I was too busy looking at Joe Talley. He was pretty messy. Through the open bathroom door I could see the top half of him. The shower was still on and turned too hot so that steam drifted around him. He lay on his back with his legs still in the shower and the big knife was stuck through his throat at an angle so that the tip of it came out under his ear.

The girl made a dive for the door and I caught her in time, whirled her back, picked her up bodily and threw her onto the bed. "Be good," I said. She lay there and stared at me. I opened her purse, took out cigarettes, lit one. I looked around the room. The search had been pretty complete. The bottle on the bureau. Two glasses had been used. The third was still clean, still upside down on the tray. I poured some of the defunct's bourbon, a liberal dose, took it over and pushed Anne's legs out of the way so I could sit on the bed.

"I could use some of that," she said in a wheedling tone.

"Tell me some things and maybe you'll get some."

"Why did you kill him, honey?" I knew she hadn't. I knew she didn't have time to do it. But she didn't know I knew.

Her eyes darkened curiously. "I'm asking you that, mister."

"I'm turning you in to the local cops. I think they have cells with dirt floors. I think the jailers will give me a vote of thanks for putting something like you in there. The bugs are bad, but they'll keep you entertained."

"You can't bluff me, mister. Who are you?"

"How did you get here so fast from National City? You and Torran."

"Who's Torran? Somebody I ought to know?"

"From way back," I said.

"Why did you kill Joe Talley, mister?"

I took another pull at the drink. Her eyes kept flicking to the glass and now and then she'd lick her underlip.

"We're going around in circles, Anne. I didn't kill him. And I know you didn't. But I do know who did. Interested?"

She sat up, pulled her knees up, hugged them. "Who?"

"I'll give you a little. You give me a little first."

She shut her eyes for a long three seconds. "We got here fast because there was a light plane staked out for us at Ensenada."

"A girl killed him. A Mexican girl wearing a white dress and carrying a big red purse. She was pretty. He brought her back here from the beach around noon. They both looked a little high."

Still hugging her knees, she said five or six words that she shouldn't have known. Her lips writhed like bloody worms as she said them.

I asked, "Where's Torran?"

Suddenly a thought seemed to strike her.

Her eyes went wide. She scrambled off the bed, took one hesitant step toward the door and then stood there. "Look, I just realized that maybe . . ."

"Go ahead and talk. Get it off your chest," I told her. "I know that you and Joe Talley planned to hijack Torran's take and you crossed Torran by sending the wire to Brankis. I know which bus Torran took dressed as a fat lady, and I know the place he tossed the getup out of the gray Buick, and I know how you honked at the bus."

It was meant to shake her. It did. Her face went white again. She sat down beside me on the bed.

"Who are you?"

"I'm just a guy interested in three hundred and seventy thousand dollars, sweet."

She ran her fingertips along the back of my hand. "If I could trust you, mister."

"How do you mean?"

"Wouldn't I be a damn fool if I steered you to that money and then you took it all?"

I nodded gravely. "You'd grab it all for yourself if you could, wouldn't you?"

She looked at me. "I need help. Joe was going to help. I'm afraid he talked to the wrong people. I'm afraid he was killed by somebody who wants the money."

"Where's Torran?"

"How can I trust you?"

"You can't. But I think you're on a spot where you're going to have to trust somebody."

She turned into my arms and caught her hand strongly at the back of my neck and kissed me. She could be considered an expert. The kiss was as smarting hot as the sauce that came with the one meal I had in Mexico City.

"It's nice," I said casually, "but it isn't worth three hundred and seventy thousand." I blocked the slap she threw at me and watched her as she went over to the bureau.

She picked up the bottle and tilted it high. Her throat worked convulsively for five long swallows. She lowered the bottle, said, "Haaaah", tilted it high again and took three more swallows. She wiped her wet mouth on the back of her hand, leaving a smear of deep red.

"I've got to tell you," she said, "because I've got to have help. Torran is sick. He got sick in National City, and he's been running a hell of a high fever. He's out of his head sometimes. That made it simple for me to contact Joe as soon as we landed. Joe made the arrangement for a house up the beach, a small place walled in and private. Torran's there. The bad thing was not knowing how to get the money away from him. It's all crammed into a huge money belt. Even sick like that, I couldn't risk it. And I'm not killing anybody, even for that amount of money.

"Joe has contacts. He got some sedative and handed it to me early this morning. I couldn't get it down Torran until noon.

"When he was out, I got the belt off him. I know it isn't safe to stay here. I can't get it out of Mexico without Joe's help. So I hid it in the house and came to get Joe and tell him. Now I'm afraid to go back there, because if Joe talked to the wrong people and there's another group after that money, they'll be at the house now. If you come back with me and help me get the money, and help me get it to El Salvador, I'll give you seventy thousand."

"Half, sweet."

"One hundred thousand. No more. Final offer." The liquor had gotten into her bloodstream. Her lips looked swollen and she weaved slightly.

"Half, and be good, or I'll take it all."

She leered at me. "Maybe we could stick together, huh? Your

money is my money?" She laughed. It looked funny to see her standing there laughing, because behind her I could see Joe Talley's hand, palm upward, the steam curling around it.

She turned toward the bottle. I got there first. She cursed me. She clawed at my face and I slapped her so hard her eyes went off focus. Then she turned sweet. "You gotta help me, honey," she said. "Gee, I don't know your name."

"Russ, sweet. Be good. Stand by the door. There's prints to get rid of. That heat is going to make time of death tough for them to determine."

I cleaned up and we left. A man was standing up the walk talking to a woman who stood in front of the neighboring cabaña. I turned back toward the door, waved, and said, "See you later, boy."

Her face and eyes were empty as we got into the cab. She gave the address "Ocho Calle Revocadera."

"You know the language?"

"Twenty words, Russ."

I held my hands low and took a look at the automatic. It was a toy. Twenty-five caliber. Curly designs etched into the steel. The clip was full. The cab took fifteen minutes to put us by the gate in the wall around the house. She sat in the cab and started to tremble. "I'm scared," she said in a low tone.

I held the door and she got out. I paid the driver and the cab went away from there. I looked at the gate. There was a chain for a padlock, but no padlock. I slipped the catch and pushed it open. The lawn was deep green, unkempt. Flowers straggled in wild confusion along the side of the pink stone house.

"What room is he in?"

She was shivering again. "In . . . in the back."

"Did you lock the place up?"

"Yes."

I took a look at the side door. The wood was splintered and pieces of the brass lock lay on the stone step. I pushed her to one side, kicked the door open and went in fast, whirling on balance, the way I had been taught. The hallway was empty, dim. I listened. The house was silent.

"Come in," I whispered. She came in obediently. She was chewing on her lip. The liquor was sweating its way out of her.

"Where did you hide it?" I whispered, my lips close to her ear.

"You'll take me with you, Russ?"

"Of course."

"Promise."

"I promise."

"Come on, then." She walked with extreme caution. I followed her. It was hard to walk silently on the gayly patterned tile floor. She peered into the next room and then walked in. Suspended from the ceiling was a huge fixture, like a fruit bowl. She pointed up at it. I picked up the antique Spanish chair from its position near the door and put it silently under the fixture. She put her hand on my shoulder and stepped up onto the chair, reached her hands up and around the edge of the fixture.

The flick of movement was off to the side. I turned, firing as I turned, my snapping shot drowned by the resounding smash of a heavier weapon. He stood gaunt in the doorway, wearing only pajama pants, his eyes glittering and feverish, black stubble on his face, his lips cracked and caked with white.

As the muzzle swung toward me, I saw the tiny holes appearing in his naked chest, all left of center. His left. The little automatic shot well. He tried to hold onto the doorway and steady the weapon. He trembled with effort but he could not stay the slow sagging of the muzzle. When he fired it, it was aimed at the tile. It smashed tile, whirred by my head and chunked into the wall behind me. His knees made a clocking sound on the tile and he folded awkwardly onto his face, getting one hand up but not far enough.

I turned toward Anne Richardson. Both her hands were clamped on the rim of the light fixture and her feet were still on the chair. But her knees sagged so that all her weight was on her hands, and on the fixture. It pulled free of the ceiling and she came down with it, hitting cruelly against the heavy arm of the chair, tumbling off onto the floor while the glass splashed into all corners of the room.

I knelt by her and turned her over gently and saw where the bullet had entered, just below the bare midriff, dead center, ranging upward. She gave me an odd little smile and said, "Tell . . . tell them I . . ." Then she chopped her heels at the floor so hard she broke the straps of both cork-soled shoes and they came off. She arched up a few inches and dropped back and died. I wondered what I was supposed to tell them.

I went to the front door and listened. There was no traffic in the road. The nearest beach house was four hundred yards away, and the sound of the surf was loud.

Torran was dead. That look of affability was gone in death. He looked weak, vicious, cruel. He looked like a punk, a dirty small-time killer. I searched the house. The kitchen was small. The girl in the white dress lay with her head under the sink, face down, the big red purse under her stomach, her white dress high on the bare strong brown thighs. The slug had made an evil mess of the back of her head. Her companion, a dark man I had never seen before, was one eighth alive. At least he was breathing. His pulse had a flutter like the wings of a captive moth. He had two in the belly.

When Torran had regained the belt, he had put it where a sick person could be expected to put it. Under his pillow. I opened it. Each compartment was hard as a stone with money. It was crammed in so tightly the belt would have to be cut to get it out without tearing it.

I looked at it. All the money in the world. Fresh money, still in the mint wrappers. All the money in the world for all the things in the world. I sat on the bed that smelled of fever and sickness in the room with the drawn blinds and ran my fingertips back and forth across the visible edges of the stacks of bills. I thought of crazy but possible things.

It was done very, very neatly. It was done the way experts do it. A gardener was working in front of my cabaña at the Hotel de las Americas. Another man was coming down the path with a covered tray. I unlocked the door and went in. When I was three steps inside the room the gardener shoved the muzzle of the weapon through the screen of the side window. The waiter tossed napkin and tray aside, kept the light machine gun the napkin had covered. He held it centered on the small of my back. At the same instant the third man stepped out of my bathroom and covered me with a professional-looking revolver.

I raised my arms and stood there. With no accent at all the man in front of me said, "Sit down and hold onto your ankles."

I did as directed. They took the gun first. Then they took the money belt off me. They put the gun and the money belt on the bed. They seemed to be waiting for someone. I felt better. I had a lovely idea. "Police?" I asked. My voice sounded like something crawling up the side of a wall.

"But of course," the English-speaking one said.

We all waited. Broughton came in. The white caterpillar eyebrows showed no surprise, no elation. He looked like the deacon standing at the end of the pew waiting for the collection plate to be handed back.

"You saved us some trouble, Gandy," he said.

"Glad I could help."

"We didn't find Brankis until yesterday. We've gotten excellent cooperation from the Mexican authorities."

"Put that in your report, Broughton."

He nodded. "I will. You nearly made it, Gandy. One day later . . ."

"My hard luck, I suppose," I said. "Can I get up on my feet?"

He nodded. I got up. He showed expression for the first time. I was something low, dirty and evil. Something you'd find under a wet rock. Something he wanted to step on.

"We're taking you back," he said.

"Kind of you, sir."

I grinned at him. I gave him a big broad grin and he turned away from it. I was laughing inside. I was laughing so hard I hurt. Let him have his fun. Sooner or later he was going to find out about the wire I sent before returning to my cabaña – that wire to Washington Bureau Headquarters, giving the case code name, reporting recovery, requesting instructions.

You see, it looked like all the money in the world, but sometimes even that isn't enough.

THE MURDERING KIND!

Robert Turner

1

It started off just like any other Friday night. I left my office in the Emcee Publishing Company building on Forty-Sixth Street at five-oh-five. I went across the street to the quiet, dim little bar in the Hotel Marlo where every Friday night for the past year or so, I'd been stopping off after work for a dry Manhattan. I felt good. I had that Friday-payday glow of satisfaction that you get when you've got a good tough week's work behind you, money in your pocket and two free days at home with Fran and the kids ahead of you.

I wasn't looking for any trouble. I would have the one drink, leave the Marlo and make the five thirty-seven Express bus to Jersey. I'd meet Johnny Haggard on the bus, and we'd bull it all the way home about our jobs and what we were going to do about the crab grass on our so-called lawns. Johnny lives next door to me in Greenacres, a new development just outside of Wildwood in North Jersey. There are plenty of acres there, but not much of it green, what with the thin layer of topsoil the builders used over all that fill. Anyhow.

No trouble. No excitement. Nothing different. Everything the same as usual. That's what I thought . . . But a couple of things happened.

The Marlo is a small, old, side-street residential hotel. The bar is tiny, very dimly lighted, quiet, with no jukebox and usually not very crowded. Sometimes I'm the only one in there having a drink at five-ten. But not tonight. There was a girl there, all alone at the bar when I came in.

There was nothing special about her at first glance. And that's all I did, at first, was glance at her. Believe me. Listen, I've been married ten years and I appreciate a good-looking woman the same as the next guy. I kid with the guys and sometimes with Fran, just to needle her a little, about stepping out and fooling around. You know. But you also know it's talk with most of us guys. After all, a man's got a swell wife, a couple of fine kids, a nice home. You can't have everything. So you make up your mind to that and forget about the things you don't have.

Herb, the tall, gloomy-looking bartender at the Marlo, saw me come in the door and had my Manhattan half made by the time I got onto one of the leather barstools. I sat there, savoring the first lemon-peel-tart smooth burn of the drink in my mouth, trickling down my throat, and looked at myself in the backbar mirror. I was not the only one. The girl at the other end of the bar was looking at my reflection, too. Our eyes met. She let them hold for a moment and then dropped her gaze, almost shyly.

Some girls can do a lot with their eyes. This one could. I don't know how to explain it. Her eyes were very dark, extremely widely set, kind of intense and brooding-looking. With that one look she seemed to say: "You seem interesting to me. I think I could get to like you. If you study me closely I think you'll feel the same way. And if you spoke to me, if you did it nicely, not in a wise-guy way, I wouldn't brush you off. But *you'll* have to make the approach. I wouldn't dare." You know what I mean?

So using the backbar mirror, I looked her over more carefully. She wasn't well dressed. She was wearing a trench coat, with the back of the collar turned up and no hat. Her hair was thick and blonde and hung gracefully about her shoulders but that's all you could say about it. Her nose was a little too broad and her mouth too wide and full-lipped, but somehow those features seemed to fit just right with the dark, brooding eyes and although she wasn't striking, she was a damned attractive girl. The quiet type. The kind who wouldn't want a lot of money spent on her, who would be content to just sit and have a couple of drinks with a guy and talk and maybe go to a movie or something . . . You can see the way my mind was working.

I'd almost finished the Manhattan when our eyes met in the mirror again and this time, they held longer and I got the feeling that both of us were trying to tear our gaze away and couldn't.

It was as though we were looking very deep into each other, hungrily. And then when she finally yanked her gaze away, I felt shaken and a little giddy, as though this was my third Manhattan instead of my first.

I glanced sideways at her and she had her legs angled off the stool and crossed. She was wearing high heels, not extreme, but enough to give her naturally gracefully curved legs what seemed like extra length and sleekness. I suddenly realized that my heart was pounding too hard, and so were the pulses in my wrist.

Herb the bartender went down to the girl, seeing she'd finished her drink. He asked her if she'd like another. She hesitated and then caught my glance in the backbar mirror again and turned quickly away and said, "Yes, please." Her voice was soft, husky, almost a whisper.

I knew then that I'd better get out of there, fast. All kinds of crazy thoughts and ideas were going through my head. I drained my glass, started to get up and somebody swatted me on the back. I wheeled angrily to look into Ronny Chernow's handsome, grinning face.

"Hi, Kip," he said. "Living dangerously, I see. Sitting in a cozy little bar, drinking cocktails and flirting with a pretty girl! Ah, you sly old dogs, you quiet ones, you never can tell about your type."

I got very red. I started to tell Chernow that in the first place I wasn't flirting, in the second place I was only thirty-one years old, at least a couple of years younger than he was. But he wasn't even looking at me. He was staring at the girl at the end of the bar and smiling at her. He was looking at her the way guys like Ronny Chernow always look at girls, as though she wasn't wearing anything; patronizingly, as though he was thinking: *You're not too bad, Baby. Maybe I'll give you a great big break and go after you!*

But the girl wasn't paying any attention to him. Chernow turned back to me. He took hold of my arm. "Hey, you're not running off so soon. Have another drink with me. Or will Momma spank you if you miss that first bus home?"

What can you say to a remark like this? If you deny it, then go, you make it sound true, anyhow. I thought about the girl at the bar. She was listening to this. The loud way Chernow always talked, she couldn't help it.

I knew what Ronnie Chernow really thought about me: I was stuffy, not a sport, a guy who never had any fun, was regimented, never varied his routine – a man on a treadmill, going like hell but never getting anywhere. I didn't care what Chernow thought about me. But I cared what *I* thought. And suddenly, crazily, I wondered if he was right. I had to prove that he wasn't.

"Okay, Ronny," I said. "*If* you're buying. I hear you're a tight man with a buck."

That got him. Chernow was always talking about how much money he made and spent. *"Me?"* he said. "What are you talking about? Why, I spend more in one—" Then he stopped and grinned, realizing I'd turned the needle around on him. "Okay, Kip," he said.

While Herb made the second Manhattan, I looked at the clock. It was five-twenty. By now, I should have been a block away, on my way home, on the way to that five-thirty-seven Express. I knew now that I was going to miss it. It was the damnedest feeling. Maybe it was silly, but I felt a little sick and scared, apprehensive. In the five years we'd been living in Wildwood, I hadn't missed that bus. I'd never stayed in town one night, even. Now that I realized that, it seemed a little ridiculous. At the same time I felt a slight exultation, a sort of breaking loose feeling, of strange freedom. I drained half of the Manhattan at one gulp. I looked at Ronny Chernow in the mirror behind the bar.

He was big, handsome, in a red-faced, square-jawed sort of way. His carefully tousled, boyishly curly hair made him look younger than he was. A lot of the girls in our office were crazy about him. He was the vigorous, aggressive, breezy type and he was always kidding around with the girls and always letting hints drop to other guys in the place that he'd dated a number of them and found them vulnerable.

He was the business manager of Emcee Publications and I don't know what he made, but it must have been somewhere around ten thousand a year. But he spent and dressed as though his salary was three times that. Being single, though, with nobody else's way to pay through life but his own, I guess he could do that.

It was hard to like the man. He was big-mouthed and overpowering. But it was just as hard not to admire him. He was everything that I was not and I thought about that, sitting here. At least Ronny Chernow had color. I was drab. His kind of life was excitement. Mine was boredom, monotony. Men like Chernow felt sorry for worms like me.

I began to rebel against that. I told myself: *I'm going to have a little change. I deserve it. I'm way overdue. I'll show this big, handsome jerk next to me that I can have fun, too. I'll call Fran and tell her I won't be home until late. I'll stay here, have another drink or two and then go someplace for dinner. Later, I'll go to the fights at the Garden.*

"Ronny," I said. "You're a real round-town boy. Where's a good place to have dinner? I'm staying in town tonight."

His thick handsome brows rose as though I'd said I was going out to stick up a bank. "What!" he said. "You're finally going to break away from Momma's apron strings? Congratulations, kid. I'd just about given you up. Maybe you are human, after all." He slapped me on the back again. "Where you going? Got a date?"

I began to enjoy this. I wanted it to last a little longer. I began to almost like Chernow. "Now, look," I said and winked at him. "Have I asked you where you're going tonight, who you're going to be with? Does Gimbels tell Macy's. It's none of my business. Maybe this isn't any of yours."

He looked dubious but didn't press the point. We finished our drinks and Chernow said: "Well, since you don't have to run, let's do this again." He flipped his empty glass with the back of his forefinger.

I didn't answer. I looked at the clock. It was five-thirty. I should call Fran. Somehow I dreaded that. That would be the final break with my routine. I hated to make it. Yet I had to call her. Then I remembered that she wouldn't be expecting me until six-thirty. She wouldn't leave to meet the bus at Wildwood until six-twenty. I still had plenty of time for that call. I watched Herb make two more drinks. Then I looked toward the glass and saw the girl at the end of the bar staring at me again. Chernow noticed, too.

"Hey!" he said. "That baby is giving you the eye. If she even half looked at me like that, I'd be down there sitting on her lap by now."

"Well," I said, sarcastically, "you're the Casanova type, anyhow."

He missed the sarcasm. "Listen," he said. His eyes appraised me. "You could do all right, too, if you'd give yourself half a chance. You're a good-looking guy – a little on the slim side, but not bad. You're too timid, though. Women like aggressive guys. You gotta go after them. You—"

"Hey!" I broke in. He was beginning to embarrass me. "Not to change the subject, but did you find out from the advertising department how come we lost that second cover ad?"

"They've switched to the Tripub Comics group for the next six months. But they'll be back as soon as Tri's circulation drops and you can goose ours up again. How about getting on the ball and doing that, huh, kid?"

"Sure," I began to burn a little. As editor of Emcee's Comic magazine group, I was responsible for circulation. "That's easy. Just get the old man to allow me five bucks a page more for the artists and a dollar a page more for the writers. Better art and better stories are what the kids are buying. I do the best I can on the lousy budget I got."

"I suppose," Chernow finished his drink, swung around on his stool. He was looking at the legs of the girl at the end of the bar. He made a whistling sound. "Man, look at those legs!" he said. "Kip, kid, if you don't make that before you leave here, I'll disown you . . . Well, I got to run. Have a good time, boy. Live dangerously!"

I waved and in the bar mirror, watched him breeze out of the place. I told myself to hell with him. The next time I caught the eye of the girl at the end of the bar, I smiled. She looked frightened and turned her eyes right away.

"Herb," I said. He came toward me, wiping his hands on his bar apron, his amber eyes doleful. "Herb, ask the lady if she'll have a drink on me. At the end of the bar there."

The bartender's dolorous voice said: "You sure you want to do that, Mr Morgan? I mean, I know it's none of my business, but . . ." He broke off, half apologetically.

Something like a bell of warning seemed to toll inside my head. But I was looking at myself in the bar. Like Chernow had said, I wasn't a bad-looking guy. And that third Manhattan had hit home. I wasn't drunk but I was feeling – well – aggressive, cocky.

"Don't be silly, Herb," I said. "See if the lady'd like a drink."

He ambled down to the other end of the bar, spoke to the girl. I watched her in the mirror. She registered a little surprise, a little confusion, just the right amount of each, very cutely. I didn't hear what she said, but saw Herb start to mix a martini, then take it down to her. She looked at me in the bar mirror, raised the glass and formed the words, "Here's luck," with her full lips.

I said: "Herb, make me another drink. I've got to make a phone call." It was a quarter to six, now. I couldn't put it off any longer. I went through into the lobby to the phone booths. I called Fran, told her I'd been detained at the office, but was leaving now.

"I haven't looked at the schedule yet, Baby," I said. "So I don't know which bus I'll be able to get at this time. I'll call you from Wildwood and you can run out. Okay?"

"Kip," Fran said. "Are you all right?"

My heart skipped a couple of beats for no reason at all. "Sure. Of course I'm all right. What do you mean?"

"You haven't been drinking?"

I didn't answer for several seconds. Then I said: "Well, I stopped off and had a couple with Ronny Chernow. Why, I don't sound drunk, do I?"

She giggled. "No, silly. But you never call me 'Baby'. It sounded funny, coming from you."

"Oh," I said. "Well, I'll see you later."

"Okay," she said. "Okay, *Baby!*" She hung up.

I realized as soon as I left the phone booth that the instant I'd spoken to Fran, I'd forgotten all about my resolve to stay in town for dinner and the fights. At the sound of her voice I'd instinctively reverted to my role of the faithful home-loving husband. Routine had won out. I shrugged. It was probably just as well. Away from the dim lighting of the bar and the sight of the girl sitting there all alone, I realized that I just wasn't cut out for that sort of thing, let's face it. I would go back, finish that last drink I'd ordered and take off for the bus terminal.

Back in the Marlo bar, as I passed behind the girl at the end, she half turned, said, huskily: "Thanks for the drink. Why don't you bring yours over here? I mean, it's silly for the two of us not to talk."

I got kind of choked up. My heart felt too big and thick inside my chest; I was sure she could hear it. I was suddenly glad that I'd made that mistake on the phone and committed myself about going home, now. If I hadn't, I'd probably take this girl up on her invitation. The way the sound of her voice hit me, the impact her eyes had upon me – well – a guy is only human.

I said: "Uh – thanks – but I've got to run, now. Some other time."

I went to my own end of the bar, gulped down the Manhattan, gagging on it a little. When I set the empty glass down, I misjudged the distance, set it down a little too hard. I knew then that I was a little tight. I knew when I got outside it was going to hit me. I turned away from the bar and the girl spoke again:

"How about letting me buy you one, before you go? I mean, I don't want to be obligated. Please? Pretty please?"

This time her voice didn't get under my skin. It even annoyed me a little. She seemed suddenly overanxious and the soft huskiness had become harsh with the almost desperation tone of her voice now. And that repeated 'I mean' business grated, too. I was glad this was almost over and I'd had sense enough to get out from under before it was too late.

I had to pass her again to go out through the lobby exit. I said, almost abruptly: "No. No thank you. Next time. Good night." She half swung around on the stool as I started past and I had a nervous intuition that she was going to jump off the stool, confront me, block my exit, try to stop me from leaving. But she didn't.

I got out into the lobby and she must have been moving on tiptoe because I wasn't aware that she'd followed me out until she was right up beside me. She hooked her left arm through mine. At the same time I felt something hard being jammed against my right ribs. The arm hooked in mine pulled me forcibly to a stop. I looked at her. Out here in the bright light of the small hotel lobby, she didn't look so good. Her eyes were still beautiful but now their intensity, their broodingness looked sullen, almost angry. Lipstick was too thick on her wide mouth. Under the powder and rouge, her skin was coarse, grainy. But she was smiling up at me, invitingly. At least it would look that way to somebody else. But it didn't to me. Her face was too tight. The smile was too forced.

"Just a min—"

"Shut up, stupid," she cut me off. She was whispering, through her teeth, without breaking the smile. "I've got a gun in your ribs and if you make me, I'll use it right here. I could get away before anyone even realized what happened. Understand? Do as I say."

I wanted to laugh and at the same time a chill ran all over me. This was ridiculous. I was Kip Morgan, managing editor of the Comic Magazine Group at Emcee Publications, Inc., right across the street. I had never been arrested in my life. I bad never known any woman like this before. All my friends were respectable. And this was New York City, at the dinner hour. This was the Hotel Marlo, right in the public lobby, with the desk clerk and a bellhop only a few yards away and a portly old gentleman sitting in a lobby chair only a few feet away. This was all crazy.

"Are you kidding?" I said. "You . . ." I let my voice trail off. I was looking down at her other hand and it was thrust inside the trenchcoat where nobody could see it. The hand that was holding a gun, she said, against my ribs. I began to know, right then, that she wasn't kidding.

"Just walk with me slowly, toward the elevator. Don't say anything. Don't make any commotion or try to signal anyone. Don't try to break away. Behave yourself and you won't get hurt. I promise."

Sickness suddenly twisted at my stomach. I knew what it was, now. This was payday. It was a Friday and the Fifteenth. Payday for almost everybody in New York City. This was some kind of a new holdup gimmick. I thought of the hundred and twenty-five dollars in cash I had in my pocket. A full week's take-home. A whole week of getting up every morning at six-thirty and not getting home until almost seven at night. A week of deadliness and cajoling artists and script writers into getting their stuff in on time, of making out vouchers, and editing scripts and going over silverprints and a million other little chores and details.

A hundred and twenty-five bucks. And a mortgage payment due on the house. And food money next week for Fran. The new suit for young Stevie. The party dress for little June.

Fury seared through me. And shame. Fury because this girl was going to try and steal my money, that money that meant so many things to so many people. Shame because she was obviously cheap and vicious and I'd almost let myself be led on into taking her out. Because I hadn't gone home at the usual time, like someone sensible, because I'd let myself be jived into an extra drink.

I started to wrench violently away from her, then to grab her and howl for help. But she must have felt me tense. We were in front of the elevator, now. The gun ground deep into my ribs, hurting. She whispered. "You'd die, instantly. You wouldn't have a chance. Don't be a jerk. Be good for just a few more minutes and you'll be alive tomorrow."

The violent anger faded. Losing the money wouldn't hurt Fran and the kids half as much as it would their losing me. "Okay," I said. "But I think you've got the wrong guy. I'm broke. I deposited my money in the bank this noon." It was a last desperate play. It didn't work.

The elevator door opened and she whispered: "Be quiet, now."

We got in the elevator. The operator hardly glanced at us. A guy and a gal, arm in arm, getting into an elevator. What was that to get excited about? The girl, undoubtedly, was registered here. So she was taking a friend to her room. It was early in the evening. What was wrong with that?

Neither of us spoke after she said, "Fourteen" to the operator.

I remembered, crazily, that the fourteenth floor in all hotels is really the thirteenth. It's supposed to be less unlucky that way. It wasn't for me.

We got out and she guided me to the left, down the corridor. I heard the elevator door slam shut behind us. There was no sound in the whole hotel. Even our footsteps were muffled on the carpeting. I began to get really scared. The hollow of my spine got wet with sweat and my shirt stuck back there. Perspiration trickled coldly down my ribs, too. I thought once again, desperately, of yanking away, making a break. But at the same instant I realized that the girl would be even less likely to hesitate about killing me up here, with no witnesses. No . . . My chance was gone. If there'd ever been any chance.

2. The Patsy

She stopped in front of 1409 and still holding that gun in my ribs, she crossed her other hand over to the right side pocket and extracted the hotel key. The door opened easily and she unhooked my arm, pulled the gun out from under her coat and shoved me inside. There was a short hallway and the room at the other end was lighted. The gun at my spine forced me along, into that room.

There was a man sitting there. I had never seen him before in my life. But he seemed to know me. He said: "Hello, Morgan."

He was slouched in a green, leather-covered easy chair. A cigarette dangled from one of his slim, pale, long-fingered hands. Streamers of smoke went straight up. He was small and very thin, but not gangsterish-looking. Not in the movie tradition, anyhow. His hair was crew-cropped, a mousy brown color. His ears looked too large for his narrow, bony skull. He had level, gray, intelligent-looking eyes and they weren't shifty at all. They held my gaze, almost amusedly. But his mouth was what told me I was in for a hard time. It was tiny and pursed tightly as though he was mad at somebody and all tense and strung-up, even though he was sitting there so at ease and relaxed.

Still looking at me, he said to the girl: "What the hell took you so long, Viv?"

She stood off to one side still holding the gun. "Broth-*er!*" she said. "What a Sunday-school boy. I did everything. Everything but go over and sit on his lap. I would have done that, but that spaniel-faced old barkeep didn't seem too crazy about what I was up to. Anyhow, I couldn't get him to bite. He was running right out on me and I had to practically kidnap him, right in the lobby. And brother, don't think that didn't make me nervous!"

That was funny. I'd never even given a thought to the fact that she'd probably been just as scared as I was down there. I said, suddenly: "Look, what's this all about? If you want my money, I'll give it to you. You'd take it, anyhow. But, please take it easy. I – I've got a wife and kids." My voice broke and I felt sick, ashamed, pleading, begging with these people. But I'd have gotten down on my knees to them, right then, if it would have helped me get out of there any faster.

"Money," the man in the chair said. He laughed. It was a quick, sputtering sound. "Sure, we'll take your money. Throw me your wallet."

I reached inside my jacket pocket and took out the wallet, tossed it to him. "I'd like the wallet back."

He took out the sheaf of bills, riffled through them. He tossed the wallet back to me. "Over a hundred bucks more," he said to the girl, "Vivian, I've got the papers all ready. You keep that gun on him. But if there's any trouble, watch what you're doing. Don't shoot me by mistake."

He reached down to the armchair-side old-fashioned radio, and I saw that it was already lit up, turned on. He twisted the volume knob slowly and an orchestra playing a popular song grew louder and louder until it was almost deafening in the room. He said to Vivian:

"Now, if you have to shoot, it won't be so noticeable. Nor when he hollers. I think he'll holler real good."

With the racket of the radio, I could only half hear what he said. But my mind filled in the rest of it. I was suddenly confused and I felt cold and ill the way you do when you've got a fever and you have to get up out of bed at night. I was weak as a child.

I tried to figure what this was all about but I couldn't make it.

I looked toward the hotel room desk and saw that it was covered with papers. The man got up out of the chair. He said: "Vivian, get behind him with that shooter and ease him over to the desk."

She jabbed the muzzle of the gun against my spine and I stepped toward the desk. "Morgan," the man said. His voice got taut, his words clipped. "Morgan, I'm going to ask you to sign something. I hope you refuse. I hope you try to give us trouble. Because then we'll have to make you sign it. And that's what I'd like to have to do."

I looked at him and he held his hand out toward me, his skinny, white, long-fingered hands. In the pinkish palms he held two rolls of nickels. He closed his fingers around them. His knuckles stood out sharply. With the weight of those nickels in them, those knuckles would make his fists like gnarled clubs. There was suddenly a roaring in my ears and my heart seemed to be up and choking in my throat. I hadn't been in a fight, been hit by a fist, since I was a kid. And only twice, then. I'd always hated fist fights. I'd avoided them. It made me ill to hit somebody else and to feel another's fist making that sickly smack noise against my own face was worse.

Turning away from him, I looked down at the top paper on the desk. It was a letter on Emcee Publishing Company letterhead stationery. My eyes seemed to ache and I had trouble reading. I kept wiping the flat of my hands up and down my trousers but they still stayed slick with sweat. The letter was dated today. It said:

To Whom It May Concern:

For the past year I have steadily and regularly been embezzling company funds. All told, I have taken nearly $50,000. This was done with the aid and connivance of Miss Elizabeth Tremayne, of the Business Department. How, will be obvious, Monday, when the books are examined.

The money has all been spent on gambling on horses and in bad stock market investments. I'd hoped to win or earn the money back and prevent eventual discovery, but this did not work out.

For all the trouble and disillusion this is going to cause, I am truly sorry.

I herewith, also append a list of the dozen or more different signatures I used on the company checks, to remove any doubt that I've been the culprit.

(Signed)

Under this was a list of signatures, names I didn't even recognize. But as I looked at this letter, it flashed through my mind what this was all about. Emcee Publication's fiscal year started on Monday. A complete auditing would be made. Whoever *had* been embezzling knew their time was up and they couldn't avoid discovery. I was going to be the fall guy – in advance.

Something hit me in the cheek and for a moment I didn't feel any pain. Only shock and a slight dizziness. But the blow whirled me around. Something hit me in the stomach. I bent way over, took a stumbling step forward, my legs apart, and almost fell. I'd never felt so sick to my stomach. Yet all I could do was make gagging sounds. I couldn't seem to get any breath. As though from a great distance, down a long, wind-rushing tunnel I heard someone say: "Sign that letter."

The sickness left. I straightened up. The girl behind me said: "Give him a chance, Smitty. Don't bang up his face."

I stood there sucking in breath, trying to focus my eyes. I leaned on the desk, with both hands, looked down at that letter. That letter! I couldn't sign that, no matter what they did to me. I couldn't take the rap for somebody else's crookedness.

I thought of the whispering and sniggering there'd be at the Emcee offices, Monday, after news of that letter spread around . . . "That Kip Morgan," they'd say. "Who'd ever have thought it? But they say those quiet guys are the ones you've got to watch out for. Listen, I'll bet some dame got plenty of that dough, too!" . . . I could see the newspaper headlines, especially in the Wildwood Press:

LOCAL MAN CONFESSES $50,000 THEFT!

I thought of my neighbours, of my kids going to school and the other kids pointing at them, whispering. I knew how cruel kids could be about things like that.

I wouldn't do it. To hell with them. I wasn't going to sign it.

Smitty hit me again. His weighted, sharp-knuckled fist caught me in the kidney. I went twisting over to one side like a stagger-drunk. Pain ran all through me in little flashes of fire, then ran all together in a balled-up flame of aching agony all up my left side and back. I felt tears hot and blurry in my eyes, then running down my cheeks. I looked at Smitty. His wide-set gray eyes were crinkled at the corners as though he was grinning. But his little kewpie doll mouth stayed the same; it showed no expression.

"You're a real hero, aren't you?" he said. "That's beautiful. I like heroes."

He came toward me. And I suddenly didn't care about the girl with the gun behind me. Let her shoot me. Let them kill me. At least the pain would be over. Then they could never make me sign that letter. I swung at him with every ounce of strength I had left. He picked the blow off with his left arm like a lovetap. He took hold of me with his left hand, by the shirt front. His right hand whip-snapped back and forth across my cheeks and mouth, stinging hard. I felt the salty blood in my mouth.

Then his balled, weighted fist hit me in the stomach again. I don't remember falling. But I was on the floor, staring down at the green wall-to-wall rug. I saw Smitty's feet in front of me. He wore patent leather shoes, like dancing pumps, with small black leather bows on them. Then his feet disappeared. There was pain – vast, searing pain all through my ribs as he kicked me.

I cursed. I called him every filthy word I'd ever heard. I was crying, sobbing with rage and pain. I said: "Why are you doing this to me? Why, why? I never did anything to you! Stop it! Please, please stop!"

"For a thousand bucks we're doing it," Smitty said. I could hear him quite plainly in the momentary lull between the end of a song on the radio and the commercial. "For a grand I'd kick hell out of my own mother. So it's nothing personal, understand. But you'd better sign that letter."

The radio music blasted out again. I felt somebody grab me under the arms, lift me. Somehow I got my feet together under me and stood. But not for long. My knees seemed to have no bones in them. I fell backward and sat down on the edge of the bed. I leaned over and put my face in my hands, then looked at the smear of blood on my fingers.

There was suddenly a terrible noise and excruciating pain in my ear. It wasn't until later that I realized he'd slapped me over the ear with his cupped hand. For a moment, I couldn't even hear the radio. I rocked in agony and blubbered. I called to Fran to help me. I kept calling her name. It didn't do any good. Smitty kept slapping and cuffing me and when I'd fall over on my side onto the bed, his fist would wallop into my ribs or kidneys.

After a while there was just a void of pain. I got numb all over, didn't think, didn't react. And then I realized he wasn't hitting me any more. I looked up through tear-fogged eyes at him and knew that as long as I didn't react he'd ease up on me. At the same time, sharp thoughts seemed to flash suddenly through my brain. I felt filled with cunning. I told myself: "I can outsmart this guy. I can be crooked, too. I can double-deal *him!* Okay, I'll sign their damned letter. I've been stupid. What difference does it make? This is only Friday night and I've got my office keys. I've got until Monday morning. I can prove my innocence. What good is that piece of paper? I can show my cuts and bruises, prove that I was forced to sign it. I'll go right to the police and I'll help them find out who it was really stole that money.

Leering at Smitty and Vivian, I got up from the bed. I reached out toward the desk. "All – all right," I said. "I'll sign."

I started to walk toward the desk but my legs gave out. Smitty had to put his arm around me, hold me up until I got to the desk, could lean on it with one hand. I picked up the pen. I signed their confession for them. I had hardly put the pen down when Smitty hit me in the temple. There was an explosion of multicolored lights. There was darkness. Then blinding light again. On and off. On and off.

I wasn't completely out. I was aware of being dragged along the floor by hands under my armpits. I could hear voices. I could hear that the radio had been turned off. But I couldn't move. There was a tingling all through my arms and legs the same as you get when you lie on one arm and it goes numb. I heard Smitty swear. He said: "Shut the window again, Viv. We can't do it, now. There's a damn cop standing in that doorway right across the street."

"So what?" she said. "He isn't looking up here. We can get him dumped out and the cop won't know anything about it until he hits the pavement. We'll be gone by then."

"Don't be stupid. Suppose he *does* just happen to glance up while we're easing him out the window. We'd never get out of the hotel."

Oh, yes, I'd been very clever, very cunning, to sign that confession for them. So clever, so brilliant – so stupified with pain, I hadn't realized they couldn't let me live. I was going to be a "suicide". That would tie in beautifully with the confession. How could they let me live to contest the thing?

Some of the numbness left my arms and legs. I realized I was huddled in a heap against the wall under the hotel-room window. I thought of the way it would look out that window, down fourteen – no thirteen – flights. I thought about air rushing past me, taking my breath away as I'd fall, wheeling, turning, over and over. I thought of the sound I'd make, hitting the pavement down there.

"Why doesn't the fat fool go, get out of that doorway?" Vivian said. "Of all the fool places for a cop to stand around and kill time!"

Please, I begged, *Please, God, don't let him move. Don't let him move, make him stay there. Right there!*

"Listen," Vivian said. "Turn the radio on again. You can shoot him. Make it look like *he* did it, himself. I'm getting nervous. I want to get this over with and get out of here."

"Oh, sure," Smitty said. "With this gun. It can be traced, you goon. That's no good. There's got to be some other way. That damned cop looks like he's settled for the night over there."

There was silence for a moment. I felt my leg twitch and jerk, uncontrollably. Vivian said: "Hurry up. He's coming to, again."

I lay very still. I got cramped from the huddled position they'd let my limp figure fall into. But I didn't move again.

"His wrists," Vivian said, "We can break a glass. A sharp piece of glass and cut the veins in his wrists."

Smitty thought about that. I got afraid they would hear the thunder of my heart, know I was listening. Then Smitty said: "No. First place, the police would wonder about him being all bruised up. Going out the window, that wouldn't have been noticed or thought anything of. Besides, the bleeding would take too long. We'll wait. That cop's got to leave sometime."

It came to me quite clearly, then, what I had to do. I didn't like the idea. I wasn't brave about it. I just didn't have any choice. It came to me that as far as they were concerned, I was already dead. There was no question but what they were going to kill me, by one method or another, sooner or later. They had to.

Knowing that I was going to die, anyhow, I suddenly knew that I'd make it as tough as possible for them, at least make a fight for it. Being shot wouldn't be any worse than being tossed out that window. I braced both hands against the wall and lunged away from it, scrabbled to my feet, staggering back away from them. I was weak and trembling. Both Vivian and Smitty looked at me in surprise. Vivian still held the gun.

"Well," Smitty said. "Snookums woke up." He put his hands in his pockets, took out the rolls of nickels. "I'll have to rock him off to sleep again."

I started backing away, slowly, toward the door. I saw Vivian raise the revolver, saw her fingers tighten, whiten, around it. I heard Smitty say: "Don't use that gun. We don't have to. The radio's off. They'd hear a shot all through the hotel. And there'd be no powder burns. It wouldn't look like suicide. I'll take care of him."

He came at me fast, half running. I whirled and got to the corner of the room where it turned into the hall leading to the door. I stopped and swung around again. He was almost on me and his own momentum was too much for him to stop. I hit him. I swung with all my might, from the knees. The blow smashed into his cheeks. But nothing happened. He just swayed and looked at me with a sort of puzzled look in those wide-set, level gray eyes. I knew then that I was too weak to hurt him much.

I knew then that this was going to be like a dream I often had, where I was fighting somebody and I kept hitting them, hitting them, but nothing happened and they didn't seem to be hurt. They'd keep laughing at me. This was going to be like that. For one crazy moment I thought that maybe all this was just part of some nightmare. Maybe I'd awaken any moment and find myself at home in bed, with Fran curled up warmly beside me.

Then I heard Vivian say: "Get out of the way, Smitty. I've got to shoot him. We can't let him get away!" She sounded hysterical.

That was when I swung again. This time my fist hit Smitty on the point of the jaw and he staggered backward until his legs hit the edge of the bed and he sat down on it. I went down the hall toward the door, sprinting. I got the door open and looked back and saw Vivian turn the corner of the room and level the gun at me. The door slammed shut, blocking off the picture of that snarling, feline face of hers. I didn't think of direction. I just turned to the left and ran and turned a corner of the hall and saw ahead of me on the right a door marked Fire Exit. I went through it and stopped. If they came after me, they'd assume that I'd gone down the stairs. So I went up. I went up two flights, three steps at a time, on my tiptoes, making as little noise as possible. At the top, I sprawled, exhausted, against the wall and listened. There was no sound from the fire stairs at all. Only the sound of my own labored breathing.

I went through into the sixteenth floor hallway, made my way to the elevator, rang the bell. It seemed like hours before the indicator crawled up to fourteen. I held my breath to see if it would stop there. It didn't. It came on up to sixteen. The elevator operator, a middle-aged man with a hawk nose and glasses, peered at me curiously as I got in.

"Listen," I said. "If you get a buzz at the fourteenth floor, don't stop. Please. It – it's a matter of life and death."

I looked at the indicator bank and so did he. We both saw there was no signal to stop at fourteen. I leaned against the wall of the elevator and for the first time became really aware of the throbbing aches in my ribs and kidneys and at my left temple. There was a welt there from Smitty's knuckles. I took out a handkerchief and wet it with my tongue, wiped some of the blood away from my lips. There wasn't much. My lip was cut on the inside, was a little puffy.

"What happened?" the operator asked. He looked at me with that curious but unemotional expression that spectators at an accident always have.

"I–I had some trouble, that's all," I said. Sure. Just some trouble. Beaten up, almost thrown out of a window, but for the intervention of some kind providence. I got to trembling again, thinking about it.

The elevator reached the main floor and I walked, wobbledy-legged, across the lobby to the desk. The clerk, a needle-thin man with great horned-framed glasses and a pointed nose said, "Yes, sir?" without hardly looking at me.

I took a deep breath. Down here in the brightly lighted, rather ancient and shoddy austerity of this hotel lobby, what I was going to have to say would sound melodramatic, ridiculous. I said. "You'd better send the house officer up to room fourteen-o-nine. I just escaped from there after being beaten up and robbed and almost killed. I—"

I stopped. A sickening shock went through me. I had forgotten that letter of confession I'd signed. Smitty and Vivian still had that. I looked up at the desk clerk again. He was peering at me as though I'd just crawled out of the woodwork. "Are you – uh – *sure*, sir?" he said.

"Look." I took out my blood-smeared handkerchief and showed it to him. I curled back my upper lip with one finger so he could see the cut there. I pointed to my temple and the lump right in front of my ear. I said: "A girl accosted me here in the lobby and forced me up to her room at gunpoint. There was a man there and he—"

"Here in *this* lobby?" the clerk cut in. "What room was this, sir?"

I told him. I got sore. "Are you going to send the house dick up there or do I have to call outside police? I want you to hurry. They've probably left that room already as it is. But check it anyhow. And they can't get out of this hotel without my seeing them. I'll stay here with a cop until they *do* try to get out."

The desk clerk was looking over his file card. "Room fourteen-o-nine," he said. "We don't have a girl registered for that room. It – well – I suppose it *could* be a girl. The name is K. Morgan. No baggage. Paid one day, in advance."

"Morgan," I repeated after him. "That's *my* name. Let me see the registry."

He showed it to me. The signature was a reasonable facsimile of my own.

They hadn't made any mistake. They'd registered the room in my name. It would look like I'd taken it with the express purpose of leaping fom the window, killing myself. At the same time I realized that they probably had another room of their own, on the same floor, that they could flee to, hide out in, if anything went wrong.

"Do you remember what the person looked like who registered for that room?" I said.

The clerk shook his head, looked at the registration. "Whoever it was, signed in at noon. I didn't come on until four P.M."

I watched the clerk pick up a desk phone, heard him ask for 1409. He waited quite a while, then hung up. "Nobody answers," he said.

"Of course not. They've gone."

But they were still in the hotel. I thought: *I'll have them call the police. We'll go to every room on the fourteenth floor. If we don't find them, we'll go through every room in the hotel. We'll get them.*

Then I realized that wasn't bright. Supposing I did find them. I couldn't prove anything. There were two of them, their words against mine. Even Herb, the bartender, recognizing that the girl was the one who'd been in the bar with me, left when I did, wouldn't prove anything. That was out.

I got a better idea. I told the clerk: "Never mind. Skip it. I'll handle it myself."

I turned away from the desk and went out onto the street. I crossed the street and got into a darkened doorway over there, where I could watch the hotel exit. I stood there. This would be better. One or both of them would have to leave the hotel sometime. They would have to report to whoever had hired them to do this to me. I'd follow, find out who it was. Then I'd really have something to work on. But maybe they wouldn't go to their boss. They might telephone him or her and report on what had happened. Well, that was a chance I'd have to take.

While I waited, I went over the whole thing in my mind. I got the setup pretty clearly. They were trying to frame me for the embezzlement, so it must've been worked in a way that would have been possible for me to accomplish. There was only one way that was possible. I didn't actually handle any company cash. But I got the checks for other people and mailed them to them. To our artists and writers. Hundreds of thousands of dollars a year in checks.

The procedure was this. I had to voucher for a script or art work when it was turned in, as managing editor of the comics magazine group. The business office made out checks for those vouchers and the individual checks in turn were given back to me to mail to the artists and writers. The average writer's check for a single script was sixty to seventy dollars. The average artist's check was for twenty dollars a comic-book page, which meant their checks averaged about one hundred and sixty dollars. We paid editorial bills twice a week. It would be a comparatively simple thing for me, in connivance with somebody in the business office, to make out vouchers to phoney names, for scripts and/or art work that hadn't even been done, a couple of times a week. Then, when I got the checks, to sign them with the name they were made out to, then double-endorse them with another phoney name, with which I'd already established a bank account, and deposit them to that account.

Liz Tremayne, the bookkeeper, if working with me on this deal, could easily cover for me on the books, until the end of the fiscal year when the regular annual auditing took place.

I had never thought of this possibility to defraud Emcee Publications out of thousands of dollars before. But I thought of it now. Plenty. The more I thought of it, the more I realized how badly that confession would make things look for me.

But since I hadn't done this, I had to figure out who had. Nobody but me handled checks and vouchers in the editorial department. Almost anybody in the business office could have worked the deal. All they had to do was get hold of a stack of editorial voucher forms from the stock room, learn to forge my handwriting, and – working with Liz Tremayne, who kept books and made out the checks – they wouldn't even have to be too clever with that. But how about the people who signed the checks? Wouldn't they get suspicious over a couple of extra checks being there twice a week?

The checks bore two signatures, M. C. Malkom's, the president's, and the authorized counter-signature, which would be Ronny Chernow's, as head of the Business Office. Chernow! Since Emcee Publications put out other books besides comics – Confession magazines and a string of pulps – there would probably be twenty or thirty checks to be signed twice a week.

Mr Malkom probably never even looked at them, but went through them and signed them one right after the other as fast as he could. Especially since the checks always went up for his final signature close to five o'clock in the afternoon. But Chernow wouldn't rush through those checks, signing them, without examining them. That was part of his job, to double check on things like that, make sure a mistake hadn't been made and two checks made out in error for the same material.

That did it. I knew then that Ronny Chernow was the one who had been working this embezzlement deal, who had decided to frame me for it. It all stacked up. Chernow, himself, gambled, played the market a lot. I'd seen the newspapers on his desk, turned to the racing entries and the market listings, many times. This was the answer to how he lived a life that would seem to take three times his salary.

I thought, then, too, about Liz Tremayne, the bookkeeper. She was a girl you could not figure. She was tall and neat, but you could never tell much about her figure. She always wore loose-fitting dresses or severely tailored suits. She wore double-lensed glasses and little if any makeup. She wore her brown hair pulled back into a severe bun. I remembered that she had nice features, but the way she dressed and wore her hair, you'd never notice that. She impressed everyone as being a very plain, unattractive girl. No sex appeal at all.

Yet, I also remember now, a long time ago, hearing Ronny Chernow, standing with a bunch of other men from the office by the water cooler one day, watching Liz Tremayne go past.

Ronny had said: "You see all that protective coloration? But it doesn't fool me. Put some makeup on that baby, fix her hair right, get her into the right dresses and take those horrible glasses off and I'll bet she'd knock your eyes out. And *that* kind – once you break through that icy surface – man, oh, man!"

We'd all thought Ronny was crazy, then. But I saw now where he could be right. And that tied in with Liz helping him out with this deal. The quiet, plain, bookish type like that often went crazy for a man who was a complete opposite like Chernow. Especially once he'd started paying a lot of attention to her, began softening her up. And a woman in love with a man, often would do anything for him.

So there it was. Now what was I going to do with it? Chernow was my man. He knew I stopped in at the Marlo bar for a cocktail every Friday night. He'd hired Vivian and Smitty to do a job on me. He'd had her planted in the bar, then came in, himself, to put the finger on me, so she wouldn't make any mistake and get the wrong guy. He'd even suckered me into staying for another drink, when I was ready to leave, tried to plant the idea in my mind of making a play for Vivian. It all tied in, nicely.

3. Ugly Duckling

ACROSS the street was a barber shop, with a clock in the window. The time was 8:10. It hardly seemed possible that all this had happened in only a couple of hours. It seemed like I'd been up half the night, already. And then I remembered Fran. She'd be expecting me home. I should have been there, even, before this. She'd get upset, worried. I had to call her. But I wondered what I could tell her. The truth would drive her crazy with anxiety. I'd have to make up something to tell her.

I decided not to wait any longer for Vivian and Smitty to leave the hotel. Now I knew who was behind all this, I didn't necessarily need them; I walked down to the corner, entered a cigar store and called Fran. While I was waiting for her to answer, I counted the money I had in my pocket. I'd taken a five-dollar bill from my pay, this noontime, put that in my pocket and placed the rest of my cash in my wallet. Smitty had gotten that. Lunch and the drinks tonight had left me with a dollar bill and a few cents change from the five.

Fran came on and sounded relieved at hearing from me. I told her that as I was leaving the bar with Chernow, we'd bumped into a couple of other men from the office. They were going to the fights at the Garden, I told her and one of them had an extra ticket, so I decided to go along. I said I hadn't been able to get to a phone before. I hoped she wouldn't mind.

"Of course not, darling," Fran said. "Just don't be too late. And have fun!"

I hung up and sat there for a moment. Yeah. Have fun. I was going to have a lot of fun.

I left the cigar store and stood out on the street in front of it. I looked down Forty-Sixth Street toward Broadway. It was a long alley of flickering neon lights. I hadn't been in New York at night like this for years. But if I saw it every night, I think it would have affected me the same way. New York, even the Times Square area, is a business world by day. It's speed, turmoil, excitement. But it's in black and white. After dark the whole thing changes.

The pace doesn't slow, but now it's in full color and the moving neon lights heighten the effect of continual action. Reality, ugliness, is gone. You don't notice the dirt-littered gutters, the unpainted buildings, the grimy bricks and windows. Manhattan by day is a businesswoman, crisp, efficient, an executive, stern, no time for anything but making money: a salesman, loud, swaggering, confident. By night the town's an exciting, painted woman of the evening; a young girl out on her first New York date; an actor between performances, out on the street in costume and greasepaint.

You stand in a midtown side street at night and all your values change. The pulsing nightlife around you gets into your own bloodstream. Obligations, duties, ideals, slip away. Life is a carnival. Perspectives change. Nothing counts, suddenly, but laughing, singing, drinking, dancing. You need a pretty girl, to look at the promise in her eyes, to watch her tongue moisten her red lips, to watch her teeth shine in the saying; you want to feel that girl in your arms as the chrome-like polish and smoothness of a name band stirs the rhythm in you both; you want to get drunk, where all is beautiful, all gaiety, fast funny talk, and none of it will ever end and there will be no morning, no hangover, no regret.

In spite of what I'd been through this evening, and the jam I was still in, I felt all that, for a moment. I could imagine what it would do to some people, *living* in all that, going out into it night after night. Because you weren't a part of it – and little of it was for nothing, you had to buy it – unless you had money in your pockets. Lots of money. I could imagine that this was what had happened to Ronny Chernow and perhaps Liz Tremayne, too.

But I forced all that out of my mind. I had to get this evening over with. I had to get Ronny Chernow, get that signed statement of confession back and get him arrested for all he'd done. That was a big order.

What would happen if I went straight to Chernow, now, confronted him with the whole thing? He'd laugh at me, deny it, say I was drunk. Or possibly he would kill me. Or Vivian and Smitty, his hired help would either be there, or get there after I arrived. No. That was out. I had to learn more, first, at least.

I remembered that the confession I'd been forced to sign implicated Liz Tremayne. I didn't doubt but what she'd been in on all this with Chernow. But I could not figure his mentioning her in the confession. Monday, when the whole thing came out, she'd be on the spot, too. She certainly wouldn't protect Chernow, then. There was only one answer to that. She'd been killed, probably, with another note and with the murder made to look like suicide, also. That would round it out nicely for Chernow. If that hadn't happened yet, it would soon. If it hadn't happened yet, I could save Liz's life. Once she saw the way her partner was double-crossing her, she'd turn on him, substantiate my story. If she was still alive.

I went back into the cigar store, called Liz Tremayne. There was no answer. But I had to find out whether she was dead yet or not. Her address was on West End Avenue and I took a subway up there. It was an old, run-down apartment building, still bearing some trace of its glory days in the faded and torn canopy over the front and in the fat, whiskey-flushed doorman in his soiled uniform. There was no switchboard, but I learned from the mailboxes that Miss Elizabeth Tremayne lived in Apartment 3 M.

There had been no police cars in front of the place, no sign of excitement. I figured I'd gotten a break, that she was still alive. I rang the bell outside of her apartment. There was the click of high heels across the floor inside and the door cracked open. Then it was thrown wide. The girl who stood there didn't look like the Liz Tremayne of Emcee Publications, Inc. Business Office. In fact, for a flashing second I didn't even recognize her.

The hair that was always pulled into a tight, unattractive bun at the back, now flowed softly, silkily about her shoulders. It had been just washed and treated with some kind of light rinse and it looked alive and all full of shiny highlights. It was a honey color, instead of just brown.

Liz was wearing makeup, tonight. Her lips were smoothly painted and glistening. There were artfully blended touches of color at her high cheekbones. Without glasses, her eyes were beautiful. They were a flame-blue, in striking contrast to the thick, black, spiky lashes and the thin, dark, neatly formed arch of the brows above them.

She was wearing a blace lace and silk negligée, trimmed with what looked to me like pink angora. It was just held together by a belt in the front. She had everything necessary to wear something like that. What Ronny Chernow had said about her that day long ago, was true in spades. This Liz Tremayne knocked you out, all right. I couldn't get my breath that first moment of looking at her.

"Kip!" she said. She didn't even sound like the same girl I'd seen around the office for several years. When she'd changed her appearance she'd apparently altered her whole personality. "Kip Morgan, what are you doing here?"

I'd wanted to see what emotions registered in her eyes when she first recognized me. But it didn't work out. I wasn't looking at her eyes. When my gaze did finally rise to her face, she was smiling, puzzled.

"Something's happened," I said. "I – we'd better not talk out here."

"Of course," she said. "Come on in."

She stepped aside and I moved past her, down a short hallway and into the living room. The room was large, high-ceilinged. It was furnished more like a studio than an apartment. Instead of a sofa there was a studio conch. There was no matching furniture, no upholstered chairs. There were two leather-covered lounge chairs and several straight-backed ones. There were scatter rugs on the floor and prints of good paintings decorated the blue-tinted walls. Between two enormous windows was a ceiling-high bookcase, with every other shelf decorated with knick-knacks, instead of books. I turned to Liz Tremayne.

"How well do you know Ronny Chernow?" I demanded.

She blinked. The color on her cheekbones seemed to darken. She held her hands clasped in front of her. Her voice was distant, cool, when she said: "What's this all about? You have no right to come barging in here, uninvited, questioning me about my private life!"

"All right," I said. I gave it to her right between the eyes. "Chernow has been embezzling Emcee Publications out of thousands of dollars for a full year. You've been his accomplice. I have proof, so don't try to deny it."

She fell back away from me as though I'd slapped her. She went deadly pale and now the spots of rouge on her cheeks stood out like red poker chips. Her hands clenched together until the knuckles stood out whitely.

"You must be insane!" she said. "Making an accusation like that! What in the world's the matter with you, Kip? What's made you say – or even think a thing like – embezzling funds? How?" She glanced toward the door of another room, a reflex action, but then caught it and turned her gaze quickly back to me again.

I got a crawling feeling up my spine. Supposing Ronny Chernow, when he heard from his gun-goons – Vivian and Smitty – that I'd escaped, had anticipated me, come straight here. He could be hiding in that room, right now, waiting to kill me himself, not trusting to hirelings this time.

I took a big, gulping breath and without waiting, or giving myself a chance to get really scared, I whirled around Liz Tremayne and walked to that room. While I was fumbling inside the door for the light switch, Liz leaped at me, tried to yank me away. But she was too late. My fingers found the wall switch and the room flooded with light. Liz stood trying to pull me away from the doorway.

It was a bedroom, furnished with cheap maple furniture. There was nobody hiding there. But on the bed were two expensive alligator leather suitcases and a woman's purse. I started toward them and Liz grabbed my shoulder, wheeled me around, got in front of me, blocking me off.

"You have no right!" she half screamed. "This is *my* apartment.

Get out of here! Get out! I'll call the police – have you thrown out!"

She was strong. She kept pushing me back toward the doorway to the living room, away from those bags on the bed. She was so strong, she kept throwing me off balance, gradually forcing me out of the room. It was no time to be gentlemanly. I grabbed her by the wrists and flung her with every bit of strength in me, away from me. She went spinning and hit the wall with her back, jarring her, so that hair fell down over one eye. She leaned back against the wall, her head forward and lowered a little, her beautiful eyes, frightened, angry, blurred with tears, looking up at me through the thick black lashes. She was half sobbing.

"Call the police?" I said. "Go ahead. I'm going to do it, anyhow, when I get through here. Now, stay away from me. If you interfere, I'll have to knock you out." Big, tough Kip Morgan, a real rough cookie – when he was up against an unarmed girl. But I had to do it.

I went over to the bed and snapped open one of the suitcases. It was filled with women's clothing. On the top, lying face down, was a framed photograph. I turned it over and looked down into a portrait of smirking, handsome Ronny Chernow, dressed like Mr John K. Rockabilt. I put it back down, shut the suitcase. I picked up the purse, opened it. Along with all the usual feminine junk, there was an airlines envelope, containing two one-way flight tickets to Mexico City. I put them back, then tossed the purse back onto the bed.

"You and Ronny were running out on the whole thing, eh?" I said. "To Mexico."

She was still leaning against the wall. The tears had finally squeezed out of her eyes and were running down her cheeks. She pushed the hair back from her forehead and shook her head. Her gaze dropped away from mine, fell to the floor.

"How did you find out about it, Kip? We – we thought we had plenty of time. Until Monday, at least, maybe longer. Where's Ronny? Have the police got him?"

She could have been acting, but I didn't think so. There was a whipped tone to her voice. And the packed bags and the airline tickets told of her innocence. She was getting the big double-deal from Chernow and didn't even know it. Yet. She was being made a patsy, too, right along with me.

"I don't know where Ronny is!" I told her. "How'd I find out about this? Because Chernow paid a guy and a girl to lure me to a hotel room. They beat me into signing a confession that *I'd* been the one taking the money, pulling that phoney check racket for the past year. Then they were going to throw me out of the window. It would look as though I'd committed suicide. You and Ronny Chernow would have been beautifully cleared. Neither of you would have had a thing to worry about Monday morning."

Her eyes widened. "But – but I don't understand. Why didn't Ronny tell me about all this? He told me that because I was implicated there wasn't any way of framing it on anyone else. We – we talked about that. We discussed trying to put it all onto you. Kip. But Ronny said we couldn't – not and keep in the clear. He still had over five thousand left when he sold out what was left of his stocks. He said with just a few thousand we could live well for a few months in Mexico and that he had some connections down there, that there was plenty of money to be made down there for a man with brains and looks and personality. So we were going to run for it. By now, I didn't care. I–I was just glad that it was over . . . I–I guess he must have made a last minute change in plans and figured some way to put it onto you and still keep me in the—"

"No," I cut in on her. "He didn't. He planned it this way right from the beginning, Liz. I forgot to tell you. *Your* name *was* mentioned in that confession letter I was forced to sign. It fully implicated you. The only one Ronny Chernow kept in the clear was himself. The way he was going to do that was to kill you, too. Another suicide. That would tie it all up."

She shook her head violently from side to side. Her mouth was slack, her eyes wild, trapped-looking. "No!" she cried. "You're wrong! It couldn't be that. Ronny wouldn't do that to me!" Her voice broke. "He loves me. We were going to be married in Mexico! You're wrong, wrong, all wrong!"

"He never loved you," I told her. "Or he wouldn't have gotten you into this in the first place. A guy like Chernow isn't capable of love, not real love. He liked you – he went for you – big, maybe. But not any more, Liz. He got tired of you. He was through with you. He wanted to get rid of you. This gave him an out on that, too."

She had her face in her hands, now. Her soft, silky, honey-colored hair hung over her hands as she bent her head. I couldn't hear her sobbing but I could see her shoulders shaking. I could see a vein standing out in her throat. She was pitiful. I felt a little sorry for her.

"Liz," I said softly. "How could you get mixed up in a thing like this – with a big-mouthed, phoney louse like Chernow? How do these things happen?"

After a moment she got control of herself. She looked at me, her eyes raw-red from crying, her makeup smeared. "How?" she said. Her voice was ragged, bitter. "All right, I'll tell you how. Maybe you'll feel sorry for me. Maybe you'll figure some way to give me a break."

She told me. The beginning was an old story. Ronny Chernow was her boss. They worked late together a couple of nights. He bought her dinner. They had some drinks. It went on from there. She'd never known a man like Chernow, before. She was impressed, awed, overwhelmed by the way he dressed and the way he spent money, the places he took her.

"Places girls who work for a living, who are drab and plain, dream about, see in the movies, read about in the papers and that's all," she said. "The most expensive nightclubs. The clubhouse at Belmont. Flashy gambling places over in New Jersey. And Ronny – he was so smart about everything. He taught me how to fix myself up, how to dress. He made me – *pretty!* So that I felt as good as any of the women in those places. He drove me around in a Cadillac – a Caddy, Kip!"

"Didn't you wonder where he got the money, how he did all that on his salary?" I asked.

"He told me he was very lucky at gambling and played the market shrewdly," she said. "Listen, every night I was in such a dream world, I didn't think, didn't care *how* it was happening. Do you question miracles? Of course, in the daytime, at the office, I'd go back to my old personality. Ronny said it would be better that way, wouldn't cause any talk."

Then she told me how he trapped her. They went to Atlantic City for a weekend. He took a fifty-dollar-a-day hotel suite. He lost several hundred dollars at the race track there. When it was all over, he told her about the four fake artist's checks that he'd put through and held out and cashed, how it was a plan he'd

long had in mind. He told Liz Tremayne that she was going to
have to cover for him.

At first she refused. She was horrified, sick over it. But he
cajoled and threatened. He said if she didn't cooperate with him
and he got caught, he'd involve her, anyhow. He told her that it
would just be this once and there was no possible way of it being
found out for nearly a year. She gave in, then. She covered for
him. Then she was trapped and it became a regular thing.

"I knew we were going to have to face the music at the end,"
she finished. "But by then I didn't care, Kip. I didn't care. I
was so damned in love with the man that I didn't care about
anything. Do you understand, Kip . . . But now he's – done this
– to me!"

She started to cry again, but suddenly jerked convulsively
all over. She cut off the weeping. She forced a little half-smile
around her mouth. The negligée was half falling away from one
shoulder but she didn't do anything about it, even though she
was conscious of the way I was staring. I couldn't help it. Even
now, after all this, she was still breathtakingly beautiful.

"Kip," she said. She started slowly toward me. "Kip, I–I can't
go to prison. I–I just *can't!* Kip, I never noticed before, but
you're handsome, too. And you're clever. You've got personality,
too, Ronny Chernow isn't the only one. You'd make out fine
in Mexico, too. I'd help you, Kip; help you a *lot!* We'd make a
striking couple!"

"Don't be crazy, Liz," I said. "I've got a wife, a family. Are
you out of your mind? Stay away from me. It's no good, Liz."

But she kept walking, slowly, provocatively, her hands running
down over her own hips, pulling the negligée tautly over them,
lowering it from the shoulder some more. Watching her, little
electric shocks started shooting all through me. My breath
seemed to catch and hurt in my chest. Her eyes had cleared
from the crying spell, now. Her teeth were very white and even
against the red lips as she smiled.

"Mexico, Kip," she whispered. "You must've had dreams,
too. I – I've got five hundred dollars in cash in my purse. That's
worth a lot more in Mexico. We've already got the ticket. The
plane leaves at seven in the morning. You're going with me, Kip.
We'll both put all the past behind us – all of it. We'll start over."

I tried to back away from her, but my legs bumped against

the bed. She came right up close against me. The faintly musky scent of her filled my nostrils, my whole head. I began to tremble. She pressed against me and her long, carmine-nailed fingers grasped my lapels.

"Just you and me, Kip," she said, her voice so low and throaty I couldn't have heard it if her lips hadn't been only an inch or so away from mine.

Her hands slid from my lapels up around my neck, then to the back of my head. They pulled my head toward her. Her mouth burned against mine and the lights in the room seemed to pinwheel. All thought, all reason went up in a burst of flame in my brain.

I found myself holding onto her by the upper arms, my fingers digging into their soft flesh.

And then the whole thing exploded. It was a muffled explosion, like clapping two thickly gloved hands together hard. Liz Tremayne went limp and, still gripping her upper arms, I was half pulled over with her. I looked at her face. Her eyes stared up at me, wide open and completely blank and horrible.

Her mouth hung slack and wet. I looked over her head toward the doorway.

Ronny Chernow was standing there. He was holding one of the pillows from the studio couch bent over double across one of his hands. For a second I wondered what he was doing with it. Then I saw the smoke wisping out from under the folded pillow. I couldn't see the gun at all but I knew it was there.

My hands eased from Liz Tremayne's arms and she went down to her knees and then toppled over onto one side. There was a very tiny black hole in the back of the negligée, near the left shoulder blade. Red shiny stuff was beginning to ooze out of it onto the floor.

"She's quite a gal, eh, Morgan," Chernow said. "She can really turn it on, can't she? She was giving you full voltage. I taught her that stuff, Morgan. And all you jerks in the office thought she was such a pot, not worth a play. How wrong can you get?"

"Very," I said. "Very wrong, Chernow. As wrong as you've gotten. Now, you've just committed murder on top of everything else."

Ronny Chernow's thick, masculine brows raised. His hair

was still curly and tousled, boyishly. He was still the expensively dressed, handsome, arrogant man-about-town. If you didn't look too closely. But now I could see the glassy gleam in his eyes, and there was a brutal twist to his thin, well-shaped lips. There was a nervous tic at one corner of his mouth. Maybe he didn't realize yet but this was all having an effect on him.

"You've got it wrong," he said. He gave a quiet, confident laugh. "*I* haven't killed anybody. I didn't embezzle all that money. I didn't sign that confession that's in the mail right now, will be in old Malkom's hands, Monday morning. I didn't come here and shoot Liz . . . *You* did all those things, Morgan. Don't you see the way it is?"

I saw. There was only one way it could be, now. He was going to kill me, too. When Liz and I were found, coupled with the letter of confession, it would be a fairly simple thing for the police to figure. They'd find the plane tickets, figure we'd planned to skip, together. But at the last minute we'd had an argument, a fight about something. I'd killed Liz, then shot myself. That was the way the whole thing was going to figure.

4. Smitty Pays a Visit

I watched Ronny Chernow start toward me. He looked terribly big. Much bigger than he'd ever seemed to me before. He kept holding the couch pillow folded over the gun in his hand.

"Stand still, Morgan," he said. The smile was gone from his face. His lips were flattened against his teeth. The tic at the corner of his mouth was leaping crazily.

Sure, I thought, stand still so that you can get close enough so that there'll be powder burns on my shirt front. But I couldn't seem to make myself move. I felt frozen, carved out of stone. I looked down on Liz Tremayne, sprawled there, her legs twisted under her awkwardly. She looked like a broken rag doll. I wondered if she was having any of those dreams now.

There it is, I told myself. There's that other life you missed by getting married and settling down. There's Miss Manhattan At Night-time. There's your glittering, crowded smoky hotspots and the throbbing, pulsing music and riding through the night in an open Caddy convertible, with a beautiful girl beside you.

There's the easy, crazy, enticing, live-for-the-moment way. Lying there dead with a bullet in her back ... And coming toward you, a killer, with all those turning, tossing, conscience-stricken nights behind him, with the cruel desperation etched into his face, with fear like little maggots in his brain all the time.

He had all that stuff. He didn't settle for your life, the drudgery, monotony, the bills, the skipping the new suits and the beautiful shirts and ties because there was another baby coming, the long bus trip back and forth, kids squalling or sick or worrisome in some other way. But look at him. On the ragged edge of mania. He can't keep killing and killing.

"That's right," Chernow said in the quietest voice I'd ever heard him use. "Stand nice and still. Nice – and – still . . ."

I had to stop watching him come toward me. My eyes swiveled to an electric clock on the dresser. I watched the second hand sweep around, knocking off the remaining seconds of my life. It was quarter to ten. I wondered what Fran was doing. The kids would be in bed. Fran would be out in the kitchen probably, ironing. Or else she'd be watching television in the living room, remembering things about the programs to tell me about when I got home. Or maybe she was over at the Haggards next door, gabbing with Helene, or playing Canasta. When I got home, she'd have the latest community gossip, and she'd brag about how much she'd won from the Haggards ... *When I got home?*

Ronny Chernow was only a step away from me, now. Quicksilver seemed to run all through me. The freeze left me. I screamed it: "I'm not going to die! I won't! *I won't!"*

I lunged toward him, slammed into him, knocked him off balance. There was a clicking sound. It wasn't until long later that I realized the gun had jammed on him, that possibly material of the cushion had caught the hammer or something. Right now I only wondered why didn't he shoot – get it over with. Why didn't I hear that muffled clap of sound again and feel the hurt and burn of the bullet striking me, the flood of pain or the nothingness or whatever it was happened when a bullet pumps into your heart and you die.

At the same time, I got halfway past him before he wrenched the gun – from the cushion, tossed the cushion to the floor. I could hear someone shouting, screaming, cursing. For a second I didn't even realize it was my own voice. Then, as I started toward the door, I looked back. Chernow was right behind me. He had the gun raised. It was a small, nickel-plated revolver. He caught me with the barrel right across the top of the forehead. I went off balance and staggered, crashed against the wall and went down. My eyes wouldn't focus. The walls and ceiling of the room were tilting, tipping, rolling lazily around and around my head.

As though from a great distance, I heard someone pounding fiercely on the door and rattling the knob. I tried to get to my feet to hold onto the wall. But it kept wheeling away from me. Finally it slowed and stopped. I leaned against that wall, sort of crawled up it and got to my feet. I shook my head, looked around. Liz Tremayne was still on the floor, dead. The nickel-plated revolver was lying near her feet. There was now a terrible thumping, shattering noise coming from the door, outside, leading to the hallway. I looked for Chernow but he wasn't there.

I walked over and picked up the revolver from the floor. I didn't have any clear idea why. I was still dazed. But I must have reasoned that I was in danger, needed protection. A gun was protection. Still holding it, I staggered out into the living room, just as the front door of the apartment crashed open and a man half fell inside.

He was short and bull-shouldered. He was wearing a T-shirt and a pair of wrinkled, soiled slacks. His arms were thick and muscular and black with hair. His square-jawed, beetle-browed face looked nervous, hesitant.

"What's going on in here?" he said. "I heard screaming and before that what sounded like a shot. I live next door. Where's Miss Tremayne?"

I started to jerk my thumb toward the bedroom, to say, "In there – dead." But something stopped me. This thing was getting worse instead of better. Sure, Ronny Chernow had fouled-up on killing me. I was still alive. But there was still that confession he had mailed, there was still a dead woman – the one mentioned in the confession – in that other room, dead by the gun which I held in my hand. Chernow was gone. He was out of it. There was only me. And the neighbor from next door to testify to the police about breaking in and finding me with the murder gun in my hand.

I said. "You back up, feller and get the hell out of here,

quick!" I jerked the gun toward him. He turned and squeezed back out past that half broken-in door like a snake slithering out of a trap.

I knew he'd go back to his own flat, call the police. I could hear other doors opening along the hall, voices questioning about the commotion. I jammed the revolver into my pocket, headed for the open window that Chernow had gone through. I went out and down the fire escape the same way as he had. I dropped from the bottom rung into an alley, my feet stinging. I ran out into the side street and kept running until I reached Broadway and a subway kiosk.

The people standing on the subway platform, waiting for a train, quieted me a little, helped me to calm down, to think. They all looked so normal, so bored and average. Just regular people, with regular everyday troubles. No murders for them, no beautiful girls, nobody trying to kill them, no thrills, excitement. Maybe some of them were worried about debts, or somebody sick, or how they would break down Mr So-and-so's sales resistance. Stuff like that. Once I must have looked that way, too. But not any more.

I caught some of the people staring at me. I stepped over to a gum machine, stared into the mirror. There was a dull red, swollen welt across my forehead just below the hairline, where the gun barrel had struck me. My upper lip still looked puffed. But it was really the expression in my eyes that had made people stare at me. My eyes looked harrassed, desperate, almost wild. They were deeply ringed underneath and bloodshot.

I turned away and tried to figure what I had to do, what would be best. There didn't seem to be any best. It was all bad. If I went to the police, told them the whole story, they'd hold me. They'd get Ronny Chernow. He'd deny everything. They'd hold me until Monday morning, at least. The news would get out. The story would break in the newspapers. Fran would go crazy with fear and doubt and worry. Monday morning they'd go over the books and the phoney vouchers that Chernow had made out, to get his checks every week. Those vouchers he'd have had to keep, to jibe with the regular monthly check of the books by old man Lesvich in the accounting department. They—

Those vouchers! They were my way out! Handwriting experts could prove they were forged, that I hadn't written them. It struck me like a jolt of white-hot lightning. Those vouchers would clear me of this whole thing.

But then I realized that after failing to kill me, Ronny Chernow would realize that, too. Chernow was as smart, if not smarter, than I. He'd go and get those vouchers – if he didn't already have them. Chances were, he did not. With me dead, he wouldn't have needed them. I stuck my hand into my pocket, feeling for the office keys. They weren't there. They were gone. I realized that Smitty and Vivian must have taken them, after they'd knocked me cold up in the hotel room.

A subway train roared in and I got on. It seemed to crawl down to Fiftieth Street. When it finally got there and I started running down toward Forty-Sixth and working over toward Sixth Avenue, it seemed that I wasn't really running at all. Again it was like a nightmare – the one where your feet are glued in mud, or for some other reason you're running like crazy, but not making any progress. But then I was there. I was pounding on the locked glass front door of our building. Inside, I could see the night register stand and the padded chair where Floyd, the night elevator man and watchman, always sat. He wasn't there. I kept pounding and rattling on the door, going crazy, sweat beginning to roll along my ribs.

This went on for what seemed like ten minutes but was probably only two or three. Then I saw bent old Floyd and his bushy white hair ambling jerkily along the hallway toward the door. When he opened it, I pushed inside. He looked at me, half curiously, half resentfully, for all the racket I'd caused and for disturbing him. His eyes were still full of sleep.

"Has anyone else been here in the last hour or so, Floyd?" I asked. "Mr Chernow. You know, the big red-faced man, with curly hair, always well dressed. Was he here?"

Floyd looked up at the ceiling. He dug through this thick shock of white hair and scratched at his head. Then he looked at me again. He yawned. "Wouldn't rightly know, son," he said. "Not if he had his keys, anyhow. I ain't let nobody in since seven o'clock, but you. But, then, I was down cellar just now – uh – fixing up things, so I wouldn't know."

What he'd been fixing down cellar was his ear. He'd been pounding it. I'd seen the old couch he had down there. But I didn't say anything. I pushed past him toward the elevator. At night they run the freight elevator, which is self-operating. I stopped before boarding it. I said:

"Floyd, this is important. Get it straight. If Mr Chernow, the man I just described, comes here while I'm upstairs, you phone up there and let me know. Then call the police."

Floyd said: "Sure thing. I – the police?"

"That's right," I said. "You do as I say and don't ask any questions. This is important."

I got into the cold elevator, worked the cable until it brought me up to the business offices on the fifth floor. I got off. It was pitch-dark up there. I switched the reception-room light on, walked to the inner office door. It was unlocked. I walked inside and switched on the overhead lights there. I stood for a moment, looking around at the empty desks and covered-up typewriters. It looked strange at night like this, the office unoccupied. There was a musty smell to the place with all the windows closed.

I looked at the desk where Liz Tremayne sat and I got kind of choked up. For a second I seemed to see her sitting there, her hair pulled back in that tight, ugly bun, those double-lensed glasses on her, as she bent over her ledgers. The girl with the dreams – the Jekyll-Hyde girl. Dead now at the city morgue. On a slab, with an assistant coroner probing for the greasy hunk of lead in her back.

Yeah, and with every cop in the city looking for a man answering my description, to pin that killing onto me. I had to get going.

The file cabinets stood in a row against the wall, over by the glass-enclosed office with the lettering on the door that said: RONALD CHERNOW, *Business Manager*. I went quickly through two or three files, before I came to the right one. It was labeled: *Editorial Vouchers*. It took me another five minutes or so to wade through batches of vouchers from the Pulp, Confession and Comics Group section, before I found the ones I wanted. Or where they should have been. They were gone.

Panic-stricken, my hands tore through the whole file again. Then once more slowly. All the vouchers for the past year were gone. Gone. The realization that I was too late slid over me like a weighted wet blanket. I half fell against the filing cabinet, my stomach banging the drawer back in.

I recognized the voice right away, even though it was subdued for Ronny Chernow. He said: "I didn't hit you hard enough, did I? I thought the police would have you by now."

I spun around. He was over by the receptionist's switchboard. A bulky briefcase with his initials on it rested on the floor next to the switchboard. Chernow had another gun in his hand. This one was an automatic, bluish-black, snubnose, ugly-looking.

"I heard the elevator coming up," he said. "I switched off all the lights. I thought it was probably Floyd making a check of the building. I never thought you'd be bright enough – or is it dumb enough – to come here."

I looked down at his briefcase. "You have the vouchers in there, don't you? With me in the hands of the police, come Monday morning, and nobody could prove a thing against you, could they? It would be my story against yours. With my signature on a confession, and those airplane tickets in Liz's purse, making your story look much better."

"Exactly," he said. "Now you're going with me, Morgan. We'll go down in the elevator, and leave by the back way so Floyd doesn't see us, through the cellar. Come on, Morgan. Let's go."

The only thing I could figure by that was that he still had it in mind to kill me in some way to make it look like a suicide. Perhaps push me in front of a subway train, something like that. Perhaps he no longer even planned to kill me at all, but just wanted to make sure I didn't interfere with him getting out of the building with those vouchers. Outside, perhaps, he would let me go, knowing that eventually the police would pick me up. I didn't know. But I couldn't take any chances on any of that. I was sick of this whole thing. I was up to the ears with it. I wanted it to be over and I wanted out.

He apparently had no idea I was armed. When he bent to pick up the briefcase, he took his eyes off me for a moment. My hand dug into the right jacket pocket, pulled out the revolver. I pointed it right at him and squeezed the trigger. Nothing happened. It was still jammed. I swore and threw the gun at him.

Then there was the shot. It echoed thunderingly loud in the empty office. I stiffened all over. I waited for the flood of pain that I knew was going to come. Instinctively I balled my fist and jammed it into my stomach. I sucked my lips between my teeth and started to bite on them. But the hurting didn't come. I'd once heard that when you get shot badly, you don't feel it the first instant. You're numbed with shock. I figured that was the truth.

And then I noticed that I was down on my knees. What felt like a cherry-hot poker went through my shoulder. I clamped a hand up there, just over the right breast and felt the hole in my suit as I went over onto my face. But I didn't black out. I lay very still, waiting for the second shot that would finish me. It came – louder, more choking, more deafening than the first. I didn't feel that one, either. Then I heard a voice and I knew why I wouldn't ever feel that second bullet. I hadn't gotten it.

I was sprawled on my side, to one side of a desk. I could look under the desk and I saw that Ronny Chernow was on the floor, too. He was on his belly, and inching himself along, clawing his way with both hands, dragging himself toward a pair of black patent-leather shoes with tiny, shiny black bows on the toes. I heard the man called Smitty say:

"You can't renege on me, Chernow, you big overdressed punk!" Smitty piled a gutter name on top of that. "When I called you and told you what happened, you said that was tough. Me and Vivian wouldn't get our fee for botching the job. I started to tell you we'd better, that we did half the job anyhow, got that guy to sign the confession for you and put it in the mail. But you didn't give me a chance. You hung up on me, after telling me where I could go for my grand. You didn't think there was anything we could do about it, did you? You don't know me very well. Chernow. I don't like welchers."

Chernow, crawling along the office floor, almost got to Smitty's patent-leather shiny shoes. He reached for them. Smitty stepped inside the reach and kicked Chernow in the face.

"You were just driving off in that big Caddy of yours when I got to your apartment, Chernow," Smitty said. "I followed you. I followed you every place. Even here. I got in with the keys I took from that other guy, that Morgan guy's pocket. I've been waiting for a nice quiet place to do this to you. No witnesses or nothing. I was just going to do it when you heard the elevator and put the lights out. So I waited."

Under the desk, I watched Smitty bend over Chernow and when Chernow reached for his throat, Smitty slammed him across the temple with his gun butt. It made a sickening sound. I gagged and covered my mouth with my hand, praying

Smitty wouldn't hear me. I didn't move. I watched Smitty take Chernow's wallet from inside his jacket pocket. He pulled out a thick sheaf of bills, thumbed through them.

"Nice," he said. "What a break. Nearly five thousand, all in hundreds and fifties. This is a much better fee than you promised, Mister Chernow. It looks like Vivian and me are going to take a nice little trip. Florida, maybe. We've always wanted to go to Florida, even in the spring."

He kicked Chernow again and when the other man didn't move, Smitty walked out of the office into the reception room, slamming the door behind him. I heard the old freight elevator wheezing and clanking as he went down.

I tried to get up, now. I got hold of a corner of the desk and tried to pull myself up. I didn't make it. I got freezing cold and sweat poured from me. I shook like a bird dog. Knife-shoots of pain stabbed through my shoulder and the feel of the sticky, wet blood there turned my stomach.

I kept trying to pull myself to my feet and not making it. Finally, I got smart. I saw a telephone cord looped down from the desk. I grabbed it, yanked the instrument down clattering to the floor. I dialed the O and when the operator came on, I said: "Police!"

She didn't seem to hear me. She kept repeating: "Operator! Operator!" I must have said "Police!" a dozen times before I realized that no sound was coming through my lips.

Then I tried to shout at the top of my lungs. The words came out in a hoarse, rasping whisper. But she heard me. She heard me give her the address and the floor number. But I didn't hear what she said. I was suddenly swimming in a sea of inky blackness.

When the lights came on again, I was in a hospital bed. I started to sit up, but there was a mule-kick of pain through my shoulder that stopped me. I fell back on the pillow. One of the men was tall, spare-built. He had a bald head, except for a thin rim of iron-gray hair just around the ears.

"Take it easy, Morgan," he said. "Everything's all right. We caught Smitty Smithers and Vivian Engles at the airport. They were going to Florida. But if Chernow dies they'll be going to a hotter place. And his chances aren't good. All we want from you is a few statements, right now, Morgan. Can you talk for a while?"

I grinned up at him. "I could talk forever," I said. "And probably will. Go ahead. Shoot."

There were a lot of questions. They'd gotten most of the story from Smitty and Vivian and the dying Chernow. But I was able to fill in a lot for them, to explain how the embezzlement had been handled. When they were through, I found I was so weak I could hardly talk. And I felt sleepy again. They said they'd see me again in the morning. I smiled weakly, mumbled: "Somebody – call – my wife."

They said that somebody already had and I dozed off. When I awakened again, Fran was there. She was sitting beside the bed, holding my hand. She smiled and said: "How do you feel, Kip?"

"Oh, boy!" I said. "Like a million. Let's jump rope or climb trees or something." I felt all scooped out. My shoulder was throbbing and my head was keeping time with it and every one of my nerve ends seemed to be jangling.

A middle-aged nurse came in, smiled at both of us and said: "I'm sorry. It's time for his medicine." She handed me two pills and a glass of water. I swallowed them and washed them down. The water tasted brackish. But in a few moments the throbbing in my shoulder and head eased. The nerves stopped jangling.

"Kip," Fran said. "I've heard the whole story several times already, but I still can't – can't hardly believe it. *You*, Kip!"

"Yeah," I said. "Me! Were you worried about me, Fran?"

"No," she said. "I was over at Haggards. Helene cheated as usual, but I ended up winning. I won—"

"Two dollars and eighty cents," I finished. Fran always won or lost that amount, to within a few pennies. It was really phenomenal.

"Two sixty-seven," she corrected.

I looked at her and grinned. She was wearing a plain, round little piece of blue felt that looked like a beany and had cost eight dollars. I remembered how I'd beefed about it. She needed a permanent but still her hair was pretty. It was just plain brown, with some strands of gray in it, but it was nice. She had her lipstick on a little crooked and there was a faint tracery of lines in her face and she looked very tired, but still cute. She was wearing her powder-blue suit and for a woman with two children, I had to admit she still had one helluva figure.

"You know, Kip," she was saying, "in spite of what happened tonight, I think it would be a good idea for you to take a night off once in a while. I thought about it after you called the last time and said you were staying in town. I realized how awfully tiresome and monotonous it must be for you never to have a night off away from me and the kids."

I started to protest vehemently until I saw the twinkle in her eyes.

"Kip," she said, softly. "Those girls you got mixed up with, tonight. Were they very pretty – very young and pretty?"

"Good God, no!" I told her. "They were hags, both of them." I knew that was what she wanted me to tell her. I grinned.

Another nurse came into the room and went around to the foot of the bed to look at my chart. She was a young bleached blonde, and beautiful, a little doll, with her big blue eyes and a shape that even the crisp white uniform couldn't hide. She smiled over the chart at me and winked. I closed my eyes and rubbed the sight of her out of my brain.

"She was very attractive," Fran said in a moment and I knew the blonde nurse was gone.

"Nah!" I whispered. I was getting terribly sleepy again. I could hardly keep my eyes open. "She was a mess, a horror! Besides, after tonight, I *hate* pretty women."

"Is that *so*, Kip Morgan?" Fran said. "Where does that leave me? What am I, just a dowdy little housewife?"

I looked up at her. It was funny, the sleepier I got and the more I looked at Fran, the prettier she became. I mean *really* pretty. You know, from inside of her, like. I reached out and took her hand. I said. "They must've given me sump'n. Can't – stay – awake . . . You goin' – stay here – with me . . . Right here?"

"Yes, darling," she said. "All right. Helene Haggard is staying over at the house."

Her voice droned on and I wanted to tell her thanks for coming and for staying here with me and for being so pretty and being my wife and all, but I guess I went to sleep instead.

CIGARETTE GIRL

James M. Cain

I'd never so much as laid eyes on her before going in this place, the *Here's How*, a nightclub on Route 1, a few miles north of Washington, on business that was 99 percent silly, but that I had to keep to myself. It was around 8 at night, with hardly anyone there, and I'd just taken a table, ordered a drink, and started to unwrap a cigar, when a whiff of perfume hit me, and she swept by with cigarettes. As to what she looked like, I had only a rear view, but the taffeta skirt, crepe blouse, and silver earrings were quiet, and the chassis was choice, call it fancy, a little smaller than medium. So far, a cigarette girl, nothing to rate any cheers, but not bad either, for a guy unattached who'd like an excuse to linger.

But then she made a pitch, or what I took for a pitch. Her middle-aged customer was trying to tell her some joke, and taking so long about it the proprietor got in on the act. He was a big, blond, guy, with kind of a decent face, but he went and whispered to her as though to hustle her up, for some reason apparently. I couldn't quite figure it out. She didn't much seem to like it, until her eye caught mine. She gave a little pout, a little shrug, a little wink, and then just stood there, smiling.

Now I know this pitch and it's nice, because of course I smiled back, and with that I was on the hook. A smile is nature's freeway: it has lanes, and you can go any speed you like, except you can't go back. Not that I wanted to, as I suddenly changed my mind about the cigar I had in my hand, stuck it back in my pocket, and wigwagged for cigarettes. She nodded, and when she came over said: "You stop laughing at me."

"Who's laughing? Looking."

"Oh, of course. That's different."

I picked out a pack, put down my buck, and got the surprise of my life: she gave me change. As she started to leave, I said "You forgot something, maybe?"

"That's not necessary."

"For all this I get, I should pay."

"All what, sir, for instance?"

"I told you: the beauty that fills my eye."

"The best things in life are free."

"On that basis, fair lady, some of them, here, are tops. Would you care to sit down?"

"Can't."

"Why not?"

"Not allowed. We got rules."

With that she went out toward the rear somewhere, and I noticed the proprietor again, just a short distance away, and realized he'd been edging in. I called him over and said: "What's the big idea? I was talking to her."

"Mister, she's paid to work."

"Yeah, she mentioned about rules, but now they got other things too. Four Freedoms, all kinds of stuff. Didn't anyone ever tell you?"

"I heard of it, yes."

"You're Mr *Here's How*?"

"Jack Conner, to my friends."

I took a V from my wallet, folded it, creased it, pushed it toward him. I said: "Jack, little note of introduction I generally carry around. I'd like you to ease these rules. She's cute, and I crave to buy her a drink."

He didn't see any money, and stood for a minute thinking. Then: "Mister, you're off on the wrong foot. In the first place, she's not a cigarette girl. Tonight, yes, when the other girl is off. But not regular, no. In the second place, she's not any chiselly-wink, that orders rye, drinks tea, takes the four bits you slip her, the four I charge for the drink – and is open to propositions. She's class. She's used to class – out West, with people that have it, and that brought her East when they came. In the third place she's a friend, and before I eased any rules I'd have to know more about you, a whole lot more, than this note tells me.

"Pleased to meet you and all that, but as to who you are, Mr Cameron, and what you are, I still don't know—"

"I'm a musician."

"Yeah? What instrument?"

"Any of them. Guitar, mainly."

Which brings me to what I was doing there. I do play the guitar, play it all day long, for the help I get from it, as it gives me certain chords, the big ones that people go for, and heads me off from some others, the fancy ones on the piano, that other musicians go for. I'm an arranger, based in Baltimore, and had driven down on a little tune detecting. The guy who takes most of my work, Art Lomak, the band leader, writes a few tunes himself, and had gone clean off his rocker about one he said had been stolen, or thefted as they call it. It was one he'd been playing a little, to try it and work out faults, with lyric and title to come, soon as the idea hit him. And then he rang me, with screams. It had already gone on the air, as 20 people had told him, from this same little honky-tonk, as part of a 10 o'clock spot on the Washington FM pick-up. He begged me to be here tonight, when the trio started their broadcast, pick up such dope as I could, and tomorrow give him the low-down.

That much was right on the beam, stuff that goes on every day, a routine I knew by heart. But his tune had angles, all of them slightly peculiar. One was, it had already been written, though it was never a hit and was almost forgotten, in the days when states were hot, under the title *Nevada*. Another was, it had been written even before that, by a gent named Giuseppe Verdi, as part of the *Sicilian Vespers*, under the title *O Tu Palermo*. Still another was, Art was really burned, and seemed to have no idea where the thing had come from. They just can't get it, those big schmalzburgers like him, that what leaks out of their head might, just once, have leaked in. But the twist, the reason I had to come, and couldn't just play it for laughs, was: Art could have been right. Maybe the lilt *was* from him, not from the original opera, or from the first theft, *Nevada*. It's a natural for a 3/4 beat, and that's how Art had been playing it. So if that's how they were doing it here, instead of with *Nevada*'s 4/4, which followed the Verdi signature, there might still be plenty of work for the lawyers Art had put on it, with screams, same like to me.

Silly, almost.

Spooky.

But maybe, just possibly, right.

So Jack, this boss character, by now had smelled something fishy, and suddenly took a powder, to the stand where the fiddlers were parked, as of course the boys weren't there yet, and came back with a Spanish guitar. I took it, thanked him, and tuned. To kind of work it around, in the direction of Art's little problem, and at the same time make like there was nothing at all to conceal, I said I'd come on account of his band, to catch it during the broadcast, as I'd heard it was pretty good. He didn't react, which left me nowhere, but I thought it well to get going.

I played him *Night and Day*, no Segovia job, but plenty good, for free. On "Day and Night", where it really opens up, I knew things to do, and talk suddenly stopped among the scattering of people that were in there. When I finished there was some little clapping, but still he didn't react, and I gave thought to mayhem. But then a buzzer sounded, and he took another powder, out toward the rear this time, where she had disappeared. I began a little beguine, but he was back. He bowed, picked up his B, bowed again, said: "Mr Cameron, the guitar did it. She heard you, and you're in."

"Will you set me up for two?"

"Hold on, there's a catch."

He said until midnight, when one of his men would take over, she was checking his orders. "That means she handles the money, and if she's not there, I could just as well close down. You're invited back with her, but she can't come out with you."

"Oh. Fine."

"Sir, you asked for it."

It wasn't quite the way I'd have picked to do it, but the main thing was the girl, and I followed him through the OUT door, the one his waiters were using, still with my Spanish guitar. But then, all of a sudden, I loved it, and felt even nearer to her.

This was the works of the joint, with a little office at one side, service bar on the other, range rear and centre, the crew in white all around, getting the late stuff ready. But high on a stool, off by herself, on a little railed-in platform where waiters would have to pass, she was waving at me, treating it all as a joke. She called down: "Isn't this a balcony scene for you? You have to play me some music!"

I rattled into it quickly, and when I told her it was *Romeo and Juliet*, she said it was just what she'd wanted. By then Jack had a stool he put next to hers, so I could sit beside her, back of her little desk. He introduced us, and it turned out her name was Stark. I climbed up and there we were, out in the middle of the air, and yet in a way private, as the crew played it funny, to the extent they played it at all, but mostly were too busy even to look. I put the guitar on the desk and kept on with the music. By the time I'd done some *Showboat* she was calling me Bill and to me she was Lydia. I remarked on her eyes, which were green, and showed up bright against her creamy skin and ashy blonde hair. She remarked on mine, which are light, watery blue, and I wished I was something besides tall, thin, and red-haired. But it was kind of cute when she gave a little pinch and nipped one of my freckles, on my hand back of the thumb.

Then Jack was back, with champagne iced in a bucket, which I hadn't ordered. When I remembered my drink, the one I *had* ordered, he said Scotch was no good, and this would be on him. I thanked him, but after he'd opened and poured, and I'd leaned the guitar in a corner and raised my glass to her, I said: "What's made him so friendly?"

"Oh, Jack's always friendly."

"Not to me. Oh, no."

"He may have thought I had it coming. Some little thing to cheer me. My last night in the place."

"You going away?"

"M'm-h'm."

"When?"

"Tonight."

"That's why you're off at 12?"

"Jack tell you that?"

"He told me quite a lot."

"Plane leaves at 1. Bag's gone already. It's at the airport, all checked and ready to be weighed."

She clinked her glass to mine, took a little sip, and drew a deep, trembly breath. As for me, I felt downright sick, just why I couldn't say, as it had all to be strictly allegro, with nobody taking it serious. It stuck in my throat a little when I said: "Well – happy landings. Is it permitted to ask which way that plane is taking you?"

"Home."

"And where's that?"

"It's – not important."

"The West, I know that much."

"What else did Jack tell you?"

I took it, improvised, and made up a little stuff, about her high-toned friends, her being a society brat, spoiled as usual, and the heavy dough she was used to – a light rib, as I thought. But it hadn't gone very far when I saw it was missing bad. When I cut it off, she took it. She said: "Some of that's true, in a way. I was – fortunate, we'll call it. But – you still have no idea, have you, Bill, what I really am?"

"I've been playing by ear."

"I wonder if you want to know?"

"If you don't want to, I'd rather you didn't say."

None of it was turning out quite as I wanted, and I guess maybe I showed it. She studied me a little and asked: "The silver I wear, that didn't tell you anything? Or my giving you change for your dollar? It didn't mean anything to you, that a girl would run a straight game?"

"She's not human."

"*It means she's a gambler.*"

And then: "Bill, does that shock you?"

"No, not at all."

"I'm not ashamed of it. Out home, it's legal. You know where that is now?"

"Oh! *Oh!*"

"Why oh? And *oh*?"

"Nothing. It's – Nevada, isn't it?"

"Something wrong with Nevada?"

"No! I just woke up, that's all."

I guess that's what I said, but whatever it was, she could hardly miss the upbeat in my voice. Because, of course, that wrapped it all up pretty, not only the tune, which the band would naturally play for her, but her too, and who she was. Society dame, to tell the truth, hadn't pleased me much, and maybe that was one reason my rib was slightly off key. But gambler I could go for, a little cold, a little dangerous, a little brave. When she was sure I had really bought it, we were close again, and after a nip on the freckle her fingers slid over my hand. She said play her *Smoke* – the smoke she had in her eyes. But I didn't, and we just sat there some little time.

And then, a little bit at a time, she began to spill it: "Bill, it was just plain cock-eyed. I worked in a club, the Paddock, in Reno, a regular institution. Tony Rocco – Rock – owned it, and was the squarest bookie ever – why he was a Senator, and civic, and everything. And I worked for him, running his wires, practically being his manager, with a beautiful salary, a bonus at Christmas, and everything. And then wham, it struck. This federal thing. This 10 percent tax on gross. And we were out of business. It just didn't make sense. Everything else was exempted. Wheels and boards and slots, whatever you could think of, but us. Us and the numbers racket, in Harlem and Florida and Washington."

"Take it easy."

"That's right, Bill. Thanks."

"Have some wine?"

". . . Rock, of course, was fixed. He had property, and for the building, where the Paddock was, he got $250,000 – or so I heard. But then came the tip on Maryland."

That crossed me up, and instead of switching her off, I asked her what she meant. She said: "That Maryland would legalize wheels."

"What do you smoke in Nevada?"

"Oh, I didn't believe it. And Rock didn't. But Mrs Rock went nuts about it. Oh well, she had a reason."

"Dark, handsome reason?"

"I don't want to talk about it, but that reason took the Rocks for a ride, for every cent they got for the place, and tried to take me too, for other things beside money. When they went off to Italy, they thought they had it fixed, he was to keep me at my salary, in case Maryland *would* legalize, and if not, to send me home, with severance pay, as it's called. And instead of that—"

"I'm listening."

"I've said too much."

"What's this guy to you?"

"Nothing! I never even saw him until the three of us stepped off the plane – with our hopes. In a way it seemed reasonable. Maryland has tracks, and they help with the taxes. Why not wheels?"

"And *who* is this guy?"

"I'd be ashamed to say, but I'll say this much: I won't be a kept floozy. I don't care who he thinks he is, or—"

She bit her lip, started to cry, and really shut up then. To switch off, I asked why she was working for Jack, and she said: "Why not? You can't go home in a barrel. But he's been swell to me."

Saying people were swell seemed to be what she liked, and she calmed down, letting her hand stay when I pressed it in both of mine. Then we were really close, and I meditated if we were close enough that I'd be warranted in laying it on the line, she should let that plane fly away, and not go to Nevada at all. But while I was working on that, business was picking up, with waiters stopping by to let her look at their trays, and I hadn't much chance to say it, whatever I wanted to say. Then, through the IN door, a waiter came through with a tray that had a wine bottle on it. A guy followed him in, a little noisy guy, who said the bottle was full and grabbed it off the tray. He had hardly gone out again, when Jack was in the door, watching him as he staggered back to the table. The waiter swore the bottle was empty, but all Jack did was nod.

Then Jack came over to her, took another little peep through the window in the OUT door, which was just under her balcony, and said: "Lydia, what did you make of him?"

"Why – he's drunk, that's all."

"You notice him, Mr Cameron?"

"No – except it crossed my mind he wasn't as tight as the act he was putting on."

"Just what crossed *my* mind! How could he get that drunk on a split of Napa red? What did he want back here?"

By now, the waiter had gone out on the floor and came back, saying the guy wanted his check. But as he started to shuffle it out of the bunch he had tucked in his vest, Jack stopped him and said: "He don't get any check – not till I give the word. Tell Joe I said stand by and see he don't get out. *Move!*"

The waiter had looked kind of blank, but hustled out as told, and then Jack looked at her. He said: "Lady, I'll be back. I'm taking a look around."

He went, and she drew another of her long, trembly breaths. I cut my eye around, but no one had noticed a thing, and yet it semed kind of funny they'd all be slicing bread, wiping glass, or fixing cocktail setups, with Jack mumbling it low out of the side of his mouth. I had a creepy feeling of things going on, and my mind took it a little, fitting it together, what she had said about the bag checked at the airport, the guy trying to make her, and most of all, the way Jack had acted, the second she showed with her cigarettes, shooing her off the floor, getting her out of sight. She kept staring through the window, at the drunk where he sat with his bottle, and seemed to ease when a captain I took to be Joe planted himself pretty solid in a spot that would block off a runout.

Then Jack was back, marching around, snapping his fingers, giving orders for the night. But as he pressed the back door, I noticed his hand touched the lock, as though putting the catch on. He started back to the floor, but stopped as he passed her desk, and shot it quick in a whisper: "He's out there, Lydia, parked in back. This drunk, like I thought, is a finger he sent in to stop you, but he won't be getting out for the airport, right now."

"Will you call me a cab, Jack?"

"Cab? I'm taking you."

He stepped near me and whispered: "Mr Cameron, I'm sorry, this little lady has to leave, for—"

"I know about that."

"She's in danger—"

"I've also caught on to that."

"From a no-good imitation goon that's been trying to get to her here, which is why I'm shipping her out. I hate to break this up, but if you'll ride with us, Mr Cameron—"

"I'll follow you down."

"That's right, you have your car. It's Friendship Airport just down the road."

He told her to get ready, while he was having his car brought up, and the boy who would take her place on the desk was changing his clothes. Step on it, he said, but wait until he came back. He went out on the floor and marched past the drunk without even turning his head. But she sat watching me. She said: "You're not coming, are you?"

"Friendship's a little cold."

"But not mine, Bill, no."

She got off her stool, stood near me and touched my hair. She said: "Ships that pass in the night pass so close, so close." And then: "I'm ashamed, Bill. I'd have to go for this reason. I wonder, for the first time if gambling's really much good." She pulled the chain of the light, so we were half in the dark. Then she kissed me. She said: "God bless and keep you, Bill."

"And you, Lydia."

I felt her tears on my cheek, and then she pulled away and stepped to the little office, where she began putting a coat on and tying a scarf on her head. She looked so pretty it came to me I still hadn't given her the one little bouquet I'd been saving for the last. I picked up the guitar and started *Nevada*.

She wheeled, but what stared at me were eyes as hard as glass. I was so startled I stopped, but she kept right on staring. Outside a car door slammed, and she listened at the window beside her. Then at last she looked away, to peep through the Venetian blind. Jack popped in, wearing his coat and hat, and motioned her to hurry. But he caught something and said, low yet so I could hear him: "Lydia! What's the matter?"

She stalked over to me, with him following along, pointed her finger, and then didn't say it, but spat it: "He's the finger – that's what's the matter, that's all. He played *Nevada*, as though we hadn't had enough trouble with it already. And Vanny heard it. He hopped out of his car and he's under the window right now."

"Then OK, let's go."

I was a little too burned to make with the explanations, and took my time, parking the guitar, sliding off, and climbing down, to give them a chance to blow. But she still had something to say, and to me, not to him. She pushed her face up to mine, and mocking how I had spoken, yipped. "Oh! . . . *Oh!* OH!" Then she went, with Jack. Then I went, clumping after.

Then it broke wide open.

The drunk, who was supposed to sit there, conveniently boxed in, while she went slipping out, turned out more of a hog-calling type, and instead of playing his part, jumped up and yelled: "Vanny! *Vanny!* Here she comes! She's leaving! VANNY!"

He kept it up, while women screamed all over, then pulled a gun from his pocket, and let go at the ceiling, so it sounded like the field artillery. Jack jumped for him and hit the deck, as his feet shot from under him on the slippery wood of the dance floor. Joe swung, missed, swung again, and landed, so Mr Drunk went down. But when Joe scrambled for the gun, there came this voice through the smoke: "Hold it! As you were – and leave that gun alone."

Then hulking in came this short-necked, thick-shouldered thing, in Homburg hat, double-breasted coat, and white muffler, one hand in his pocket, the other giving an imitation of a movie gangster. He said keep still and nobody would get hurt, but "I won't stand for tricks." He helped Jack up, asked how he'd been. Jack said: "Young man, let me tell you something—"

"How you been? I asked."

"Fine, Mr Rocco."

"Any telling, Jack – I'll do it."

Then, to her: "Lydia, how've *you* been?"

"That doesn't concern you."

Then she burst out about what he had done to his mother, the gyp he'd handed his father, and his propositions to her, and I got it, at last, who this idiot was. He listened, but right in the middle of it, he waved his hand toward me and asked: "Who's this guy?"

"Vanny, I think you know."

"Guy, are you the boyfriend?"

"If so I don't tell you."

I sounded tough, but my stomach didn't feel that way. They had it some more, and he connected me with the tune, and seemed to enjoy it a lot, that it had told him where to find her, on the broadcast and here now tonight. But he kept creeping closer, to where we were all lined up, with the drunk stretched on the floor, the gun under his hand, and I suddenly felt the prickle, that Vanny was really nuts, and in a minute meant to kill her. It also crossed my mind, that a guy who plays the guitar has a left hand made of steel, from squeezing down on the strings, and is a dead sure judge of distance, to the last eighth of an inch.

I grabbed for my chord and got it.

I choked down on his hand, the one he held in his pocket, while hell broke loose in the place, with women screaming, men running, and fists trying to help. I had the gun hand all right, but when I reached for the other he twisted, butted, and bit, and for that long I thought he'd get loose, and that I was a gone pigeon. The gun barked, and a piledriver hit my leg. I went down. Another gun spoke and he went down beside me. Then there was Jack, the drunk's gun in his hand, stepping in close, and firing again.

I blacked out.

I came to, and then she was there, a knife in her hand, ripping the cloth away from the outside of my leg, grabbing napkins, stanching blood, while somewhere ten miles off I could hear Jack's voice, as he yelled into a phone. On the floor right beside me was something under a tablecloth.

That went on for some time, with Joe calming things down and some people sliding out. The band came in, and I heard a boy ask for his guitar. Somebody brought it to him, and then, at last, came the screech of sirens, and she whispered some thanks to God.

Then, while the cops were catching up, with me, with Jack, and what was under the cloth, we both went kind of haywire, me laughing, she crying, and both in each other's arms. I said: "Lydia, Lydia, you're not taking that plane. They legalize things in Maryland, one thing specially, except that instead of wheels, they generally use a ring."

THE GETAWAY

Gil Brewer

Vincenti lit a fat joint, took a big toke, then glanced sideways at the wheelman of the silver Continental Mark IV. Vincenti was loose. He was always loose. He had a job to do and would be paid well. He was a heavy and he only worked to contract.

"Nervous?" the paunchy, red-faced driver asked. He wore medium blue with a plum maroon tie.

Vincenti did not answer. He took another deep toke and chewed on the acrid smoke. Tall, slim, impeccably groomed in pearl gray, with eyes like slate, he somehow resembled a statue.

The wheelman's name was Morganza. He was also the finger. His hair looked like a wet, blue-black cap, and there was something anxious in his pale eyes.

"I'd be nervous," he said.

"You are."

"I mean if I was you."

"I wouldn't doubt that."

Vincenti's voice was silken. It appealed to women, along with everything else about the man, and he enjoyed that fact.

They were on Franklin and mid-afternoon Tampa traffic moved glitteringly, sedately. Then Morganza made a sharp right and slowed the flash car. They drew to the curb.

Vincenti's practiced finger flicked the roach out the window. He was patient. He had to be.

"It's that loan company, across there. Acme," Morganza said. He coughed lightly and checked his wrist where gold gleamed. "Due – right now."

Vincenti watched the Acme Loan entrance. His nose was a blade and his chin held a deep cleft. He sighed and yearned for

Vegas with some fresh broad. Well, it would come later, after he returned to LA.

The grass had given him a small lift.

Suddenly Morganza said, "Here it is, you."

Vincenti looked quickly towards the Acme Loan.

An enormous man in eye-shattering white, slow-moving, ponderous but with the provoking grace of an elephant, still young, shoved from the Acme entrance into the street. Another man, short, reed-like, gripping a tan straw hat, was with him. They stood there on the sidewalk. The short man gestured ubiquitously, while the big man grew like a tree.

Morganza opened his door and stepped out.

"Which the hell one?" Vincenti's voice was flat, like tepid tea.

"Biggie," Morganza jerked, and was gone, melting into the afternoon.

Vincenti lifted long legs and slid over beneath the wheel, planting his feet. He waited, watching the big man.

So, this was Nemo Lucelli, god of the Gulf Coast, with wormy fingers that fatted into Miami's guts, palpated Jacksonville, and saw to the Bahamas skim. Overlord of Florida crime, glutting on everything from prostitution and narcotics to illegal Florida gambling; twisting the coat-tails of governors, senators, and shipping magnates. It was reported authoritatively that his Mexican connection was the fatted calf itself. And anachronistic Murder Inc. was nothing to Lucelli's bloodbath.

The Big Nemo . . . but Vincenti hadn't figured him this big in girth.

The National Syndicate wanted Nemo wasted.

Vincenti knew he would be able to retire for maybe three years after this job, able to thoroughly feed his own ravening appetites. Women. Young girls.

He tightened his teeth, his slate-colored eyes checking every corner for *soldatos*, bodyguards, the lieutenants of Lucelli's regime. The Tampa hierarchy did not know Vincenti and would not make him. Morganza was from Chi, with *capo* Ringotti. Morganza would already be at Tampa International, a fly duck.

A quick-moving soldier opened a Caddy limousine door, and Lucelli lurched towards the shiny car, leaving the short fellow still gesticulant.

Vincenti knew that car would be slug-proof.

A door slammed. Vincenti saw the fat man in white lift a glass from a portable bar in the limo. Then the Caddy purred into traffic.

Vincenti knew it had to be obtuse.

Now was the word. Or as close to *now* as conditions would permit. Make the damn hit and get out.

Vincenti quickly lit a previously rolled joint, took a vigorous toke, and skunked after the Cad, holding his breath, experiencing a tingle in his solar plexus. This was the biggest hit he'd ever attained, and he was playing it to rule . . . the rule cooked up on the cross-country jet flight.

Hit – *now*. No maps. No clockwork. No shenanigans.

It had to be *hit now*, because Lucelli's fortress could be creepy, and there was the ever-gnawing probability that winds would blow news of this top-brass execution decision.

There was *always* a long tongue, no matter how the odds looked.

Vincenti toked the fat joint deeply, holding the narcotic smoke, the red ember sputtering. Ordinarily he spent days, sometimes weeks, on a hit – planning, scheming, checking every angle. Not this time. No time was this time.

He knew he had to be high. It was in and hit and run.

Desperation was beginning to drive him now.

He worked at desperation. He was a pro. His card was death and the deal was no shuffle, no cut.

They were approaching West Shore Boulevard, the limo blurringly smooth at a sixty clip.

Traffic was heavy.

The afternoon sighed, turned, and rolled over towards four o'clock. Black palm fronds fingered the yellow haze like cemetery hands.

Abruptly the limousine crawled into a circular drive rimmed with glistening poplars and silk oaks, slowed to gleam and glitter in the shadows of a portico fronting a small yellow-stone cottage – small by Lucelli's standards, Vincenti mused, firing another joint. Actually the cottage was a minor mansion.

Still . . . it didn't look like home ground, for some reason.

He tooled the outside lane slowly, turning to check. Sure enough, Lucelli was out of the limo and the big car was pulling away in the drive.

Vincenti checked the rear-view mirror, holding his breath.

The Cad crept back onto the boulevard and increased speed.

Lucelli was alone back there at the yellow-stone cottage.

Vincenti wheeled the Continental to the right, down a curving red-brick street shaded with ancient water oaks.

He couldn't believe it! He couldn't!

The *now* was in solid.

Curtly, then, the professional took over. He sped down the block, turned fast right again, marking where the yellow-stone cottage would stand on the boulevard.

He parked at the curb, allowed his right hand to check the spring-holstered, silenced Luger beneath his left arm, then just sat there a moment.

The quiet-looking stone home to the right, behind fastidious dark green Florida poppy hedge, seemed uninhabited. Vincenti had the salesman's antennae about matters like that.

Anyway, it was *now* – not later.

He lit still another joint, left the car, and walked rapidly along the outside poppy hedge that bordered a blue-gravel drive. He glanced neither right nor left. He held smoke in his lungs and the afternoon was a cinema screen, flickering impossible paradise.

The large homes on either side were set distantly.

He approached a yellow-stone wall. The cottage where Lucelli had stopped took up, in grounds, obviously most of the block. The place with the hedges was a cheapie.

He flicked the roach away, touched the wall, and with a smooth leap elbowed the rim.

He clung there, taking it in – a kidney-shaped swimming pool under silk oaks, the water like green ice. Walls. Footpaths. Flowers in bloom. A mocking blue jay.

Glass doors open on glitter and shadow.

Nobody. No sound other than the blue jay.

Then ... soft music. Bartok. Vincenti prided himself on a secret vice. Lucelli the Slaughterhouse, attending Bartok?

He sniffed – sniffed again. Musk. Incense. Lucelli. *Avanti.* Nemo Lucelli!

A white shape moved through velvet-red shadows inside the cottage.

Vincenti went up the wall, and down into a horseshoe flowerbed of yellow roses. He barely landed here before he was running lightly, silently, around the pool, past canvas deck chairs, luxuriously padded chaises, across a broad flagged patio with a half-finished drink on a redwood table, and over to the glass doors.

He could feel his heart astounding his chest. He was sweating now, as he let the Luger fit into his palm, and gripped the cool butt, fingering cold steel.

"Who is it?" The voice was fat, hoarse, and deep, from inside the cottage.

Vincenti whapped the Luger's sliding blue-steeled breech open with an oily click, and leaped between the glass doors.

Everything happened at once. The music. The jay screaming. Nemo Lucelli standing there like an elephant in a white terry-cloth robe, belted around the enormous girth, a fat, manicured hand with a square-cut diamond, holding a martini glass, a woman's voice:

"What is it – Nemo?"

Vincenti said, "Hello."

Nemo Lucelli backed through an alcove into a sprawling, shadowed living room with huge hassocks and a fireplace. He paused against a glass cocktail table, his mouth working around unspoken words.

"They said you broke word," Vincenti told Lucelli. "They said to waste you."

"Wait—" Lucelli said.

His drink spilled on the thick gold rug.

Vincenti emptied the Luger. It made gasping sounds. Crimson blossoms appeared across Lucelli's chest. He gave a tremendous leap backwards and crashed down on the glass-topped cocktail table, shattering the plate.

He was dead. His eyes were open.

The jay screamed. The music softly curtained the diminishing afternoon as Vincenti released the spent clip from the Luger and slapped a fresh one in its place.

"Nemo?"

The woman's voice again, up and to the left, coming near.

She burst into the room, saw the hulk covered by terry cloth amid the jagged shards of broken glass, the blood. She put one hand to her mouth and bit knuckle. Then she flung coppery red hair out of one eye and stared at Vincenti.

"Hello and good-bye," Vincenti said.

He lifted the Luger.

"You fool!" the girl who was more than mere woman said. She whirled and spat on the bloody body of Nemo Lucelli. "I wanted him dead! Don't kill me – think, you fool!"

Vincenti frowned, staring at this girl.

She was beautiful, with long, flowing red hair. She wore a black swimsuit – a bikini – that was revealing enough to make a man hold his breath. Tall, she was, firm-breasted, long-thighed, with broad red lips, large blue eyes – a wish, a promise.

"Who are you?" Vincenti said.

"Not now – not here." She spoke rapidly. "There's no time. They're coming back, don't you see? Nemo sent them for some brandy." She paused, put both hands to her cheeks. "You kill me, you'll never get away – they'll know somebody else did this. I know what to do – let me do it. I hated him! I was bought and paid for. Everybody knows it. They'll think I did this. They know it's been coming. Don't you see – here – they're here now!"

She pointed towards a front window. Beyond the sound of the music was the sound of a car's wheels on gravel, and Vincenti saw gleams and glitters out there in the silky shade from the limo's paint job.

The girl snatched up a red robe from a chair.

"Where's your car, you idiot – hurry!"

Thinking how it had to be the weed, Vincenti grabbed her hand and turned running, dragging her – because truly it was good in this direction, too – this girl was his alibi.

If he made it.

"Where?" she gasped.

He said nothing, holstered the Luger, thinking how they would believe she had killed Lucelli. He grabbed the Luger from its holster again, thinking, You forgot, you fool! It's that damned Acapulco Gold.

He flung the Luger into the pool with a splash that shattered the icy green, and they ran through the flower beds to the yellow-stone wall.

"Hey!"

It was a shout from back in the cottage.

"It's them," the girl whispered, cringing against Vincenti.

Vincenti did not hesitate. He grasped her around the smooth, plump thighs and lifted her quickly to the top of the wall.

"Drop down," he said, scrambling after her.

There were shouts from inside the cottage.

Vincenti slipped over the wall just as somebody fired in his direction. Chips of shattered stone flew in the afternoon.

"Run for the street – my car," he told the girl, thrusting her ahead.

"They climbed the wall!" a man shouted from behind.

They made the Continental.

"Let me drive," the girl said. "There's only one place to go – my plane at the St Petersburg-Clearwater Airport. This area'll be crawling. It's our only chance."

"Get in," Vincenti told her. "I'm driving." He was also thinking fast. She was right. Word would go out. *Soldatos* would be everywhere, watching for her and whoever was with her. They would be at every entrance to the city, every highway would soon be covered. There was only the one chance: with her.

They were away fast, with the girl directing him on back routes. It was all Vincenti could do to hold the speed down, and there was a snarl of discouragement in his chest, but it began to lessen with each mile. This girl – this girl was something to consider – a beauty – and with quick brains, too.

Lucelli was dead. He would have plenty of money. This girl would have plenty, too – it was a fast deal and a good one.

Soon they were out of Tampa on the Courtney-Campbell Causeway, headed for Route 19. Vincenti began to relax a touch, but he did not let up on the accelerator. He knew anything could happen. Lucelli's web could reach out . . .

"What's your name?" he asked the girl, trying to think about more comforting things.

"Anette," she said.

"Okay, Anette. Looks as if we'll be together for a time. But where'll we go?" He hesitated, then took a shot at it. "I'm from LA."

"My money's in Vero Beach – that's where I live. I was just visiting Nemo at one of his castles, see? We'll fly my Cessna to Vero – agreed?"

"Then where?"

"There's only one where. Europe. We'll head for Miami, and

fly to England first. It's the only way, and it can be damned thin. Nemo rules – ruled this state." She slid closer to Vincenti. "What's your name?"

He told her.

"But what's your first name?"

"Harry."

"Gee, I dig that – Harry."

He allowed himself to comfort her somewhat by placing one hand on her knee, while visions danced in his head.

Sugar plums, he thought. Sweet sugar plums.

Presently they reached the St Pete-Clearwater Airport. In less than fifteen minutes they were seated in Anette's four-seat Cessna; a beautiful ship, colored red, white, and yellow – sleek in the early twilight.

They came down the runway with Anette at the controls. She had asked him if he could fly.

"I leave that up to pilots."

"Vero, here we come," she said, and they were airborne.

Vincenti took his first clean breath of freedom. There was little chance of being caught now. He had done his job. Lucelli was dead. He would collect payment by cable in London. He had his passport with him. He was always ready for anything.

They winged above Tampa Bay. The waters, in the last of the sunlight, looked as if studded with diamonds. He saw the vast span of the Howard Frankland Bridge up ahead, cars like ants speeding along the whiteway.

He lit two joints and passed her one.

She smiled at him and took a big toke.

"Hey," he said suddenly. "You're going down – we're flying pretty damned low."

"Want to show you how pretty it can be. Then, after, we'll get to know each other. There's an automatic pilot, see? Nemo had it installed for me. I'm setting it now."

They were flying at tremendous speed towards the looming bridge span.

Vincenti did not want to show his tight fright to this girl. She was truly something.

She pushed the throttle up all the way, and turned to smile at him again.

"This grass is good stuff," she said.

He said, just to make words, "You didn't tell me your last name."

She stood up, stepped over, and slipped beside him. But she seemed somehow stiff and sober.

"Well, honey," she said. "My last name's Lucelli." She looked straight into his eyes and ruffled the back of his hair. "I'm Nemo Lucelli's daughter. You see, now? And you're one of us. You know how it is, avenging a death in the family." Excitement was in her eyes. "That's how it is, honey – Harry Vincenti!"

He stared at her as the words registered. Fear stabbed him. He hurled her aside. She sprawled to the deck.

"Lucelli," he heard himself say.

Tears rushed into the girl's eyes. "I *loved* my father. But you wouldn't dig that, you pig!" She screamed it. "He was a great, kind man. I loved him. You killed him. I'll die for him!"

He struck her across the mouth, then whirled to look through the windshield. The bridge loomed dead ahead. He dove for the controls.

The plane smashed into the bridge and exploded with a shattering roar of flame.

Harry Vincenti crashed headlong through the windshield. He arced through the air like a limber rag doll and sprawled sliding in a bloody path in the far second lane of traffic.

He was dead before the big semi ran over him, but it didn't really matter.

PREVIEW OF MURDER

Robert Leslie Bellem

1. Date with a Recluse

It was a cheap, frowsy hotel in a cheap shoddy neighborhood a good distance south of Hollywood Boulevard. It was standing like a tired harridan on the east side of the street so that the setting sun in the west painted its shabby brick facade the color of old blood that nobody wanted any more.

Over the entrance faded gilt lettering said "Chaple Arms," which could have been a misspelling of "Chapel" or might be the proprietor's name. The cars parked along the curb in front were old, worn-out models in need of polish they would never get, with dented fenders and recap tires any self-respecting junk dealer would have sneered at.

Drifting past in second gear, I watched a mangy alley cat in the doorway, licking its chops and working on a bird it had killed. That was the only visible movement, the only sign of life. It was just as much a sign of death, if you thought about it from the bird's viewpoint: only the bird was beyond caring. The Chaple Arms didn't seem to care, either. It was that kind of hotel. One more stain on the steps couldn't possibly matter.

The voice on the phone that afternoon hadn't matched any of this. Asking me to come here at six sharp, it had sounded austere and dignified, with culture and education back of it. And money. It had sounded like a lot of money.

In the private detective business you develop a sort of extra sense which reacts to subtle nuances like that. So I was disappointed when I copped a glimpse of the Chaple Arms. It wasn't a place where money lived. Maybe it had been, once, a long time ago. Could be. But now it was a fleabag.

I looked at my strap-watch. Five of six. I drove my jalopy to the next corner and made a U-turn, wheeled back and found a berth almost directly across the street from the tawdry brick building. At three of six I ankled past the alley cat, noticed that the bird was all gone except a few wing feathers, and barged into a dingy lobby that smelled as unclean as it looked.

The linoleum on the floor was worn through in spots by the feet of trudging years, showing that it had been laid on an original installation of white tiles. There were two overstuffed chairs against the right-hand wall, as wrinkled and sagging as the bags under a sick man's eyes, and on the left there was a short, stained marble-top counter with a desk clerk behind it, pigeonholing folded circulars into a rectangular wooden tier of square open-front letterboxes.

His black alpaca coat was shiny with age, freckled with small gray flakes the exact shade of his hair. His back was toward me and he didn't look around when I spoke to him.

So I spoke again, louder. "Hey, you with the dandruff on your shoulders," I said.

He kept right on stuffing circulars into pigeonholes. Then I lamped two little twisted black wires running down along his collar, and I leaned over the counter and nudged him on the spine with my forefinger. Leaning over the counter made me feel pretty sure no laundry would ever be able to take the grease stains from the front of my clothes. Touching the clerk with my finger made me feel as if I would never wash my hands clean again, no matter how much soap and water I used.

He jumped slightly and turned around, and the little twisted wires ran from a button in his ear to a black plastic box hooked heavily to his breast pocket. He had a face like crinkled parchment and eyes as sadly apologetic as a cocker spaniel's. He jiggled something on the plastic box, a switch that clicked audibly.

"Wear a hearing aid," he said in a powdery voice. "Generally keep it turned off to save the batteries. You scared me a rifle, poking me like that."

"Sorry, old-timer," I said. "Although I should think you'd be used to it if you keep your back to the customers all the time."

"Got me a little mirror on the wall." He jerked a thumb. "Usually watch it so's nobody sneaks up on me, but I guess I kind of forgot this time. Preoccupied." He let a small sigh dribble past lips as loose as dangling rubber bands. "Something I could do for you?"

"I want to see a guy that lives here – name of Fullerton. Joseph T. Fullerton."

"Nobody sees Joseph T. Fullerton, mister. Nobody ain't seen Joseph T. Fullerton in nine, ten years to my knowledge. Not even the maids which brush up his rooms. You prolly think I'm kidding you, but I ain't."

"I've got an appointment," I said.

For all that meant to him he might as well have had his hearing aid switched off. "For six o'clock," I added. "It's six now, even up."

"No offense, mister, but I just plain don't believe you."

"About it being six o'clock?"

"About you having no appointment to see Mr Fullerton. Like I said, nobody sees him. Nobody at all. He don't allow it."

"I'm Nick Ransom," I said patiently, and took a card out of my wallet to prove it. I put the card on the counter. "Somebody calling himself Joseph T. Fullerton phoned me at my office this afternoon and asked me to be here at six sharp. Maybe it was a rib, but that voice didn't sound like a practical joker's. You might give Fullerton a jingle and check on it. That is, if there really is a Joseph T. Fullerton registered here."

"Orders is never to disturb him under no circumstances." With mild curiosity he read my card, his rubber-band lips moving as he spelled out the words. "Nick Ransom. Confidential Investigations. That's be kind of a cop, wouldn't it?"

"Private."

He made with another dribbling sigh.

"Nothing like this ain't never happened before since I been working here." He moved to a small old-fashioned switchboard and peered at it, picked up a fragment of pale blue paper that had scribbling on it. "Well, I be danged. Day man must of left this for me and I never seen it when I come on duty at five. Says somebody named Nick Ransom is to be tooken straight up to Mr Fullerton."

"Yeah," I said. I set fire to a gasper.

*   *   *

He shook his head wearily. More dandruff snowed down on the alpaca coat's shoulders.

"Reason I never noticed it, they ain't been no calls go through the board since I come on shift. Danged day man shouldn't of left it tucked behind the keys that way. He ought to of told me."

"So now you know," I said. "And it's two minutes past six. I don't like to keep a client waiting."

"Course not. Dumb me, making you stand around."

He hit a tap-bell under the counter. It had a clean, tinkly sound that broke across the lobby and lost itself, discouraged, against musty velour draperies on the opposite wall. There followed a whirring hiccuppy noise from somewhere in the rear, and an antique elevator creaked jerkily down an open grillwork shaft. Its wrought iron gate slid open, rattling on worn grooves, and a kid in his early twenties stepped out smartly.

"Pete," the clerk said, "show this here gent up to Three-seventeen."

Pete's glimmers widened. He was a tall punk, not quite up to my six feet plus but slender and lithe and broad of shoulder in a nondescript uniform a size too small for his build. He probably had inherited it from a whole series of predecessors, but he wore it with a nice jauntiness that certainly didn't belong in a joint like the Chaple Arms.

He had wavy brown hair and even white teeth, and an uncompromising jaw that went well with the humorous up-quirk at the corners of his lips.

"Maybe I'd better borrow that ear gadget of yours," he said, and grinned. "I'd have sworn you said Three-seventeen."

"I did say Three-seventeen," the clerk told him.

"But that's—"

"Fullerton's, yeh. And Fullerton don't never have no callers. He does now."

"Right-o," Pete said. "This way, sir."

He led me toward the elevator.

Just as I was stepping into the cage, the clerk at the counter lifted his powdery voice.

"Hey, mister." He beckoned me, and I went back to him. "You wouldn't want to spare me one of them cigarettes of yours, I don't suppose?" he said. "Not that I'm awful partial to cigarettes. Cigars is my preference, only I'm a mite strapped this week, and—"

I dug a four-bit piece out of my jeans, gave it to him. "Buy yourself a perfecto."

"Criminity. Fifty cents! Biggest tip I taken in for more'n a year. Thanks." He leaned forward. "Confidential, mister, the real reason I called you back, I wondered would you do me a little favor."

"Such as?"

"If you *do* get to see Joseph T. Fullerton, I'd sure love to hear what he really looks like. Ain't never seen him myself, and I got a bump of curiosity a mile high."

"I'll give you a verbal portrait," I said, and went over to the elevator again.

The good-looking Pete clanged the door shut and pulled a rope, and the cage moved upward in little jerky bumps, like hiccups. Midway between the first and second floors I dredged out another half-dollar and spun it around my thumb.

"Speaking of Fullerton," I said.

"Were we speaking of Mr Fullerton, sir?"

The punk quirked a smile at me.

"Discreet bellhops in a trap like this," I said. I put away the four-bit piece and started toying with a folded dollar bill. "Been working here long, son?"

"Four years. Putting myself through college. USC." He eyed the folded buck as we creaked past the second-floor landing. "You were asking about Fullerton?"

"Uh-huh. He's a recluse, I gather."

"A mild word for it. Nobody ever sees him. When the maids tidy up he hides in a sort of closet he's got rigged as a tuckaway. The help take him his meals. I get his supper from a place around the corner and leave it in his living room."

"But you've never met him?"

"I've talked to him through his hideaway door, is all. Third floor, sir." He clanged the cage open and pointed. "Three-seventeen is just past that turn in the corridor." Then, when I handed him the dollar: "Thanks, sir. Want to know something?"

"That was my last loose buck, Buster."

He grinned. "This is for free." The grin got turned off like a spigot. "I don't think you're going to like visiting Mr Fullerton. It's a spooky experience until you get used to it. Lots of luck, sir."

2. Talk with a Corpse

I walked along the hallway with the elevator's ancient hesitant creaks dwindling down behind me. Presently I came to a door and bunted it with my knuckles, then stepped aside, just in case Joseph T. Fullerton happened to be the kind of hermit with homicidal eccentricities such as shooting guns through thin wooden paneling.

"Nick Ransom out here!" I said loudly. "By appointment."

"You're five minutes late."

There was something vaguely familiar in this voice, a texture my subconscious mind picked up and fingered and tried to recognize. It was a voice of the same general timbre and intonation as that of the guy who had phoned me, yet different and somehow more natural, as if, over the wire, he had disguised his delivery just a little so it wouldn't strike a responsive echo in my memory.

Now, though, he didn't seem to care if I caught hep. It bothered me because I couldn't place it, and for some reason I couldn't savvy I felt a shiver crawling down my back, the way you do when you dream something not too pleasant at night.

"Come in," it said. "It's unlocked for you."

I grasped the knob and it turned in my hand. I pushed on the portal but nothing happened; it didn't give.

"Opens outward. I forgot to tell you. Special arrangement of mine. Pull."

Whoever he was, he was no stranger to me. I combed through my mental card-index file but the thing eluded me, like trying to pin down a shadow. I pulled, and the door swung smoothly on oiled hinges. I barged into a room that had nobody in it but me, and the empty room spoke my name.

It said, "Hello, Nick. I understand you've quit the stunting racket and gone into private detective work," in the voice of a man I had known a long time ago; a man buried and gone these past fourteen years or more. The empty room said, "It's good to see you again, Nick," and the voice belonged to a dead man.

I could remember, and see and hear it all now, those years ago – and I knew.

I was standing on the sidelines of a movie set, out of camera range, watching two guys who were going to be blasted to bits the next minute – not make-believe blasted for a spool of film, but actually and horribly blown apart like chopped meat. That was fourteen years ago, but the fourteen years faded and vanished like a lap dissolve shot so that time was telescoped and the past merged into the present, the present became the past.

I was on a cavernous sound stage at Paragon Pix seeing a sequence in rehearsal, a sequence destined never to be played because in another sixty seconds the leading man would be a corpse. He would be the late lamented Ronald Barclay, as handsome a ham as ever starred in the flickering tintypes.

Barclay was tall and swarthy, with the brand of boudoir eyes that made matrons swoon and their daughters crave to leave home. He had dark wavy hair with touches of frost at the temples which he refused to let the makeup department do anything about, and he was built like a Roman gladiator. In private life he carried a baseball bat to beat off the women who tried to surrender their all at his shrine.

I watched him there on the set, rehearsing a brief piece of business for a close-up, a bit of action which I myself would duplicate later in a long shot. That long shot was where the peril would be, and since Paragon Pix couldn't afford to risk Barclay's million-dollar good looks, I was the stunt expert they had hired to double for him in the hazard scene.

Not that I considered it especially hazardous. According to the scenario he was to pick up a cigarette box from a table and open it, whereupon a bomb which the villain had planted in the box would blow up like a cannon cracker. Of course the explosion wouldn't show in the close-up. The director would cut out the scene just as Barclay lifted the gadget.

Then I would step in and replace him while the camera was moved some distance away. I would lift the lid of the box, and a small charge of flashlight powder would ignite in such a way that I couldn't get burned if I remembered to be careful and hold my hands in the right position.

The special effects department would subsequently doctor the footage, intensify the size of the flame-flash, and a loud boom would be dubbed onto the sound track. Meanwhile, the initial close-up had to be timed out with Barclay himself going through the motions.

I watched as a prop man walked on-stage and placed the cigarette box in position. I saw Barclay reach for it ahead of schedule as if idly curious to inspect it. There came a thunderous roar that shook the set. *Ker-blaaam!*

With my ears ringing and my glimmers smarting, half-blinded, I plunged forward from the sidelines, hearing behind me the shouts of the director and his camera crew, the screams of the script girl, the stunned oaths of carpenters and grips and juicers milling around in momentary panic. I reached the crumpled, unconscious forms of Ronald Barclay and the property man who had been standing too close to him when the blast went off. I bent down and beat out the flames that were charring their ripped and red-stained clothes.

Five minutes later I helped load both men into the ambulance that came wailing onto the lot from a nearby hospital. I couldn't help thinking that the ambulance might have been toting my own gory fragments instead of theirs if the bomb had waited until my turn had come to handle it.

Barclay kicked the bucket before the internes could hoist him onto an operating table. His subsequent funeral was a nine-day wonder even for Hollywood, where nine-day wonders seldom last more than a day and a half.

The prop man wasn't so lucky. He lived. Permanently maimed, he survived his injuries and eventually dropped out of the news, out of sight. Nobody cared; nobody bothered to fasten official blame on him for accidentally loading the mock bomb with dynamite instead of harmless flashlight powder.

Besides, he had paid for his blunder. It cost him two legs and an arm. You don't prosecute a basket case who can't fight back. You just let him fade into oblivion.

Fourteen years . . .

In my mind those years slowly stretched out into proper perspective, resumed their long endless shape of days and weeks and months. I snapped back to the present, and I was no longer a stunt expert on that cavernous Paragon sound stage. I was now a private dick in the drab living room of a fleabag called the Chaple Arms. I was here by the request of a telephone voice and listening to that same disembodied voice coming from nowhere; hearing it and remembering it, remembering that the last time I'd heard it was just before a property cigarette box exploded.

But it wasn't the voice of the bomb crippled prop man, who had lived. It was the voice of Ronald Barclay, the handsome star, who had died.

It was a trick, natch. It had to be a trick. Some dizzy jerk with a perverted sense of humor was needling me, giving me a bad time. I glowered around the room at the cheap window curtains, the shabby-genteel mission furniture, the threadbare carpet and dingy walls.

A heavy-set bozo glowered back at me from over near a corner – a tall, scowling character in tweeds, with a truculent glint in his peepers. He was my own reflection in a full-length mirror set into a closet door. Nobody else was around.

"Now just one condemned minute," I snarled. "I can go along with a gag as well as the next slob. But—"

"It's no gag, Nick," Ronald Barclay's voice said. "And you needn't be so jittery. I'm behind the mirror. It's one of those new-fangled two-way glasses. I can see out through it, but all you can see is yourself." There was a brief chuckle, not entirely mirthful. "I'm talking through a hole in the wall. You can't find it, though, because it's covered with wallpaper."

"That's where you usually find vermin in a drop like this," I said. "Behind the wallpaper. And quit explaining your dime-store hocus-pocus magic act in Ronald Barclay's voice. Barclay was sort of a friend of mine in the old days, as friendly as a star ever gets with a mere stunt man, and he's dead. I don't like it. Stop imitating him."

"I can't stop, because I'm not imitating him, and because I'm not dead. I'm alive and I'm Ronald Barclay." Bitterness was in that. "Have a drink, Nick. I left a bottle of Scotch on that table behind you. Vat 69. That's your brand, as I recall."

Sure it was my brand. I picked up the bottle and let some of its mellow lightning slide down my throat. I needed it. My nerves were jumpy.

"Everybody in Hollywood knows the kind of Scotch I prefer," I growled. "That proves nothing."

"Do you remember the time I went on a brannigan and you took me to your apartment and kept me there three days to sober me up for a new picture I was starting?"

I stiffened. I had never told a living soul about that crazy episode. Nobody else knew it except Barclay himself, unless he had blabbed it to some third party before he died.

I was getting confused. Dead men can't talk from behind mirrors. I took another swig from the bottle and exhaled the aroma around a test question.

"What kind of pajamas did I loan you to wear? What color?"

"You didn't. Your spare pajamas were all in the laundry. You borrowed a nightgown from a girl in the next apartment. It was a cerise chiffon."

I strangled. "You *are* Barclay! Come out of hiding. I want to look at you."

"Nobody looks at me, Nick. Not even you. Nobody's looked at me since I moved in here after the hospital released me. Nobody ever will."

"But – but—"

"It was really the prop man who died, Nick. His name was Joc Fullerton, in case you've forgotten. He died, and I lived. A little piece of me lived. No legs. One arm. Half a face." There was a catch in the voice, almost like a sob. Then it steadied. "I was a vain man, Nick, remember? When I found out I was going to live and look like a butchered frog, I couldn't take it. Not as Ronald Barclay I couldn't."

I stared at the mirror. All I saw was my own optics bulging like oysters being squeezed from two fists.

"Women had worshipped me," Barclay's voice said. "Now if they saw me it would be with horror and loathing. I didn't want that. I didn't want sympathy. I wanted to die, but the doctors wouldn't let me die, curse them. So I cooked up a scheme."

"I get it," I said thickly. "You arranged to have the property man, Joe Fullerton, buried in your name. And you took his. It was a trade, a switch. You couldn't stand being a maimed Ronald Barclay, but a crippled Fullerton you could adjust to. You bribed the right people, and – good glory, it's fantastic!"

"On the contrary, it was fairly simple. Fullerton had no family; neither had I. Who'd know the difference? I didn't have to bribe anybody. Fullerton was blasted beyond recognition. So was I. Even the fingerprints of my one remaining hand had been destroyed. No fingerprints. No teeth in my mouth for dental chart comparisons. No mouth, period – until the plastic surgeons built me something I could use for a mouth, such as it is."

"You mean you just kept insisting you were Fullerton and the hospital staff believed you?"

"Yes. Luckily the real Fullerton had an accident policy – twenty thousand dollars for the loss of two limbs, forty for the loss of three. I collected the forty thousand and moved to the Chaple Arms. I've been here ever since."

"Come on out," I said earnestly. "I want to see you."

"Nobody sees me, Nick. How often must I say it?"

"So you're in a wheelchair," I said. "Which is why your door opens outward, so you can get away in case of fire. So you're a no-legged guy with a missing arm and a face that would give dames the screaming meemies. But I'm no dame; I'm a friend of yours. I want to see you. I can take it."

"No." His voice sharpened. "And don't come any closer to this closet. It wouldn't do you any good. There's no knob on the outside. And if you smash the glass I'll kill you. I've got one good hand and it's holding a gun, and I'd kill anybody who looked at me. I'm not fooling, Nick. Don't force me to do something I wouldn't want to do!"

3. Dead Man's Diary

Ronald Barclay sounded sincere and a little hysterical, and maybe a touch demented along with it. Only a loony guy would do what he had done, live the way he had been living. And if he really had a roscoe he was as dangerous as sparks in a gunpowder factory.

I backed off, gave the Vat 69 another fast belt.

"Okay," I said, "so you don't want to be looked at. And for fourteen years you've pretended to be deceased. That much I'll buy. As an amateur psychologist I might even understand it. But why did you ask me to come here? And after keeping your secret all these years, why let me in on it now?"

"Because I trust you. And I need a favor."

"What favor?"

"I want you to be my decoy."

"I don't get that," I said.

He said through the hole in the wall: "Decoy. Lure. Bait."

"I still don't get it."

"I'm asking you to entice a certain person here to my rooms. I don't care what pretext you use. That I leave up to your judgment. Just so you fetch him here and leave him."

"So it's a him, not a her," I said. "Maybe if I stick around long enough I'll learn even more. Don't let me hurry you, pal. I have the evening free."

"You have a sarcastic tongue, too. You always had. Don't rush me, Nick. Let me tell it my way. This man I want brought here to me . . . What's the matter with you?"

"Nothing. Go ahead. I'm listening."

"Why have you got your head cocked to one side like that?"

"I told you I was listening." I was, too. Not only to Ronald Barclay's voice, but to something else that might have been only my imagination. "Go on with your story. You've got a reason for wanting a certain character lured here. What's the reason and who is the guy?"

"He's the man who murdered me," Barclay said, and at the same instant I whipped out the .32 automatic I always pack in an armpit rig, hurled my tonnage across the room.

I didn't plunge toward the mirrored closet. I catapulted at the door to the outer corridor. If there's anything that broils me to a crisp it's an eavesdropper. And I'd already had enough weirdness and mystification for one afternoon.

The trick door gave me trouble because I forgot it opened outward. I grasped the knob, twisted it, pulled, and almost dislocated my wrist with the sudden yank. Then I remembered to push.

I pushed. I bounced over the threshold into the musty hallway with its dead, rancid smells, and there was nobody in sight. There was nothing except gloomy, thickening shadows as dusk gathered. I might as well have peered up and down the passages of an abandoned morgue. The silence was a thing you could practically pick up and rub in your fingers.

I went back into the room and pulled the door shut after me. I had the jitters. I had the kind of shakes you get from talking to an invisible dead man who was alive enough and crazy enough to belong in a padded cell.

I needed another snort of the crazy man's Scotch but I didn't take it because my brain felt too fuzzy as it was. Next thing I knew I would be having delirium tremens. Maybe I already had delirium tremens.

I should have stayed out there in the hall while I had the chance. I should have copped a fast scram. I should have gone home where I could try to forget I'd ever been in a joint called the Chaple Arms. But no, I had to barge on back into the room.

Barclay's voice came through the wallpaper-covered speaking hole. It sounded grim.

"You took your life in your hands pulling that caper, Nick. For a minute I thought you were trying to get at me. I almost shot you through this mirror. What was the idea? What spooked you?"

"I realize the risk now," I said sourly. "But I thought I'd heard somebody outside stealing an earful." I holstered my heater. "Evidently I was haywire. And for pipe's sake quit yacking at me about shooting through the mirror. You're giving me a complex." I made a resentful mouth at the looking glass. "If you want me to leave, say the word. I'll go quietly; I'd be glad to. I'm getting so I don't like it here, if I ever did."

"I apologize, Nick. I'm sorry. And I don't want you to leave. Not just yet."

I did want to leave, but I didn't say so.

"And another thing," was what I said. "Just before I dived at the door you spouted a line of dizzy dialogue about the man who murdered you. Let's stop making with that kind of double talk. Nobody murdered you, because you're still alive. Taking your word for it, of course. Consequently—"

"Alive! You can't call anyone in my condition alive."

"All I know about your condition is what you've told me. Have you shown yourself? No."

"I don't intend to," he said harshly. "As for the murder part, call it a maimed man's sardonic figure of speech. In my own estimation I'm worse than dead, but skip it. There *was* a man who got killed, though, remember? A prop man. Joseph T. Fullerton, whose name I stole. How do you classify that?"

"An accident."

"Wrong. It was murder. Premeditated murder, as cold and calculated as slaughtering cattle in a packing house." He hesitated a second. "Nick, on that picture with the explosion sequence, do you recall the director?"

"Sure," I said. "Emil Heinrich. A kraut. He's big stuff now. He climbed slow, but he climbed high. Head man of Paragon Pix. He's come a long way. What about him?"

"He'd just been married a short while to an extra girl named Marian Lodge. Pretty, but not a brain in her head."

"He's still married to her," I said. "And she's still pretty. And she still hasn't got a brain in her head. So what?"

"Heinrich thought I was on the make for her."

"Were you?"

"My home-wrecking was strictly on the screen. You know that. I never looked at her sidewise, but Heinrich had notions. He actually accused me, once. I laughed at him." The voice went brittle, metallic. "I laughed at him. Heaven help me."

"Make your point," I said.

The short hairs were beginning to prickle at the nape of my neck and I felt that shiver going down my spine, crawling inch by inch like a bad dream.

There was a rustling noise behind the wallpaper. "Yesterday I was getting ready to discard an old trunk, Nick. A trunk that belonged to Joe Fullerton, part of his stuff that was moved here with me when I took his name, assumed his identity. I'd rummaged through it before, thrown away the things of his I didn't need, then I'd used it to store junk of my own. But yesterday I decided to get rid of it. I emptied it out."

"And?"

"I discovered a false bottom compartment I'd never noticed before. It had a book in it, a diary. Fullerton's private diary. I wouldn't know why a man would want to keep a thing like that. Diaries are for women, I always thought. But Fullerton had one. Made daily entries – up to the day before he was killed."

"All right, build it up. Make me wait for the punch line."

"This is serious, Nick, not funny. I'm going to read you part of the last page Fullerton wrote. Listen. 'Twice yesterday I found Heinrich messing around my props. He didn't see me watching him, but I saw things I'm going to take up with the union if this keeps up. What right has a kraut director got to butt in on the property department? If he thinks I'm not capable of measuring a load of flashlight powder in a cigarette box let him take it up with the producer. Let him tell the brass hats in the front office. Next time I catch him poking around that prop bomb I'm going to raise a mess, job or no job. Up to now I've kept my mouth shut, but he better lay off. I don't like outsiders fooling with my private can of flash powder, either'."

I said in a choked voice, "Is that all?"

"Isn't it enough, Nick? After fourteen years I know what really happened! Heinrich was jealous of me. He tampered with the cigarette-box bomb. In spite of Fullerton's watchfulness and suspicions he succeeded in fixing it to go off prematurely, when I picked it up. And he substituted something powerful for the harmless flash powder that was supposed to be in it."

"Now wait. You're just guessing. You're not sure he did that."

"All right, so I'm guessing. Theorizing. But it adds."

He couldn't convince me.

"Not necessarily," I said. "Maybe I was the one he was after. Maybe he had a grudge against me, for some reason I can't figure. After all, I was the stunt man who was scheduled to let the thing explode in my hands."

"Originally, that's true. Unknown to you, though, Heinrich altered the script just a little. An important little. When we started rehearsing the scene he rearranged the action so that you wouldn't be first to handle the cigarette box. He directed me to pick it up and pry open the lid for that close-up. He told me it was a dummy box; harmless. And certainly I had no reason to disbelieve him.

"He said he would then cut the scene, let you double for me in the following long shot, and go on with the action from there. He was smooth, Nick. He sold it to me and I never suspected what was coming. You know how it worked out. I picked up the real bomb and it went bang. And all these years I thought it was a mischance, an accident – until I found the prop man's diary. Then I knew Heinrich had planned to kill me."

I dredged out a gasper, set fire to it. The smoke burned my gullet like acid, like the fumes of blasting powder, like the hot sting that had scorched my nostrils fourteen years ago on a Paragon sound stage when I had beat out the flames charring the crimson-stained clothing of two crumpled shapes who once had been husky, healthy men.

"You can't make it stick, pal," I said. "Not on the diary of a guy dead and buried all this time."

"There's no statute of limitations on homicide, Nick."

"All right, give it to the cops and see what happens. They'd slip you the big nix. Insufficient proof, for one thing. All you can offer is unsupported surmise. And Emil Heinrich is a powerful hombre these days. A bozo in his position packs weight." I put my coffin nail in an ash-tray, snubbed it out, and had a swig from the Scotch bottle. "You'd wind up before a rigged lunacy commission. They'll say you're off your rocker. Fourteen years of hiding your ugliness from the world drove you out of your mind."

"Do you think that?"

I hedged. "Never mind what I think. The main point is, you could wind up in a room with soft walls."

"Not while I've got one hand to hold a gun."

"Back at that again," I said.

"And anyhow, I don't plan to go to the police. I want Heinrich here. I want a private showdown with him."

"Oh-oh," I said. "No, thanks. Include me out. I'm no assassin. I'm not even an assistant assassin. If you're looking for homicide help, get another boy."

His voice went smooth, persuasive. "Don't let my gun talk put wrong ideas in your head. I'm not going to kill him. He's worth a lot more to me alive. Alive and successful and prosperous. Do you think forty thousand dollars can last forever? Most of the money I got from Joe Fullerton's insurance policy has been spent. And I'm too settled here to relish the idea of being moved to an almshouse. I don't want charity, and I refuse to be a public charge. I simply want to talk to Heinrich."

"Blackmail, eh? A shakedown."

"That's a little crude. I want to sell him the Fullerton diary for enough cash to see me through the rest of my life. Is that unfair?"

4. Kill and Vanish

Such guff as this I didn't swallow. It was too transparent, too obvious. Barclay had bumpery on his mind and I wanted no part of that. By the same token you can't come right out and say no to a potential madman with a gat in his clutch. It was a situation calling for finesse.

I lied diplomatically.

"Hmmm-m-m," I said. "Just a financial transaction, huh? That's different." I moved easily toward the door.

"Where are you going?" he asked uneasily.

"To do what you asked. To arrange to lure Heinrich here."

"You're really going to help me?"

"Anything for a pal," I said, and pushed the portal open.

It resisted me. Something was against it, outside in the hall. Something with weight that didn't want to yield.

I shoved with all my hundred and ninety pounds of heft, suddenly and explosively. From the mirrored closet behind me came a displeased oath. Barclay must have thought I was taking a runout on him.

And I was. Or anyhow that had been my intention until I smacked the corridor door wide open and knocked somebody sprawling on the hallway's thin-worn carpet. Then I changed my mind, because I had finally nailed my eavesdropper.

He was the deaf desk-clerk, with the parchment face, from downstairs. The door batted him all the way across the passage and he fetched up against the opposite wall, huddled, flopping, a bag of bones in a black alpaca coat. I grabbed him, dragged him back and pulled him into the room.

It was pretty dark now, but not too dark for me to see a wheel-chair rolling toward me. The mirrored closet gaped wide, and the fragment of man who used to be Ronald Barclay was out of his hiding place. Maybe my unexpected maneuver with the door had brought him forth because of curiosity. Or maybe he'd had an idea of pursuing me, guessing that I was going to scram and leave him in the lurch.

He might even have figured a double-cross and decided to gun me in the back. I don't know and I never found out. I didn't have time to ask him.

I only knew that in the gloom of nightfall he didn't look so hideous. Sitting in the wheelchair, he had a blanket over his lap so you couldn't actually tell that his legs were missing. Without the lights turned on, his face could have passed for a face, for it was a pale blur above a white shirt even paler and blurrier.

One sleeve was empty, pinned to the chest. The other had an

arm in it which ended in a stubby hand, the hand being busy propelling the chair by its wheel-rim. That was swell. As long as it was busy it couldn't do anything about the nickel-plated .38 revolver resting on the blanketed lap.

That's what I thought.

The pale blur of face spouted harsh curses. "You tricked me!" he raved. "You tricked me out of the closet so you could look at me."

"Stow it." I was leaning over the desk clerk. "This lad was listening, and—"

The sky came down and hit me on the noggin. All the stars in the heavens fell with the sky and danced in my optics, and all at once I was pitching down a long black tunnel that gulped me like a raw oyster. My head came off and floated away. It wasn't a head, it was a balloon, and somebody had cut the string. It drifted on a rising current, and the current became a whirlpool of pain filled with India ink.

Blooey. I didn't even feel the floor when it bounced me . . .

There was one dim light in the room, and two eyes fastened on me. I didn't like them. They were too wide open, too glassy. Eyes are supposed to blink once in a while. These didn't. They regarded me with the cold impassive speculation of a fish three days on ice. Expressionless. Unsympathetic.

The devil with them. I wanted sympathy. My skull throbbed like an ulcer in a movie producer's stomach. I was an ill man. I was a sick dick and I didn't like being stared at.

Ronald Barclay hadn't liked it either, I reflected dourly. And when he didn't like a thing he was a man who resented it the hard way. For a one-armed guy he certainly packed a wallop. It takes a hefty bash to put me down for the count, but he had what it takes. I decided I was lucky he had only whammed me with a .38. If it had been a .45 it would probably have finished me.

As it was, I had a lump on top of my conk the size of second base and I was lying on the floor, sniffing the dust of the thin carpet and looking into a pair of cold cod-fish glims belonging to somebody sprawled a couple of feet ferninst me. I didn't mind the character being so close, but that steady mackerel focus gave me the fantods.

I got more than the fantods when it slowly dawned on me that the bozo wasn't breathing.

He had a vacant, expressionless face as wrinkled as parchment, as colorless as wax candles. There was a wired button in one ear and a switched-off plastic box hanging from his alpaca coat, but he wasn't using the equipment as a hearing aid. He was the desk clerk, and he was defunct. He couldn't be anything else, the way his left temple was crushed in.

I whispered something silently.

The fog cleared out of my brain and I tabbed a wheelchair beyond the clerk's lifeless husk. The last time I'd seen that wheelchair it had contained Ronald Barclay. Now it contained nobody. It was just an empty wheelchair.

I sat up and waited for nausea to hit me the way it does when you've got a minor concussion and move too fast. My head vibrated like strings on a hockshop banjo and my stomach churned.

As soon as it stopped churning I lurched to my feet. Astonishingly, I didn't fall down again. For a guy with a cracked plate, this was a major accomplishment. I felt well enough to hip a quick dram from that fifth of Vat 69 on the table, and then I felt even better. I dug inside my coat, unshipped my roscoe and was back in business. I prowled the apartment.

First I looked in the closet behind the trick mirror. It was a big roomy space, dark as the inside of a rubber boot until I used the beam of my pencil flash. Barclay wasn't there. When I moved to the bedroom he wasn't in there, either. I drew another blank in the bathroom – no Barclay. Par for the course. But in a padlocked alcove between bedroom and bath I stumbled onto all the clues a snoop would ever need.

The padlock was duck soup for the pick I carry on my keyring, and the alcove was actually a miniature workshop. It had a wooden bench with precision lathes, motors, tools, strips and bars and hunks of metal that looked like aluminium or duralumin. It had an assortment of chromium steel coil springs, leather straps and the oddest looking hinges and pivots I'd ever gandered.

The corners of the alcove were piled with contraptions too beautifully fashioned to be called junk, but too outlandish to be called anything else. Some of the things had ball-and-socket couplings with mechanical latching devices. Others were whittled of wood and padded with leather to turn a harness-

and-saddlemaker green with envy. It was a museum collection, a handicraft exhibit meriting booth space at an exposition. It had probably cost Ronald Barclay ten or twelve solitary and laborious years out of his life, and it was worth maybe seven dollars for scrap.

I heard footfalls.

I whirled, skulked silently back to the living room in time to hear a doorknob click and see it turn. I brought up my cannon and snicked off the safety.

The door swung outward and a tall, wide-shouldered punk ankled into the room – a punk with brown hair in crisp waves and an uncompromising chin as substantial as a granite cornerstone. He had a stethoscope clasped around his neck and dangling down onto his manly chest, but he was no doctor. Doctors don't wear second-hand bellhop uniforms a size too small for them.

"Hi, Pete," I said, and drew a bead on him. I was proud of myself for remembering that Pete was what the desk clerk had called him. "Freeze, please."

He didn't jump all the way out of his brogans, but he gave it the old college try. He goggled at my gat, backed against a wall and froze as instructed.

"Hey!" he strangled.

I kept him covered. "Just a formality, Pete. I'm a little nervous. For all I knew it might have been Frankenstein's monster coming in. It might have been Jack the Ripper. It could have been anybody, but it turns out to be a combination bellhop and elevator jockey wearing a stethoscope. The stethoscope confuses me. Let's hear about it."

"You – you're alive!"

"Yeah." I gestured to the desk clerk crumpled on the floor in a motionless lump. "But he's not. Explain the stethoscope, please. Talk it up."

Pete regarded me with bewilderment. "I thought you were dead. When I found you a minute ago, you looked like it."

"Ah. So you've been in here before."

"Certainly. That's why I rushed out to get my stethoscope. To try you for heartbeats. You didn't seem to have a pulse."

"Don't tell me you're a sawbones in your spare time?"

"I'm studying to be one." He was as dignified as only a young guy who takes himself seriously can be. "I'm in my final semester of pre-med. Winthrop is the name, Peter Warren Winthrop." His rugged jaw firmed and his kisser showed no good-humored quirk at the corners. "Just because I wear this monkey suit and accepted a dollar tip from you, don't get wrong ideas."

"I get many wrong ideas," I said.

5. Murder on the Make

Putting away my rod, I flashed Pete a fast swivel at my private badge. It didn't seem to be much of a surprise to him.

"Okay, son," I said. "You were in here a moment ago. Why?"

"I was looking for old Duffy," Pete said.

"Him?" I flicked a glance at the deceased bozo.

Pete nodded. "He wasn't at his desk and the switchboard had a buzz. I thought perhaps he'd slipped upstairs without calling for the elevator, so I ran my car up here to Three, the top, and started scouting the halls. Duffy had a bit of listening at doors occasionally. Wood makes a good sound conductor when you put a hearing aid microphone against the panels. So I noticed this particular door open and looked in."

"You saw what?"

"You and Duffy were on the floor. He was dead. I wasn't sure about you, so I went for my stethoscope."

"That's all?"

"Yes, sir. Except the wheelchair, of course."

"Nobody was in it when you first looked?"

"Nobody." He frowned. "I assume it's Mr Fullerton's chair. But if so, where's Fullerton?"

"That's what I'm wondering," I said. "And his name isn't Fullerton; it's Barclay. Not that it matters to you. What does matter is, he's gone. He was here, but he isn't here now. You didn't tab anybody going down the stairs?"

"I did not. Although the stairway is nowhere near my elevator, so that doesn't spell anything." He frowned again. "But if Fullerton, or Barclay or whatever his name is – if he uses a wheelchair he must be crippled. That's an assumption on my part, of course, for I never laid eyes on him. But presuming he *is* a cripple—"

"He's one-armed and legless."

"You mean you saw him?"

"Unfortunately, yes."

"Then if he's like you say, how could he get out of his wheelchair and go down two flights of steps?" Pete's peepers narrowed and suspicion slid into them. Suspicion of me. "And who murdered Duffy?"

"The answer is in an alcove between the bedroom and bath," I said. "Barclay experimented in prosthetics. He dabbled at inventing artificial limbs. That's why I asked if you saw anybody scramming. He must have had a set of gams he could get around on."

"I – see."

"You didn't think I croaked Duffy and abolished Barclay down the drainpipes and clouted myself unconscious, did you? You needn't answer that. I can guess how you figured it, only you figured it wrong. Now where's a phone?"

He pointed to a hand-set on a stand. "But you can't go through the switchboard because Duffy isn't there to give you a line."

"Poor old guy," I said. "He probably never got to spend that four bits for a perfecto. But at least he satisfied his curiosity about what the lodger in Three-seventeen looked like. He saw him. And the price he paid was much too high."

I shooed Pete out into the hall, followed him, shut the door behind us.

"Let's go, chum," I said. "I've got dialing to do and connections to make. There's a maniac killer on the loose and he's thirsting for revenge, gunning for a movie mogul. This is a thing for the cops."

It was for the cops, all right, but the cops wouldn't have it. That cost them another bump-off before the night ended.

And it came near installing me in a coffin. Sometimes when my sleep is restless I can still feel those fingers closing like metal bands around my throat. Those are the nights I get up and drink myself very, very drunk . . .

My coupe could do eighty with a tail wind. On a downgrade it might even nudge ninety. I held it to fifty, though, because the last thing I wanted was a ticket for speeding. Not that the ticket would bother me, but you don't like to be delayed by motorbike bulls when you're trying to reach a guy and warn him he's a ripe target for a madman's bullet.

I whammed west on Sunset to Highland, north on Highland past Hollywood Boulevard and aimed for the hills above that. The multicolored lights of Los Angeles spread out behind and below me like a vast carpet of glowing embers, infernal, patterned in blotchy angles and lines that merged and dimmed against the far infinity of horizon and night.

Ahead, the convoluted hills rose darkly to a star-flecked sky, with here and there a pinprick twinkle on a knoll or cliffside, as if the crests had stretched far up and seized some of the stars to wear for diamonds. Lights in the windows of hilltop houses always look that way from a distance, and in Hollywood it's considered swanky indeed to live in a district hilltop house.

That was why Emil Heinrich lived in one. Heinrich was big stuff.

I tooled my crate along a curving roadway and climbed. What I had to do was a cop job, but the cops wouldn't handle it. They were a pack of dopes, particularly my old friend Ole Brunvig of the Homicide Squad. In my mind's ear I could still hear the echo of Brunvig's grainy, dyspeptic voice when I called him up from the lobby of the Chaple Arms.

"Nick Ransom, yeah," I said. "There's been a kill. A desk clerk, name of Duffy, made the mistake of looking at Ronald Barclay, and Barclay extinguished him. Now Barclay's on the prowl to pull another bump."

"He – what?"

I repeated it. "Barclay croaked this clerk named Duffy and now he's out gunning for—"

"Stop kidding me. How can the clerk be out gunning for somebody if he's croaked?"

"Not the clerk!" I yelped. "He's defunct. It's Barclay who's on the loose, getting ready to kill again. The name he's been using is Joseph T. Fullerton, but he's really Ronald Barclay." This sounded a little complex, but I let it go. "You remember Barclay. He used to be the hottest ham in the Paragon roster."

"Oh. That Barclay. For a moment you had me puzzled." Sudden peevishness sprouted through the sarcasm. "Sure I remember Ronald Barclay. He died fourteen years ago. Killed by an explosion on a sound stage. So now his ghost is horsing around Hollywood and you want him pinched for murder, hey?"

"Yes, but he's not a ghost. He's alive, and he's got a roscoe and he's on the prowl for the guy who put him in his grave."

"Now cut that out!" Brunvig blew his lid. "If he's alive, nobody put him in his grave. If he was in his grave, he isn't alive. Lay off the drunken comedy."

"It's not comedy and I'm sober," I said hotly. "Barclay is not dead. He never was. His funeral was phony. The explosion cost him both legs and an arm, but it didn't really kill him. I'm telling you he knocked me senseless a little while ago and bumped a hotel clerk named Duffy and then walked out while I was too unconscious to stop him."

"Oho. He walked out." Brunvig's voice rose to a shrill scream of rage, through which you could hear the gnashing of teeth. "He walked out. He's got no legs, but he walked out. All right, Sherlock, that tears it. I've had enough."

"Listen," I said. "You don't understand!"

"I understand plenty. You're intoxicated. You're fried up to the scalp. Okay, you've had your fun with me. Now go to bed and sleep it off before I get sore and jerk your license." Violently he hung up in my ear.

You couldn't blame him too much. Try to convince anybody that a screen star dead fourteen years is actually alive. Try to make a skeptical cop believe there's a legless, one-armed bozo walking around packing murder in his pocket, hunting the party whose bomb had blasted him to a living death. You had to see it, as I'd seen it, to know it was true. Otherwise it sounded as screwy as an opium smoker's dream.

So I got nowhere with Brunvig. I rang him back and he refused to talk to me. He wouldn't even take the call.

That dumped it spang in my lap, which was what I deserved. It was my own fault. I should have made a getaway from Barclay's suite when I'd had the chance, should have tipped the law to come slap a straitjacket on him when I first realized he was dangerously insane.

Instead, I'd turned my back on him so he could bash me. Worse, I'd dragged a poor old deaf yuck into the room and got him conked to his ancestors. I felt almost as guilty as if I'd killed Duffy myself.

Any way you looked at it, Barclay was now my personal responsibility. It was up to me to track him down, collar him before he slew any more citizens. Finding him shouldn't be too difficult, I concluded. He had an obsession, a fixed idea. He craved vengeance on Emil Heinrich, therefore he would make a beeline for Heinrich's opulent igloo in the Hollywoodland hills, probably by taxi. This called for a chase sequence, yoicks and tally-ho in a thundering hurry.

Not that I cared about Heinrich. If he had actually gimmicked the cigarette-box bomb fourteen years ago it was high time retribution caught up with him. It had to be legal retribution, though, and not meted out by a maniac with a penchant for murdering innocent bystanders. I didn't want any more dead guys like Duffy weighing on my conscience.

So I left Peter Warren Winthrop, bellhop, elevator jockey and medical student, holding down the fort at the Chaple Arms. I posted him in the frowsy, unclean lobby and ordered him to keep phoning Homicide until he persuaded them to send a tech squad and a meat basket for Duffy's remainders.

"Stay with it, son, and don't take no for an answer," I said.

Then I blipped out to my bucket and lit a shuck for high ground.

Now, ten minutes later, I twisted my tiller, scooted around a series of curves that slanted upward in tilted coils like rope a careless giant had tossed away. And presently I came to my destination.

Heinrich had a layout in keeping with his lofty position as head cheese of a major studio. It was a cubistic stucco affair on three different levels, as if the architect had melted it and let it drip down the face of the hill until it congealed there in an unsymmetrical jumble of gray blocks.

An abrupt driveway angled to a parking area in front of the garage, which might have held ten Cadillacs if you squeezed them in with a shoe-horn. From this terraced plateau, monolithic steps led up to the next level. You didn't really need an alpenstock to make the climb.

At the top of the steps there was a flat expanse, part patio, part lawn, part flagstones, part garden and part swimming pool. Lake Michigan was bigger than the swimming pool. Skirting it, you came to the house itself, its main entrance recessed in a sort of embrasure. By that time you were ready for artificial respiration.

I thumbed the bell-push, waited for my pulse to get back down out of the stratosphere. By and by the chrome-plated door opened and a stuffed shirt in butler's livery inspected me with the cordial sunny warmth of December in Siberia.

"Yes, sir?" He let the words slide past his sinuses, like a repressed whinny.

"Mr Heinrich," I said, and briefly flashed my badge.

"The master is not at home, sir. And if I may say so, sir, I find your approach to be most crude in its subterfuge."

"Hah?"

"The badge, sir. A special, I believe. Not a genuine police shield at all." He leered at me. "You are not the only impostor who has tried to obtain an interview on false credentials. Most of them pretend to be gas meter readers, telephone repairmen and termite inspectors. I give you credit for more originality," he added grudgingly. "But the fact remains that actors, musicians and scenario writers seeking employment with Paragon must see Mr Heinrich at the studio, not at his residence. Good night, sir."

6. Body on the Lam

As that butler said "good night" he started to close the door in my face, very politely, very properly. And very firmly.

I leaned against its velvety chromium surface, just as politely and twice as firmly. I'm a patient guy, but I was fed up with people giving me the brushoff. I reached around the edge of the portal, harvested a fistful of the butler's livery and hauled him up close to me. I thrust my kisser two inches from his, so he could smell the Scotch on my breath.

"Pal," I said, "I'm coming in. If you insist on it I'll trudge the length of you like a welcome mat, but I'm coming in. I've got to talk to Heinrich and I've got to have permission to prowl the property. Do you take me to your boss right now or shall we wrestle for it?"

"He – he's not home!" he squawked, flapping like a hen laying a square egg. "Let go of me!"

I shook him a little, just enough to make his tonsils rattle.

"Don't lie to me, baby. There's a killer loose. He's looking for your employer and he's toting a thirty-eight for a divining rod. Take me to Heinrich. Pronto."

"He's out. There's no-nobody home except Mrs Heinrich and myself. The rest of the household staff have the evening off. You let g-go of me or I'll call the p-police!"

"I wish you would," I said grimly. "Maybe they'll listen to you. They wouldn't to me."

Still holding him, I shoved him backward into a reception hall that needed only a layer of turf to make it a polo field.

"But first take me to Mrs Heinrich," I said. "That's assuming you were levelling about her hubby not being home." I kicked the door shut behind me, listened for the click that satisfied me the latch had snapped. "Meanwhile, don't let anybody else in. Except the cops, of course. I wasn't fooling about a killer being loose."

He flapped some more. "You c-can't—"

"Don't be tiresome," I said. "I'll even let you announce me to the lady. Nick Ransom is the handle. Maybe she'll remember me from the days when she was an extra named Marian Lodge and I was a stunt man around the lots."

"But – but Mrs Heinrich doesn't like to be disturbed during her star bath."

"Star bath?"

"Like a sun bath, only at night. Something about the cosmic rays. She read it in a book."

I took this in stride. The night was so full of whacky events I was growing calloused to it. And Marian always had a bird-brain.

"We'll disturb her anyhow," I said. "Get going."

Muttering, he led me along the reception hall to a corridor, and along that to a stairway, and up this to a level which seemed to project outward into empty space. Actually it was a glassed-in-solarium with the domed roof rolled open; a basking room built out over the cliffside with no visible means of support, ending on a sheer drop down into the next precinct.

The butler cleared his throat apologetically, spoke my name and scuttled away with his coat-tails dipping lint. He never did phone Headquarters, the heel. He was all bluff and no hole card.

I stood there trying to adjust my eyes to the dark. There was movement on something that might be a chaise longue. You couldn't quite tell in the blackness. The movement was white, though. Fascinatingly white. And a drawling she-male voice said:

"Nick Ransom, of all people. This *is* a surprise. Imagine, after all these years. And just as rugged as ever."

I went toward her, wondering how she could spot my ruggedness in a room as dark as the bottom of the La-Brea tar pits. Presently my glimmers got their second wind and there was just enough starlight to show me the shapely outlines of a jane on a daybed. Just to make sure, I lit a match on my thumbnail.

Then I said: "Yipe!" and my flabbergasted exclamation blew out the flame.

The doll was Marian Lodge, all right; Marian Heinrich, now. Brunette, statuesque, relaxed, and utterly uninhibited.

She laughed. "Shocked, Nick? That's out of character."

"Yeah, but I wasn't expecting—"

"To get the full benefit of star bath rays you must have them flow over you like sea foam. All over you. Over all of you. Come sit by me, darling."

"No," I said firmly, "I'll talk from here. It's serious, and I want to keep my mind on it."

"Silly boy." Silk whispered intimately and a zipper wheeked. "Now you can be serious. Come kiss me hello."

I sidled closer, cautiously.

"That was years ago. Before you got married. Speaking of husbands—"

"Let's not." She sat up, snared my fingers, tugged me down on the cushions. "Husbands bore me. Especially mine."

"Where is he tonight?"

"Out chasing, I suppose. As usual. Don't worry, he won't bother us. He never gets home until late. Kiss me."

I could be as persistent as she was. "Any way of getting hold of him by phone?"

"Heaven forbid." She hauled at my wrist. "I'm so glad you came to see me, Nick. Like old times."

Old times, my elbow. I'd been on two mild parties with her and she wanted to build it up to a feature production. In technicolor. What she was doing with my captured hand would have made a wooden Indian throw away his cigars. I was no wooden Indian, though. I was a private eye hunting a homicidal madman. "Cut it out, tutz," I said. "I want to ask you something."

"The answer is yes. Now kiss me."

"Remember Ronald Barclay?"

"Do I! Mmm-mmm. I adored that man. Kiss me."

By main strength, I got my fingers away from her. "Did he ever make a pass at you?"

"No." She sighed regretfully. "Darn it."

"But your husband was jealous of him, wasn't he?"

"I wish you'd stop reminding me of my husband at a time like this. For all I care he can drop dead."

This startled me. It made two people who yearned for Heinrich to pass away. Heinrich was not a popular guy.

"You might be surprised if he did die, hon," I said. "Tonight. With a hole in the head. A bullet-hole, that is."

She snagged my other hand and was reckless with it. Her sultry breath danced along my cheek. She was driving me crazy.

"Silly. You don't have to shoot him," she murmured. "I won't even tell him you were here."

"I didn't say *I'd* shoot him!" I choked. "I meant . . . Hey, cut it out. Quit it."

Star glow dropped little glints in her sleek black hair and her lips were a dark flutter of challenge and demand. But whatever I was going to do about it never got done, because just then a voice full of adenoids whinnied at us from the solarium entrance.

A butler is handy to have around, sometimes.

"I beg pardon," the butler said. "There's a person at the door who insists upon seeing Mr Ransom."

I leaped up to my feet. In the same motion I unholstered my fowling piece. If this was Ronald Barclay trying to trick me out where he could use me for a clay pigeon, slugs were going to fly through the blue California night.

"Describe him," I said.

"He's rather young, sir. And tall. He gave his name as Peter Warren Winthrop, and when I refused to admit him he asked me to convey a message to you. Something to the effect, sir, that Duffy has disappeared."

I made a record getting downstairs to see Peter Warren Winthrop. He had plenty to say and not much breath to say it with.

"It's the truth, Ransom, so help me," Pete Winthrop said. His athletic shoulders twitched under a gabardine topcoat and he sounded like a guy who has experienced a profound shock, like encountering a herd of polka-dotted zebras. "I know it's hard to believe. I could scarcely believe it myself. But it's true."

We were outdoors, pacing the patio flagstones. Behind us, Heinrich's cubistic wigwam was buttoned up tighter than a bald man's scalp, and I'd warned the butler to keep it that way when I ankled out to parley with the Chaple Arms bellhop. Keeping step with him now, and holding to the thick shadows, I had my gat in my grasp and my peepers peeled for possible peril.

"How'd you discover it, son?" I said.

"I – I had put through another call to your friend Brunvig at Homicide Headquarters, but as soon as I mentioned your name to him and said I was phoning to report the same murder you had told him about, he slammed up on me. Then I got an idea."

"Yeah?"

He nodded, and told me about it. "I decided I would go out and try to find any kind of policeman – you know, a motorcycle officer or radio prowl car cop, maybe even a flatfoot pounding a beat. Anybody with a badge and a little authority. But first I wanted to make sure none of the tenants up on three would wander into Three-seventeen and see Duffy's corpse and throw the whole house into a panic. I couldn't remember whether we had left the door of the suite open or closed, locked or unlocked."

"So you went up there."

"Yes. And he was gone. Duffy, I mean. Vanished. Not a trace of him. Do you realize what that means? It means that Fullerton, or Barclay as you called him – it means he was there in the hotel all the time. Hiding some place. Hiding while you and I went down and started phoning from the lobby." The punk shivered visibly in his topcoat. "You'd gone away and left me there with a killer. And he had moved Duffy's body as soon as the coast was clear."

"Moved it where?"

"How should I know? Not in any of the broom closets or linen pantries. I looked. I was scared, but I looked anyhow. But I didn't try any of the rooms. We've got a full house, everything occupied. I couldn't very well start knocking on doors, asking guests to let me in so I could search for a dead man. I didn't know *what* to do. Then I figured I'd better come here and tell you about it. I figured you might have some angles."

"All I ran into was curves," I said dourly.

I was thinking of Marian Heinrich and her star bath. She would do no more star bathing tonight. Thick, sinister clouds were drifting in from Santa Monica, sullen and ominous, wrapping up the stars in black cotton batting. You couldn't see the surrounding hills, you couldn't even see the flagstones you were walking on. All you could see was a mental image of something maniacal and monstrous, something on artificial legs stalking you through a darkness as thick as oatmeal cooked in a vat of dye.

"He was clever," Pete Winthrop said. "Nobody can prove he murdered Duffy if Duffy's corpse can't be found. The cops will never believe your story, now. Which gives him a clear field to ambush Heinrich."

"Not while we do sentry duty," I said.

"We?"

"Beat it if you're yellow," I growled. "I'll do what has to be done."

"I didn't mean it that way," he said apologetically. "I was just flattered to think you wanted me." Impressed. Boyish. A punk with a chance to assist a private dick and overwhelmed by it. And a little uncertain, too. "Mightn't it be a good idea to phone the law again and try to persuade them to send somebody to help us stand guard?"

7. Fingers of Guilt

We had paced all the way back to the front door by that time, Peter and I. And as if in answer to his suggestion, the portal opened not more than half an inch.

"Mr Ransom, sir," came through the opening in a shaky whinny.

"Close that door and keep it locked!" I rasped.

"Y-yes, sir," the butler said. "But I thought you should be informed that I fear I delayed too long in attempting to call the police as you originally suggested. Our line seems to be dead, sir." The door swung shut and the latch clicked.

"Golly!" Pete Winthrop made a gulping noise in his gullet. "A dead phone. A cut wire. Barclay's here – on the grounds!"

I gave him a shove. "Scatter. Stay up here on the patio level. Keep moving. I'll patrol down along the driveway and garage. That way I'll be set in case he tries to dry-gulch Heinrich coming home in his car. I don't suppose you've got a heater?"

"Heater?"

"Gun."

"No."

"Barclay has, so watch out. Don't jump him if you see him."

"What *shall* I do?"

"Yell for me and duck for cover. Don't let him get you in the open."

We separated, and I went catfooting down the long monolithic stairway. There was one thing in our favor – the rear of the estate was walled in by a precipitous hill, barricading it against approach or escape. You couldn't get in that way unless you used a block and tackle or descended by parachute. You couldn't get out without a helicopter.

This made my strategy valid. The lower-level driveway was the only entrance, and the only exit. And the house itself was practically impregnable when its doors and windows were locked. Clenching my cannon, I was ready for the payoff.

Silence pressed down around me. With the coming of the clouds, even the hillside crickets had quit being chirpy. I kept listening for anything that might sound like the metallic clank of artificial legs in motion, the scrape of soles on cement paving.

Away back in the recesses of my think-tank something bothered me, something that refused to be dragged out so I could inspect it. It was an evasive wisp, a fragment that played hide-and-seek with my subconscious. I felt the same way about it that I'd felt when I had first heard an empty room speak my name with Ronald Barclay's voice. Haunted, uncomfortable.

I had a curious sensation that Barclay didn't exist, that he never had existed; that everything had been a figment of my imagination. But the throbbing lump on top of my noggin contradicted any such nonsense.

Barclay had been real enough. Figments of the imagination don't slug you to dreamland, and they don't croak poor old deaf guys like Duffy. And I had glimpsed the maimed ham with my own optics. I had lamped him in his wheelchair, definitely legless under the lap blanket, definitely one-armed, with a shirt sleeve pinned up emptily.

"Ransom!"

The shout came hoarsely from above, and then I heard a series of scuffling sounds, the violent rustling of underbrush. I leaped for the steps, took them three at a time, catapulted across lawn and patio toward those continuing noises.

Hard by the tiled area bordering the swimming pool there was a row of clumped hydrangea bushes. I couldn't see them stirring, but I heard them.

Flying blind, I plunged forward – and overshot the mark.

Something reached out, tripped me. As I stumbled, a heavy and panting burden landed on my back with an impact that drove me down on all fours like a bear. I didn't lose my roscoe, but for all the good it did me I might as well have pitched it into the pool. The hand that held it was pressed knuckle-deep in loam and I couldn't raise it, couldn't even move it.

Weight crushed me, flattened me, and then fingers clamped around my throat from behind. They were hot, inexorable fingers as relentless as steel springs.

They throttled me, pressing against my jugular and carotid artery, collapsing my gullet and robbing my bellows of air. I bucked and arched my spine and sunfished like a rodeo bronc, but all I threw was snake-eyes. I didn't throw my rider.

Then I didn't throw anything. I got thrown. I was propelled headlong into the swimming pool and I sank like an anchor.

They say a drowning gee sees his whole life pass by him in a series of flashback montage memories. Not me. I just saw the scenes of the past few hours. Plummeting downward in cold water, I reviewed everything that had happened.

My head stopped throbbing and my mind sharpened like a razor on a hone. I saw the cat eating a bird on the steps of the Chaple Arms. I saw Ronald Barclay's hotel suite, the trick mirror in the closet door, the little padlocked alcove workshop where he had dabbled in prosthetics. I saw the defunct Duffy lying with his temple crushed in, a button fastened in one ear and wires running down to a switched-off hearing gadget he would never need again.

I saw a legless figure in a rolling wheelchair, a one-armed form with a vague blur of face and a gat in his lap, and the voice of a guy I'd once considered my friend. I had the memory of a kraut director named Heinrich who had climbed to the top of the cinema heap, slowly but implacably, until he was chief poo-bah of a major studio.

And I saw a voluptuous and uninhibited quail, featherbrained, black of hair and gorgeously white of skin, lolling in a darkened solarium taking a star bath, letting her lovely contours soak up cosmic rays while she expressed a fervent wish that her hubby would drop dead.

I hit bottom. And, as I hit, I found all the answers. A fine time to be finding answers, when you're drowning at the bottom of a swimming pool.

On the other hand, when you're a murderer and you've strangled a guy and dumped him in the deep six, you'll likely stand by to see if he floats to the surface again. That's so you can shoot him, bludgeon him or shove him under to make certain he dies – if he's not already dead. Naturally, if he's dead he'll stay beneath the water and you needn't worry about him any more.

I stayed under water.

I wasn't deceased. I wasn't even unconscious. But I knew if I came up for air I would be a goner. The instant my conk popped out it would be a bull's-eye, either for a bullet or a fractured skull if I happened to be within reaching distance of the pool's edge. I realized this even while my lungs were bursting and every muscle struggled to impel me off the bottom.

I fought it. I reverted to my stunting days when I could stay immersed as long as the scenario demanded. I held my breath, got my feet planted solidly on the slippery tile floor of the immense pool and slowly started walking. Very slowly, so I couldn't create surface ripples. And keeping my mental fingers crossed, hoping I was headed in the right direction.

My soles detected a slant – downward.

I reversed myself. My ears were pounding now, and my chest was full of molten metal that seared and burned like a blast furnace. But I had learned which way the pool's bottom tilted, and I was heading for the shallow end. All I needed was another minute.

Too bad Emil Heinrich was such a big shot at Paragon Pix. Too bad he had so much dough. If he had been less wealthy his swimming pool would be smaller. I could reach the shallow part sooner. But no, Heinrich had to be in the top chips. Try that on your philosophy. A guy earned too much geet, and because of it people died.

I couldn't hold my breath any longer.

I let some of it out and it streamed up over my head like an immense balloon. Like a drifting blister. Like bubble gum. It popped and broke on the surface. I could hear it.

Okay, killer. You happy now? You know what that air-bubble spells. You've murdered me. That was the last of my air. Now you can go away. I'm on the bottom and I'm croaked.

Oh, yeah? That's what you think.

The pool's floor slanted more abruptly. I kept walking. I got my cigarette holder out of my inside coat pocket. It was a plastic cigarette holder with silver filigree. A client had given it to me one time, by way of showing gratitude. I never use it, except when I'm trying to impress other clients. Cigarette holders are an affectation. I like to inhale my poison straight.

Nice cigarette holder. Not as long as a symphony conductor's baton, but long enough. A hollow tube, slightly flared at one end; a mouthpiece on the other.

Shallow water now. Still deep enough to cover me, but shallow. Careful now. Keep at least six inches of water over your head, Ransom, old boy. Don't break the surface.

I stuck the holder in my mouth and poked its opposite end out of the pool. I blew through it, cleared it.

Then I breathed through it. I breathed air. Wonderful element, air. Puts oxygen in your blood and hair on your chest. I breathed air through the plastic tube, and nobody knew it. Nobody could see me. To all intents and purposes I was a cadaver at the bottom of the water. For a cadaver I was feeling pretty spry.

I kept breathing, not moving. No telling how long it would be before I dared take a chance and scramble out onto dry land. I couldn't tell who was watching, any more than the watcher could tell I was alive. I breathed, and waited. I waited and breathed.

Nobody lives forever. I walked and broke water and found the hand rails of a ladder and got my feet on the rungs, hauled myself to the bordering tiles. No gunshots. No swat on the steeple. Nothing but darkness and the squishing of my shoes and the splashy *drip-drip-drip* from my ruined tweeds.

That, and distant bitter dialogue, and a motor idling lazily on the driveway down below.

The motor had a rich hollow chuckle from its exhaust, like an Indian tomtom in a rain barrel. It sounded healthy and powerful and expensive. It sounded like five miles to the gallon, provided the driver did a lot of coasting.

The masculine voices sounded sore.

I skittered to the steep concrete escarpment the Heinrich menage used for an outdoor stairway and probed my way down through a night that was just as dark as it had ever been. On the parking area this side of the driveway there was something that could have been a Cadillac, a Packard, a Lincoln or a streamlined Diesel locomotive.

Its rear end was pointing inward, twin tail-lights and amber back-up lights glowing like a Christmas tree. Apparently the guy at the wheel had come up the drive and then jockeyed the massive heap around so he could back into the garage and be ready for a fast straight-ahead takeoff in the morning.

His head lamps made the driveway and parking level as bright as a movie set under sun arcs, but he wasn't at his tiller now. He had got out and walked around to open the garage doors, and I recognized him in the red-and-amber glow of his stern lights. He was Emil Heinrich, short, dumpy, potbellied, with a face like a full moon. His wife had said he wouldn't be home until late, but he had fooled her.

He was talking in a thick, guttural monotone to somebody who lurked in the shadows at the sedan's far side.

"Zo. You want me to bay you one hundred thousandt tollars for dis diary. The diary of a dead man, agguzing me of murter. You zay you vill turn me ofer to the law if I revuze. Pah! Id iss ridiculous. I vill gif you one thousandt tollars cash, vich I habben to haf in mein bocket for small change. One thousandt, for your nuisanz walue." He spat. "Take id or leaf id."

"I'll take it as first payment."

I knew that voice. How well I knew that voice! Resonant. Determined. I didn't have to gander its owner, hidden around the far side of the sedan. Hearing it was enough.

Heinrich reached into a coat pocket as if to bring forth the promised lettuce. He made a mistake. A bad mistake. He dragged a roscoe out instead.

Flame lanced out around the sneezing *ka-chow!* of gunfire. It wasn't Heinrich's gun that fired, though. He never got around to it. He lurched, took three mincing steps backward, crossed his ankles awkwardly and twisted as he fell. After he fell he didn't even move.

8. Last Kill, Last Chase

Catapulting down the remaining steps, I was unable to draw a bead on the killer because the chuckle-purring sedan was in the way. I had my own heater ready, but I couldn't use it. A car door slammed. The chuckle-purr snarled into a roar. Rear tires spun, screeched, got traction. The sedan made like jet propulsion going down the driveway.

I snapped a cap at where I thought its gas tank ought to be. Nothing happened. My rod had been too long under water. The cartridge must have been just slightly defective, enough to let the powder get soaked.

I swore, ejected it, jacked another shell into the firing chamber and tried again. But by that time the getaway crate had careened onto the road and was gone. The gat jumped in my fist and my slug went *pee-yowp!* against the opposite cliff. Clean miss.

Then I wasted time. I bent down in the darkness, inspected Heinrich's porky poundage. His wife had got her wish. She was a widow now. Scratch one studio executive. A tunnel that only a .38 could make was drilled all the way through his chest. No matter how important you are in Hollywood, a .38 slug in your heart brings you down to size.

The nickel-plated revolver on Ronald Barclay's legless lap had been .38 caliber. That was the final clue.

I lunged to my coupé where I'd parked it over to one side of the garage apron. Unfortunately, I'd left it headed inward. Now I had to get it started, get it horsed around in the opposite direction. That wasted more time. I finally made it and went thundering down the driveway, around the bend into the road. Then I widened out, fed my clattering cylinders all the coal they would take. I made knots. I bored a hole in the night that the night would never repair.

Down out of the hills, a siren cut loose behind me and a red spotlight stabbed my rear-view mirror.

I pulled over. A prowl car drew abreast. I bounced out, rushed to the cop chariot and yodeled:

"Boys, you've got a passenger!" I flashed my badge, piled into the police buggy. "Let's go! And get me Lieutenant Ole Brunvig on your two-way short wave. Brunvig of Homicide. This is murder."

The cops bought it. I must have sounded plenty sincere. They believed me. The one sitting alongside the driver cut in his transmitter, talked to his hand mike. Presently Brunvig's voice rasped in the cowl speaker.

I snaked the hand mike away from the cop and made with the words. Terse words that boiled out of me like Mount Vesuvius in eruption. After a while the loud-speaker snapped back at me. I had a date with Brunvig at the Chaple Arms.

The prowl car picked up velocity. The guy at the wheel was good. He sent only three pedestrians scampering up palm trees. He took only the first skin of red paint off a passing Pacific Electric bus. He should have been a barber. He could shave you with his front fender and never leave a whisker.

Ole Brunvig's official bucket was just pulling up in front of the Chaple Arms as we screamed to a halt behind him. Up ahead, a sedan was parked – a new, streamlined monster that didn't belong to this neighborhood at all. It made the rest of the heaps on the street look like scrap iron. And the sedan was Emil Heinrich's.

I leaped to the sidewalk, grabbed Ole's arm and yanked him into the flea-bag hotel's dingy lobby without missing a stride. There was nobody holding down the greasy, marble-topped desk. I ducked around back of it, found a chart for the rectangular tier of wooden letterboxes.

"One-thirty-nine!" I yeeped. "Ground floor. Come on!"

Brunvig hadn't had a chance to say anything. He still didn't. He just unlimbered his cannon and kept pace with me around a rear hallway to the door I wanted. I pointed at the keyhole.

"Okay," he grunted. "If I get busted back to harness for this, I'll reach down your throat and yank you inside out." Then, expertly, he shot the lock to splinters.

I hit the portal a mighty lick and went sailing into a small, cheerless room.

"This is all of it, punk," I said to Peter Warren Winthrop. "You're through. You're through being a bellhop, elevator operator and medical student. And you're through killing people."

He straightened up from a Gladstone bag he had been hastily packing.

"What?"

"Playing stupid will buy you nothing," I said. "The giveaway was when you throttled me, dunked me in the pool. Up until then I hadn't suspected you. My attention was all on Ronald Barclay. I'd sensed something haywire about the Barclay theory, but I couldn't nail it down. Then you choked me, hurled me to a watery grave – at which juncture the finger pointed straight at you. A lot of fingers. Ten of them, to be exact."

"What the devil are you talking about?"

"I'm talking about two hands closing around my throat. One set of fingers pressing my carotid artery, and the other set digging into my jugular vein on the opposite side of my neck. Then I knew it couldn't be Barclay who had jumped me, because he was a one-armed guy. And the fingers strangling me were real. Human. Alive. Hot. Not one real hand and one artificial. Both hands were genuine. That eliminated Barclay."

"This is all Greek to me," he said.

I sneered at him. "It was to me, too, until I savvied the clue of the ten fingers. Then everything else clicked into place. I remembered pushing Barclay's living-room door open, and encountering resistance – the pressure of somebody leaning against it outside in the hall. I remembered giving it a shove, and bouncing poor old Duffy across the corridor so that he landed like a sack of bones.

"At the time I thought he'd been eavesdropping. But eavesdroppers don't lean against doors when you catch them at it. They turn and run for cover."

"So what?"

"So the next time I saw Duffy he was deceased of a cracked superstructure. And his hearing aid was switched off, which didn't spell anything to me at the time. It did later, though, when I began adding things up. With his ear gadget turned off to save the batteries, he couldn't have been listening at the door."

The punk shifted uneasily. "I don't get what you're driving at. It sounds like a lot of hogwash."

"Yeah?" I said. "Well, how about this? You followed me up to Heinrich's igloo in the Hollywoodland hills, ostensibly to inform me that Duffy's corpse had vanished. But I hadn't told you I was going to the Heinrich stash. I never mentioned Heinrich's name to you. And you couldn't have heard me say it when I phoned Lieutenant Brunvig at Headquarters, because Brunvig cut me off before I brought Heinrich into the conversation. Yet you trailed me, found me. How?"

"Why, I – I – that is, I—"

"*You* were the eavesdropper," I said. "Not Duffy. You, Peter Warren Winthrop. That accounts for the stethoscope. A stethoscope is a handy listening device. Plug it in your ears and put the diaphragm end against a wall or a door and you can hear whatever is being said inside a room. Know what I think? I think you listened to everything Ronald Barclay told me. You found out who he was. And what he had on Emil Heinrich – which was plenty, from a blackmailer's viewpoint. You probably wondered how you could make use of the information to line your own pockets. And while you listened, Duffy came upstairs and caught you with your stethoscope to the door."

He turned a little pallid around the fringes. I had him winging now.

"Poor old Duffy," I said. "He saw you eavesdropping, and you slugged him to keep him from raising a row. Maybe you didn't mean to kill him – I wouldn't know about that. But you did kill him. You crushed his temple. Then you took a powder, leaving his body propped against the door. That was the pressure I felt when I shoved it open. The resistance was Duffy's dead weight. When I bounced him across the hall he was already defunct, although I didn't suspect it. And in the gloom and dusk I didn't notice the depression in his skull."

"Now see here—"

"Having murdered one guy, you were in up to your ears." I ignored his attempted interruption. "And you saw a chance for a fortune in shakedown dough. You pranced into the room as I dragged Duffy over the threshold. Ronald Barclay wheeled his chair out of the closet at the same instant. I thought he was the one who slugged me senseless, but now I know it must have been you.

"You bashed me. Then you croaked Barclay. He was a defenseless cripple and you cooled him, pilfered his thirty-eight and the diary. You toted his remainders out of the room to make it look as if he'd left under his own steam."

The punk made a raucous sound.

"Sheepdip," he said.

"Sure, sheepdip," I said. "I swallowed it. Because I found

an alcove where he'd experimented in making artificial legs, I actually believed he had walked out. I was a fool. I should have realized that was impossible. He dabbled in prosthetics, yes; but everything he made was junk. Useless.

"So anyhow you came back, perhaps thinking you'd killed me as well as Duffy and Barclay. I surprised you by being alive and on my feet, with a gun aimed at you. I'll give you credit – you played it smart. I had the drop on you, and you made the best of a bad situation. Later you got a nice break when the cops refused to come to the hotel. That forced me to lone-wolf it out to Heinrich's tepee. It left you alone, gave you time to arrange new plans."

"Such as?" he blustered.

"Such as moving Duffy's corpse, hiding it where you had already hidden Barclay's," I said. "I doubt you ever made a telephone call to Police Headquarters."

Ole Brunvig growled: "Right. He didn't."

"Okay," I said to the punk. "With your two victims stashed out of sight, you trailed me from inside. You also cut their phone line. Then, when we separated, you faked a fracas on the upper level, drew me in and thought you bumped me. Now you had a free hand to intercept Heinrich when he came home. You could demand a hundred grand blackmail for a diary that might convict him of a kill fourteen years ago."

I paused. "The fact that Heinrich offered to buy it makes me think that he *did* gimmick the bomb that croaked a prop man and maimed Barclay. I'm not too sorry you knocked him off. If that had been the only murder you pulled tonight I'd be inclined to say the devil with it. But you cooled Duffy and Barclay, and they didn't deserve it."

"Can you prove any of this?"

"I can try," I said, and ankled to a closet on my left, yanked it open.

Two stiffs fell out. One of them wore a hearing aid. Duffy. The other had one arm and no legs. Barclay.

Winthrop's hand went into the Gladstone he had been packing. It came up with a nickel-plated .38 fowling piece, the rod he had stolen from Ronald Barclay when he glommed the Fullerton diary.

Long before he could trigger the gat, though, Ole Brunvig

cut loose with his service revolver. There were two sharp thunderclap barks, spaced so closely together they sounded almost like one. Winthrop yowled like a banshee and slammed against the wall with ketchup spurting from both shoulders.

Brunvig showed his teeth. "Now he knows what it's like to be maimed. Look at that bag, Sherlock, and see if you can find the diary."

I found it. And Peter Warren Winthrop took his shattered shoulders to the gas chamber the following month.

Sometimes I wonder if Marian Heinrich still indulges in star baths. One of these nights I'm going up in the hills to see.

FOREVER AFTER

Jim Thompson

It was a few minutes before five o'clock when Ardis Clinton unlocked the rear door of her apartment, and admitted her lover. He was a cow-eyed young man with a wild mass of curly black hair. He worked as a dishwasher at Joe's Diner, which was directly across the alley.

They embraced passionately. Her body pressed against the meat cleaver, concealed inside his shirt, and Ardis shivered with delicious anticipation. Very soon now, it would all be over. That stupid ox, her husband, would be dead. He and his stupid cracks – all the dullness and boredom would be gone forever. And with the twenty thousand insurance money, ten thousand dollars double-indemnity . . .

"We're going to be so happy, Tony," she whispered. "You'll have your own place, a real swank little restaurant with what they call one of those intimate bars. And you'll just manage it, just kind of saunter around in a dress suit, and—"

"And we'll live happily ever after," Tony said. "Just me and you, baby, walking down life's highway together."

Ardis let out a gasp. She shoved him away from her, glaring up into his handsome empty face. "Don't!" she snapped. "Don't say things like that! I've told you and told you not to do it, and if I have to tell you again. I'll—!"

"But what'd I say?" he protested. "I didn't say nothin'."

"Well . . ." She got control of herself, forcing a smile. "Never mind, darling. You haven't had any opportunities and we've never really had a chance to know each other, so – so never mind. Things will be different after we're married." She patted his cheek, kissed him again. "You got away from the diner, all right? No one saw you leave?"

"Huh-uh. I already took the stuff up to the steam-table for Joe, and the waitress was up front too, y'know, filling the sugar bowls and the salt and pepper shakers like she always does just before dinner. And—"

"Good. Now, suppose someone comes back to the kitchen and finds out you're not there. What's your story going to be?"

"Well . . . I was out in the alley dumping some garbage. I mean—" he corrected himself hastily, "maybe I was. Or maybe I was down in the basement, getting some supplies. Or maybe I was in the john – the lavatory, I mean – or—"

"Fine," Ardis said approvingly. "You don't say where you were, so they can't prove you weren't there. You just don't remember where you were, understand, darling? You might have been any number of places."

Tony nodded. Looking over her shoulder into the bedroom, he frowned worriedly. "Why'd you do that now, honey? I know this has got to look like a robbery. But tearin' up the room now, before he gets here—"

"There won't be time afterwards. Don't worry, Tony. I'll keep the door closed."

"But he might open it and look in. And if he sees all them dresser drawers dumped around, and—"

"He won't. He won't look into the bedroom. I know exactly what he'll do, exactly what he'll say, the same things that he's always done and said ever since we've been married. All the stupid, maddening, dull, tiresome—!" She broke off abruptly, conscious that her voice was rising. "Well, forget it," she said, forcing another smile. "He won't give us any trouble."

"Whatever you say," Tony nodded docilely. "If you say so, that's the way it is, Ardis."

"But there'll be trouble – from the cops. I know I've already warned you about it, darling. But it'll be pretty bad, worse than anything you've ever gone through. They won't have any proof, but they're bound to be suspicious, and if you ever start talking, admitting anything—"

"I won't. They won't get anything out of me."

"You're sure? They'll try to trick you. They'll probably tell you that I've confessed. They may even slap you around. So if you're not absolutely sure . . ."

"They won't get anything out of me," he repeated stolidly. "I won't talk."

And studying him, Ardis knew that he wouldn't.

She led the way down the hall to the bathroom. He parted the shower curtains, and stepped into the tub. Drawing a pair of gloves from his pocket, he pulled them onto his hands. Awkwardly, he fumbled the meat cleaver from beneath his shirt.

"Ardis. Uh – look, honey."

"Yes?"

"Do I have to hit you? Couldn't I just maybe give you a little shove, or—"

"No, darling," she said gently. "You have to hit me. This is supposed to be a robbery. If you killed my husband without doing anything to me, well, you know how it would look."

"But I never hit no woman – any woman – before. I might hit you too hard, and—"

"Tony!"

"Well, all right," he said sullenly. "I don't like it, but all right."

Ardis murmured soothing endearments. Then, brushing his lips quickly with her own, she returned to the living room. It was a quarter after five, exactly five minutes – but *exactly* – until her husband, Bill, would come home. Closing the bedroom door, she lay down on the lounge. He negligee fell open, and she left it that way, grinning meanly as she studied the curving length of her thighs.

Give the dope a treat for a change, she thought. Let him get one last good look before he gets his.

Her expression changed. Wearily, resentfully, she pulled the material of the negligee over her legs. Because, of course, Bill would never notice. She could wear a ring in her nose, paint a bull's eye around her navel, and he'd never notice.

If he had ever noticed, just once paid her a pretty compliment . . .

If he had ever done anything different, ever said or done anything different at all – even the teensiest little bit . . .

But he hadn't. Maybe he couldn't. So what else could she do

but what she was doing? She could get a divorce, sure, but that was all she'd get. No money; nothing with which to build a new life. Nothing to make up for those fifteen years of slowly being driven mad.

It's his own fault, she thought bitterly. I can't take any more. If I had to put up with him for just one more night, even one more hour . . . !

She heard heavy footsteps in the hallway. Then, a key turned in the doorlatch, and Bill came in. He was a master machinist, a solidly built man of about forty-five. The old-fashioned gold-rimmed glasses on his pudgy nose gave him a look of owlish solemnity.

"Well," he said, setting down his lunch bucket. "Another day, another dollar."

Ardis grimaced. He plodded across to the lounge, stooped, and gave her a half-hearted peck on the cheek.

"Long time no see," he said. "What we havin' for supper?"

Ardis gritted her teeth. It shouldn't matter, now; in a few minutes it would all be over. Yet somehow it *did* matter. He was as maddening to her as he had ever been.

"Bill . . ." She managed a seductive smile, slowly drawing the negligee apart. "How do I look, Bill?"

"Okay," he yawned. "Got a little hole in your drawers, though. What'd you say we was havin' for supper?"

"Slop," she said. "Garbage. Trash salad with dirt dressing."

"Sounds good. We got any hot water?"

Ardis sucked in her breath. She let it out again in a kind of infuriated moan. "Of course, we've got hot water! Don't we always have? Well, don't we? Why do you have to ask every night?"

"So what's to get excited about?" he shrugged. "Well, guess I'll go splash the chassis."

He plodded off down the hall. Ardis heard the bathroom door open, and close. She got up, stood waiting by the telephone. The door banged open again, and Tony came racing up the hall.

He had washed off the cleaver. While he hastily tucked it back inside his shirt, Ardis dialed the operator. "Help," she cried weakly. "Help . . . police . . . murder!"

She let the receiver drop to the floor, spoke to Tony in a whisper. "He's dead? You're sure of it?"

"Yeah, yeah, sure I'm sure. What do you think?"

"All right. Now, there's just one more thing . . ."

"I can't, Ardis. I don't want to. I—"

"Hit me," she commanded, and thrust out her chin. "Tony, I said to hit me!"

He hit her. A thousand stars blazed through her brain, and disappeared. And she crumpled silently to the floor.

. . . When she regained consciousness, she was lying on the lounge. A heavy-set man, a detective obviously, was seated at her side, and a white-jacketed young man with a stethoscope draped around his neck hovered nearby.

She had never felt better in her life. Even the lower part of her face, where Tony had smashed her, was surprisingly free of pain. Still, because it was what she should do, she moaned softly; spoke in a weak, hazy voice.

"Where am I?" she said. "What happened?"

"Lieutenant Powers," the detective said. "Suppose you tell me what happened, Mrs Clinton."

"I . . . I don't remember. I mean, well, my husband had just come home, and gone back to the bathroom. And there was a knock on the door, and I supposed it was the paper-boy or someone like that. So—"

"You opened the door and he rushed in and slugged you, right? Then what happened?"

"Well, then he rushed into the bedroom and started searching it. Yanking out the dresser drawers, and—"

"What was he searching for, Mrs Clinton? You don't have any considerable amount of money around, do you? Or any jewelry aside from what you're wearing? And it wasn't your husband's payday, was it?"

"Well, no. But—"

"Yes?"

"I don't know. Maybe he was crazy. All I know is what he did."

"I see. He must have made quite a racket, seems to me. How come your husband didn't hear it?"

"He couldn't have. He had the shower running, and—"

She caught herself, fear constricting her throat. Lieutenant Powers grinned grimly.

"Missed a bet, huh, Mrs Clinton?"

"I – I don't know what you're—"

"Come off of it! The bathtub's dry as an oven. The shower was never turned on, and you know why it wasn't. Because there was a guy standing inside of it."

"B-but – but I don't know anything. I was unconscious, and—"

"Then, how do you know what happened? How do you know this guy went into the bedroom and started tearing it apart? And how did you make that telephone call?"

"Well, I . . . I wasn't completely unconscious. I sort of knew what was going on without really—"

"Now, you listen to me," he said harshly. "You made that fake call of yours – yes, I said *fake* – to the operator at twenty-three minutes after five. There happened to be a prowl car right here in the neighborhood, so two minutes later, at five-twenty-five, there were cops here in your apartment. You were unconscious then, more than an hour ago. You've been unconscious until just now."

Ardis' brain whirled. Then, it cleared suddenly, and a great calm came over her.

"I don't see quite what you're hinting at, lieutenant. If you're saying that I was confused, mixed up – that I must have dreamed or imagined some of the things I told you – I'll admit it."

"You know what I'm saying! I'm saying that no guy could have got in and out of this place, and done what this one did, in any two minutes!"

"Then the telephone operator must have been mistaken about the time," Ardis said brightly. "I don't know how else to explain it."

Powers grunted. He said he could give her a better explanation – and he gave it to her. The right one. Ardis listened to it placidly, murmuring polite objections.

"That's ridiculous, lieutenant. Regardless of any gossip you may have heard, I don't know this, uh, Tony person. And I most certainly did not plot with him or anyone else to kill my husband. Why—"

"He says you did. We got a signed confession from him."

"Have you?" But of course they didn't have. They might have found out about Tony, but he would never have talked. "That hardly proves anything, does it?"

"Now, you listen to me, Mrs Clinton! Maybe you think that—"

"How is my husband, anyway? I do hope he wasn't seriously hurt."

"How *is* he?" the lieutenant snarled. "How would he be after gettin' worked over with—" He broke off, his eyes flickering. "As a matter of fact," he said heavily, "he's going to be all right. He was pretty badly injured, but he was able to give us a statement and—"

"I'm so glad. But why are you questioning me, then?" It was another trick. Bill had to be dead. "If he gave you a statement, then you must know that everything happened just like I said."

She waited, looked at him quizzically. Powers scowled, his stern face wrinkling with exasperation.

"All right," he said, at last. "All right, Mrs Clinton. Your husband is dead. We don't have any statement from him, and we don't have any confession from Tony."

"Yes?"

"But we know that you're guilty, and you know that you are. And you'd better get it off your conscience while you still can."

"While I still can?"

"Doc" – Powers jerked his head at the doctor. At the man, that is, who appeared to be a doctor. "Lay it on the line, doc. Tell her that her boyfriend hit her a little too hard."

The man came forward hesitantly. He said, "I'm sorry, Mrs Clinton. You have a – uh – you've sustained a very serious injury."

"Have I?" Ardis smiled. "I feel fine."

"I don't think," the doctor said judiciously, "that that's quite true. What you mean is that you don't feel anything at all. You couldn't. You see, with an injury such as yours—"

"Get out," Ardis said. "Both of you get out."

"Please, Mrs Clinton. Believe me, this isn't a trick. I haven't wanted to alarm you, but—"

"And you haven't," she said. "You haven't scared me even a little bit, mister. Now, clear out!"

She closed her eyes, kept them closed firmly. When, at last, she reopened them, Powers and the doctor – if he really had been a doctor – were gone. And the room was in darkness.

She lay smiling to herself, congratulating herself. In the

corridor outside, she heard heavy footsteps approaching; and she tensed for a moment. Then, remembering, she relaxed again.

Not Bill, of course. She was through with that jerk forever. He'd driven her half out of her mind, got her to the point where she couldn't have taken another minute of him if her life depended on it. But now . . .

The footsteps stopped in front of her door. A key turned in the lock, the door opened and closed.

There was a clatter of a lunchpail being set down; then a familiar voice – maddeningly familiar words:

"Well. Another day, another dollar."

Ardis' mouth tightened; it twisted slowly, in a malicious grin. So they hadn't given up yet! They were pulling this one last trick. Well, let them; she'd play along with the gag.

The man plodded across the room, stooped, and gave her a half-hearted peck on the cheek. "Long time no see," he said. "What we havin' for supper?"

"Bill . . ." Ardis said. "How do I look, Bill?"

"Okay. Got your lipstick smeared, though. What'd you say we was having for supper?"

"Stewed owls! Now, look, mister. I don't know who you—"

"Sounds good. We got any hot water?"

"Of course, we've got hot water! Don't we always have? Why do you always have to ask if – if –"

She couldn't go through with it. Even as a gag – even someone who merely sounded and acted like he did – it was too much to bear.

"Y-you get out of here!" she quavered. "I don't have to stand for this! I *c-can't* stand it! I did it for fifteen years, and—"

"So what's to get excited about?" he said. "Well, guess I'll go splash the chassis."

"Stop it! *STOP IT!*" Her screams filled the room . . . silent screams ripping through silence. "He's – you're dead! I know you are! You're dead, and I don't have to put up with you for another minute. And – and – !"

"Wouldn't take no bets on that if I was you," he said mildly. "Not with a broken neck like yours."

He trudged off toward the bathroom, wherever the bathroom is in Eternity.

THE BLOODY TIDE

Day Keene

1. Out of the Jug

Morning was slow in coming. I'd waited for it a long time. Three years the man said. And three years I had done without any nonsense about parole or executive clemency.

I was washed and dressed and waiting when the rising siren blew. As McKenny, the screw on our tier, clomped down the steel catwalk to pull the master switch, he paused in front of my cell and grinned:

"This is the day, eh, Charlie?"

The lump in my throat was so big all I could do was nod.

Breakfast wasn't much better. The pock marks in the plaster of the mess hall bothered me. I knew them for what they were. If it hadn't been for Swede, I could be dead instead of going out this morning. I could be with Mickey and Saltz. I could be down in solitary with the other ringleaders of the riot. I could even be with Swede.

The thought cost me my appetite. When we finally filed out of the mess hall a front-of-the-prison guard asked if my name was Charlie White. When I said it was, he led the way to a small room in the administration building. The clothes I'd signed for the day before were hanging on a wire hanger.

"When you're dressed," he said, "turn the things you're wearing now over to the supply clerk. Then go straight down the hall to the warden's office." He laughed. "That is, unless you want to keep your denim as a souvenir."

I said, "No, thank you. I don't want any souvenirs. All I want of this is a faint recollection."

"Then stay out of trouble," he told me.

The warden had my dossier on his desk. He looked from it to me and said, "I'd planned to talk to you, White. You're several cuts above the average man we get here and I don't want to see you back. But right now you're so filled with self-pity and feeling, so pushed around that nothing I could say would do a bit of good."

He laid a typed receipt, a sealed envelope, a small sheaf of bills, and some silver on the corner of his desk. "So if you'll sign a receipt for the one hundred and twenty-six dollars and fifty cents that is credited to your account, I'll keep my mouth shut and let someone else do the talking."

That would probably be Father Reilly. The priest had given me the only news I'd had of Beth. I knew she was clerking in a store in Palmetto City. I knew she knew about Zo. But if Beth had filed suit for divorce, I hadn't been served with the papers.

"Goodbye and good luck, White," the warden concluded the interview.

I started to crack, "Thanks for nothing," but something stopped me. Perhaps it was the fact I had plenty for which to thank him. The warden had leaned over backwards to see that the attempted break hadn't earned me any bad time.

The same guard took me in tow again. But we weren't headed for the chaplain's office. It was the first time I had been in a death house. I didn't like it.

Swede was sitting on the edge of a desk in a small windowless conference room. He looked much the same as he always had except his tan was gone, the lines in his face were deeper, and his eyes seemed even bluer.

The guard said I had ten minutes, and closed and locked the door. The lump in my throat grew still larger. Ten minutes wasn't long enough to even start thanking the old man for what he'd done for me. I'd have been in the attempted break up to my eyes if Swede hadn't landed a hard right on my jaw that had belted me back on my cot unconscious.

When I'd come to again, Mickey and Saltz were dead, and Swede had picked up the big tab for caving in a guard's head.

"*Stay out of this, kid,*" he'd warned me, "*You only got six months to go. I got life and ninety-nine years.*"

Swede sucked hard at his cigarette as if with time running out on him he wanted to enjoy every puff to the maximum. "Ten minutes," he said, "isn't long. So let me do the talking, kid. Would you say I was a Holy Joe?"

The lump in my throat let go and I laughed nervously.

"Then keep that in mind," Swede said. "You and me are a lot alike, Charlie. We both like the water. We've both made a good living on and out of it. But were we content with that? No." He gestured with his cigarette.

"That's why I asked the warden if I could talk to you. A man does a lot of thinking when he gets in one of these quick-fry joints. And it all boils down to this: A man hauls in the fish he baits for and at the depth at which he fishes."

He lighted a cigarette from the butt of the one he was smoking. "In the old days it was different. A man had to depend on himself and there was a lot of wide open space for him to do it in. But times have changed. After years of sailing by guess, society has set out certain buoys and markers." He asked if I had a silver dollar. There was one in the silver the warden had given me. Swede traced the lettering on the head side with a finger. "*E Pluribus Unum.* Know what that means, Charlie?"

I said, "Something about one for all or all for one."

Swede shook his head. "No. It means *one out of many.* And that's you and me, Charlie. And the screw who brought you here. And the warden. And the guy who's going to fry me tonight. We're all just one out of many. And you've got to swim with the school and keep its rules or — Well, look what's happened to me. Look what happened to you when you tried to sail on your own.

"As rackets go, you had a good one. But let's add up the score. On the debit side it cost you your wife, your boat, and got you three years in the can. On the profit side you had a dozen roaring good drunks in *Habana*, a fancy dame, and the false knowledge that you were smarter than your fellow fishing-boat captains. There were no lulls in your business. You brought in a good load every time. Okay. How much dough have you got?"

I told him. "One hundred and twenty-six dollars and fifty cents."

Swede hooted. "For three years of your time. There are guys netting mullet out of Naples, and Palmetto City for that matter, who are making that much in one night. But netting mullet is hard work. So is fishing the grouper banks. And you and me had to be wise guys. You hear from your wife yet?"

I said I had not.

"Well," Swede admitted. "I don't know why you should. A man can starve a dame. He can cuss her. He can beat her every night and twice on Sunday and she'll still think he's her personal Marshall plan in a silver champagne bucket. But only if she knows she's the only woman in his life."

He went on before I could speak.

"But are you willing to admit you made a mistake and cut bait or fish? No. You're so rotten filled with self-pity and hate, it's a shame." He snuffed out his cigarette. "I know how you feel, Charlie. I've got a temper, too. That's one of the reasons I'm here." He read my mind. "But don't do it. Killing your former partner because he ran out on you when the law stepped in, will only bring you back here. And I mean *here*."

Swede lighted a third cigarette. "Look. When you came back from that mess over there in '45 or '46 you'd been living in a bloody tide for four years. Life meant nothing. A thousand lives meant nothing. We had a similar red tide in the Gulf while you were gone. Fish died by the tens of millions. The shores and tide flats were heaped so high with dead fish they stunk. Everyone swore things would never be the same again.

"But they are. The water gradually cleared and the fish began to spawn again. Nature is building back. And that's what you've got to do, Charlie. Forget this. You're in clean water again. If you're smart, you'll stay there. Get a job fishing on shares. Swab out a charter boat if you have to. Then when you get something to offer her, find your wife. Get down on your knees if you have to and beg her to forgive you and come home."

I said that sounded like good advice.

Swede looked at me a long minute, then snuffed out his cigarette. "But you aren't going to take a damn word of it. Okay, kid. It's your funeral."

The guard opened the door. "That's it."

"I've been wasting my time," Swede told him. He walked out of the room without offering to shake hands. "I won't bother to say goodbye. It's just *auf Wiedersehen*, Charlie. I'll try to save a quart and a blonde for you down there."

*   *   *

I walked back through the yard with the guard and out the front door of the prison. It was the same sun on the outside of the wall but it was brighter somehow. It almost blinded me. I stood on the steps for a moment looking at the cars in the parking lot and flipping a mental coin.

If Beth was waiting for me, I'd follow Swede's advice. If she wasn't, I was off to the races. I'd identify, locate, and kill *Señor Peso* if I had to call for the quart and the blonde that Swede had promised to save.

Señor Peso was obviously a *nom de plume* and a cover. It sounded like a gag. The prosecutor had made much of that fact at my trial. But it was the only name I had.

Swede lost. Beth wasn't waiting – but Zo was. I walked over to the yellow jeepster she was driving and her voice reached out and caressed me.

"Hello, honey. Am I glad to see you." Zo lifted her lips to be kissed. "I've been waiting out here since daybreak."

Her lips were clinging. Her fingers dug into my back. After three years in a cell, it was like kissing a jet plane. I said:

"You shouldn't kiss strange men like that. You won't go to heaven."

She wrinkled her nose at me. "Who wants to go to heaven? And since when are you a stranger?" She slid over on the seat. "Get in, honey. You drive."

I said, "What? Without a driver's license? You want me to break the law?"

She thought that was very funny. "Okay. I'll drive." When I still didn't get into the jeepster, she fished in her purse for the Havana bank pass book that had been in her possession when the law had swooped down on me. "And don't jump to false conclusions. No one let you down. The big shot couldn't show up at your trial. It would have jeopardized the whole setup." She handed me the pass book.

I had lied to Swede. I wasn't broke. I was filthy. And I was still important to the gang. Every month I had spent in a cell, someone, *Señor Peso* presumably, had deposited one thousand dollars to my account. The last figure showed $36,124.00.

Zo asked, "Feel better?"

The Devil came up behind me and pushed. *To hell with Beth. To hell with everything*, I thought. *To hell with trying to kill Señor*

Peso. In his way the guy had played square with me. Why should I try to goose into his grave an egg who laid so many golden pesos?

I got into the jeepster and Zo pulled out of the parking lot and headed south on Florida 16 into Starke. I asked her where we were headed. She said:

"Over to the West Coast. I've engaged a double cabin on a little cove just above Dead Man's Bay. But we won't be there long. One of the boys will put in with a converted Tarpon Springs sponge boat in the next few days and take us on to Havana and Shrimp Cay. That all right with you?"

Her head was bare. She was wearing a strapless sun dress that made her shoulders look like they were made of rich cream. Heat and palm trees, the slap of blue waves, and Zo. It sounded good to me.

"Yeah. Sure. That's fine," I told her.

She pulled to the side of the road and handed me an opened bottle of rum. Then, the same devil who was pushing me lighting twin candles in her eyes, she kissed me, hard. "Okay. Until then. You drink and dream, I'll drive . . ."

It was afternoon when we reached the cabin. We'd stopped twice to eat. Once in Gainesville and once in Cross City. I'd also picked up another bottle of rum. After being away from it so long, it hit me almost as hard as Zo's kisses.

The cabin, when we reached it, was a pleasant blur in a stand of slash pine on an isolated section of the shore. A rutted sand road led back to it. As nearly as I could tell, the nearest house was a mile away. The gulf looked the same as it always had, blue and endless and inviting.

It gave me an idea. If I wanted to stay with the party, I had to get some coffee in and some water on me. I told Zo, "I'm going to dunk the body. Put some coffee on, will you, babe?"

She laughed. "You're out of training, honey. But go ahead. You do just that. I figured you might want to swim and you'll find some trunks in the bedroom closet."

She got busy at the stove and I staggered on into the bedroom. Zo had told me we'd be alone, but as I closed the bedroom door I could have sworn I heard someone say:

"You got him, eh?"

I opened the door and asked her, "Who was that?"

At the time it didn't seem important. I closed the door again and tried to hang up my coat but I was so high I hung it upside down and an envelope fell out and skittered across the floor. I recognized it as the envelope the warden had given me along with my discharge papers and what money I had coming. Sitting on the bed I tore it open, and two tens and a five dollar bill fell out. Forcing my eyes to focus, I read:

> *Sweetheart,*
> *I'd be there when you get out if I could possibly manage it but I have to hang on to my job. So, as a substitute, in case you are broke, I am enclosing my last week's salary for train fare. I love you and I'm waiting.*
> *We'll start all over.*
> *Beth*

It was the type of letter Beth would write. Beth loved me and she was waiting. And here I was all mixed up with Zo again. I was still so long that Zo called:

"What's the matter? You aren't sick, are you, honey?"

I told her the truth. "Yeah. Plenty." I got a grip on the rum and tried to do some straight thinking. With Beth out of my life forever, nothing would ever be right again. The money and excitement and Zo were poor substitutes for what I really wanted. Beth was my wife. She was my life. I loved her.

I fished my coat from the door and staggered back into the living room. "So I'm a heel," I told Zo. "I'm sorry. But you and I are washed up as of now. I'm going back to Palmetto City and my wife."

She wanted to know if I was kidding.

I said I was never more serious.

She wasn't so pretty now. Her black eyes narrowing to slits, she spat, "You're either drunk or crazy. How much can you make commercial fishing or running a charter boat?"

I said, "Even so. I'm going back to Palmetto City and Beth and get a job and open the old house and raise five or six red-headed kids and be disgustingly honest."

Her eyes opening wide, she screamed, "No. Don't!"

I thought she was screaming at me. She wasn't. The blow came from one side and behind me. I turned in time to see a blur of white face through the fog of pain that was reaching up to engulf me. Then the leaded butt of a gaff hook used as a club landed a second time, and I floated out into space on a red tide.

Just as I passed the last buoy marking the channel of consciousness I thought I heard the flat slap of a pistol. Then a black roller swept me under.

2. Sprouting Wings

The tarpon was huge, two hundred pounds or more, the largest I'd ever hooked. He broke water a dozen times while I was playing him. I was bathed in sweat. My arms and shoulders felt like they had been pounded with a mallet by the time I got him within ten feet of the boat. Then he really went crazy.

With a series of high-powered jolts like the current they were going to shoot into Swede, he lashed into a flurry of frenzy that almost tore the rod out of my hands. I eased the star drag too late. He didn't want any part of where he was and streaked off into the blue, snapping the wire leader as if it had been string.

I looked over the edge of the cruiser to see what had frightened him. A twenty-foot shark looked back. I was still trying to figure out who had tied the shark under my boat, when he tried to climb into the cockpit with me and I beat at him frantically with my fists.

It was the sharpness of the pain that knifed the fog away. With the first of returning consciousness I lay, gasping, looking up into the dark, thinking what a screwy dream it had been.

The tied shark was an old gag. All of the guides on the waterfront had used it at one time or another to give their charter passengers a thrill. A six-foot shark tied under a cruiser could make a two-pound trout fight like a fifty-pound blue marlin.

Then, one by one the shattered pieces of reality began to fall into place like the curlicues of a gigantic jigsaw puzzle.

I was lying on the floor of the cabin on the shore of Dead Man's Bay. I'd just read the letter from Beth and told Zo I was going back to my wife when an unidentified party, presumably male, had popped out of nowhere and beaten me half to death with the loaded butt of a gaff hook.

It didn't make sense to me. I had no illusions about Zo. She'd never sprout any wings. I hadn't asked her how she'd lived during the three years I'd been in prison. It hadn't mattered. A jealous boyfriend was the obvious answer. But why in the name of time should he pop up and try to beat in my brains when I'd just announced I was going back to my wife?

Then I thought of the voice I'd heard when I'd gone into the bedroom.

"*You got him, eh?*"

Zo had denied there was a voice. But there obviously had been. In the light of what had happened, it began to look like she had contracted to deliver me to the cabin on Dead Man's Bay like so much beef.

On the other hand, she had screamed, "*No. Don't!*" just prior to the first blow.

I gave up trying to think and got to my feet. The interior of the cabin was as black as a fish wholesaler's heart. I tried to find the light switch and, failing, struck a match instead.

According to the alarm clock on the mantel I had been out for hours. It only lacked a few minutes of midnight. The rum bottle was standing on the table. I rinsed my mouth with a drink. Then, striking another match, I walked on into the bedroom – and wished I hadn't.

Zo was lying on the bed, her eyes wide open and staring at the ceiling. But they weren't seeing anything. I struck another match and looked closer. She was cold. The flat slap of a pistol I had heard had been meant for her. She had been dead as long as I had been unconscious.

I lighted a third match and looked around the room. The sense of unreality persisted. A chair had been tipped just so. A shattered rum bottle lay by the side of the bed. Another had drained out its contents on the rug.

Catching sight of a dark object in her hand, I bent over the bed and looked at it. It was the leaded gaff hook with which I had been slugged.

I walked out into the other room and found my coat. The pistol with which she had been killed was in my right-hand coat pocket.

I could see the scene as described by the papers. A recently released con and his moll had rented the cabin to celebrate his release. A drunken brawl had ensued and during it I had killed her.

There was a metallic "pong" as the alarm clock on the

mantel passed the hour. A hundred and some odd miles away, in Raiford, Swede was taking the big jump. He knew all the answers now.

"*Here. And I mean right here,*" he had told me.

Swede had been right about a lot of things. If only I'd listened to him. If only I'd opened the letter from Beth before I had met Zo.

The match burned down and burned my fingers. I didn't feel it. This was murder and I was tagged. I walked out the door and stood on the screened-in porch. The night was black but filled with stars. The tide was out and the sweet-sour smell of the tide flats filled the air. I'd never wanted so much to live or felt I had so much to live for. I thought of what I'd told Zo.

"*Even so. I'm going back to Palmetto City and Beth and get a job and open the old house and raise five or six red-headed kids and be disgustingly honest.*"

That was a laugh. The only place I was going was back to Raiford. A half-dozen guards had seen me get into the jeepster. The waitresses at both Gainesville and Cross City would testify that they had seen us together and I had been drinking heavily.

The jeepster was still in front of the cabin. The smart thing for me to do would be to drive to the nearest phone and call the state patrol and get it over. No one would believe my story. I couldn't describe the guy I'd seen. He was as vague as my testimony concerning *Señor Peso.*

The big veins in my temple began to pound. *Señor Peso.* The guy was beginning to haunt me. If it hadn't been for him, I'd still be operating the *Beth II* out of Bill's Boat Basin as a deep-sea charter cruiser. It had been his voice on the phone the time I'd been behind in my payments that had started off all of the fireworks.

"*This is Señor Peso, Captain White. How would you like to make a quick five thousand dollars?*"

How would I like to drop a mullet net around ten ton of pompano? All I had to do for the money was meet the *Andros Ancropolis*, a converted sponge boat, eighty miles out in the gulf and bring in a few small waterproof packages that fit easily in my bait well. I didn't know what was in them. I was afraid to ask. I needed that five thousand bad.

That had been the beginning. A trip to Veracruz had followed. Then one to Pinar del Rio. Then one to Havana where I'd met

Zo. After that I was in so deep it hadn't mattered. I met who I was ordered to meet, took what I was ordered to get, and brought it back to various points ranging from drops in the Ten Thousand Islands as far north at Palmetto City with a few trips up the bay to Tampa.

I only made one restriction. I refused to run wetbacks. I hadn't spent three years of my life in the navy fighting for the so-called American way of life only to turn around and smuggle in for pay the very guys who were trying to destroy it.

After the one proposition along that line, *Señor Peso* hadn't mentioned the subject again. All of the Coast Guard boys knew me. The older officers had known my father. I never had any trouble getting clearance papers. No one ever stopped me. Until that last time.

Then only my good service record, a purple heart, all the cash I had in the bank, the confiscation of my new boat, and me pleading guilty to assault with a deadly weapon during the fracas that followed the boarding, had saved me from a long Federal rap. That trip, my bait well had been filthy with forty grand worth of Swiss watches and French perfumes on which no duty had been paid.

But I still hadn't ever met *Señor Peso*. All my instructions had come by phone. My money came in the mail, in cash. And once the law had laid its arm on me, he had run out on me cold. When the prosecution had asked me for whom I was running the stuff, all I could offer was a mythical *Señor Peso*. It was a wonder I hadn't gotten life.

Not that it mattered now. Zo was dead and I was tagged. And if he hadn't come forward before, I couldn't expect *Señor Peso* to come out in the open now. Staring up at the stars, I remembered the dead girl's words at the prison.

"And don't jump to false conclusions. No one let you down. The big shot couldn't show up at your trial. It would have jeopardized the whole setup."

It sounded logical. He'd made good to the tune of $36,000.00. Zo with her talk of Havana and a converted sponger putting in had obviously been under instructions that – if they had been carried out – would have proven profitable to me. No. I couldn't blame *Señor Peso* for this. This was a personal affair between the dead girl and myself and the man who had killed her.

The night was cool. I put on my coat and lighted a cigarette just as a pair of headlights turned off the highway a quarter of a mile away and bounced down the rutted sand road toward the cabin. I kicked the screen door open and walked out and stood with my hand on the butt of the gun in my pocket, in the shadow of a big slash pine fifty feet from the wooden porch.

The car was blue and white, a state patrol car, with two uniformed troopers in it. They skirted the yellow jeepster and parked in front of the porch.

Getting out, one of them said, "It looks quiet enough to me. Probably a false alarm."

"Probably," his partner agreed. He flicked the car's searchlight around among the trees, missing me by inches. Then he pointed it at the shoreline. "Lonely sort of place, though." He was a bit impatient with his partner. "Well, go ahead. Bang on the door. Wake 'em up and ask 'em if anyone screamed."

His partner banged the screen door. "State Police."

When no one answered, he opened the screen and walked in, sweeping a path before him with his flashlight. A moment later I heard him whistle. Then the lights in the bedroom came on and he shouted to his partner:

"Hey. Come in here, Jim. That fisherman who called the barracks wasn't whoofing. Some dame was screaming all right. But she isn't screaming now. She's dead."

So much was clear. The man who had killed Zo had waited as long as he could, hoping her body would be discovered. When it wasn't, he'd called the State Patrol. He really wanted to pin this thing on me and he didn't want me to get too far away before the law stepped in.

I hoped the trooper would leave his keys in the car. He didn't. Sliding out from behind the wheel, he clipped his keys on his belt before drawing his gun and striding into the cabin.

I inched over toward the jeepster. A few minutes before I'd been considering calling the State Patrol and turning myself in. Now I was damned if I would. I didn't want to go back to Raiford. I didn't want to die. At least not without seeing Beth and telling her I was sorry.

The ignition key was still in the jeep. Keeping it between me and the cabin, I walked the length of the patrol car, raised the hood as quietly as I could and yanked out a handful of wires.

Then I walked back and climbed in the jeepster, crossed my fingers and kicked it over. Over the roar of the motor, I heard one of the troopers say:

"What the hell?"

Then I'd spun the jeepster in a sharp U-turn that threw up a screen of sand and was bouncing down the rutted road with both troopers shouting after me and spraying the back of the car and the windshield with lead.

I made the highway without being hit and into a little town on the north bank of a river. I had, at the most, a five- or ten-minute start. I'd put the patrol car temporarily out of action, but their two-way radio was still working. It would only be a matter of minutes before roadblocks would be set up and every law-enforcement officer in Dixie, Bronson, Alachua, Marion and Citrus counties would be alerted for a killer driving a new yellow jeepster.

A tired-looking tourist driving a mud-splattered '48 with Iowa license plates was just pulling out of the town's only filling station as I passed it. I drove on to the edge of town and the bridge across the river. There was a small gap between the black-and-white guard rail and the bridge.

Pointing the jeepster at the gap, I rammed down the gas and hopped out. It hit the gap dead-center and disappeared with a splintering of wood and a screech of metal. A moment later there was a great splash. The '48 behind me braked to a stop and the tourist stuck his head out the window.

"Holy smoke," he said. "What happened, fellow? Did your car go out of control?"

"No," I told him. "I did." I opened the door on the far side, climbed in beside him, and rammed the nose of the gun that had killed Zo in his ribs. "Look," I said, "I have a date with a roadblock where this road joins US 19. That is, unless I get there first. How fast will this crate go?"

He looked at the gun in his ribs and swallowed hard. "Well," he admitted, "I've had it up to ninety. And my foot wasn't all the way to the floor."

I said, "Then put it there. As of now."

3. Close Call

It could be the law would figure out I was in Palmetto City. If it did, it wasn't my fault. I'd left a trail only a snake with Saint Vitus dance could follow. I hadn't doubled back once but I'd done a lot of twisting and changing of means of transportation. I'd kissed the Iowa tourist goodbye at Inglis after giving him the impression I had a boat waiting for me in Withlacoochee Bay. From there I'd picked up a ride on a fruit truck as far as Dunnellon and US 41. I'd taken a bus from there to Tampa and spent most of the day buying new clothes piecemeal.

When I'd finished buying slacks and a sport coat and a loud gabardine shirt and washing the blood from the back of my head, I looked a lot more like a northern tourist than I did a local boy who'd spent most of his life on the water.

The Tampa papers were filled with the thing. The headline on the evening paper read:

EX-CONVICT MURDERS SWEETHEART

The story was about as I expected. The way the law figured it, Zo and I had staged a drunken party to celebrate my release. During it, we had quarreled and I killed her. I was, variously reported, seen north near Tallahassee, boarding a forty-foot sloop in Withlacoochee Bay, and hopping a south-bound freight at Dunnellon.

But the law was merely confused, not stupid. Once they sifted out the false reports, the net would begin to tighten. And Beth was in Palmetto City. The chances were there was a stake-out right now on the house in which she was living.

I'd taken a plane from Tampa to Palmetto City. But I didn't dare take a cab from the airport to the return address she had given on her letter. I had been born in the town. I'd lived there most of my life. I knew all the cab drivers. All of them knew me. I also knew the law. Ken Gilly, a kid with whom I had gone to school, was now a lieutenant in charge of the detective bureau.

Getting out of the airport as fast as I could without attracting attention, I strolled past the dark ball park and out to the mole in the bay where, night or day, there were always a dozen or so northern tourists fishing. It was dark on the mole and as good a place to kill time as any.

My plans were all tentative. I wanted to talk to Beth. I wanted to tell her I was sorry things turned out as they had for us. Then I wanted to talk to one or two of the boys who still berthed their fishing cruisers at Bill's Boat Basin. One of them, Matt Heely, owed me plenty. And I was willing to call it square for a free trip to Shrimp Cay.

It was too late for me to turn honest now. Once there I'd attempt to contact *Señor Peso* through channels and see what he had in mind when he had sent Zo to re-establish contact with me. If he decided I was too hot to be of any use to him, there was still the thirty-six grand in my Havana bank account. And a man had to be pretty stupid if he couldn't have one hell of a time drinking himself to death on thirty-six thousand dollars anywhere south of the Tropic of Cancer.

The tide was in. The moon was right. You could have caught fish with dough-balls and a bent pin. At one o'clock I interrupted the excited shoe clerk from Chicago who was pulling in pig-fish, about the size of the ones I usually used as bait for snook, and who was teaching me how to fish, telling him that while it all was very interesting I thought I would turn in.

The return address on Beth's letter was less than a mile from the mole. It proved to be a small white frame garage apartment on a palm tree- and bougainvillea-tangled alley on the south-east side of town, not far from the store in which she was clerking. It was a hell of a place for the wife of a man who'd made the money I'd made to live in. Shame heated the collar of my sport shirt. Swede had been right about the bloody tide, too. I must have been out of my mind to treat Beth the way I had.

Of course she could be living in the big old house on the island across the deep water channel from the mainland. But she couldn't live there and work in town. The only way it could be reached was by boat. Unless she had rented the old place to bring in a little additional income, the chances were that nothing but snakes and raccoons and rabbits and field mice had lived on the island for three years.

There was no police car in front or in the alley. Keeping close to the wall, I climbed the stairs and rapped lightly on the door.

Either Beth wasn't asleep or she was sleeping lightly. Almost immediately she asked, "Yes? Who is it?"

I took a deep breath and told her. "Charlie."

A moment of silence followed. Then slippered feet scuffed across the floor and only a screen door separated us. A single beam of moonlight, flooding in through a hole in the vine that almost covered the porch, spotlighted her white face. I'd forgotten she was so pretty. Even with her cheeks stained with tears and dark lines under her eyes, she was beautiful. And one time she had loved me and I had thrown her away for a mess of Zo.

Pressing her nose against the screen she said, "You shouldn't have come here, Charlie. The police were here not two hours ago and I promised Ken Gilly I'd call him if you did contact me."

I said, "Then you know?"

She brushed a lock of red hair away from her forehead. "Yes. I know. It was in the papers."

I got it off my chest with a rush. "I didn't do it, Beth. I didn't kill her. And I didn't open your letter, I didn't realize what it was, until after I'd reached the cabin. When I did read it, I told Zo I was coming back to Palmetto and you. And that was when it happened. Someone slugged me and shot Zo."

She said, "And you expect me to believe that?"

I asked, "Have I ever lied to you, Beth?"

She thought a moment. "No. That's one thing you've never done." She unhooked the screen. "Come in. Come in before one of the neighbors sees you."

Inside the room I tried to take her in my arms but she pushed me away.

"No. I want time to think. This may change things for both of us. What do you intend to do now, Charlie?"

I told her.

Beth said, "In other words, if you can evade the law and get out of the country, you're going right back in the same old racket. You're going to work for this *Señor Peso* again."

I asked her what else I could do.

She told me. "Be a man. If you didn't kill that girl there must be some way we can prove it."

I asked her, "How?"

She shook her head. She was standing so close to me that

one of her curls brushed my face. It was all I could do to keep from digging both of my hands in her hair and pulling her to me. "I don't know," she admitted. Then, woman-like, she persisted, "But there must be some way. Perhaps Mr Clifton could help us."

He was the guy she worked for. I'd never liked him. Few of the local people did, even if they did trade in his store. A cocky little Yankee, he'd come to Palmetto City twenty years before and built an idea into the biggest business in town. He wouldn't be undersold. If a fellow merchant ran a loss leader costing from two cent, Clifton would lose five to get the business. And he had.

From a two-by-four dry-goods store he'd branched out into a block-square four-story-high merchandise carnival, handling everything from apples to zithers. If you couldn't buy it at Clifton's, it wasn't for sale.

I asked, "Why should he help us?"

Beth was frank about it. "Mr Clifton's in love with me. He's asked me to marry him. He even offered to buy the old house out on the island so I'd have some money and wouldn't have to work while I made up my mind whether or not to divorce you."

I said, "Oh, yeah?"

Beth put me back in my place. "*You* should get sore."

The strain was beginning to get me. I sat down on the edge of the bed and buried my head in my hands. "Okay, honey," I admitted. "I'm sorry. I haven't got a beef. Not with the way I've loused up our lives."

She sat down on the bed beside me. "Kiss me, Charlie."

I said that after the way I'd treated her I shouldn't think she'd want me to. Her lips inches from mine, she repeated, "I asked you to kiss me, Charlie."

I took her face in my hands and kissed her. But it wasn't the way I kissed Zo. It was more like I'd kissed her in front of the altar after the Reverend Paul had finished marrying us and the world was going to be our oyster. She was something sweet and beautiful and fragile. She was good. She was something that had been missing out of my life for a long time.

When I lifted my face, her eyes were shining in the dark and patting my cheek with one hand she kissed me back of her own accord. "It's going to be all right, honey," she told me. "I don't know how we'll do it. But we will *make* it right."

A car purred to a stop in the alley. Heavy feet began to climb the stairs. A moment later there was a light knock on the door.

Standing up in front of me, Beth asked, "Yes?"

"It's Ken again, Beth," Gilly told her. "I'm sorry to disturb you but I thought you ought to know. Charlie's been traced to a men's store in Tampa where he bought a complete new outfit. We're setting up roadblocks on the causeway and all roads leading into Palmetto City."

"Oh," Beth said. "Oh."

Ken sounded tired. "I wish the guy hadn't headed back this way. Heaven knows I don't want to make the pinch. Charlie's my friend. But what can I do?"

Beth suggested. "Maybe he didn't do it, Ken. Maybe he didn't kill that girl."

Lieutenant Gilly was skeptical. "Yeah. Maybe. And maybe some day filet of grunt will sell for as much as snapper fingers. Well, Tampa only being sixty miles away, I thought I'd let you know. You want me to post a guard in the alley?"

Beth's fingers tightened on mine. "No. I don't think that will be necessary, Ken. Even if Charlie should come here I don't think he'd hurt me."

"No," Gilly agreed. "Well, it's just as well. I can use every man I have on the roadblocks. But if he should slip through and come here, you let me know now, Beth."

He clumped on back down the stairs. A moment later the police cruiser purred off into the night. I could feel the cold sweat start on my cheeks. The boys were beginning to haul in the net – and I was in it. It wouldn't be long now.

Beth sat back on the bed, all business. "No one ever comes in here but me, and I was going to suggest you stay here until after I'd talked to Mr Clifton. Now that's out. When you don't show up at the blocks, they're going to know you got through and someone is bound to suggest the police search this apartment. There's only one logical place for you to stay."

I asked her where that was.

She said, "Out at the house. You know it and the island better than anyone else. An army couldn't find you there if you didn't want them to. Now, tell me the whole thing from the minute you were released from prison yesterday morning."

I gave her a play-by-play description. But I still didn't like the Clifton angle and said so. "You say the guy loves you. You say he's asked you to divorce me and marry him. Well, what's his reaction going to be when you tell him I'm in town? He's going to reach for his phone and call the cops. The guy is a bargain hunter. And it's a lot cheaper for him to turn me in to be burned than it is for him to pay for a divorce."

Beth said I wasn't doing Mr Clifton justice. He was really a very fine and a very honorable man. She shook her curls in my face. "Besides I'm not going to tell him you're in town. You have to admit he is smart?"

I said I did.

Beth continued. "All I am going to tell him is that I don't think you killed that girl and ask his advice on how to go about hiring a private detective to prove it."

It didn't sound too bad. The guy was smart. And Beth was right about the island. I could hide out on it indefinitely. "Well, okay," I agreed. "But how are you going to contact me?"

She said she would find some way to do so without making Ken Gilly suspicious. "After all, it's our house. I have a right to go out there anytime I want to. Maybe I want to put it in shape to be sold."

I asked her when she'd been out there last.

She said, "Not since shortly after your trial. For a long time I didn't care what happened to it. Now, if we can straighten out this mess you're in, we're going back there to live."

I got up to go while the going was good and Beth walked to the door with me. "I love you, Charlie."

I said that went double. I felt some better. I felt a lot better. But we still had a long row to hoe. I didn't see how anyone could possibly prove I hadn't killed Zo.

I wanted to stay. I knew Beth wanted me to. But Ken Gilly was nobody's fool. When I didn't show at the roadblocks he'd know I had slipped into town before they had been established and would put a stake-out on Beth's apartment without telling her anything about it.

Beth kissed me at the screen door. "I'll be out – soon. With good news to report."

Keeping close to the wall and out of the moonlight, I tiptoed sideways down the stairs to the alley and made my way towards the nearest street. I'd gone perhaps twenty yards from the foot of the stairs when the big guy stepped out from behind the bole of a pineapple palm.

"You there," he stopped me. "What's your name? And what are you doing prowling an alley at two o'clock in the morning?"

My first thought was, *Ken left a stake-out after all.*

I thought fast: I didn't know the man. He was obviously new to the force, at least since I'd been sent to Raiford. If he took me in, I was dead. I still had the murder gun in my pocket. They'd burn me like they'd burned Swede. My only chance was to bluff and run.

"Why, my name is Olson," I lied. I tried to feint him off guard by making him look where I was pointing. "I live in that house back there, officer. And I'm on my way downtown to try to locate an all-night drugstore."

"Oh," he said. "I see."

There was a glint of silver in the moonlight. I thought at first he was throwing a gun on me. Then his arm reversed itself and started up in a familiar arc and I knew what he had in his hand. Backing a step, I let it rip air where my belly had been.

Then, stepping in before he could recover his balance, I smashed a hard right to his jaw that smacked him off his feet and his head into an empty garbage can with sufficient force to make it ring like a bell-buoy.

He was out, cold. Striking a match I leaned over him. I still didn't know him. But whoever he was I doubted if he was an officer of the law. If he was, he was the first cop I'd ever seen who carried a six-inch fish knife.

Then the light in the window of the apartment just over my head came on and some old dame asked nervously:

"What was that? Who's that out there in the alley?"

I said, "Me-arrh."

"Oh," she said. "Bad kitty."

Then I tiptoed out of there fast before she stopped to think that kitty cats didn't strike matches.

4. Dead Man's Bay

The water was warm but the air was cold. The tide had changed and was going out. The pull of it was terrific. It had been three years since I'd done any swimming. I thought when I reached mid-channel that the tide was going to sweep me out into the gulf. As it was, I lost one of my shoes off the length of plank on which I had piled my clothes and which I was pushing ahead of me.

It would have been much easier to steal a boat. But I knew how most bait-camp men were. They hated to lose a boat almost as badly as a wife. A good boat cost two hundred dollars. You could get married for five. And I didn't want to direct any attention to the island.

The knife man worried me. Who was he? How had he known I would be coming down that alley? Why had he tried to kill me? He wasn't the man who had killed Zo. That much I knew. It hadn't been his voice that had said, "*You got him, eh?*" Nor was he the man who had slugged me with the butt of the gaff hook. He was a much larger man whose muscles strained the shoulders of his coat. If he had swung the gaff, it would have caved in my head.

As the low-lying trees grew to their proper place in the night sky, I felt for bottom and found it. The storms of the last three years hadn't changed the coast line of the island, not on the lee side at least. The deep water extended to within a few feet of the shore. I waded up on to the sand and slapped and tramped myself dry and warm before I put on my clothes.

Now, I was really home. My rotting nets, unused since before I had gone into the Service, still hung on their long drying racks. A half-dozen hulks and stove-in row-boats lay buried in the sand, including the bare ribs of the fifty-foot bottom that had been my father's boat. I was glad the old man was dead. I was the first of our family to do time and the disgrace would have broken his heart.

Dressed, I turned for a last look at the mainland. It was a good mile and a half across the channel. I couldn't see the running lights of any boats. My passage, so far as I knew, had been unobserved.

I padded, barefoot, up the weed-overgrown path toward the

house, hoping I didn't step on a snake. The path was a jungle of vines. I wiggled my way through them, being careful not to disturb them any more than I had to. I didn't know how long I would have to stay on the island. And when both his roadblocks and stake-out failed, Gil would undoubtedly make a perfunctory search of the home place.

Then I thought of something both Beth and I had forgotten – food. Unless there were some canned goods in the pantry, food was going to be a problem. But I'd face that when I came to it. As long as I knew I was going to live, I could live on fish and rabbits if I had to.

The house itself was set well back from the shore in a clearing that we had farmed from time to time. Now the ground was sour and overrun with saw palmetto. Even in the waning moonlight I could see the fifteen-foot wide porch across the front was sagging badly in spots, supported only by the thick-trunked red and purple bougainvillea and flame vine that had been old before I was born.

I picked an orange from a tree and tried to suck it but the grove was as sour as the garden. I wondered why Clifton had offered to buy the place from Beth. Probably out of pity or in the hope of buttering her up so she would say yes to his proposal. The old place was out of the world. I mean that literally.

No one but a typical cracker fishing family or a pair of kids as much in love as Beth and I had been would want to live in such a place. And the rest of the island was as bad. It was still as wild as it had been when the wreckers had been a power in Key West and Billy Bowlegs had terrorized gulf shipping.

I walked up the stairs to the porch. Coiled in a pool of moonlight, a ten-button rattlesnake watched me from the shredded canvas of a once-expensive chaise longue I had given Beth when we'd first been married.

I opened the door and went in. The big front room smelled old and musty. By striking a match I found a lamp with some oil in it and lit it. Even as old and decrepit as it was, after three years in a six by eight cell, the house looked good to me. At least here I could breathe. There were some canned goods in the pantry but not much, enough perhaps for three or four meals.

The more I thought about Beth asking Mr Clifton to suggest a good private detective to prove I hadn't killed Zo, the screwier it sounded. If the guy was really in love with her, he wasn't going to cut off his prospects by sweeping the legal sand spurs out of her husband's path to her side.

When she contacted me, I'd suggest she try to arrange passage for us both and meet me somewhere down in the Caribbean. I was pretty certain that Matt Heely would run us down, for a fresh piece of change, if not for the money he owed me. Matt was as bad as I'd been. He made good money but he threw it away with both fists and was always in financial hot water when it came time to pay his insurance or the installments on his boat.

Crossing the kitchen floor, I plowed up a pine splinter with my big toe that made me see stars for a minute. The quarter-inch callouses on my feet were gone. I'd have to have shoes of some kind. Then I thought of the old pair of sneakers I'd discarded just before making my final trip down to Shrimp Cay for the load with which I'd been caught. They should be up in the attic somewhere. Beth was as bad as a magpie. She never threw anything away on the theory that some time she might find a use for it. And this was one of the times.

Holding the lamp in one hand, I padded up the back stairs to the second floor and stopped in front of the door of the bedroom that Beth and I had used. I hadn't had it on the first floor but here I had an eerie feeling that I was being watched. I opened the door and held the lamp high.

It was the same with the three other bedrooms on the floor. They were all as Beth had left them when she'd left the island, stripped to the bare mattress with the bedding folded neatly and piled at the foot of each bed. It was my nerves, nothing more. I started to light a cigarette as I climbed the stairs to the attic, then decided to conserve my supply. Cigarettes were another thing that Beth and I had forgotten.

The old house had been built by my grandfather when both labor and lumber were cheap. Rumpus rooms hadn't been thought of, but he'd finished the attic as a ballroom so he and his friends could dance when a party of boats had come out from the mainland or a rare passenger vessel, New Orleans- or Havana-bound, had dropped anchor in the deep channel.

The finished section was thirty by forty feet, paneled in rare woods, with two large dormer windows on each side and two more windows at each end. But it had been a long time since it had been used as a ballroom. The windows had been boarded up and covered with cobwebs for years. Even when I had been a small boy, the attic had become a family catch-all.

I pushed open the heavy door and walked in and a sudden gust of wind blew out the flame of my lamp. Cursing the wind, I walked a few more feet. Then setting the lamp on the bare floor I lifted the hot glass chimney, struck a match and applied it to the wick.

I wasn't alone in the attic. Sitting in built-in bunks against the wall were perhaps a dozen men, their eyes as flat and expressionless as those of the coiled rattlesnake I had seen on the chaise longue. I'd seen their faces before.

At least I'd seen similar faces in the stews of Marseille, Port Said, Sevastopol, Hamburg, and two dozen other war-torn ports. They were the faces of wanted men. Men wanted in their own countries for treason and murder and fabulous thefts. Men willing to pay a stiff price to escape the noose, the guillotine, the firing squad, and the garrote.

I straightened. "What the hell?"

A thin-faced man with a heavy accent said, "Someone make out that light."

It was the only word spoken. Another man snatched the lamp from me and extinguished it. I reached for the gun that had killed Zo and remembered it was in the pocket of my coat. And I'd left my coat in the kitchen.

Then the first of a dozen fists found me and beat me to my knees with the deadly precision of men who have nothing left to lose. I fought back to my feet and the ring of fists hemming me in gave way for a moment as I tried to pound my way to the door. Then a foot thudded into me. As I went screaming to the floor, still other feet found my head, my chin.

The huge tarpon was back on my line. Only this time, like a fool, I'd allowed the line to become entangled with my ankles and he'd pulled me over the side of the cruiser and was heading, seemingly, for the bottom of the gulf out in fifty fathoms.

I was cold. I was wet. I was strangling. I was sinking through endless fathoms of black water, towed by the huge fish. It was strange what a man would dream.

Then an alarm bell rang in my head. I wasn't dreaming.

I was drowning. It wasn't a fish pulling me down. It was a weight. I fumbled at the cord. Then I managed to open my knife and cut it.

The swift descent ended abruptly and I shot surfaceward. Just as my lungs were about to burst I broke water. I gasped a mouthful of air and sunk again, but just under the surface this time.

When my head broke water again, I turned on my back and floated. Perhaps five hundred feet away the running lights of a boat were circling and I could hear the faint throb of an underwater exhaust. I lay with my cheek to the water watching the lights. As they came toward me again I turned on my belly, ready to dive.

Then from the wheel of the boat, Matt Heely said, "Like a stone. Poor Charlie." He sounded sad.

The boat passed to port. Its stern lights grew small, then disappeared, and I was alone in the night. I tried to raise myself in the water and was partially successful. There were no short lights in sight. That meant I was a long way out in the gulf.

I turned on my back again and floated until my breathing was normal. Then I tried to find shore again and had better luck this time. Almost parallel with the water I could see a faint pinprick of light that didn't look like a waning star. I swam toward it slowly, floating frequently to rest, hoping it was the light on Quarantine Key.

I had to reach shore. I meant to. I had the whole setup now. I knew who had killed Zo. I knew why she had been sent to meet me. I knew why thirty-six thousand dollars had been credited to my account. I not only knew who had killed her, but why. More, I knew what the men were doing in the attic of the old home place and how they had gotten there.

The sky grew blacker, then faded into a dead gray. All of the stars disappeared. A light onshore wind sprang up and whipped up a froth of white caps. I swam on doggedly. The gray turned to a dirty mauve and then to a bright crimson before breaking into day. I found a drifting, mossy old plank and used it to rest on.

It had been Quarantine Light I had seen. I passed to starboard of it on an incoming tide, unobserved. The same thing happened with the Coast Guard plane making its routine morning flight. I was just another speck in an endless carpet of water.

Then the water turned a pale green and I knew I was on the outer bar. I waded a few hundred yards, then sat neck-deep on the edge of blue water for perhaps half an hour before striking out again to cover the last half-mile.

I came ashore a few hundred yards above the former luxury hotel on the beach that the government had bought and turned first into a rehabilitation center and then into a veteran's hospital. An early-rising former GI hunting for shells along the beach looked at me curiously, then decided I was a fellow patient.

"Out for an early morning swim, eh?"

I said that was right and asked him if he had a cigarette. He had and gave me one. I sucked the smoke into my lungs gratefully. Nothing had ever tasted quite so good except the cigarette I had smoked after I'd finished my part of the demolition work on Saipan.

It was perhaps six o'clock. There was no one but myself and the former GI on the beach. That much was fortunate. The law was still looking for me. And all I had on was a pair of shorts. I'd kicked off my pants and ripped off my shirt perhaps five miles out.

My new friend looked at my battered face and grinned, and I knew what he was thinking. As soon as they get a little dough together, a lot of the boys out at the hospital swarm into town and raise hell in an attempt to forget that they will never be the men that they once were. I touched my face. It was tender to the touch but the long immersion in salt water had cauterized the cuts. And if it looked like the rest of my body, it was a sight in technicolor.

His grin widened. "Kinda pitched one, eh?"

I said, "That's right. And am I going to get hell. You don't know where I can borrow some clothes, do you, buddy, just long enough to sneak by the desk?"

That was right up his alley. He'd held up a few bars himself. "Why not cop a suit from the old ward-room?" he asked. He nodded at an open ground-floor door. "You know. In where the orderlies hang up their civies when they change into whites."

I patted him on the back. "Thanks. That's an idea, fellow."

There was a clatter of dishes in the kitchen as the help brought up breakfast, but I was alone in the locker-room. I picked out a white sport shirt and a gray gabardine suit and a pair of two-toned sport shoes that didn't fit too badly. A broad-brimmed panama hat that I could pull down over my eyes and so hide most of my face completed the ensemble. The name of the guy who owned the clothes was Phillips. His hospital pass was in a glassine case in the outer breast pocket of the coat. Making a mental note to reimburse him for the loan if I lived through the fireworks I intended to touch off, I walked down a long corridor and out the front door of the hospital.

A sleepy guard barely glanced at the pass.

"A long night, eh, fellow?" he yawned.

I agreed it had been a long night.

5. Señor Peso

Clifton's was always crowded, from eight o'clock in the morning until midnight. It was around ten when I got there. According to the headlines of the paper on the news rack next to the cigarette counter, I was still driving the cops nuts.

I hadn't attempted to crash the roadblocks set up on either side of Tampa. I hadn't been seen in Palmetto City. The general public had been alerted to watch for me. I was known to be armed, and dangerous. I was described as pale, six feet tall, weighing in the neighborhood of two hundred pounds and wearing blue slacks, a checked sport coat, and white shoes. I was probably bareheaded as I was never known to wear a hat.

I turned the pages of the paper. Swede was on page four, in a one-column two-inch box. All it said about him was that Swen (Swede) Olson, former fishing guide and convicted murderer, had been executed at midnight for killing a prison guard during an abortive attempted break. Swede's troubles were over. I though of what he'd told me in the death house.

A man hauls in the fish he baits for and at the level at which he fishes.

If that wasn't good logic, I'd eat it.

The snip back of the cigarette counter asked if I wanted to buy the paper or rent it. I laid twenty-seven cents of Phillips' change on the counter.

"Tut, tut. What if Mr Clifton should hear you? Remember

the customer is always right. But just to show you my heart is in the right place I'll take the paper and a deck of cigs."

She slammed the cigarettes on the counter. My picture was on the front page of the paper next to a picture of Beth. She'd looked straight into my face but hadn't recognized me.

I cracked the cellophane wrapper, then tapped the picture of Beth. "Now could I have some information. Where can I find this girl? I was told she worked at the cigarette counter."

The snip snapped, "She did. But right now you'll probably find her in Mr Clifton's office." She patted her blonde hair. "Not that I can see what he sees in her."

I walked back through an aisle lined with tables cluttered with merchandise to the elevator and asked to be taken to the fourth floor. No one, including the elevator operator, gave me a second look.

The office was large and modern. Behind a half-glass partition I could hear a man, presumably Clifton, saying, "But, my dear girl, I'd like to help you. You know that. But I can't see what good hiring a private detective would do. I've been talking to Lieutenant Gilly since you first mentioned the matter this morning and he says there isn't a doubt but what White killed that girl in the cabin on Dead Man's Bay."

Beth stuck to her guns. "I don't believe it."

I opened the door and walked in.

A dapper little man, perhaps five feet four, with wide-spread intelligent eyes, a high forehead and hair so black it looked like it had been dyed, Clifton waved me out of the office. "I'm sorry, sir," he said. "But whatever it is, I'm too busy to see you right now. Please come back later."

I closed the door and leaned against it.

Beth recognized me and dug a fist into her mouth to keep from screaming. "Charlie," she said finally. "What are you doing here?"

I drew a chair up to the desk and sat down. "Well, it got a little hot out on the island. In fact, quite a few things have happened since I saw you last night. And as you said maybe Mr Clifton would help us, I thought I'd come and see what he could do."

The little guy looked at me like I was something obnoxious. "Nothing. I can do absolutely nothing," he said. "As I was just telling Beth –" he corrected himself – "Mrs White, Lieutenant

Gilly says there is no doubt about your guilt and I can't afford to be involved in such a sordid matter."

Beth said, "What do you mean, 'things got a little hot out on the island'?"

I lighted a cigarette and told the story just as it had happened. When I had finished, Clifton said:

"But that's preposterous. Who were these men in your attic?"

I said I imagined they were wetbacks that *Señor Peso* had paid Matt Heely or one of the other boys working for him to smuggle in from Cuba or Mexico.

"The old house," I pointed out, "is ideally situated. A boat can bring them in. A boat can distribute them along the coast in the guise of tourists and the law never be the wiser unless one of them should be picked up accidentally. Even then, I imagine by the time they leave the house they're well equipped with fake papers. As I see it, they're just another item of profit with *Señor Peso*."

Clifton made a gesture of distaste. "That name." He lighted a cigarette and smoked it in short, quick puffs. "And you say at the end of the attack that this Matt Heely took you out into the gulf in his fishing cruiser, weighted your ankles and dropped you in?"

I said that was correct.

Now he was openly skeptical. "I don't believe it. Even if you had managed to cut the cord you couldn't have swam that far."

Beth said, "That wasn't far for Charlie. He was on a water demolition team during the war. You know. One of the boys with goggles and rubber flippers who swam in the night before the first assault wave hit a beach and blew up all the obstacles they could."

Clifton eyed me with fresh respect. "I don't know what to think or what to say," he said finally. "Just what is it you want of me, White?"

I said, "You have a cruiser down at the yacht basin. I want you and Beth to come out to the island with me and check my story. In other words I want a friend in court before I turn myself in. A responsible businessman who can back at least a portion of my story."

He thought a moment. "You think this Matt Heely could be *Señor Peso*?"

I said, "Matt could be. He's smart enough." I snuffed out

my cigarette. "If I'm right it was *Señor Peso* who killed Zo and pinned her death onto me. It was *Señor Peso* who hired a knife man to wait outside Beth's apartment last night. It was *Señor Peso* who ordered me dropped in the gulf."

He protested, "But why?"

I said that would probably come out when we found out who he was. He sat silent a long moment drumming with his fingers on his desk. Then Beth turned her smile on him and said:

"Please."

She really had the guy wrapped around her little finger. He was so nuts about her it oozed out all of his pores.

"Well, all right," he said finally. "But let's have an understanding, White. If we do go out to the island and find nothing in the old house to substantiate your fantastic story, you will turn yourself in to Lieutenant Gilly as soon as we return to the mainland and allow the law to take its course. Is that understood?"

I said it was.

He said, "Then you go ahead to the yacht basin. Mrs White and I will follow."

I passed a half a dozen cops on my way down to the basin. One or two of them glanced at me casually but none of them attempted to stop me.

His boat was a thirty-eight-footer, double cabin, with a flying bridge. He knew how to handle it, too. If he hadn't been a successful merchandiser, he'd have made a good fishing-boat captain. What's more he knew the bottom of the channel like the lines in his well-kept hand. Easing the nose of the cruiser in between the rotting pilings of what once had been a pier, he made it possible for Beth to step ashore without even getting her feet wet. I helped him tie up to a piling, then followed him ashore.

Seen in broad daylight the old house looked better than it had in the moonlight. There was nothing wrong with it or the path or the clearing that a few dollars and elbow grease wouldn't make right again.

The first place I went was the kitchen. But the coat I'd left on a chair was gone, and with it the gun that had killed Zo.

Clifton was impatient. "Well, let's get on with it," he said. "Let's see this fabulous attic."

As I led the way up the stairs, he asked if I was armed. When I said I wasn't he said:

"Then it's a good thing that I brought a gun with me." He was openly skeptical. "Heaven knows I wouldn't want to face an attic filled with wetback desperadoes without a gun."

I paused on the second floor for a deep breath, then walked up the attic stairs and threw the heavy door open. The floor was thick with dust. There were no built-in bunks against the wall. The walls were lined solidly with the antique furniture that various Whites had discarded over a period of a hundred years.

Beth began to cry.

Clifton was silent a moment. Then drawing his gun, he motioned me back down stairs to the second floor. "I was afraid it would be like this," he admitted. "But what in the name of time did you hope to gain by telling us such a fantastic story?"

I asked him why the gun.

"You're not mentally right," he said. "You can't be."

I lighted a cigarette and leaned against the jamb of one of the closed bedroom doors. "That can be," I admitted. "Heaven knows I've made a mess of my life. But tell me this, *Señor Peso*. Did you ever see a Florida attic that had been closed up for three years that wasn't covered with cobwebs?"

His voice shrill, he asked, "What was that you just called me?"

I said, "Answer my question. No. You never did. You could get the men who were in here last night out of the attic and onto the mainland. You could rip out the bunks and move the old furniture back. You could cover the floor with dust. But you couldn't replace the cobwebs. That's something only a spider can do."

He wet his lips with the tip of his tongue. "You're crazy. You're out of your mind."

I said, "We'll leave that up to the law. And while the law is at it, I want them to check your whereabouts at the time that Zo was killed. I doubt you have an alibi. You can't have. Because you were the guy who shot her and dusted me with a gaff hook."

His voice grew even shriller. "And just why should I do such a thing? What was my motive?"

I nodded at Beth. "My wife. She was the one thing you couldn't get at a bargain. You couldn't buy her. But you could buy me. That's why you sent Zo to meet me. That's why you deposited the thirty-six grand to my account. That's why you had Zo steam me up about heading straight for Cuba and Shrimp Cay. That's why you were at the cabin, to make certain she had me in tow.

"And everything went just fine until I read Beth's letter and told Zo it was no dice, that I was heading back to Palmetto City and Beth. It was you to whom Zo cried out just before you shot her. Shot her because you saw another way to accomplish your purpose. With me back in a cell at Raiford waiting to be burned for murder, I couldn't very well return to Beth. And, in time, you knew you'd get what you wanted."

He laughed. "A jury would howl at that story."

I said, "Okay. Let's test it. Let's go back to the mainland. I'll tell my story and you tell yours."

He shook his head. "No. I'm afraid we can't do that. I'm a prominent man in Palmetto City and my business enemies would be certain to try to make capital of this."

I said, "You mean you're afraid that the Feds might look at your invoices and begin to wonder where you're getting some of your goods that you're able to sell for less than your fellow merchants pay for it wholesale. Hell. It's been right in front of my nose all the time. No one but you could be *Señor Peso*."

The little man sighed. Then looking at Beth he said, "I'm sorry."

"Sorry for what?" she asked him.

He said, "That I can't allow such a scurrilous story as this to be bruited about. I'm very sorry, my dear. I'd hoped to make you very happy. But now –" He thumbed the safety of his gun.

I said, "It won't wash, Clifton. One dame on a gun is enough. Besides, just how do you intend to explain our bodies?"

His eyes overly bright, he said, "That's simple. I'll tell the police the fantastic story you told me. Then I'll tell them when I called you a liar, you saw that you were trapped and shot your wife and committed suicide."

It was still as death in the old second-floor hallway. A chorus of dust particles were dancing in the sunlight streaming in the front window. Clifton lifted the gun in his hand and the door of the bedroom behind me opened and Ken Gilly stepped out in the hall saying:

"I wouldn't, Mr Clifton. With all your dough, you've got a

much better chance hiring a high-priced lawyer." Ken cocked the big gun in his own hand. "Of course if you insist."

Around us the doors of the other bedrooms opened. There was an officer in each one, one of them a police stenographer who was still scrawling curlicues on his pad.

Clifton wasn't a fool. He dropped his gun. "You win," he said looking at me. "You're smarter than I gave you credit for being." He looked at Ken. "Well, let's get back to the mainland so I can contact my lawyers." His smile was thin. "But you haven't a damn thing on me but some foolish conversation."

Putting his gun away, Ken rubbed thoughtfully at the knuckles he had bruised beating at least a portion of the truth out of Matt Heely after I had gone to him with my story, directly from the hospital.

"Oh, I don't know," he said slowly. "A little of this, a little of that. A guy talks here. A guy talks there. And the first thing you know, it builds into a conviction." He waved his hand at the stairs. "Take Mr Clifton away, boys. We're going to give him a bargain, board and lodging free for nothing."

When they had gone, Ken turned to me, offered me his hand.

"Welcome, Charlie." He brushed my nose with the tip of one finger. "But keep that clean now, fellow. Hear me?"

I said I did and intended to.

Then he was gone and Beth and I were alone and she was in my arms.

"I love you, love you so, Charlie," she whispered.

Swede had been right about a lot of things. He'd told me:

"*A man can starve a dame. He can cuss her. He can beat her every night and twice on Sunday and she'll still think he's her personal Marshall plan in a silver champagne bucket. But only if she knows she's the only woman in his life.*"

I hadn't known how really big a lump in the throat could be. All I could say was her name. But that was all right with Beth. She understood. The bloody tide was over for both of us. There was nothing ahead but clear sailing in clean water.

She lifted her face to mine. "Hey, you, Mister Man. Remember me? How's about a kiss?"

And that was all right with me, too.

DEATH COMES GIFT-WRAPPED

William P. McGivern

Sergeant Burt Moran was a tall man with hard flat features and eyes that were cold and dull, like those of a snake. He was that comparatively rare thing among cops, a man equally hated by crooks and by his fellow officers. Operators on both sides of the law forgot their differences and came to agreement on one point at least: that Moran was a heel by any or all standards.

Moran was a bully who shook down petty crooks for a few bucks whenever he got the chance. But he left the big boys alone. He lacked the imagination to serve them and, consequently, he never got in on the important payoff. There would have been some dignity in being a big grafter, but Moran grubbed for his few extra dollars the hard way, the cheap way, the way that earned him nothing else but contempt.

There was a streak of savage brutality in him that caused the underworld to mingle their contempt with a certain fear. Moran had killed six men in the line of duty, three of whom were unarmed at the time, and another who had died after Moran had worked him over with a sap for fourteen hours. The story of the men he'd killed wasn't told because a corpse is an unsatisfactory witness. Moran knew this. He knew all about killing.

Now, at two o'clock in the morning, in the cheap room of a cheap hotel, Moran was going to learn about murder. He had to commit a murder because of something new in his life, something that he had always sneered at in the lives of other men.

Moran was in love. And he had learned that love, like anything else, costs money.

He stood just inside the doorway of the room and watched the scrawny, thin-faced man who was staring at him from the bed. The man was Dinny Nelson, a small-time bookie who, Moran knew, carried all his assets in a hip wallet.

Dinny brushed a hand over his sleep-dulled features and said, "What's the pitch, Moran? You got no right busting in here."

Moran drew his gun and leveled it at Dinny. He knew what would happen with crystal clarity, not only to Dinny and the portions of his body hit by the heavy slugs, but after that, to Dinny's corpse, to the police department and to himself, Moran. It was an old story to him. He had killed six men in the line of duty and he knew the way everything worked. No one would doubt his story.

Dinny saw his fate in Moran's face. He began to beg in a cracked voice. "No, no, you can't," he said. "There's no reason to kill me – I ain't done nothing. Don't."

Moran fired three shots and they were very loud in the small, thin-walled room. Dinny's body jack-knifed with the impact of the slugs, rolled from the bed to the floor. He didn't live long. Moran watched expressionlessly as Dinny's limbs twisted spasmodically, then became rigid and still. Underneath Dinny's body the roses in the faded pattern of the rug bloomed again, bright and scarlet.

There was two thousand three hundred and thirty dollars in Dinny's wallet. Moran left thirty. The money made a comfortable bulge against his leg as he sauntered to the phone . . .

While the coroner did his work and two lab technicians went over the room, Moran told his story to Lieutenant Bill Pickerton, his immediate superior at Homicide.

"Tonight I seen him taking bets in the lobby," Moran said. "This was eleven. I started across to him but he seen me and ducked into the bar and then out to the street. So I drifted away. Around two I came back, came right up here to his room. I told him to get dressed but the fool went for me. I had to shoot him."

Lieutenant Pickerton rubbed his long jaw. "This stinks worse than your usual stuff, Moran. You could have handled him with your fists. He doesn't have a gun."

Moran shrugged. "Why should I risk getting beat over the head with a chair or something?"

Pickerton looked at him with active dislike. "Okay, turn in a written report tomorrow morning. The old man won't like this, you know."

"To hell with the old man," Moran said. "He wants us to bring 'em in with a butterfly net, I suppose."

"All right," Pickerton said. He paid no more attention to Moran, but studied the body and the room with alert, careful eyes.

Downstairs, Moran hailed a cab and gave the driver the address of the Diamond Club. He stared out the window at the dark streets of the Loop, his impassive face hiding the mirth inside him.

When Moran had realized that a nightclub singer couldn't be impressed by a cop's salary, he had looked around in his dull, unimaginative fashion for a way to get some money. Nothing had occurred to him for quite a while. Then the idea came, the idea that a cop could literally get away with murder.

After he got that much, the rest was easy. He had picked Dinny because he wasn't big-time, but big enough as far as money went. Now it was all over and he had the money. There would be a routine investigation of course, but there was no one to come forward with Dinny's version of what had happened. Therefore, the department would have to accept Moran's story. They might raise hell with him, threaten him some, but that didn't matter.

Moran's hand touched the unfamiliar bulge of money in his pocket and a rare smile touched the corner of his mouth. It didn't matter at all.

He paid off the driver in front of the Diamond Club on Randolph Street and walked past the head waiter with a familiar smile. The head waiter smiled cordially, for Moran's visits to the club had been frequent over the past two months, dating from the time Cherry Angela had joined the show.

Moran found a corner table and watched the girl singing at the mike. This was Cherry Angela. The blue spot molded her silver evening dress to her slim, pliant body, revealing all the curving outlines. She wore her platinum hair loose, falling in soft waves to her shoulders, and her eyes and features were mocking as she sang an old, old story about a man and a woman.

Moran forgot everything watching the girl. And there was an expression of sullen hunger on his face.

She came to his table after the number and sat down with lithe grace. "Hi, copper," she said, and her voice was amused. "Like my song?"

"I liked it," Moran said.

Her lean face was mocking. "I should do a black-flip from sheer happiness, I suppose. Would a beer strain your budget?"

"Go ahead," Moran said, flushing. "I've spent plenty on you, baby."

"You tired of it?" she said lightly.

Moran put his hands under the table so she wouldn't see their trembling. She was in his blood like nothing else had ever been in his life. But he got nothing from her but mockery, or sarcasm that shriveled him up inside.

He knew that she let him hang around for laughs, enjoying the spectacle of a forty-year-old flatfoot behaving like an adolescent before her charms. For just a second then he wanted to tell her what he had done tonight, and about the money in his pocket. He wanted to see her expression change, wanted to see respect for him in her eyes.

But he resisted that impulse. Fools bragged. And got caught. Moran wasn't getting caught.

Some day he'd have her where he wanted. Helpless, crawling. That was what he wanted. It was a strange kind of love that had driven Moran to murder.

He took her home that night but she left him at the doorway of her apartment. Sometimes, if he'd spent a lot of money, she let him come up for a nightcap, but tonight she was tired.

Leaving her, Moran walked the five miles to his own apartment, hoping to tire himself out so that he could sleep without tormenting himself with visions of what she might be doing, or who she might be with.

But once in bed, he knew the walk hadn't helped. He was wide awake and strangely nervous. After half an hour of tossing he sat up and snapped on the bed lamp. It was five-thirty in the morning, and he had a report to make on the murder in about four hours. He needed sleep, he needed to be rested when he told his story, and thinking about that made sleep impossible.

He picked the evening paper from the floor, glanced over the news. There was a murder on page one, not his, but somebody else's. He thought about his murder then and realized with a slight shock of fear that it had been on his mind all the time. It was the thing keeping him from sleep. Not Cherry Angela.

He frowned and stared out the window at the gray dawn. What was his trouble? This killing tonight was just like the others. And they hadn't bothered him. There must be a difference somewhere, he decided. It came to him after a while. The others had been killings. This one was murder. And the difference was that murder made you think.

Moran lay back in the bed, but he didn't go to sleep. He kept thinking.

At ten after eleven Moran had finished his report. He read it over twice, frowning with concentration, then took it down to Lieutenant Bill Pickerton's office.

There was someone with Pickerton, a young man with mild eyes and neatly combed hair. He was sitting beside Pickerton's desk, and the two men were talking baseball.

Pickerton nodded to Moran, said, "This is Don Linton from the commissioner's office, Moran."

Moran shook hands with Linton and put his report before Pickerton. Pickerton handed it to Linton. Linton said, "Excuse me," put on rimless glasses and bent his head to the report.

Moran lit a cigarette and dropped the match in Pickerton's ashtray. He guessed that Linton was here to look into the Dinny Nelson killing. His eyes were hot from his sleepless night and he was irritable.

"Is that all you want?" he asked Pickerton.

Linton answered. He said, "No. I've got a few questions. Have a chair, Sergeant."

Pickerton remained silent.

Moran sat down, trying to control the heavy pounding of his heart. They had nothing on him. It was his word, the word of a cop, and it was the only word they'd get.

"Okay, this seems clear," Linton said. He put his glasses away, studied Moran directly. "I'm from the commissioner's office, Moran. The commissioner wants me to ascertain that the shooting of Dinny Nelson was justified. Let's start with this. You're a homicide sergeant, assigned to roving duty in the Loop. Why did you make it your business to go to Nelson's room to arrest him on a gambling charge?"

Moran was ready for that one. He explained that he'd seen Dinny taking bets in the hotel lobby, that it seemed a pretty flagrant violation, so he'd decided to pick him up, even though it wasn't his beat.

Moran's voice was steady as he talked. All of this was true. He *had* seen Dinny taking a bet, had tried to pick him up, and Dinny had given him the slip. On that ground Moran felt confident.

"Okay," Linton said casually. "Now according to our information Dinny Nelson usually carried a sizeable amount of cash with him. But there was just thirty dollars on his body after you shot him. Got any ideas about that, Sergeant?"

"No," Moran said.

There was silence. Pickerton and Linton exchanged a glance. Then Linton put his fingertips together precisely and looked at Moran. "Did you leave the hotel room at any time after the shooting? I mean did you step out and leave the body alone?"

"No," Moran said. He wondered what Linton was getting at.

"You see, there was a bellhop on the floor at the time. He had brought some aspirin up to a woman. He has a record for theft and it occurred to us that if you left the room for any length of time, he might have slipped in, stolen the money and left before you returned."

"I didn't leave the room," Moran said. He felt scared. They might be telling the truth, but he doubted it. They were setting a trap, leaving an opening for him to dive into. A man guilty and scared would grab any out. Moran wet his lips and kept quiet. Crooks who got caught got scared. They started lying, blundered, and hung themselves talking. That wouldn't happen to him. They had his story.

Linton asked him then why he hadn't subdued Dinny with his fists. That was better. That was the sort of stuff he expected. Half an hour later Linton said he had enough, and Moran walked to the door. He was sweating. He was glad to get out. Linton might look like a law student, but his mind was sharp, strong like a trap.

As he reached the door, Linton said, "By the way, you know Cherry Angela, don't you?"

Moran's hand froze on the knob. He turned and his body was stiff and tense. "Yeah," he said. His voice wasn't steady.

Linton looked pleasantly interested, that was all. "I've heard

her sing," he said. "And I heard you were a friend of hers."
He said nothing else, volunteered no other information, but
continued to watch Moran with a polite expression.

Moran stood uncertainly for a moment, then nodded quickly
to the two men and went out to the elevators. Waiting for a car,
he wondered how Linton knew he was a friend of Cherry's.
They must already have done some checking into his activities.
Moran lit a cigarette and wasn't surprised to notice that his
fingers were trembling . . .

That day was hell. He couldn't sleep, and food tasted like
sawdust. Also, he kept thinking, turning everything over in his
mind a thousand times. That made him tense and jumpy.

That night Moran went to the Diamond Club for Cherry's
early show. When he walked through the archway he saw her
sitting at a corner table with a man. There was a champagne
bottle beside them in an ice bucket and they were talking very
seriously. Moran felt a bitter anger and unconsciously his hands
balled into fists.

He started toward their table, moving deliberately. This is the
time for a showdown, he thought. I'll chase that punk out of
here and have it out with her.

Then he recognized the young man with her, and the shock
of that recognition sent a cold tremor through his body.

It was Linton, the investigator from the commissioner's office.

Moran's face felt hot and stiff. He turned clumsily, hoping
they hadn't seen him, and went back across the room, forcing
himself to walk casually.

But splintered thoughts were flicking into his mind with
frightening intensity. What was Linton doing here? What was
Cherry telling him? More important, what was Linton asking her?

Ignoring the head waiter's puzzled smile, Moran hurried out
of the club. He walked a block quickly before his heart stopped
hammering and he was able to think. He knew he had behaved
foolishly. He should have gone to her table, said hello and sat down.
Any change in his normal routine would look suspicious now.

Lighting a cigarette, he realized that he must see Cherry
tonight, find out what Linton had been after. He retraced his
steps until he came to a doorway about fifty feet from the
entrance of the Diamond Club. There he stopped and prepared

to wait. For he had to be sure that Linton was gone before going in to see Cherry.

It was a long wait.

The last show ended, noisy customers streamed out, but still Linton had not appeared. Moran's throat was dry from too many cigarettes, and his eyes burned from lack of sleep. But he waited, a deep shadow in the doorway.

Then Linton appeared and Moran cursed bitterly under his breath. For Cherry was with him, bundled up in furs and chattering so that her voice carried along the street to him.

The doorman went out in the street to hail them a cab. There were plenty of cabs out and that was a break. Linton and Cherry climbed into one, and Moran hurried down the block from the club and caught the next cruiser. He told the driver to follow Linton's cab and it led them to Cherry's apartment.

Moran ordered his driver to stop half a block away. He watched while Cherry and Linton got out and went into her building. But their cab waited and in a few seconds Linton appeared again and drove away.

Moran let out a relieved sigh. He paid off his cab and walked slowly along the darkened street until he came abreast of Cherry's entrance. For a second he hesitated, wetting his lower lip uncertainly. It was stupid for him to barge in on Cherry now. It would look as if he were afraid, guilty.

But he felt he had to know what Linton had wanted. That was the only way he could release the tight, aching feeling in his stomach. He made up his mind and turned into her entrance.

She opened the door in answer to his knock, her eyes widening with surprise. "Well, it's a small world," she said. "I just left one of your buddies."

"I know," Moran said, and stepped inside. She had changed into a green robe and as she turned he saw the flash of her legs, slim, smooth and bare. But they didn't distract him now.

"What did he want?" he said watching her closely.

"The copper?" She shrugged and went to a table for a cigarette. "What does any copper want? Information."

He walked to her side and suddenly all the twisted feeling he had for her crystalized to hatred. She was so cool, so bored and indifferent, while he was ready to crack in pieces from the pressure inside him.

Raising his thick hand he struck the cigarette from her mouth with brutal force. She staggered, face whitening with shock and anger. But he caught her shoulders and jerked her close to him.

"Now," he said, in a low hard voice. "You talk, baby. What did that guy want?"

"You're hurting me," she said, breathing angrily. "He wanted to know about you. Now let me go."

"What did you tell him?" he asked hoarsely.

She turned from him and sat down on the couch. "I didn't tell him anything," she said, rubbing her bruised shoulders. "Now you can get the hell out of here. No guy pushes me around, Moran."

"Forget that," Moran said. "I didn't mean to get rough. But I'm in a jam, baby. I had to shoot a guy last night and the old women in the commissioner's office are on my tail. They're trying to frame me, and that's why that guy Linton was snooping around you."

Cherry's lean face was interested. She said, "Did you kill the guy, Moran?"

"I shot him. He went for me and I shot him, that's all."

"Oh," she said. She smiled. "You wouldn't do anything original, I guess. Nothing that might put an extra buck in your pocket."

"I get along on my pay," Moran said.

"And your friends have to, too," she said. "That's why you haven't got any, I suppose."

"I didn't get anything out of shooting the guy," Moran said. That was smart. Not talking, not bragging. Guys talked to dames, then the dames talked. That wasn't for Moran.

Cherry grinned ruefully and leaned back against the fat pillows on the couch. There was one light in the room, a lamp on an end table that caught lights in her loose blonde hair and accentuated the soft curves of her body. Yawning, she put her legs onto the couch. The green robe parted, revealing her slim calves in the soft light. She didn't seem to notice.

She was smiling, but there was a hard light in her eyes. "Tell me, Moran," she said, "how does it feel to kill a man?"

Moran swallowed heavily. He couldn't wrench his eyes from her long bare legs, or stop the sudden drumming in his temples.

When he spoke, his voice was dry. "It's like anything else you do, like smoking a cigarette or buying a paper, that's all."

She sighed. "You're such a clod, Moran. You're like a big heap of dough that's turning sour."

He came closer to her. "I could be different with you," he said. "You drive me crazy, baby."

She laughed with real amusement. "In the Casanova role you're a riot."

"Damn you," he said hoarsely.

She laughed again and sat up, putting her feet on the floor. "Let's break this up," she said. "You're a jerk and always will be, Moran. I might have liked you a little if you were smart, or if you had a spare buck to spend on a girl, but as you stand you're hopeless. So beat it, will you? And stop hanging around the club."

"Now wait," Moran said. His anger broke, melted away. "You don't mean that. I'll go, but let me see you again."

Her voice was hard. "No. You're all through. Beat it."

Moran stood beside her, reached for her hand. "What would you think if I was smart, if I did have a little dough?"

"I don't want to play twenty questions," she said coldly.

"This is no gag," he said. When he saw interest in her face, he slid on the couch beside her and began speaking rapidly, the words spilling out in a rush. "I got a little dough," he said. "I got it from Dinny Nelson last night. He was the guy I shot. I blew him out like a candle, then took his bundle. It's all yours, baby, for anything you want. But we got to play it quiet until I get a clean bill from the commissioner's office. You see that, don't you?"

"Are you on the stuff?" she said. "Is this story coming out of a pipe?"

"No, no it's on the level," he said. "I did it for you, baby. I shot hell out of him and got the dough. And I'm in the clear."

"Let's see the dough," she said skeptically.

He took the roll from his pocket. He had kept it on him because there was no safer place. Now he spread it in her lap and watched her face. She fingered the money gently and gradually a little smile pulled at her lips. "I might change my ideas about you," she said at last.

"Sure you will," Moran said eagerly. "I'm okay, baby. You'll see."

"I kind of want to find out," she said, grinning at him. "Want to excuse baby a minute?"

He watched her as she walked to the bedroom door. Something tightened in him as he saw the way her shoulders tapered gracefully to her slender waist, and the way her hips moved under the silken robe. She turned at the doorway and winked at him, and he saw the gleam of her long legs before she disappeared.

It was worth it, Moran thought exultantly. He felt happy for the first time since the murder. This was going to make it all right, and the tight ache inside him melted away and he knew it was gone for good.

He lit a cigarette and leaned back against the cushions, closing his eyes. Linton could go to hell, and so could Pickerton. They had nothing on him, now or ever.

He opened his eyes when he heard the click of the doorknob. Straightening up, he crushed out a cigarette and got to his feet, a grin on his face.

The bedroom swung open and Moran's heart lurched sickeningly.

Lieutenant Pickerton walked into the room, a gun in his hand. The gun was pointed at Moran's stomach.

"You're all through," he said.

Moran stood still, the grin pasted on his face, his mind frozen in the paralysis of panic. He tried to speak but no words came out, and the noise he made was like the grunt of an animal.

There was the sound of a key in the front door and then Linton came in, gun in hand.

He glanced at Pickerton. "You get it all?"

"The works," Pickerton nodded.

Linton came to Moran's side, deftly slipped the gun from his shoulder holster. "You're under arrest for the murder of Dinny Nelson," he said formally. "Anything you say may be used against you. As you know," he added dryly.

"Yeah, I know," Moran said numbly. Linton's words, the old familiar words, released him from paralysis.

Cherry appeared in the bedroom doorway, stepped around Pickerton and entered the room. She picked up a cigarette and smiled. Her fingers moved to the mark on her cheek where he had struck her.

Then she looked at Moran. "They wanted me to get you to talk," she said. "I wasn't going to, because I'm no informer. I might have warned you that Pickerton was hiding in the bedroom, but after you hit me, I had to pay you back."

"That was just one of the stupid things you did," Pickerton said. He shook his head disgustedly. "What made you think you were smart enough to get away with murder? Your speed is the little stuff, Moran."

Moran wet his lips. "What did I do wrong?" he asked. He didn't know what was happening to him but he felt weak and drained.

Pickerton glanced at Linton. "You tell him," he said.

"We had nothing on you," Linton said, "except your bad record, and the fact that Dinny's money had been taken. But you acted from the start in a suspicious manner. During our first talk you were nervous, sweating. Later you came to the Diamond Club, but when you saw me with Cherry, you turned and got out. We saw you, of course.

"Pickerton came here to Cherry's apartment because we knew you'd come here. A smart man wouldn't have. I took Cherry home, drove off. You immediately barged into the building and I came back and followed you up here."

He glanced at Cherry, then back at Moran. "You were too nervous to be subtle with her, or to go easy. You pushed her around and that did what we hadn't been able to do, convinced her to help us. She played you like a sucker. You spilled everything to her, which is the thing only a fool would have done. Fortunately for us, Moran, you're a fool." His face became curious. "A cop should have known better. Didn't you stop to think at all?"

"I was thinking about the murder," Moran said slowly. "It was on my mind. That left no room for any thinking about the smart thing to do."

Pickerton took his arm and started him toward the door.

Linton walked over and shook hands with Cherry. "Thanks for the help," he said. He hesitated, then smiled. "I'd like to see you some time when I'm off duty."

Cherry pulled the robe tight around her slim waist. "Any old time – just any old time."

Linton grinned. "I'll call you."

He took Moran's other arm and the three men went out the door.

Moran walked like a dead man.

THE GIRL BEHIND THE HEDGE

Mickey Spillane

The stocky man handed his coat and hat to the attendant and went through the foyer to the main lounge of the club. He stood in the doorway for a scant second, but in that time his eyes had seen all that was to be seen; the chess game beside the windows, the foursome at cards and the lone man at the rear of the room sipping a drink.

He crossed between the tables, nodding briefly to the card players, and went directly to the back of the room. The other man looked up from his drink with a smile. "Afternoon, Inspector. Sit down. Drink?"

"Hello, Dunc. Same as you're drinking."

Almost languidly, the fellow made a motion with his hand. The waiter nodded and left. The inspector settled himself in his chair with a sigh. He was a big man, heavy without being given to fat. Only his high shoes proclaimed him for what he was. When he looked at Chester Duncan he grimaced inwardly, envying him his poise and manner, yet not willing to trade him for anything.

Here, he thought smugly, *is a man who should have everything yet has nothing. True, he has money and position, but the finest of all things, a family life, was denied him.* And with a brood of five in all stages of growth at home, the inspector felt that he had achieved his purpose in life.

The drink came and the inspector took his, sipping it gratefully. When he put it down he said, "I came to thank you for that, er . . . tip. You know, that was the first time I've ever played the market."

"Glad to do it," Duncan said. His hands played with the glass, rolling it around in his palms. He eyebrows shot up suddenly, as though he was amused at something. "I suppose you heard all the ugly rumors."

A flush reddened the inspector's face. "In an offhand way, yes. Some of them were downright ugly." He sipped his drink again and tapped a cigarette on the side table. "You know," he said. "If Walter Harrison's death hadn't been so definitely a suicide, you might be standing an investigation right now."

Duncan smiled slowly. "Come now, Inspector. The market didn't budge until after his death, you know."

"True enough. But rumor has it that you engineered it in some manner." He paused long enough to study Duncan's face. "Tell me, did you?"

"Why should I incriminate myself?"

"It's over and done with. Harrison leaped to his death from the window of a hotel room. The door was locked and there was no possible way anyone could have gotten in that room to give him a push. No, we're quite satisfied that it was suicide, and everybody that ever came in contact with Harrison agrees that he did the world a favor when he died. However, there's still some speculation about you having a hand in things."

"Tell me, Inspector, do you really think I had the courage or the brains to oppose a man like Harrison, and force him to kill himself?"

The inspector frowned, then nodded. "As a matter of fact, yes. You *did* profit by his death."

"So did *you*," Duncan laughed.

"Ummmm."

"Though it's nothing to be ashamed about," Duncan added. "When Harrison died the financial world naturally expected that the stocks he financed were no good and tried to unload. It so happened that I was one of the few who knew they were as good as gold and bought while I could. And, of course, I passed the word on to my friends. Somebody had might as well profit by the death of a . . . a rat."

Through the haze of the smoke Inspector Early saw his face tighten around the mouth. He scowled again, leaning forward in his chair. "Duncan, we've been friends quite a while. I'm just cop enough to be curious and I'm thinking that our late Walter Harrison was cursing you just before he died."

Duncan twirled his glass around. "I've no doubt of it," he said. His eyes met the inspector's. "Would you really like to hear about it?"

"Not if it means your confessing to murder. If that has to happen I'd much rather you spoke directly to the DA."

"Oh, it's nothing like that at all. No, not a bit, Inspector. No matter how hard they tried, they couldn't do a thing that would impair either my honor or reputation. You see, Walter Harrison went to his death through his own greediness."

The inspector settled back in his chair. The waiter came with drinks to replace the empties and the two men toasted each other silently.

"Some of this you probably know already, Inspector," Duncan said . . .

"Nevertheless, I'll start at the beginning and tell you everything that happened. Walter Harrison and I met in law school. We were both young and not too studious. We had one thing in common and only one. Both of us were the products of wealthy parents who tried their best to spoil their children. Since we were the only ones who could afford certain – er – pleasures, we naturally gravitated to each other, though when I think back, even at that time, there was little true friendship involved.

It so happened that I had a flair for my studies whereas Walter didn't give a damn. At examination time, I had to carry him. It seemed like a big joke at the time, but actually I was doing all the work while he was having his fling around town. Nor was I the only one he imposed upon in such a way. Many students, impressed with having his friendship, gladly took over his papers. Walter could charm the devil himself if he had to.

And quite often he had to. Many's the time he's talked his way out of spending a weekend in jail for some minor offense – and I've even seen him twist the dean around his little finger, so to speak. Oh, but I remained his loyal friend. I shared everything I had with him, including my women, and even thought it amusing when I went out on a date and met him, only to have him take my girl home.

In the last year of school the crash came. It meant little to me because my father had seen it coming and got out with his fortune increased. Walter's father tried to stick it out and went under. He was one of the ones who killed himself that day.

Walter was quite stricken, of course. He was in a blue funk and got stinking drunk. We had quite a talk and he was for quitting school at once, but I talked him into accepting the money from me and graduating. Come to think of it, he never did pay me back that money. However, it really doesn't matter.

After we left school I went into business with my father and took over the firm when he died. It was that same month that Walter showed up. He stopped in for a visit, and wound up with a position, though at no time did he deceive me as to the real intent of his visit. He got what he came after and in a way it was a good thing for me. Walter was a shrewd businessman.

His rise in the financial world was slightly less than meteoric. He was much too astute to remain in anyone's employ for long, and with the Street talking about Harrison, the Boy Wonder of Wall Street, in every other breath, it was inevitable that he open up his own office. In a sense, we became competitors after that, but always friends.

Pardon me, Inspector, let's say that I was his friend, he never was mine. His ruthlessness was appalling at times, but even then he managed to charm his victims into accepting their lot with a smile. I for one know that he managed the market to make himself a cool million on a deal that left me gasping. More than once he almost cut the bottom out of my business, yet he was always in with a grin and a big hello the next day as if it had been only a tennis match he had won.

If you've followed his rise then you're familiar with the social side of his life. Walter cut quite a swath for himself. Twice, he was almost killed by irate husbands, and if he had been, no jury on earth would have convicted his murderer. There was the time a young girl killed herself rather than let her parents know that she had been having an affair with Walter and had been trapped. He was very generous about it. He offered her money to travel, her choice of doctors and anything she wanted . . . except his name for her child. No, he wasn't ready to give his name away then. That came a few weeks later.

I was engaged to be married at the time. Adrianne was a girl I had loved from the moment I saw her and there aren't words enough to tell how happy I was when she said she'd marry me.

We spent most of our waking hours poring over plans for the future. We even selected a site for our house out on the Island and began construction. We were timing the wedding to coincide with the completion of the house and if ever I was a man living in a dream world, it was then. My happiness was complete, as was Adrianne's, or so I thought. Fortune seemed to favor me with more than one smile at the time. For some reason my own career took a sudden spurt and whatever I touched turned to gold, and in no time the Street had taken to following me rather than Walter Harrison. Without realizing it, I turned several deals that had him on his knees, though I doubt if many ever realized it. Walter would never give up the amazing front he affected."

At this point Duncan paused to study his glass, his eyes narrowing. Inspector Early remained motionless, waiting for him to go on.

"Walter came to see me," Duncan said. "It was a day I shall never forget. I had a dinner engagement with Adrianne and invited him along. Now I know that what he did was done out of sheer spite, nothing else. At first I believed that it was my fault, or hers, never giving Walter a thought . . .

Forgive me if I pass over the details lightly, Inspector. They aren't very pleasant to recall. I had to sit there and watch Adrianne captivated by this charming rat to the point where I was merely a decoration in the chair opposite her. I had to see him join us day after day, night after night, then hear the rumors that they were seeing each other without me, then discover for myself that she was in love with him.

Yes, it was quite an experience. I had the idea of killing them both, then killing myself. When I saw that that could never solve the problem I gave it up.

Adrianne came to me one night. She sat and told me how much she hated to hurt me, but she had fallen in love with Walter Harrison and wanted to marry him. What else was there to do? Naturally, I acted the part of a good loser and called off the engagement. They didn't wait long. A week later they were married and I was the laughing stock of the Street.

Perhaps time might have cured everything if things hadn't turned out the way they did. It wasn't very long afterwards that

I learned of a break in their marriage. Word came that Adrianne had changed and I knew for a fact that Walter was far from being true to her.

You see, now I realized the truth. Walter never loved her. He never loved anybody but himself. He married Adrianne because he wanted to hurt me more than anything else in the world. He hated me because I had something he lacked . . . happiness. It was something he searched after desperately himself and always found just out of reach.

In December of that year Adrianne took sick. She wasted away for a month and died. In the final moments she called for me, asking me to forgive her; this much I learned from a servant of hers. Walter, by the way, was enjoying himself at a party when she died. He came home for the funeral and took off immediately for a sojourn in Florida with some attractive showgirl.

God, how I hated that man! I used to dream of killing him! Do you know, if ever my mind drifted from the work I was doing I always pictured myself standing over his corpse with a knife in my hand, laughing my head off.

Every so often I would get word of Walter's various escapades, and they seemed to follow a definite pattern. I made it my business to learn more about him and before long I realized that Walter was almost frenzied in his search to find a woman he could really love. Since he was a fabulously wealthy man he was always suspicious of a woman wanting him more than his wealth, and this very suspicion always was the thing that drove a woman away from him.

It may seem strange to you, but regardless of my attitude, I saw him quite regularly. And equally strange, he never realized that I hated him so. He realized, of course, that he was far from popular in any quarter, but he never suspected me of anything else save a stupid idea of friendship. But as I had learned my lesson the hard way, he never got the chance to impose upon me again, though he never really had need to.

It was a curious thing, the solution I saw to my problem. It had been there all the time, I was aware of it being there, yet using the circumstances never occurred to me until the day I was sitting on my veranda reading a memo from my office manager. The note stated that Walter had pulled another coup in the market and had the Street rocking on its heels. It was one of those times when any variation in Wall Street reflected the economy of the country, and what he did was undermine the entire economic structure of the United States. It was with the greatest effort that we got back to normal without toppling, but in doing so a lot of places had to close up. Walter Harrison, however, had doubled the wealth he could never hope to spend, anyway.

As I said, I was sitting there reading the note when I saw her behind the window in the house across the way. The sun was streaming in, reflecting the gold in her hair, making a picture of beauty so exquisite as to be unbelievable. A servant came and brought her a tray, and as she sat down to lunch I lost sight of her behind the hedges and the thought came to me of how simple it would all be.

I met Walter for lunch the next day. He was quite exuberant over his latest adventure, treating it like a joke.

I said, "Say, you've never been out to my place on the Island, have you?"

He laughed, and I noticed a little guilt in his eyes. "To tell you the truth," he said, "I would have dropped in if you hadn't built the place for Adrianne. After all . . ."

"Don't be ridiculous, Walter. What's done is done. Look, until things get back to normal, how about staying with me a few days. You need a rest after your little deal."

"Fine, Duncan, fine! Anytime you say."

"All right, I'll pick you up tonight."

We had quite a ride out, stopping at a few places for drinks and hashing over the old days at school. At any other time I might have laughed, but all those reminiscences had taken on an unpleasant air. When we reached the house I had a few friends in to meet the fabulous Walter Harrison, left him accepting their plaudits and went to bed.

We had breakfast on the veranda. Walter ate with relish, breathing deeply of the sea air with animal-like pleasure. At exactly nine o'clock the sunlight flashed off the windows of the house behind mine as the servant threw them open to the morning breeze.

Then she was there. I waved and she waved back. Walter's head turned to look and I heard his breath catch in his throat.

She was lovely, her hair a golden cascade that tumbled around her shoulders. Her blouse was a radiant white that enhanced the swell of her breasts, a gleaming contrast to the smooth tanned flesh of her shoulders.

Walter looked like a man in a dream. "Lord, she's lovely!" he said. "Who is she, Dunc?"

I sipped my coffee. "A neighbor," I said lightly.

"Do you . . . do you think I could get to meet her?"

"Perhaps. She's quite young and just a little bit shy and it would be better to have her see me with you a few times before introductions are in order."

He sounded hoarse. His face had taken on an avid, hungry look. "Anything you say, but I have to meet her." He turned around with a grin. "By golly, I'll stay here until I do, too!"

We laughed over that and went back to our cigarettes, but every so often I caught him glancing back toward the hedge with that desperate expression creasing his face.

Being familiar with her schedule, I knew that we wouldn't see her again that day, but Walter knew nothing of this. He tried to keep away from the subject, yet it persisted in coming back. Finally he said, "Incidentally, just who is she?"

"Her name is Evelyn Vaughn. Comes from quite a well-to-do-family."

"She here alone?"

"No, besides the servants she has a nurse and a doctor in attendance. She hasn't been quite well."

"Hell, she looks the picture of health."

"Oh, she is now," I agreed. I walked over and turned on the television and we watched the fights. For the sixth time a call came in for Walter, but his reply was the same. He wasn't going back to New York. I felt the anticipation in his voice, knowing why he was staying, and had to concentrate on the screen to keep from smiling.

Evelyn was there the next day and the next. Walter had taken to waving when I did and when she waved back his face seemed to light up until it looked almost boyish. The sun had tanned him nicely and he pranced around like a colt, especially when she could see him. He pestered me with questions and received evasive answers. Somehow he got the idea that his importance warranted a visit from the house across the way. When I told him that to Evelyn neither wealth nor position meant a thing he looked at me sharply to see if I was telling the truth. To have become what he was he had to be a good reader of faces and he knew that it *was* the truth beyond the shadow of a doubt.

So I sat there day after day watching Walter Harrison fall helplessly in love with a woman he hadn't met yet. He fell in love with the way she waved until each movement of her hand seemed to be for him alone. He fell in love with the luxuriant beauty of her body, letting his eyes follow her as she walked to the water from the house, aching to be close to her. She would turn sometimes and see us watching, and wave.

At night he would stand by the window not hearing what I said because he was watching her windows, hoping for just one glimpse of her, and often I would hear him repeating her name slowly, letting it roll off his tongue like a precious thing.

It couldn't go on that way. I knew it and he knew it. She had just come up from the beach and the water glistened on her skin. She laughed at something the woman said who was with her and shook her head so that her hair flowed down her back.

Walter shouted and waved and she laughed again, waving back. The wind brought her voice to him and Walter stood there, his breath hot in my face. "Look here, Duncan, I'm going to go over and meet her. I can't stand this waiting. Good Lord, what does a guy have to go through to meet a woman?"

"You've never had any trouble before, have you?"

"Never like this!" he said. "Usually they're dropping at my feet. I haven't changed, have I? There's nothing repulsive about me, is there?"

I wanted to tell the truth, but I laughed instead. "You're the same as ever. It wouldn't surprise me if she was dying to meet you, too. I can tell you this . . . she's never been outside as much as since you've been here."

His eyes lit up boyishly. "Really, Dunc. Do you think so?"

"I think so. I can assure you of this, too. If she does seem to like you it's certainly for yourself alone."

As crudely as the barb was placed, it went home. Walter never so much as glanced at me. He was lost in thought for a long time, then: "I'm going over there now, Duncan. I'm crazy about that girl. By God, I'll marry her if it's the last thing I do."

"Don't spoil it, Walter. Tomorrow, I promise you. I'll go over with you."

His eagerness was pathetic. I don't think he slept a wink that night. Long before breakfast he was waiting for me on the veranda. We ate in silence, each minute an eternity for him. He turned repeatedly to look over the hedge and I caught a flash of worry when she didn't appear.

Tight little lines had appeared at the corner of his eyes and he said, "Where is she, Dunc? She should be there by now, shouldn't she?"

"I don't know," I said. "It does seem strange. Just a moment." I rang the bell on the table and my housekeeper came to the door. "Have you seen the Vaughns, Martha?" I asked her.

She nodded sagely. "Oh, yes, sir. They left very early this morning to go back to the city."

Walter turned to me. "Hell!"

"Well, she'll be back," I assured him.

"Damn it, Dunc, that isn't the point!" He stood up and threw his napkin on the seat. "Can't you realize that I'm in love with the girl? I can't wait for her to get back!"

His face flushed with frustration. There was no anger, only the crazy hunger for the woman. I held back my smile. It happened. It happened the way I planned for it to happen. Walter Harrison had fallen so deeply in love, so truly in love that he couldn't control himself. I might have felt sorry for him at that moment if I hadn't asked him, "Walter, as I told you, I know very little about her. Supposing she is already married."

He answered my question with a nasty grimace. "Then she'll get a divorce if I have to break the guy in pieces. I'll break anything that stands in my way, Duncan. I'm going to have her if it's the last thing I do!"

He stalked off to his room. Later I heard the car roar down the road. I let myself laugh then.

I went back to New York and was there a week when my contacts told me of Walter's fruitless search. He used every means at his disposal, but he couldn't locate the girl. I gave him seven days, exactly seven days. You see, that seventh day was the anniversary of the date I introduced him to Adrianne. I'll never forget it. Wherever Walter is now, neither will he.

When I called him I was amazed at the change in his voice.

He sounded weak and lost. We exchanged the usual formalities; then I said, "Walter, have you found Evelyn yet?"

He took a long time to answer. "No, she's disappeared completely."

"Oh, I wouldn't say that," I said.

He didn't get it at first. It was almost too much to hope for. "You . . . mean you know where she is?"

"Exactly."

"Where? Please, Dunc . . . where is she?" In a split second he became a vital being again. He was bursting with life and energy, demanding that I tell him.

I laughed and told him to let me get a word in and I would. The silence was ominous then. "She's not very far from here, Walter, in a small hotel right off Fifth Avenue." I gave him the address and had hardly finished when I heard his phone slam against the desk. He was in such a hurry he hadn't bothered to hang up . . ."

Duncan stopped and drained his glass, then stared at it remorsefully. The Inspector coughed lightly to attract his attention, his curiosity prompting him to speak. "He found her?" he asked eagerly.

"Oh yes, he found her. He burst right in over all protests, expecting to sweep her off her feet."

This time the inspector fidgeted nervously. "Well, go on."

Duncan motioned for the waiter and lifted a fresh glass in a toast. The inspector did the same. Duncan smiled gently. "When she saw him she laughed and waved. Walter Harrison died an hour later . . . from a window in the same hotel."

It was too much for the inspector. He leaned forward in his chair, his forehead knotted in a frown. "But what happened? Who was she? Damn it, Duncan . . ."

Duncan took a deep breath, then gulped the drink down.

"Evelyn Vaughn was a hopeless imbecile," he said.

"She had the beauty of a goddess and the mentality of a two-year-old. They kept her well tended and dressed so she wouldn't be an object of curiosity. But the only habit she ever learned was to wave bye-bye . . ."

ONE ESCORT – MISSING OR DEAD

Roger Torrey

1

The ad was so screwy I didn't want anything to do with it. But Miss Bryce was both worried and willing to pay me for the trip. Once more I looked over the unusual advertisement.

WILL THE LADY WHO LEFT THE YALE MAN CALL FOR HIM AT DARNELL'S TAVERN ON THE SAWMILL RIVER PARKWAY.

We left the car in the parking lot, and on my way to the door I said:

"This is a gag, Miss Bryce – and it didn't miss. You're falling for it."

She was getting her own way and so she was feeling a little happier.

"You wait and see," she told me. "There's something wrong. You just wait and hear what they say."

With that we went into the place.

It was very nice and the girl pointed this out to me with: "D'ya think I'd made a mistake about being here? I know what you're thinking – that I was drunk and got mixed up. But I'll even show you the booth we were in. It's *this* way."

She took my arm and led me to a booth about halfway down the dance floor. A waiter broke away from the bar and headed down our way. The floor was bigger than most places like that have, and the bar was at the end of the place. Booths all around the floor, with tables for two spotted out in front of them. And even as far away from the bar as we were I could see it was stocked with good liquor and a lot of it.

In other words the place had class.

The waiter came up and the girl leaned across and whispered: "That's one of them! One of those I talked with."

He was a tough-looking mug, and he came up as though he grudged having to give us the service. He was looking at me and paying no attention to the girl. I told him I wanted straight rye and water, and Miss Bryce said: "A Martini, please."

He looked at her then – one of those so-here-you-are-again looks.

"That's right, friend," I told him. "It's the same lady! How about the drinks?"

I watched him talking to the barman then, while the Martini was being mixed and when the order was being put on a tray.

The girl was speaking again: "You see? He knew me."

"Well, why shouldn't he? You told me you'd been talking to him about this missing man. He'd hardly forget a thing like that."

"I should have gone to the police," Miss Bryce said.

"Why didn't you?"

"Well – well, because."

"That's a swell reason," I began, and stopped because the waiter was back with the tray and with a check for the drinks already on it. He stood there, and when I didn't do anything about it he said: "There's the check."

I told him I saw it.

"I just got told not to serve this lady any more drinks," the waiter explained.

"Who told you?" I asked.

He jerked his head toward the barman and didn't answer.

I said: "If there's one thing I love it's a snooty waiter. This is a public place, isn't it? The lady isn't drunk, is she? So you'll serve us drinks and like it or I'll find out the reason why."

"I just do what I'm told," he said to that. And I retorted: "That's what I want, so where's the argument? If I tell you we want a drink you get it."

He turned his head then and beckoned for the barman, who came out from around his plank with one hand under his apron.

He was as hard-looking as the waiter, but he had a nice soft voice. He used it, saying: "Trouble, Luigi?"

The waiter said: "The guy's giving me an argument. I told him no more drinks for the gal and he gives me an argument."

The barman said to me: "Look, Mister! I don't know you and I don't want any trouble. But I'm running this place and I'll not serve that girl another drink."

"Why not?"

He came up right to the edge of the booth table and said: "Well, I'll tell you. She came up here just after I went on shift, and she gives us a story about leaving her boyfriend here. She claims she was in here night before last with him. She also claims that I was on the bar and that Luigi was, the one that served them. Now I was working that night. And so was Luigi.

"We just changed to day shift today. She wasn't in here or we'd have seen her. We haven't got any missing boys around here. The girl's maybe a friend of yours, but she can't come in here with a screwy story like that and get drinks served her. She made a scene, Mister. She called me a liar and she called Luigi a liar. So no drinks. Is that plain?"

Luigi said: "She's just nuts, is all."

I said to the barman: "You all through with the speech?"

"Why?" he asked.

"Because, if you are, get back to that bar and make us another drink. One for me and one for the lady. Now move!"

He did. Faster than I thought he would and entirely in the wrong direction. Toward me instead of toward the bar. I saw the light shine on the brass on his hand as he took it out from under his apron and rolled away from it, but I didn't have a chance. I was sitting down and cooped, with that booth table catching me at the knees.

The barman caught me on the cheek with the first lick. I didn't know where the second one landed until I woke up sitting in the seat of my own car with the Bryce girl alongside me. She had as nice a set of hysterics as I ever saw in my life. And it took me about a minute to decide my jaw wasn't fractured, and to find that my gun had been slipped out of its clip and hadn't been put back.

I didn't argue. I remembered we'd passed a gas station down the road and I drove back there in a hurry . . .

It seemed the best thing to do at the time and in the circumstances.

The boys at the station were not only nice, but curious. I managed to cut the Bryce girl off before she could tell them anything she shouldn't have. My story was that I'd stopped to pick up a hiker and that the guy had tried to bat me down and take my car, and that I'd shoved him off the running board.

The story went over, but I was praying no highway cop would come by and ask me leading questions. Fooling nice kids like those station boys and fooling a tough cop are two different things. I got the blood off my face and the girl quieted down. As I turned the car back toward town, she said: "Now what do you think? And what are you going to do about it?"

"I think you've got something. We were all alone there, and if you'd only been a little dopey they'd have never turned you down for drinks. You were with somebody, weren't you, and you were sober. And that slugging match came up too fast to be on the up and up.

"And taking my gun wasn't the right thing to do on just an ordinary little bounce, like I shouldn't have been given. That's a public place and they're supposed to serve the public. So maybe you've got something there. Maybe this boyfriend of yours is really missing from the place, after all. Maybe you *were* right. Maybe you *were* there."

"We were there all right. What are you going to do about it?"

The answer was so plain I thought she'd figured it out for herself. I said: "Why, I'm going to stop at the State Police station and tell the boys what happened. So will you. Then I'll swear to a warrant and we'll go back there with a bunch of cops while they shake the place down properly.

"I could pick up a cop along the road here, but it's better to go to headquarters and do it right. We've got such a screwy story they'll probably want to check on me before they'll go for it."

"We can't do that," Miss Bryce said.

"Why can't we? If nothing else, I want my gun back."

Miss Bryce then told me why we couldn't go to the cops on the thing.

2

It seemed that she and this missing boy, whose name was George Harper, were engaged to be married, but that they'd had a struggle getting that way. George was a wild kid, and papa and mama Bryce didn't think he'd do the right thing by their little daughter. He'd been in a couple of jams for drunken driving and his folks once had had to pay him out of a girl jam. Both families had money, or so I gathered.

The girl insisted that going to the cops was out. That I'd have to work it out in some way so there'd be no notoriety. She didn't want her folks to hear of it.

They'd been in this place the night before. And they hadn't been supposed to be in any place where liquor was sold because George was on strict probation.

For that matter, he was on probation with the cops as well. He wasn't supposed to take even one drink and drive his car. That promise was the only thing that had saved his driver's licence.

They'd got in an argument over the kid's drinking. The girl had given him back some sort of a class pin that seemed to mean a lot to her and then had walked out on him.

We came to the police barracks about then, and I parked just the other side of it while we went over it.

I said: "Look, Miss Bryce! This is all well and good. But if you're really worried about this boy the cops are the people to tell it to. They've got authority and I haven't. I'm not going to take a chance on losing my licence by busting into that place without a bunch of cops and a search warrant behind me. On top of that I've just found out it's too hard on the face and eyes."

"How much?" she asked.

Which is what I'd been working for. The more I thought it over, the less I wanted to go to the cops with a screwy story like the one I had . . .

I didn't go back until ten that night and I didn't go back alone. I took Whitey Malone with me, and I had a spare gun and a sap as well as Whitey. I figured I shouldn't take too much of a beating with all three, because Whitey, at one time, had been better than a fair middleweight. He was a little punchy, but he did what he was told to do – and that's what I wanted. I parked the car behind a bunch of others.

"So you got it?" I said. "I go in first and you drift in behind me. Wherever I park, you park near. If I get in a beef, you know what to do."

"Sure, Joe," Whitey answered. "And if nothing happens and you give me the nod I sort of wander around and look the joint over. That right?"

"That's right. Now you've got money and you're supposed to buy a drink often enough for it to look good, but don't get tight. If it comes to a brawl I'll have a tough enough time getting out by myself, without having to dig you out from under a table and carry you on my back."

"Don't fret," he said, sounding hurt, "I don't get loopy when I'm working."

I knew a lot better, but I was hoping he'd hold up that night. It was the stuff in bottles that had beaten him in the ring, not the men he'd fought.

So that's the way we went in, and we found the place about half full.

I headed for the bar the first thing. If the lad who had given me the bounce had told me the truth he and his waiter pal had been off shift for some time. And the only chance I had for trouble would be that one or the other was hanging around. If that was the case I wanted to find it out right at the start, because I wanted to look around a bit and I wanted Whitey to do the same.

But the two barmen who were working then were strangers and I saw no trace of the waiter named Luigi. I took a couple of drinks at the plank, then gave Whitey the nod and sat down at a table where I could watch the dancing. Whitey drooped an eyelid at me and headed toward the back and the men's lounge.

And he was still back there when the cigarette girl came by, with her cute little tray and her cute little uniform.

"Cigarettes, Mister?"

I'd have bought them anyway, but I was a cinch when I saw the pin that held her uniform blouse together. I'd had the Bryce girl give me a description of the pin she'd given back to the boyfriend, and if this wasn't the one it was a dead ringer. I paid for the cigarettes with a five-dollar bill.

"If I told you to keep the change, would you get a cut on it?" I asked.

The girl was pretty and she was smart. She nodded her head and said: "That's the boss just going behind the bar."

I looked at the boss and saw what she meant. He was little and hard-looking and the type who wouldn't let a dime out of his hands unless he was getting two dimes in return. And I knew how most cigarette girls have to turn in their tips.

I said: "Look! He's watching. I'll take the change back and meet you by the ladies' lounge. I'll pass it to you there. If you can't get rid of it back there you're not as smart as I think you are."

"What's the idea?" she asked, all the time counting me out the change. She wasn't in any hurry about it. The girl kept smiling and nodding and acting like cigarette girls are supposed to act with customers who are spending money.

I put on the same kind of an act, and said: "You know something it's worth twenty dollars to me to find out. The five is just so you'll meet me and let me tell you what it is."

"Watch when I go back," she told me. "You come back in about five minutes. I like to talk about things like twenty bucks, Mister."

I could tell by the way she acted that she figured I was on the make. It made me a little sore to be picked for a masher. But I'd walked into it and I was getting a chance to talk with the girl and that was what I was working for. She made her rounds and went out in the back. I waited the five minutes and went the same way.

The bar went about halfway across the back of the building, and the swinging doors to the kitchen opened at one end of it. Past this door was an open hall with a shaded sign on each side of it. One read: *LADIES*, the other *GENTLEMEN*. On the other side of the bar was another hall, but this one was curtained and there was no sign of any kind by it.

I took it for granted it would lead back to dressing-rooms for the floor show that was advertised as being on three times nightly. To be truthful I wasn't worrying about it much. I was thinking I'd stumbled on a lead to my missing George Harper if I worked it right and got any kind of break.

As I went down my hall I saw the girl waiting for me. It was quite dark, so dark that I could scarcely make out the dim outlines of the girl.

She said: "Okay, hot shot! Spring it fast! I've got to get back on the floor. I'm not through work until four."

I gave her the change from the five and said: "I'm law. I want to know where you got that pin that's holding your blouse together. I'm willing to pay for the information, and if I don't get it I'm willing to take you out of here right now. Not at four o'clock, but right now."

"Tough, eh?" she said, sounding very thoughtful about it.

"Tough enough."

She proved half smart right then. She said: "You're private law, if you're any law at all. No regular cop would pay for what he could get for nothing. Listen. I get through here at four and I ride back with some of the boys in the band. My name's Mary Ames, and I live on West Seventieth. Can you remember the address?"

I said I could and she gave it to me.

She said: "I can't talk now. I haven't got time. And I haven't got guts enough, either, Mister. You wait for me outside my place. I'll be there about a quarter to five at the latest. And I'm not doing this for the twenty."

"What for then?" I asked.

She said: "You wouldn't understand."

And with that the door of the men's lounge opened and two men came out. And after them a third.

The first one was the bartender who'd heaved me out of the place that afternoon. The second was a dapper little man about half the barman's size. The third was Whitey Malone. With the light from the open door on them they were in a spot where I could get a good look. And I looked even as I ducked so that the barman wouldn't recognise me.

I even looked long enough to see the little man with him had a scarred neck. The scar ran from just back of his ear down into his collar. The barman and his pal ducked into a door right across the hall from the one they'd come out of – a door that in that shadow I hadn't even seen. Whitey turned away toward the bar and dance floor.

I said to the girl: "Who was the big guy?"

"Oh!" she said worriedly. "Did he see us?"

I told her that I didn't think it likely; that we were probably too much in shadow. I didn't tell her that if that barman had seen me he'd have probably tried to repeat the afternoon performance, because I certainly didn't have either the time or the wish to go into that right then.

"You be in front of my place at that time," she said. "Hurry back now. I've got to go. Please! You don't know the chance I'm taking."

I said again that I'd be waiting for her and went back in the bar and dance place. As soon as I got Whitey's eye I nodded toward the door and paid my bar check and went out. Whitey followed me in more of a hurry than I thought he'd be in. I asked him if he'd found out anything.

"Just that you were talking to a girl in that back hall," he told me. "That's all."

"Did you see me?"

"Sure – not plain, but plain enough."

That gave me something to think about while I was driving back into town.

3

It wasn't until I'd been waiting a half-hour too long that I really started to worry. And at half-past five I started back alone. I had a notion to stop for Whitey, but all he was good for was a stand-up and knock-down fight. And I had a hunch it wasn't going to be anything like that.

I was right. Plenty right. I left my car way this side of the place, before I came to the bridge which was at least a half-mile this side of the tavern. I went up through the brush at the side of the road, too, making the sneak as quiet as I could. But, just the same, I barely put my head out of the bushes, and where I could see the place, when somebody shot at it.

It wasn't any mistake, either. It wasn't anybody potting at what he thought was a rabbit with a small-calibre rifle. The weapon was a heavy pistol. And when I ducked my head like a turtle and went back in the brush they tried for a lucky break and emptied the gun just by guess in my general direction.

By the time they got it unloaded I was getting away from there fast. I didn't have any reason at all to shoot back, even if I did have a dirty idea about it. And that wasn't enough. I stopped for breath and heard them chasing me.

One of them shouted: "He went this way, Sam."

The voice was over at the side, so I kept on heading down the general direction of the road, to where I'd left my car. And I pretty near got caught – because they figured I'd go that way and almost cut me off.

If they hadn't I wouldn't have found the car. I got to the bridge with them close enough behind so that I knew I'd never make it across without being seen. And I had the choice of making a target of myself or getting wet.

I took the latter. Ducking under the bridge with my gun out, I was ready to pop anybody who came in under there after me. The two of them who were chasing me stood right over me and talked it over.

One was the barman I'd had the trouble with. I knew his voice. The other belonged to a stranger, or at least I didn't recognise it. The barman spoke, and it was all I could do to understand him because he was out of breath.

"The skunk got away. It's the same guy, I tell you. The one I gave the heave-ho to this afternoon."

The other one said: "You damn fool! How d'ya know that? And if it was, why didn't you let him walk into something? What in hell did you start blasting at him for?"

The barman insisted: "It's the same guy. He was snooping around tonight, too, I tell you. It was him talking to Mary."

"It was probably some damn fool drunk wandering around the woods. Maybe some guy who ran out of gas and came up to the place looking for a borrow."

"He wouldn't come up through the brush, would he?"

The other man thought this over and finally admitted it wasn't likely.

Then he said: "To hell with it! If the guy tries to pull the cops in they'll laugh at him. He hasn't got anything except an idea. If they come up and say anything we'll tell 'em the guy must either be crazy or drunk. The place is clear."

"It is not."

"Why not?"

"Maury!"

The other man laughed. "Maury'll be okay! Don't you fret about Maury."

They left, and I let down the hammer of my gun and looked around. I was in mud to my waist and in water up to my knees. But what I was looking at was the back end of a convertible coupé sticking up out of the water just under the overhang of the bridge. The car was just about on its nose, with the back end far enough out of water for me to see it was a new green car.

And Miss Bryce had told me her missing boyfriend was driving a new green convertible . . .

The cops took it as a routine case because I didn't try to make anything else out of it. My story was that I had a leaking connection on my car radiator and stopped at the creek to fill up so I could limp into town and a garage. That I'd just stumbled on the convertible in that way.

That left the Bryce girl clear out of the picture, as far as the cops and the newspapers were concerned. The State Police sergeant said: "Anybody in it?"

I said I was afraid to look and that if there'd been anybody in the car they were certainly dead by that time. The car had been in the creek for some time.

"How d'ya know that?" he said.

"Because the creek's muddy, as you can see by looking at me. The water was clear around the car."

"Then why couldn't you see if there was anybody in it?"

I explained again that the car was tipped. Of course by that time he'd sent a pair of troopers to investigate the thing. It was just a natural police suspicion that was causing the questioning. Not that it made me feel much easier, knowing this.

Then I really got sick. Another trooper came in and said:

"They've checked that identification on the girl I found, sergeant. Her name was Ames, all right. She lived on West Seventieth at the same address as was on the letter in her purse. The city police just called in."

I hadn't said anything before and now I couldn't. The cops don't like it when you only tell half a story and sometimes they do things about your licence for the holding out. I looked

Roger Torrey

interested, and the sergeant said: "We picked up a girl alongside the road about an hour ago. She'd been thrown out of a car, it looked like. Another damn fool kid who let herself get picked up by strangers."

"Local girl?"

He shrugged and said: "New York. At least that's where she lived. The cops there just checked on it and verified it."

That was that. Darnell's Tavern wasn't even in the picture, though the city police would no doubt find out the girl had worked there. And when they found it out the people at the tavern would just say the girl left with some man they didn't know. The cops would put it down as a killing and let it go at that. Which is all they could do, knowing nothing about what had happened.

About then the two troopers who'd been sent to look at the car in the creek came back. They told the sergeant the car was empty and that they'd looked around and seen no evidence of anyone being hurt.

The sergeant sent the police wrecker after the car. I went back to the city to get some sleep – and to try for an idea that would break the thing up and still leave me in the clear with the police. I'd made up my mind that I was going to tell the police what I knew about the mess, client or no client – promise or no promise – if I didn't think of something by that afternoon.

The worst part of the whole business was that there was no proof of a thing. The Bryce girl had a screwy story and nothing to back it up. My story about having the date with the dead girl had no proof back of it – any more than my story about being shot at did. The cops would naturally think that young Harper had run his car off the road while drunk.

They'd believe he had left it rather than report it to the police. For if Harper went to jail on a drunken driving charge he would certainly have lost not only his licence but have spent a little time in jail.

The people at Darnell's would just blandly deny the whole thing. And the cops would believe them, because there was a logical answer to everything that left Darnell's entirely out of the thing.

There was a good chance of young Harper having been murdered. But there was no question at all about the Ames girl being killed to keep her from talking to me.

That's why I put the blame for her death where it belonged – on my own shoulders.

I live in an apartment hotel, a small one where the doors are locked each night at one. That's when the clerk closes up shop and the bell boys take over. Whitey Malone called me at four and said he was coming over – so Whitey gets credit for saving my life. He'd just walked in, looking very unhappy. I'd telephoned down for ice and soda to go with the whisky I already had when there was a knock on the door. Whitey was nearest it.

I said: "That'll be the ice, now. Open it, will you, Whitey?"

Whitey opened it and Luigi, the one who'd first refused to serve a drink to the Bryce girl at Darnell's, walked in. Back of him came the little man with the scarred neck, the one I'd seen with the barman the night before. Both of them had guns, and Whitey and I backed away.

"Over against the window!" Luigi ordered.

My gun was on the dresser, out of its clip. The man with the scar picked it up and started to slide it in his side coat pocket.

"Nice gun, Luigi!" he said. "The dope knows guns, I guess."

Whitey said: "I thought it was you, Maury! I thought it was you!"

The man with the scar looked Whitey over very carefully.

Whitey gave him a feeble grin and said: "If I was in trunks and didn't have quite so much fat around my belly you'd know me."

Maury said: "Whitey Malone, by hell!"

Recognising Whitey had taken his mind away from his business a second – and in that second Whitey moved in. Maury was handicapped by having one hand in his pocket and he'd dropped his gun muzzle a little in addition. And Whitey had always been fast. He slid in ahead and slammed the little man in the stomach. The little man expelled a whoosh and doubled over.

Then Luigi slammed his gun barrel against the side of Whitey's head. Whitey went down on top of the little man with the scar, but by that time I had both hands on Luigi's gun wrist.

4

He was shouting: "Let go! Let go!" and was pulling away and trying to get his wrist free. At the same time he was hitting me in the face with his free hand. He was off balance and all that, but it wasn't doing me any good.

My face was still sore from the beating I'd taken the afternoon before, and this was giving him too much of an edge. We wrestled around until we got close to where Whitey Malone and Maury, the scarred man, were on the floor. Then somebody got me by an ankle and yanked.

I went down to the floor, but I took Luigi's arm down with me – still holding to it with both wrists. Then I looked past Luigi's leg and saw the bell boy standing in the door, with a trayful of ice and soda and with his mouth wide open.

I yelled: "Get help! Help!"

It was the scarred man who had me by the ankle, because he said: "Hold tight, Luigi: I'll get him!"

I could also hear the bell boy out in the hall, shouting: "Help! Help! Help!"

If I'd let go of Luigi's wrist I'd have been shot. I had to take a chance on what the little man was going to do, and what he did was rap me on the head with his gun. But he was about half lying on me and had to reach up to hit. So all it did was make me let go of Luigi's wrist and fall on my face. I could hear, but I couldn't move.

Luigi said: "I'll get him right!"

The little man said: "Get the hell out of here! That hall's going to be full in a minute."

Then I heard them go out the door.

It seemed like it took me forever to get my face from the floor, but it couldn't have been long. I twisted my head and there was my own gun in reach. Getting it, I reached the door in time to see Luigi and the little man just at the elevator. Luigi was half in it. The little man was the best target and so I picked him and let go. He went inside and the doors slammed.

I said: "I missed! Missed him!"

I got to the telephone to call the desk and could get no answer. The operator was probably listening to everybody on the floor telling her about the fracas. If she had any brains she'd probably already have called the cops. I put the phone down and Whitey Malone said:

"Argh-gh-gh!"

Whitey was trying to sit up and wasn't doing well at it. I got him up on the bed and felt his head, where the gun had clipped him. But I couldn't find any sign of a fracture. Then one of the biggest cops I ever saw in my life dashed in with a gun in his hand.

"Hey, you! Hands up!" he commanded.

I said: "Don't be a fool! I'm going to call a doctor for my friend."

The cop said: "There's one downstairs. You killed that guy, didn't you?"

"I missed him, I thought."

"You missed him like hell! You shot his guts out all over the inside of the elevator."

"What about the other one?"

"He got away. You got a gun?"

"On the dresser."

He backed away from me until he got my gun. Then he said, a little friendlier: "What in hell happened, boy?"

Whitey's eyes opened then. He looked as if he was around enough to understand what I was saying.

I said: "I'm damned if I know. The two guys came in with guns. My friend here took a swing at one of them and then the battle started. I shot at one, but I thought I missed."

"You hit centre. Who were they?"

"I don't know."

"What d'ya mean, you don't know. A couple of guys don't just walk in and start trouble with a strange guy, do they?"

"They did, didn't they?"

"You're a shamus?"

"Licence in my wallet. That's on the dresser, too."

He looked at my licence. I finally got the desk and told them to send the doctor up. By the time he arrived there were a lot more policemen, the manager of the hotel, two newspapermen inside, with a dozen others trying to get in.

It would have taken a hall to take care of the crowd that wanted to join us. But when I mentioned that to the cops they chased everybody out.

I thought that was so they could question Whitey and me with a little peace and quiet. But I was all wrong. That was to give themselves a chance for rough stuff, if they decided any was necessary – but Whitey and I fooled them.

We didn't know either of the men. We didn't know what they wanted to do a thing like that for. We'd never seen either of them before.

In fact, we didn't know a thing.

We spent the next two days in jail and in different cells. But Whitey had the idea, and I wasn't worrying about him saying anything. In fact there wasn't a lot he *could* say. He knew nothing at all about the girl being found dead. I hadn't had a chance to tell him about that.

Whitey didn't know about my early-morning trip back, and about me being shot at and having to hide under the bridge. He wouldn't have talked anyway – he's not the talking kind.

The dead man was Maury Cullen, and he was a bad one. Cullen had served time for everything from plain robbery to manslaughter. He'd spent more time in jail than he had outside, if you counted the time he'd spent in reform schools while yet a kid. That was the only reason there wasn't more trouble about it – the only thing that kept my licence for me.

I left Whitey at my place when I met the Bryce girl. I'd called her house the minute I left the station. Finally I got the girl after going through a performance that made me think I was trying to talk with a railroad president.

I said: "This is Joe Shannon, Miss Bryce. I'd like to see you."

"I've been trying to get in touch with you," she said. "I've called your office at least a dozen times a day."

"There's been a little trouble."

"You mean – you mean that George is in trouble."

"I mean that I'm in trouble. Or don't you read the papers?"

"Well, no. I don't pay much attention to them. What happened?"

I told her I couldn't talk to her over the phone and asked her to set a place to meet me. She suggested the Plaza. And when I laughed she told me she often met people there. I gave her the name of a halfway decent bar and restaurant on the wrong side of town. She agreed to meet me there in an hour.

And she did. She came in looking flustered. The minute we were in a booth, she leaned across to me and said:

"I've almost gone crazy. Haven't you heard a thing about him?"

"You might as well get ready to take it on the chin, kid. I'm afraid there's no news as yet. And this time no news is bad news."

"I thought about that. I mean about George maybe being kidnapped."

"That racket's been out since the government men took over, Miss Bryce. I don't mean that he was kidnapped. It's worse than that, I'm afraid."

The girl got white and asked me if I meant he was killed. I said that was it exactly, waiting for her to break down all over the place, but she did exactly the opposite.

She said: "But why?"

Her face was so white that the makeup stood out on it in patches. But her voice was even and no louder than it had been.

I said: "I don't know. Did he have much money on him?"

"Very little. He just had an allowance, you know, and he was careless with money."

"Then I can't tell you, though I'm beginning to get an idea. It's nothing I can go to the cops with."

Then she said something that made me so mad I could hardly talk.

"If it's more money you want, Mr Shannon, I can pay it."

"There's been a girl killed over this mess," I said. "On top of that I've killed a man and spent the last couple of days in jail over it, even if I'm loose now. I damn near got killed myself, and a man who was working with me almost got the same. I've been beaten up and shot up and chivvied around by the cops, and you talk to me about money. Will your money bring back that girl?"

"I'm sorry," said Miss Bryce. "What should I do?"

"If you've got any pull at all, or know anybody who has, you can find out who put that blind ad in the paper. The ad that started this. They're not supposed to give out that information, but maybe you could get it for me. And if you've got the nerve you can go down to the morgue with me and look at all the unidentified bodies of men around the age of this George Harper.

"If he was killed and all marks cut out of his clothes, or if he'd been stripped, that's where he'd be. If I knew him by sight I wouldn't need you. Unless you want to tell his people the story."

"Why break it to them that way?" she asked. "And, besides, we're not sure yet. George had two little moles on his chest, and he weighed one hundred and sixty-two pounds. He was twenty-two. His hair was blond and his eyes were blue."

"That won't be enough."

She didn't change the expression on her face a bit as she said: "He had a birthmark – a strawberry mark I think you call it, on his left thigh. It was very large. As big as that."

She made a big circle on the table.

I said: "Okay, I'll go down and look while you try and find who put that ad in the paper. I'll phone you back in two hours, say. At your house. And listen! If I go through with this and get into trouble, will you tell the cops about it? I mean if I fix it so there's nothing to kick back on you or on the boy?"

"Why of course," she said, looking surprised. "It's only that I don't want to make trouble for my people and his."

We left it that way.

<h1 style="text-align:center">5</h1>

There was nothing doing at the morgue except that I damn near passed out while looking for the Harper boy's body. I'd told the cop in charge that my brother was missing and that I was worried. I gave a vague description that tallied a little with the one the girl gave me. The attendant took me around and showed me every man they'd taken into the place during the last three days.

On the third tray they pulled out of the wall was Maury Cullen – the man I'd shot. They'd done a P. M. on him and sewed him up with a swell cross-stitch, but I could see what my slug had done to him. He'd probably been dead before the elevator got to the ground floor.

The attendant said: "I don't suppose this one would be your brother, Mister, but to make sure you'd better look. He's a little older than the way you say it, but it could be."

I said: "No, but the guy looks a little familiar."

He looked at me and said: "It gets you, looking at these stiffs.

That is, at first. I'm sort of used to it. But at that I don't eat my lunch in here."

The place didn't smell like any lunch room to me and I said so. It smelled of iodine and chloride of lime and formaldehyde, but all that wasn't enough to kill the other smells. The attendant explained it with: "Some of these guys are taken out of the river after they've been in too long. Some of the others are found a little late. We freeze 'em and all that, but you can't kill all of it."

I got out of the place just in time to keep from being sick.

Miss Bryce said: "If he wasn't there that means there's still a chance, doesn't it, Mr Shannon?"

"I'm afraid it's slight," I told her. "What about that ad?"

"I got a friend of mine who knows a columnist down there to ask about it. It was a girl named Mary Ames who put it in. Does that help you any?"

"Quite a bit!" Then I told her that I'd keep in touch with her.

I hung up the phone, feeling even sicker than I had at the morgue. I remembered what the girl had said when I'd mentioned the twenty dollars I was going to give her for the information. She'd said she wasn't telling me anything because of the twenty, and I'd asked her why she was talking then. She'd said I wouldn't understand – and I hadn't then.

Finding about the ad gave me the answer. The kid had been sticking around and she'd seen he was going to get into trouble. She had tried to get him out of there without telling him anything that would hurt the place too much.

I didn't understand this last – but I had a notion I would in a very short time. In fact, just after Darnell's closed after that night's business.

That's when I planned on crashing the place.

We went in at half-past four. Just Whitey and I. We waited until the band boys had packed up and left and until most of the stragglers were gone. But we didn't wait long enough for any of the help to leave. I mean kitchen help and waiters and bar men. I didn't know who was wrong and who was right in the place. And I didn't want any of the wrong ones to get away.

The doors were locked, of course, so we went in through a window we opened on the dressing-room side of the place. I went in first. Then Whitey passed me the gun I'd made for him during the afternoon and followed it.

It was a good gun, but not handy for housebreaking. I'd gone into a second-hand shop and picked up one of the best guns the Winchester people ever made – an 1897 model twelve-gauge shotgun. That's the one with the hammer.

The new hammerless pumps are quieter and maybe they work a little smoother. But those old hammer guns never hung up and there was never a question about 'em being ready for action. All you have to do is pull the hammer back and pull the trigger.

I'd taken a hacksaw and cut the barrel off just in front of the pump grip. There were five shells in the barrel and another in the chamber, and all loaded with number one buck shot. That's the size that loads sixteen in a shell, and for close-range work that's just dandy. They're big enough to blow a man to hell and back, and there's enough of them to spread out and take in a lot of territory.

It was the logical weapon for Whitey, because he didn't know any more about a pistol than a cat knows about heaven. And he'd shot a rifle and shotgun a few times.

And he was out for blood. It wasn't that he'd been roughed up in my room at the time I killed Maury Cullen – because that didn't bother him. That was just a piece of hard luck to him. When I'd been knocked out and my gun taken from me no doubt the barman had rolled me and found my address and had remembered it.

Whitey had just happened to be calling when they came after me. It wasn't that. It was the girl being killed that was getting him crazy. And he was getting crazy, no mistake. He was a little punchy anyway, from a few too many fights, and when he got excited it hit him.

I whispered: "Now remember! I make the play, if there's one made. Wait for me and back me up. Don't start it."

He mumbled: "The dirty skunks!"

I went out to the front and peeked through the curtain shutting off the hall from the main room. There were still a few people finishing up their last drinks. But the lights had been cut and the bar was closed, and only one waiter was in evidence.

Quite a lot of noise came from the kitchen, and I figured

they'd be following the usual roadhouse custom of eating after the guests had left. So I went back to where I'd left Whitey and his shotgun.

"We're getting a break!" I said. "I think they'll all be together in the kitchen. Let's find the door."

Somebody found it for us. We were going down the hall toward the back of the place when a door opened just ahead of us and somebody stepped out. I could hear dishes rattle and heard somebody laugh. The man who'd opened the door turned away from us without seeing us, letting the door slam shut behind him.

He didn't get far. I didn't know who he was or whether he was right or wrong, but I wasn't taking any chances. I caught him just as he started to open another door. When he turned his head to see who was running up to him I slammed him across the jaw with the side of my gun. It's no trick – you just palm it and swing.

Down he went and I took a look in the room. It was empty and I went back to Whitey, who was just outside the kitchen door. Whitey was breathing through his nose, like he used to do in the ring.

I said: "Let's go!" and opened the door into the kitchen.

And I was in, with Whitey and the shotgun right on my heels, before anybody even looked around.

It wasn't the way I'd have put 'em if I'd had the placing. There were two guys in white aprons over in front of a big range. One man in a waiter's uniform was just in back of them. The barman who'd first slugged me was sitting at a kitchen table, alongside the one the dead girl had pointed out as being the boss.

Another waiter was leaning across the table and telling them something they were laughing over. One other waiter was right in back of them, and two men were sitting at the same table with their backs to us.

They didn't stay that way. The waiter saw by the look on the tough barman's face that something was behind him, and he swung. So did the two men by him.

The odds were all wrong and I was glad the shotgun idea had occurred to me. Nine of them and two of us – but the shotgun evened it a bit.

I said: "Everybody over against the wall. Jump!"

I moved the muzzle of my gun a little, and Whitey croaked: "Move!"

The two cooks and two of the waiters started to move. But they never had time to get to the wall. All hell broke loose – like I was hoping it would. The big barman stood up and brought a gun up from where he'd pulled it under the protection of the table. I shot him as near centre as I could. When he didn't fall I did it again.

He tottered and looked at his boss, just in time to see the front of the man's face go out the back of his neck. I swear it looked like that. Whitey's shotgun just blew his face off at that distance. One of the men who'd been sitting with their backs to us fell off his chair. He started to crawl under the table, but the other one stood up, dragging at a gun he must have been carrying in a hip pocket holster.

I took time and did it right. I lined the sights of my gun on the pit of his stomach and let go. Then he doubled up and fell straight toward me. He landed on his face, without even putting his hands out to break his fall.

Whitey's shotgun blasted out again. The waiter on our side of the table went back through the air at least three feet. It was as if there'd been a rope around his middle and somebody had yanked. Then the man who'd ducked under the table shot. I sat down on the floor without knowing how I got there. Whitey shot twice. There was a lot of thumping noise coming from under the table and no more shooting.

The two cooks and the waiters who were left were against the wall, but only two of them were standing with their hands up. The other two were sitting on the floor holding their hands on their legs and howling blue murder.

Whitey said: "You hurt bad, Joe?"

The slug I'd taken had gone through the fleshy part of my leg. I didn't think it had touched the bone because I could move my foot and not hear anything grate.

I said: "I don't think so. Tell those guys over against the wall to come over to me one at a time. I'll shake 'em down and you watch it."

Whitey said: "To hell with it. They're in this, too. They get the same."

I don't know yet whether he was bluffing or meant it, or was just a little crazy with excitement and didn't realize what he was doing. Anyway, he raised the shotgun and the men by the wall screamed at him not to do it. I shouted the same thing.

"Go out in front and collect everybody," I said. "Bring 'em in, customers and all. They see that shotgun and they'll mind you."

Whitey went out of the service door. He came back in a moment with a puzzled look and a bottle of whisky.

"There's nobody there and the front door's wide open," he said. "I thought you could use a drink."

I had the bottle up to my mouth when the big barman – the one I'd first shot – started to move. He'd fallen ahead, so that his head and upper body were across the table. Now he raised his head and looked at me, saying: "I *knew* I should have taken you and that girl out of the way that first time you came in. My name's Ames – I was married to Mary."

Then he put his head down again, but it didn't stay there. He slipped down on the floor, moving gradually at first, then hitting the floor with a bang.

Whitey said to the four men by the wall: "Well, you guys going to talk, or do I turn loose on you?"

They talked with that, and I didn't blame them. A dumb man would have found speech if he'd looked at Whitey and that shotgun, because Whitey certainly looked as though he wanted to use it.

I heard all about it in the hospital. It was a good hospital, too, and I had a private room. With the Bryce girl's father footing the bills.

Whitey said: "Yeah, the state cops found Harper's body back in the woods. One of them damn waiters showed 'em where to look. The kid got looping drunk and kept wandering around the place. Finally he walked into Maury Cullen and his two pals who were hiding out.

"The barman and Maury and his pals grabbed the kid, but they didn't knock him off right then. They held him down in the hideout room, in the basement of the joint. That's what the spot was doing as a side-line – hiding out guys who were plenty hot and willing to pay for a place to stay."

"That's what the cops said."

Whitey went on: "Well, the gal didn't want to turn in her husband, even if she wasn't living with him. She gets the idea that if somebody come looking for Harper they'd get scared and turn him loose. They didn't – they knocked him on the head and buried him instead. He'd been nice to the girl – he'd even given her his frat pin after his girlfriend had given it back to him. That killing got the girl. She wanted to squawk, but she was scared of her husband."

"She was going to talk to me," I said.

"But she wasn't going to let her husband know about it," Whitey explained. "He caught her and they knocked her off. Anyway, the whole gang were in the hideout racket and they're all going up. You know, Joe, I should have told you about Maury, but I didn't have the guts. I knew the guy the minute I saw him in the can.

"He was a bad one years ago. He'd come to me when I was fighting and wanted me to throw a fight. That's why I didn't want to tell you, see? I figured you'd think maybe I was crooked or something. Say! You going to get in trouble with the cops over this?"

"Hell, no!" I told him. "Bryce got everything cleared. The cops act like I've got a medal coming. They figured it cleared out a bad bunch they didn't know about. And then, Bryce pulls a lot of weight. It's all okay."

"Swell, Joe," Whitey said, beaming at me.

"Tell me something," I said.

"Sure, Joe."

"Did you throw that fight that Maury Cullen wanted you to throw?"

Whitey stared at me and said: "Why – hell, yes! D'ya think I'm nuts?"

DON'T BURN YOUR CORPSES BEHIND YOU

William Rough

1. One Corpse – Well Done

Slabbe lowered his after-lunch quart of beer long enough to rake in the busy telephone. "Yeah?"

Homicide Lieutenant Carlin answered. "That grifter you're looking for, Max Lorenz – we got him."

Slabbe changed the location of eight ounces of beer. "I should put you cops on retainer."

"Oh, you pay your license."

"Sure it's him, Pat? Five feet eight, a hundred and sixty pounds, light complected—"

Carlin cackled: "Dark complected now."

Slabbe's big hand on the telephone hardened a bit. "That so," he murmured.

"He was burned up," Carlin said. "He went over Bleeker's Canyon in a jalopy and it caught fire. Some Oybay Outscays found it this morning, what was left of it. Lorenz was in it – what was left of him."

Slabbe's meatblock face registered as much expression as a meatblock. "Accident, huh?"

"Am I a whirlwind?"

"They post him yet?"

"Doing it now."

"I'll be down."

Slabbe drank to the last drop, left his office and walked for ten minutes and entered City Hall. The morgue was in the basement. He filled his lungs with the relatively sweet corridor air before turning the knob of the autopsy room door, held his breath, nodding to Carlin, a rangy, slope-shouldered cigar-smoker in blue serge, and squinted at the charred stuff on one of the three guttered tables.

He said: "Dark complected is right."

Carlin never used a word when a grunt would do.

A pathologist who had rolled up his sleeves but hadn't bothered to don a gown said to another who was acting as medical stenographer: "It's a male. Been dead a while. Today's Wednesday, two o'clock. Say about Monday afternoon or night. Five feet eight'll do. Can't guess the weight much from the ashes."

Carlin tilted the stub of his cigar close under his long bony nose to mask the smells. "What else, doc?"

"Some lung tissues in fair shape. Tell you if he was breathing when the fire started."

"Suppose you do that." Carlin looked at Slabbe. "Any reason for him to have got knocked off?"

"No-o-o."

Carlin snorted. "When you say it like that, you might mean—" He stopped; his snort had yanked the cigar stub from under his nostrils and he'd sucked in a good lungful. He gagged, covered it, whitening. He started for the door, controlling himself, then peeked at another operating table bearing something that had been picked off a tide flat and upon which the median incision had not yet been stitched. He ran.

"Sensitive for a cop," murmured the pathologist.

"Don't worry about him," Slabbe said. "He can back me up any day."

"He shouldn't mind just one," the pathologist said. "Monday we had – how many was it, Joe?" he asked the other medic.

"Twenty-six. Twenty passengers and the crew."

Slabbe nodded. A Lockheed Constellation had cracked up on the take-off Monday at the airport and burst into flames. Everyone aboard had perished.

Slabbe pointed a frankfurter-thick finger at the operating table "That his thigh?"

The pathologist peered. "Yeah."

"Bullet in it?"

"See for yourself."

"Hard to tell," Slabbe said. "How about an X-ray? A slug, even if it was there, could fall out or melt up. There's supposed to be one in his left thigh, though."

"Oh, this is the right one. Here's the left."

"Still can't tell," Slabbe shrugged. "Check it, will you? Check too, if he was pushed around, slugged or like that before he died. A good sock knocks loose fat deposits and the blood takes 'em to the lungs, right?"

The medic looked up sharply. "How did you know?"

"Read it in a book," Slabbe said. He left.

Carlin had his pacing area of the corridor blue with cigar smoke. He grimaced. "I helped out with those bodies at the airport Monday and didn't even flutter, but today I had kidneys for lunch. Come on upstairs."

In his gopher-hole-sized office upstairs in the Homicide Bureau he went to the window and nursed two tall green bottles of ale in off the outside sill. He dealt one to Slabbe, fished for an opener.

Slabbe absently uncapped his bottle with his teeth. "How did you make him, Pat?" he asked. "Car license?"

"You're gonna bust your teeth some day." Carlin caught foam. "Yeah," he said. "The jalopy had a Pennsylvania license tag and I phoned Harrisburg and it was registered in Lorenz's name Saturday: '41 Chevvy, two-door sedan. What was he up to?"

"Well, I can't just say."

"That's dandy."

"Don't pop off now. He was a grifter and that's for sure, so he didn't just come here for the mountain air; but why he did come, I don't know. He got out of Lewisburg Saturday, which accounts for him buying a jalopy in Pennsylvania. This is good ale."

"What little bird told you this?" Carlin murmured.

"No little bird, an old buzzard – the New York manager of the Zenith Detective Agency. How come I had the weather eye out for Lorenz is I got a sort of tie-in with Zenith. No retainer, no contract or anything, understand. It's just that I passed along some dope on a guy they had on one of their readers once and they sent me a check for fifty bucks and said I was an alert investigator that they'd remember if ever they were interested in this neck of the woods again. So last week they wanted a line on Lorenz and called me. They don't want him for anything he *did*, they just want to keep him spotted for whatever he *might* do. Big outfits like Zenith find it pays to get there first sometimes."

"Don't educate me," Carlin sniffed.

Slabbe drank. "They probably had a plant at Lewisburg and found out that Lorenz was heading this way, and the old buzzard in the New York office remembers that I'm an alert investigator—"

"You said that."

"If I don't, who will? Anyhow, I didn't find out what Lorenz was up to here. I didn't even see the guy in the flesh."

"You saw the flesh, though. What was his rap in Lewisburg for?"

Slabbe held up an open palm, not quite as heavy and gray as a small granite grave marker. "The Zenith telegram didn't say. All it said was he was about forty, probably armed, always dangerous. Five feet eight, a hundred and sixty pounds, light complected, blond, natural teeth, brown eyes, a limp in the left leg from a slug in the thigh picked up in a heist of some kind, years back. I told the medics to X-ray for the slug."

Carlin stopped drinking abruptly. "You think it ain't him?"

Slabbe's shoulders moved like ponderous sides of beef, in a shrug that said nothing. "Today's Wednesday. He was sprung Saturday morning. It would take time to buy the jalopy and transfer the tags and about ten hours to drive here from Lewisburg. He could have hit here late Saturday night or Sunday morning, but I put some lines out as soon as I got the Zenith telegram Saturday and none of my people saw him . . . or so they say. That's why I contacted you and asked did you spot any strangers in town."

Slabbe put his bottle on the scarred desk. "The doc says Lorenz fluffed off Monday. Maybe the guy wasn't in a hurry to get here. Maybe he got drunked up along the road to celebrate and took his time, and never got to town at all. We should find out if he was in and did his stuff, whatever it was, and was on the way out again when he piled up, or if he was just heading in. Which way was the car going?"

Carlin's dark eyes were as gloomy as his voice. "No can tell. Bleeker's Canyon is a seventy-foot drop from the road. A car turns over going down and you can't say where it was heading unless skid marks show on the road, which they don't. The guard rail is gone in a couple spots and there's curves that if you come around too fast, blooie. The fire sure as hell made smoke and a blaze, though, but nobody reported it."

"Lonely stretch there," Slabbe reminded. "You might see smoke in the daytime, but the way the road overhangs the cliff along there, at night you wouldn't see any flames unless you had your head out the car window and had giraffe blood in your neck."

Slabbe got his bulk vertical again, tossed a gumdrop into the air and caught it on his tongue. "I'll talk to my people again. Maybe with Lorenz dead, they'll remember something."

"You'll also phone Zenith and say that the circumstances of Lorenz's death are highly suspicious, that the local police are baffled and that the services of an alert investigator are for hire."

"You're a cynical so-and-so, Pat," Slabbe said mildly, and went back to his office and did it.

The voice of the Zenith Detective Agency's New York City manager, one Enoch Oliver, purred as smoothly over the wire as one of the phone company's dynamos. It informed Slabbe that it would be most gratifying indeed if Max Lorenz were really kaput – but by all means to make sure.

Lorenz had first attracted Zenith's attention in 1922 when he burgled a New Jersey warehouse protected by them. He was committed to the New Jersey state reformatory May 8, 1922, and paroled December 20, 1925.

On August 12, 1928, he was committed to Elmira reformatory from Dutchess County, N.Y., for five years, for grand larceny. He was transferred to Dannemora, Auburn and Clinton prisons, being paroled from the latter March 10, 1931. Declared delinquent of parole, he was returned to Sing Sing September 16, 1931, transferred to Clinton and reparoled July 7, 1932. He was again declared delinquent of parole December 9, 1932, and returned to Sing Sing where he made an unsuccessful attempt to escape.

Transferred back to Clinton and paroled November 22, 1933, he was taken in custody by Dutchess County officers and sentenced to five years for burglary. Again he was paroled, on September 23, 1935.

He was arrested February 9, 1936, by Troy police for the Saratoga Springs headquarters, charged with grand larceny and the possession of a concealed weapon in connection with a hot car setup. He went the circuit of prisons and was released by commutation November 19, 1940.

"Busy little bee, wasn't he?" Slabbe told the phone.

Mr Oliver agreed absently, concluded the biography with: "In June 1942, Lorenz was arrested in Pennsylvania in connection with black market operations in nylon hose, sentenced September 12 to from four to seven years in Lewisburg, from which penitentiary he was released July 6, 1946."

A Zenith man planted in Lewisburg for the express purpose of welcoming strayed sheep back into a world of light – and incidentally learning their attitude and plans for the future, when possible – had tried to shake Lorenz's hand at the pen gate. He'd got the hand but in the stomach, together with Lorenz's "Scram, gum heel! You don't have nothing on me and you ain't gonna get nothing. You won't even see me around in a couple days."

Being the usual fearless type of Zenith operative, the man had oozed along in Lorenz's wake, nonetheless, had seen him buy the '41 Chevvy, had talked with the used-car dealer, learning that Lorenz hadn't been at all critical of the car, though he'd paid cash. Lorenz had said that he wanted a car for only a few days and then the hell with it.

While the tags were being transferred, Lorenz had gone to a respectable enough saloon and taken on a cargo of gin and bitters. At one point he had asked for a road map and had drawn a pencil line on it from Lewisburg to Treverton, and this was how the Zenith operative – snitching the map later – had surmised Lorenz's destination.

Slabbe clucked admiringly at the Zenith sleuth's ingenuity and inquired if the man had by any chance checked back with prison officials to learn who had visited Max Lorenz lately, and so on.

Mr Oliver said quietly: "We have been established in this business since 1872, Mr Slabbe."

"Excuse it," Slabbe said.

"It's excused," Mr Oliver murmured. "Lorenz's last visitor, on June 28, just eight days before he was released, was a man who operates a private detective agency in your town, Mr Slabbe."

Slabbe sat up.

"The name is Jacob George," Mr Oliver continued, "and it was he who deposited five hundred dollars with the warden to be paid to Lorenz upon his release, which, of course, explains how Lorenz was able to buy an automobile for cash. The price, incidentally, was three hundred and seventy-five dollars plus the cost of transferring the license tags."

Slabbe managed something about Zenith being quite a neat outfit. Mr Oliver passed this and purred that perhaps with this information in his possession Mr Slabbe might now do a bit more than he had in the past few days, if he hoped to be considered an alert investigator by the Zenith Detective Agency. The phone clicked.

Slabbe swore quietly but emphatically, jiggled the phone, gave a number and demanded of the female voice that answered: "Where's Jake, Susie?"

"I don't know, Benjie. Probably on a toot, the poor guy. Hasn't been in since Monday afternoon."

" 'Cause why?"

" 'Cause a client that was going to pay heavy got killed in that plane wreck Monday."

"Who?"

"We-ell, it's confidential."

"Look, Susie kid, you know me. Tell me. There's a guy dead over this, and if Jake hasn't showed since Monday . . . well, you better tell me."

"Benjie! You don't think—"

"Talk, cookie."

"Gee, yeah! Jake was working for Mr John Nola. He was tracing somebody for him for weeks. He had a big expense account and last week he was up to Lewisburg and said the job was practically cinched if his party showed up when he was sprung."

"Did the party show? Was he about five-eight, light complected, a limp in the left leg?"

"*Yes!* He came to the office about three o'clock Monday afternoon and he saw Jake and went right out. Jake called him Lorenz. On the way out he whispered to me: 'I'm taking him to Nola's home and we collect.' And about an hour later Mr Nola called and said Jake's job was done and that he'd put a check for a thousand dollars in the mail next morning. I called around for Jake, caught him at Fudge Burke's and told him. He said we'd celebrate that night, only a little later it came over the radio that Mr Nola was one of the passengers in the plane wreck and I guess when Jake heard that Nola had burned up and wouldn't be putting the check in the mail after all, Jake got burned up, too, and . . . Ooo, I don't mean it like it *sounds!*"

"Keep your snood on, honey. And I'll call you back."

Slabbe called seven numbers, said each time, "Seen Jake George?" and received four "Naws," one negative grunt and two "No, dearies." He called City Hall, reminded Carlin that this constituted cooperating with authority and relayed his information.

"We'll put him on the air," Carlin said. "What are you going to do?"

"See Fudge Burke," Slabbe said and went there.

2. The Bitter and the Sweet

It was a block-long edifice which, besides serving as rendezvous and clearing house for the underworld, rendered various public services, starting with juke jive for the kiddies and working up to pool, bowling, bingo, a night spot complete with craps and roulette and geisha girls.

One wall of Fudge's executive-type office on the third floor was slotted one-way glass overlooking the casino and bar. Slabbe handed over his compact .38 to an expert at the metal door and waded through the sponge-rubber-cushioned oriental rug, nodded genially to the candy man.

Fudge flapped a plump hand at one of the red leather club chairs. His dumpy body was a marshmallow. His face was a buttered bon-bon, topped with a puddle of chocolate syrup for hair. He said: "Trouble?"

Slabbe said, "Information."

"Candy?" Fudge pushed a hammered copper dish an eighth of an inch toward Slabbe. "Drink?" He flapped a soft hand at his private bar. Slabbe looked over the bottles of various nectars and liqueurs, shook his grizzled head.

Fudge said: "Such as?"

"Max Lorenz," Slabbe said. "Ex-con. See him here?"

The soft brown raisins of Fudge Burke's eyes moved lovingly over the hammered copper dish. He selected a chocolate-covered cherry and nestled it in his cheek, sucked experimentally.

He said: "I don't keep customers by advertising 'em."

Slabbe agreed solemnly, but pointed out: "He's cooked though, and that makes a difference. You can talk when they're dead, can't you?"

Fudge caressed the jowl that held the cherry. "I guess," he said and spoke to the watcher on duty at the one-way glass. "Seen a Max Lorenz, Slip?"

Slip didn't turn. "I'd say no even if I did, but I didn't."

"Know him?" Slabbe pressed.

"I would if I'd seen him here. Ten minutes after a stranger comes in down there, he ain't a stranger or he ain't in no longer. If he don't make himself satisfactory, he goes out."

Slabbe said to Fudge: "Slip isn't on twenty-four hours. How about the other watchers? Maybe they saw Lorenz."

"Charley's sick and Slip and Dink Quint have been on alone for ten days," Fudge said. "Dink'll be here later. You can ask him."

There was the sound of Slabbe's hand sand-papering his gray-bristled jaw line. He said: "Tough about John Nola going in that plane crack-up, Monday."

Fudge said delicately: "He was only one out of twenty-six. Why so tough about him?"

"Oh, prominent man and stuff," Slabbe said. "His silk company gives work to about eighteen hundred men. Son a hero in the Pacific. Didn't know Nola myself, did you?"

"To see," Fudge yawned. "The hero pays his dues here regular. Blackjack and craps player. Can't settle down, I guess, after what he went through. Maybe he's here now. Is he, Slip?"

Slip didn't turn. "Yeah. At the bar with that Reed biscuit. She's a lotta woman, but built."

Slabbe looked through the one-way glass at a couple half turned to face each other at the gleaming bar below. She was a lot of woman, he agreed. She was at least five feet eleven, a red-lipped brunette, an Amazon princess.

It was a job to look heroic beside her, but the livid scar on Prentice Nola's right cheek and his fierce blue eyes and the combination of sun-whitened hair and black bushy beard got him by.

"Looks more than twenty-seven, don't he?" Slip commented. "The beard hides all but that one scar. He was a pilot. He was strafing some Jappies on a move and cracked right up into them. Busted his legs but got a gun going and held 'em till his buddies come up. Nervous as hell. He can drink two bottles of Scotch and walk away from 'em. He just come from the old man's funeral."

"Never saw the girl before," Slabbe decided.

"Her first time here was Saturday night," Slip said. "She's staying at the Carleton Arms, registered from New York City. She picked the hero up, only he thinks he picked her up. Watch when she turns her head."

Slabbe watched, grunted. "What a beaut. Somebody must've hit that left eye with a roundhouse. She get it here?"

"G'wan, we don't let stuff like that happen here. She come in with it Monday night, says she bumped into a something, but not a fist. Barney McPhail, the houseman at the Carleton Arms, says no commotion around her except wolves she brushes off like nothing. Ruby Reed. New York City. We don't worry so much about babes as guys."

Slabbe tongued his gum out of a cavity and got it going again, said, "Thanks," and started for the door. Then he murmured: "Seen Jake George lately?"

Fudge Burke said: "Well, well. That's what you want, eh?"

"Guess I wasn't so cute," Slabbe sighed.

The chocolate broke and Fudge tilted his head back to let the cherry syrup ooze down a favorite channel. He smacked his lips, started scouting for another cherry and said: "Tell you what, Slabbe, come back when Dink's here. He saw Jake George. He'll tell you all he knows. He'll tell you when Jake was in last, what he ate and drank, who he went out with, what happened to him, all of it."

Slabbe's gray eyes were opaque. "Cooperation with a capital C. How come?"

For just a second Fudge's candy-eaten teeth showed. Then he turned it into a grin and chuckle. "Well, like you said when you came in . . . when they're dead you can talk."

"Yeah." Slabbe took a step, stopped. He did a double take. He licked his lips. "I heard it right, what you said?"

Fudge nodded.

"Then Jake's dead?"

Fudge nodded again.

Slabbe took a breath. "What—"

Fudge flapped his hand at him. "Don't heckle *me*. I told you Dink'll tell you. He'll be here at eight."

Slabbe glanced at his railroader's watch. It was three-thirty. "Eight o'clock, hell," he growled. "Where's Dink now?"

"Give 'em an inch and they want – Hell with it!" Fudge snapped. "Fairview Hotel."

Halfway through the metal door Slabbe caught himself, held out his hand to the guard. "Gimme my gun back."

Slabbe got out of the elevator in the casino and headed for the bar. At three-thirty in the afternoon a mere handful of fifty-odd citizens were anaesthetizing themselves. Slabbe jostled a half-dozen aside and came up beside Prentice Nola's football shoulders.

He said: "You're in a mood, Mr Nola, but this is important. Can I talk to you?"

The flick of the blue eyes was sharp enough to shave with, then dull. "A character," Prentice Nola said to his and Ruby Reed's reflections in the bar mirror. "A little man mountain who says I'm in a mood." He sipped his Scotch and soda. "Take off."

"I like Fred Allen, personally," Slabbe said. "But you're funny, too. So are dead men. So is life. So's your old man."

He moved back from the bar, fast, behind Nola. His hands made clamps on Nola's biceps, which were hard-packed as cables. It looked like a friendly gesture, but Nola couldn't move. Slabbe was set in case the bearded youngster put a knee against the bar and heaved backwards, but it didn't happen.

Nola said: "The longer you hold me, the harder I'll hit you when you let go."

"I take it back about your old man. It slipped," Slabbe said.

He looked at Ruby Reed. She was ready for something but waiting for the right spot. "Talk to him," Slabbe told her. "This is kid stuff. Two guys are dead so far. I'm a private dick."

Ruby's lips, red as red, parted ever so slightly. "It's absurd, Prentice, but let's not have a scene."

"OK?" Slabbe asked Nola.

Some of the tension went out of Nola's arms. "Let me drink," he said. Slabbe let him, waiting, then moved back alongside him on the left. The purple mouse on Ruby's left eye was several days old but still something to behold.

Nola said: "Spit it out. I'm still in that mood."

Slabbe nodded. "Your father hired a detective named Jake George. Maybe you know why."

"I don't."

"Ever hear of Max Lorenz?"

"No."

"OK. I'll be seeing you."

Nola's hand was the clamp this time, on Slabbe's right wrist, "No, you don't, big boy."

Slabbe started to use the necessary twist and foot-pounds to release his wrist without quite fracturing Nola's thumb, then stopped. The reason he stopped had nothing to do with the ex-pilot, it had to do with Ruby Reed. Her perfectly madeup face, stark white against the contrast of her upswept ebony hair, was showing no expression whatever – which was, of course, the giveaway.

Nola was saying: "I didn't pull my weight while the old man was alive, but maybe this did something to me. Maybe I'm interested in something – for the first time since they invalided me out."

Slabbe mumbled something, stared into the bar mirror. Ruby's green eyes were on him. Her lips moved, formed the words, "See me later." Slabbe winked into the mirror.

Prentice Nola snapped: "Why would my father have employed a detective?"

"That's what I asked you," Slabbe said. "Would I ask what I know?"

Nola's blue eyes burned at him. Softly, he said: "Men ask what they know to find out if anybody else knows. Especially dicks, big boy."

"Not this trip, junior," Slabbe said easily. "How close were you to your father?"

"None of your damn business, big boy."

"I can find out somewhere else."

"I'm scared."

Slabbe grimaced. "We should have a camera and sound truck. About here the director would say, 'Cut.' Let go of my wrist and get back on your bottle. Put milk in it. That's for babies."

Nola began to breathe the least bit deeper. The pupils of his eyes got small. Almost delicately, he released Slabbe's wrist, slid off the barstool.

Slabbe warned: "Five bouncers will be on top of us."

Ruby said huskily: "Prentice, stop!"

The words were repeated, and in a female voice, but not Ruby's. In a tinkling voice, a voice clear as tiny bells in a fine Swiss watch. "Prentice, stop that!" it said.

Prentice winced, looked over his shoulder as if there might be a chance he was hearing things, saw that he wasn't and moaned softly: "Good Lord, Aunt Serena, why didn't you bring the servants too?"

"Don't be rude, Prentice." The tinkling voice had the clarity of ice, now. "I'm sure this is a charming place to mourn your father, but you're coming home."

Slabbe looked at her. Her ancient, rustling black taffeta with lace at the throat suggested another century. Her white hair under its black bonnet might have been a powdered wig. Her companions might have been a retinue of lady-in-waiting and footmen. They were instead a little-girl-sized ash-blonde, a slender, tired-faced young man and a brute in chauffeur's livery.

The latter just stood there, yellow-flecked hazel eyes alert. The tired-faced young man put a hand on Prentice Nola's shoulder, said, "Come on, chum," and then saw Ruby Reed's green eyes gleaming on him and was done for – literally. His thin, high-cheekboned face was no longer merely tired – it was dead.

"Prentice is so confused," murmured the ash-blonde. "I know how he feels, I had nothing to live for, either, till Bill came." Her soft gray eyes went to the dead-faced young man.

Prentice mocked: "My Lord, sweetness and light at Fudge Burke's."

"Shut up, Prentice," ordered the tinkling voice. "Don't be sentimental, Ione," it told the blonde. "Start him moving, William," it prodded the object of Ruby's predatory gleam – not missing it at all.

It was then Slabbe's turn. "May I ask who you are?" the old woman murmured. "You were about to fight with Prentice, weren't you? You'd make mincemeat of him."

Slabbe tongued his chewing gum into a cavity, suspecting that it would offend. "I'm a private detective, ma'am. Benjamin Slabbe."

"Indeed. Prentice isn't involved with the law? He became intoxicated one night and forged his father's name to a check, but that was settled in the family, and he didn't do it again."

Prentice snarled: "Thank you, Aunt Serena!"

"Tchah! You can't keep things from detectives, you jackanapes." Her eyes were black moist olives, thirty years younger than the rest of her. She said to Slabbe: "I am Serena Yates, John Nola's wife's sister. You know Prentice. This is Ione Nola and William Teel, her fiancé. We've just buried John. We think Prentice should come home with us for the afternoon, at least. You're not arresting him?"

"No, ma'am," Slabbe said. "I only asked him if he knew why his father hired a detective named Jake George."

"I see. Did he know?"

"He said not. More likely – maybe – uh, perhaps you—"

"More likely I know?" Miss Yates provided. "No. I ran my brother-in-law's home for him, raised his children, practically, but I was not in his confidence about any monkey business. I'll be happy to talk with you later. Right now, we're leaving . . . Prentice, you're ready?" The black eyes seemed to notice Ruby Reed for the first time.

Prentice grimaced and performed the introduction. "Miss Reed. Yes, Aunt Serena, a casual acquaintance." Prentice patted Ruby's not-thin arm. "Excuse it, sugar. I'll see you later."

"By all means bring Miss Reed along," Miss Yates said abruptly. Everyone stared. Bill Teel's dead face threw off its paralysis to twitch protestingly.

Ruby was off her stool, chin up, sails set. "I'd love to come," she cooed.

"Of course, my child," Miss Yates said, black eyes gliding the length of Ruby's statuesque figure with no more interest than a python might have in its prey. She turned and the brute in chauffeur's livery took her arm solicitously.

Slabbe stood aside. As Ruby Reed glided past him, he whispered: "What time?"

Her lips didn't move. "Forget it."

Slabbe watched them leave, the little old lady in black on the arm of the hulking chauffeur, followed by Ione Nola and Bill Teel and The Drunk and The Body. He tried to dip up an appropriate rhyme or moral or parable, plodded to a phone booth.

He informed Carlin: "Ruby Reed at the Carleton Arms Hotel knows Max Lorenz, but don't pressure her yet – I got her dated whether she likes it or not. She came to Fudge Burke's place the first time Saturday night and picked up Prentice Nola, a drinker and gambler, who once forged a check on his pop. Doesn't seem like anything Jake George would have been called in on, though. He's dead, says Fudge Burke. How d'yuh like that?"

"Geez!"

"The docs find a slug in Lorenz's thigh?"

"No. They found false teeth in his mouth, though."

"So then it ain't Lorenz," Slabbe grunted morosely. "Zenith said he has natural teeth."

"Yeah. This burned guy had a skull fracture, too, before the fire started. The fracture killed him and the fact that there was time enough for some fat to travel to the lungs shows the guy was dead before the car went over the cliff. It's homicide."

"And Jake George had false teeth," Slabbe said. "And he left his office Monday with Lorenz. Lorenz dumped Jake into Bleeker's figuring Jake would be identified as him. It adds. Lorenz told the Zenith plant in Lewisburg that he wouldn't even see him around in a couple days. He told the used-car dealer he only wanted the jalop for a few days. He had it rigged, huh, Pat? . . . Hey, you there?"

Carlin grunted peevishly. "Yeah, I'm here. Stuck here. If I could get a civil service job, I'd leave here in three minutes."

"I know. It just goes to show you," Slabbe consoled.

"Show me what?"

"I dunno. Can't think of anything symbolic. How about checking the speedometer in Lorenz's car? We know he drove here from Lewisburg. See if the miles say he went anywhere else, huh?"

"What's about Jake George?"

"I'm checking that right now."

"Where can I catch you?"

"Wherever somebody burns a corpse behind 'em."

Evening chill laced the late April sunlight and toilers who had beat the time clock a little shuttled through the streets, as Slabbe stepped out of a cab in front of a moldy but not resigned brick building called the Fairview Hotel, and ferried his gray-tropical-worsted-clad bulk across the lobby. He wore the same weight clothing all year around, without topcoat, changed every day, but was not the best customer a tailor could have in the pressing department. About June he changed his gray winter hat for a white Panama.

The lobby was as large and as full as the ace of diamonds, the pip being a youth of sixty who drew salary as desk clerk. He gave Slabbe the number of Dink Quint's room, not ungraciously, not too hungrily and did not look too disappointed when there was no more to the transaction. Slabbe entered an automatic elevator, pressed the 5 button and braced himself as engineering noises clanked above and below him and the cage took off. On 5 he got out gingerly and rapped on Dink Quint's door.

A dry, tired whisper eddied from beyond the door, repeated itself several times before Slabbe's ears organized it. It was saying: "Come in. Come on in. For crissakes, are you deaf? Come in."

Slabbe tested the door, found it unlocked and filled it for a second and then was in a fairly spacious hotel cell. Dry, tired eyes checked him over. The whispering vocal chords sighed, and Dink Quint slid a small-wristed pale hand from under his pillow, made himself more comfortable under four blankets, reached for an eye-cup on the table beside his bed and began filling it with eye-wash from a blue bottle. Five colors stabbed and slashed each other in his silk pajamas.

"Snazzy pajumpers there," Slabbe admired. "Steal 'em from a Jap? I guess Fudge called and said I was coming?"

"I don't sleep with the door open," Dink husked and sat up and threw a shot into each eye. He was five feet three, a good hundred pounds after a steak dinner, with tiredness living closer to him than his skin – except when he was on duty in front of the one-way glass in Fudge Burke's office. Then he missed nothing.

Slabbe looked for a chair, dismissed the contraption as unfit for heavy duty and balanced himself for a stand.

He said: "Shoot then."

Dink put down his eye-cup, jacked a cigarette between his dry, tired lips and turned his thin face sideways so he didn't have to lift the match farther than necessary. He began to talk.

"Jake George came into Fudge's place Monday afternoon about three-thirty and had two shots and two beers while he was waiting for a sandwich: pickled tongue. He ate it and had a couple more drinks. He was killing time. He was ready to shove off again when he got a phone call."

"That was his secretary, Susie," Slabbe nodded.

"Yeah, a little after four o'clock. Well, when he was coming from the phone booth, all smiles, a guy steps up to him and his smiles go away, and I see the guy has a rod on Jake. In his pocket, the rod was, but I see stuff like that."

"Who was the guy?"

"So I says to Fudge – he was eating a candied apple – 'Fudge, a guy just put a rod on Jake George and took him out. Does he get away with it?' Fudge says, 'See what's up, Dink – Slip'll take over.' I chase after Jake and the guy, follow them. The guy has a car. He makes Jake drive."

"Who was the guy?"

"Jeez, you got patience! Ike Veech."

Slabbe's lips pulled back as if he were going to whistle between his teeth. "Ike Veech," he said softly, "wouldn't kill his old lady for less than a C-note. Where'd he ride Jake to!"

"Lilac Lake," Dink said. "A cabin up there. Going into it, he cut Jake down."

"Hard enough to kill him?"

"No, not then," Dink said judiciously. "He just rocked him to sleep and then cooked himself some supper. Boy, it made me hungry." Dink sighed. "I hung around a long time, and it was bacon he made: I smelled it."

"OK, OK."

"After dark about eight o'clock another guy drove up to the cabin and went in. Him, I don't see clear. No moon or nothing, and they had the curtains pulled. Say another hour, and the two of them bring Jake out, not on his feet, and put him in the back of Ike's car. He was no more Jake then. You can tell by the sag and slop of 'em when they're meat."

Slabbe wet his lips. "Uh-huh?"

"The other guy jumps in his car and starts off. I figure he's my pigeon now and go after him. But – you dumb slob!" Dink screeched, with the first show of vitality in his voice. "You let him follow you here!"

Slabbe was stone. There was life in Dink's murky hazel eyes now, bright life, life that wanted to stay life. Dink's cigarette glowed cherry red, though the rest of him, except for the eyes, was rigid.

There was no need for Slabbe to look around. He said woodenly. "Who is it? Ike?"

Dink didn't move. The door behind Slabbe closed delicately. "It's me, yeah," said Ike Veech's twang. "Nuh-uh, don't turn yet."

3. Death at the Door

There was a gliding, stealthy sound behind Slabbe. A hand gentle as air moved over him, found his armpit clip, whisked out the compact .38 he carried. The air stirred again as Veech drew back. The .38 hit the floor.

"You can turn now, not fast," he said through his nose. He added reprovingly: "You never were mouthy, Dink. How come?"

Slabbe pivoted, but slowly. Ike Veech's dapper shoulders were against the door. The .32 in his gray-gloved hand was carelessly assured, his shiny patent leather slippers were flat on the floor. His dark liquid eyes roved only as much as necessary between Slabbe and Dink on the bed.

Slabbe defended himself to Dink. "He wasn't on me when I came in."

"Why, no," Ike Veech, agreed sympathetically. "A guy built like you ain't hard to trail, though."

"Lissen, Ike," Dink said fast. "I don't talk unless Fudge says so, see? And he knows I know, and you don't walk in on him, brother. He takes care of his guys, too. You better take it easy with me."

"What's the color, Dink?" Veech chuckled.

"White! Go to hell! I'm just telling you. Give it to me and see. Fudge'll have Slip and Tommy and Pointer run you down even in South America."

"Shuddup!"

"Sure!"

"Why didn't you shuddup right along? A rat's a rat."

"—you!" Dink said. "Fudge liked Jake George. I don't know why. Maybe Jake sent him a box of candy once. He told me to tell Slobby here what I seen, so I tell him. I didn't tell him about the guy with you 'cause I didn't make him. Like I was just saying, I start after him when he pulls out after helping you dump Jake in your car. Only my jalopy is parked away from the cabin so's you wouldn't hear me start up, and while I'm running for it, your partner gets a start. I try for about five miles but don't catch him, then I come back to the cabin to see what you're gonna do with Jake's body, only by then you're gone too. That's a lot I know, isn't it? And would I tell it in court? You don't have to touch me—"

"Shuddup!" Ike Veech stirred the air with his gun barrel, in Slabbe's direction. "He goes. That's for sure."

Dink let his pillow have him again. His teeth chattered just a little, stopped. He might have been a bit tireder than normally, but the difference was too slight for Slabbe to judge. He knew Dink had talked his way out of it, though. Dink knew, too.

He said wearily to Ike Veech: "Not here. Not now. Take him out."

Veech frowned, cocked his pearl-gray fedora back on crisp black curls with a casual twist of the gun barrel. "It has to be here," he decided. "I wouldn't fool with him in an elevator or like that."

"Not with *me* here!" Dink squeaked. "The johns would put me through the wringer. I'm not taking that."

Veech's voice snarled: "Get out, then!"

"I'm not dressed."

"*Get* dressed!"

"Yeah. OK. Watch him now."

Dink flung his blankets aside, came to sitting position, swiveled to get his feet over the edge of the bed. And while he did this, his scrawny wrist disappeared under his pillow and he brought it around, pillow and all, and shot three times like that.

Two of his slugs missed Ike Veech completely. One of them, the second probably, took Veech in the midsection.

Slabbe was on the floor.

Veech cursed loud and bitterly. He emptied his gun at Dink.

He was curdling at the knees, though. Slabbe didn't know it and got his hand on his .38 and turned it up, butt braced on the floor. He shot twice, held the third because he saw, by then, that Veech's gun was pointing at nothing but the ceiling. Presently Veech's head and open eyes were, too.

Dink still had the pillow in his lap, only now he was trying to hold something together with it. It was smouldering, and little curls of acrid smoke twisted into his face. They were not dispelled by any breathing for an interval.

Slabbe got to a knee, stood, reached to slap the pillow out.

Dink wouldn't – or couldn't – let it go. His voice had never been tireder. "It wasn't Fudge that liked Jake George," he said. "It was me. Jake helped me get a divorce and put my kid in a good school, years ago. That's why I sang. If I'd-uh had guts, I'd-uh gone into that cabin. Honest, I didn't think they were gonna g-give it to him, though."

Slabbe stopped trying to pull the pillow away. There was no flame in it and Dink didn't seem to mind.

Slabbe said: "You didn't make the guy Ike was working with?"

"Honest, no. The car, though, I know it good. A twelve-cylinder Caddy. That bigshot's, John Nola. You can take it from there, huh?"

Dink bent in the middle over the pillow.

Carlin's dark eyes smouldered on the burnt pillow which a medical examiner had pried away from Dink Quint's middle. He said: "Damned if it wouldn't have been another corpse burned behind you, at that." His cigar jutted suspiciously Slabbe's way. "Did you smell this coming?"

"I read it in Dink's palm, yeah," Slabbe said. "Don't be that way. I told you just how it happened."

"Don't you always – *afterwards?*"

"Let's eat, Pat."

"You stay right where you are!"

"C'mon, I'll buy."

"You'll . . . Well, OK then." Carlin issued instructions to his squad, stepped long legs over Ike Veech's body by the door. Slabbe followed. They went to a chophouse, ordered.

"I hated to do that," Slabbe said. "Shoot Veech, I mean. He could have busted it wide open for us, maybe, if he knew why he helped kill Jake George. I wonder did he, though."

"Gun for hire was all he was," Carlin shrugged. "Lorenz just picked him up to do a job."

"Lorenz, huh?" Slabbe mused. "You think it was Lorenz in that Caddy that came to the cabin to meet Veech?"

"Don't *you?*"

Slabbe's shrug was as informative as the booth walls.

"He ain't saying," Carlin informed his steak. "Here's my end: Jake George traces Max Lorenz for John Nola, puts five hundred bucks on the line with the warden for Lorenz to come here soon as he's sprung. Lorenz does that – incidentally, we accounted for him along the way."

Slabbe looked up.

Carlin said: "He kept on drinking after he left Lewisburg and Sunday night a Statie flagged him down up the line, shooed him into a tourist place to sleep it off. Lorenz left the tourist place Monday morning about eleven, which would put him down in town just about three."

"Uuh," Slabbe said in congratulation.

"So he went straight to Jake George's office and Jake took him to Nola. Then Jake left and went over to Fudge Burke's to buy himself a drink on the deal. I'd say that Lorenz came together with Nola and then got Ike Veech to take care of Jake. Don't ask why yet. Jake was a mouth that might have shot off, maybe. Anyway, Ike Veech took Jake up to Lilac Lake and waited further orders. Chances are that he had Lorenz's Chevvy to work with, right? So that night Lorenz shows up in Nola's Caddy. They scrag Jake and put him in the Chevvy and take him to Bleeker's Canyon, douse the jalop with gas and roll it over. Pick a hole in it."

"Nola," Slabbe said. "Upstanding citizen, pillar of the community and so on. He wouldn't be in it."

"Nuts. He wouldn't *have* to be in on the killing, I'll give you, because he was burned up in that plane when it took off at four o'clock Monday afternoon, while Jake wasn't killed till that night. Maybe *because* Nola died, Jake died. Maybe with Nola out of the way by a pure accident, Lorenz had whatever it is all to himself and wanted to close mouths. Yeah, why not? The first order to Veech was only to hustle Jake up to the lake. It wasn't until Lorenz showed up at night that Jake got killed. See, with Nola alive Lorenz was only going to keep Jake shut up for a while. With Nola dead, he decides to shut Jake permanent."

"Chew that canary good before you swallow it," Slabbe advised. "Did you check the speedometer readings on the Chevvy? Was it burned too bad?"

Carlin leered. "I only got two hands and a dozen guys on the squad. It's being done. I already telegraphed the used-car guy to see what the reading was when Lorenz took over the car, or if the speedometer was turned back. That's a waste of money – I never saw a used-car guy yet that didn't turn 'em back."

Slabbe sandpapered his jaw line. "While you didn't have anything else to do this aft' I guess you checked on Nola some, huh?"

"Dry up, you comic," Carlin spat. "I want to enjoy this steak . . . Yeah, like you said, he was okay from A to izzard. He lived here all his life and was the kind of guy who doesn't even go through stop signs. How he tied in with Max Lorenz maybe a tea-leaf reader could tell us."

"We could see if he had made his plane reservation in advance or if he grabbed it at the last minute," Slabbe said. "If he jumped on a plane without warning, it could mean he learned something from Lorenz that made him travel. Where was the plane heading, Pat?"

"Just New York City. Everybody was checked into their seats, too, the plane took off on time, four o'clock and all the corpses were accounted for. What I don't get is—"

"Don't try thinking yet," Slabbe cut in. "We haven't got enough, we'll just get ballixed up. Why don't you come along with me and meet the people?"

Carlin made a weighing sound through his long bony nose.

"You're damned polite – when you know I'm going to stick closer to you than your hat anyhow!"

Way out in Treverton Heights was money: wide boulevards, wider lawns, tall trees, taller houses, brighter stars, cleaner air, soundless – and a beat cop who said, "Yes, sir. Good evening, sir," when Carlin cut his black departmental sedan into the curb and called: "Hey, you."

Slabbe said: "Can I chew gum in this neighborhood, Officer?"

"Of course, sir."

Carlin grimaced. "Take off your disguise, Flaherty."

"Oh! Good evening – I mean, Hi, Lieutenant. What's up?"

"Chisel any meals in the Nola kitchen?"

"Uh—"

"Relax. I had a tour up here myself, once."

"Well, yessir."

"OK. Gossip with us."

"About the Nolas, Lieutenant? Well, they just had a death in the family."

"We know. Who all lives there?"

"Just Miss Yates, Mr Prentice, Miss Ione and Bill Teel now – and the servants."

Slabbe clucked at the sprawling white colonial-style mansion, silvery in the moonlight. "You could make a dozen apartments in that left wing alone."

"Who's Bill Teel?" Carlin asked.

"War buddy of Prentice's," Flaherty said. "Nice-looking guy about twenty-six, only the war made him look older. He's going to marry Ione, and that makes 'em both lucky. Her first boyfriend got it in Germany and she walked around here without eyes for months, the old battle-axe just as bad – uh, I mean Miss Yates. Then Prentice brought Bill Teel home and the girl fell for him and everything's okey-doke. I guess him being a returned soldier and her other boyfriend being a soldier that wasn't coming back, it was easy for her to what'chacallit."

"Transfer her affections," Slabbe said. "You say Miss Yates was busted up too?"

"On account of Ione, yeah. You'd think she was the kid's real mother, and, well—" Flaherty dropped his voice confidentially –

"this is just kitchen talk now, but there are some that say Miss Yates *could* be Ione's right old lady, at that."

Carlin said: "Pour Mrs Flaherty another cup of tea, and let's get cozy."

"Aw, Lieutenant, you asked for gossip, didn't you? They say that years ago it was a toss-up as to whether John Nola would marry Miss Yates or her sister, Agnes, the one he did marry. Then when Ione was on the way, *both* the sisters went to France and came back after the baby was born and then right soon Mrs Nola died and Miss Yates stayed on at the house ever since, taking care of everything. And John Nola never got hitched again, so what do you think?"

Carlin said sourly: "I think that's just fine, a lot to go up against them with."

Slabbe asked: "Ever see Jake George around the Nola stadium here, Flaherty?"

The beat cop said no, he was on duty nights mostly.

"Monday night then," Slabbe said, "you might've seen the Nola Caddy breeze in and out, huh?"

"Heck, there were lots of bigshot cars in and out here Monday night, friends coming to sympathize about Mr Nola and all."

Carlin said: "All the folks at home then?"

"Yessir."

"Except," Carlin sniffed, "that with cars in and out, any of them could have been in and out in them."

Flaherty shuffled. "I guess, sir."

Slabbe held up two criss-crossed fingers thicker than the knot in an old-fashioned giant pretzel, and asked hopefully: "A light-complected guy, Flaherty, five-eight, limp in the left leg; make him around here anytime?"

"A grifter?" Flaherty asked.

Slabbe leaned forward. "You got it."

Flaherty shook his head ponderously. "Nope, nobody like that."

Carlin groaned. "Go for a walk, Flaherty."

He jack-knifed bony legs out of the sedan, complaining to Slabbe: "These kind of people are very tough or dumb. I don't know just what to fish for, except to find out if one of them knows why Nola wanted Max Lorenz."

Slabbe followed him up a flagged walk that was almost a

double-lane driveway. He observed the lawns, trees, shrubbery and outlying buildings. "Good place to play cowboys and Indians."

A dark, bulking shadow drifted in behind them, said: "Yeah. Which one of you is Tonto and which is the Lone Ranger?"

Neither Slabbe or Carlin looked around. They kept walking. Slabbe said conversationally: "Without looking, I'd say this is the chauffeur."

Carlin said: "A college man?"

"Dartmouth or Dannemora," Slabbe agreed.

The voice behind them said sneeringly: "You read that in *Murder, My Sweet.*"

Slabbe said: "The book was called *Farewell, My Lovely.* You're thinking of the picture. You saw me at Fudge Burke's place. This is Carlin, Homicide."

"He doesn't need a sheriff's star on his chest. What are you heckling these people for? Prentice is a lush. Ione's in love with love. Bill Teel's weak with a touch of malaria, and Miss Yates will tell you to go to hell."

"Let her tell us herself," Carlin snapped.

"John Nola didn't take any of them into his confidence," the chauffeur said, shoulder to shoulder with them now, but considerably taller.

"He did you, though, I guess," Carlin sneered.

"Yeah, he did me, though, you guess."

"Just a second, Pat." Slabbe stopped, faced the chauffeur. In the dark their silhouettes could have doubled for part of the scenery: Slabbe for one of the fuller evergreens, the chauffeur for a medium-sized oak.

Slabbe said genially: "I always like to hear small talk in the evening. What's your name, bo?"

"Mister Alan Hurst to you, big boy."

"You heard Prentice call me that. Ernie Hurst any relative of yours? Ernie and I had adjoining suites in the tank once."

"My brother."

Slabbe studied the man's heavy face, thick neck, powerful shoulders. "You don't look much like Ernie. He's about as wide as a hatchet blade."

"Yeah," Hurst said. "My old man took one look at me and bought an electric ice box."

"You got a record?" Slabbe asked.

"A record of clean living, thank you."

"Turn it on, then."

"As one citizen to another, you could go dip your head in shellac," Hurst said. "To give the people inside a break, OK, I'll tell you! I took eight or nine hundred lickings from my old man, then gave him a daisy and took off. Ernie stayed, and maybe that's why he's such a runt. I bummed around, then Miss Yates caught me snitching pears off one of those trees in the back. She gave me a break. I was sixteen. I've been the chauffeur around here for fifteen years. I got a bad heart, believe it or scratch, so I wasn't in the Army. A chauffeur gets close to his boss, so I know why Mr Nola wanted Max Lorenz, and it doesn't have anything to do with the rest of the tribe."

Slabbe nudged Carlin. "I could go a bottle of beer while we hear this."

"Huh?" Carlin said. "Oh, sure. But there ain't a saloon in this neighborhood."

"Come on, I'll buy," the chauffeur said. He started across the lawn toward the garage. Slabbe winked at Carlin. They fell in: two longs and a short.

4. Land of Silk and Money

Alan Hurst said: "You Dick Tracys want Max Lorenz, right?"

Slabbe and Carlin exchanged glances over their beer bottles. Carlin said to Hurst: "Go ahead."

"You want to know why John Nola wanted Lorenz, too, right?" Hurst asked. "Go ahead, you both grunt together now."

Carlin scowled. "We could do this downtown, too, if you're so big for your pants."

"I'm pale," Hurst said. He lounged back in a well-worn, leather-upholstered rocker, his yellow-flecked hazel eyes amused at Slabbe and Carlin, across the room. They were in his spacious quarters on the second floor of the Nola garage – bedroom, bath and roomy sitting room.

Hurst stretched long black-putteed legs in front of him, yawned absently and undid the top couple buttons of his gray tunic. "You won't find Lorenz in a hurry, if at all," he said reflectively. He removed his visored cap and ruffled thick dark brown hair with a paddle-sized hand.

Slabbe chewed gum solemnly, suggested to Carlin: "Let's go halfway with him, Pat."

"Nuts," Hurst said. "You don't have to do me favors. I'm doing you one. I'll be handing you stuff that it would take you months to get on your own – if you *ever* got it."

Carlin's bony nose came forward. "Get to the point, son, get to the point."

"Gladly, sir, he said," Hurst mocked. "I know how you johns work, so I want a concession."

Carlin snapped: "What does that crack mean?"

Hurst shrugged. "Just that you're interested in getting your own chores done, not some other cops' in some other town or county or state."

"Yeah?" Carlin challenged.

"Oh, relax," Hurst said. "I'd hate to be hanging since the last time you were to Sunday School."

"I knew it," Carlin said thickly. "Wasting our time." He started to get up.

"Wait," Hurst frowned. "I'm saying what I'm saying—"

"Trouble is you're not saying *nothing!*" Carlin spat.

"I will," Hurst returned. "But only because the old girl up at the house there gave me a fair shake when anyone else would have seen me in reform school and now I can do her a favor back for it."

"Miss Yates, huh?" Slabbe said. "Then she's in it?"

"She is like hell. Ione's in it. I mean Bill Teel's in it, not Miss Yates."

"Clear as hell, ain't it?" Carlin sneered.

Hurst's wide dark face tightened. "Give me a chance, I'm getting there. Miss Yates is nuts about Ione, so anything that hurts the kid hurts her, that's all."

Slabbe nodded. "And anything that hurts Teel hurts Ione and that hurts Miss Yates, that it?"

Hurst nodded in return. Carlin said: "Well, we got together for a second."

"Grow up, will you?" Hurst drawled. "OK, I'll pull out the stops. Here it is – Ione's boyfriend got it in the war and she's always been a romantic drip and she almost blew her top. She was in a fog for months—"

Slabbe murmured: "Is Ione really Miss Yates' daughter?"

"I don't know. I guess. What's the odds?" Hurst shrugged. "She loves her like her own, which is the thing. Anyway, then Prentice came home with Bill Teel and Ione fell for him. So it was OK for a while. Teel seemed like a swell guy. He knew something about the silk business and pitched right in and really did a job. He did what the old man hoped Prentice would do, I'd say. You know, take the business to heart and so on."

"Nola liked Teel?" Slabbe asked.

"Yeah, at first. I'm coming to that. Nola thought Teel was OK. The guy was a returned soldier and all that, and he was making good. The hitch came when the date was set for Teel and Ione to marry. The old man must have figured it was time to know a little more about Teel."

Carlin smacked his lips. "So Nola hired Jake George to look Teel up."

Hurst nodded easily, though his yellow-flecked eyes were veiled. "That was a couple weeks back. Jake George poked around – how do you go about tracing a guy? Look up his record in the service if you can, see where he enlisted, talk to draft board, huh? Me, I'd just go through the guy's stuff and look for letters and addresses and so on."

"You could do it a couple ways," Slabbe encouraged. "Jake did, hey? Got a line on the boy?"

"Yeah. Traced him back to a silk mill in Scranton, Pennsylvania, which explains how he knew something about the business in the first place."

Slabbe rubbed some wrinkles out of his lightweight gray trousers along the thigh. "Now we start to tie in a little," he said. "Max Lorenz was picked up in Pennsylvania for this last rap in a black-market nylon setup. Nylons mean silk. Teel worked with silk. Carry on."

The big chauffeur took his time over a swallow of beer almost as copious as Slabbe could manage. "Well, Teel was in on that black-market deal, whatever it was," he said. "His name was Walter Evans then and he was a foreman in the shipping department in this Scranton mill, and Max Lorenz got to him

– this is all what Jake George reported to Nola, understand? When the setup blew up on them, Teel lammed and joined the army under the name he's using now. Lorenz took a rap, but didn't split on Teel, so I honest-to-God don't think the Scranton cops or the Feds could make a case against Teel without Max's testimony if it comes down to it – which is why I don't mind telling it to you upstanding officials."

"You couldn't stop being cute for a second, could you?" Carlin said. "No, I guess not. What next?"

The dark skin on Hurst's wide cheekbones and jaw tightened till it almost glistened, but his voice was quiet enough. "John Nola decided Teel was nobody to marry Ione. But he knew how nuts Ione was about Teel and that she wouldn't listen to reason. So he told Jake George to get to Max Lorenz in the pen and grease Max to give out with whatever was needed to hang a rap on Teel. Nola figured if he put Teel in the can, Ione wouldn't be able to marry him at least till his term was up and by that time maybe she'd be over him – or maybe he figured that so long as he had enough on Teel to send him over he could scare Teel into bailing out. Got that?"

"Got more beer?" Slabbe said.

Hurst got up. His stride, going and coming from the refrigerator, was sinuous as a huge dark cat's. He dealt out more bottles.

He said: "But Lorenz wouldn't deal through a go-between. He had to see Nola personally and get as big a price as the tariff would bear. That's why he came here when he was sprung. He came here and talked to Nola Monday afternoon just before I drove Nola to the airport. I don't think they came together on a price, though, because Nola was sore."

"Did you see the plane crack up?" Slabbe asked.

Hurst shook his head. "No. I carried Nola's bag to it and put him on, then went back to the car. The plane and me took off at the same time. As soon as I got back here, though, it came over the local radio that the plane had burned. Miss Yates sent me back to the airport to make sure there was no hope, then I got Prentice at Fudge Burke's and we got an undertaker."

Carlin scowled. "If Nola didn't hit a bargain with Lorenz, how come he told Jake George's secretary that he'd put a check for Jake in the mail? That sounded like he was satisfied."

354 *William Rough*

Hurst gave Carlin a long, sideways glance. "I wouldn't expect a cop to get it right off. Take time."

Slabbe mused. "Whether they hit it off or not, Lorenz would tell Nola to call off Jake, huh?"

"Sure Lorenz had Nola weejied into a corner," Hurst said. "Who could finger Teel for Nola? Only Lorenz. Suppose Lorenz said now you play ball with me or I'll keep quiet till *after* your daughter marries this bum, and *then* I'll sing – and how would an upstanding pillar of the community like that?"

The chauffeur nodded knowingly. "See, Lorenz had Nola on the short end and could afford to drag it out, only being a riffler he'd naturally want to get rid of anybody in the deal who smelled like copper, meaning Jake George. Lorenz probably said: 'Pay this peeper off and make sure he's satisfied and then we'll talk business.' "

"Bushwah!" Carlin exploded.

Hurst wasn't bothered. "You always say that, just on general principles. Your patsy there is thinking it fits." He nodded at Slabbe.

Slabbe said: "I'm not just checking the framework. Anything's possible. So Nola calls Jake George off the case. Then what?"

"Then Nola shoves off in that plane wreck," Hurst said, "and it's all Lorenz's baby. It's the life of Reilly for him from there in."

"Yeah?" Carlin said.

"Why not?" Hurst countered. "Lorenz has it on Teel. Teel's going to marry Ione. She inherits at least half of Nola's estate. Lorenz can blackmail Teel till 1996."

The phone rang. Hurst answered it, said, "Yes, Miss Yates," hung up and buttoned his tunic again, adjusted his cap. "They want the car. Miss Reed is leaving," he explained. "Anyhow, I've spilled it and that's all the hospitality I have on hand." He nodded at the empty beer bottles.

"What's *your* angle?" Carlin said. "And what about Jake George?"

"Lorenz must have knocked George off," Hurst shrugged. "Jake was the only other guy in the world that knew about it – except me, and Lorenz didn't know I knew – and Lorenz didn't want Jake mixing in and maybe trying to squeeze out a few dibs himself. My angle is only to save Miss Yates grief, like I said in the first place, by saving Ione grief, which means letting Bill

Teel alone. Why not, you guys? You can't make a case against him without Lorenz splits on him and maybe not even then. And Lorenz won't be around here for a good stretch. He'll wait till Ione and Teel are married and then try to bleed them – only maybe this time I'll have something to talk over with him." Hurst's eyes glistened a little. "How about it? If you find Jake George's body, you'll see it fits."

"Maybe we already found it," Carlin said sourly.

"You don't say. Where?"

"Guess."

Slabbe said absently: "In Bleeker's Canyon, burned to a crisp in Lorenz's Chevvy."

Hurst's face showed nothing. Not Carlin's. His started to redden, and the nostrils of his bony nose flared. He opened his mouth, but after Slabbe's quick wink he closed it again.

"So what about it?" Hurst pressed. "Lay off Teel. He's straight now, or I don't know guys. He went through a war, and there *are* people who learn their lesson."

Carlin had to take it out on somebody. He said nastily: "Like you, I suppose. You're the little fixer-upper because the old girl caught you snitching pears once and let you go. In a pig's eye! What *did* she catch you at, punk?"

If it had been two strides from Hurst's position to Carlin's chair, the slope-shouldered detective would have had clawed hands on his neck. He pawed for his sap.

It was three strides, though, and the huge chauffeur made a tremendous effort and caught himself. He was breathing hard. His yellow-flecked eyes were small and shiny. Deep in his chest, he said at the sap: "You think that thing could stop me?"

Slabbe made the floor vibrate, going toward the door.

Carlin yelped: "Hey!"

"Hey, hell!" Slabbe grunted. "While you jokers were waltzing there, I heard shots from the house."

There were two wet marks on Ruby Reed's lime-green suit. She was on her back in front of the main door to the Nola home. Her green eyes were open and the bruise on the left one was no particular color at all now, just darker than the rest of her white skin.

Her black hair was scarcely disarranged. Her long shapely

legs were not twisted awkwardly, but it was not a posed tableau: her skirt was swirled higher than a photographer would have arranged it.

For a second Slabbe's heavy face might have shown a bit more gray granite than usual, then he was again chewing gum stolidly, "I guess I don't get to keep that date with you, baby," he murmured.

"Who done it?" Carlin cursed softly, dark eyes everywhere. He bit his lips, barked at the people in the wash of light from the open door, "OK, I sound like a hayseed, but who saw it, or something?"

There was no immediate answer. Prentice and Ione Nola and Miss Yates and Bill Teel stood close to each other, elbows touching. Behind them servants fidgeted and whispered. Alan Hurst stepped toward the old lady in black taffeta, breathing heavily. "You don't have to stay here, Miss Yates," he said.

"Cut it!" Carlin snapped.

Hurst's wide shoulders swung back viciously. Then his hazel eyes widened and he put a hand against the house to support himself. Miss Yates' black eyes snapped to him. Her tinkling voice ordered: "Take Alan inside, Joseph – it's his heart again," and a butler sidled around her and took Hurst's elbow.

Miss Yates transferred her glance to Teel's haggard face. He looked older than she did. "What happened, William?" she said. "What's wrong with your arm?"

Carlin rammed a cigar under his long nose. "I'll handle this, thank you. Yeah, what *is* wrong with your arm, bo?"

Teel took his brown eyes off Ruby, sent them straight ahead to look at something a thousand miles away, and said without any inflection whatever: "I was standing in front of the door with her, waiting for Alan to bring the car around. Someone shot at us. I got hit in the arm."

"Bill!" Ione Nola squealed and pawed at him.

"Shuddup!" Carlin bit. "He'll live." He looked at Teel's tired mouth and empty eyes and his lips peeled back a trifle wolfishly. "For a while, anyhow. Hear me, son? This is a very, very old gag, maybe."

Black taffeta rustled. The tinkling voice sounded like icicles breaking against one another. "I presume you represent the police," Miss Yates said to Carlin. "It's fortunate that you should be on hand at this time, *un*fortunate that you know only a single technique; intimidation."

Prentice Nola scratched his beard. "Tell him, Aunt Serena," he leered.

Carlin struggled with a mouthful of marbles.

Slabbe touched his gray hat deferentially. "Sorry, ma'am. If you people would just say where you were and if you heard the shots, and so on, you could go inside."

"Thank you, Mr Slabbe," Miss Yates said. "Bill was with Miss Reed, of course, as he's admitted. Prentice, you may be sure, was no farther from a brandy decanter than necessary."

"*Merci*, darling," Prentice mocked. "I was indeed imbibing in my room on the second floor. I heard the shots and looked over my balcony railing, saw Ruby sprawled here and came down."

Miss Yates said: "Ione, where were you?"

The pint-sized ash-blonde turned her head from Teel long enough to say, "Dressing," and turned back again. Her little-girl's fingers touched Teel's gray cheek.

"I was also in my room," Miss Yates said. "I heard the shots and also looked over my balcony railing and saw what had happened and came down. May I offer a suggestion?"

"Yes'm," Slabbe said.

"Then I suggest you scour this vicinity for a medium-sized man who limps on his left leg."

Carlin's cigar gave a downward tilt as his mouth opened. "*What?*"

Miss Yates said coolly: "I can't say if Prentice was using his eyes when he was on his balcony, but I was. And I saw such a man run east over the lawn."

Slabbe looked quickly at Prentice, whose jaw was twitching and whose eyes were ugly on the old woman.

Slabbe shifted back to Teel. "We know about you, son," he said quietly. "Did you see who it was? Was it Max Lorenz? It's OK. We know you know him."

Teel's mouth opened three times for one word. When it came, it was: "Yes."

Slabbe caught Carlin's eye, jerked his head toward the door. Carlin scowled, said generally: "OK, you can go inside."

"Oh, my book!" Ione Nola cried. She pointed at a slender volume that was lying near Ruby's outstretched hand. "I loaned it to her. Bill gave it to me. I thought if she and Prentice were in love, she'd be thrilled to read—"

"Be quiet, Ione," Miss Yates ordered. "Go inside."

Slabbe stooped and picked up the book. It fell open at a well-marked page.

One eye on Ione, he read:

> *How do I love thee? Let me count the ways.*
> *I love thee to the depth and breadth and height*
> *My soul can reach, when feeling out of sight*
> *For the ends of Being and ideal Grace.*
> *I love thee to the level of every day's*
> *Most quiet need, by sun and candlelight.*
> *I love thee freely, as men strive for Right;*
> *I love thee purely, as they turn from Praise . . .*

Carlin raged. "What the – that's enough! Cut that out!"

Slabbe paid him no attention. He was watching Ione's starry eyes. She said: "Isn't it marvelous, Bill?" to Teel. "That's the way I feel for you and—"

"Ione! Inside!" The tinkling voice was sharp. Miss Yates caught the girl's elbow, turned her to the door. Teel started to follow, his shoulders sagging.

"Not you," Carlin snapped at him. "You stick here, I know all about you, boy. I don't know why you'd knock this dish off, but you could have. Two shots for her and one for yourself and heave the rod into the shrubs over there and say you saw Lorenz do it. You and me got a session coming up."

Slabbe took three steps backwards, saw that Carlin wasn't paying attention, turned and plodded toward the street. He went to the Carleton Arms Hotel and cornered the houseman, Barney McPhail.

"You're stuck for a hotel bill, chum," he told the well-dressed, dapper handshaker. "Miss Ruby Reed. Dead. Shot. No more wolves will bother her. Who did?"

McPhail flicked the starboard end of a black waxed mustache delicately, pale eyes expressionless. "She registered here, 507, Saturday afternoon from New York City. So far as 1 know, she didn't have any visitors or calls. I can check."

"Suppose you do," Slabbe encouraged.

McPhail did. Miss Reed had had no phone calls or visitors that anyone remembered, and such things were generally remembered in a lush thirty-five-story inn like the Carleton Arms.

"How'd she get the shiner?" Slabbe asked.

Barney McPhail did not look embarrassed, having learned poise in his day, but he squirmed just a little. "I hope nothing's going to come of that, Slabbe," he murmured. "It wouldn't exactly be the job, but it would hurt my stock around here. A guy got into her suite and slugged her – she *said*."

"You don't buy it?" Slabbe asked.

"We-ell, I don't know. It could have happened, but she's a type – was, huh? – that would sue, or threaten to, and she didn't. She was willing to let it pass, said she wouldn't even have mentioned it if another guest hadn't heard her scream and reported it."

"What was the story, Barney?"

McPhail's neat shoulders moved a deprecating quarter inch. "She was on her way into her suite Monday afternoon about five. She opened the door and a guy's fist smashed her. She screamed, didn't see the guy clear. He ran. Another guest coming from his room saw the guy's back, called for help. I went up. Nothing missing from the Reed kid's room. She said let it go. Should *I* argue?"

"How about mail for her?" Slabbe pressed.

"I'll check."

McPhail did it again. There had been no mail for Miss Reed. There might have been a telegram, a desk clerk thought. The records would show it. The records showed it. Miss Reed had received a telegram Monday afternoon. There was no copy of it on file here. There would be one in the telegraph company's office. Slabbe left and went to his office and used the telephone to call the New York office of the Zenith Detective Agency.

5. A Matter of Minutes

Late though it was – nine o'clock – the purring voice of Mr Enoch Oliver over the wire assured Slabbe that he was not being inconvenienced, that it was his custom when working with less experienced investigators than regularly employed by Zenith to remain at the office in case the less experienced investigators needed moral support and/or the aid of a more experienced investigator.

Slabbe grunted under his breath, "You and the President!" Into the phone, he said: "Was there a woman involved in the last trick Max Lorenz went over for?"

"I have the file on my desk," Mr Oliver said. "I'll summarize the information it contains. There were eight people involved. The ring leaders were Max Lorenz, Walter Evans and his wife, Ruby Reed Evans, a night club singer who contacted wealthy women who wanted nylons and who may have married Evans for the express purpose of enticing him to divert the necessary materials from the silk company for which he worked. Lorenz was apprehended. Evans and his wife vanished. Lorenz refused to implicate them, and they were considered small fry and not traced."

Slabbe licked his lips sanguinely. "Maybe they're not small fry today. The girl was just shot. The guy was with her. He's using the name of William Teel now, and with the wife dead he can marry money and have his own silk company."

Mr. Oliver was polite about this, but purringly reminded Slabbe once again that the person whom Zenith considered it worthwhile to spend money on was one Max Lorenz. Was he dead or wasn't he?

Slabbe grimaced. "I'll tell you that after you have your Wheaties in the morning, Ollie, old kid. Sweet dreams."

Slabbe telephoned City Hall and had an interesting conversation with the laboratory technician who had examined the burned Chevvy, and then got connected with the detective bureau and used Carlin's name to instruct them to find out this and that about the telegram which Ruby Reed had received at the Carleton Arms Hotel Monday afternoon.

Having done this, he felt he should also tell Carlin about it. First, he called Abe Morse and Charlie Somers, boys who took his money occasionally, and ordered them to idle away a few hours in the vicinity of the Nola home. He then got Carlin on the wire there, gnawed off the cap of a quart of beer and enjoyed it leisurely while Carlin bawled him out.

"OK, I was a bad boy," Slabbe said, finally. "There were just

enough miles on Lorenz's Chevvy for him to have got here
from Lewisburg, with maybe eight or ten over for riding around
town. Lilac Lake is a dozen miles out, so Lorenz's car wasn't up
there and can't be the one Ike Veech was using. By itself, that
doesn't sound like much, but here's another thing: there was no
ignition key in Lorenz's Chevvy and the switch was off. The car
was started by fiddling with the wires on the distributor, get it?"

Carlin's voice altered. "Which means that Lorenz wasn't the
guy who rolled the heap into Bleeker's Canyon, because if he
did it, since the car was his, the ignition would be switched on
and the key would be on hand."

"Yeah."

"That's dandy."

"Isn't it, though? Can you make anything stick on Teel, Pat?
Did you find the gun Ruby was shot with so that he could have
done it like you said – shot her and himself and heaved it?"

"No, dammit. I still got guys searching the grounds for it.
Teel sticks to his story. They got the family lawyer on hand,
and he told them all to clam up – as if he had to. There ain't no
reason why Teel would kill Ruby that I see. Prentice either, or
anybody else, though they could have. Any one of 'em could
have sneaked out of the house by a back or side door and let
her have it and then said they were in their room, or something.
Only Prentice swears he only knew Ruby from Saturday night
when he picked her up at Fudge Burke's."

"What does Teel say?" Slabbe asked.

"Nothing."

"He's your boy, Pat. Ruby Reed was his wife."

Carlin evidently had no expletive on tap strong enough for
the occasion. He was silent while Slabbe explained.

Then he said softly: "I'll face up to him with it. It ought to
be good."

"Watch how Ione takes it," Slabbe advised. "Teel could have
got hold of the Caddy to drive up to the lake Monday night, too.
Let him know that."

"Yeah. This is going to hold. Maybe it's going to put Teel and
Max Lorenz in it together. Why not? We already got Teel and
the old lady on record as saying it was Lorenz who shot Ruby.
OK, they're stuck with it. Teel found out that Nola was bringing
Lorenz here to upset his apple cart. Teel got to Lorenz first, told

him to ride with him instead of Nola and there'd be more in the end. Maybe Lorenz didn't sign on the dotted line right off, but as soon as Nola was dead in the plane wreck he teamed up with Teel. Sure. Lorenz contacted Ruby when he was sprung, told her to come here and he'd meet her. She was the clincher, Teel's wife. Only when Lorenz threw in with Teel, then Ruby wasn't needed."

"See if the DA thinks it's enough," Slabbe encouraged.

"I'll do just that," Carlin promised.

"Check. I'll see you downtown. You bringing him right down?"

"Soon as I can," Carlin said. "This gang gives me the willies."

Slabbe hung up and opened the refrigerator by his desk, treated himself to another quart of beer, waiting. When the phone rang again and a detective said, "Here's what that telegram said," Slabbe reached for a pencil and scratch pad. It wasn't necessary, however. The message was short enough to remember easily.

The detective quoted: " 'See John Nola for your end.' No signature. The thing was handed in at the airport Monday afternoon at three-fifty."

Slabbe's gray eyes were opaque. He put the telephone back into its cradle and sat without taking his hand off it for five minutes. When he was ready again, he used it to call the airport. He learned that the wrecked plane had been cleared by the control tower on last Monday at exactly 3:50 p.m., and that John Nola had made his reservation two days in advance. He called Jake George's secretary, Susie Caston, who lived within a half dozen blocks of his office.

Ten minutes later she was there, a small blonde woman, no longer young, her face limp as the dyed rabbit fur on the collar of her three-year-old cloth coat.

Slabbe got up and fathered her into a chair, making grunting, sympathetic sounds. He studied her empty brown eyes, avoided them as he said: "I guess there's not much doubt about Jake, honey. He wouldn't want you to take on, though"

"Did you – find him?" Her voice was dead.

"I don't think so. Not yet. It could be him in a car that burned up, but maybe not. It depends on you a lot, honey."

"Me?"

"On your memory, anyhow," Slabbe nodded, "Just relax. You want to help, don't you?"

"I want to see the man who killed Jake."

Slabbe squeezed her shoulder, returned to his reinforced chair. Casually he said: "Remember what time John Nola called Monday afternoon to tell you he'd be putting a check in the mail?"

Her hands were together in her lap. She sat stiffly, lips ragged. "It's important, isn't it? Then I can't say for sure. It was about an hour after Jake went out with the blond man who limped. I think they went out about three. That would make it about four, but I can't be sure."

Slabbe slid his spittoon out from under his desk, dropped his gum into it. "You'll be sure, honey," he promised. "We're going to make you sure. We'll do a complete coverage, but take it easy. Don't strain. This has to stand up in court."

"All right," she said dully.

Slabbe got a scratch pad handy. "Just to get organized, we'll start with Sunday night. Where were you, honey? What did you do? What time did you get home? What time did you go to bed? Did you read or something before you fell asleep? Go ahead now. Don't leave anything out, but don't hurry."

She started. There was no emotion in her voice, little interest. Slabbe was patient.

"Now for Monday morning," he said. "Everything you did, honey. What time did you get up? Did you get right out when the alarm went off, or did you turn over for another minute?"

"I got right up. My alarm is set for seven o'clock."

"What did you do first? What do you always do?"

"Wash—"

"OK, then what? Make your own breakfast? What did you have? What bus or streetcar did you take? Remember the driver? Remember the elevator boy at Jake's office building who took you up? Did he say good morning? Take it, honey. You can remember every single second if you work it right."

"Yes. I can, can't I?"

"You bet you can," Slabbe said. "If you get ahead of yourself don't be afraid to go back. I'm writing it all down in order. Spit it out, honey, spit it out."

Susie Caston went on. She spoke faster now. She began

to wrinkle her brow. Her eyes got life back into them. She talked over Monday morning, every minute of it. Her voice gathering strength and interest. "It's like living it over again, Benjie," she said. "I can almost feel the temperature of the office that day. It was cold, I remember. There was something wrong with the radiator. I called the superintendent three times. He said he'd send a plumber up. The plumber came about three-thirty—"

"Uh-uh, not too fast," Slabbe cut in. "We're only at the morning yet. Don't jump ahead. Don't try to tell something that happened before something else. One at a time, honey, one at a time. What about lunch?"

"Twelve-thirty to one-thirty," she responded promptly. "I walked downstairs. The elevator was on the top floor. I went out the front door, went east down Main Street, north on Fifth. I went to the Acme lunchroom. I had a grilled cheese sandwich, two olives with it, lemon sponge pie, a cup – no, two cups of cocoa. I smoked two cigarettes. Going back to the office . . ."

Slabbe filled in his chart. As nearly as possible, every minute was accounted for in chronological order.

"Yes," Susie cried, "it was just three o'clock when that man came in, a few seconds before. I can hear the City Hall clock sometimes when the wind is right. He came in and said, 'Where's the boss?' and I got up and went into Jake's office, and the clock was striking three times. Jake looked past me into the outer office and saw the man and jumped up and yelled: 'Come in, Lorenz; come right in. Beat it, Susie.' But they weren't together more than five minutes when they came out again, headed for the door. That was when Jake whispered to me: 'I'm taking him to Nola's home and we collect.' "

"On the ball now, honey," Slabbe warned. "Keep it coming. Were you standing up or sitting down when they left? Did you look at your watch? How did you pass the time?"

"I was typing when they went out. I finished four letters. It was after three then. I wanted to get done to hear Marty and Hazel on the radio. That's that program that's on every day at three-thirty."

Slabbe cut in. "How long is the program?"

"Fifteen minutes. They advertise a soap powder."

"Did you get it on?"

"Yes. I remember, I turned it on while I was still typing, and I kept going till the announcer was done with the first commercial. Then I leaned back and listened."

"And Nola hadn't called yet?"

"No. The program was over. The plumber came before Mr Nola called. He came just at the end of the program with tools. And I said, 'Don't you start making noise till I hear this.' He said, 'Lady, I knock off at four o'clock, so I've got fifteen minutes to stop you squawking about how cold it is.' "

Susie's eyes were intent now. She wasn't in Slabbe's office. She was back in Jake George's office Monday afternoon at 3:45. She said: "Then the commercial started again and I told the plumber to bring the roof down if he wanted to. He went to work. I typed another letter, that took at least ten minutes. Then the telephone rang and it was Mr Nola. I yelled at the plumber: 'Stop that for just a second please.' And he stopped, and I talked to Mr Nola and—"

Slabbe had stopped listening. This was what he wanted. The plumber would be another witness.

"How am I doing, Benjie?" Susie asked.

"You *did*, baby," Slabbe assured her. "There's no doubt it was him, is there? You know his voice?"

"Oh, yes, I talked to him often. I'll swear it was him."

"And a jury will believe you, honey," Slabbe said grimly.

"But Benjie, what's it all about?"

"Just that it must have been five minutes to four when John Nola called you, honey, and the plane that cracked up took off at ten minutes to four."

Susie goggled. "Well, then . . . he . . . I mean."

"You bet." Slabbe sat down again. "He was never on that plane."

6. Hot and Heavy

Slabbe was again alone in his office at eleven o'clock when Charlie Somers called to say: "That big chauffeur took off in the Nola Caddy as soon as Carlin pulled his boys out. Abe Morse is tailing him."

"That's your shift in, then," Slabbe said. "I'll pay you in the a.m."

He got City Hall on the wire, told Carlin: "Come on over, Pat. We're gonna go places."

Carlin arrived promptly. His dark eyes were glittering. "You told me to take Teel down just for monkey business, didn't you?"

Slabbe shrugged apologetically. "Well, he was logical, wasn't he? It looked good, too, and it took you and your gang away from the Nola joint so they could operate some more. That's what they're doing, only they have company. Abe Morse is working."

"Who's 'they'?" Carlin demanded.

"Just Hurst, so far," Slabbe said. "Drink some beer. I don't think he'll be going far, but we gotta wait for Abe to put him in somewhere and get to a phone. How did Ione Nola take it when you let it out that Teel was Ruby's hubby?"

Carlin folded his long form into a chair, grimaced. "It was touch and go. I didn't know for a second whether she'd claw my eyes out or fold up and we'd have to send for a nut doctor."

"Uh-huh?" Slabbe was interested.

"It hit her hard, all right. Her face started to bust up. Then the old lady, Miss Yates, did a Marines to the rescue and started telling her that she loved Teel, didn't she, and the charges against him were preposter-something, and here was where her love was going to be tested, and like that."

"And Ione pulled out of it?"

Carlin nodded. "Yep. She's more nuts about the guy than ever. Dames are nuts."

"You braced Teel with the Caddy being at Lilac Lake Monday night?"

"Sure. He wouldn't talk. He has the oldest face on a guy of twenty-seven I ever saw."

"He has good reason to, I'd say," Slabbe mused. "Murders going on around him, on his account, and him not having much, if anything to do with them, but still needing to keep his lip buttoned."

Carlin leveled a finger longer and bonier than his nose at Slabbe. "Just let's hear you explain this."

The phone rang.

Slabbe grinned. "You'll get it on a platter." He answered

the phone. Abe Morse's husky voice said: "Benjie? I put this chauffeur into a cabin up here at Lilac Lake. I'm down the road at a gas station. He's alone and he put a pot of coffee on the stove, so I took a chance on phoning."

"Slide back there, but don't let him get his mitts on you, kid. He didn't go there just to drink coffee. We'll be up. How do we make the right cabin?"

"Turn left at the breast of the dam, left again a hundred yards on. It's a big log place, all by itself. My jalopy'll be off in a little grove of pine trees."

Slabbe hung up. "OK Leftenant," he told Carlin. They drove to Lilac Lake, left at the breast of the dam, left again a hundred yards on. There wasn't much moon, no stars. The air off the black-looking water was chill. Slabbe's breath made frosty clouds when he said, "There's the pine grove," and swung ponderously to peer.

Carlin eased the departmental sedan off the road. The tires made whispering sounds on pine needles, a winter old. They found Abe Morse's car, but not Abe. They prowled ahead on foot, found the cabin, a solid two-story structure in the log cabin tradition, but with nothing phony about the logs. The place was a fort.

"The caddy's gone," Slabbe frowned. "Cripes, I hope Hurst didn't clip Abe."

"I hope you get your hope," Carlin grunted. "No lights inside now. No coffee, I can smell. When these trees get full of leaves, I'll bet it's black as hell in here."

Slabbe squeezed the lieutenant's arm for silence – and got it, complete silence, with only the intangible, non-noise sound of a large body of water nearby.

"Take a chance on a light for a second, Pat," Slabb suggested. "The road's dirt. Ought to be tire marks."

"Yeah," Carlin said a second later. "Car came in, didn't go out."

"He made coffee and drove on past the cabin, huh?" Slabbe said. "Suppose I slip down on foot and you go back for the sedan?"

It wasn't necessary. A shadow darker than the rest glided up to them. Abe Morse's husky voice said: "He's about a quarter of a mile down the road. He's looking for something in a gully off to the right. I got the distributor cap off the Caddy. Was that right?"

"It wasn't wrong." Slabbe chuckled.

"Looking for something in a gully?" Carlin scowled. "What the hell for?"

"A body, is my guess," Slabbe said. He went ahead, faster now. Carlin cursed and stumbled. "Give me a good concrete city street," he complained. "What's that?"

"Tree toads in the woods," Abe Morse husked. "An owl over there in that chestnut tree. See it?"

"The tree or the owl?" Carlin said sarcastically. "I wouldn't know one from the other."

Alan Hurst's flashlight was suddenly a giant white firefly below them to the right. He was in a gully fifty feet deep, fifty yards across, that ran beside the road. Slabbe squatted and pulled Carlin down beside him so that their silhouettes did not stand out.

"It's not so steep going down from here, but look at the other side," he said. "It's a face of rock. He'll have to come back up this way or cut left or right down there and plough a hundred yards before he can break clear. How about one of you guys at each end? I'll go down right here."

Abe Morse slipped away without question. Carlin spat and burped, but finally loped off. Slabbe went down, crab-style, feet first on his heels, palms and beam. The chauffeur's flash was swinging methodically, covering every square foot of the undergrowth as he worked through the gully. He found what he was looking for just as Slabbe came up behind him.

Hurst was breathing fast, but stopped and gave a little grunt of triumph as his flash centered on his find: a man's body. The man was on his back. His clothing showed that he'd been out in the weather for days. Slabbe recognized his features: Jake George.

Hurst hesitated no longer. He caught the man's arm, started to lift him as easily as a sack of feathers. He stopped, frowned, let the arm go again. He picked up a basketball-sized rock, poised it over the dead man's pasty face.

Slabbe said: "Don't do it, son."

It was a mistake. Slabbe was shambling forward, but he shouldn't have spoken. Or he should at least have clipped Hurst first.

The chauffeur swung easily, smoothly, catlike, and shot-putted his rock at the first thing he saw moving, which was Slabbe. Man, beast or devil smacking into Slabbe once he was under way would have come off second best, but not rock. It took him on the left shoulder and let him know about it. It stopped him, swung him with more, though less localized push, than a .45 Colt slug. He spun so that his back was toward Hurst when the chauffeur cut his flash and leaped away.

Slabbe closed his teeth against the pain, lurched around and shambled after Hurst. The chauffeur's longer legs made it an uneven contest. He was twenty yards ahead of Slabbe and gaining.

Slabbe opened his mouth to shout to Carlin and Abe Morse, but decided against it. If Hurst knew there were reinforcements handy, he might go to earth in the undergrowth. As it was, he was certainly trying for the Caddy – which was now without a distributor cap.

Slabbe tried for the car, too. Since he had just come down, while Hurst had been here for a while, he was a bit better oriented. When he started clawing up the slope to the road, he was sure he was lined up with the Caddy, while Hurst, off to the right, would have to run back this way once he made the road.

Slabbe's left hand and arm were numb. His right hand tore on the rocks he clutched at, felt warm and sticky. The slope was just a blur, he could have closed his eyes and made just as good time. He heard the scrambling sliding sound made by rocks and dislodged earth by both himself and his quarry. His lungs were bellows sucking air through his open mouth, drying his lips and tongue and throat till he wanted to gag. He rolled over the hump and was on the road again. Hurst's footfalls were approaching, thumping on the dirt. Slabbe peered for the dark shape of the Caddy. He saw double – but it was no illusion. There *were* two cars there. Headlights slashing suddenly into the night proved it. A tinkling voice proved it. In Fudge Burke's place the voice had sounded clearly as tiny bells in a fine Swiss watch. Out here, with sky and trees to background it, it was a carillon.

"Here, Alan!" it cried. "In here! Quickly!"

7. Fire to the Finish

Hurst could have made it – but didn't. It wasn't his lungs or his legs that gave out. It was his heart. One second he was running freely in a long, loping stride. The next he lurched. The next after, he crumpled.

Slabbe was down on one knee. He shifted his gun from its line on where Hurst had been to the tires of the car with the blazing headlights. But that wasn't necessary either. Miss Yates was not leaving, she was hurrying to Alan Hurst. Slabbe saw her kneel beside him. Her bonnet had fallen off and her white hair was silvery in the wash of the automobile headlights. There was no need for Slabbe to hurry.

When he had dusted himself off, righted his hat and swabbed blood from his right hand, he went over. Miss Yates was rising. She trembled a little.

"Dead?" Slabbe asked.

She nodded, turned. Slabbe took her arm. "I think there's coffee in the cabin. Who owns the place?"

"It was John Nola's. We thought we could intimidate that detective, Jake George, or buy him off if we held him a prisoner here for a while, but when Alan talked to the man Monday night, he saw there was only one way."

Slabbe nodded. "So Hurst and Ike Veech killed Jake, put the body in Veech's car and Veech drove down here to the gully and dumped it in. They didn't think then that it would be found soon or that it would make much difference, anyhow. Let's go into the cabin."

She offered no resistance. The only sound was the rustling of her black taffeta skirt and Slabbe's breathing coming back to normal.

There was a smell of coffee inside the cabin. Slabbe hesitated, then saw that she was through, and went to the kitchen. He brought coffee back to where she sat in front of a huge fieldstone fireplace. Her pale face was as unruffled as her fine white hair, but her hands twitched ever so slightly.

Slabbe said: "It was all for love of Ione. M'm, and hate of Nola probably."

The voice did not tinkle now, it was too low. "I did hate John

Nola. I loved him at first and even after he married my sister and Prentice was born. Then he said that he still loved me. Ione is my child, mine and his. Knowing it practically killed John's wife, my sister, but even after she was dead he wouldn't marry me – perhaps it was *because* she died over our affair. So then I hated him."

"Love and hate," Slabbe said. "They complicate things. You wanted Ione to marry Bill Teel?"

"Yes."

"Even though you must have learned or guessed that he was a phony?"

Serena Yates lifted her chin. "When Bill Teel brought life to my daughter's eyes again after the months she spent in a crazy dream world of grief and escape, I knew he was good for her. I wouldn't have cared if he were a freak – but he isn't. He became infatuated with a girl once, a Ruby Reed, and married her and she enticed him into a criminal enterprise. He learned from his mistake. I've watched him these past months, and he's building solidly and honestly for a good life."

"Only John Nola couldn't see him?" Slabbe said.

The old woman's black smooth eyes were venomous. "John Nola thought people are black or white, with no in-between. Teel was all bad or all good. John said all bad, and he had a strange, perverse love of Ione. He didn't want her to marry a criminal. The fool was so insensitive that in spite of knowing what he'd done to me he scoffed at the notion that betrayal by a loved one can make a woman warped and bitter, if not actually mad. I know it can," she said bitingly. "Ione had transferred everything she'd felt for her first boy to Bill. If he had let her down—"

"But just pulling a trick a couple years ago wouldn't have thrown her if she was so nuts about him," Slabbe interrupted.

The black eyes studied him. "You're quite right. A woman in his past would have done it, though – I thought. Bill told me openly and frankly that he had already been married and not divorced when I encouraged him to love Ione. *I* told him not to tell her. I was wrong there, but my child was coming to life again and I wouldn't risk anything that might change her. And then as she loved Bill more and more and believed that she was the only one he had ever loved, it became even more dangerous, to my way of thinking, to tell her that another woman had been first in his life."

"To your way of thinking," Slabbe said. "You put that in yourself. You see you were wrong there, too. She knows now that Teel was married to Ruby. She took it, didn't she? She didn't crack."

The old lady bowed her head.

Slabbe said: "You can't keep your kid from getting bumped, lady. Everybody gets bumped. Most everybody takes it, too. They stand on their feet. They gotta. It's not *your* way of thinking that counts for them, it's their own way. Believe different and look what happens. Rather than let John Nola give your kid a bump, you killed him."

"In cold blood," Serena Yates said.

"Drink your coffee," Slabbe murmured. "You'll have to make a statement when Lieutenant Carlin gets here. Let me go over it with you."

He sandpapered his jawline, sighed. He said: "John Nola meant to expose Teel. He hired Jake George. Jake got a line on Teel, an old black market rap hanging over him. Nola may have been pig-headed, like you say, but he knew a mere criminal charge that maybe wouldn't even stick wouldn't be enough to make Ione throw Teel down. He told Jake to dig some more, look for a woman in Teel's past. Jake heard of a wife, but couldn't trace her. He went to Max Lorenz to see if Lorenz knew where she was. Lorenz did and would tell for a price. That was John Nola's scheme: put Teel's wife up against him in front of Ione."

"And break her heart," Serena Yates said harshly.

"It didn't break," Slabbe said simply.

"Thank God. That's why telling you the truth is good, at last. You'll see that Ione and Bill had no part of it and let them alone."

Slabbe said: "Your chauffeur was nuts about you. He killed for you."

"I caught him burgling our house when he was only sixteen years old and gave him a job. I killed John Nola, though, and Ruby Reed, too. I wouldn't have let Alan touch Jake George if I'd guessed what would happen."

Slabbe shrugged. "Hurst knew a little about how cops operate. He knew you can't just wet your toes in a murder deal, you gotta jump in feet first. He took a Brody on telling us as much of the truth as possible, hoping we'd check just so far and be satisfied, not tie Ruby Reed in with Teel. But I knew she had to fit somewhere the second she showed that she knew Max Lorenz, at Fudge Burke's. The telegram Lorenz sent her from the airport showed they were definitely connected. He told her to meet him here to make money, but didn't tell her the score because she, as the wife, would have been in the driver's seat. It was just coincidence that she picked up Prentice at Fudge Burke's. Maybe not. She was the type to go for the rich pups and Prentice hangs out at Fudge's. So long as they both were in the place at the same time, they were bound to get together. It was one between the eyes for Bill Teel when he walked in there today and spotted her."

"It was – what do you say? – a bad break." The old lady's lips were tight. "If Prentice hadn't met her, and she hadn't seen Bill, she would have given up waiting for Max Lorenz after a few days and probably never have returned to Treverton."

"Loves and hates, women and breaks," Slabbe murmured. "Did you try to buy her?"

"Of course."

"And her price?"

"Prentice."

Slabbe sighed. "It would be, wouldn't it? She'd keep mum about Teel if you helped her to marry Prentice."

Serena Yates' black eyes were icy. "I knew her type. We never could have been sure of her – and Prentice wouldn't have had her, anyhow."

"She had to go," Slabbe agreed. "No time like the present, either. When she walked out the door with Teel, you slipped out another door and shot her. You're not so good with a gun. You pinked Teel."

"I am good with a gun. I meant to wound him to divert suspicion from him," the old lady said calmly.

"And when you claimed you'd seen a man who limped run over the lawn, he had no choice but to back you up. He wasn't in it, no – only up to his gizzard. How did he know you'd killed Nola? Was he there when you did it?"

The white head shook slowly. "I called him Monday to try to bargain with Lorenz. I overheard John and Lorenz in the study

Monday afternoon. I called Bill at once, told him to catch Lorenz when Lorenz left the house and promise to pay him more *not* to produce Ruby than John was paying him to do it. Bill was outside when Lorenz left. He was in the car with him, drove to the airport with him. But Lorenz hated Bill because Bill hadn't been apprehended in the black market thing. He laughed at Bill and wrote that telegram to Ruby right in front of him, bragged that Ruby was already here in town and would go straight to Nola the minute she received the telegram. Bill phoned back to the house to me when Lorenz boarded the plane. Bill saw the plane crack up from the phone booth and blurted out what had happened."

Slabbe said: "How come that Nola let Lorenz have the plane reservation?"

"Because Lorenz said he wouldn't reveal Ruby's whereabouts till he was safely out of town. He was a conniving criminal type who thought John might, once he'd got his information, call in the police and try to get back the price he'd paid Lorenz. When Lorenz said that he'd wire John the minute he arrived in New York, John said he'd see that Lorenz got there as soon as possible and gave him the plane reservation."

Serena Yates' smooth eyes opened as wide as possible, but the pupils were small and black and perfectly motionless. "Yes," she said and her tinkling voice was metallic. "Bill was talking to me on the telephone. He said that the plane had just taken off, that Lorenz had telegraphed Ruby at the Carleton Arms, what could we do? Then he cried, 'My God, the plane cracked up! It's a mass of flame! No one has a chance!' "

Her teeth gleamed. "Lorenz was dead. John Nola was in his study. *He* was the one who should have been on that plane. What did it matter about Lorenz? He'd sent a telegram. Ruby would appear. Why couldn't it have been John? Why, I asked myself – why couldn't it *still* be John?"

Her coffee cup grated on the saucer. Her bloodless lips were not those of a white-haired old lady. "I shouted at Bill, 'Go to her hotel! Stop her from reading that telegram! Do anything! I'll reason with John Nola!' "

Slabbe said: "Teel got into Ruby's suite and accepted the telegram when it was sent up. She walked in on him before he could get away, though, and he slugged her. You slugged Nola – only harder."

"With a poker," she said. "Just once. He was in his big chair at the fireplace. I picked up the poker. I hit him with twenty years of hatred. He *was* supposed to be dead in the plane – he was dead then!"

"Just get rid of him now, was all you had to do," Slabbe said. "Hurst comes in here."

"Yes. I needed help. Alan worshipped me. I called him. He said if John was supposed to have been burned up – then *burn* him up. And if Max Lorenz's body was going to be identified as John's, then why not have John's identified as Lorenz's?"

"Lorenz had been driving a car," Slabbe nodded. "A chauffeur would think of that. Lorenz's car must be at the airport. Hurst went there, but the ignition key wasn't in it. He monkeyed with the distributor wires and got it going, came back to the house, put Nola's body in. That night he fired the car and rolled it into Bleeker's Canyon. But there was Jake George, too."

"Alan thought of him at once, but he couldn't be in two places at the same time. He called a man named Ike Veech to kidnap Jake George and bring him here. He called Veech again today after we saw you at Fudge Burke's and told him to pick you up and see if you were making any progress."

Slabbe said: "You were afraid that Jake George was a chiseler who might try to blackmail Teel and Ione after they married. But Jake was OK, just a peeper trying to get along, but honest. You couldn't let him go after pulling shennigans on him." Slabbe's voice was thin. "For that, you don't bother me a bit, lady."

She looked away.

Slabbe moved his sore shoulder ponderously. "Your original plan was to burn Nola's body in Lorenz's Chevvy and have it identified as Lorenz. You didn't intend Jake George's body to turn up until after the investigation of the burned body was old and cold. The two catches were that we knew how to identify Lorenz from a bullet in his thigh – and so knew it couldn't have been him who burned in the Chevvy – and Ruby Reed spotted Bill Teel."

Slabbe squinted somberly. "With us nosing around about the burned body and Ruby in a spot to tip the cart, you and Hurst cooked a new deal. You figured that we thought Lorenz was still alive. So why not foster that illusion? Kill Ruby and blame it on Lorenz.

"Of course if we were to go on believing the burned guy was Jake George, then Hurst had to make sure Jake's body wouldn't turn up or at least wouldn't be identifiable as Jake when it did get found. I'd deliberately let it out to Hurst that we figured the body in the Chevvy was Jake's and then put a couple of my people out to watch Hurst's move. He came up here tonight to beat Jake's face in with a rock."

Slabbe found his chewing gum, used it moodily for a second. "John Nola taking that plane right at the time he'd talked to Lorenz wasn't kosher. Nola's main ambition right then was to expose Teel; he would have said to hell with whatever his trip was for. Then I remembered that Susie had said Nola had called her just about the time the plane took off. It was worth a workout and it paid. Nola couldn't have been on the plane. Who was then? Who would send that telegram to Ruby? Max Lorenz, of course. So he was the one on the plane. Then where was John Nola? Why not him in the burned Chevvy? And who would have killed him to stop him from exposing Teel and hurting little Ione? I didn't have to guess, lady."

Slabbe shook his grizzled head. He marveled: "When you let Hurst tell most of the truth about Teel, you counted on the fact that no dumb cop would imagine anything so goofy as that this had all started rolling because a screwy old woman had raised her daughter dizzy enough to go bats because her boyfriend had once married a tramp."

Serena Yates clenched her coffee cup as if to throw it. She didn't. One by one, her fingers lost their strength and the black fire in her eyes consumed itself. She tried to set the cup down. It fell and broke. She stared at the pieces. Her face worked. "May I go upstairs to the bathroom?" she said.

"Uh-uh," Slabbe refused. "After Carlin hears it, you can do it – kill yourself, you mean, don't you?"

She stood up and without haste held the white lace at her throat free with one hand and removed a small revolver from her bosom with the other.

"Yes, kill myself," she said. "Not you, too, I hope."

Slabbe didn't move. "Nope, not me, lady."

He watched her climb the open staircase, her gun steady. She stood at the top, gripping the rustic banister.

"The bedroom doors are made of seasoned logs," she said.

"The locks are bolts which cannot be shot loose. There are no ladders available, so you won't be able to reach the second floor from outside."

For just a second her eyes, black as ever but no longer smooth, looked off at something that wasn't in the cabin. Then she opened a bedroom door.

"And there are large emergency lamps filled with kerosene in each bedroom," she said. She closed the door.

Slabbe tried what there was. It wasn't much. Even when Carlin and Abe Morse came it wasn't much. Abe dashed for the nearest village for what fire apparatus was on hand, but that wasn't much either.

Slabbe stood beside Carlin outside, watching the licking brilliance at a second-story window. He wondered if, for a second, he saw a vacant face at the window, but there was too much smoke to be sure.

A CANDLE FOR THE BAG LADY

Lawrence Block

He was a thin young man in a blue pinstripe suit. His shirt was white with a button-down collar. His glasses had oval lenses in brown tortoiseshell frames. His hair was a dark brown, short but not severely so, neatly combed, parted on the right. I saw him come in and watched him ask a question at the bar. Billie was working afternoons that week. I watched as he nodded at the young man, then swung his sleepy eyes over in my direction. I lowered my own eyes and looked at a cup of coffee laced with bourbon while the fellow walked over to my table.

"Matthew Scudder?" I looked up at him, nodded. "I'm Aaron Creighton. I looked for you at your hotel. The fellow on the desk told me I might find you here."

Here was Armstrong's, a Ninth Avenue saloon around the corner from my Fifty-seventh Street hotel. The lunch crowd was gone except for a couple of stragglers in front whose voices were starting to thicken with alcohol. The streets outside were full of May sunshine. The winter had been cold and deep and long. I couldn't recall a more welcome spring.

"I called you a couple times last week, Mr Scudder. I guess you didn't get my messages."

I'd gotten two of them and ignored them, not knowing who he was or what he wanted and unwilling to spend a dime for the answer. But I went along with the fiction. "It's a cheap hotel," I said. "They're not always too good about messages."

"I can imagine. Uh. Is there someplace we can talk?"

"How about right here?"

He looked around. I don't suppose he was used to conducting his business in bars but he evidently decided it would be all right to make an exception. He set his briefcase on the floor and seated himself across the table from me. Angela, the new day-shift waitress, hurried over to get his order. He glanced at my cup and said he'd have coffee, too.

"I'm an attorney," he said. My first thought was that he didn't look like a lawyer, but then I realized he probably dealt with civil cases. My experience as a cop had given me a lot of experience with criminal lawyers. The breed ran to several types, none of them his.

I waited for him to tell me why he wanted to hire me. But he crossed me up.

"I'm handling an estate," he said, and paused, and gave what seemed a calculated if well-intentioned smile. "It's my pleasant duty to tell you you've come into a small legacy, Mr Scudder."

"Someone's left me money?"

"Twelve hundred dollars."

Who could have died? I'd lost touch long since with any of my relatives. My parents went years ago and we'd never been close with the rest of the family.

I said, "Who – ?"

"Mary Alice Redfield."

I repeated the name aloud. It was not entirely unfamiliar but I had no idea who Mary Alice Redfield might be. I looked at Aaron Creighton. I couldn't make out his eyes behind the glasses but there was a smile's ghost on his thin lips, as if my reaction was not unexpected.

"She's dead?"

"Almost three months ago."

"I didn't know her."

"She knew you. You probably knew her, Mr Scudder. Perhaps you didn't know her by name." His smile deepened. Angela had brought his coffee. He stirred milk and sugar into it, took a careful sip, nodded his approval. "Miss Redfield was murdered." He said this as if he'd had practice uttering a phrase which did not come naturally to him. "She was killed quite brutally in late February for no apparent reason, another innocent victim of street crime."

"She lived in New York?"

"Oh, yes. In this neighborhood."

"And she was killed around here?"

"On West Fifty-fifth Street between Ninth and Tenth avenues. Her body was found in an alleyway. She'd been stabbed repeatedly and strangled with the scarf she had been wearing."

Late February. Mary Alice Redfield. West Fifty-fifth between Ninth and Tenth. Murder most foul. Stabbed and strangled, a dead woman in an alleyway. I usually kept track of murders, perhaps out of a vestige of professionalism, perhaps because I couldn't cease to be fascinated by man's inhumanity to man. Mary Alice Redfield had willed me twelve hundred dollars. And someone had knifed and strangled her, and –

"Oh, Jesus," I said. "The shopping-bag lady."

Aaron Creighton nodded.

New York is full of them. East Side, West Side, each neighborhood has its own supply of bag women. Some of them are alcoholic but most of them have gone mad without any help from drink. They walk the streets, huddle on stoops or in doorways. They find sermons in stones and treasures in trashcans. They talk to themselves, to passers-by, to God. Sometimes they mumble. Now and then they shriek.

They carry things around with them, the bag women. The shopping bags supply their generic name and their chief common denominator. Most of them seem to be paranoid, and their madness convinces them that their possessions are very valuable, that their enemies covet them. So their shopping bags are never out of their sight.

There used to be a colony of these ladies who lived in Grand Central Station. They would sit up all night in the waiting room, taking turns waddling off to the lavatory from time to time. They rarely talked to each other but some herd instinct made them comfortable with one another. But they were not comfortable enough to trust their precious bags to one another's safekeeping, and each sad crazy lady always toted her shopping bags to and from the ladies' room.

Mary Alice Redfield had been a shopping-bag lady. I don't know when she set up shop in the neighborhood. I'd been living in the same hotel ever since I resigned from the NYPD and separated from my wife and sons, and that was getting to be quite a few years now. Had Miss Redfield been on the scene that long ago? I couldn't remember her first appearance. Like so many of the neighborhood fixtures, she had been part of the scenery. Had her death not been violent and abrupt I might never have noticed she was gone.

I'd never known her name. But she had evidently known mine, and had felt something for me that prompted her to leave money to me. How had she come to have money to leave?

She'd had a business of sorts. She would sit on a wooden soft-drink case, surrounded by three or four shopping bags, and she would sell newspapers. There's an all-night newsstand at the corner of Fifty-seventh and Eighth, and she would buy a few dozen papers there, carry them a block west to the corner of Ninth and set up shop in a doorway. She sold the papers at retail, though I suppose some people tipped her a few cents. I could remember a few occasions when I'd bought a paper and waved away change from a dollar bill. Bread upon the waters, perhaps, if that was what had moved her to leave me the money.

I closed my eyes, brought her image into focus. A thickset woman, stocky rather than fat. Five-three or -four. Dressed usually in shapeless clothing, colorless gray and black garments, layers of clothing that varied with the season. I remembered that she would sometimes wear a hat, an old straw affair with paper and plastic flowers poked into it. And I remembered her eyes, large guileless blue eyes that were many years younger than the rest of her.

Mary Alice Redfield.

"Family money," Aaron Creighton was saying. "She wasn't wealthy but she had come from a family that was comfortably fixed. A bank in Baltimore handled her funds. That's where she was from originally, Baltimore, though she'd lived in New York for as long as anyone can remember. The bank sent her a check every month. Not very much, a couple of hundred dollars, but she hardly spent anything. She paid her rent—"

"I thought she lived on the street."

"No, she had a furnished room a few doors down the street from where she was killed. She lived in another rooming house on Tenth Avenue before that but moved when the building was sold. That was six or seven years ago and she lived on Fifty-fifth Street from then until her death. Her room cost her eighty dollars a month. She spent a few dollars on food. I don't know what she did with the rest. The only money in her room was a coffee can full of pennies. I've been checking the banks and there's no record of a savings account. I suppose she may have spent it or lost it or given it away. She wasn't very firmly grounded in reality."

"No, I don't suppose she was."

He sipped at his coffee. "She probably belonged in an institution," he said. "At least that's what people would say, but she got along in the outside world, she functioned well enough. I don't know if she kept herself clean and I don't know anything about how her mind worked but I think she must have been happier than she would have been in an institution. Don't you think?"

"Probably."

"Of course she wasn't safe, not as it turned out, but anybody can get killed on the streets of New York." He frowned briefly, caught up in a private thought. Then he said, "She came to our office ten years ago. That was before my time." He told me the name of his firm, a string of Anglo-Saxon surnames. "She wanted to draw a will. The original will was a very simple document leaving everything to her sister. Then over the years she would come in from time to time to add codicils leaving specific sums to various persons. She had made a total of thirty-two bequests by the time she died. One was for twenty dollars – that was to a man named John Johnson whom we haven't been able to locate. The remainder all ranged from five hundred to two thousand dollars." He smiled. "I've been given the task of running down the heirs."

"When did she put me into her will?"

"Two years ago in April."

I tried to think what I might have done for her then, how I might have brushed her life with mine. Nothing.

"Of course the will could be contested, Mr Scudder. It would be easy to challenge Miss Redfield's competence and any relative could almost certainly get it set aside. But no one wishes to challenge it. The total amount involved is slightly in excess of a quarter of a million dollars—"

"That much."

"Yes. Miss Redfield received substantially less than the income which her holdings drew over the years, so the principal kept growing during her lifetime. Now the specific bequests she made total thirty-eight thousand dollars, give or take a few hundred, and the residue goes to Miss Redfield's sister. The sister – her name is Mrs Palmer – is a widow with grown children. She's hospitalized with cancer and heart trouble and I believe diabetic complications and she hasn't long to live. Her children would like to see the estate settled before their mother dies and they have enough local prominence to hurry the will through probate. So I'm authorized to tender checks for the full amount of the specific bequests on the condition that the legatees sign quitclaims acknowledging that this payment discharges in full the estate's indebtedness to them."

There was more legalese of less importance. Then he gave me papers to sign and the whole procedure ended with a check on the table. It was payable to me and in the amount of twelve hundred dollars and no cents.

I told Creighton I'd pay for his coffee.

I had time to buy myself another drink and still get to my bank before the windows closed. I put a little of Mary Alice Redfield's legacy in my savings account, took some in cash, and sent a money order to Anita and my sons. I stopped at my hotel to check for messages. There weren't any. I had a drink at McGovern's and crossed the street to have another at Polly's Cage. It wasn't five o'clock yet but the bar was doing good business already.

It turned into a funny night. I had dinner at the Greek place and read the *Post*, spent a little time at Joey Farrell's on Fifty-eighth Street, then wound up getting to Armstrong's around ten-thirty or thereabouts. I spent part of the evening alone at my usual table and part of it in conversation at the bar. I made a point of stretching my drinks, mixing my bourbon with coffee, making a cup last a while, taking a glass of plain water from time to time.

But that never really works. If you're going to get drunk you'll manage it somehow. The obstacles I placed in my path just kept me up later. By two-thirty I'd done what I had set out to do. I'd made my load and I could go home and sleep it off.

I woke around ten with less of a hangover than I'd earned and no memory of anything after I'd left Armstrong's. I was in my own bed in my own hotel room. And my clothes were hung neatly in the closet, always a good sign on a morning after. So I must have been in fairly good shape. But a certain amount of time was lost to memory, blacked out, gone.

When that first started happening I tended to worry about it. But it's the sort of thing you can get used to.

It was the money, the twelve hundred bucks. I couldn't understand the money. I had done nothing to deserve it. It had been left to me by a poor little rich woman whose name I'd not even known.

It had never occurred to me to refuse the dough. Very early in my career as a cop I'd learned an important precept. When someone put money in your hand you closed your fingers around it and put it in your pocket. I learned that lesson well and never had cause to regret its application. I didn't walk around with my hand out and I never took drug or homicide money but I certainly grabbed all the clean graft that came my way and a certain amount that wouldn't have stood a white glove inspection. If Mary Alice thought I merited twelve hundred dollars, who was I to argue?

Ah, but it didn't quite work that way. Because somehow the money gnawed at me.

After breakfast I went to St Paul's but there was a service going on, a priest saying Mass, so I didn't stay. I walked down to St Benedict the Moor's on Fifty-third Street and sat for a few minutes in a pew at the rear. I go to churches to try to think, and I gave it a shot but my mind didn't know where to go.

I slipped six twenties into the poor box. I tithe. It's a habit I got into after I left the department and I still don't know why I do it. God knows. Or maybe He's as mystified as I am. This time, though, there was a certain balance in the act. Mary Alice Redfield had given me twelve hundred dollars for no reason I could comprehend. I was passing on a ten percent commission to the church for no better reason.

I stopped on the way out and lit a couple of candles for various people who weren't alive anymore. One of them was for the bag lady. I didn't see how it could do her any good, but I couldn't imagine how it could harm her, either.

*　　　*　　　*

I had read some press coverage of the killing when it happened. I generally keep up with crime stories. Part of me evidently never stopped being a policeman. Now I went down to the Forty-second Street library to refresh my memory.

The *Times* had run a pair of brief back-page items, the first a report of the killing of an unidentified female derelict, the second a follow-up giving her name and age. She'd been forty-seven, I learned. This surprised me, and then I realized that any specific number would have come as a surprise. Bums and bag ladies are ageless. Mary Alice Redfield could have been thirty or sixty or anywhere in between.

The *News* had run a more extended article than the *Times*, enumerating the stab wounds – twenty-six of them – and described the scarf wound about her throat – blue and white, a designer print, but tattered at its edges and evidently somebody's castoff. It was this article that I remembered having read.

But the *Post* had really played the story. It had appeared shortly after the new owner took over the paper and the editors were going all out for human interest, which always translates out as sex and violence. The brutal killing of a woman touches both of those bases, and this had the added kick that she was a character. If they'd ever learned she was an heiress it would have been page three material, but even without that knowledge they did all right by her.

The first story they ran was straight news reporting, albeit embellished with reports on the blood, the clothes she was wearing, the litter in the alley where she was found and all that sort of thing. The next day a reporter pushed the pathos button and tapped out a story featuring capsule interviews with people in the neighborhood. Only a few of them were identified by name and I came away with the feeling that he'd made up some peachy quotes and attributed them to unnamed nonexistent hangers-on. As a sidebar to that story, another reporter speculated on the possibility of a whole string of bag-lady murders, a speculation which happily had turned out to be off the mark. The clown had presumably gone around the West Side asking shopping-bag ladies if they were afraid of being the killer's next victim. I hope he faked the piece and let the ladies alone.

And that was about it. When the killer failed to strike again the newspapers hung up on the story. Good news is no news.

*   *   *

I walked back from the library. It was fine weather. The winds had blown all the crap out of the sky and there was nothing but blue overhead. The air actually had some air in it for a change. I walked west on Forty-second Street and north on Broadway, and I started noticing the number of street people, the drunks and the crazies and the unclassifiable derelicts. By the time I got within a few blocks of Fifty-seventh Street I was recognizing a large percentage of them. Each mini-neighborhood has its own human flotsam and jetsam and they're a lot more noticeable come springtime. Winter sends some of them south and others to shelter, and there's a certain percentage who die of exposure, but when the sun warms the pavement it brings most of them out again.

When I stopped for a paper at the corner of Eighth Avenue I got the bag lady into the conversation. The newsie clucked his tongue and shook his head. "The damnedest thing. Just the damnedest thing."

"Murder never makes much sense."

"The hell with murder. You know what she did? You know Eddie, works for me midnight to eight? Guy with the one droopy eyelid? Now he wasn't the guy used to sell her the stack of papers. Matter of fact that was usually me. She'd come by during the late morning or early afternoon and she'd take fifteen or twenty papers and pay me for 'em, and then she'd sit on her crate down the next corner and she'd sell as many as she could, and then she'd bring 'em back and I'd give her a refund on what she didn't sell."

"What did she pay for them?"

"Full price. And that's what she sold 'em for. The hell, I can't discount on papers. You know the margin we got. I'm not even supposed to take 'em back, but what difference does it make? It gave the poor woman something to do is my theory. She was important, she was a businesswoman. Sits there charging a quarter for something she just paid a quarter for, it's no way to get rich, but you know something? She had money. Lived like a pig but she had money."

"So I understand."

"She left Eddie seven-twenty. You believe that? Seven hundred and twenty dollars, she willed it to him, there was this lawyer come around two, three weeks ago with a check. Eddie

Halloran. Pay to the order of. You believe that? She never had dealings with him. I sold her the papers, I bought 'em back from her. Not that I'm complaining, not that I want the woman's money, but I ask you this: Why Eddie? He don't know her. He can't believe she knows his name, Eddie Halloran. Why'd she leave it to him? He tells this lawyer, he says maybe she's got some other Eddie Halloran in mind. It's a common Irish name and the neighborhood's full of the Irish. I'm thinking to myself, Eddie, schmuck, take the money and shut up, but it's him all right because it says in the will. Eddie Halloran the newsdealer is what it says. So that's him, right? But why Eddie?"

Why me? "Maybe she liked the way he smiled."

"Yeah, maybe. Or the way he combed his hair. Listen, it's money in his pocket. I worried he'd go on a toot, drink it up, but he says money's no temptation. He says he's always got the price of a drink in his jeans and there's a bar on every block but he can walk right past 'em, so why worry about a few hundred dollars? You know something? That crazy woman, I'll tell you something, I miss her. She'd come, crazy hat on her head, spacy look in her eyes, she'd buy her stack of papers and waddle off all businesslike, then she'd bring the leftovers and cash 'em in, and I'd make a joke about her when she was out of earshot, but I miss her."

"I know what you mean."

"She never hurt nobody," he said. "She never hurt a soul."

"Mary Alice Redfield. Yeah, the multiple stabbing and strangulation." He shifted a cud-sized wad of gum from one side of his mouth to the other, pushed a lock of hair off his forehead and yawned. "What have you got, some new information?"

"Nothing. I wanted to find out what you had."

"Yeah, right."

He worked on the chewing gum. He was a patrolman named Andersen who worked out of the Eighteenth. Another cop, a detective named Guzik, had learned that Andersen had caught the Redfield case and had taken the trouble to introduce the two of us. I hadn't known Andersen when I was on the force. He was younger than I, but then most people are nowadays.

He said, "Thing is, Scudder, we more or less put that one out of the way. It's in an open file. You know how it works. If we get new information, fine, but in the meantime I don't sit up nights thinking about it."

"I just wanted to see what you had."

"Well, I'm kind of tight for time, if you know what I mean. My own personal time, I set a certain store by my own time."

"I can understand that."

"You probably got some relative of the deceased for a client. Wants to find out who'd do such a terrible thing to poor old Cousin Mary. Naturally you're interested because it's a chance to make a buck and a man's gotta make a living. Whether a man's a cop or a civilian he's gotta make a buck, right?"

Uh-huh. I seem to remember that we were subtler in my day, but perhaps that's just age talking. I thought of telling him that I didn't have a client but why should he believe me? He didn't know me. If there was nothing in it for him, why should he bother?

So I said, "You know, we're just a couple weeks away from Memorial Day."

"Yeah, I'll buy a poppy from a Legionnaire. So what else is new?"

"Memorial Day's when women start wearing white shoes and men put straw hats on their heads. You got a new hat for the summer season, Andersen? Because you could use one."

"A man can always use a new hat," he said.

A hat is cop talk for twenty-five dollars. By the time I left the precinct house Andersen had two tens and a five of Mary Alice Redfield's bequest to me and I had all the data that had turned up to date.

I think Andersen won that one. I now knew that the murder weapon had been a kitchen knife with a blade approximately seven and a half inches long. That one of the stab wounds had found the heart and had probably caused death instantaneously. That it was impossible to determine whether strangulation had taken place before or after death. That *should* have been possible to determine – maybe the medical examiner hadn't wasted too much time checking her out, or maybe he had been reluctant to commit himself. She'd been dead a few hours when they found her – the estimate was that she'd died around midnight and the body wasn't reported until half-past five. That wouldn't have ripened her all that much, not in winter weather, but most likely her personal hygiene was nothing to boast about, and she was just a shopping-bag lady and you couldn't bring her back to life, so why knock yourself out running tests on her malodorous corpse?

I learned a few other things. The landlady's name. The name of the off-duty bartender, heading home after a nightcap at the neighborhood after-hours joint, who'd happened on the body and who had been drunk enough or sober enough to take the trouble to report it. And I learned the sort of negative facts that turn up in a police report when the case is headed for an open file – the handful of nonleads that led nowhere, the witnesses who had nothing to contribute, the routine matters routinely handled. They hadn't knocked themselves out, Andersen and his partner, but would I have handled it any differently? Why knock yourself out chasing a murderer you didn't stand much chance of catching?

In the theater, SRO is good news. It means a sellout performance, standing room only. But once you get out of the theater district it means single room occupancy, and the designation is invariably applied to a hotel or apartment house which has seen better days.

Mary Alice Redfield's home for the last six or seven years of her life had started out as an old Rent Law tenement, built around the turn of the century, six stories tall, faced in red-brown brick, with four apartments to the floor. Now all of those little apartments had been carved into single rooms as if they were election districts gerrymandered by a maniac. There was a communal bathroom on each floor and you didn't need a map to find it.

The manager was a Mrs Larkin. Her blue eyes had lost most of their color and half her hair had gone from black to gray but she was still pert. If she's reincarnated as a bird she'll be a house wren.

She said, "Oh, poor Mary. We're none of us safe, are we, with the streets full of monsters? I was born in this neighborhood and I'll die in it, but please God that'll be of natural causes. Poor Mary. There's some said she should have been locked up, but Jesus, she got along. She lived her life. And she had her check coming in every month and paid her rent on time. She had her own money, you know. She wasn't living off the public like some I could name but won't."

"I know."

"Do you want to see her room? I rented it twice since then. The first one was a young man and he didn't stay. He looked all right but when he left me I was just as glad. He said he was a sailor off a ship and when he left he said he'd got on with another ship and was on his way to Hong Kong or some such place, but I've had no end of sailors and he didn't walk like a sailor so I don't know what he was after doing. Then I could have rented it twelve times but didn't because I won't rent to colored or Spanish. I've nothing against them but I won't have them in the house. The owner says to me, Mrs Larkin he says, my instructions are to rent to anybody regardless of race or creed or color, but if you was to use your own judgment I wouldn't have to know about it. In other words he don't want them either but he's after covering himself."

"I suppose he has to."

"Oh, with all the laws, but I've had no trouble." She laid a forefinger alongside her nose. It's a gesture you don't see too much these days. "Then I rented poor Mary's room two weeks ago to a very nice woman, a widow. She likes her beer, she does, but why shouldn't she have it? I keep my eye on her and she's making no trouble, and if she wants an old jar now and then whose business is it but her own?" She fixed her blue-gray eyes on me. "You like your drink," she said.

"Is it on my breath?"

"No, but I can see it in your face. Larkin liked his drink and there's some say it killed him but he liked it and a man has a right to live what life he wants. And he was never a hard man when he drank, never cursed or fought or beat a woman as some I could name but won't. Mrs Shepard's out now. That's the one took poor Mary's room, and I'll show it to you if you want."

So I saw the room. It was kept neat.

"She keeps it tidier than poor Mary," Mrs Larkin said. "Now Mary wasn't dirty, you understand, but she had all her belongings. Her shopping bags and other things that she kept in her room. She made a mare's nest of the place, and all the years she lived here, you see, it wasn't tidy. I would keep her bed made but she didn't want me touching her things and so I let it be cluttered as she wanted it. She paid her rent on time and made no trouble otherwise. She had money, you know."

"Yes, I know."

"She left some to a woman on the fourth floor. A much younger woman, she'd only moved here three months before Mary was killed, and if she exchanged a word with Mary I couldn't swear to it, but Mary left her almost a thousand dollars. Now Mrs Klein across the hall lived here since before Mary ever moved in and the two old things always had a good word for each other, and all Mrs Klein has is the welfare and she could have made good use of a couple of dollars, but Mary left her money instead to Miss Strom." She raised her eyebrows to show bewilderment. "Now Mrs Klein said nothing, and I don't even know if she's had the thought that Mary might have mentioned her in her will, but Miss Strom said she didn't know what to make of it. She just couldn't understand it at all, and what I told her was you can't figure out a woman like poor Mary who never had both her feet on the pavement. Troubled as she was, daft as she was, who's to say what she might have had on her mind?"

"Could I see Miss Strom?"

"That would be for her to say, but she's not home from work yet. She works part-time in the afternoons. She's a close one, not that she hasn't the right to be, and she's never said what it is that she does. But she's a decent sort. This is a decent house."

"I'm sure it is."

"It's single rooms and they don't cost much so you know you're not at the Ritz Hotel, but there's decent people here and I keep it as clean as a person can. When there's not but one toilet on the floor it's a struggle. But it's decent."

"Yes."

"Poor Mary. Why'd anyone kill her? Was it sex, do you know? Not that you could imagine anyone wanting her, the old thing, but try to figure out a madman and you'll go mad your own self. Was she molested?"

"No."

"Just killed, then. Oh, God save us all. I gave her a home for almost seven years. Which it was no more than my job to do, not making it out to be charity on my part. But I had her here all that time and of course I never knew her, you couldn't get to know a poor old soul like that, but I got used to her. Do you know what I mean?"

"I think so."

"I got used to having her about. I might say Hello and Good morning and Isn't it a nice day and not get a look in reply, but even on those days she was someone familiar to say something to. And she's gone now and we're all of us older, aren't we?"

"We are."

"The poor old thing. How could anyone do it, will you tell me that? How could anyone murder her?"

I don't think she expected an answer. Just as well. I didn't have one.

After dinner I returned for a few minutes of conversation with Genevieve Strom. She had no idea why Miss Redfield had left her the money. She'd received $880 and she was glad to get it because she could use it, but the whole thing puzzled her. "I hardly knew her," she said more than once. "I keep thinking I ought to do something special with the money, but what?"

I made the bars that night but drinking didn't have the urgency it had possessed the night before. I was able to keep it in proportion and to know that I'd wake up the next morning with my memory intact. In the course of things I dropped over to the newsstand a little past midnight and talked with Eddie Halloran. He was looking good and I said as much. I remembered him when he'd gone to work for Sid three years ago. He'd been drawn then, and shaky, and his eyes always moved off to the side of whatever he was looking at. Now there was confidence in his stance and he looked years younger. It hadn't all come back to him and maybe some of it was lost forever. I guess the booze had him pretty good before he kicked it once and for all.

We talked about the bag lady. He said, "Know what I think it is? Somebody's sweeping the streets."

"I don't follow you."

"A cleanup campaign. Few years back, Matt, there was this gang of kids found a new way to amuse theirselves. Pick up a can of gasoline, find some bum down on the Bowery, pour the gas on him and throw a lit match at him. You remember?"

"Yeah, I remember."

"Those kids thought they were patriots. Thought they

deserved a medal. They were cleaning up the neighborhood, getting drunken bums off the streets. You know, Matt, people don't like to look at a derelict. That building up the block, the Towers? There's this grating there where the heating system's vented. You remember how the guys would sleep there in the winter. It was warm, it was comfortable, it was free, and two or three guys would be there every night catching some Z's and getting warm. Remember?"

"Uh-huh. Then they fenced it."

"Right. Because the tenants complained. It didn't hurt them any, it was just the local bums sleeping it off, but the tenants pay a lot of rent and they don't like to look at bums on their way in or out of their building. The bums were outside and not bothering anybody but it was the sight of them, you know, so the owners went to the expense of putting up cyclone fencing around where they used to sleep. It looks ugly as hell and all it does is keep the bums out but that's all it's supposed to do."

"That's human beings for you."

He nodded, then turned aside to sell somebody a *Daily News* and a *Racing Form.* Then he said, "I don't know what it is exactly. *I* was a bum, Matt. I got pretty far down. You probably don't know how far. I got as far as the Bowery. I panhandled, I slept in my clothes on a bench or in a doorway. You look at men like that and you think they're just waiting to die, and they are, but some of them come back. And you can't tell for sure who's gonna come back and who's not. Somebody coulda poured gas on me, set me on fire. Sweet Jesus."

"The shopping-bag lady—"

"You'll look at a bum and you'll say to yourself, 'Maybe I could get like that and I don't wanta think about it.' Or you'll look at somebody like the shopping-bag lady and say, 'I could go nutsy like her so get her out of my sight.' And you get people who think like Nazis. You know, take all the cripples and the lunatics and the retarded kids and all and give 'em an injection and Goodbye, Charlie."

"You think that's what happened to her?"

"What else?"

"But whoever did it stopped at one, Eddie."

He frowned. "Don't make sense," he said. "Unless he did the one job and the next day he got run down by a Ninth Avenue bus, and it couldn't happen to a nicer guy. Or he got scared. All that blood and it was more than he figured on. Or he left town. Could be anything like that."

"Could be."

"There's no other reason, is there? She musta been killed because she was a bag lady, right?"

"I don't know."

"Well, Jesus Christ, Matt. What other reason would anybody have for killing her?"

The law firm where Aaron Creighton worked had offices on the seventh floor of the Flatiron Building. In addition to the four partners, eleven other lawyers had their names painted on the frosted glass door. Aaron Creighton's came second from the bottom. Well, he was young.

He was also surprised to see me, and when I told him what I wanted he said it was irregular.

"Matter of public record, isn't it?"

"Well, yes," he said. "That means you can find the information. It doesn't mean we're obliged to furnish it to you."

For an instant I thought I was back at the Eighteenth Precinct and a cop was trying to hustle me for the price of a new hat. But Creighton's reservations were ethical. I wanted a list of Mary Alice Redfield's beneficiaries, including the amounts they'd received and the dates they'd been added to her will. He wasn't sure where his duty lay.

"I'd like to be helpful," he said. "Perhaps you could tell me just what your interest is."

"I'm not sure."

"I beg your pardon?"

"I don't know why I'm playing with this one. I used to be a cop, Mr Creighton. Now I'm a sort of unofficial detective. I don't carry a license but I do things for people and I wind up making enough that way to keep a roof overhead."

His eyes were wary. I guess he was trying to guess how I intended to earn myself a fee out of this.

"I got twelve hundred dollars out of the blue. It was left to me by a woman I didn't really know and who didn't really know me. I can't seem to slough off the feeling that I got the money for a reason. That I've been paid in advance."

"Paid for what?"

"To try and find out who killed her."

"Oh," he said. "*Oh*."

"I don't want to get the heirs together to challenge the will, if that was what was bothering you. And I can't quite make myself suspect that one of her beneficiaries killed her for the money she was leaving him. For one thing, she doesn't seem to have told people they were named in her will. She never said anything to me or to the two people I've spoken with thus far. For another, it wasn't the sort of murder that gets committed for gain. It was deliberately brutal."

"Then why do you want to know who the other beneficiaries are?"

"I don't know. Part of it's cop training. When you've got any specific leads, any hard facts, you run them down before you cast a wider net. That's only part of it. I suppose I want to get more of a sense of the woman. That's probably all I can realistically hope to get, anyway. I don't stand much chance of tracking her killer."

"The police don't seem to have gotten very far."

I nodded. "I don't think they tried too hard. And I don't think they knew she had an estate. I talked to one of the cops on the case and if he had known that he'd have mentioned it to me. There was nothing in her file. My guess is they waited for her killer to run a string of murders so they'd have something more concrete to work with. It's the kind of senseless crime that usually gets repeated." I closed my eyes for a moment, reaching for an errant thought. "But he didn't repeat," I said. "So they put it on a back burner and then they took it off the stove altogether."

"I don't know much about police work. I've been involved largely with estates and trusts." He tried a smile. "Most of my clients die of natural causes. Murder's an exception."

"It generally is. I'll probably never find him. I certainly don't expect to find him. Just killing her and moving on, hell, and it was all those months ago. He could have been a sailor off a ship, got tanked up and went nuts and he's in Macao or Port-au-Prince by now. No witnesses and no clues and no suspects and the trail's three months cold by now, and it's a fair bet the killer doesn't remember what he did. So many murders take place in blackout, you know."

"Blackout?" He frowned. "You don't mean in the dark?"

"Alcoholic blackout. The prisons are full of men who got drunk and shot their wives or their best friends. Now they're serving twenty-to-life for something they don't remember. No recollection at all."

The idea unsettled him, and he looked especially young now. "That's frightening," he said. "Really terrifying."

"Yes."

"I originally gave some thought to criminal law. My Uncle Jack talked me out of it. He said you either starve or you spend your time helping professional criminals beat the system. He said that was the only way you made good money out of a criminal practice and what you wound up doing was unpleasant and basically immoral. Of course there are a couple of superstar criminal lawyers, the hotshots everybody knows, but the other ninety-nine percent fit what Uncle Jack said."

"I would think so, yes."

"I guess I made the right decision." He took his glasses off, inspected them, decided they were clean, put them back on again. "Sometimes I'm not so sure," he said. "Sometimes I wonder. I'll get that list for you. I should probably check with someone to make sure it's all right but I'm not going to bother. You know lawyers. If you ask them whether it's all right to do something they'll automatically say no. Because inaction is always safer than action and they can't get in trouble for giving you bad advice if they tell you to sit on your hands and do nothing. I'm going overboard. Most of the time I like what I do and I'm proud of my profession. This'll take me a few minutes. Do you want some coffee in the meantime?"

His girl brought me a cup, black, no sugar. No bourbon, either. By the time I was done with the coffee he had the list ready.

"If there's anything else I can do—"

I told him I'd let him know. He walked out to the elevator with me, waited for the cage to come wheezing up, shook my hand. I watched him turn and head back to his office and I had the feeling he'd have preferred to come along with me. In a day or so he'd change his mind, but right now he didn't seem too crazy about his job.

*   *   *

The next week was a curious one. I worked my way through the list Aaron Creighton had given me, knowing what I was doing was essentially purposeless but compulsive about doing it all the same.

There were thirty-two names on the list. I checked off my own and Eddie Halloran and Genevieve Strom. I put additional check marks next to six people who lived outside of New York. Then I had a go at the remaining twenty-three names. Creighton had done most of the spadework for me, finding addresses to match most of the names. He'd included the date each of the thirty-two codicils had been drawn, and that enabled me to attack the list in reverse chronological order, starting with those persons who'd been made beneficiaries most recently. If this was a method, there was madness to it; it was based on the notion that a person added recently to the will would be more likely to commit homicide for gain, and I'd already decided this wasn't that kind of a killing to begin with.

Well, it gave me something to do. And it led to some interesting conversations. If the people Mary Alice Redfield had chosen to remember ran to any type, my mind wasn't subtle enough to discern it. They ranged in age, in ethnic background, in gender and sexual orientation, in economic status. Most of them were as mystified as Eddie and Genevieve and I about the bag lady's largesse, but once in a while I'd encounter someone who attributed it to some act of kindness he'd performed, and there was a young man named Jerry Forgash who was in no doubt whatsoever. He was some form of Jesus freak and he'd given poor Mary a couple of tracts and a Get Smart – Get Saved button, presumably a twin to the one he wore on the breast pocket of his chambray shirt. I suppose she put his gifts in one of her shopping bags.

"I told her Jesus loved her," he said, "and I suppose it won her soul for Christ. So of course she was grateful. Cast your bread upon the waters, Mr Scudder. Brother Matthew. You know there was a disciple of Christ named Matthew."

"I know."

He told me Jesus loved me and that I should get smart and get saved. I managed not to get a button but I had to take a couple of tracts from him. I didn't have a shopping bag so I stuck them in my pocket, and a couple of nights later I read them before I went to bed. They didn't win my soul for Christ but you never know.

I didn't run the whole list. People were hard to find and I wasn't in any big rush to find them. It wasn't that kind of a case. It wasn't a case at all, really, merely an obsession, and there was surely no need to race the clock. Or the calendar. If anything, I was probably reluctant to finish up the names on the list. Once I ran out of them I'd have to find some other way to approach the woman's murder and I was damned if I knew where to start.

While I was doing all this, an odd thing happened. The word got around that I was investigating the woman's death, and the whole neighborhood became very much aware of Mary Alice Redfield. People began to seek me out. Ostensibly they had information to give me or theories to advance, but neither the information nor the theories ever seemed to amount to anything substantial, and I came to see that they were merely there as a prelude to conversation. Someone would start off by saying he'd seen Mary selling the *Post* the afternoon before she was killed, and that would serve as the opening wedge of a discussion of the bag woman, or bag women in general, or various qualities of the neighborhood, or violence in American life, or whatever.

A lot of people started off talking about the bag lady and wound up talking about themselves. I guess most conversations work out that way.

A nurse from Roosevelt said she never saw a shopping-bag lady without hearing an inner voice say *There but for the grace of God.* And she was not the only woman who confessed she worried about ending up that way. I guess it's a specter that haunts women who live alone, just as the vision of the Bowery derelict clouds the peripheral vision of hard-drinking men.

Genevieve Strom turned up at Armstrong's one night. We talked briefly about the bag lady. Two nights later she came back again and we took turns spending our inheritances on rounds of drinks. The drinks hit her with some force and a little past midnight she decided it was time to go. I said I'd see her home. At the corner of Fifty-seventh Street she stopped in her tracks and said, "No men in the room. That's one of Mrs Larkin's rules."

"Old-fashioned, isn't she?"

"She runs a daycent establishment." Her mock-Irish accent

was heavier than the landlady's. Her eyes, hard to read in the lamplight, raised to meet mine. "Take me someplace."

I took her to my hotel, a less decent establishment than Mrs Larkin's. We did each other little good but no harm, and it beat being alone.

Another night I ran into Barry Mosedale at Polly's Cage. He told me there was a singer at Kid Gloves who was doing a number about the bag lady. "I can find out how you can reach him," he offered.

"Is he there now?"

He nodded and checked his watch. "He goes on in fifteen minutes. But you don't want to go there, do you?"

"Why not?"

"Hardly your sort of crowd, Matt."

"Cops go anywhere."

"Indeed they do, and they're welcome wherever they go, aren't they? Just let me drink this and I'll accompany you, if that's all right. You need someone to lend you immoral support."

Kid Gloves is a gay bar on Fifty-sixth west of Ninth. The decor is just a little aggressively gay lib. There's a small raised stage, a scattering of tables, a piano, a loud jukebox. Barry Mosedale and I stood at the bar. I'd been there before and knew better than to order their coffee. I had straight bourbon. Barry had his on ice with a splash of soda.

Halfway through the drink Gordon Lurie was introduced. He wore tight jeans and a flowered shirt, sat on stage on a folding chair, sang ballads he'd written himself with his own guitar for accompaniment. I don't know if he was any good or not. It sounded to me as though all the songs had the same melody, but that may just have been a similarity of style. I don't have much of an ear.

After a song about a summer romance in Amsterdam, Gordon Lurie announced that the next number was dedicated to the memory of Mary Alice Redfield. Then he sang.

> *She's a shopping-bag lady who lives on*
> *the sidewalks of Broadway*
> *Wearing all of her clothes and her years*
> *on her back*

Toting dead dreams in an old paper sack
Searching the trashcans for something she
lost here on Broadway –
Shopping-bag lady . . .

You'd never know but she once was an
actress on Broadway
Speaking the words that they stuffed in
her head
Reciting the lines of the life that she led
Thrilling her fans and her friends and her
lovers on Broadway –
Shopping-bag lady . . .

There are demons who lurk in the corner
of minds and of Broadway
And after the omens and portents and
signs
Came the day she forgot to remember her
lines
Put her life on a leash and took it out
walking on Broadway –
Shopping-bag lady . . .

There were a couple more verses and the shopping-bag lady in the song wound up murdered in a doorway, dying in defense of the "tattered old treasures she mined in the trashcans of Broadway." The song went over well and got a bigger hand than any of the ones that had preceded it.

I asked Barry who Gordon Lurie was.

"You know very nearly as much as I," he said. "He started here Tuesday. I find him whelming, personally. Neither overwhelming nor underwhelming but somewhere in the middle."

"Mary Alice never spent much time on Broadway. I never saw her more than a block from Ninth Avenue."

"Poetic license, I'm sure. The song would lack a certain something if you substituted Ninth Avenue for Broadway. As it stands it sounds a little like 'Rhinestone Cowboy.' "

"Lurie live around here?"

"I don't know where he lives. I have the feeling he's Canadian.

So many people are nowadays. It used to be that no one was Canadian and now simply everybody is. I'm sure it must be a virus."

We listened to the rest of Gordon Lurie's act. Then Barry leaned forward and chatted with the bartender to find out how I could get backstage. I found my way to what passed for a dressing room at Kid Gloves. It must have been a ladies' lavatory in a prior incarnation.

I went in there thinking I'd made a breakthrough, that Lurie had killed her and now he was dealing with his guilt by singing about her. I don't think I really believed this but it supplied me with direction and momentum.

I told him my name and that I was interested in his act. He wanted to know if I was from a record company. "Am I on the threshold of a great opportunity? Am I about to become an overnight success after years of travail?"

We got out of the tiny room and left the club through a side door. Three doors down the block we sat in a cramped booth at a coffee shop. He ordered a Greek salad and we both had coffee.

I told him I was interested in his song about the bag lady.

He brightened. "Oh, do you like it? Personally I think it's the best thing I've written. I just wrote it a couple of days ago. I opened next door Tuesday night. I got to New York three weeks ago and I had a two-week booking in the West Village. A place called David's Table. Do you know it?"

"I don't think so."

"Another stop on the K-Y circuit. Either there aren't any straight people in New York or they don't go to nightclubs. But I was there two weeks, and then I opened at Kid Gloves, and afterward I was sitting and drinking with some people and somebody was talking about the shopping-bag lady and I had had enough Amaretto to be maudlin on the subject. I woke up Wednesday morning with a splitting headache and the first verse of the song buzzing in my splitting head, and I sat up immediately and wrote it down, and as I was writing one verse the next would come bubbling to the surface, and before I knew it I had all six verses." He took a cigarette, then paused in the act of lighting it to fix his eyes on me. "You told me your name," he said, "but I don't remember it."

"Matthew Scudder."

"Yes. You're the person investigating her murder."

"I'm not sure that's the right word. I've been talking to people, seeing what I can come up with. Did you know her before she was killed?"

He shook his head. "I was never even in this neighborhood before. *Oh*. I'm not a suspect, am I? Because I haven't been in New York since the fall. I haven't bothered to figure out where I was when she was killed but I was in California at Christmastime and I'd gotten as far east as Chicago in early March, so I do have a fairly solid alibi."

"I never really suspected you. I think I just wanted to hear your song." I sipped some coffee. "Where did you get the facts of her life? Was she an actress?"

"I don't think so. Was she? It wasn't really *about* her, you know. It was inspired by her story but I didn't know her and I never knew anything about her. The past few days I've been paying a lot of attention to bag ladies, though. And other street people."

"I know what you mean."

"Are there more of them in New York or is it just that they're so much more visible here? In California everybody drives, you don't see people on the street. I'm from Canada, rural Ontario, and the first city I ever spent much time in was Toronto, and there are crazy people on the streets there but it's nothing like New York. Does the city drive them crazy or does it just tend to draw crazy people?"

"I don't know."

"Maybe they're not crazy. Maybe they just hear a different drummer. I wonder who killed her."

"We'll probably never know."

"What I really wonder is *why* she was killed. In my song I made up some reason. That somebody wanted what was in her bags. I think it works as a song that way but I don't think there's much chance that it happened like that. Why would anyone kill the poor thing?"

"I don't know."

"They say she left people money. People she hardly knew. Is that the truth?" I nodded. "And she left me a song. I don't even feel that I wrote it. I woke up with it. I never set eyes on her and she touched my life. That's strange, isn't it?"

*　　*　　*

Everything was strange. The strangest part of all was the way it ended.

It was a Monday night. The Mets were at Shea and I'd taken my sons to a game. The Dodgers were in for a three-game series which they eventually swept as they'd been sweeping everything lately. The boys and I got to watch them knock Jon Matlack out of the box and go on to shell his several replacements. The final count was something like 13–4. We stayed in our seats until the last out. Then I saw them home and caught a train back to the city.

So it was past midnight when I reached Armstrong's. Trina brought me a large double and a mug of coffee without being asked. I knocked back half of the bourbon and was dumping the rest into my coffee when she told me somebody'd been looking for me earlier. "He was in three times in the past two hours," she said. "A wiry guy, high forehead, bushy eyebrows, sort of a bulldog jaw. I guess the word for it is underslung."

"Perfectly good word."

"I said you'd probably get here sooner or later."

"I always do. Sooner or later."

"Uh-huh. You okay, Matt?"

"The Mets lost a close one."

"I heard it was thirteen to four."

"That's close for them these days. Did he say what it was about?"

He hadn't, but within the half hour he came in again and I was there to be found. I recognized him from Trina's description as soon as he came through the door. He looked faintly familiar but he was nobody I knew. I suppose I'd seen him around the neighborhood.

Evidently he knew me by sight because he found his way to my table without asking directions and took a chair without being invited to sit. He didn't say anything for a while and neither did I. I had a fresh bourbon and coffee in front of me and I took a sip and looked him over.

He was under thirty. His cheeks were hollow and the flesh of his face was stretched over his skull like leather that had shrunk upon drying. He wore a forest-green work shirt and a pair of khaki pants. He needed a shave.

Finally he pointed at my cup and asked me what I was drinking. When I told him he said all he drank was beer.

"They have beer here," I said.

"Maybe I'll have what you're drinking." He turned in his chair and waved for Trina. When she came over he said he'd have bourbon and coffee, the same as I was having. He didn't say anything more until she brought the drink. Then, after he had spent quite some time stirring it, he took a sip. "Well," he said, "that's not so bad. That's okay."

"Glad you like it."

"I don't know if I'd order it again, but at least now I know what it's like."

"That's something."

"I seen you around. Matt Scudder. Used to be a cop, private eye now, blah blah blah. Right?"

"Close enough."

"My name's Floyd. I never liked it but I'm stuck with it, right? I could change it but who'm I kidding? Right?"

"If you say so."

"If I don't somebody else will. Floyd Karp, that's the full name. I didn't tell you my last name, did I? That's it, Floyd Karp."

"Okay."

"Okay, okay, okay." He pursed his lips, blew out air in a silent whistle. "What do we do now, Matt? Huh? That's what I want to know."

"I'm not sure what you mean, Floyd."

"Oh, you know what I'm getting at, driving at, getting at. You know, don't you?"

By this time I suppose I did.

"I killed that old lady. Took her life, stabbed her with my knife." He flashed the saddest smile. "Steee-rangled her with her skeeee-arf. Hoist her with her own whatchacallit, petard. What's a petard, Matt?"

"I don't know, Floyd. Why'd you kill her?"

He looked at me, he looked at his coffee, he looked at me again.

He said, "Had to."

"Why?"

"Same as the bourbon and coffee. Had to *see*. Had to taste it and find out what it was like." His eyes met mine. His were very large, hollow, empty. I fancied I could see right through them to the blackness at the back of his skull. "I couldn't get my mind away from murder," he said. His voice was more sober now, the mocking playful quality gone from it. "I tried. I just couldn't do it. It was on my mind all the time and I was afraid of what I might do. I couldn't function, I couldn't think, I just saw blood and death all the time. I was afraid to close my eyes for fear of what I might see. I would just stay up, days it seemed, and then I'd be tired enough to pass out the minute I closed my eyes. I stopped eating. I used to be fairly heavy and the weight just fell off of me."

"When did all this happen, Floyd?"

"I don't know. All winter. And I thought if I went and did it once I would know if I was a man or a monster or what. And I got this knife, and I went out a couple nights but lost my nerve, and then one night – I don't want to talk about that part of it now."

"All right."

"I almost couldn't do it, but I couldn't *not* do it, and then I was doing it and it went on forever. It was *horrible*."

"Why didn't you stop?"

"I don't know. I think I was afraid to stop. That doesn't make any sense, does it? I just don't know. It was all crazy, insane, like being in a movie and being in the audience at the same time. Watching myself."

"No one saw you do it?"

"No. I threw the knife down a sewer. I went home. I put all my clothes in the incinerator, the ones I was wearing. I kept throwing up. All that night I would throw up even when my stomach was empty. Dry heaves, Department of Dry Heaves. And then I guess I fell asleep, I don't know when or how but I did, and the next day I woke up and thought I dreamed it. But of course I didn't."

"No."

"And what I did think was that it was over. I did it and I knew I'd never want to do it again. It was something crazy that happened and I could forget about it. And I thought that was what happened."

"That you managed to forget about it?"

A nod. "But I guess I didn't. And now everybody's talking about her. Mary Alice Redfield, I killed her without knowing her name. Nobody knew her name and now everybody knows it and it's all back in my mind. And I heard you were looking for me, and I guess, I guess . . ." He frowned, chasing a thought around in his mind like a dog trying to capture his tail. Then he gave it up and looked at me. "So here I am," he said. "So here I am."

"Yes."

"Now what happens?"

"I think you'd better tell the police about it, Floyd."

"Why?"

"I suppose for the same reason you told me."

He thought about it. After a long time he nodded. "All right," he said. "I can accept that. I'd never kill anybody again. I know that. But – you're right. I have to tell them. I don't know who to see or what to say or, hell, I just—"

"I'll go with you if you want."

"Yeah. I want you to."

"I'll have a drink and then we'll go. You want another?"

"No. I'm not much of a drinker."

I had it without the coffee this time. After Trina brought it I asked him how he'd picked his victim. Why the bag lady?

He started to cry. No sobs, just tears spilling from his deep-set eyes. After a while he wiped them on his sleeve.

"Because she didn't count," he said. "That's what I thought. She was nobody. Who cared if she died? Who'd miss her?" He closed his eyes tight. "Everybody misses her," he said. "Everybody."

So I took him in. I don't know what they'll do with him. It's not my problem.

It wasn't really a case and I didn't really solve it. As far as I can see I didn't do anything. It was the talk that drove Floyd Karp from cover, and no doubt I helped some of the talk get started, but some of it would have gotten around without me. All those legacies of Mary Alice Redfield's had made her a nine-day wonder in the neighborhood. It was one of those legacies that got me involved.

Maybe she caught her own killer. Maybe he caught himself,

as everyone does. Maybe no man's an island and maybe everybody is.

All I know is I lit a candle for the woman, and I suspect I'm not the only one who did.

BLACK PUDDING

David Goodis

They spotted him on Race Street between Ninth and Tenth. It was Chinatown in the tenderloin of Philadelphia and he stood gazing into the window of the Wong Ho restaurant and wishing he had the cash to buy himself some egg-foo-yung. The menu in the window priced egg-foo-yung at eighty cents an order and he had exactly thirty-one cents in his pocket. He shrugged and started to turn away from the window and just then he heard them coming.

It was their footsteps that told him who they were. There was the squeaky sound of Oscar's brand-new shoes. And the clumping noise of Coley's heavy feet. It was nine years since he'd heard their footsteps but he remembered that Oscar had a weakness for new shoes and Coley always walked heavily.

He faced them. They were smiling at him, their features somewhat greenish under the green neon glow that drifted through after-midnight blackness. He saw the weasel eyes and buzzard nose of little Oscar. He transferred his gaze to the thick lips and puffed-out cheeks of tall, obese Coley.

"Hello, Ken." It was Oscar's purring voice, Oscar's lips scarcely moving.

"Hello," he said to both of them. He blinked a few times. Now the shock was coming. He could feel the waves of shock surging towards him.

"We been looking for you," Coley said. He flipped his thick thumb over his shoulder to indicate the black Olds 88 parked across the street. "We've driven that car clear across the country."

Ken blinked again. The shock had hit him and now it was past and he was blinking from worry. He knew why they'd been looking for him and he was very worried.

He said quietly, "How'd you know I was in Philly?"

"Grapevine," Oscar said. "It's strictly coast-to-coast. It starts from San Quentin and we get tipped off in Los Angeles. It's a letter telling the Boss you been paroled. That's three weeks ago. Then we get letters from Denver and Omaha and a wire from Chicago. And then a phone call from Detroit. We wait to see how far east you'll travel. Finally we get the call from Philly, and the man tells us you're on the bum around Skid Row."

Ken shrugged. He tried to sound casual as he said, "Three thousand miles is a long trip. You must have been anxious to see me."

Oscar nodded. "Very anxious." He sort of floated closer to Ken. And Coley also moved in. It was slow and quiet and it didn't seem like menace but they were crowding him and finally they had him backed up against the restaurant window.

He said to himself, *They've got you, they've found you and they've got you and you're finished.*

He shrugged again. "You can't do it here."

"Can't we?" Oscar purred.

"It's a crowded street," Ken said. He turned his head to look at the lazy parade of tenderloin citizens on both sides of the street. He saw the bums and the beggars, the winos and the ginheads, the yellow faces of middle-aged opium smokers and the grey faces of two-bit scufflers and hustlers.

"Don't look at them," Oscar said. "They can't help you. Even if they could, they wouldn't."

Ken's smile was sad and resigned. "You're so right," he said. His shoulders drooped and his head went down and he saw Oscar reaching into a jacket pocket and taking out the silver-handled tool that had a button on it to release a five-inch blade. He knew there would be no further talk, only action, and it would happen within the next split second.

In that tiny fraction of time, some gears clanged to shift from low to high in Ken's brain. His senses and reflexes, dulled from nine years in prison, were suddenly keen and acutely technical and there was no emotion on his face as he moved. He moved very fast, his arms crossing to shape an X, the left hand flat and rigid and banging against Oscar's wrist, the right hand a fist that caught Coley in the mouth. It sent the two of them staggering backward and gave him the space he wanted and he darted through the gap, sprinting east on Race Street toward Ninth.

As he turned the corner to head north on Ninth, he glanced backward and saw them getting into the Olds. He took a deep breath and continued running up Ninth. He ran straight ahead for approximately fifteen yards and then turned again to make a dash down a narrow alley. In the middle of the alley he hopped a fence, ran across a backyard, hopped another fence, then a few more backyards with more fence-hopping, and then the opened window of a tenement cellar. He lunged at the window, went in head-first, groped for a handhold, couldn't find any, and plunged through eight feet of blackness on to a pile of empty boxes and tin cans. He landed on his side, his thigh taking most of the impact, so that it didn't hurt too much. He rolled over and hit the floor and lay there flat on his belly. From a few feet away a pair of green eyes stared at him and he stared back, and then he grinned as though to say, *Don't be afraid, pussy, stay here and keep me company, it's a tough life and an evil world and us alleycats got to stick together*.

But the cat wasn't trusting any living soul. He let out a soft meow and scampered away. Ken sighed and his grin faded and he felt the pressure of the blackness and the quiet and the loneliness. His mind reached slowly for the road going backward nine years . . .

It was Los Angeles, and they were a small outfit operating from a first-floor apartment near Figueroa and Jefferson. Their business was armed robbery and their work-area included Beverly Hills and Bel-Air and the wealthy residential districts of Pasadena. They concentrated on expensive jewelry and wouldn't touch any job that offered less than a ten-grand haul.

There were five of them, Ken and Oscar and Coley and Ken's wife and the Boss. The name of the Boss was Riker and he was very kind to Ken until the possession of Ken's wife became a need and then a craving and finally an obsession. It showed in Riker's eyes whenever he looked at her. She was a platinum-blonde dazzler, a former burlesque dancer named Hilda. She'd been married to Ken for seven months when Riker reached the point where he couldn't stand it any longer and during a job in Bel-air he banged Ken's skull with the butt end of a revolver. When the police arrived, Ken was unconscious on the floor and later in the hospital they asked him questions but he wouldn't answer. In the courtroom he sat with his head bandaged and they asked him more questions and he wouldn't answer. They gave him five-to-twenty and during his first month in San Quentin he learned from his lawyer that Hilda had obtained a Reno divorce and was married to Riker. He went more or less insane and couldn't be handled and they put him in solitary.

Later they had him in the infirmary, chained to the bed, and they tried some psychology. They told him he'd regain his emotional health if he'd talk and name some names. He laughed at them. Whenever they coaxed him to talk, he laughed in their faces and presently they'd shrug and walk away.

His first few years in Quentin were spent either in solitary or the infirmary, or under special guard. Then, gradually, he quieted down. He became very quiet and in the laundry-room he worked very hard and was extremely cooperative. During the fifth year he was up for parole and they asked him about the Bel-Air job and he replied quite reasonably that he couldn't remember, he was afraid to remember, he wanted to forget all about it and arrange a new life for himself. They told him he'd talk or he'd do the limit. He said he was sorry but he couldn't give them the information they wanted. He explained that he was trying to get straight with himself and be clean inside and he wouldn't feel clean if he earned his freedom that way.

So then it was nine years and they were convinced he'd finally paid his debt to the people of California. They gave him a suit of clothes and a ten-dollar bill and told him he was a free man.

In a Sacramento hash-house he worked as a dishwasher just long enough to earn the bus-fare for a trip across the country. He was thinking in terms of the town where he'd been born and raised, telling himself he'd made a wrong start in Philadelphia and the thing to do was go back there and start again and make it right this time, really legitimate. The parole board okayed the job he'd been promised. That was a healthy thought and it made the bus-trip very enjoyable. But the nicest thing about the bus was its fast engine that took him away from California, far away from certain faces he didn't want to see.

Yet now, as he rested on the floor of the tenement cellar, he could see the faces again. The faces were worried and frightened and he saw them in his brain and heard their trembling voices. He heard Riker saying, "They've released him from Quentin. We'll have to do something." And Hilda saying, "What can we do?" And Riker replying, "We'll get him before he gets us."

He sat up, colliding with an empty tin can that rolled across the floor and made a clatter. For some moments there was quiet and then he heard a shuffling sound and a voice saying, "Who's there?"

It was a female voice, sort of a cracked whisper. It had a touch of asthma in it, some alcohol, and something else that had no connection with health or happiness.

Ken didn't say anything. He hoped she'd go away. Maybe she'd figure it was a rat that had knocked over the tin can and she wouldn't bother to investigate.

But he heard the shuffling footsteps approaching through the blackness. He focused directly ahead and saw the silhouette coming towards him. She was on the slender side, neatly constructed. It was a very interesting silhouette. Her height was approximately five-five and he estimated her weight in the neighborhood of one-ten. He sat up straighter. He was very anxious to get a look at her face.

She came closer and there was the scratchy sound of a match against a matchbox. The match flared and he saw her face. She had medium-brown eyes that matched the color of her hair, and her nose and lips were nicely sculptured, somewhat delicate but blending prettily with the shape of her head. He told himself she was a very pretty girl. But just then he saw the scar.

It was a wide jagged scar that started high on her forehead and crawled down the side of her face and ended less than an inch above her upper lip. The color of it was a livid purple with lateral streaks of pink and white. It was a terrible scar, really hideous.

She saw that he was wincing, but it didn't seem to bother her. The lit match stayed lit and she was sizing him up. She saw a man of medium height and weight, about thirty-six years old, with yellow hair that needed cutting, a face that needed shaving, and sad lonely grey eyes that needed someone's smile.

She tried to smile for him. But only one side of her mouth could manage it. On the other side the scar was like a hook that pulled at her flesh and caused a grimace that was more anguish than physical shame. Such a pretty girl. And so young. She couldn't be more than twenty-five. Well, some people had all the luck. All the rotten luck.

The match was burned halfway down when she reached into the pocket of a tattered dress and took out a candle. She went through the process of lighting the candle and melting the base of it. The softened wax adhered to the cement floor of the cellar and she sat down facing him and said quietly, "All right, let's have it. What's the pitch?"

He pointed backward to the opened window to indicate the November night. He said, "It's chilly out there. I came in to get warm."

She leaned forward just a little to peer at his eyes. Then, shaking her head slowly, she murmured, "No sale."

He shrugged. He didn't say anything.

"Come on," she urged gently. "Let's try it again."

"All right." He grinned at her. And then it came out easily. "I'm hiding."

"From the Law?"

"No," he said. "From trouble."

He started to tell her about it. He couldn't understand why he was telling her. It didn't make sense that he should be spilling the story to someone he'd just met in a dark cellar, someone out of nowhere. But she was company and he needed company. He went on telling her.

It took more than an hour. He was providing all the details of events stretched across nine years. The candlelight showed her sitting there, not moving, her eyes riveted to his face as he spoke in low tones. Sometimes there were pauses, some of them long, some very long, but she never interrupted, she waited patiently while he groped for the words to make the meaning clear.

Finally he said, " – It's a cinch they won't stop, they'll get me sooner or later."

"If they find you," she said.

"They'll find me."

"Not here."

He stared at the flickering candle. "They'll spend money

to get information. There's more than one big mouth in this neighborhood. And the biggest mouths of all belong to the landlords."

"There's no landlord here," she told him. "There's no tenants except me and you."

"Nobody upstairs?"

"Only mice and rats and roaches. It's a condemned house and City Hall calls it a firetrap and from the first floor up the windows are boarded. You can't get up because there's no stairs. One of these days the City'll tear down this dump but I'll worry about that when it happens."

He looked at her. "You live here in the cellar?"

She nodded. "It's a good place to play solitaire."

He smiled and murmured. "Some people like to be alone."

"I don't like it," she said. Then, with a shrug, she pointed to the scar on her face. "What man would live with me?"

He stopped smiling. He didn't say anything.

She said, "It's a long drop when you're tossed out of a third-story window. Most folks are lucky and they land on their feet. I came down head first, cracked my collar-bone and got a fractured skull, and split my face wide open."

He took a closer look at the livid scar. For some moments he was quiet and then he frowned thoughtfully and said, "Maybe it won't be there for long. It's not as deep as I thought it was. If you had it treated—"

"No," she said. "The hell with it."

"You wouldn't need much cash," he urged quietly. "You could go to a clinic. They're doing fancy tricks with plastic surgery these days."

"Yeah, I know." Her voice was toneless. She wasn't looking at him. "The point is, I want the scar to stay there. It keeps me away from men. I've had too many problems with men and now, whenever they see my face, they turn their heads the other way. And that's fine with me. That's just how I want it."

He frowned again. This time it was a deeper frown and it wasn't just thoughtful. He said, "Who threw you out of the window?"

"My husband." She laughed without sound. "My wonderful husband."

"Where is he now?"

"In the cemetery," she said. She shrugged again, and her tone was matter-of-fact. "It happened while I was in hospital. I think he got to the point where he couldn't stand to live with himself. Or maybe he just did it for kicks, I don't know. Anyway, he got hold of a razor and cut his own throat. When they found him, he was very, very dead."

"Well, that's one way of ending a marriage."

Again she uttered the soundless laugh. "It was a fine marriage while it lasted. I was drunk most of the time. I had to get drunk to take what he dished out. He had some weird notions about wedding vows."

"He wasn't faithful to you?"

"Oh! It wasn't that. No. He went out of his way to throw me into the company of other men. At first I thought it was odd, but then I found that it was deliberate, calculated. He expected me to compromise myself and then he'd demand money and if I didn't cooperate he'd beat me. It was a hell of a thing to happen to anyone with any decent ideals. I don't like blackmail – even now. But then it was mental torture to me. So I got it in the neck either way. I used to have bad dreams about it, and I mean bad. I still have them sometimes, so then I need sweet dreams, and that's when I reach for the pipe."

"The pipe?"

"Opium," she said. She said it with fondness and affection. "Opium." There was tenderness in her eyes. "That's my new husband."

He nodded understandingly.

She said, "I get it from a Chinaman on Ninth Street. He's a user himself and he's more than eighty years old and still in there pitching, so I guess with O it's like anything else, it's all a matter of how you use it." Her voice dropped off just a little and her eyes were dull and sort of dismal as she added, "I wish I didn't need so much of it. It takes most of my weekly salary."

"What kind of work you do?"

"I scrub floors," she said. "In nightclubs and dance-halls. All day long I scrub the floors to make them clean and shiny for the night-time customers. Some nights I sit here and think of the pretty girls dancing on them polished floors. The pretty girls with flowers in their hair and no scars on their faces—" She broke it off abruptly, her hand making a brushing gesture as though to disparage the self-pity. She stood up and said, "I gotta go out to do some shopping. You wanna wait here till I come back?"

Without waiting for his answer, she moved across the cellar toward a battered door leading to the backyard. As she opened the door, she turned and looked at him. "Make yourself comfortable," she said. "There's a mattress in the next room. It ain't the Ritz Carlton exactly, but it's better than nothing."

He was asking himself whether he should stay there.

He heard her saying, "Incidentally, my name is Tillie."

She stood there waiting.

"Kenneth," he said. "Kenneth Rockland."

But that wasn't what she was waiting for. Several moments passed, and then somehow he knew what she wanted him to say.

He said, "I'll be here when you come back."

"Good." The candlelight showed her crooked grin, a grimace on the scarred face. But what he saw was a gentle smile. It seemed to drift toward him like a soothing caress. And then he heard her saying. "Maybe I'll come back with some news. You told me it was two men. There's a chance I can check on them if you'll tell me what they look like."

He shook his head. "You better stay out of it. You might get hurt."

"Nothing can hurt me," she said. She pointed her finger at the wreckage of her face. Her tone was almost pleading as she said, "Come on, tell me what they look like."

He shrugged. He gave a brief description of Oscar and Coley. And the Olds 88.

"Check," Tillie said. "I don't have 20–20 but I'll keep them open and see what's happening."

She turned and walked out and the door closed. Ken lifted himself from the floor and picked up the candle. He walked across the cement floor and the candle showed him a small space off to one side, a former coal-bin arranged with a mattress against the wall, a splintered chair and a splintered bureau and a table stacked with books. There was a candleholder on the table and he set the candle on it and then he had a look at the books.

It was an odd mixture of literature. There were books dealing with idyllic romance, strictly from fluttering hearts and soft moonlight and violins. And there were books that probed much deeper, explaining the scientific side of sex. There was one book in particular that looked as though she'd been concentrating on it. The pages were considerably thumbed and she'd used a pencil to underline certain paragraphs. It was clear that she was faced with the hell of a personal problem she was trying to solve intelligently and couldn't.

He shook his head slowly. He thought, *It's a damn shame . . .*

And then, for some unaccountable reason, he thought of Hilda. She flowed into his mind with a rustling of silk that sheathed the exquisite contours of her slender torso and legs. Her platinum-blonde hair was glimmering and her long-lashed green eyes were beckoning to say, Come on, take my hand and we'll go down Memory Lane.

He shut his eyes tightly. He wondered why he was thinking about her. A long time ago he'd managed to get her out of his mind and he couldn't understand what had brought her back again. He begged himself to get rid of the thought, it was a white-hot memory that disturbed him profoundly. Without sound he said, *Goddamn her.*

And suddenly he realized why he was thinking of Hilda. It was like a curtain lifted to reveal the hidden channels of his brain. He was comparing Hilda's physical perfection with the scarred face of Tillie. His eyes were open and he gazed down at the mattress on the floor and for a moment he saw Hilda on the mattress. She smiled teasingly and then she shook her head and said, *Nothing doing.* So then she vanished and in the next moment it was Tillie on the mattress but somehow he didn't feel bitter or disappointed; he had the feeling that the perfection was all on Tillie's side.

He took off his shoes and lowered himself to the mattress. He yawned a few times and then he fell asleep.

A voice said, "Kenneth—"

He was instantly awake. He looked up and saw Tillie. He smiled at her and said, "What time is it?"

"Half-past five." She had a paper bag in her hand and she was taking things out of the bag and putting them on the table. There was some dried fish and a package of tea leaves and some cold fried noodles. She reached deeper into the bag and took out a bottle containing colorless liquid.

"Rice wine," she said. She set the bottle on the table. Then again she reached into the bag and her hand came out holding a cardboard box.

"Opium?" he murmured.

She nodded. "I got some cigarettes, too." She took a pack of Luckies from her pocket, opened the pack and extended it to him.

He sat up and put a cigarette in his mouth and used the candle to light it. He said, "You going to smoke the opium?"

"No, I'll smoke what you're smoking."

He put another cigarette in his mouth and lit it and handed it to her.

She took a few drags and then she said quietly, "I didn't want to wake you up, but I thought you'd want to hear the news."

He blinked a few times. "What news?"

"I saw them," she said.

He blinked again. "Where?"

"On Tenth Street." She took more smoke into her mouth and let it come out of her nose. "It was a couple hours ago, after I come out of the Chinaman's."

He sat up straighter. "You been watching them for two hours?"

"Watching them? I been with them. They took me for a ride."

He stared at her. His mouth was open but no sound came out.

Tillie grinned. "They didn't know I was in the car."

He took a deep breath. "How'd you manage it?"

She shrugged. "It was easy. I saw them sitting in the car and then they got out and I followed them. They were taking a stroll around the block and peeping into alleys and finally I heard the little one saying they might as well powder and come back tomorrow. The big one said they should keep on searching the neighborhood. They got into an argument and I had a feeling the little one would win. So I walked back to the car. The door was open and I climbed in the back and got flat on the floor. About five minutes later they're up front and the car starts and we're riding."

His eyes were narrow. "Where?"

"Downtown," she said. "It wasn't much of a ride. It only took a few minutes. They parked in front of a house on Spruce near Eleventh. I watched them go in. Then I got out of the car—"

"And walked back here?"

"Not right away," she said. "First I cased the house."

Silly Tillie, he thought. *If they'd seen her they'd have dragged her in and killed her.*

She said, "It's one of them little old-fashioned houses. There's a vacant lot on one side and on the other side there's an alley. I went down the alley and came up on the back porch and peeped through the window. They were in the kitchen, the four of them."

He made no sound, but his lips shaped the word. "Four?" And then, with sound, "Who were the other two?"

"A man and a woman."

He stiffened. He tried to get up from the mattress and couldn't move. His eyes aimed past Tillie as he said tightly, "Describe them."

"The man was about five-ten and sort of beefy. I figure about two hundred. He looked about forty or so. Had a suntan and wore expensive clothes. Brown wavy hair and brown eyes and—"

"That's Riker," he murmured. He managed to lift himself from the mattress. His voice was a whisper as he said, "Now let's have the woman."

"She was something," Tillie said. "She was really something."

"Blonde?" And with both hands he made a gesture begging Tillie to speed the reply.

"Platinum blonde," Tillie said. "With the kind of a face that makes men turn round and stretch their necks to look at. That kind of a face, and a shape that goes along with it. She was wearing—"

"Pearls," he said. "She always had a weakness for pearls."

Tillie didn't say anything.

He moved past Tillie. He stood facing the dark wall of the cellar and seeing the yellow-black play of candlelight and shadow on the cracked plaster. "Hilda," he said. "Hilda."

It was quiet for some moments. He told himself it was wintertime and he wondered if he was sweating.

Then very slowly he turned and looked at Tillie. She was sitting on the edge of the mattress and drinking from the bottle of rice wine. She took it in short, measured gulps, taking it down slowly to get the full effect of it. When the bottle was half empty she raised her head and grinned at him and said, "Have some?"

He nodded. She handed him the bottle and he drank. The Chinese wine was mostly fire and it burned all the way going down and when it hit his belly it was electric hot. But the climate it sent to his brain was cool and mild and the mildness showed in his eyes. His voice was quiet and relaxed as he said, "I thought Oscar and Coley made the trip alone. It didn't figure that Riker and Hilda would come with them. But now it adds. I can see the way it adds."

"It's a long ride from Los Angeles," Tillie said.

"They didn't mind. They enjoyed the ride."

"The scenery?"

"No," he said. "They weren't looking at the scenery. They were thinking of the setup here in Philly. With Oscar putting the blade in me and then the funeral and Riker seeing me in the coffin and telling himself his worries were over."

"And Hilda?"

"The same," he said. "She's been worried just as much as Riker. Maybe more."

Tillie nodded slowly. "From the story you told me, she's got more reason to worry."

He laughed lightly. He liked the sound of it and went on with it. He said, through the easy laughter, "They really don't need to worry. They're making it a big thing and it's nothing at all. I forgot all about them a long time ago. But they couldn't forget about me."

Tillie had her head inclined and she seemed to be studying the sound of his laughter. Some moments passed and then she said quietly, "You don't like black pudding?"

He didn't get the drift of that. He stopped laughing and his eyes were asking what she meant.

"There's an old saying," she said. "Revenge is black pudding."

He laughed again.

"Don't pull away from it," Tillie said. "Just listen to it. Let it hit you and sink in. Revenge is black pudding."

He went on laughing, shaking his head and saying, "I'm not in the market."

"You sure?"

"Positive," he said. Then, with a grin, "Only pudding I like is vanilla."

"The black tastes better," Tillie said. "I've had some, and

I know. I had it when they told me he had done away with himself."

He winced slightly. He saw Tillie getting up from the mattress and moving towards him. He heard her saying, "That black pudding has a wonderful flavor. You ought to try a spoonful."

"No," he said. "No, Tillie."

She came closer. She spoke very slowly and there was a slight hissing in her voice. "They put you in prison for nine years. They cheated you and robbed you and tortured you."

"That's all past," he said. "That's from yesterday."

"It's from now." She stood very close to him. "They're itching to hit you again and see you dead. They won't stop until you're dead. That puts a poison label on them. And there's only one way to deal with poison. Get rid of it."

"No," he said. "I'll let it stay the way it is."

"You can't," Tillie said. "It's a choice you have to make. Either you'll drink bitter poison or you'll taste that sweet black pudding."

He grinned again. "There's a third choice."

"Like what?"

"This." And he pointed to the bottle of rice wine. "I like the taste of this. Let's stay with it until it's empty."

"That won't solve the problem," Tillie said.

"The hell with the problem." His grin was wide. It was very wide and he didn't realize that it was forced.

"You fool," Tillie said.

He had the bottle raised and he was taking a drink.

"You poor fool," she said. Then she shrugged and turned away from him and lowered herself to the mattress.

The forced grin stayed on his face as he went on drinking. Now he was drinking slowly because the rice wine dulled the action in his brain and he had difficulty lifting the bottle to his mouth. Gradually he became aware of a change taking place in the air of the cellar; it was thicker, sort of smokey. His eyes tried to focus and there was too much wine in him and he couldn't see straight. But then the smoke came up in front of his eyes and into his eyes. He looked down and saw the white clay pipe in Tillie's hand. She was sitting on the mattress with her legs crossed, Buddha-like, puffing at the opium, taking it in very slowly, the smoke coming out past the corners of her lips.

The grin faded from his face. And somehow the alcohol-mist was drifting away from his brain. He thought, *She smokes it because she's been kicked around.* But there was no pity in his eyes, just the level look of clear thinking. He said to himself, *There's only two kinds of people in this world, the ones who get kicked around and the ones who do the kicking.*

He lowered the bottle to the table. He turned and took a few steps going away and then heard Tillie saying, "Moving out?"

"No," he said. "Just taking a walk."

"Where?"

"Spruce Street," he said.

"Good," she said. "I'll go with you."

He shook his head. He faced her and saw that she'd put the pipe aside. She was getting up from the mattress. He went on shaking his head and saying, "It can't be played that way. I gotta do this alone."

She moved toward him. "Maybe it's goodbye."

"If it is," he said, "there's only one way to say it."

His eyes told her to come closer. He put his arms around her and held her with a tenderness and a feeling of not wanting to let her go. He kissed her. He knew she felt the meaning of the kiss, she was returning it and as her breath went into him it was sweet and pure and somehow like nectar.

Then, very gently, she pulled away from him. She said, "Go now. It's still dark outside. It'll be another hour before the sun comes up."

He grinned. It was a soft grin that wasn't forced. "This job won't take more than an hour," he said. "Whichever way it goes, it'll be a matter of minutes. Either I'll get them or they'll get me."

He turned away and walked across the cellar toward the splintered door. Tillie stood there watching him as he opened the door and went out.

It was less than three minutes later and they had him. He was walking south on Ninth, between Race Street and Arch, and the black Olds 88 was cruising on Arch and he didn't see them but they saw him, with Oscar grinning at Coley and saying, "There's our boy."

Oscar drove the car past the intersection and parked it on the north side of the Arch about twenty feet away from the corner. They got out and walked toward the corner and stayed close to the brick wall of the corner building. They listened to the approaching footsteps and grinned at each other and a few moments later he arrived on the corner and they grabbed him.

He felt Coley's thick arm wrapped tight around his throat, pulling his head back. He saw the glimmer of the five-inch blade in Oscar's hand. He told himself to think fast and he thought very fast and managed to say, "You'll be the losers. I made a connection."

Oscar hesitated. He blinked puzzledly. "What connection?"

He smiled at Oscar. Then he waited for Coley to loosen the armhold on his throat. Coley loosened it, then lowered it to his chest, using both arms to clamp him and prevent him from moving.

He made no attempt to move. He went on smiling at Oscar, and saying, "An important connection. It's important enough to louse you up."

"Prove it," Oscar said.

"You're traced." He narrowed the smile just a little. "If anything happens to me, they know where to get you."

"He's faking," Coley said. Then urgently, "Go on, Oscar, give him the knife."

"Not yet," Oscar murmured. He was studying Ken's eyes and his own eyes were somewhat worried. He said to Ken, "Who did the tracing?"

"I'll tell that to Riker."

Oscar laughed without sound. "Riker's in Los Angeles."

"No he isn't," Ken said. "He's here in Philly."

Oscar stopped laughing. The worry deepened in his eyes. He stared past Ken, focusing on Coley.

"He's here with Hilda," Ken said.

"It's just a guess," Coley said. "It's gotta be a guess." He tightened his bear-hug on Ken. "Do it, Oscar Don't let him stall you. Put the knife in him."

Oscar looked at Ken and said, "You making this a quiz game?"

Ken shrugged. "It's more like stud poker."

"Maybe," Oscar admitted. "But you're not the dealer."

Ken shrugged again. He didn't say anything.

Oscar said, "You're not the dealer and all you can do is hope for the right card."

"I got it already," Ken said. "It fills an inside straight."

Oscar bit the edge of his lip. "All right, I'll take a look." He had the knife aiming at Ken's chest, and then he raised it and moved in closer and the tip of the blade was touching Ken's neck. "Let's see your hole-card, sonny. All you gotta do is name the street and the house."

"Spruce Street," Ken said. "Near Eleventh."

Oscar's face became pale. Again he was staring at Coley.

Ken said, "It's an old house, detached. On one side there's a vacant lot and on the other side there's an alley."

It was quiet for some moments and then Oscar was talking aloud to himself, saying, "He knows, he really knows."

"What's the move?" Coley asked.

He sounded somewhat unhappy.

"We gotta think," Oscar said.

"This makes it complicated and we gotta think it through very careful."

Coley muttered a four-letter word. He said, "We ain't getting paid to do our own thinking. Riker gave us orders to find him and bump him."

"We can't bump him now," Oscar said. "Not under these conditions. The way it stacks up, it's Riker's play. We'll have to take him to Riker."

"Riker won't like that," Coley said.

Oscar didn't reply. Again he was biting his lip and it went on that way for some moments and then he made a gesture toward the parked car. He told Coley to take the wheel and he'd sit in the back with Rockland. As he opened the rear door he had the blade touching Ken's side, gently urging Ken to get in first. Coley was up front behind the wheel and then Oscar and Ken occupied the rear seat and the knife in Oscar's hand was aimed at Ken's abdomen.

The engine started and the Olds 88 moved east on Arch and went past Eighth and turned south on Seventh. There was no talk in the car as they passed Market and Chestnut and Walnut. They had a red light on Locust but Coley ignored it and went through at forty-five.

"Slow down," Oscar said.

Coley was hunched low over the wheel and the speedometer went up to fifty and Oscar yelled, "For Pete's sake, slow down. You wanna be stopped by a red car?"

"There's one now," Ken said, and he pointed toward the side window that showed only the front of a grocery store. But Oscar thought it might really be a side street with a police car approaching, and the thought was in his brain for a tiny fraction of a second. In that segment of time he turned his head to have a look. Ken's hand moved automatically to grab Oscar's wrist and twist hard. The knife fell away from Oscar's fingers and Ken's other hand caught it. Oscar let out a screech and Ken put the knife in Oscar's breast just over his heart. The car was skidding to a stop as Ken stabbed Oscar to finish him. Coley was screaming curses and trying to hurl himself sideways and backwards toward the rear seat and Ken showed him the knife and it didn't stop him. Ken ducked as Coley came vaulting over the top of the front seat, the knife slashing upward to catch Coley as he came on. It buried itself deep enough into his breast to reach the heart and left Coley collapsed with his legs still over the front seat and his body sprawling across the lifeless form of Oscar in the back.

"I'm dying," Coley gurgled. "I'm—" That was his final sound. His eyes opened very wide and his head snapped sideways and he was through for this night and all nights.

Ken opened the rear door and got out. He had the knife in his pocket as he walked with medium-fast stride going south on Seventh to Spruce. Then he turned west on Spruce and walked just a bit faster. Every now and then he glanced backward to see if there were any red cars but all he saw was the empty street and some alley cats mooching around under the street lamps.

In the blackness above the roof-tops the bright yellow face of the City Hall clock showed ten minutes past six. He estimated the sky would be dark for another half-hour. It wasn't much time, but it was time enough for what he intended to do. He told himself he wouldn't enjoy the action, and yet somehow his mind was suffused with a kind of anticipatory satisfaction. It looked like Tillie had been right about that black pudding.

He quickened his pace just a little, crossed Eighth Street and Ninth, and walked faster as he passed Tenth. There were no lit windows on Spruce Street but as he neared Eleventh the moonlight blended with the glow of a street lamp and showed him the vacant lot. He gazed across the empty space to the wall of the old-fashioned house.

Then he was on the vacant lot and moving slowly and quietly toward the rear of the house. He worked his way to the sagging steps of the back porch, saw a light in the kitchen window, climbed two steps and three and four and, peering through the window, saw Hilda.

She was alone in the kitchen, sitting at a white-topped table and smoking a cigarette. There was a cup and saucer on the table, the saucer littered with coffee-stained cigarette butts. As he watched, she got up from the table and went to the stove to lift a percolator off the fire and pour another cup of coffee.

She moved with a slow weaving of her shoulders and a flow of her hips that was more drifting than walking. He thought, *She still has it, that certain way of moving around, using that body like a long-stemmed lily in a quiet breeze. That's what got you the first time you laid eyes on her. The way she moves. And one time very long ago you said to her, "To set me on fire, all you have to do is walk across a room." You couldn't believe you were actually married to that hothouse-prize, that platinum-blonde hair like melted eighteen-karat, that face, she still has it, that body, she still has it. It's been nine years, and she still has it.*

She was wearing bottle-green velvet that set off the pale green of her eyes. The dress was cut low, went in tight around her very narrow waist and stayed tight going down all the way past her knees. She featured pearls around her throat and in her ears and on her wrists. He thought, *You gave her pearls for her birthday and Christmas and you wanted to give her more for the first wedding anniversary. But they don't sell pearls in San Quentin. All they sell is plans for getting out. Like lessons in how to crawl through a pipe, or how to conceal certain tools, or how to disguise the voice. The lessons never paid off, but maybe now's the time to use what you learned. Let's try Coley's voice.*

His knuckles rapped the kitchen door, and his mouth opened to let out Coley's thick, low-pitched voice saying, "It's me and Oscar."

He stood there counting off the seconds. It was four seconds and then the door opened. It opened wide and Hilda's mouth opened wider. Then she had her hand to her mouth and she was stepping backward.

"Hello, Hilda." He came into the kitchen and closed the door behind him.

She took another backward step. She shook her head and spoke through the trembling fingers that pressed against her lips. "It isn't—"

"Yes," he said. "It is."

Her hand fell away from her mouth. The moment was too much for her and it seemed she was going to collapse. But somehow she managed to stay on her feet. Then her eyes were shut tightly and she went on shaking her head.

"Look at me," he said. "Take a good look."

She opened her eyes. She looked him up and down and up again. Then, very slowly, she summoned air into her lungs and he knew she was going to let out a scream. His hands moved fast to his coat pocket and he took out Oscar's knife and said quietly, "No noise, Hilda."

She stared at the knife. The air went out of her without sound. Her arms were limp at her sides. She spoke in a half-whisper, talking to herself. "I don't believe it. Just can't believe it—"

"Why not?" His tone was mild. "It figures, doesn't it? You came to Philly to look for me. And here I am."

For some moments she stayed limp. Then, gradually, her shoulders straightened. She seemed to be getting a grip on herself. Her eyes narrowed just a little, as she went on looking at the silver-handled switch-blade in his hand. She said, "That's Oscar's knife—?"

He nodded.

"Where is Oscar?" she asked. "Where's Coley?"

"They're dead." He pressed the button on the handle and the blade flicked out. He said, "It's a damn shame. They wouldn't be dead if they'd let me alone."

Hilda didn't say anything. She gave a little shrug, as though to indicate there was nothing she could say. He told himself it didn't make sense to wait any longer and the thing to do was put the knife in her heart. He wondered if the knife was sharp enough to cut through ice.

He took a forward step, then stopped. He wondered what was holding him back. Maybe he was waiting for her to break, to fall on her knees and beg for mercy.

But she didn't kneel and she didn't plead. Her voice was matter-of-fact as she said, "I'm wondering if we can make a deal."

It caught him off balance. He frowned slightly. "What kind of deal?"

"Fair trade," she said. "You give me a break and I'll give you Riker."

He changed the frown to a dim smile. "I've got him anyway. It's a cinch he's upstairs sound asleep."

"That's fifty percent right," she said. "He's a very light sleeper. Especially lately, since he heard you were out of Quentin."

He widened the smile. "In Quentin I learned to walk on tiptoe. There won't be any noise."

"There's always noise when you break down a door."

The frown came back. "You playing it shrewd?"

"I'm playing it straight," she said. "He keeps the door locked. Another thing he keeps is a .38 under his pillow."

He slanted his head just a little. "You expect me to buy that?"

"You don't have to buy it. I'm giving it to you."

He began to see what she was getting at. He said, "All right, thanks for the freebee. Now tell me what you're selling."

"A key," she said. "The key to his room. He has one and I have one. I'll sell you mine at bargain rates. All I want is your promise."

He didn't say anything.

She shrugged and said, "It's a gamble on both sides. I'll take a chance that you'll keep your word and let me stay alive. You'll be betting even-money that I'm telling the truth."

He smiled again. He saw she was looking past him, at the kitchen door. He said, "So the deal is, you give me the key to his room and I let you walk out that door."

"That's it." She was gazing hungrily at the door. Her lips scarcely moved as she murmured, "Fair enough?"

"No," he said. "It needs a tighter contract."

Her face was expressionless. She held her breath.

He let her hold it for a while, and then he said, "Let's do it so there's no gamble. You get the key and I'll follow you upstairs. I'll be right in back of you when you walk into the room. I'll have the blade touching your spine."

She blinked a few times.

"Well?" he said.

She reached into a flap of the bottle-green velvet and took out a door-key. Then she turned slowly and started out of the kitchen. He moved in close behind her and followed the platinum-blonde hair and elegant torso going through the small dining-room and the parlor and toward the dimly lit stairway. He came up at her side as they climbed the stairs, the knife-blade scarcely an inch away from the shimmering velvet that covered her ribs.

They reached the top of the stairs and she pointed to the door of the front bedroom. He let the blade touch the velvet and his voice was a whisper saying, "Slow and quiet. Very quiet."

Then again he moved behind her. They walked slowly toward the bedroom door. The blade kissed the velvet and it told her to use the key with a minimum of sound. She put the key in the lock and there was no sound as she turned the key. There was only a slight clicking sound as the lock opened. Then no sound while she opened the door.

They entered the room and he saw Riker in the bed. He saw the brown wavy hair and there was some grey in it along the temples. In the suntanned face there were wrinkles and lines of dissipation and other lines that told of too much worry. Riker's eyes were shut tightly and it was the kind of slumber that rests the limbs but not the brain.

Ken thought, *He's aged a lot in nine years; it used to be mostly muscle and now it's mostly fat.*

Riker was curled up, his knees close to his paunch. He had his shoes off but otherwise he was fully dressed. He wore a silk shirt and a hand-painted necktie, his jacket was dark grey cashmere and his slacks were pale grey high-grade flannel. He had on a pair of argyle socks that must have set him back at least twenty dollars. On the wrist of his left hand there was a platinum watch to match the large star-emerald he wore on his little finger. On the third finger of his left hand he had a three-karat diamond. Ken was looking at the expensive clothes and the jewelry and thinking, *He travels first-class, he really rides the gravy train.*

It was a bitter thought and it bit deeper into Ken's brain. He said to himself, *Nine years ago this man of distinction beat you up and left you for dead. You've had nine years in Quentin and he's had the sunshine, the peaches-and-cream, the uninterrupted and desirable company of the extra-lovely Mrs Riker while you lived alone in a cell –*

He looked at the extra-lovely Mrs Riker. She stood motionless at the side of the bed and he stood beside her with the switchblade aiming at her velvet-sheathed flesh. She was looking at the blade and waiting for him to aim it at Riker, to put it in the sleeping man and send it in deep.

But that wasn't the play. He smiled dimly to let her know he had something else in mind.

Riker's left hand dangled over the side of the bed and his right hand rested on the pillow. Ken kept the knife aimed at Hilda as he reached toward the pillow and then under the pillow. His fingers touched metal. It was the barrel of a revolver and he got a two-finger hold on it and eased it out from under the pillow. The butt came into his palm and his middle finger went through the trigger-guard and nestled against the back of the guard, not touching the trigger.

He closed the switchblade and put it in his pocket. He stepped back and away from the bed and said, "Now you can wake up your husband."

She was staring at the muzzle of the .38. It wasn't aiming at anything in particular.

"Wake him up," Ken murmured. "I want him to see his gun in my hand. I want him to know how I got it."

Hilda gasped and it became a sob and then a wail and it was a hook of sound that awakened Riker. At first he was looking at Hilda. Then he saw Ken and he sat up very slowly, as though he was something made of stone and ropes were pulling him up. His eyes were riveted to Ken's face and he hadn't yet noticed the .38. His hand crept down along the side of the pillow and then under the pillow.

There was no noise in the room as Riker's hand groped for the gun. Some moments passed and then there was sweat on Riker's forehead and under his lip and he went on searching for the gun and suddenly he seemed to realize it wasn't there. He focused on the weapon in Ken's hand and his body began to quiver. His lips scarcely moved as he said, "The gun – the gun—"

"It's yours," Ken said. "Mind if I borrow it?"

Riker went on staring at the revolver. Then very slowly his head turned and he was staring at Hilda. "You," he said. "You gave it to him."

"Not exactly," Ken said. "All she did was tell me where it was."

Riker shut his eyes very tightly as though he was tied to a rack and it was pulling him apart.

Hilda's face was expressionless. She was looking at Ken and saying, "You promised to let me walk out—"

"I'm not stopping you," he said. Then, with a shrug and a dim smile, "I'm not stopping anyone from doing what they want to do." And he slipped the gun into his pocket.

Hilda started for the door. Riker was up from the bed and lunging at her, grabbing her wrist and hurling her across the room. Then Riker lunged again and his hands reached for her throat as she tried to get up from the floor. Hilda began to make gurgling sounds but the noise was drowned in the torrent of insane screaming that came from Riker's lips. Riker choked her until she died. And even then he stayed where he was and went on screaming at her.

Ken stood there, watching it happen. His mind absorbed and recorded every detail of the scene. He thought, *Well, they wanted each other, and now they got each other*.

He walked out of the room and down the hall and down the stairs. As he went out of the house he could still hear the screaming. On Spruce, walking toward Eleventh, he glanced back and saw a crowd gathering outside the house and then he heard the sound of approaching sirens. He waited there and saw the police cars stopping in front of the house, the policemen rushing in with drawn guns. Some moments later he heard the shots and he knew that the screaming man was trying to make a getaway. There was more shooting and suddenly there was no sound at all. He knew they'd be carrying two corpses out of the house.

He turned away from what was happening back there, walked along the curb toward the sewer-hole on the corner, took Riker's gun from his pocket and threw it into the sewer. In the instant that he did it, there was a warm sweet taste in his mouth. He smiled, knowing what it was. Again he could hear Tillie saying, "Revenge is black pudding."

Tillie, he thought. And the smile stayed on his face as he walked north on Eleventh. He was remembering the feeling he'd had when he'd kissed her. It was the feeling of wanting to take her out of that dark cellar, away from the loneliness and the opium. To carry her upward toward the world where they had such things as clinics, with plastic specialists who repaired scarred faces.

The feeling hit him again and he walked faster.

A MATTER OF PRINCIPAL

Max Allan Collins

It had been a long time since I'd had any trouble sleeping. Probably Vietnam, and that was gunfire that kept me awake. I've never been an insomniac. You might think killing people for a living would give you restless nights. Truth is, those that go into that business simply aren't the kind who are bothered by it much.

I was no exception. I hadn't gone into retirement because my conscience was bothering me. I retired because the man I got my contracts through got killed – well, actually I killed him, but that's another story – and I had enough money put away to live comfortably without working, so I did.

The A-frame cottage on Paradise Lake was secluded enough for privacy, but close enough to nearby Lake Geneva to put me in contact with human beings, if I was so inclined, which I rarely was, with the exception of getting laid now and then. I'm human.

There was also a restaurant nearby, called Wilma's Welcome Inn, a rambling two-story affair that included a gas station, modest hotel accommodations and a convenience store. I'd been toying with the idea of buying the place, which had been slipping since the death of Wilma; I'd been getting a little bored lately and needed something to do. Before I started putting people to sleep, I worked in a garage as a mechanic, so the gas station angle appealed to me.

Anyway, boredom had started to itch at me, and for the past few nights I'd had trouble sleeping. I sat up all night watching satellite TV and reading paperback westerns; then I'd drag around the next day, maybe drifting to sleep in the afternoon just long enough to fuck up my sleep cycle again that night.

It was getting irritating.

At about three-thirty in the morning on the fourth night of this shit, I decided eating might do the trick. Fill my gut with junk food and the blood could rush down from my head and warm my belly and I'd get the fuck sleepy, finally. I hadn't tried this before because I'd been getting a trifle paunchy, since I quit working, and since winter kicked in.

In the summer I'd swim in the lake every day and get exercise and keep the spare tire off. But in the winter I'd just let my beard go and belt-size, too. Winters made me fat and lazy and, now, fucking sleepless.

The cupboard was bare so I threw on my thermal jacket and headed over to the Welcome Inn. At this time of night the convenience store was the only thing open, that and one self-serve gas pump.

The clerk was a heavy-set brunette named Cindy from nearby Twin Lakes. She was maybe twenty years old and a little surly, but she worked all night, so who could blame her.

"Mr Ryan," she said, flatly, as I came in, the bell over the door jingling.

"Cindy," I said, with a nod, and began prowling the place, three narrow aisles parallel to the front of the building. None of the snacks appealed to me – chips and crackers and Twinkies and other preservative-packed delights – and the frozen food case ran mostly to ice-cream sandwiches and popsicles. In this weather, that was a joke.

I was giving a box of Chef Boyardee lasagna an intent once-over, like it was a car I was considering buying, when the bell over the door jingled again. I glanced up and saw a heavy-set man – heavy-set enough to make Cindy look svelte – with a pockmarked face and black-rimmed glasses that fogged up as he stepped in.

He wore an expensive topcoat – tan, a camel's hair number you could make payments on for a year and still owe – and his shoes had a bright black city shine, barely flecked with ice and snow. His name was Harry Something, and he was from Chicago. I knew him, in another life.

I turned my back. If he saw me, I'd have to kill him, and I was bored, but not that bored.

Predictably, Harry Something went straight for the potato chips; he also rustled around the area where cookies were shelved. I risked a glimpse and saw him, not two minutes after he entered, with his arms full of junk food, heading for the front counter.

"Excuse me, miss," Harry Something said, depositing his groceries before Cindy. His voice was nasal and high-pitched; a funny, childish voice for a man his size. "Could you direct me to the sanitary napkins?"

"You mean Kotex?"

"Whatever."

"The toiletries is just over there."

Now this was curious, and I'll tell you why. I had met Harry Something around ten years before, when I was doing a job for the Outfit boys. I was never a mob guy, mind you, strictly a freelancer, but their money was as good as anybody's. What that job was isn't important, but Harry and his partner Louis were the locals who had fucked up, making my outsider's presence necessary. Harry and Louis had not been friendly toward me. They had threatened me, in fact. They had beaten the hell out of me in my hotel room, when the job was over, for making them look bad.

I had never taken any sort of revenge out on them. I occasionally do take revenge, but at my convenience, and when a score strikes me as worth settling. Harry and Louis had really just pushed me around a little, bloodied my nose, tried to earn back a little self-respect. So I didn't hold a grudge. Not a major grudge. Fuck it.

As to why Harry Something purchasing Kotex in the middle of the night at some backwoods convenience store was curious, well, Harry and Louis were gay. They were queens of crime. Mob muscle who worked as a pair, and played as a pair.

I don't mean to be critical. To each his own. I'd rather cut my dick off than insert it in any orifice of a repulsive fat slob like Harry Something. But that's just me.

And me, I'm naturally curious. I'm not nosy, not even inquisitive. But when a faggot buys Kotex, I have to wonder why.

"Excuse me," Harry Something said, brushing by me.

He hadn't seen my face – he might not recognize me, in any case. Ten years and a beard and twenty pounds later, I wasn't as easy to peg as Harry was, who had changed goddamn little.

Harry, having stocked up on cookies and chips and Kotex, was now buying milk and packaged macaroni and cheese and provisions in general. He was shopping. Stocking up.

And now I knew what he was up to.

I nodded to surly Cindy, who bid me goodbye by flickering her eyelids in casual contempt, and went out to my car, a blue sporty Mazda I'd purchased recently. I wished I'd had the four-wheel drive, or anything less conspicuous, but I didn't. I sat in the car, scooched down low; I did not turn on the engine. I just sat in the cold car in the cold night and waited.

Harry Something came out with two armloads of groceries – Kotex included, I presumed – and he put them in the front seat of a brown rental Ford. Louis was not waiting for him. Harry was alone.

Which further confirmed my suspicions.

I waited for him to pull out onto the road, waited for him to take the road's curve, then started up my Mazda and glided out after him. He had turned left, toward Twin Lakes and Lake Geneva. That made sense, only I figured he wouldn't wind up either place. I figured he'd be out in the boonies somewhere.

I knew what Harry was up to. I knew he wasn't exactly here to ski. That lardass couldn't stand up on a pair of skis. And he wasn't here to go ice-fishing, either. A city boy like Harry Something had no business in a touristy area like this, in the off-season – unless Harry was hiding out, holing up somewhere.

This would be the perfect area for that.

Only Harry didn't use Kotex.

He turned off on a side road, into a heavily wooded area that wound back toward Paradise Lake. Good. That was very good.

I went on by. I drove a mile, turned into a farmhouse gravel drive and headed back without lights. I slowed as I reached the mouth of the side road, and could see Harry's tail lights wink off.

I knew the cabin at the end of that road. There was only one, and its owner only used it during the summer; Harry was either a renter, or a squatter.

I glided on by and went back home. I left the Mazda next to the deck and walked up the steps and into my A-frame. The nine millimeter was in the nightstand drawer. The gun hadn't been shot in months – Christ, maybe over a year. But I cleaned and oiled it regularly. It would do fine.

So would my black turtle-neck, black jeans, black leather bomber jacket, and this black moonless night. I slipped a .38 revolver in the bomber jacket right side pocket, and clipped a hunting knife to my belt. The knife was razor-sharp with a sword point; I sent for it out of the back of one of those dumb-ass ninja magazines – which are worthless except for mail-ordering weapons.

I walked along the edge of the lake, my running shoes crunching the brittle ground, layered as it was with snow and ice and leaves. The only light came from a gentle scattering of stars, a handful of diamonds flung on black velvet; the frozen lake was a dark presence that you could sense but not really see. The surrounding trees were even darker. The occasional cabin or cottage or house I passed was empty. I was one of only a handful of residents on Paradise Lake who lived year-round.

But the lights were on in one cabin. Not many lights, but lights. And its chimney was trailing smoke.

The cabin was small, a traditional log cabin like Abe Lincoln and syrup, only with a satellite dish. Probably two bedrooms, a living room, kitchenette and a can or two. Only one car – the brown rental Ford.

My footsteps were lighter now; I was staying on the balls of my feet and the crunching under them was faint. I approached with caution and gun in hand and peeked in a window on the right front side.

Harry Something was sitting on the couch, eating barbecue potato chips, giving himself an orange-mustache in the process. His feet were up on a coffee table. More food and a sawed-off double-barrel shotgun were on the couch next to him. He wore a colorful Hawaiian shirt; he looked like Don Ho puked on him, actually.

Hovering nervously nearby, was Louis, a small, skinny, bald ferret of a man, who wore jeans and a black shirt and a white tie. I couldn't tell whether he was trying for trendy or gangster, and frankly didn't give a shit, either way.

Physically, all the two men had in common was pockmarks and a desire for the other's ugly body.

And neither one of them seemed to need a sanitary napkin, though a towelette would've come in handy for Harry Something. Jesus.

I huddled beneath the window, wondering what I was doing here. Boredom. Curiosity. I shrugged. Time to look in another window or two.

Because they clearly had a captive. That's what they were doing in the boonies. That's why they were stocking up on supplies at a convenience store in the middle of night and nowhere. That's why they were in the market for Kotex. That's what I'd instinctively, immediately known back at the Welcome Inn.

And in a back window, I saw her. She was naked on a bed in the rustic room, naked but for white panties. She was sitting on the edge of the bed and she was crying, a black-haired, creamy-fleshed beauty in her early twenties.

Obviously, Harry and Louis had nothing sexual in mind for this girl; the reason for her nudity was to help prevent her fleeing. The bed was heavy with blankets, and she'd obviously been keeping under the covers, but right now she was sitting and crying. That time of the month.

I stood in the dark in my dark clothes with a gun in my hand and my back to the log cabin and smiled. When I'd come out into the night, armed like this, it wasn't to effect a rescue. Whatever else they were, Harry and Louis were dangerous men. If I was going to spend my sleepless night satisfying my curiosity and assuaging my boredom by poking into their business, I had to be ready to pay for my thrills.

But the thing was, I recognized this young woman. Like Harry, I spent a lot of hours during cold nights like this with my eyes frozen to a TV screen. And that's where I'd seen her: on the tube.

Not an actress, no – an heiress. The daughter of a Chicago media magnate whose name you'd recognize, a guy who inherited money and wheeled-and-dealed his way into more, including one of the satellite super-stations I'd been wasting my eyes on lately. The Windy City's answer to Ted Turner, right down to boating and womanizing.

His daughter was a little wild, frequently seen in the company of rock stars (she had a tattoo of a star – not Mick Jagger, a five-pointed *star* star – on her white left breast, which I could see from the window) and was a Betty Ford clinic drop-out. Nonetheless, she was said to be the apple of her daddy's eye, even if that apple was a tad wormy.

So Harry and Louis had put the snatch on the snatch; fair enough. Question was, was it their own idea, or something the Outfit put them up to?

I sat in the cold and dark and decided, finally, that it just didn't matter who or what was behind it. My options were to go home, and forget about it, and try (probably without any luck) to get some sleep; or to rescue this somewhat soiled damsel in distress.

What the hell. I had nothing better to do.

I went to the front door and knocked.

No answer.

Shit, I knew somebody was home, so I knocked again.

Louis cracked open the door and peered out and said, "What is it?" and I shot him in the eye.

There was the harsh, shrill sound of a scream – not Louis, who hadn't had time for that, but the girl in the next room, scared shitless at hearing a gunshot, one would suppose.

I paid no attention to her and pushed the door open – there was no night latch or anything – and stepped over Louis, and pointed the nine millimeter at Harry, whose orange-ringed mouth was frozen open and whose bag of barbecue potato chips dropped to the floor, much as Louis had.

"Don't, Harry," I said.

I could see in Harry's tiny dark eyes behind his thick black-rimmed glasses that he was thinking about the sawed-off shotgun on the couch next to him.

"Who the fuck . . ."

I walked slowly across the rustic living room toward the couch; in the background, an old colorized movie was playing on their captive's daddy's super-station. I plucked the shotgun off the couch with my left hand and tucked it under my arm.

"Hi, Harry," I said. "Been a while."

His orange-ringed mouth slowly began to work and his eyes began to blink and he said, "Quarry?"

That was the name he'd known me by.

"Taking the girl your idea, or are you still working for the boys?"

"We . . . we retired, couple years ago. God. You killed Louis. Louis. You killed Louis . . ."

"Right. What were you going to put the girl's body in?"

"Huh?"

"She's obviously seen you. You were obviously going to kill her, once you got the money. So. What was the plan?"

Harry wiped off his orange barbecue ring. "Got a roll of

plastic in the closet. Gonna roll her up in it and dump her in one of the gravel pits around here."

"I see. Do that number with the plastic right now, for Louis, why don't you? Okay?"

Tears were rolling down Harry's stubbly pockmarked cheeks. I didn't know whether he was crying for Louis or himself or the pair of them, and I wasn't interested enough to ask.

"Okay," he said thickly.

I watched him roll his partner up in the sheet of plastic, using duct tape to secure the package; he sobbed as he did it, but he did it. He got blood on his Hawaiian shirt; it didn't particularly show, though.

"Now I want you to clean up the mess. Go on. You'll find what you need in the kitchen."

Dutifully, Harry shuffled over, got a pan of warm water and some rags, and got on his knees and cleaned up the brains and blood. He wasn't crying anymore. He moved slow but steady, a fat zombie in a colorful shirt.

"Stick the rags in the end of Louis' plastic home, would you? Thank you."

Harry did that, then the big man lumbered to his feet, hands in the air, and said, "Now me, huh?"

"I might let you go, Harry. I got nothing against you."

"Not . . . not how I remember it."

I laughed. "You girls leaned on me once. You think I'd kill a person over something that trivial? What kind of guy do you think I am, Harry?"

Harry had sense enough not to answer.

"Come with me," I said, and with the nine millimeter's nose to Harry's temple, I walked him to the door of the bedroom.

"Open it," I said.

He did.

We went in, Harry first.

The girl was under the covers, holding the blankets and sheets up around her in a combination of illogical modesty and legitimate fear.

Her expression melted into one of confusion mingled with the beginnings of hope and relief when she saw me.

"I've already taken care of the skinny one," I said. "Now

Harry and me are going for a walk. You stay here. I'm going to get you back to your father."

Her confusion didn't leave, but she began to smile, wide, like a kid Christmas morning seeing her gifts. Her gift to me was dropping the blankets and sheets to her waist.

"Remember," I said. "Stay right there."

I walked Harry out, pulling the bedroom door shut behind me.

"Where are her clothes?"

He nodded to a closet. Same one he'd gotten the plastic out of.

"Good," I said. "Now let's go for a walk. Just you and me and Louis."

"Loo . . . Louis?"

"Better give Louis a hand, Harry."

Harry held the plastic-wrapped corpse in his arms like a B-movie monster carrying a starlet. The plastic was spattered with blood, but on the inside. Harry looked like he was going to cry again.

I still had the sawed-off shotgun under my arm, so it was awkward, getting the front door open, but I managed.

"Out on the lake," I said.

Harry looked at me, his eyes behind the glasses wary, glancing from me to his plastic-wrapped burden and back again.

"We're going to bury Louis at sea," I said.

"Huh?"

"Just walk, Harry. Okay? Just walk."

He walked. I followed behind, nine millimeter in one hand, sawed-off in the other. Harry in his Hawaiian shirt was an oddly comic sight, but I was too busy to be amused. Our feet crunched slightly on the ice. No danger of falling in. Frozen solid. Kids ice-skated out here. But not right now.

We walked a long way. We said not a word, until I halted him about mid-way. The black starry sky was our only witness.

"Put him down, Harry," I said. The nine millimeter was in my waistband; the shotgun was pointed right at him.

He set his cargo gently down. He stood looking gloomily down at the plastic shroud, like a bear contemplating its own foot caught in a trap.

I blasted both barrels of the shotgun; they blew the quiet night apart and echoed across the frozen lake and rattled the world.

Harry looked at me, stunned.

"What the fuck . . .?"

"Now unroll Louis and toss him in," I said, standing near the gaping hole in the ice. "I'm afraid that plastic might float."

Horrified, the big man did as he was told. Louis slipped down the hole in the ice and into watery nothingness like a turd down the crapper.

"Slick," I said, admiringly.

"Oh Jesus," he said.

"Now you," I said.

"What?"

I had the nine millimeter out again.

"Jump in," I said. "Water's fine."

"Fuck you!"

I went over quickly and pushed the big son of a bitch in. He was flailing, splashing icy water up on me, as I put six bullets in his head, which came apart in pieces, like a rotten melon.

And then he was gone.

Nothing left but the hole in the ice, the water within it making some frothy reddish waves that would die down soon enough.

I gathered the weapons and the plastic and, folding the plastic sheet as I walked, went back to the cabin.

This was reckless, I knew. I shouldn't be killing people who lived on the same goddamn lake I did. But it was winter, and the bodies wouldn't turn up for a long time, if ever, and the Outfit had used this part of the world to dump its corpses since Capone was just a mean street kid. Very little chance any of this would come back at me.

Nonetheless, I had taken a risk or two. I ought to get something out of it, other than killing a sleepless night.

I got the girl's clothes and went in and gave them to her. A heavy-metal T-shirt and designer jeans and Reeboks.

"Did you kill those men?" she said, breathlessly, her eyes dark and glittering. She had her clothes in her lap.

"That's not important. Get dressed."

"You're wonderful. You're goddamn fucking wonderful."

"I know," I said. "Everybody says the same thing. Get dressed."

She got dressed. I watched her. She was a beautiful piece of ass, no question. The way she was looking at me made it clear she was grateful.

"What can I do for you?" she said, hands on her hips.

"Nothing," I said. "You're on the rag."

That made her laugh. "Other ports in a storm."

"Maybe later," I said, and smiled. She looked like AIDs-bait to me. I could be reckless, but not that reckless.

I put her in my car. I hadn't decided yet whether or not to dump the brown rental Ford. Probably would. I could worry about that later. Right now, I needed to get her to a motel.

She slept in the car. I envied her, and nudged her awake when we reached the motel just inside the Illinois state line.

I'd already checked in. I ushered her in to the shabby little room, its floor space all but taken up by two twin beds, and she sat on the bed and yawned.

"What now?" she said. "You want your reward?"

"Actually, yes," I said, sitting next to her. "What's your father's number?"

"Hey, there's time for that later . . ."

"First things first," I said, and she wrote the number out on the pad by the phone.

I heard the ring, and a male voice said, "Hello?"

I gave her the receiver. "Make sure it's your father, and tell him you're all right."

"Daddy?" she said. She smiled, then she made a face. "I'm fine, I'm fine . . . the man you sent . . . what?"

She covered the receiver, eyes confused again. "He says he didn't send anybody."

I took the phone. "Good evening, sir. I have your daughter. As you can hear, she's just fine. Get together one-hundred-thousand dollars in unmarked, nonsequential tens, twenties and fifties, and wait for the next call."

I hung up.

She looked at me with wide eyes and wide-open mouth.

"I'm not going to kill you," I said. "I'm just turning a buck."

"You bastard!"

I put the duct tape over her mouth, taped her wrists behind her and taped her ankles too, and went over and curled up on the other bed, nine millimeter in my waistband.

And slept like a baby.

CITIZEN'S ARREST

Charles Willeford

It was fairly late in the afternoon when I stopped at Gwynn's Department Store on my way home to look at some new fishing tackle. Gwynn's is the best store in the entire city; there are three full floors of everything imaginable. So I always took my time shopping at Gwynn's; a man who's interested in the outdoors can spend several hours in there just looking around.

My back was to the man at the counter – the thief, I should say – because I was looking at the shotguns in the rack behind the locked glass doors. He must have seen me, of course, but he didn't know, I suppose, that I could see his reflection in the glass doors as he stood at the next counter. There was no clerk in the immediate vicinity; there were just the two of us in this part of the store on the ground floor. Casually, as I watched him in the polished glass, he snatched the heavy lighter off the counter and slipped it into the deep right-hand pocket of his green gabardine raincoat.

I was pretty well shocked by this action. As a kid, I had pilfered a few things from ten-cent stores – pencils and nickel key-rings, and once a twenty-five-cent "diamond" ring – but this was the first time in my life I had ever seen anybody deliberately *steal* something. And it was an expensive table lighter: $75 not counting tax. Only a minute or two before I had examined the lighter myself, thinking how masculine it would look on the desk in my office or on the coffee table in a bachelor's apartment. Of course, as a married man, I couldn't afford to pay that much money just for a cigarette lighter, but it was a beautiful piece of work, a "conversation piece", as they say in the magazine ads. It was a chromium-plated knight in armor about six inches tall.

When you flipped up the visor on the helmet a butane flame flared inside the empty head, and there was your light. There had been a display of these lighters in shining armor on the gift counter, and now, as the big man sauntered toward the elevators, there was one less.

If I'd had time to think things over I am inclined to believe now that I would have ignored the theft. As I've always said, it was none of my business, and nobody wants to get involved in a situation that is bound to be unpleasant, but at that particular moment a young clerk appeared out of nowhere and asked me if I needed any help. I shook my head, and pointed my chin in the general direction of the elevators.

"Do you see that man over there in the green raincoat? I just saw him take one of those knight table lighters off the counter and put it into his pocket."

"Do you mean he stole it?" he asked, in a kind of stage whisper.

"No." I shook my head again. "I didn't say that. All I said was that he put the lighter into his pocket and then walked over to the elevators."

The big man entered the elevator, together with a teenaged boy who badly needed a haircut, and the operator clanged the door closed.

The clerk, who couldn't have been more than twenty-two or three, cleared his throat. "I'm afraid, sir, that this sort of thing is a little out of my province. Would you mind talking to our floor manager, Mr Levine?"

I shrugged in reply, but there was a sinking sensation in my stomach all the same. By mentioning the theft I had committed myself, and now I knew that I had to go through with it no matter how unpleasant it turned out to be.

The clerk soon returned with Mr Levine, a squat bald man in his early forties. He wore a plastic name tag and a red carnation on the left lapel of his black silk suitcoat.

I briefly explained the theft to Mr Levine. He pursed his lips, listened attentively, and then checked out my story by going over to the glass case of shotguns to prove to himself that the gift counter was reflected perfectly in the polished surface.

"Would you be willing, Mr—?"

"Goranovsky."

"Would you be willing, Mr Goranovsky, to appear in court as a witness to this shoplifting? Providing, of course, that such is the case."

"What do you mean, if such is the case? I told you I saw him take it. All you have to do is search him, and if you find the lighter in his raincoat – in the right-hand pocket – the case is cut and dried."

"Not exactly, sir. It isn't quite that simple." He turned to the clerk, whose eyes were bright with excitement, and lowered his voice. "Call Mr Sileo, and ask him to join us here."

The clerk left, and Mr Levine steepled his fingers. "Mr Sileo is our security officer," he explained. "I don't want you to think that we don't appreciate your reporting this matter, Mr Goranovsky, because we do, but Gwynn's can't afford to make a false accusation. As you said, there was no clerk in the vicinity at the time, and it's quite possible that the gentleman might have gone off to search for one."

I snorted in disgust. "Sure, and if he can't find one on the second floor, maybe he'll find one on the third."

"It's possible," he said seriously, ignoring my tone of voice. "Legally, you see, no theft is involved unless he actually leaves the store without paying for the item. He can still pay for the lighter, or put it back on the counter before he leaves."

"Sure, I see. Why not forget the whole thing? I'm sorry I brought the matter up."

"No, please. I merely wanted to explain the technical points. We'll need your cooperation, and it's Mr Gwynn's policy to prosecute shoplifters; but you can't make charges without an airtight case and a reliable witness. If we arrest him within the store, all the man has to say is that he was looking for a clerk, and there isn't anything we can do about it. He very well may be looking for a clerk. If such is the case, we could very easily lose the goodwill of a valuable customer."

"I understand; I'm a businessman myself. In fact, I hope I'm wrong. But if I'm not, you can count on me to appear in court, Mr Levine. I've gone this far."

We were joined by Mr Sileo. He was slight, dark, and businesslike. He looked more like a bank executive than a detective, and I had a hunch that he had an important job of some kind with Gwynn's, that he merely doubled as a security officer. In a businesslike manner, he quickly and quietly took charge of the situation.

I was directed to stand by the elevators and to point out the thief when he came down. Mr Levine was stationed in the center aisle, and Mr Sileo took up his post by the Main Street entrance. If, by chance, the shoplifter turned right after leaving the elevator – toward the side exit to 37th Street – Mr Levine could follow him out, and Mr Sileo could dart out the main door and circle around the corner to meet the man outside on 37th Street. Mr Sileo explained the plan so smoothly, I supposed it was some kind of standing procedure they had used effectively before. The eager young clerk, much to his disgust, was sent back to work by Mr Levine, but he wasn't needed.

To my surprise, when I looked at my watch, only ten minutes had passed since I reported the theft. The next ten minutes were much longer as I waited by the elevators for the man in the green raincoat to reappear. He didn't look at me as he got off, and I pointed him out by holding my arm above my head, as Mr Sileo had directed, and then trailed the man down the wide corridor at a safe distance. I wondered if he had a gun, and at this alarming thought I dropped back a little farther, letting Mr Levine get well ahead of me. Mr Sileo, who had picked up my signal, went out the front door as soon as it became apparent that the man was going to use the Main Street exit. I could see Mr Sileo through the glass door as he stood on the front sidewalk; he was pretending to fumble a cigarette out of his pack. A moment later, just about the time I reluctantly reached the Main Street doorway myself, Mr Levine and Mr Sileo were escorting the big man back inside the store.

I couldn't understand the man's attitude; he was smiling. He had a huge nose, crisscrossed with prominent blood veins, and he had a large mouth, too, which probably looked bigger than it was because of several missing teeth.

The four of us moved silently down the right side aisle a short distance to avoid blocking the doorway. For a strained moment nobody said anything.

"I'm sorry, sir," Mr Sileo said flatly, but pleasantly, "but this gentleman claims that you took a desk lighter off the counter and put it into your pocket without paying for it."

I resented the offhand way Mr Sileo had shifted all of the

responsibility onto me. The big man shrugged and, if anything, his genial smile widened, but his bluish white eyes weren't smiling as he looked at me. They were as cold and hard as glass marbles.

"Is that right?" He chuckled deep in his throat. "Is this the lighter you mean?" He took the chrome-plated knight out of his raincoat pocket.

"Yes," I said grimly, "that's the one."

He unbuttoned his raincoat and, after transferring the lighter to his left hand, dug into his pants pocket with his right.

"This," he said, handing a slip of paper to Mr Sileo, "is my receipt for it."

Mr Sileo examined the receipt and then passed it to Mr Levine. The floor manager shot me a coldly furious look and returned the slip of paper to the man. The thief reached into his inside jacket pocket for his checkbook. "If you like," he said, "you can look at the checkstub, as well."

Mr Sileo shook his head, and held his hands back to avoid taking the checkbook. "No, sir, that's quite all right, sir," he said apologetically.

Mr Levine made some effusive apologies for the store which I thought, under the circumstances, were uncalled for – but the big man cut him off in the middle of a long sentence.

"No harm done," he said good-naturedly, "none at all. In your place, I'd have checked, too. In all probability," he qualified his remark.

"It was my mistake," I said, finally. "I'm sorry you were inconvenienced." And then, when neither Mr Levine nor Mr Sileo said anything to me, and the big man just stood there – grinning – I turned on my heel and left the store, resolving, then and there, never to spend another dime in Gwynn's as long as I lived.

There had been no mistake. I had seen the man take the lighter, and there had been no clerks anywhere near us at the time. I stood beside my car at the curb, filled with frustration as I ran things all over again in my mind. A trick of some kind had been pulled on the three of us, but how the man had worked it was beyond my comprehension. I opened the door on the sidewalk side and slid across the seat. As I fastened my seat belt, a meaty hand opened the door and the big man in the green raincoat grinned in at me. He held out the shining knight for my inspection.

"Want to buy a nice table lighter, buddy?" he said, chuckling deep in his throat. I can let you have it without any tax."

I swallowed twice before I replied. "I knew you stole the lighter, but how did you get the receipt?"

"Will you buy the lighter if I tell you?"

"No, damn you; I wouldn't give you ten cents for it!"

"Okay, Mr Do-Gooder," he said cheerfully, "I'll tell you anyway. This morning there were several lighters on the counter, and I bought one of them at ten a.m. After stashing the first one in a safe place, I came back late this afternoon and got this one free. Unfortunately, you happened to see me pick it up. The receipt I got this morning, however, served me very well for the second. The store stays open until nine-thirty tonight, and I had planned to come back after dinner and get another one. So long as I took them one at a time, one receipt is as good as three, if you get my meaning. So the way I figure it, you ought to buy this one from me because I can't come back tonight for my third lighter. You cost me some money, fella."

"I've got a good mind to go back in and tell Mr Sileo how you worked it."

"Really? Come on, then. I'll go in with you."

"Get the hell out of here!"

He chuckled, slammed the door, and walked away.

My fingers trembled as I lit a cigarette. There was no mistaking my reaction now – I was no longer frustrated, I was angry. If the man had been my size – or smaller – I would have chased after him and knocked out the remainder of his front teeth. I also considered, for a short moment, the idea of telling Mr Levine how he had been cheated. All they had to do was to inventory their remaining lighters (there couldn't be too many of them in stock, an expensive item like that) and they would soon find out that they were one short. But after the cold way they had treated me, I didn't feel like telling them anything.

A policeman's head appeared at the car window. "Is this your car, sir?"

"Of course."

"Will you get out, please, and join me on the sidewalk?" He

walked around the front of the car and I unfastened my seat belt and slid back across the seat; I was more than a little puzzled.

"Take a look," he said, pointing at the curb when I joined him on the sidewalk. "You're parked well into the red zone."

"That isn't true," I said indignantly. "Only the front bumper's in the zone; my wheels are well behind the red paint. There's supposed to be a little leeway, a limit of tolerance, and I'm not blocking the red zone in any way—"

"Don't argue with me, sir," he said wearily, taking a pad of tickets out of his hip pocket. "Ordinarily, I'd merely tell you to repark or move on, but this time I'm giving you a ticket. A good citizen in a green raincoat reported your violation to me at the corner just now, and he was a gentleman who had every right to be sore. He said he told you that you were parked in the red zone – just as a favor – and you told him to go to hell. Now, sir, what is your name?"

SLEEPING DOG

Ross Macdonald

The day after her dog disappeared, Fay Hooper called me early. Her normal voice was like waltzing violins, but this morning the violins were out of tune. She sounded as though she'd been crying.

"Otto's gone." Otto was her one-year-old German shepherd. "He jumped the fence yesterday afternoon and ran away. Or else he was kidnapped – dognapped, I suppose is the right word to use."

"What makes you think that?"

"You know Otto, Mr Archer – how loyal he was. He wouldn't deliberately stay away from me overnight, not under his own power. There must be thieves involved." She caught her breath. "I realize searching for stolen dogs isn't your métier. But you *are* a detective, and I thought, since we knew each other . . ." She allowed her voice to suggest, ever so chastely, that we might get to know each other better.

I liked the woman, I liked the dog, I liked the breed. I was taking my own German shepherd pup to obedience school, which is where I met Fay Hooper. Otto and she were the handsomest and most expensive members of the class.

"How do I get to your place?"

She lived in the hills north of Malibu, she said, on the far side of the county line. If she wasn't home when I got there, her husband would be.

On my way out, I stopped at the dog school in Pacific Palisades to talk to the man who ran it, Fernando Rambeau. The kennels behind the house burst into clamor when I knocked on the front door. Rambeau boarded dogs as well as trained them.

A dark-haired girl looked out and informed me that her husband was feeding the animals. "Maybe I can help," she added doubtfully, and then she let me into a small living room.

I told her about the missing dog. "It would help if you called the vets and animal shelters and gave them a description," I said.

"We've already been doing that. Mrs Hooper was on the phone to Fernando last night." She sounded vaguely resentful. "I'll get him."

Setting her face against the continuing noise, she went out the back door. Rambeau came in with her, wiping his hands on a rag. He was a square-shouldered Canadian with a curly black beard that failed to conceal his youth. Over the beard, his intense, dark eyes peered at me warily, like an animal's sensing trouble.

Rambeau handled dogs as if he loved them. He wasn't quite so patient with human beings. His current class was only in its third week, but he was already having dropouts. The man was loaded with explosive feeling, and it was close to the surface now.

"I'm sorry about Mrs Hooper and her dog. They were my best pupils. He was, anyway. But I can't drop everything and spend the next week looking for him."

"Nobody expects that. I take it you've had no luck with your contacts."

"I don't have such good contacts. Marie and I, we just moved down here last year, from British Columbia."

"That was a mistake," his wife said from the doorway.

Rambeau pretended not to hear her. "Anyway, I know nothing about dog thieves." With both hands, he pushed the possibility away from him. "If I hear any word of the dog, I'll let you know, naturally. I've got nothing against Mrs Hooper."

His wife gave him a quick look. It was one of those revealing looks that said, among other things, that she loved him but didn't know if he loved her, and she was worried about him. She caught me watching her and lowered her eyes. Then she burst out, "Do you think somebody killed the dog?"

"I have no reason to think so."

"Some people shoot dogs, don't they?"

"Not around here," Rambeau said. "Maybe back in the bush someplace." He turned to me with a sweeping explanatory gesture. "These things make her nervous and she gets wild ideas. You know Marie is a country girl—"

"I am not. I was born in Chilliwack." Flinging a bitter look at him, she left the room.

"Was Otto shot?" I asked Rambeau.

"Not that I know of. Listen, Mr Archer, you're a good customer, but I can't stand here talking all day. I've got twenty dogs to feed."

They were still barking when I drove up the coast highway out of hearing. It was nearly forty miles to the Hoopers' mailbox, and another mile up a blacktop lane that climbed the side of a canyon to the gate. On both sides of the heavy wire gate, which had a new combination padlock on it, a hurricane fence, eight feet high and topped with barbed wire, extended out of sight. Otto would have to be quite a jumper to clear it. So would I.

The house beyond the gate was low and massive, made of fieldstone and steel and glass. I honked at it and waited. A man in blue bathing trunks came out of the house with a shotgun. The sun glinted on its twin barrels and on the man's bald head and round brown, burnished belly. He walked quite slowly, a short, heavy man in his sixties, scuffing along in huarachas. The flabby brown shell of fat on him jiggled lugubriously.

When he approached the gate, I could see the stiff gray pallor under his tan, like stone showing under varnish. He was sick or afraid, or both. His mouth was profoundly discouraged.

"What do you want?" he said over the shotgun.

"Mrs Hooper asked me to help find her dog. My name is Lew Archer."

He was not impressed. "My wife isn't here, and I'm busy. I happen to be following soybean futures rather closely."

"Look here, I've come quite a distance to lend a hand. I met Mrs Hooper at dog school and—"

Hooper uttered a short, savage laugh. "That hardly constitutes an introduction to either of us. You'd better be on your way right now."

"I think I'll wait for your wife."

"I think you won't." He raised the shotgun and let me look into its close-set, hollow round eyes. "This is my property all the way down to the road, and you're trespassing. That means I can shoot you if I have to."

"What sense would that make? I came out here to help you."

"You can't help me." He looked at me through the wire gate with a kind of pathetic arrogance, like a lion that had grown old in captivity. "Go away."

I drove back down to the road and waited for Fay Hooper. The sun slid up the sky. The inside of my car turned oven-hot. I went for a walk down the canyon. The brown September grass crunched under my feet. Away up on the far side of the canyon, an earthmover that looked like a crazy red insect was cutting the ridge to pieces.

A very fast black car came up the canyon and stopped abruptly beside me. A gaunt man in a wrinkled brown suit climbed out, with his hand on his holster, told me that he was Sheriff Carlson, and asked me what I was doing there. I told him.

He pushed back his wide cream-colored hat and scratched at his hairline. The pale eyes in his sun-fired face were like clouded glass inserts in a brick wall.

"I'm surprised Mr Hooper takes that attitude. Mrs Hooper just came to see me in the courthouse. But I can't take you up there with me if Mr Hooper says no."

"Why not?"

"He owns most of the county and holds the mortgage on the rest of it. Besides," he added with careful logic, "Mr Hooper is a friend of mine."

"Then you better get him a keeper."

The sheriff glanced around uneasily, as if the Hoopers' mailbox might be bugged. "I'm surprised he has a gun, let alone threatening you with it. He must be upset about the dog."

"He didn't seem to care about the dog."

"He does, though. *She* cares, so *he* cares," Carson said.

"What did she have to tell you?"

"She can talk to you herself. She should be along any minute. She told me that she was going to follow me out of town." He drove his black car up the lane. A few minutes later, Fay Hooper stopped her Mercedes at the mailbox. She must have seen the impatience on my face. She got out and came toward me in a little run, making noises of dismayed regret.

Fay was in her late thirties and fading slightly, as if a light frost had touched her pale gold head, but she was still a beautiful woman. She turned the gentle force of her charm on me.

"I'm dreadfully sorry," she said. "Have I kept you waiting long?"

"Your husband did. He ran me off with a shotgun."

Her gloved hand lighted on my arm, and stayed. She had an electric touch, even through layers of cloth.

"That's terrible. I had no idea that Allan still had a gun."

Her mouth was blue behind her lipstick, as if the information had chilled her to the marrow. She took me up the hill in the Mercedes. The gate was standing open, but she didn't drive in right away.

"I might as well be perfectly frank," she said without looking at me. "Ever since Otto disappeared yesterday, there's been a nagging question in my mind. What you've just told me raises the question again. I was in town all day yesterday so that Otto was alone here with Allan when – when it happened." The values her voice gave to the two names made it sound as if Allan were the dog and Otto the husband.

"When what happened, Mrs Hooper?" I wanted to know.

Her voice sank lower. "I can't help suspecting that Allan shot him. He's never liked any of my dogs. The only dogs he appreciates are hunting dogs – and he was particularly jealous of Otto. Besides, when I got back from town, Allan was getting the ground ready to plant some roses. He's never enjoyed gardening, particularly in the heat. We have professionals to do our work. And this really isn't the time of year to put in a bed of roses."

"You think your husband was planting a dog?" I asked.

"If he was, I have to know." She turned toward me, and the leather seat squeaked softly under her movement. "Find out for me, Mr Archer. If Allan killed my beautiful big old boy, I couldn't stay with him."

"Something you said implied that Allan used to have a gun or guns, but gave them up. Is that right?"

"He had a small arsenal when I married him. He was an infantry officer in the war and a big-game hunter in peacetime. But he swore off hunting years ago."

"Why?"

"I don't really know. We came home from a hunting trip in British Columbia one fall and Allan sold all his guns. He never said a word about it to me but it was the fall after the war ended, and I always thought that it must have had something to do with the war."

"Have you been married so long?"

"Thank you for that question." She produced a rueful smile. "I met Allan during the war, the year I came out, and I knew I'd met my fate. He was a very powerful person."

"And a very wealthy one."

She gave me a flashing haughty look and stepped so hard on the accelerator that she almost ran into the sheriff's car parked in front of the house. We walked around to the back, past a freeform swimming pool that looked inviting, into a walled garden. A few Greek statues stood around in elegant disrepair. Bees murmured like distant bombers among the flowers.

The bed where Allan Hooper had been digging was about five feet long and three feet wide, and it reminded me of graves.

"Get me a spade," I said.

"Are you going to dig him up?"

"You're pretty sure he's in there, aren't you, Mrs Hooper?"

"I guess I am."

From a lath house at the end of the garden, she fetched a square-edged spade. I asked her to stick around.

I took off my jacket and hung it on a marble torso where it didn't look too bad. It was easy digging in the newly worked soil. In a few minutes, I was two feet below the surface, and the ground was still soft and penetrable.

The edge of my spade struck something soft but not so penetrable. Fay Hooper heard the peculiar dull sound it made. She made a dull sound of her own. I scooped away more earth. Dog fur sprouted like stiff black grass at the bottom of the grave.

Fay got down on her knees and began to dig with her lacquered fingernails. Once she cried out in a loud harsh voice, "Dirty murderer!"

Her husband must have heard her. He came out of the house and looked over the stone wall. His head seemed poised on top of the wall, hairless and bodiless, like Humpty Dumpty. He had that look on his face, of not being able to be put together again.

"I didn't kill your dog, Fay. Honest to God, I didn't."

She didn't hear him. She was talking to Otto. "Poor boy, poor boy," she said. "Poor, beautiful boy."

Sheriff Carlson came into the garden. He reached down into

the grave and freed the dog's head from the earth. His large hands moved gently on the great wedge of the skull.

Fay knelt beside him in torn and dirty stockings. "What are you doing?"

Carlson held up a red-tipped finger. "Your dog was shot through the head, Mrs Hooper, but it's no shotgun wound. Looks to me more like a deer rifle."

"I don't even own a rifle," Hooper said over the wall. "I haven't owned one for nearly twenty years. Anyway, I wouldn't shoot your dog."

Fay scrambled to her feet. She looked ready to climb the wall. "Then why did you bury him?"

His mouth opened and closed.

"Why did you buy a shotgun without telling me?"

"For protection."

"Against my dog?"

Hooper shook his head. He edged along the wall and came in tentatively through the gate. He had on slacks and a short-sleeved yellow jersey that somehow emphasized his shortness and his fatness and his age.

"Mr Hooper had some threatening calls," the sheriff said. "Somebody got hold of his unlisted number. He was just telling me about it now."

"Why didn't you tell me, Allan?"

"I didn't want to alarm you. You weren't the one they were after, anyway. I bought a shotgun and kept it in my study."

"Do you know who they are?"

"No. I make enemies in the course of business, especially the farming operations. Some crackpot shot your dog, gunning for me. I heard a shot and found him dead in the driveway."

"But how could you bury him without telling me?"

Hooper spread his hands in front of him. "I wasn't thinking too well. I felt guilty, I suppose, because whoever got him was after me. And I didn't want you to see him dead. I guess I wanted to break it to you gently."

"This is gently?"

"It's not the way I planned it. I thought if I had a chance to get you another pup—"

"No one will ever take Otto's place."

Allan Hooper stood and looked at her wistfully across the

open grave, as if he would have liked to take Otto's place. After a while, the two of them went into the house.

Carlson and I finished digging Otto up and carried him out to the sheriff's car. His inert blackness filled the trunk from side to side.

"What are you going to do with him, Sheriff?" I asked.

"Get a vet I know to recover the slug in him. Then if we nab the sniper, we can use ballistics to convict him."

"You're taking this just as seriously as a real murder, aren't you?" I observed.

"They want me to," he said with a respectful look toward the house.

Mrs Hooper came out carrying a white leather suitcase which she deposited in the back seat of her Mercedes.

"Are you going someplace?" I asked her.

"Yes. I am." She didn't say where.

Her husband, who was watching her from the doorway, didn't speak. The Mercedes went away. He closed the door. Both of them had looked sick.

"She doesn't seem to believe he didn't do it. Do you, Sheriff?"

Carlson jabbed me with his forefinger. "Mr Hooper is no liar. If you want to get along with me, get that through your head. I've known Mr Hooper for over twenty years – served under him in the war – and I never heard him twist the truth."

"I'll have to take your word for it. What about those threatening phone calls? Did he report them to you before today?"

"No."

"What was said on the phone?"

"He didn't tell me."

"Does Hooper have any idea who shot the dog?"

"Well, he did say he saw a man slinking around outside the fence. He didn't get close enough to the guy to give me a good description, but he did make out that he had a black beard."

"There's a dog trainer in Pacific Palisades named Rambeau, who fits the description. Mrs Hooper has been taking Otto to his school."

"Rambeau?" Carlson said with interest.

"Fernando Rambeau. He seemed pretty upset when I talked to him this morning."

"What did he say?"

"A good deal less than he knows, I think. I'll talk to him again."

Rambeau was not at home. My repeated knocking was answered only by the barking of the dogs. I retreated up the highway to a drive-in where I ate a torpedo sandwich. When I was on my second cup of coffee, Marie Rambeau drove by in a pickup truck. I followed her home.

"Where's Fernando?" I asked.

"I don't know. I've been out looking for him."

"Is he in a bad way?"

"I don't know how you mean."

"Emotionally upset."

"He has been ever since that woman came into the class."

"Mrs Hooper?"

Her head bobbed slightly.

"Are they having an affair?"

"They better not be." Her small red mouth looked quite implacable. "He was out with her night before last. I heard him make the date. He was gone all night, and when he came home, he was on one of his black drunks and he wouldn't go to bed. He sat in the kitchen and drank himself glassy-eyed." She got out of the pickup facing me. "Is shooting a dog a very serious crime?"

"It is to me, but not to the law. It's not like shooting a human being."

"It would be to Fernando. He loves dogs the way other people love human beings. That included Otto."

"But he shot him."

Her head drooped. I could see the straight white part dividing her black hair. "I'm afraid he did. He's got a crazy streak, and it comes out in him when he drinks. You should have heard him in the kitchen yesterday morning. He was moaning and groaning about his brother."

"His brother?"

"Fernando had an older brother, George, who died back in Canada after the war. Fernando was just a kid when it happened and it was a big loss to him. His parents were dead, too, and they put him in a foster home in Chilliwack. He still has nightmares about it."

"What did his brother die of?"

"He never told me exactly, but I think he was shot in some

kind of hunting accident. George was a guide and packer in the Fraser River Valley below Mount Robson. That's where Fernando comes from, the Mount Robson country. He won't go back on account of what happened to his brother."

"What did he say about his brother yesterday?" I asked.

"That he was going to get his revenge for George. I got so scared I couldn't listen to him. I went out and fed the dogs. When I came back in, Fernando was loading his deer rifle. I asked him what he was planning to do, but he walked right out and drove away."

"May I see the rifle?"

"It isn't in the house. I looked for it after he left today. He must have taken it with him again. I'm so afraid that he'll kill somebody."

"What's he driving?"

"Our car. It's an old blue Meteor sedan."

Keeping an eye out for it, I drove up the highway to the Hoopers' canyon. Everything there was very peaceful. Too peaceful. Just inside the locked gate, Allan Hooper was lying face down on his shotgun. I could see small ants in single file trekking across the crown of his bald head.

I got a hammer out of the trunk of my car and used it to break the padlock. I lifted his head. His skin was hot in the sun, as if death had fallen on him like a fever. But he had been shot neatly between the eyes. There was no exit wound; the bullet was still in his head. Now the ants were crawling on my hands.

I found my way into the Hoopers' study, turned off the stuttering teletype, and sat down under an elk head to telephone the courthouse. Carlson was in his office.

"I have bad news, Sheriff. Allan Hooper's been shot."

I heard him draw in his breath quickly. "Is he dead?"

"Extremely dead. You better put out a general alarm for Rambeau."

Carlson said with gloomy satisfaction, "I already have him."

"You have him?"

"That's correct. I picked him up in the Hoopers' canyon and brought him in just a few minutes ago." Carlson's voice sank to a mournful mumble. "I picked him up a little too late, I guess."

"Did Rambeau do any talking?"

"He hasn't had a chance to yet. When I stopped his car, he

piled out and threatened me with a rifle. I clobbered him one good."

I went outside to wait for Carlson and his men. A very pale afternoon moon hung like a ghost in the sky. For some reason, it made me think of Fay. She ought to be here. It occurred to me that possibly she had been.

I went and looked at Hooper's body again. He had nothing to tell me. He lay as if he had fallen from a height, perhaps all the way from the moon.

They came in a black county wagon and took him away. I followed them inland to the county seat, which rose like a dusty island in a dark green lake of orange groves. We parked in the courthouse parking lot, and the sheriff and I went inside.

Rambeau was under guard in a second-floor room with barred windows. Carlson said it was used for interrogation. There was nothing in the room but an old deal table and some wooden chairs. Rambeau sat hunched forward on one of them, his hands hanging limp between his knees. Part of his head had been shaved and plastered with bandages.

"I had to cool him with my gun butt," Carlson said. "You're lucky I didn't shoot you – you know that, Fernando?"

Rambeau made no response. His black eyes were set and dull.

"Had his rifle been fired?"

"Yeah. Chet Scott is working on it now. Chet's my identification lieutenant and he's a bear on ballistics." The sheriff turned back to Rambeau. "You might as well give us a full confession, boy. If you shot Mr Hooper and his dog, we can link the bullets to your gun. You know that."

Rambeau didn't speak or move.

"What did you have against Mr Hooper?" Carlson said.

No answer. Rambeau's mouth was set like a trap in the thicket of his beard.

"Your older brother," I said to him, "was killed in a hunting accident in British Columbia. Was Hooper at the other end of the gun that killed George?"

Rambeau didn't answer me, but Carlson's head came up. "Where did you get that, Archer?"

"From a couple of things I was told. According to Rambeau's wife, he was talking yesterday about revenge for his brother's death. According to Fay Hooper, her husband swore off guns when he came back from a certain hunting trip after the war. Would you know if that trip was to British Columbia?"

"Yeah. Mr Hooper took me and the wife with him."

"Whose wife?"

"Both our wives."

"To the Mount Robson area?"

"That's correct. We went up after elk."

"And did he shoot somebody accidentally?" I wanted to know.

"Not that I know of. I wasn't with him all the time, understand. He often went out alone, or with Mrs Hooper," Carlson replied.

"Did he use a packer named George Rambeau?"

"I wouldn't know. Ask Fernando here."

I asked Fernando. He didn't speak or move. Only his eyes had changed. They were wet and glistening-black, visible parts of a grief that filled his head like a dark underground river.

The questioning went on and produced nothing. It was night when I went outside. The moon was slipping down behind the dark hills. I took a room in a hotel and checked in with my answering service in Hollywood. About an hour before, Fay Hooper had called me from a Las Vegas hotel. When I tried to return the call, she wasn't in her room and didn't respond to paging. I left a message for her to come home, that her husband was dead.

Next, I called R.C.M.P. headquarters in Vancouver to ask some questions about George Rambeau. The answers came over the line in clipped Canadian tones. George and his dog had disappeared from his cabin below Red Pass in the fall of 1945. Their bodies hadn't been recovered until the following May, and by that time they consisted of parts of the two skeletons. These included George Rambeau's skull, which had been pierced in the right front and left rear quadrants by a heavy-caliber bullet. The bullet had not been recovered. Who fired it, or when or why, had never been determined. The dog, a husky, had also been shot through the head.

I walked over to the courthouse to pass the word to Carlson. He was in the basement shooting gallery with Lieutenant Scott, who was firing test rounds from Fernando Rambeau's .30/30 repeater.

I gave them the official account of the accident. "But since

George Rambeau's dog was shot, too, it probably wasn't an accident," I said.

"I see what you mean," Carlson said. "It's going to be rough, spreading all this stuff out in court about Mr Hooper. We have to nail it down, though."

I went back to my hotel and to bed, but the process of nailing down the case against Rambeau continued through the night. By morning, Lieutenant Scott had detailed comparisons set up between the test-fired slugs and the ones dug out of Hooper and the dog. I looked at his evidence through a comparison microscope. It left no doubt in my mind that the slugs that killed Allan Hooper and the dog Otto had come from Rambeau's gun.

But Rambeau still wouldn't talk, even to phone his wife or ask for a lawyer.

"We'll take you out to the scene of the crime," Carlson said. "I've cracked tougher nuts than you, boy."

We rode in the back seat of his car with Fernando handcuffed between us. Lieutenant Scott did the driving. Rambeau groaned and pulled against his handcuffs. He was very close to the breaking point, I thought.

It came a few minutes later when the car turned up the lane past the Hoopers' mailbox. He burst into sudden fierce tears as if a pressure gauge in his head had broken. It was strange to see a bearded man crying like a boy, and whimpering, "I don't want to go up there."

"Because you shot him?" Carlson said.

"I shot the dog. I confess I shot the dog," Rambeau said.

"And the man?"

"No!" he cried. "I never killed a man. Mr Hooper was the one who did. He followed my brother out in the woods and shot him."

"If you knew that," I said, "why didn't you tell the Mounties years ago?"

"I didn't know it then. I was seven years old. How would I understand? When Mrs Hooper came to our cabin to be with my brother, how would I know it was a serious thing? Or when Mr Hooper asked me if she had been there? I didn't know he was her husband. I thought he was her father checking up. I knew I shouldn't have told him – I could see it in his face the minute after – but I didn't understand the situation till the other night, when I talked to Mrs Hooper."

"Did she know that her husband had shot George?"

"She didn't even know George had been killed. They never went back to the Fraser River after 1945. But when we put our facts together, we agreed he must have done it. I came out here next morning to get even. The dog came out to the gate. It wasn't real to me – I was drinking most of the night – it wasn't real to me until the dog went down. I shot him. Mr Hooper shot my dog. But when he came out of the house himself, I couldn't pull the trigger. I yelled at him and ran away."

"What did you yell?" I said.

"The same thing I told him on the telephone: 'Remember Mount Robson.'"

A yellow cab, which looked out of place in the canyon, came over the ridge above us. Lieutenant Scott waved it to a stop. The driver said he'd just brought Mrs Hooper home from the airport and wanted to know if that constituted a felony. Scott waved him on.

"I wonder what she was doing at the airport," Carlson said.

"Coming home from Vegas. She tried to call me from there last night. I forgot to tell you."

"You don't forget important things like that," Carlson said.

"I suppose I wanted her to come home under her own power."

"In case she shot her husband?"

"More or less."

"She didn't. Fernando shot him, didn't you, boy?"

"I shot the dog. I am innocent of the man." He turned to me: "Tell her that. Tell her I am sorry about the dog. I came out here to surrender the gun and tell her yesterday. I don't trust myself with guns."

"With darn good reason," Carlson said. "We know you shot Mr Hooper. Ballistic evidence doesn't lie."

Rambeau screeched in his ear, "You're a liar! You're all liars!"

Carlson swung his open hand against the side of Rambeau's face. "Don't call me names, little man."

Lieutenant Scott spoke without taking his eyes from the road. "I wouldn't hit him, Chief. You wouldn't want to damage our case."

Carlson subsided, and we drove on up to the house. Carlson

went in without knocking. The guard at the door discouraged me from following him.

I could hear Fay's voice on the other side of the door, too low to be understood. Carlson said something to her.

"Get out! Get out of my house, you killer!" Fay cried out sharply.

Carlson didn't come out. I went in instead. One of his arms was wrapped around her body; the other hand was covering her mouth. I got his Adam's apple in the crook of my left arm, pulled him away from her, and threw him over my left hip. He went down clanking and got up holding his revolver.

He should have shot me right away. But he gave Fay Hooper time to save my life.

She stepped in front of me. "Shoot me, Mr Carlson. You might as well. You shot the one man I ever cared for."

"Your husband shot George Rambeau, if that's who you mean. I ought to know. I was there." Carlson scowled down at his gun, and replaced it in his holster.

Lieutenant Scott was watching him from the doorway.

"You were there?" I said to Carlson. "Yesterday you told me Hooper was alone when he shot Rambeau."

"He was. When I said I was there, I meant in the general neighborhood."

"Don't believe him," Fay said. "He fired the gun that killed George, and it was no accident. The two of them hunted George down in the woods. My husband planned to shoot him himself, but George's dog came at him and he had to dispose of it. By that time, George had drawn a bead on Allan. Mr Carlson shot him. It was hardly a coincidence that the next spring Allan financed his campaign for sheriff."

"She's making it up," Carlson said. "She wasn't within ten miles of the place."

"But you were, Mr Carlson, and so was Allan. He told me the whole story yesterday, after we found Otto. Once that happened, he knew that everything was bound to come out. I already suspected him, of course, after I talked to Fernando. Allan filled in the details himself. He thought, since he hadn't killed George personally, I would be able to forgive him. But I couldn't. I left him and flew to Nevada, intending to divorce him. I've been intending to for twenty years."

Carlson said: "Are you sure you didn't shoot him before you left?"

"How could she have?" I said. "Ballistics don't lie, and the ballistic evidence says he was shot with Fernando's rifle. Nobody had access to it but Fernando and you. You stopped him on the road and knocked him out, took his rifle and used it to kill Hooper. You killed him for the same reason that Hooper buried the dog – to keep the past buried. You thought Hooper was the only witness to the murder of George Rambeau. But by that time, Mrs Hooper knew about it, too."

"It wasn't murder. It was self-defense, just like in the war. Anyway, you'll never hang it on me."

"We don't have to. We'll hang Hooper on you. How about it, Lieutenant?"

Scott nodded grimly, not looking at his chief. I relieved Carlson of his gun. He winced, as if I were amputating part of his body. He offered no resistance when Scott took him out to the car.

I stayed behind for a final word with Fay. "Fernando asked me to tell you he's sorry for shooting your dog."

"We're both sorry." She stood with her eyes down, as if the past was swirling visibly around her feet. "I'll talk to Fernando later. Much later."

"There's one coincidence that bothers me. How did you happen to take your dog to his school?"

"I happened to see his sign, and Fernando Rambeau isn't a common name. I couldn't resist going there. I had to know what had happened to George. I think perhaps Fernando came to California for the same reason."

"Now you both know," I said.

THE WENCH IS DEAD

Fredric Brown

1

A fuzz is a fuzz is a fuzz when you awaken from a wino jag. God, I'd drunk three pints of muscatel that I know of and maybe more, maybe lots more, because that's when I drew a blank, that's when research stopped. I rolled over on the cot so I could look out through the dirty pane of the window at the clock in the hockshop across the way.

Ten o'clock said the clock.

Get up, Howard Perry, I told myself. Get up, you B.A.S. for bastard, rise and greet the day. Hit the floor and get moving if you want to keep that job, that all-important job that keeps you drinking and sometimes eating and sometimes sleeping with Billie the Kid when she hasn't got a sucker on the hook. That's your life, you B.A.S., you bastard. That's your life for a while. This is it, this is the McCoy, this is the way a wino meets the not-so-newborn day. You're learning, man.

Pull on a sock, another sock, pants, shirt, shoes, get the hell to Burke's and wash a dish, wash a thousand dishes for six bits an hour and a meal or two a day when you want it.

God, I thought, did I really have the habit? Nuts, not in three months. Not when you've been a normal drinker all your life. Not when, much as you've always enjoyed drinking, it's always been in moderation and you've always been able to handle the stuff. This was just temporary.

And I had only a few weeks to go. In a few weeks I'd be back in Chicago, back at my desk in my father's investment company, back wearing white shirts, and B.A.S. would stand for Bachelor of Arts in Sociology. That was a laugh right now, that degree. Three months ago it had meant something – but that was in Chicago, and this was LA, and now all it meant was bastard. That's all it had meant ever since I started drifting.

It's funny, the way those things can happen. You've got a good family and a good education, and then suddenly, for no reason you can define, you start drifting. You lose interest in your family and your job, and one day you find yourself headed for the Coast.

You sit down one day and ask yourself how it happened. But you can't answer. There are a thousand little answers, sure, but there's no *big* answer. It's easier to worry about where the next bottle of sweet wine is coming from.

And that's when you realize your own personal B.A.S. stands for bastard.

With me, LA had been the end of the line. I'd seen the *Dishwasher Wanted* sign in Burke's window, and suddenly I'd known what I had to do. At pearl-diver's wages, it would take a long time to get up the bus fare back to Chicago and family and respectability, but that was beside the point. The point was that after a hundred thousand dirty dishes there'd *be* a bus ticket to Chicago.

But it had been hard to remember the ticket and forget the dishes. Wine is cheap, but they're not giving it away. Since I'd started pearl-diving I'd had grub and six bits an hour for seven hours a day. Enough to drink on and to pay for this dirty, crumby little crackerbox of a room.

So here I was, still thinking about the bus ticket, and still on my uppers on East Fifth Street, LA. Main Street used to be the tenderloin street of Los Angeles and I'd headed for it when I jumped off the freight, but I'd found that the worst district, the real Skid Row, was now on Fifth Street in the few blocks east of Main. The worse the district, the cheaper the living, and that's what I'd been looking for.

Sure, by Fifth Street standards, I was being a pantywaist to hold down a steady job like that, but sleeping in doorways was a little too rugged and I'd found out quickly that panhandling wasn't for me. I lacked the knack.

I dipped water from the cracked basin and rubbed it on my face, and the feel of the stubble told me I could get by one more day without shaving. Or anyway I could wait till evening so the shave would be fresh in case I'd be sleeping with Billie.

Cold water helped a little but I still felt like hell. There were empty wine bottles in the corner and I checked to make sure they were completely empty, and they were. So were my pockets, except, thank God, for tobacco and cigarette papers. I rolled myself a cigarette and lighted it.

But I needed a drink to start the day.

What does a wino do when he wakes up broke (and how often does he wake otherwise?) and needs a drink? Well, I'd found several answers to that. The easiest one, right now, would be to hit Billie for a drink if she was awake yet, and alone.

I crossed the street to the building where Billie had a room. A somewhat newer building, a hell of a lot nicer room, but then she paid a hell of a lot more for it.

I rapped on her door softly, a little code knock we had. If she wasn't awake she wouldn't hear it and if she wasn't alone she wouldn't answer it.

But she called out, "It's not locked; come on in," and she said "Hi, Professor," as I closed the door behind me. "Professor" she called me, occasionally and banteringly. It was my way of talking, I guess. I'd tried at first to use poor diction, bad grammar, to fit in with the place, but I'd given it up as too tough a job. Besides, I'd learned Fifth Street already had quite a bit of good grammar. Some of its denizens had been newspapermen once, some had written poetry; one I knew was a defrocked clergyman.

I said, "Hi, Billie the Kid."

"Just woke up, Howie. What time is it?"

"A little after ten," I told her. "Is there a drink around?"

"Jeez, only ten? Oh well, I had seven hours. Guy came here when Mike closed at two, but he didn't stay long."

She sat up in bed and stretched, the covers falling away from her naked body. Beautiful breasts she had, size and shape of half grape-fruits and firm. Nice arms and shoulders, and a lovely face. Hair black and sleek in a page-boy bob that fell into place as she shook her head. Twenty-five, she told me once; and I believed her, but she could have passed for several years less than that, even, now without make up and her eyes still a little puffy from sleep. Certainly it didn't show that she'd spent three years as a B-girl, part-time hustler, heavy drinker. Before that she'd been married to a man who'd worked for a manufacturing jeweler; he'd suddenly left for parts unknown with a considerable portion of his employer's stock, leaving Billie in a jam and with a mess of debts.

Wilhelmina Kidder, Billie the Kid, my Billie. Any man's Billie if he flashed a roll, but oddly I'd found that I could love her a little and not let that bother me. Maybe because it had been that way when I'd first met her over a month ago; I'd come to love her knowing what she was, so why should it bother me? What she saw in me I don't know, and didn't care.

"About that drink," I said.

She laughed and threw down the covers, got out of bed and walked past me naked to the closet to get a robe. I wanted to reach for her but I didn't; I'd learned by now that Billie the Kid was never amorous early in the morning and resented any passes made before noon.

She shrugged into a quilted robe and padded barefoot over to the little refrigerator behind the screen that hid a tiny kitchenette. She opened the door and said, "God damn it."

"God damn what?" I wanted to know. "Out of liquor?"

She held up over the screen a Hiram Walker bottle with only half an inch of ready-mixed Manhattan in it. Almost the only thing Billie ever drank, Manhattans.

"As near out as matters. Honey, would you run upstairs and see if Mame's got some? She usually has."

Mame is a big blonde who works behind the bar at Mike Karas' joint, The Best Chance, where Billie works as B-girl. A tough number, Mame. I said, "If she's asleep she'll murder me for waking her. What's wrong with the store?"

"She's up by now. She was off early last night. And if you get it at the store it won't be on ice. Wait, I'll phone her, though, so if she *is* asleep it'll be me that wakes her and not you."

She made the call and then nodded. "Okay, honey. She's got a full bottle she'll lend me. Scram."

I scrammed, from the second floor rear to the third floor front. Mame's door was open; she was out in the hallway paying off a milkman and waiting for him to receipt the bill. She said, "Go on in. Take a load off." I went inside the room and sat down in the chair that was built to match Mame, overstuffed. I ran my fingers around under the edge of the cushion; one of Mame's men friends might have sat there with change in his pocket. It's surprising how much change you can pick up just by trying any overstuffed chairs or sofas you sit on. No change this time, but I came up with a fountain pen, a cheap dime-store-looking one. Mame had just closed the door and I held it up. "In the chair. Yours, Mame?"

"Nope. Keep it, Howie, I got a pen."

"Maybe one of your friends'll miss it," I said. It was too cheap a pen to sell or hock so I might as well be honest about it.

"Nope, I know who lost it. Seen it in his pocket last night. It was Jesus, and the hell with him."

"Mame, you sound sacrilegious."

She laughed. "Hay-*soos*, then. Jesus Gonzales. A Mex. But when he told me that was his handle I called him Jesus. And Jesus was *he* like a cat on a hot stove!" She walked around me over to her refrigerator but her voice kept on. "Told me not to turn on the lights when he come in and went over to watch out the front window for a while like he was watching for the heat. Looks out my side window too, one with the fire escape. Pulls down all the shades before he says okay, turn on the lights." The refrigerator door closed and she came back with a bottle.

"Was he a hot one," she said. "Just got his coat off – he threw it on that chair, when there's a knock. Grabs his coat again and goes out my side window down the fire escape." She laughed again. "Was that a flip? It was only Dixie from the next room knocking, to bum cigarettes. So if I ever see Jesus again it's no dice, guy as jumpy as that. Keep his pen. Want a drink here?"

"If you'll have one with me."

"I don't drink, Howie. Just keep stuff around for friends and callers. Tell Billie to give me another bottle like this back. I got a friend likes Manhattans, like her."

When I got back to Billie's room, she'd put on a costume instead of the robe, but it wasn't much of a costume. A skimpy Bikini bathing suit. She pirouetted in it. "Like it, Howie? Just bought it yesterday."

"Nice," I said, "but I like you better without it."

"Pour us drinks, huh? For me, just a quickie."

"Speaking of quickies," I said.

She picked up a dress and started to pull it over her head. "If you're thinking that way, Professor, I'll hide the family treasures. Say, that's a good line; I'm getting to talk like you do sometimes."

I poured us drinks and we sat down with them. She'd stepped into sandals and was dressed. I said, "You've got lots of good lines, Billie the Kid. But correct me – was that lingerie instead of a bathing suit, or am I out of date on fashions?"

"I'm going to the beach today, Howie, for a sun-soak. Won't go near the water so why not just wear the suit under and save changing? Say, why don't you take a day off and come along?"

"Broke. The one thing to be said for Burke as an employer is that he pays every day. Otherwise there'd be some dry, dry evenings."

"What you make there? A fin, maybe. I'll lend you a fin."

"That way lies madness," I said. "Drinks I'll take from you, or more important things than drinks. But taking money would make me—" I stopped and wondered just what taking money from Billie would make me, just how consistent I was being. After all, I could always send it back to her from Chicago. What kept me from taking it, then? A gal named Honor, I guess. Corny as it sounds, I said it lightly. "I could not love thee, dear, so much, loved I not Honor more."

"You're a funny guy, Howie. I don't understand you."

Suddenly I wanted to change the subject. "Billie, how come Mame doesn't drink?"

"Don't you know hypes don't like to drink?"

"Sure, but I didn't spot Mame for one."

"Hype with a big H for heroin, Howie. Doesn't show it much, though. I'll give you that."

"I haven't known enough junkies to be any judge," I said. "The only one I know for sure is the cook at Burke's."

"Don't ever try it, Howie. It's bad stuff. I joy-popped once just to see what it was like, but never again. Too easy to get to like it. And Howie, it can make things rough."

I said, "I hear your words of wisdom and shall stick to drink. Speaking of which—" I poured myself another.

2

I got to the restaurant – it's on Main, a block from Fifth – at a quarter after eleven, only fifteen minutes late. Burke was at the stove – he does his own cooking until noon, when Ramon comes on – and turned to glare at me but didn't say anything.

Still feeling good from the drinks, I dived into my dishwashing. The good feeling was mostly gone, though, by noon, when Ramon came on. He had a fresh bandage on his forehead; I wondered if there was a new knife wound under it. He already had two knife scars, old ones, on his cheek and on his chin. He looked mean, too, and I decided to stay out of his way. Ramon's got a nasty temper when he needs a jolt, and it was pretty obvious that he needed one. He looked like a man with a kingsize monkey, and he was. I'd often wondered how he fed it. Cooks draw good money compared to other restaurant help, but even a cook doesn't get enough to support a five or six cap a day habit, not at a joint like Burke's anyway. Ramon was tall for a Mexican, but he was thin and his face looked gaunt. It's an ugly face except when he grins and his teeth flash white. But he wouldn't be grinning this afternoon, not if he needed a jolt.

Burke went front to work the register and help at the counter for the noon rush, and Ramon took over at the stove. We worked in silence until the rush was over, about two o'clock.

He came over to me then. He was sniffling and his eyes were running. He said, "Howie, you do me a favor. I'm burning, Howie, I need a fix, quick. I got to sneak out, fifteen minutes."

"Okay, I'll try to watch things. What's working?"

"Two hamburg steak dinners on. Done one side, five more minutes other side. You know what else to put on."

"Sure, and if Burke comes back I'll tell him you're in the can. But you'd better hurry."

He rushed out, not even bothering to take off his apron or chef's hat. I timed five minutes on the clock and then I took up the steaks, added the trimmings and put them on the ledge, standing at an angle back of the window so Burke couldn't see that it was I and not Ramon who was putting them there. A few minutes later the waitress put in a call for stuffed peppers, a pair; they were already cooked and I didn't have any trouble dishing them.

Ramon came back before anything else happened. He looked like a different man – he would be for as long as the fix lasted. His teeth flashed. "Million thanks, Howie." He handed me a flat pint bottle of muscatel. "For you, my friend."

"Ramon," I said, "you are a gentleman and a scholar." He went back to his stove and started scraping it. I bent down out of sight to open the bottle. I took a good long drink and then hid it back out of sight under one of the tubs.

Two-thirty, and my half-hour lunch break. Only I wasn't hungry. I took another drink of the muskie and put it back. I could have killed it but the rest of the afternoon would go better if I rationed it and made it last until near quitting time.

I wandered over to the alley entrance, rolling a cigarette. A beautiful bright day out; it would have been wonderful to be at the beach with Billie the Kid.

Only Billie the Kid wasn't at the beach; she was coming toward me from the mouth of the alley. She was still wearing the dress she'd pulled on over the bathing suit but she wasn't at the beach. She was walking toward me, looking worried, looking frightened.

I walked to meet her. She grabbed my arm, tightly. "Howie. Howie, did you kill Mame?"

"Did I – *what?*"

Her eyes were big, looking up at me. "Howie, if you did, I don't care. I'll help you, give you money to get away. But—"

"Whoa," I said, "Whoa, Billie. I didn't kill Mame. I didn't even rape her. She was okay when I left. What happened? Or are you dreaming this up?"

"She's dead, Howie, murdered. And about the time you were there. They found her a little after noon and say she'd been dead somewhere around two hours. Let's go have a drink and I'll tell you what all happened."

"All right," I said. "I've got most of my lunch time left. Only I haven't been paid yet—"

"Come on, hurry." As we walked out of the alley she took a bill from her purse and stuffed it into my pocket. We took the nearest ginmill and ordered drinks at a booth at the back where we weren't near enough anyone to be heard. The bill she'd put in my pocket was a sawbuck. When the waitress brought our drinks and the change I shoved it toward Billie. She shook her head and pushed it back. "Keep it and owe me ten, Howie. You might need it in case – well, just in case." I said, "Okay, Billie, but I'll pay this back." I would, too, but it probably wouldn't be until I mailed it to her from Chicago and it would probably surprise the hell out of her to get it.

I said, "Now tell me, but quit looking so worried. I'm as

innocent as new-fallen snow – and I don't mean cocaine. Let me reconstruct my end first, and then tell yours. I got to work at eleven-twenty. Walked straight there from your place, so it would have been ten after when I left you. And – let's see, from the other end, it was ten o'clock when I woke up, wouldn't have been over ten or fifteen minutes before I knocked on your door, another few minutes before I got to Mame's and I was up there only a few minutes. Say I saw her last around twenty after ten, and she was okay then. Over."

"Huh? Over what?"

"I mean, you take it. From when I left you, about ten minutes after eleven."

"Oh. Well, I straightened the room, did a couple things, and left, it must have been a little after twelve on account of the noon whistles had blown just a few minutes ago. I was going to the beach. I was going to walk over to the terminal and catch the Santa Monica bus, go to Ocean Park. Only first I stopped in the drugstore right on the corner for a cup of coffee. I was there maybe ten–fifteen minutes letting it cool enough to drink and drinking it. While I was there I heard a cop car stop near but I didn't think anything of it; they're always picking up drunks and all.

"But while I was there, too, I remembered I'd forgot to bring my sunglasses and sun-tan oil, so I went back to get them.

"Minute I got inside the cops were waiting and they asked if I lived there and then started asking questions, did I know Mame and when I saw her last and all."

"Did you tell them you'd talked to her on the phone?"

"Course not, Howie. I'm not a dope. I knew by then something had happened to her and if I told them about that call and what it was about, it would have brought you in and put you on the spot. I didn't even tell them you were with me, let alone going up to Mame's. I kept you out of it.

"They're really questioning everybody, Howie. They didn't pull me in but they kept me in *my* own room questioning me till just fifteen minutes ago. See, they really worked on me because I admitted I knew Mame – I had to admit that 'cause we work at the same place and they'd have found that out.

"And of course they knew she was a hype, her arms and all; they're checking everybody's arms and thank God mine are okay. They asked me mostly about where we worked, Mike's. I think they figure Mike Karas is a dealer, what with Mame working for him."

"Is he, Billie?"

"I don't know, honey. He's in some racket, but it isn't dope."

I said, "Well, I don't see what either of us has to worry about. It's not our – My God, I just remembered something."

"What, Howie?"

"A guy saw me going in her room, a milkman. Mame was in the hall paying him off when I went up. She told me to go on in and I did, right past him."

"Jesus, Howie, did she call you by name when she told you to go on in? If they get a name, even a first name, and you living right across the street—"

I thought hard. "Pretty sure she didn't, Billie. She told me to go in and take a load off, but I'm pretty sure she didn't add a Howie to it. Anyway, they may never find the milkman was there. He isn't likely to stick his neck out by coming to them. How was she killed, Billie?"

"Somebody said a shiv, but I don't know for sure."

"Who found her and how come?"

"I don't know. They were asking me questions, not me asking them. That part'll be in the papers, though."

"All right," I said. "Let's let it go till this evening, then. How's about this evening, Billie, are you going to The Best Chance anyway?"

"I *got* to, tonight, after that. If I don't show up, they'll want to know why and where I was and everything. And listen, don't you come around either, after hours tonight or in the morning. You stay away from that building, Howie. If they find that milkman they might even have him staked out watching for you. Don't even walk *past*. You better even stay off that block, go in and out the back way to your own room. And we better not even see each other till the heat's off or till we know what the score is."

I sighed.

I was ten minutes late reporting back and Burke glared at me again but still didn't say anything. I guess I was still relatively dependable for a dishwasher, but I was learning.

I made the rest of the wine last me till Baldy, the evening shift dishwasher, showed up to relieve me. Burke paid me off for the day then, and I was rich again.

3

Someone was shaking me, shaking me hard. I woke to fuzz and fog and Billie the Kid was peering through it at me, looking really scared, more scared than when she'd asked me yesterday if I'd killed Mame.

"Howie, wake up." I was in my own little shoebox of a room, Billie standing by my cot bending over me. I wasn't covered, but the extent of my undressing had been to kick off my shoes.

"Howie, listen, you're in trouble, honey. You got to get out of here, back way like I come in. Hurry."

I sat up and wanted to know the time.

"Only nine, Howie. But hurry. Here. This will help you." She screwed off the top of a half-pint bottle of whisky. "Drink some quick. Help you wake up."

I took a drink and the whisky burned rawly down my throat. For a moment I thought it was going to make me sick to my stomach, but then it decided to stay down and it did clear my head a little. Not much, but a little.

"What's wrong, Billie?"

"Put on your shoes. I'll tell you, but not here."

Luckily my shoes were loafers and I could step into them. I went to the basin of water, rubbed some on my face. While I washed and dried and ran a comb through my hair Billie was going through the dresser; a towel on the bed, everything I owned piled on it. It didn't make much of a bundle.

She handed it to me and then was pulling me out into the hallway, me and everything I owned. Apparently I wasn't coming back here, or Billie didn't think I was.

Out into the alley, through to Sixth Street and over Sixth to Main, south on Main. A restaurant with booths, mostly empty. The waitress came over and I ordered coffee, black. Billie ordered ham and eggs and toast and when the waitress left she leaned across the table. "I didn't want to argue with her in front of you, Howie, but that food I ordered is for you; you're going to eat it all. You got to be sober."

I groaned, but knew it would be easier to eat than to argue with a Billie the Kid as vehement as this one.

"What is it, Billie? What's up?"

"Did you read the papers last night?"

I shook my head. I hadn't read any papers up to about nine o'clock and after that I didn't remember what I'd done or hadn't. But I wouldn't have read any papers. That reminded me to look in my pockets to see what money I had left, if any. No change, but thank God there were some crumpled bills. A five and two ones, when I pulled them out and looked under cover of the table. I'd had a little over nine out of the ten Billie had given me to buy us a drink with, a little under five I'd got from Burke. That made fourteen and I'd spent seven of it somehow – and God knows how since I couldn't possibly have drunk that much muskie or even that much whisky at Fifth Street prices. But at least I hadn't been rolled, so it could have been worse.

"They got that milkman, Howie," Billie was saying. "Right off. He'd given Mame a receipt and she'd dropped it on that little table by the door so they knew he'd been there and they found him and he says he'll know you if he sees you. He described you too. You thinking straight by now, Howie?"

"Sure I'm thinking straight. What if they *do* find me? Damn it, I didn't kill her. Didn't have any reason to. They can't do any more than question me."

"Howie, haven't you ever been in trouble with cops? Not on anything serious, I guess, or you wouldn't talk like that. That milkman would put you right on the scene at close to the right time and that's all they'd want. They got nobody else to work on.

"Sure they'll question you. With fists and rubber hoses they'll question you. They'll beat the hell out of you for days on end, tie you in a chair with five hundred watts in your eyes and slap you every time you close them. Sure they'll question you. They'll question you till you wish you *had* killed Mame so you could tell 'em and get it over with and get some sleep. Howie, cops are tough, mean bastards when they're trying to pin down a murder rap. This is a murder rap, Howie."

I smiled a little without meaning to. Not because what she'd been saying was funny, but because I was thinking of the headlines if they did beat the truth out of me, or if I had to tell all to beat the rap. *Chicago Scion in Heroin Murder Case*. Chicago papers please copy.

I saw the hurt look on Billie's face and straightened mine. "Sorry," I said. "I was laughing at something else. Go on."

But the waitress was coming and Billie waited till she'd left. She shoved the ham and eggs and toast in front of me. "Eat," she said. I ate.

"And that isn't all, Howie. They'll frame you on some other charge to hold you. Howie, they might even frame you on the murder rap itself if they don't find who else did it. They could do it easy, just take a few little things from her room – it had been searched – and claim you had 'em on you or they were in your room. How'd you prove they weren't? And what'd your word be against a cop's? They could put you in the little room and gas you, Howie. And there's something else, too."

"Something worse that *that*?"

"I don't mean that. I mean what they'd do to me, Howie. And that'd be for *sure*. A perjury rap, a nice long one. See, I signed a statement after they questioned me, and that'd make it perjury for me if you tell 'em the truth about why you went up to see Mame. And what else could you tell them?"

I put down my knife and fork and stared at her. I hadn't been *really* worried about the things she'd been telling me. Innocent men, I'd been telling myself, aren't framed by the cops on murder charges. Not if they're willing to tell the truth down the line. They might give me a bad time, I thought, but they wouldn't hold me long if I leveled with them. But if Billie had signed a statement, then telling them the truth was out. Billie was on the wrong side of the law already; they *would* take advantage of perjury to put her away, maybe for several years.

I said, "I'm sorry, Billie. I didn't realize I'd have to involve you if I had to tell them the truth."

"Eat, Howie. Eat all that grub. Don't worry about me; I just mentioned it. You're in worse trouble than *I* am. But I'm glad you're talking straight; you sound really awake now. Now you go on eating and I'll tell you what you've got to do.

"First, this milkman's description. Height, weight and age fairly close but not exact on any, and anyway you can't change that. But you got to change clothes, buy new ones, because Jesus, the guy got your clothes perfect. Blue denim shirt cut off above elbows, tan work pants, brown loafers. Now first thing when you leave here, buy different clothes, see?"

"All right," I said. "How else did he describe me?"

"Well, he thought you had blond hair and it's a little darker than that, not much. Said you needed a shave – you need one worse now – and said you looked like a Fifth Street bum, a wino maybe. That's all, except he's sure he could identify you if he ever saw you again. And that's bad, Howie."

"It is," I said.

"Howie, do you want to blow town? I can lend you – well, I'm a little low right now and on account of Karas' place being watched so close I won't be able to pick up any extra money for a while, but I can lend you fifty if you want to blow town. Do you?"

"No, Billie," I said. "I don't want to blow town. Not unless you want to go with me."

God, what had made me *say that?* What had I meant by it? What business had I taking Billie away from the district she knew, the place where she could make a living – if I couldn't – putting her further in a jam for disappearing when she was more or less a witness in a murder case? And when I wanted to be back in Chicago, back working for my father and being respectable, within a few weeks anyway.

What had I meant? I couldn't take Billie back with me, much as I liked – maybe loved – her. Billie the Kid as the wife of a respectable investment man? It wouldn't work, for either of us. But if I hadn't meant that, what the hell *had* I meant?

But Billie was shaking her head. "Howie, it wouldn't work. Not for us, not right now. If you could quit drinking, straighten out. But I know – I know you can't. It isn't your fault and – oh, honey, let's not talk about that now. Anyway, I'm *glad* you don't want to lam because – well, because I *am.* But listen –"

"Yes, Billie?"

"You've got to change the way you look – just a little. Buy a different colored shirt, see? And different pants, shoes instead of loafers. Get a haircut – you need one anyway so get a short one. Then get a hotel room – off Fifth Street. Main is okay if you stay away from Fifth. And shave – you had a stubble when that milkman saw you. How much money you got left?"

"Seven," I said. "But that ought to do it. I don't need *new* clothes; I can swap with uncle."

"You'll need more than that. Here." It was a twenty.

"Thanks, Billie. I owe you thirty." Owe her thirty? Hell, how much did I owe Billie the Kid already, outside of money, things money can't buy? I said, "And how'll we get in touch with one another? You say I shouldn't come to your place. Will you come to mine, tonight?"

"I – I guess they won't be suspicious if I take a night off, Howie, as long as it wasn't that first night. Right after the – after what happened to Mame. All right, Howie. You know a place called The Shoebox on Main up across from the court house?"

"I know where it is."

"I'll meet you there tonight at eight. And – and stay in your room, wherever you take one, till then. And – and try to stay sober, Howie."

4

It shouldn't be hard, I thought, to stay sober when you're scared. And I was scared, now.

I stayed on Main Street, away from Fifth, and I did the things Billie had suggested. I bought a tan work shirt, and changed it right in the store where I bought it for the blue one I'd been wearing. I stopped in the barber school place for a fourbit haircut and, while I was at it, a two-bit shave. I had one idea Billie hadn't thought of; I spent a buck on a used hat. I hadn't been wearing one and a hat makes a man look different. At a shoe repair shop that handled used shoes I traded in my loafers and a dollar fifty for a pair of used shoes. I decided not to worry about the trousers; their color wasn't distinctive.

I bought newspapers; I wanted to read for myself everything Billie had told me about the murder, and there might be other details she hadn't mentioned. Some wine too, but just a pint to sip on. I was going to stay sober, but it would be a long boring day waiting for my eight o'clock date with Billie the Kid.

I registered double at a little walk-up hotel on Market Street around the corner from Main, less than a block from the place of my evening date. She'd be coming with me, of course, since we wouldn't dare go to her place, and I didn't want there to be even a chance of trouble in bringing her back with me. Not that trouble would be likely in a place like that but I didn't want even the minor trouble of having to change the registration from single to double if the clerk saw us coming in, not for fifty cents difference in the price of the room.

I sipped at the wine slowly and read the papers. The *Mirror* gave it the best coverage, with pictures. A picture of Mame that must have been found in her room and that had been taken at least ten years ago – she looked to be in her late teens or early twenties – a flashlight shot of the interior of her room, but taken after her body had been removed, and an exterior of The Best Chance, where she'd worked. But, even from the *Mirror*, I didn't learn anything Billie hadn't told me, except Mame's full name and just how and when the body had been discovered. The time had been 12:05, just about the time Billie was leaving from her room on the floor below. The owner of the building had dropped around, with tools, to fix a dripping faucet Mame (Miss Mamie Gaynor, 29) had complained about the day before. When he'd knocked long enough to decide she wasn't home he'd let himself in with his duplicate key. The milkman's story and the description he'd given of me was exactly as Billie had given them.

I paced up and down the little room, walked the worn and shabby carpet, wondering. Was there – short of the sheer accident of my running into that milkman – any danger of my being picked up just from that description? No, surely not. It was accurate as far as it went, but it was too vague, could fit too many men in this district, for anyone to think of me in connection with it. And now, with a change of clothes, a shave, wearing a hat outdoors, I doubted if the milkman would recognize me. I couldn't remember his face; why would he remember mine? And there was no tie-in otherwise, except through Billie. Nobody but Billie knew that I'd even met Mame. The only two times I'd ever seen her had been in Billie's place when she'd dropped in while I was there, once for only a few minutes, once for an hour or so. And one other time I'd been up to her room, that time to borrow cigarettes for Billie; it had been very late, after stores and bars were closed.

The fact that I'd disappeared from my room in that block? That would mean nothing. Tomorrow a week's rent was due;

the landlord would come to collect it, find me and my few possessions gone, and rent it again. He'd think nothing of it. Why should he?

No, now that I'd taken the few precautions Billie had suggested, I was safe enough as long as I stayed away from her building.

Why was I hiding here now, then?

The wine was gone and I wanted more. But I knew what shape I'd be in by eight o'clock if I kept on drinking it, starting at this hour of the morning.

But I'd go nuts if I stayed here, doing nothing. I picked up the papers, read the funny sheets, a few other things. Back in the middle of one of them a headline over a short item caught my eye, I don't know for what reason. *Victim in Alley Slaying Identified*.

Maybe my eye had first caught the name down in the body of the story, Jesus Gonzales. And Mame's jittery guest of the night before her death had been named Jesus Gonzales.

I read the story. Yesterday morning at dawn the body of a man had been found in an areaway off Winston Street near San Pedro Street. He had been killed with a blunt instrument, probably a blackjack. As he had been robbed of everything he was carrying, no identification had been made at first. Now he had been identified as Jesus Gonzales, 41, of Mexico City, DF. He had arrived in Los Angeles the day before on the SS *Guadalajara*, out of Tokyo. His passport, which had been left in his room at the Berengia Hotel, and other papers left with it, showed that he had been in the Orient on a buying trip for a Mexico City art object importing firm in which he was a partner, and that he was stopping in Los Angeles for a brief vacation on his return trip.

Mame's Jesus Gonzales? It certainly looked that way. The place and time fitted; less than two blocks from her room. So did the time, the morning after he'd been frightened by that knock at the door and had left unceremoniously via the fire escape.

But why would he have hooked up with Mame? The Berengia is a swank hotel, only people with well-lined pockets stay there. Mame was no prize; at the Berengia he could have done better through his own bellhop.

Or could it be a factor that Mame was a junkie and, stopping in at The Best Chance, he'd recognized her as one and picked her for that reason? He could have been a hype himself, in need of a jolt and in a city where he had no contacts, or – and this seemed even more likely because of his just having landed from Tokyo – he'd smuggled some dope in with him and was looking for a dealer to sell it. The simplest and safest way to find a dealer would be through an addict.

It was just a wild guess, of course, but it wasn't too wild to be possible. And damn it, Mame's Jesus Gonzales *had* acted suspiciously and he *had* been afraid of something. Maybe he'd thought somebody was following him, following him and Mame home from The Best Chance. If he was the same Jesus Gonzales who'd just been killed and robbed only two blocks from her place, then he'd been dead right in being careful. He'd made his mistake in assuming that the knocker on Mame's door was the man who'd followed him and in going down the fire escape. Maybe his *Nemesis* had still been outside the building, probably watching from across the street, and had seen him leave. And on Winston Street *Nemesis* had caught up with him.

Nice going, B.A.S., old boy, I thought. You're doing fine. It isn't every Skid-Row pearl-diver who can reconstruct a crime out of nothing. Sheer genius, B.A.S., sheer genius.

But it was something to pass the time, a lot better than staring at the wall and wishing I'd never left Chicago. Better than brooding.

All right, suppose it figured so far – then how did Mame's death tie in with it? I didn't see how. I made myself pace and concentrate, trying to work out an answer.

I felt sure Mame had been telling me the truth about Gonzales as far as she knew it, or else she would have had no reason for mentioning it at all. Whatever his ulterior motive in picking her up, whether to buy dope or to find a contact for selling it, he hadn't yet leveled with Mame before that knock came. Otherwise she wouldn't have told it casually, as she had, as something amusing.

But the killer wouldn't have known that. He couldn't have known that Mame was not an accomplice. If what he was looking for hadn't been on the person of the man he'd killed he could have figured that it had already changed hands. Why hadn't he gone back to Mame's the same night? I didn't know, but there could have been a reason. Perhaps he had and she'd gone out, locking the door and the fire-escape window. Or maybe by that time she had other company; if he had knocked she might have opened the door on the chain – and I remembered now that there was a chain on her door – and told him so. I couldn't ask Mame now what she'd done the rest of the night after her jittery caller had left.

But if Gonzales was a stranger in town, just off the boat, how would the killer have known he had brought in heroin? – or opium or cocaine; it could have been any drug worth smuggling. And the killer must have known *something*; if it had been just a robbery kill, for whatever money Gonzales was carrying, then he wouldn't have gone back and killed Mame, searched her room. He'd have done that only if he'd known something about Gonzales that made him think Mame was his accomplice.

I killed a few more minutes worrying about that and I had the answer. Maybe not *the* answer, but at least an answer that made sense. Maybe I was just mildly cockeyed, but this off-the-cuff figuring I'd been doing *did* seem to be getting somewhere.

It was possible, I reasoned, that Mame hadn't been the first person through whom Gonzales had tried to make a contact. He could have approached another junkie on the same deal, but one who refused to tell him her contact. Her? It didn't have to be a woman, but Mame had been a woman and that made me think he'd been working that way. Say that he'd wandered around B-joints until he spotted a B-girl as an addict; he could get her in a booth and try to get information from her. She could have stalled him or turned him down. Stalled him, most likely, making a phone call or two to see if she could get hold of a dealer for him, but tipping off her boyfriend instead. Killing time enough for her boyfriend to be ready outside, then telling Gonzales she couldn't make a contact for him.

And if any of that had sounded suspicious to Gonzales he would have been more careful the second try, with Mame. He'd get her to her room on the obvious pretext, make sure they were alone and hadn't been followed before he opened up. Only, between The Best Chance and Mame's room, he must have discovered that they were being followed.

Sure, it all fitted. But what good did it do me?

Sure, it was logical. It made a complete and perfect picture, but it was all guesswork, nothing to go to the cops with. Even if they believed me eventually and could verify my guesses in the long run, I'd be getting myself and Billie the Kid into plenty of trouble in the short run. And like as not enough bad publicity – my relations with Billie would surely come out, and Billie's occupation – to have my father's clients in Chicago decide I wasn't fit to handle their business.

Well, was I? Worry about the fact that you want a drink so damned bad, I told myself, that soon you're going to weaken and go down and get another bottle. Well, why not? As long as I rationed it to myself so I would be drinking just enough to hold my own and not get drunk, not until after eight o'clock anyway . . .

What time was it? It seemed like I'd been in that damned room six or eight hours, but I'd checked in at around eleven and the sun was shining straight down in the dirty areaway my window opened on. Could it be only noon? I went out to the desk and past it, looking at the kitchen-type electric clock on the wall over it as I went by. It was a quarter after twelve.

I decided to walk a while before I went back to the room with a bottle, kill some time first. God, the time I had to kill before eight o'clock. I walked around the court house and over to Spring Street. I'd be safe there.

Hell, I'd be safe anywhere, I thought. Except maybe right in that one block of Fifth Street, just on the chance the police did have the milkman staked out in or near that building. And with different clothes, wearing a hat, he probably wouldn't recognize me anyway. Billie the Kid had panicked, and had panicked me. I didn't have anything to worry about. Oh, moving out of that block, changing out of the clothes I'd been wearing, those things had been sensible. But I didn't have to quit my job at Burke's – if it was still open to me. Burke's was safe for me. Nobody at Burke's knew where I'd lived and nobody in the building I'd lived in knew where I worked.

I thought, why not go to Burke's? He'd have the sign out in the window, now that I was an hour and a half late, but if nobody had taken the job, I could give him a story why I was so late and get it back. I'd gotten pretty good at washing dishes; I was probably the best dishwasher he'd ever had and I'd been steadier than the average one. Sure, I could go back there unless he'd managed to hire a new one already.

And otherwise, what? I'd either have to look for a new job of the same kind or keep on taking money from Billie for however long I stayed here. And taking money from Billie, except in emergency, was out. That gal named Honor back in Chicago was getting to be a pretty dim memory, but I still had some self-respect.

I cut back to Main Street and headed for Burke's. The back way, so I could see if anyone was working yet in my place, and maybe ask Ramon what the score was before I saw Burke.

From the alley doorway I could see my spot was empty, dishes piling high. Ramon was busy at the stove. He turned as I walked up to him, and his teeth flashed white in that grin. He said, "Howie! Thank God you're here. No dishwasher, everybody's going nuts."

The bandage was gone from his forehead. Under where it had been were four long scratches, downward, about an inch apart.

I stared at the scratches and thought about Ramon and his monkey and Mame and *her* monkey, and all of a sudden I had a crazy hunch. I thought about how a monkey like Ramon's could make a man do anything to get a fix. I moistened my lips. Ramon's monkey might claw the hell out of his guts, but it hadn't put those four scratches on his face. Not directly.

I didn't say it, I'd have had more sense; my mouth said it. "Mame had sharp fingernails, huh?"

5

Death can be a sudden thing. Only luck or accident kept me from dying suddenly in the next second or two. I'd never seen a face change as suddenly as Ramon's did. And before I could move, his hand had hold of the front of my shirt and his other hand had reached behind him and come up with and raised a cleaver. To step back as it started down would have put me in even better position for it to hit, so I did the only thing possible; I stepped in and pushed him backward and he stumbled and fell. I'd jerked my head but the cleaver went too wild even to scrape my shoulders. And there was a thunking sound as Ramon's head hit a sharp corner of the big stove. Yes, death can be a sudden thing.

I breathed hard a second and then – well, I don't know why I cared whether he was alive or not, but I bent forward and reached inside his shirt, held my hand over where his heart should be beating. It wasn't.

From the other side of the window Burke's voice sang out, "Two burgers, with."

I got out of there fast. Nobody had seen me there, nobody was *going* to see me there. I got out of the alley without being seen, that I knew of, and back to Main Street. I walked three blocks before I stopped into a tavern for the drink I really needed *now*. Not wine, whisky. Wine's an anodyne but it dulls the mind. Whisky sharpens it, at least temporarily. I ordered whisky, a double, straight.

I took half of it in one swallow and got over the worst of it. I sipped the rest slowly, and thought.

Damn it, Howie, I told myself, you've *got* to think.

I thought, and there was only one answer. I was in over my head now. If the police got me I was sunk. B.A.S. or not, I'd have a hell of a time convincing them I hadn't committed two murders – maybe three; if they'd tied in Jesus Gonzales, they'd pin that on me, too.

Sure, *I* knew what had really happened, but what proof did I have? Mame was dead; she wouldn't tell again what she'd told me about her little episode with Jesus. Ramon was dead; he wouldn't back up my otherwise unsupported word that I'd killed him accidentally in defending myself.

Out of this while I had a whole skin, that was the only answer. Back in Chicago, back to respectability, back to my right name – Howard Perry, B.A.S., not Howard Perry, bastard, wino, suspected soon of being a psychopathic killer. Back to Chicago, and not by freight. Too easy to get arrested that way, vagged, and maybe by that time flyers would be out with my description. Too risky.

So was waiting till eight o'clock when it was only one o'clock now. I'd have to risk getting in touch with Billie the Kid sooner. I couldn't go to her place, but I could phone. Surely they wouldn't have all the phones in that building tapped.

Just the same I was careful when I got her number. "Billie," I said, "this is the Professor." That nickname wouldn't mean anything to anybody else.

I heard her draw in her breath sharply. She must have realized I wouldn't risk calling her unless something important had come up. But she made her voice calm when she answered, "Yes, Professor?"

"Something has come up," I said. "I'm afraid I won't be able to make our eight o'clock date. Is there any chance that you can meet me now instead – same place?"

"Sure, soon as I can get there."

Click of the receiver. She'd be there. Billie the Kid, my Billie. She'd be there, and she'd make sure first that no one was following her. She'd bring money, knowing that I'd decided I had to lam after all. Money that she'd get back, damn it, if it was the last thing I ever did. Whatever money she'd lend me now, plus the other two sums and enough over to cover every drink and every cigarette I'd bummed from her. But not for the love and the trust she'd given me; you can't pay for that in money. In my case, I couldn't ever pay for it, period. The nearest I could come would be by being honest with her, leveling down the line. That much she had coming. More than that she had coming but more than that I couldn't give her.

The Shoebox is a shoebox-sized place. Not good for talking, but that didn't matter because we weren't going to talk there.

She got there fifteen minutes after I did; I was on my second drink. I ordered a Manhattan when I saw her coming in the door.

"Hello, Billie," I said.

Hello, Billie. Goodbye, Billie. This is the end for us, today. It's got to be the end. I knew she'd understand when I told her, when I told her everything.

"Howie, are you in—"

"In funds?" I cut her off. "Sure, just ordered you a drink." I dropped my voice, but not far enough to make it conspicuous. "Not here, Billie. Let's drink our drink and then I've got a room around the corner. I registered double so it'll be safe for us to go there and talk a while."

The bartender had mixed her Manhattan and was pouring it. I ordered a refill on my whisky-high. Why not? It was going to be my last drink for a long while. The wagon from here on in, even after I got back to Chicago for at least a few weeks, until I was sure the stuff couldn't get me, until I was sure I could do normal occasional social drinking without letting it start me off.

We drank our drinks and went out. Out into the sun, the warm sunny afternoon. Just before we got to the corner, Billie stopped me. "Just a minute, Howie."

She ducked into a store, a liquor store, before I could stop her. I waited. She came out with a wrapped bottle and a cardboard carton. "The ready-mixed wasn't on ice, Howie, but it's all right. I bought some ice cubes too. Are there two glasses in the room?"

I nodded; we went on. There were two glasses in the room. The wagon not yet. But it wouldn't have been right not to have a last drink or two, a stirrup cup or two, with Billie the Kid.

She took charge of the two tumblers, the drinks. Poured the drinks over ice cubes, stirred them around a while and then fished the ice cubes out when the drinks were chilled.

While I talked. While I told her about Chicago, about me in Chicago, about my family and the investment company. She handed me my drink then. She said quietly, "Go on, Howie."

I went on. I told her what Mame had told me about her guest Jesus the night before she was killed. I told her of the death of Jesus Gonzales as I'd read it in the *Mirror*. I added the two up for her.

She made us another drink while I told her about Ramon, about what had happened, about how I'd just killed him.

"Ramon," she said. "He has knife scars, Howie?" I nodded. She said, "Knife scars, a hype, a chef. I didn't know his name, but I know who his woman was, a red-headed junkie named Bess, I think it's Bess, in a place just down the block from Karas' joint. It's what happened, Howie, just like you guessed it. It must have been." She sipped her drink. "Yes, Howie, you'd better go back to Chicago, right away. It could be bad trouble for you if you don't. I brought money. Sixty. It's all I have except a little to last me till I can get more. Here."

A little roll of bills, she tucked into my shirt pocket.

"Billie," I said. "I wish—"

"Don't say it, honey. I know you can't. Take me with you, I mean. I wouldn't fit, not with the people you know there. And I'd be bad for you."

"I'd be bad for you, Billie. I'd be a square, a wet blanket. I'll have to be to get back in that rut, to hold down—" I didn't want to think about it. I said, "Billie, I'm going to send you what I owe you. Can I count on your being at the same address for another week or so?"

She sighed. "I guess so, Howie. But I'll give you my sister's name and address, what I use for a permanent address, in case you ever – in case you might not be able to send the money right away."

"I'll write it down," I said. I tore a corner off the paper the bottle had been wrapped in, looked around for something to write with; I remembered the fountain pen I'd stuck in my trousers pocket at Mame's. It was still there.

I screwed off the cap. Something glittered, falling to the carpet, a lot of somethings. Shiny little somethings that looked like diamonds. Billie gasped. Then she was scrabbling on the floor, picking them up. I stared at the pen, the hollow pen without even a point, in my hand. Hollow and empty now. But there was still something in the cap, which I'd been holding so it hadn't spilled. I emptied the cap out into my hand. Bigger diamonds, six of them, big and deep and beautifully cut.

My guess had been wrong. It hadn't been heroin Gonzales had been smuggling. Diamonds. And when he'd found himself followed to Mame's, he'd stashed them there for safety. The pen hadn't fallen from his coat pocket; he'd hidden it there deliberately.

They were in two piles on the table, Billie's hands trembling a little as she handled them one at a time. "Matched," she said reverently. "My husband taught me stones, Howie. Those six big ones – over five carats each, cut for depth, not shallow, and they're blue-white and I'll bet they're flawless, all of them, because they're matched. And the fifteen smaller ones – they're matched too, and they're almost three carats apiece. You know what Karas would give us for them, Howie?"

"Karas?"

"Fifteen grand, Howie, at least. Maybe more. These aren't ordinary; they're something special. Sure, Karas – I didn't tell you everything, because it didn't matter then, when I said I thought maybe he had some racket – not dope. He handles stones, only stones. Gonzales might have heard of him, might have been trying to contact him through Mame."

I thought about fifteen thousand dollars, and I thought about going back to Chicago. Billie said, "Mexico, Howie. In Mexico we can live like kings – like a king and queen – for five years for that much."

And stop drinking, straighten out? Billie said, "Howie, shall I take these to Karas right now so we can leave quick?" She was flushed, breathing hard, staring at me pleadingly.

"Yes," I said. She kissed me, hard, and gathered them up.

At the doorway, hand on the knob. "Howie, were you kidding when you said you were in love with a girl named Honor in Chicago? I mean, is there a real girl named that, or did you just mean—?"

"I was kidding, Billie the Kid."

The door closed.

Her heels clicked down the wooden hall. I poured myself a drink, a long one, and didn't bother to chill it with ice cubes. Yes, I'd known a girl named Honor in Chicago, once, but – ... *but that was in another country, and besides, the wench is dead.*

I drank my drink and waited.

Twenty minutes later, I heard Billie's returning footsteps in the hall.

SO DARK FOR APRIL

Howard Browne

1

When I got through telling the sergeant at Central Homicide about it, he said to sit tight and not touch anything, that somebody would be right over. I told him I wouldn't even breathe any more than was absolutely necessary and put back the receiver and went into the reception room to take another look at the body.

He was at the far end of the couch, slumped in a sitting position, with his chin on his chest and an arm hanging down. A wick of iron-gray hair made a curve against the waxen skin of a high forehead, his half-open eyes showed far too much white, and a trickle of dark blood had traced a crooked line below one corner of a slack-lipped mouth. His coat hung open, letting me see a circular red stain under the pocket of a soiled white shirt. From the center of the stain protruded the brown bone handle of a switchblade knife.

I moved over to lean against the window frame and light a cigarette. It was one of those foggy wet mornings we get early in April, with a chill wind off the lake and the sky as dull as a deodorant commercial. Umbrellas blossomed along the walks eight floors below and long lines of cars slithered past with a hooded look.

I stood there breathing smoke and staring at the dead man. He was nobody I had ever seen before. He wore a handsomely tailored suit coat of gray flannel, dirty brown gabardine slacks spattered with green paint and an oil stain across one knee, and brown bench-made shoes. His shirt was open at the throat, showing a fringe of dark hair, and he wasn't wearing a tie.

The rummage-sale air of those slacks bothered me. This was no Skid Row fugitive. His nails had that cared-for look, his face, even in death, held a vague air of respectability, and they didn't trim hair that way at barber college.

I bent down and turned back the left side of his coat. The edge of a black wallet showed in the inner pocket. That was where I stopped. This was cop business. Let the boys who were paid for it paw the corpse.

A black satin label winked up at me. I put my eyes close enough to read the stitched letters in it. A C G – in a kind of Old English script. The letters seemed too big to be simply a personal monogram, but then there's no accounting for tastes.

I let the lapel drop back to the way I had found it. The dead man didn't seem to care either way. Something glistened palely between the frayed cuffs and the tops of the custom-made shoes. I said, "Huh?" out loud and bent down to make sure.

No mistake. It made no sense but there it was. The pale white shine was naked flesh.

The dead man wasn't wearing socks.

2

Detective Sergeant Lund said, "Right smack-dab through the old ticker. He never even had time to clear his throat. Not this guy."

His curiously soft voice held a kind of grim respect. He straightened up and backed away a couple of steps and took off his hat and shook rainwater from it onto the carpet and stared thoughtfully at me out of gunmetal eyes.

I moved a shoulder and said nothing. At the wicker table across the room the two plainclothes men were unshipping tape measures and flash-bulbs and fingerprint kits. Rain tapped the glass behind me with icy fingers.

"Your turn, Pine," Lund said in the same soft voice.

"He was like that when I came in," I said promptly. I looked at my strapwatch. "Exactly thirty-two minutes ago."

"How'd he get in here?"

"I usually leave the reception room unlocked, in case I have a client and the client cares to wait."

One corner of his mouth moved up faintly. "Somebody sure wanted this guy to wait, hey?"

I shrugged. He took a turn along the room and back again, hands deep in the pockets of his topcoat. Abruptly he said. "It says on your door you're a private dick. This a client?"

"No. I never saw him before."

"What's his name?"

"I don't know."

"No identification on him?"

"I didn't look. The sergeant at Central said not to."

He seemed mildly astonished. "A man dies in your office and you don't even show a little healthy curiosity? Don't be afraid of me, Pine. I haven't chewed off anybody's arm in over a week."

"I obey the law," I said mildly.

"Well, well," he said. He grinned suddenly, and after a moment I grinned back. Mine was no phonier than his. He snapped a thumb lightly against the point of his narrow chin a time or two while thinking a secret thought, then turned back to the body.

He went through the pockets with the deft delicacy of a professional dip. The blood, the knife handle, the sightless eyes meant about half as much to him as last week's laundry. When he straightened again there was a small neat pile of personal effects on one of the couch pillows and the dead man's pockets were as empty as his eyes.

The wallet was on top. Lund speared it, flipped it open. The transparent identification panels were empty, as was the bill compartment. Shoved into the latter, however, were three or four cards. Lund looked them over slowly and carefully, his thick brows drawn into a lazy V above his long, pointed nose.

"Credit cards on a couple Loop hotels," he said, almost to himself. "Plus one of these identification cards you get with a wallet. According to what it says here, this guy is Franklin Andrus, 5861 Winthrop Avenue. One business card. It calls him a sales representative for the Reliable Amusement Machine Corporation, Dayton, Ohio. No telephone shown and nobody listed to notify. Any of this mean anything to you, Mr Pine?"

"Sorry."

"Uh-huh. You ain't playing this too close, are you?"

"I'm not even in the game," I said.

"Initials in his coat don't agree with the name on these here cards. That must mean something, hey?"

I stared at the bridge of his nose. "His coat and somebody else's cards. Or his cards and somebody else's coat. Or neither. Or both."

His mouth hardened. "You trying to kid me, mister?"

"I guess that would be pretty hard to do, Sergeant."

He turned on his heel and went through the communicating door to my inner office, still carrying the wallet. He didn't bother to shut it, and through the opening I could see him reach for the phone without sitting down and dial a number with quick hard stabs of a forefinger. What he said when he got his party was too low-voiced for me to catch.

Two minutes later, he was back. He scooped up the stuff from the couch and said, "Let's talk, hey? Let's us try out that nice private office of yours."

I followed him in and drew up the Venetian blind and opened the window a crack to let out the smell of yesterday's cigarettes. On the outer ledge four pigeons were organizing a bombing raid. Lund shoved the phone and ashtray aside, dumped his collection on the desk pad and snapped on the lamp. I sat down behind the desk and watched him pull up the customer's chair across from me.

I got out my cigarettes. He took one, sniffed at it for no reason I knew of and struck a match for us both. He leaned back and hooked an arm over the chair back and put his dull gray eyes on me.

"Nice and cozy," he said. "All the comforts. Too bad they're not all like this."

"I could turn on the radio," I said. "Maybe get a little dance music."

He grunted with mild amusement. All the narrow-eyed suspicion had been tucked out of sight. He drew on his cigarette and blew a long blue plume of smoke at the ceiling. Another minute and he'd have his shoes off.

He let his gaze drift about the dingy office, taking in the Varga calendar, the filing cases, the worn tan linoleum. He said, "The place could stand a little paint, hey?"

"You drumming up business for your day off?" I asked.

That got another grunt out of him. "You sound kind of on the excited side, Pine. Don't be like that. You wouldn't be the first private boy got a customer shot out from under him, so to speak."

I felt my face burn. "He's not a customer. I told you that."

"I guess you did, at that," he said calmly. "It don't mean I have to believe it. Client getting pushed right in your own office don't look so good, hey? What the newshounds call a bad press."

I bit down on my teeth. "You just having fun, Sergeant, or does all this lead somewhere?"

"Why, we're just talking," he said mildly. "Just killing time, you might say, until the coroner shows up. That and looking over the rest of what the guy had on him."

He stuck out an untidy finger and poked at the pile. Besides the wallet, there were several small square transparent envelopes, some loose change, a pocket comb, and a small pair of gold tweezers.

He brought his eyes up to stare coldly at me, his mellow mood gone as quickly as it had arrived. He said harshly, "Let's lay off the clowning around, mister. You were working for him. I want to know doing what."

"I wouldn't bother to lie to you," I said. "I never saw the guy before in my life, I never talked to him on the phone, or got a letter from him. Period."

His sneer was a foot wide. "Jesus, you must think I'm green!"

"I'm not doing any thinking," I said.

"I hope to tell you, you aren't. Listen, I can book you, brother!"

"For what?"

"Obstructing justice, resisting an officer, indecent exposure. What the hell do you care? I'm saying I can book you!"

I didn't say anything. Some of the angry color faded slowly from his high cheeks. Finally he sighed heavily and picked up the necktie and gave it a savage jerk between his square hands and threw it down again.

"Nuts," he said pettishly. "I don't want to fight with you. I'm trying to do a job. All I want is a little cooperation. This guy just don't walk in here blind. You're a private dick, or so your door says. Your job is people in trouble. I say it's too damn big a coincidence him picking your office to get knocked off in. Go on, tell me I'm wrong."

"I'm not saying you're wrong," I said. "I'm saying what I've already said. He's a stranger to me. He could have come in here to get out of the wet or to sell me a slot machine or to just sit down and rest his arches. I admit he might have come here to hire me. It has happened, although not often enough. Maybe somebody didn't want him spilling any touchy secrets to me, and fixed him so he couldn't."

"But you never saw him before?"

"You're beginning to get the idea," I said.

"Go ahead," he said bitterly. "Crack wise. Get out the office bottle and toss off three inches of Scotch without a chaser and spit in my eye. That's the way you private eyes do it on TV eight times a night."

"I don't have an office bottle," I said.

The sound of the reception-room door opening and closing cut off what Lund was about to say. A short plump man went past the half-open door of the inner office, carrying a black bag. Lund got up without a word and went out there, leaving me where I sat.

Some time passed. Quite a lot of time. The murmur of voices from the next room went on and on. Flash bulbs made soundless explosions of light and a small vacuum cleaner whirred. I stayed where I was and burned a lot of tobacco and crossed my legs and dangled my foot and listened to the April rain and thought my thoughts.

Thoughts about a man who might still be alive if I hadn't slept an hour later than usual. A man with mismatched clothing and no socks and an empty wallet. A man who would want to go on living, even in an age when living was complicated and not very rewarding. A man who had managed for fifty-odd years to hang on to the only life he'd ever be given to live before a switchblade knife and a strong hand combined to pinch it off.

I went on sitting. The rain went on falling. It was so dark for April.

After a while the corridor door opened to let in two men in white coats. They carried a long wicker basket between them. They passed my door without looking in. There was more indistinct murmuring, then a young voice said, "Easy with them legs, Eddie," and the basket was taken out again. It was harder to carry the second time.

Sergeant Lund walked in, his face expressionless. He sat down heavily and lighted a cigarette and waved out the match and continued to hold it. He said, "Andrus died between eight-thirty and ten. The elevator man don't recall bringing him up. What time did you get here?"

"Ten-thirty, about. Few minutes either way."

"You wouldn't happen to own a switchblade knife, hey?"

"With a brown bone handle?" I said.

He bent the used match and dropped it in the general vicinity of the ashtray. "Seven-inch blade," he muttered. "Like a goddam bayonet." He put the cigarette in a corner of his mouth and left it there. "This is a real cute killing, Pine. You notice how Andrus was dressed?"

"No socks," I said.

"That isn't the half of it, brother. New coat, old pants, fancy shoes. No hat and no topcoat. In weather like this? What's the sense?"

I spread my hands. "By me, Sergeant."

"You sure you wasn't work—"

"Don't say it!" I shouted.

The phone rang. A voice like a buzz-saw asked for Lund. He grunted into the mouthpiece, listened stolidly for nearly a full minute, then said, "Yeah," twice and passed back the receiver. I replaced it and watched him drag himself out of the chair, his expression a study in angry frustration.

"I had Rogers Park send a squad over to that Winthrop Avenue address," he growled. "Not only they don't find no trace of a Franklin Andrus; they don't even find the address! An empty lot, by God! All right. Hell with it. The lab boys will turn up something. Laundry marks, cuff dust, clothing labels. It'll take 'em a day or two, but I can wait. The old routine takes time but it always works."

"Almost always," I said absently.

He glowered down across the desk at me. "One thing I hope, mister. I hope you been holding out on me and I find it out. That's going to be jake with me."

He gathered up the dead man's possessions and stalked out. A little later one of the plainclothes men slipped in with his kit and took my fingerprints. He was nice about it, explaining they were only for elimination purposes.

3

By one o'clock I was back from having a sandwich and coffee at the corner drugstore. The reception room was empty, with only a couple of used flash bulbs, some smudges of fingerprint powder here and there and the smell of cheap cigars and damp cloth to remind me of my morning visitors. Without the dead man on it, the couch seemed larger than usual. There were no bloodstains. I looked to make sure.

I walked slowly into the other room and shucked off my trench coat. From the adjoining office came the faint whine of a dentist's drill. A damp breeze crawled in at the window and rattled the cords on the blind. Cars hooted in the street below. Sounds that made the silence around me even more silent. And the rain went on and on.

I sat down behind the desk and emptied the ashtray into the waste-basket and wiped off the glass top. I put away the cloth and got out a cigarette and sat there turning it, unlighted, between a thumb and forefinger.

He had been a nice-looking man. Fifty-five at the most. A man with a problem on his mind. Let's say he wakes up this morning and decides to take his problem to a private detective. So he gets out the classified book and looks under the right heading. There aren't many, not even for a town the size of Chicago. The big agencies he passes up, maybe because he figures he'll have to go through a handful of henna-haired secretaries before reaching the right guy. Then, not too far down the column, he comes across the name Paul Pine. A nice short name. Anybody can pronounce it.

So he takes a cab or a bus and comes on down. He hasn't driven a car; no car keys and no license on him. The waiting room is unlocked but no alert gimlet-eyed private detective around. The detective is home in bed, like a man with a working wife. So this nice-looking man with a problem sits down to wait . . . and somebody walks in and sticks a quarter-pound of steel in him.

That was it. That explained everything. Everything but what his problem was and why he wasn't wearing socks and why his wallet was empty and why his identification showed an address that didn't exist.

I got up and took a couple of turns around the room. This was no skin off my shins. The boys from Homicide would have it all wrapped up in a day or so. The old routine Lund had called it. I didn't owe that nice old man a thing. He hadn't paid me a dime. No connection between us at all.

Except that he had come to me for help and got a mouthful of blood instead.

I sat down again and tried the phone book. No Franklin Andrus listed. No local branch of the Reliable Amusement Machine Corp. I shoved the book away and began to think about the articles that had come out of the dead man's pockets. Gold tweezers, a pocket comb, five small transparent envelopes, seventy-three cents in change, a dark blue necktie. There had been a department store label on the tie – Marshall Field. I knew that because I had looked while Lund was out of the room. But Field's has more neckties than Pabst has bottles. No help there.

Is that all, Pine, I thought to myself. End of the line? You mean you're licked? A nice, clean-necked, broad-shouldered, late-sleeping detective like you?

I walked the floor some more. I went over to the window and leaned my forehead against its coolness. My breath misted the glass and I wrote my name in the mist with the end of my finger. That didn't seem to help any. I went on thinking.

Maybe what *hadn't* come out of his pockets was important. No keys, for instance. Not even to his apartment. Maybe he lived in a hotel. Not even cigarettes or a book of matches. Maybe he didn't smoke. Not even a handkerchief. Maybe he didn't have a cold.

I sat down again. There had been initials in his coat. A C G. No periods and stitched professionally in fancy letters against a square of black satin. Rather large, as I recalled. Too bad I hadn't looked inside the pocket for the tailor's label. Unless . . .

This time I used the classified book. T – for Tailors – Men's. I ran through the columns to the G's. There it was, bright and shining and filled with promise. A. Cullinham Grandfils, Custom Tailor. On Michigan Avenue, in the 600 block. Right in the center of the town's swankiest shopping district.

I closed the window, climbed into my trench coat and hat and locked up. The smell of dime cigars still hung heavy in the outer office. Even the hall seemed full of it.

4

It was made to look like a Greek temple, if you didn't look too close. It had a white limestone front and a narrow doorway with a circular hunk of stained glass above that. Off to one side was a single display window about the size of a visiting card. Behind the glass was a slanting pedestal covered with black velvet and on the velvet a small square of gray cloth that looked as though it might be of cheviot. Nothing else. No price tags, no suits, no firm name spelled out in severely stylized letters.

And probably no bargain basement.

I heaved back the heavy glass door and walked into a large room with soft dusty rose walls, a vaulted ceiling, moss green carpeting, and indirect lighting like a benediction. Scattered tastefully about were upholstered chairs and couches, blond in the wood and square in the lines. A few chrome ashstands, an end table or two, and at the far end a blond desk and a man sitting behind it.

The man stood up as I came in. He floated down the room toward me, a tall slender number in a cut-away coat, striped trousers and a gates-ajar collar. He looked like a high-class undertaker. He had a high reedy voice that said:

"Good afternoon, sir. May I be of service?"

"Are you the high priest?" I said.

His mouth fell open. "I beg your pardon?"

"Maybe I'm in the wrong place," I said. "I'm looking for the tailor shop. No name outside but the number checks."

His backbone got even stiffer although I hadn't thought that possible. "This," he said in a strangled voice, "is A. Cullinham Grandfils. Are you interested in a garment?"

"A what?"

"A garment."

"You mean a suit?"

"Ah – yes, sir."

"I've got a suit," I said. I unbuttoned my coat and showed it to him. All he did was look pained.

"What I came by for," I said, "was to get the address of a customer of yours. I'm not sure but I think his name's Andrus – Franklin Andrus."

He folded his arms and brought up a hand and turned his

wrist delicately and rested his chin between his thumb and forefinger. "I'm afraid not. No. Sorry."

"You don't know the name?"

"I'm not referring to the name. What I am attempting to convey to you is that we do not give out information on our people."

I said, "Oh," and went on staring at him. He looked like the type you can bend easy. I dug out the old deputy sheriff's star I carried for emergencies like this and showed it to him, keeping the lettering covered with the ball of my thumb. He jerked down his arms and backed away as though I'd pulled a gun on him.

"This is official," I said in a tough-cop voice. "I'm not here to horse around. Do you cooperate or do we slap you with a subpoena?"

"You'll have to discuss the matter with Mr Grandfils," he squeaked. "I simply am not – I have no authority to – You'll just have to—"

"Then trot him out, Curly. I don't have all day."

"Mr Grandfils is in his office. Come this way, please."

We went along the room and through a glass door at the far end and along a short hall to another door: a solid panel of limed oak with the words A. Cullinham Grandfils, Private, on it in raised silver letters. The door was knocked on and a muffled voice came through and I was inside.

A little round man was perched in an enormous leather chair behind an acre of teakwood and glass. His head was as bald as a collection plate on Monday morning. A pair of heavy horn-rimmed glasses straddled a button nose above a tiny mouth and a chin like a ping-pong ball. He blinked owlishly at me and said, "What is it, Marvin?" in a voice so deep I jumped.

"This – ah – gentleman is the police, Mr Grandfils. He has demanded information I simply haven't the right to—"

"That will be all, Marvin."

I didn't even hear him leave.

"I can't stand that two-bit diplomat," the little man said. "He makes the bottom of my foot itch."

I didn't say anything.

"Unfortunately he happens to be useful," he went on. "The women gush at him and he gushes back. Good for business."

"I thought you only sold men's suits," I said.

"Who do you think picks them out? Take off that coat and sit down. I don't know your name."

I told him my name and got rid of the trench coat and hat and drew up a teakwood chair trimmed in silver and sat on it. He made a quarter-turn in the big chair and his glasses flashed at me in the soft light.

"Police, eh?" he said suddenly. "Well, you've got the build for it. Where did you get that ridiculous suit?"

"This ridiculous suit set me back sixty-five bucks," I said.

"It looks it. What are you after, sir?"

"The address of one of your customers."

"I see. Why should I give it to you?"

"He was murdered. The address on his identification was incorrect."

"Murdered!" His mouth dropped open, causing the glasses to slip down on his nose. "Good heavens! One of my people?"

"He was wearing one of your coats," I said.

He passed a tremulous hand across the top of his head. All it smoothed down was scalp. "What was his name?"

"Andrus. Franklin Andrus."

He shook his head immediately. "No, Mr Pine. None of my people has that name. You have made a mistake."

"The coat fitted him," I said doggedly. "He belonged in it. I might have the name wrong but not the coat. It was his coat."

He picked a silver paper-knife from the silver trimmed tan desk blotter and rapped it lightly over and over against the knuckles of his left hand. "Perhaps you're right," he said. "My coats are made to fit. Describe this man to me."

I gave the description, right down to the kidney-shaped freckle on the lobe of the left ear. Grandfils heard me out, thought over at length what I'd said, then shook his head slowly.

"In a general way," he said, "I know of a dozen men like that who come to me. The minor touches you've given me are things I never noticed about any of them. I'm not a trained observer and you are. Isn't there something else you can tell me about him? Something you've perhaps inadvertently overlooked?"

It hardly seemed likely but I thought back anyway. I said, "The rest of his clothing was a little unusual. That might mean something to you."

"Try me."

I described the clothing. By the time I was down to where the dead man hadn't been wearing socks, Grandfils had lost interest. He said coldly, "The man was obviously some tramp. None of my people would be seen on the street in such condition. The coat was stolen and the man deserved what happened to him. Frayed slacks! Heavens!"

I said, "Not much in his pockets, but I might as well tell you that too. A dark blue necktie with a Marshall Field label, a pair of gold-plated tweezers, several transparent envelopes about the size of a postage stamp, a pocket comb and some change . . ."

My voice began to run down. A. Cullinham Grandfils had his mouth open again, but this time there was the light of recognition in his eyes. He said crisply, "The coat was a gray flannel, Mr Pine?"

"Yeah?"

"Carlton weave?"

"Hunh?"

"Never mind. You wouldn't know that. Quite new?"

"I thought so."

He bent across the desk to move a key on an intercom. "Harry," he snapped into the box. "That gray flannel lounge suit we made for Amos Spain. Was it sent out?"

"A week already," the box said promptly. "Maybe ten days, even. You want I should check exactly?"

"Never mind." Grandfils flipped back the key and leaned into the leather chair and went on tapping his knuckles with the knife. "Those tweezers and envelopes did it, sir. He's an enthusiastic stamp collector. Less than a month ago I saw him sitting in the outer room lifting stamps delicately with those tweezers and putting them in such envelopes while waiting for a fitting."

"Amos Spain is his name?"

"It is."

"He fits the description I gave?"

"Physically, exactly. But not the frayed slacks and dirty shirt. Amos Spain wouldn't be found dead in such clothes."

"You want to bet?"

". . . Oh. Of course. I simply can't understand it!"

"How about an address on Spain, Mr Grandfils?"

He dug a silver-trimmed leather notebook out of a desk drawer and looked inside. "8789 South Shore Drive. Apartment

3C. It doesn't show a telephone, although I'm confident he has one."

"Married?"

He dropped the book back in the drawer and closed it with his foot. "We don't inquire into the private lives of our people, Mr Pine. It seems to me Mrs Spain is dead, although I may be wrong. I do know Amos Spain is reasonably wealthy and, I think, retired."

I took down the address and got up and put on my coat and said, "Thanks for your help, Mr Grandfils." He nodded and I opened the door. As I started out, he said:

"You really should do something about your suits, Mr Pine."

I looked back at him sitting there like one of those old Michelin tire ads. "How much," I said, "would you charge me for one?"

"I think we could do something quite nice for you at three hundred."

"For that price," I said, "I would expect two pairs of pants."

His chin began to bob and he made a sound like roosters fighting. He was laughing. I closed the door in the middle of it and went on down the hall.

5

The address on South Shore Drive was a long low yellow-brick apartment building of three floors and an English basement. A few cars were parked along a wide sweep of concrete running past the several entrances, and I angled the Plymouth into an open spot almost directly across from 8789.

The rain got in a few licks at me before I could reach the door. Inside was a small neat foyer, complete with bright brass mail boxes and an inner door. The card on the box for 3C showed the name Amos Spain.

I pressed the right button and after a longish moment a woman's voice came down the tube. "Yes?"

That jarred me a little. I hadn't actually expected an answer. I said, "Mrs Spain?"

"This is Mrs Monroe," the voice said. "Mr Spain's daughter. Are you from the post office?"

"Afraid not. I'm an officer, Mrs Monroe. Want to talk to you."

"An officer? Why, I don't believe . . . What about?"

"Not from down here, Mrs Monroe. Ring the buzzer."

"I'll do no such thing! How do I know you're a policeman? For all I know you could be a – a—"

"On a day like this? Don't be silly."

There was some silence and then the lock began to stutter. I went through and on up carpeted steps to the third floor. Halfway along a wide cheerful hallway was a partially open door and a woman in a flowered housecoat looking out at me.

She was under thirty but not very far under. She had wicked eyes. Her hair was reddish brown and there was a lot of it. Her skin was flawless, her cheekbones high, her mouth an insolent curve. She was long and slender in the legs, small in the waist, high in the breasts. She was dynamite.

I was being stared at in a coolly impersonal way. "A policeman you said. I'm fascinated. What is it you want?"

I said, "Do I get invited in or do we entertain the neighbors?"

Her eyes wavered and she bit her lip. She started to look back over her shoulder, thought better of it, then said, "Oh, very well. If you'll be brief."

She stepped back and I followed her across a tiny reception hall and on into an immense living room, with a dinette at one end and the open door to a kitchen beyond that. The living room was paneled, with beautiful leather chairs, a chesterfield, lamps with drum shades, a loaded pipe rack, a Governor Winthrop secretary, a fireplace with a gas log. Not neat, not even overly clean, but the right place for a man who puts comfort ahead of everything else.

I dropped my coat on a hassock and sat down on one of the leather chairs. Her lips hardened. "Don't get too comfortable," she said icily. "I was about to leave when you rang."

"It's a little chilly out for a housecoat," I said.

Her jaw hardened. "Just who do you think you are, busting in here and making smart remarks? You say you're a cop. As far as manners go, I believe it. Now I think I'd like to see some real proof."

I shrugged. "No proof, Mrs Monroe. I said officer, not policeman. A private detective can be called an officer without stretching too far."

"Private—" Her teeth snapped shut and she swallowed almost

convulsively. Her face seemed a little pale now but I could have imagined that. "What do you want?" she almost whispered.

"Where's Amos Spain?" I said.

"My . . . father?"

"Uh-huh."

". . . I don't know. He went out early this morning."

"He say where?"

"No." Whatever had shocked her was passing. "Tom and I were still sleeping when he went out."

"Tom?"

"My husband."

"Where's he?"

"Still asleep. We got in late. Why do you want to know where my father is?"

I said, "I think it would be a good idea if you sat down, Mrs Monroe. I'm afraid I've brought some bad news."

She didn't move. Her eyes went on watching me. They were a little wild now and not at all wicked. She wet her lips and said, "I haven't the slightest idea what you're talking about. Bad news about what?"

"About your father. He's dead, Mrs Monroe. Murdered."

"I don't believe it," she said quickly. Almost too quickly.

"He's been identified. Not much chance for a mistake."

She turned away abruptly and walked stiffly over to a lamp table and took a cigarette from a green cloisonné box. Her hand holding the match wavered noticeably but nothing showed in her face. She blew out a long streamer of smoke and came back and perched carelessly on an arm of the couch across from me. The housecoat slipped open slightly, letting me see most of the inner curve of a freshly powdered thigh. I managed to keep from chewing a hole in the rug.

"There's been some mistake, Mr Pine. Dad never had an enemy in the world. What do you suggest I do?"

I thought back to be sure. Then I was sure. I said, "The body's probably at the morgue by this time and already autopsied. Might be a good idea to send your husband over. Save you from a pretty unpleasant job."

"Of course. I'll wake him right away and tell him about it. You've been very kind. I'm sorry if I was rude."

She hit me with a smile that jarred my back teeth and stood

up to let me know the interview was over and I could run along home now and dream about her thigh.

I slid off the chair and picked up my hat and coat. While putting them on I moved over to the row of windows and looked down into the courtyard. Nobody in sight. Not in this weather. Rain blurred the glass and formed widening puddles in thin brown grass that was beginning to turn green.

I turned and said, "I'll be running along, Mrs Monroe," and took four quick steps and reached for the bedroom door.

There was nothing wrong with her reflexes, I'll say that for her. A silken rustle and the flash of flowered cloth and she was standing between me and the door. We stood there like that, breathing at each other, our faces inches apart. She was lovely and she smelled good and the housecoat was cut plenty low.

And her face was as hard as four anvils.

"I must have made a mistake," I said. "I was looking for the hall door."

"Only two doors," she said between her teeth. "Two doors in the entire apartment. Not counting the bathroom. One that lets you out and one to the bedroom. And you picked the wrong one. Go on. Get out of here before I forget you're not a cop."

On my way out I left the inner door downstairs unlocked. In case.

6

The rain went on and on. I sat there listening to it and wondering if Noah had felt this way along about the thirty-ninth day. Smoke from my fourth cigarette eddied and swirled in the damp air through the no-draft vent.

The Plymouth was still parked across from 8789, and I was in it, knowing suddenly who had killed Amos Spain and why Spain had been wearing what he wore and why he wasn't wearing what he hadn't worn. It was knowledge built piece by piece on what I had seen and heard from the moment I walked in and found the body on the couch. It was the kind of knowledge you can get a conviction with – if you have that one key piece.

The key piece was what I didn't have.

Now and then a car came into the wide driveway and stopped at one of the entrances to let somebody out or to pick somebody up. None of them was for the rat hole to which I was glued. A delivery truck dropped off a dinette set a couple of doors down and I couldn't have cared less.

I lighted another cigarette and crossed my legs the other way and thought about hunting up a telephone and calling Lund and telling him to come out and get the knife artist and sweat that key piece out in the open. Only I didn't want it that way. This was one I wanted to wrap up myself. It had been my office and my couch and almost my client, and I was the one the cops had tromped on. Not that the tromping had amounted to much. But even a small amount of police displeasure is not what you list under assets.

Another twenty minutes floated by. They would still be up there in that apartment wearing a path in the rug. Waiting, sweating blood, hanging on desperately, risking the chance that I had known more than I let on and was already out yelling for the cops.

I would have loved to know what they were waiting for.

When the break did come I almost missed it. An ancient Ford with a pleated front fender wheezed into the curb. A hatless young man in a rained-on gray uniform got out to look at the number over the entrance to 8789. He had a damp-looking cigarette pasted to one corner of his mouth and a white envelope in his left hand. The local post office dropping off a piece of registered mail.

And then I remembered Mrs Monroe's first question.

I slapped open the glove compartment and got out my gun and shoved it under the band of my trousers while I was reaching for the door. I crossed the roadway at a gallop and barged into the foyer just as the messenger took a not too clean thumb off the button for 3C. I made a point of getting out my keys to keep him from thinking Willie Sutton was loose again.

He never even knew I was in town. He said, "Post office; registered letter," into the tube and the buzzer was clattering before he had the last word out. He went through and on up the steps without a backward glance.

The door was off the latch, the way I had left it earlier. By the time the door to 3C opened, I was a few feet away staring vaguely at the closed door to 3B and trying to look like somebody's cousin from Medicine Hat. The uniformed man said, "Amos Spain?" and a deeper voice said, "I'm Mr Spain," and a signature was written and a long envelope changed hands.

Before the door could close I was over there. I said, "It's me again."

He was a narrow-chested number with a long sallow face, beady eyes, a thin nose that leaned slightly to starboard, and a chin that had given up the struggle. Hair like black moss covered a narrow head. This would be Tom Monroe, the husband.

Terror and anger and indecision were having a field day with his expression. His long neck jerked and his sagging jaw wobbled. He clutched the edge of the door, wanting to slam it but not quite daring to. The silence weighed a ton.

All this was lost on the messenger. He took back his pencil and went off down the hall, his only worry the number of hours until payday. I leaned a hand against the thin chest in front of me and pushed hard enough to get us both into the room. I shut the door with my heel, said, "I'll take that," and yanked the letter out of his paralyzed fingers. It had sealing wax along the flap and enough stamps pasted on the front to pay the national debt.

Across the room the girl in the flowered housecoat was reaching a hand under a couch pillow. I took several long steps and stiff-armed the small of her back and she sat down hard on the floor. I put my empty hand under the pillow and found a snub-nosed Smith & Wesson .32, all chambers filled and dark red nail polish on the sight. I held it loosely along my leg and said, "Well, here we are," in a sprightly voice.

Monroe hadn't moved. He stared at me sullenly, fear still flickering in his small nervous eyes. The girl climbed painfully to her feet, not looking at either of us, and dropped down on the edge of a leather chair and put her face in her hands.

The man's restless eyes darted from me to the girl and back to me again. A pale tongue dabbed furtively at lips so narrow they hardly existed. He said hoarsely, "Just what the hell's the bright idea busting in here and grabbing what don't belong to you?"

I flapped the envelope loosely next to my ear. "You mean this? Not yours either, buster."

"It belongs to my father-in-law. I simply signed for it."

"Oh, knock it off," I said wearily. "You went way out of your league on this caper, Tom. You should have known murder isn't for grifters with simple minds."

A sound that was half wail, half sob filtered through the girl's fingers. The man said absently, "Shut up, Cora." His eyes skittered over my face. "Murder? Who's talking about murder? You the one who shoved in here a while ago and told Cora about Amos Spain?"

"I wasn't telling her a thing," I said. "She knew it long before. You told her."

"You might like to try proving that," he said.

"You bet," I said. I put the gun on the couch arm and looked at the envelope. Yesterday's postmark, mailed from New York City. Addressed in a spidery handwriting, with the return address reading: *B. Jones, General Delivery, Radio City Station, New York, NY*. I ripped open the flap and shook out the contents. A plain sheet of bond paper wrapped around three odd-looking stamps. One was circular with a pale rose background and black letters. The other two were square, one orange and one blue, with the same crude reproduction of Queen Victoria on both. All three wouldn't have carried a postcard across the street.

Monroe was staring at the stamps and chewing his lip. He looked physically ill. The girl was watching me now, her fingers picking at the edge of the housecoat, her face white and drawn and filled with silent fury.

I said, "It would almost have to be stamps. I should have guessed as much two hours ago. How much are they worth?"

"How would I know?" Monroe said sulkily. "They weren't sent to me. I never saw them before."

I slid the stamps back into the envelope and put the envelope in my pocket. "You'd know, brother. If you'd kept a better eye on Amos Spain you might even have gotten away with the whole thing."

"You've got nothing on us. Why don't you just shove off?"

"I've got everything on you," I said. "Not that I deserve any credit. The Army mule could have done the job. I can give you the State Attorney's case right now."

I picked up the gun and swung it lightly between a thumb and finger and sat on the couch arm. Rain beat against the windows in a muted murmur. From the kitchen came the lurch and whine of the refrigerator motor.

"Somebody named B. Jones," I said, "gets hold of some rare stamps. Illegally. Jones knows there are collectors around who will buy stolen stamps. Amos Spain is such a collector. A deal is made by phone or letter and the stamps are mailed to Spain. In some way you two find out about it. After the stamps are in the mail, perhaps. No point in trying to get them away from Uncle Sam; but there's another way. So the two of you show up here early this morning and force your way in on old Amos, who is still in bed. You tie him up a little, let's say, and gag him, leave him on the bed and come out here in the living room to wait for the postman with the stamps.

"But Amos isn't giving up. He gets loose, dresses and goes down the fire escape. He can't be sure when you're going to open the door and look in on him, so he puts on just enough clothes to keep from being pinched for indecent exposure. That's why he wasn't wearing socks, and why his clothes were mismatched.

"But by the time he's going down the fire escape, you look in. No Amos, and the window is open. You look out, spot him running away without topcoat or hat, and out you go after him. Tackling him on the street wouldn't do at all; your only hope is to nail him in some lonely spot and knock him off. How does it sound so far, neighbor?"

"Like a lot of words," Monroe growled.

"Words," I said, "are man's best friend. They get you fed, married, buried. Shall I tell you some more about words?"

"Go to hell."

I put down the gun and lit a cigarette and smiled. "Like I told you," I said, "you've got a simple mind. But I was telling you a story. I wouldn't want to stop now, so let's get back to Amos. You see, Amos had a big problem at this stage of the game. He couldn't go to the boys in blue and tell them about you and Cora, here. Doing that could bring out the business about the stamps and get him nailed for receiving stolen property. He had to get the two of you thrown out of his apartment before the envelope showed up.

"How to do it? Hire a strong-arm boy who won't ask questions. Where do you find a strong-arm boy on a moment's notice? The phone book's got half a column of them. Private detectives. Not the big agencies; they might ask too many questions. But one of the smaller outfits might need the business bad enough to do it Amos's way. At least it's worth trying.

"So Amos gets my address out of the phone book, the nearest one to him, and comes up to hire me. He has no idea you're following him which means he's not too careful about keeping out in the open where nothing can happen to him. He comes up to my office and I'm not in yet. He sits down to wait. You walk in and leave a switch knife in him. But that's only part of your job. You've got to fix it so there'll be a delay in identifying him – enough of a delay, at least to keep the cops away from here until the mailman comes and goes. Lifting his papers may slow things down, but you want more than that. Being a crook, you make a habit of carrying around phony identification cards. You substitute these for his own, lift whatever cash Amos had on him, slip out quick and come back here. Right so far?"

The fear had gone out of Monroe's eyes and there was the first faint sign of a smirk to his thin bloodless lips. He said airily, "If this is your idea of a way to kill a rainy afternoon, don't let me stop you. Mind if I sit down?"

"I don't care if you fall down," I said. "There's a little more and then we can all sit around and discuss the election until the cops arrive. A little more, like Cora knowing my name the first time I was here this afternoon. I hadn't told her my name, you see; just that I was a private dick. But to Cora there was only one private detective – the one whose office you'd killed Amos Spain in."

Behind me a quiet voice said, "Raise your hands."

I froze. Cora Monroe's .32 was on the couch arm, no more than six inches from my hand. I could have grabbed for it – and I could get buried for grabbing. I didn't grab.

A slender stoop-shouldered man in his early forties came padding on stocking feet in front of me. He had bushy graying hair, a long intelligent face and a capable-looking hand containing a nickel-plated Banker's Special revolver. The quiet voice belonged to him and he used it again, saying, "I won't tell you again. Put up your hands."

I put them up.

He went on pointing the gun at me while knocking the .32 off the couch with a single sweep of his other hand. It bounced along the carpet and hit the wall. He said gently, "I'll take those stamps."

"You will indeed," I said. My tongue felt as stiff as Murphy, the night he fell off the streetcar. "I guess I should have looked in the bedroom after all. I guess I thought two people should be able to lift three little stamps."

"The stamps, Mr Pine." The voice wasn't as gentle this time.

"Sure," I said. I put my hand in my coat and took out the envelope. I did it nice and slow, showing him I was eager to please. I held it out as he reached for it and I slammed my shoe down on his stocking foot with every pound I could spare.

He screamed like a woman and the gun went off. Behind me a lamp base came apart. I threw a punch, hard, and the gray-haired man threw his hands one way and the gun the other and melted into the rug without a sound.

Monroe was crouched near the side wall, the girl's .32 in his hand and madness in his eyes. While he was still bringing up the gun I jerked the Police Special from under the band of my trousers and fired.

He took a week to fall down. He put his hands together high on his chest and coughed a broken cough and took three wavering steps before he hit the floor with his face and died.

Cora Monroe hadn't moved from the leather chair. She sat stiff as an ice floe off Greenland, her face blank with shock, her nails sunk in her palms. I felt a little sorry for her. I bent down and picked the envelope off the floor and shoved it deep into a side pocket. I said, "How much were they worth, Cora?"

Only the rain answered.

I found the telephone and said what had to be said. Then I came back and sat down to wait.

It was ten minutes before I heard the first wail of distant sirens.

WE ARE ALL DEAD

Bruno Fischer

1

The caper went off without a hitch except that Wally Garden got plugged.

There were five of us. My idea had been that three would be enough, figuring the less there were the bigger the cut for each. But Oscar Trotter made the decisions.

Looking at Oscar, you might take him for a college professor – one of those lean, rangy characters with amused, intelligent eyes behind horn-rimmed glasses. He sounded like one, too, when he didn't feel like sounding like somebody else. Maybe he'd been one once, among all the other things he'd ever been.

But there was no question of what he was now. He could give the toughest hood the jitters by smiling at him a certain way, and he could organize and carry out a caper better than any man I knew.

He spent a couple of weeks casing this job and then said five men would be needed, no more and no less. So there were four of us going in soon after the payroll arrived on a Friday afternoon. The fifth, Wally Garden, was cruising outside in a stolen heap.

Wally was far and away the youngest of us, around twenty-three, and he wasn't a regular. I didn't know where Oscar had picked him up; somebody had recommended him, he'd said. It must have been somebody Oscar had a lot of confidence in because Oscar was a mighty careful guy. Wally was supposed to be very good with a car, but I think what made Oscar pick him was that he was moon-faced and clear-eyed and looked like he was always helping old ladies across streets.

Protective coloration, Oscar called it. Have one appearance during the job and another while making the getaway.

So there was the kid, and Oscar Trotter who could pass for a professor, and Georgie Ross who had a wife and two children and made like a respectable citizen except for a few days a year, and Tiny who was an old-time Chicago gorilla but could have been your kindly gray-haired Uncle Tim.

As for me, I'd been around a long, long time in thirty-four years of living. I'd almost been a lawyer, once. I'd almost married a decent woman, once. I'd almost . . .

Never mind. I was thirty-four years old and had all my features in the right places, and whenever Oscar Trotter had a job I was there at his side.

Wally Garden's part was to swipe a car early in the afternoon and pick us up on a country road and drop us off at the factory and drive slowly for five hundred feet and make a U-turn and drive slowly back. He picked out a nice car – a shiny big Buick.

The factory manufactured plastic pipe. It was in New Jersey, on the outskirts of Coast City where real estate was cheap. The office of the large, low, sprawling plant was in a wing off by itself. From that wing a side door opened directly out to a two-lane blacktop road that had little traffic. There was an armed guard who arrived with the payroll and stayed until it was distributed, but he was an old man who was given that job because he couldn't work at anything else.

Oscar decided it would be a cinch. And it was.

We were in and out in seventy seconds – five seconds under the schedule Oscar had worked out. We barged in wearing caps and T-shirts and denim work pants, and we had Halloween masks on our faces and guns in our hands. Tiny had the guard's gun before the sluggish old man knew what was up. Seven or eight others were in the office, men and women, but they were too scared to cause trouble. Which was just as well. We weren't after hurting anybody if we could help it. We were after dough, and there it was on a long table in an adjoining room, in several hundred little yellow envelopes.

Seventy seconds – and we were coming out through the side door with two satchels holding the payroll, pulling off our masks and sticking away our guns before we stepped into the open air, then striding to the Buick Wally Garden was rolling over to us.

Some hero in the office got hold of a gun and started to fire it.

The newspapers next day said it was a bookkeeper who had it in his desk. One thing was sure – he didn't know a lot about how to use it. He stood at a window and let fly wildly.

None of the slugs came near us. Anyway, not at the four of us out in the open he was firing at. But he got Wally, who was still a good twenty feet away. Got him through the car window as if he'd been an innocent bystander.

The car jerked as his foot slipped off the throttle and it stalled and stopped after rolling a few more feet. Through the windshield we saw Wally slump over the wheel.

Oscar yelled something to me, but I knew what to do. Sometimes I could think for myself. I ran around to the left front door.

The shooting had stopped. No more bullets, I supposed.

Wally turned a pale, agonized face to me as I yanked open the car door. "I'm hit," he moaned.

"Shove over," I said.

He remained bowed over the wheel. I pushed him. Oscar got into the car through the opposite door and pulled him. Groaning, Wally slid along the seat. Georgie and Tiny were piling into the back seat with the satchels. There was plenty of screaming now in the office, but nobody was coming out, not even the hero. I took Wally's place and got the stalled engine started and away we went.

Sagging between Oscar and me on the front seat, Wally started to cough, shaking all over.

"Where's it hurt, son?" Oscar asked gently.

Wally pushed his face against Oscar's shoulder, the way a frightened child would against his mother's bosom.

He gasped, "I feel . . . it stabs . . . my insides . . . bleeding."

He was the only one of us wearing a jacket. Oscar unbuttoned it and pulled it back. I glanced sideways and saw blood soaking a jagged splotch on the right side of his shirt. It looked bad.

Nobody said anything.

2

Tiny sat twisted around on the back seat watching through the rear window. It wasn't what was behind us we had to worry about as much as what was ahead. Pretty soon there would be roadblocks.

We traveled three and two-tenths miles on that road, according to plan. Then I swung the Buick left, off blacktop and onto an oiled country road running through fields and woods.

It was a bright spring afternoon, the kind of day on which you took deep breaths and felt it was good to be alive. Beside me Wally Garden started to claw at his right side. Oscar had to hold his hand to keep him from making the wound worse than it was.

Again I made a left turn. This time there was no road to turn onto but only an open field. Wally screamed between clenched teeth as the rough ground jounced the car.

Beyond the field were woods – big stuff, mostly, oaks and maples, with a fringe of high shrubs. Two cars, a Ford and a Nash, were where we'd left them this morning behind the shrubs. I rolled the hot car, the Buick, quite a way in among the trees.

It was dim in there, and cool and quiet. Wally's eyes were closed; he'd stopped squirming in agony. He would have toppled over if Oscar hadn't been holding him.

"Passed out?" I asked.

"Uh-huh," Oscar said.

Getting out of the car, he eased Wally's head and shoulder down on the seat. Wally lay on his side twitching and moaning and unconscious.

The Buick was going to be left right here – after, of course, we'd wiped off all our prints. The way we planned it, we'd hang around for two–three hours before starting back to New York in the two other cars. Until then we had plenty of time on our hands. We used some of it to make a quick count of the loot in the two satchels.

When Oscar Trotter had cased the job, he'd estimated that the take would be between forty and fifty grand. Actually it was around twenty-two grand.

What the hell! After a while you get to be part realist and part cynic, if the two aren't the same thing in this rotten racket. Nothing is ever as good as you plan or hope or dream. You're doing all right if you get fifty percent, and don't lose your life or freedom while doing it.

Every now and then I'd leave the others to go over for a look at Wally. The third time I did his eyes were open.

"How d'you feel, kid?"

He had trouble speaking. He managed to let me know he was thirsty.

There wasn't any water, but Georgie had a pint of rye. Wally, lying cramped on that car seat, gulped and coughed and gulped and pushed the bottle away. I thought it probably did him more harm than good.

"I'm burning up," he moaned.

I felt his brow. He sure was.

I went over to where Oscar and Georgie and Tiny were changing their clothes beside the Nash. This would be an important part of our protective coloration – completely different and respectable clothes.

The alarm was out for five men in a Buick, at least four of whom had been seen wearing caps and T-shirts and denim pants. I felt kind of sorry for anybody within a hundred miles who would be in T-shirts and denim pants. But we wouldn't be. We'd be wearing conservative business suits and shirts and neckties, and we'd be driving two in a Ford Georgie owned legally and three in a Nash Oscar owned legally, and why would any cop at a roadblock or toll gate waste time on such honest-looking citizens?

Except that in one of the cars there would be a wounded man. This was one contingency Oscar hadn't foreseen.

I said to Tiny who was standing in his underwear, "Give me a hand with the kid. He'll be more comfortable on the ground."

Oscar stopped buttoning a freshly laundered white shirt. "Leave him where he is."

"For how long?" I said.

There was a silence. I'd put our plight into words. This was as good a time as any to face it.

Oscar tossed me a smile. About the worst thing he did was smile. It was twisted and almost never mirthful.

"Until," he said, "somebody blunders into these woods and finds him." He tucked his shirt-tail into his pants and added hopefully, "It might take days."

Wally was nobody to me. But I said, "We can't do that."

"Have you a better idea, Johnny?" Oscar said.

"You're the big brain," I said.

"Very well then." Oscar, standing among us tall and slightly stooped, took off his horn-rimmed glasses. "Gentlemen, let us consider the situation."

This was his professorial manner. He could put it on like a coat, and when he did you knew he was either going to show how bright he was or pull something dirty.

"The odds are highly favorable," he drawled, "that before midnight we four will be out of New Jersey and in New York and each safe and snug at home. But not if we're burdened by a wounded and probably dying man. We'll never make it. If by chance we do make it, what do we do with him? At the least he needs a doctor. A doctor finds the bullet wound and calls in the police. Perhaps Wally wouldn't talk. Perhaps he will. He may be delirious and not know he's talking." Oscar's smile broadened. "There's no question, gentlemen, that we'd deserve to have our heads chopped off if we stuck our necks out so far."

Tiny said uneasily, "Yeah, but we can't just leave him here to die."

"Certainly not." Oscar's eyeglasses swung gently from his fingers. "He might die too slowly or scream and attract a passing car. There is, I'm afraid, only one alternative."

All right, but why did he have to say it in that mocking, lecturing manner, and why did he have to keep smiling all the time?

Georgie was down on one knee lacing his shoes so he wouldn't have to look at anybody. Tiny was scratching his hairy chest unhappily. I was a little sick to my stomach. And Oscar Trotter smiled.

"Tiny, your knife, please," Oscar drawled. "A gun would be too noisy."

Tiny dug his switchblade knife out of a pair of pants draped over the hood of the Nash. Oscar took it from him and moved to the Buick as if taking a stroll through the woods.

I turned away. I couldn't stop him, and if I could I wouldn't have. I'd seen that kid only twice in my life before today, the first time less than a week ago. I didn't know a thing about him except his name. He was nobody at all to me. But I turned away and my hands shook as I set fire to a cigarette.

Then Oscar was coming back.

"Well, Johnny," he taunted me, "from the first you wanted less men to cut in on the loot, didn't you?"

I had an impulse to take a swing at him. But of course I didn't.

3

Much of the next three days I watched Stella jiggle about Oscar's apartment. She was a bit on the buxom side, but in a cozy-looking, cuddly-looking way. She went in for sheer, tight sweaters and little else, and she had what to jiggle with. She belonged to Oscar.

I didn't know what the dames saw in him. He was no longer young and you couldn't call him handsome by a long shot, but he always had a woman around who had both youth and looks. Like Stella, who was merely the current one. She was also a fine cook.

I was staying with them in Oscar's two-bedroom apartment on Riverside Drive. I'd come down from Boston for that New Jersey caper, and afterward there was nothing to take me back to Boston. Oscar was letting me use the spare room while I was making up my mind whether to stay in New York or push on to wherever the spirit moved me.

On that third day Oscar and I went up to the Polo Grounds to take in a ball game. When Stella heard us at the door, she came out to meet us in the foyer.

"There's a friend of yours in the living room," she told Oscar. "A Mr Brant. He's been waiting over an hour."

I stepped to the end of the foyer and looked into the living room. The meaty man sitting on the sofa and sucking a pipe was definitely no friend of Oscar's. Or of mine. He was Bill Brant, a city detective attached to the DA's office, which meant he was a kind of free-wheeling copper.

Oscar touched my arm. "I expected this. Merely the MO. I'll do the talking." He turned to Stella. "Go do your work in the kitchen."

"I haven't any. Dinner's cooking."

"Go find something to do in the kitchen," he snapped.

She flounced away, wiggling almost as much as she jiggled. But the thing is that she obeyed.

Oscar trained his women right. She was used to being sent out of the room or sometimes clear out of the apartment when business was being discussed. She was no innocent, of course, but in his book the less any woman knew the better. It might be all right to trust Stella today, but who knew what the situation would be tomorrow? So she went into the kitchen and we went into the living room.

"Well, what d'you know!" Bill Brant beamed at me. "Johnny Worth too! Another piece fits into the picture. I guess you came to town for the Jersey stickup."

"I did?" I said and went over to the portable bar for a drink. I didn't offer the cop any.

"What's this about New Jersey?" Oscar was asking.

"We're cooperating with the police over there. You're a local resident. So was Wallace Garden who was found dead in the Buick."

"You misunderstood my question." Oscar was using his mocking drawl. "I'm not interested in the jurisdictional problems of the police. I'm simply curious as to the reason for your visit."

"Come off it," Brant said. "That payroll stickup has all your earmarks."

I helped myself to another drink. I hadn't been very much worried, but now I felt better. That, as Oscar had guessed, was all they seemed to have – the MO, the modus operandi, the well-planned, perfectly timed and executed armed robbery that cops identified with Oscar.

"Earmarks!" Oscar snorted. "Do they arrest citizens for that these days?"

"No, but it helps us look in the right direction." Brant sucked on his pipe. "That killing too. It's like you not to leave loose ends, even if it means sticking a knife into one of your own boys." He twisted his head around to me. "Or did he have you do the dirty work, Johnny?"

That was one thing about Oscar, I thought – he did his own dirty work. Maybe because he enjoyed it.

Aloud I said, "What the hell are you talking about?"

Brant sighed. What had he expected, that we'd up and confess all as soon as he told us he had a suspicion? We knew as well as he did that he didn't even have enough to take us to headquarters and sweat us, and likely never would have. But he was paid to try, and he hung around another ten minutes, trying. That got him nothing, not even a drink.

After he was gone, Stella came in from the kitchen and said dinner would be ready soon.

4

Another day passed and another. I was on edge, restless. I took walks along the Drive, I dropped in on friends, I went to the movies. Then I'd come back to Oscar's apartment and there would be Stella jiggling.

Understand me. I didn't particularly hanker for her – certainly not enough to risk fooling around with anything of Oscar Trotter's. Besides, I doubted that she would play. She seemed to like me, but strictly as her husband's friend. She was completely devoted to him.

No, it was just that any juicy dame within constant eyesight made my restlessness so much harder to take.

We were playing Scrabble on the cardtable, Oscar and Stella and I, when the doorbell rang.

It was evening, around eight-thirty. Oscar, of course, was way ahead; he was unbeatable at any game that required brains. Stella was way behind. I was in the middle, where I usually found myself in everything. As it was Stella's turn to play, I went to answer the doorbell.

A girl stood in the hall – a fair-haired, blue-eyed girl in a simple gray dress and a crazy little gray hat.

"Mr Trotter?" she said.

"You're right, I'm not," I said. "He's inside."

Without being invited in, she stepped over the threshold and closed the door behind her. "Please tell him Mrs Garden would like to see him."

"Sure." I started to turn and stopped. "Garden?" I said. "Any relative of—"

I caught myself. In my racket you became cautious about naming certain names under certain circumstances, especially when you weren't supposed to know them. There were all kinds of traps.

Gravely she said, "I was Wally's wife." She put her head back. "You must be Johnny. Wally told me about you."

I gawked at her. Standing primly and trimly in the foyer, she made me think of golden fields and cool streams and the dreams of youth.

I said, "Wait here," and went into the living room. Stella was scowling at the Scrabble board and Oscar was telling her irritably to do something or pass. I beckoned to him. He rose from the cardtable and came over to me.

"Wally's wife is in the foyer," I said.

Oscar took off his eyeglasses, a sign that he was disturbed. "He never mentioned a wife to me."

"To me either. He wasn't much of a talker."

"What does she want?"

"Seems to me," I said, "our worry is what does she know. If Wally—"

And then she was in the living room. Having waited maybe thirty seconds in the foyer, she wasn't waiting any longer. She headed straight for Oscar.

"You must be Mr Trotter," she said. "I'm Abby Garden."

Abby, I thought – exactly the name for a lovely girl of twenty, if she was that old.

Oscar put his glasses back on to stare at her. He seemed as startled as I'd been that such a dish could have been the moon-faced kid's wife. But he didn't say anything to her. In fact, his nod was rather curt. Then he looked across the room at Stella.

Stella was twisted around on her chair, giving Abby Garden that feminine once-over which in a moment took in age, weight, figure, clothes, make-up. Stella didn't look enthusiastic. Which was natural enough, considering that whatever she had the other girl had better.

"Baby," Oscar said to Stella, "take a walk to Broadway and buy a pack of cigarettes."

There were cigarettes all over the apartment. At another time he might have given her the order in one word, "Blow!" but this evening he was being polite about it in front of a guest. It amounted to the same thing. Stella undulated up the length of the room, and on the way her eyes never left the girl. No doubt she didn't care for being chased out for her. But she left, all right.

Me, whenever I told a dame to do anything, she either kicked up a fuss or ignored me. What did Oscar have?

I fixed drinks for the three of us. Abby wanted a rye highball without too much ginger ale. Her hand brushed mine as she took the glass from me. That was sheer accident, but all the same my fingers tingled.

"Now then, Mrs Garden," Oscar said. His long legs stretched from the armchair in which he lounged. "What's your business with me?"

She rolled her glass between her palms. "Wally told me his share would come to thousands of dollars."

"And who," he said, "might Wally be?"

"Please, Mr Trotter." Abby leaned forward. "We can be open and above board. Wally had no secrets from me. I didn't like it when he told me he was going in on that – that robbery. He'd already done one stretch. Six months for stealing cars. Before I met him." She bit her lower lip. "I tried to stop him, but he wouldn't listen to me."

Oscar looked utterly disgusted. He had no use for a man who blabbered to anybody, including his wife. Wally may very well have endangered us all.

"So?" Oscar said.

"Oh, you needn't worry I told the police. They asked me, of course. They questioned me for hours after they found poor Wally. But I told them I knew nothing about any holdup or who was in it." She gave him a piece of a small smile. "You see, I didn't want to get into trouble. After all, if I'd known beforehand, I was a kind of accessory, wasn't I?"

"So?" Oscar said again.

"There was one detective especially – a fat man named Brant. He kept asking me if I knew you." She looked Oscar straight in the eye. "He said you killed Wally."

"Now why would I do any such thing?"

"Brant said Wally was wounded during the getaway and then you or one of the others killed him with a knife to get him out of the way."

"My dear," Oscar said, more in sorrow than in anger, "can it be possible you fell for that line?"

"Is it a line? That's what I want to know."

Oscar sighed. "I see you're not familiar with police tricks. This is a particularly shabby one. Don't you see they made up this story to induce you to talk?"

"Then he wasn't killed with a knife?"

"No, my dear. The bullet killed him. He died in my arms. Wasn't that so, Johnny?"

"Yes," I said.

5

That word was my first contribution to the conversation, and my last for another while. Nursing a Scotch-on-the-rocks, I sat on the hassock near Abby's legs. They were beautifully turned legs. I looked up at her face. She was drinking her highball, and over the rim of the glass her wide blue eyes were fixed with rapt attention on Oscar, who was, now, being a salesman.

He was as good at that as at anything else. His honeyed voice was hypnotic, telling her how he'd loved Wally like a son, how he would have given his right arm to have saved him after that dastardly bookkeeper had plugged him, how the conniving, heartless coppers were out to make her hate him and thus betray him with that fantastic yarn that he, Oscar Trotter, would either have harmed or permitted anybody else to have harmed a hair of one of his own men.

He was good, and on top of that she apparently wasn't too bright. He sold her and she bought.

"Wally always warned me not to trust a cop." She split a very warm smile between both of us. "You look like such nice men. So much nicer than that fat detective."

Oscar purred, "Then I take it we're friends, Abby?"

"Oh, yes." She put her highball glass down on the coffee table. "And in a way we're partners, aren't we? When will I get my share?"

Suddenly there was frost in the room. The cheekbones ridged Oscar's lean face.

"What share?" he said softly.

"Why, Wally's share. He earned it, didn't he?" She was completely relaxed; she was free and easy and charming. "I read in the papers that there were twenty-two thousand dollars. One-fifth of that—"

"Young lady," Oscar cut in, "are you trying to blackmail me?"

"Not at all. I simply ask for what I'm entitled to. If money is owed to a man who dies, it goes to his wife."

She said that wide-eyed and innocent-faced, her earnest manner holding no hint of threat – merely a young and probably destitute widow wanting to clean up financial matters after her husband's untimely demise.

Huh! A few minutes ago I'd thought she wasn't so bright. Now I changed my mind.

I spoke up. "She's got something there, Oscar."

"You keep out of this."

"Not this time," I said. "I suggest we each give her five hundred bucks."

Oscar pushed his fingers under his glasses to rub his eyes. Then he nodded. He had no choice. We'd be in a bad way if she were to chirp to the cops.

"How much will that come to?" Abby asked me.

"Two grand. Wally wouldn't have gotten a fifth anyway. He was only the driver. Believe me, we're being more than fair."

"I'm sure you are," she said, and gave me a smile.

This was why I'd jumped in to negotiate – to get some such smile out of her, a smile of sheer joyous gratitude. A man has already gone quite a distance with a dame who thinks she's beholden to him for money. And with this one I was after going on and on and maybe never stopping.

"Just a minute," Oscar said.

Abby and I shifted our attention from each other to him.

"Prove you're Wally's wife," he said.

"But I am."

Oscar looked stern. "I know every switch on every con game. We don't even know Wally had a wife. If he did, we don't know you were the one. Prove it."

"Why, of course," she said. "I have my marriage license and other things at home. If you want me to bring—"

"I've a better idea," I said. I wasn't one to pass up any chance when I was on the make. I got off the hassock so quickly I almost spilled what was left in my glass. "I'll go with you right now and look over whatever you have."

"That's so good of you," she said so sweetly that my heart did a complete flip.

Oscar nodded and closed his eyes. When we left, he appeared to have fallen asleep in the armchair.

6

According to the marriage license, they'd been married seven months ago by the county clerk here in New York.

I sat in the only decent chair in the place. Nearby a train rumbled on the Third Avenue El. She didn't quite live in a slum, but the difference wasn't great. There wasn't much to this room, and there was less to the bedroom and kitchen and bathroom. They were all undersized and falling apart.

Wally's cut of the loot would have meant a lot to him and her, if he'd lived through it.

I handed the marriage license back to Abby. She fed me other stuff out of the shoebox on her lap – snapshots of her and Wally, his discharge papers from the army, the deposit book of a joint savings account containing less than fifty dollars, a letter from her mother from somewhere in Iowa complaining because she'd gone and married a man named Wallace Garden whom none of the family had met.

"Good enough," I said.

"How soon will I get the money?"

"Soon as I collect it from the others. Maybe tomorrow."

"Two thousand dollars," she reminded me.

"That's right," I said.

Abby put the lid on the shoebox and carried it into the bedroom. She didn't jiggle and wiggle like Stella. Her tight, slender figure in that trim gray dress seemed to flow when in motion.

I wanted her as I hadn't wanted anybody or anything in a very long time.

Take it easy, I warned myself while waiting for her to return. I could mark myself lousy in her book by rushing. All right, she'd been married to that round-faced kid, who'd been what he'd been, meaning no better than I, and she hadn't acted particularly upset over his death. But I didn't yet know what made her tick. I only knew that she looked like moonlight and roses and that it would be wise to handle her accordingly. She was already grateful to me. She'd be a lot more grateful when I brought her the two grand. Then would be time enough to take the next step – a big step or small step, depending on how she responded.

So I was a perfect little gentleman that evening. She put up a pot of coffee and we sat opposite each other at the table and she was as pleasant to talk to as to look at. She spoke of her folks' farm in Iowa and I spoke of my folks' farm in Indiana.

When I was leaving, she went to the door with me and put her hand in mine. And she said, "I'll see you soon, Johnny."

"Do you want to see me or the money?"

"Both," she said and squeezed my hand holding hers.

I walked on a cloud clear across town and then a couple of miles uptown to Oscar's apartment. I hadn't as much as kissed her good-night, or tried to, but what of that? My hand still tingled from the feel of hers.

I laughed at myself. Johnny Worth, the cynical hard guy, acting like a love-sick schoolboy! But I laughed at myself happily.

Oscar and Stella were in bed when I let myself in. Oscar heard me and came out of his bedroom in a bath-robe.

"She was Wally's wife all right," I told him. "Tomorrow I'll go collect the dough from Georgie and Tiny."

"You seem anxious," he said with an amused twist to his mouth.

I shrugged. "We promised her."

"I can read you like a book, Johnny." He nudged my ribs with his elbow. "Make much headway with her?"

I shrugged again.

"I guess not if you're back so early," Oscar said, leering amiably. "I can't imagine what she saw in that punk Wally. She has class. Well, good hunting."

"Good-night," I said and went into my room.

7

Next afternoon I set forth to make the collection for Abby. Oscar had given me his five hundred in the morning, and of course I had my own, so that left Georgie and Tiny to go.

Georgie Ross lived out in Queens, in a neat frame house with a patch of lawn in front. His wife and two teenaged daughters hadn't any notion of how he picked up extra money to support them. His regular job, as a traveling salesman in housewares, didn't keep him very busy or bring in much income. He had time on a weekday afternoon to be mowing his lawn.

He stopped mowing when he saw me come up the street. He stood middle-aged and pot-bellied.

"For God's sake," he complained when I reached him, "you know better than to come here."

"Relax. You can say I'm a bill collector."

"Just don't come around, that's all I ask. What d'you want?"

"To collect a bill. Five C's for Wally Garden's widow."

His eyes bugged out. "You're kidding," he said. Meaning, if I knew him, not about the widow but about the money.

I told him I wasn't kidding and I told him about Abby's visit last evening.

"Listen," Georgie said, taking out a handkerchief and wiping his suddenly sweaty face, "I'm not shelling out that kind of dough for anybody's wife. I have my own family to think of. My God, do you know what my two girls cost me? Just their clothes! And my oldest, Dinah, is starting college next year. Is that expensive! I got to hang onto every penny."

"Some of those pennies were supposed to have gone to Wally."

"It's his tough luck he wasn't around to collect." He leaned against the handle of the mower. "I tell you this: we give her two grand now, she thinks she has us over a barrel and keeps coming back for more. Oscar ought to handle her different."

"How?"

"Well, he handled her husband," Georgie said.

That was a quiet, genteel street, and he fitted into it, by looking at him, the way anybody else in sight did. He resumed mowing his lawn.

I tagged after him. "Use your head, Georgie."

"You don't get one damn penny out of me."

I knew I was licked. I'd ask Oscar to try. He could persuade him if anybody could. I left Georgie plodding stolidly behind the mower.

Tiny was harder to find. He was like me, without anywhere to stay put. He was paying rent on a mangy room he'd sublet downtown, but he only slept in it. I made the rounds of the neighboring ginmills. What with lingering in this place and that and shooting the breeze with guys I knew, I didn't come across Tiny until after nine o'clock.

He was sitting wide-shouldered and gray-haired at the bar, drinking beer. He was always drinking beer.

He said, "Gee, am I glad to see you." Picking up his glass, he slid off the stool and we went to an isolated table. "I've been trying to get Oscar on the phone," he said, "but he ain't in. Stella says she don't know where he went." He glanced around. "Johnny, there's been a city dick asking me questions this afternoon. A fat guy."

"Brant?"

"Yeah, that's the name. He's got it, Johnny. He knows who was in on it and what happened to Wally and all."

I thought of Abby.

"Go on," I said.

"Remember last Wednesday when the five of us went over the route in Oscar's car? It was hot and when we came back through the Holland Tunnel from Jersey we stopped for beer on Tenth Avenue. Remember?"

"I remember."

"Somebody that knew us saw the five of us sitting in that booth together."

I let out my breath. Not Abby.

"Who was it?" I asked.

"Search me. This Brant, he wasn't telling. Some goddamn stoolie. He knew four of us – me and you, Oscar and Georgie. The one break is he hadn't never seen Wally before. Brant is one cagy cookie, but I wasn't born yesterday. I figure they showed the stoolie Wally's picture, but he wasn't sure. If he'd been sure, they'd be piling on us."

"That's right," I said. "The cops can't make any move officially unless they can link us to Wally. I saw Georgie this afternoon and he didn't mention being questioned."

"He's been by now, I guess. The way I figure, this stoolie didn't spill till today." Tiny took a slug of beer and wiped his mouth with the back of his hand. "But I don't get it, Johnny. A stoolie sees four of us and a strange guy in a beer joint. What makes this Brant so all-fired smart he can tell from that Wally was the strange guy and we was the ones did the job way over in Jersey a couple days later?"

"Because Oscar is too good."

"Come again?"

"The caper bore the marks of genius," I said, "and Oscar is a genius. Then Brant drops into Oscar's apartment a few days ago and finds me staying there, so he's got two of us tagged. Then he learns we two plus you and Georgie were drinking beer with a fifth guy who could've been Wally Garden, and he's got us all."

"The hell he has! All he's got is thoughts running in his head. He needs evidence. How'll he get it if we sit tight?"

"He won't," I said.

This was a good time to tell him about Abby. I told him.

When I finished, Tiny complained, "What's the matter with Oscar these days? First he lets us all be seen together in a beer joint—"

"I don't remember any of us objected. In fact, I remember it was your idea we stop off."

"Sure, but Oscar should know better. He's supposed to have the brains. Then he don't know the kid had a wife and would blab every damn thing to her. Where'd he pick up Wally, anyway?"

"He never told me," I said. "But there's the widow and we promised her two grand. I want five C's from you."

Tiny thought about it, and he came up with what, I had to concede, was a good question. "You said you saw Georgie this afternoon. Did he shell out?"

"Not yet."

"Expect him to?"

"Sure."

"Bet he don't?"

"Look, Oscar will get it out of him. I'm asking you."

Tiny said cheerfully. "Tell you what I'll do, Johnny. When Georgie shells out, I'll shell out."

And he looked mighty pleased with himself. He had confidence in Georgie's passion for hanging onto a buck.

8

So after chasing around for hours I had only the thousand I'd started out with. Well, that wasn't hay and the evening was young. I could bring the thousand to Abby and tell her it was part payment. She would be grateful. She would thank me. One thing could lead to another – and perhaps tonight would be the night, the beginning.

I took a hack to her place.

Through her door I heard music going full blast. I knocked.

No answer, which wasn't surprising considering all the row a hot dance band was making. I knocked louder. Same result. I turned the knob and found the door unlocked.

Abby wasn't in the living room. The bedroom and the bathroom doors were both closed. The band music, coming from a tiny table radio, stopped and a disc jockey's voice drooled. In the comparative quiet I heard a shower running in the bathroom. I sat down to wait for her to come out.

The music started up again. It was too raucous; my mood was for sweet stuff. I reached over the table to turn off the radio, and my hand brushed a pair of horn-rimmed eyeglasses. She hadn't worn them when I'd seen her, but women were vain about such things. Probably only reading glasses.

She'd stopped showering. Now with the radio off, there was no sound in the apartment. Suddenly it occurred to me that I ought to let her know she had a visitor. Thinking she was alone, she might come trotting out without anything on. I wouldn't mind, but she might, and I was still on the perfect little gentleman technique.

I went to the bathroom door and said, "Abby."

"I'll be right out."

I hadn't time to wonder why she hadn't sounded surprised to hear a man in her apartment and why at the least she hadn't asked who I was. The explanation came almost at once – from the bedroom.

"What did you say, baby?" a man called.

"I'll be right out," she repeated.

Then it was quiet again except for the thumping of my heart.

I knew that man's voice. If there was any doubt about it, there were those eyeglasses on the table. A minute ago I'd given them hardly a glance because I hadn't any reason then to take a good look to see if they were a woman's style and size. They seemed massive now, with a thick, dark frame.

The bathroom doorknob was turning. I moved away from there until the table stopped me, and Abby came out. She was wearing a skimpy towel held around her middle and not another thing.

Her body was very beautiful. But it was a bitter thing for me to see now.

She took two or three steps into the room, flowing with that wonderful grace of hers, before she realized that the man standing by the table wasn't the one who had just spoken to her from the bedroom – wasn't the one for whom she didn't at all mind coming out like this. It was only I – I who had been dreaming dreams. Her free hand yanked up and across her breasts in that age-old gesture of women, and rage blazed in her blue eyes.

"You have a nerve!" she said harshly.

Again he heard her in the bedroom and again he thought she was speaking to him. He called, "What?" and the bedroom door opened, and he said, "With this door closed I can't hear a—" and he saw me.

Oscar Trotter was without jacket and shirt, as well as without his glasses.

I had to say something. I muttered, "The radio was so loud you didn't hear me knock. I came in." I watched Abby sidling along the wall toward the bedroom, clinging to that towel and keeping her arm pressed in front of her, making a show of modesty before me, the intruder, the third man. "I didn't expect she was having this kind of company," I added.

He shrugged.

A door slammed viciously. She had ducked into the bedroom where her clothes would be. He picked up his glasses from the table and put them on.

There was nothing to keep me here. I started to leave.

"Just a minute, Johnny. I trust you're not sore."

I turned. "What do you expect me to be?"

"After all, you had no prior claim on her." Oscar smiled smugly. "We both saw her at the same time."

He stood lean and slightly stooped and considerably older than I, and dully I wondered why everything came so easily to him – even this.

"Next time," I said, "remember to lock the door."

"I didn't especially plan this. I asked her out to dinner. My intention was chiefly business. Chiefly, I say, for I must confess she had – ah – impressed me last night."

This was his high-hat manner, the great man talking down to a lesser being. Some day, I thought wearily, I'd beat him up and then he'd kill me, unless I killed him first.

"You understand," he was drawling, "that I was far from convinced that our problem with her would be solved by giving her two thousand dollars. I had to learn more about her. After dinner we came up here for a drink." That smug smile again. "One thing led to another. You know how it is."

I knew how it was – how I'd hoped it would be with me. And I knew that he had never for one single moment made the mistake of acting the little gentleman with her.

I had forgotten about the money in my pocket. I took it out and dropped it on the table.

"Georgie and Tiny weren't keen about contributing," I told him. "There's just this thousand. You've earned the right to worry about the balance."

"I doubt that it will be necessary to give her anything now. You see, I'll be paying all her bills. She's moving in with me."

"How nice," I said between my teeth. "I'll be out of there as soon as I pack my bags."

His head was bent over the money. "Take your time," he said as he counted it into two piles. "I still have to tell Stella. Any time tomorrow will do." He pushed one pile across the table. "Here's yours."

So I had my five hundred bucks back, and that was all I had. Before I was quite out of the apartment, Oscar, in his eagerness, was already going into the bedroom where Abby was.

I went out quietly.

9

That night I slept in a hotel. I stayed in bed most of the morning, smoking cigarettes and looking up at the ceiling. Then I shaved and dressed and had lunch and went to Oscar's apartment for my clothes.

I found Stella all packed and about to leave. She was alone in the apartment. I could guess where Oscar was.

"Hello, Johnny," she said. "I'm leaving for good."

She wasn't as upset as I'd expected. She was sitting in the living room with her legs crossed and taking a final drink of Oscar's liquor.

"I know," I said. "When's she moving in?"

"Tonight, I guess." She looked into her glass. "You know, the minute she walked into this room the other night I had a feeling. Something in the way Oscar looked at her."

"I'm sorry," I said.

She shrugged. "I'm not sure I am. He was too damn bossy."

I went into the guest bedroom and packed my two bags. When I came out, Stella was still there.

"Johnny," she said, "have you any plans?"

"No."

"I called up a woman I know. She owns a rooming house off Columbus Avenue. She says she has a nice furnished apartment to let on the second floor, with kitchenette and bath. She says the room is large and airy and nicely furnished. A young married couple just moved out."

"Are you taking it?"

"I think I will." She uncrossed her knees and pulled her skirt over them. "Two people can be very comfortable."

I looked at her sitting there rather primly with eyes lowered – a placid, cozy, cuddly woman with a bosom made for a man to rest his weary head on. She wasn't Abby, but Abby was a ruined dream, and Stella was real.

"You and me?" I murmured.

"If you want to, Johnny."

I picked up my bags. "Well, why not?" I said.

10

Stella was very nice. We weren't in love with each other, but we liked each other and got along, which was more than could be said of a lot of couples living together.

We weren't settled a week in the rooming house near Columbus Avenue when Oscar phoned. Stella answered and spoke to him. I dipped the newspaper I was reading and listened to her say we'd be glad to come over for a drink that evening.

I said, "Wait a minute."

She waved me silent and told Oscar we'd be there by nine. When she hung up, she dropped on my lap, cuddling the way only she could.

"Honey, I want to go just to show I don't care for him any more and am not jealous of that Abby. You're sweeter than he ever was. Why shouldn't we all still be friends?"

"All right," I said.

Oscar answered the doorbell when we got there. Heartily

he shook Stella's hand and then mine and said Abby was in the kitchen and would be out in a minute. Stella went into the kitchen to give Abby a hand and Oscar, with a hand on my shoulder, took me into the living room.

Georgie and Tiny were there. Georgie hadn't brought his wife, of course; he kept her strictly away from this kind of social circle. They were drinking cocktails, even Tiny who was mostly a beer man.

"Looks like a caper reunion," I commented dryly. "Except that there's one missing. Though I guess we could consider that his widow represents him."

There was an uncomfortable silence. Then Oscar said pleasantly, "Here, sour-puss, maybe this will cheer you up," and thrust a cocktail at me.

I took it and sipped.

Then Abby came in, bearing a plate of chopped liver in one hand and a plate of crackers in the other. She had a warm smile for me – the impersonal greeting of a gracious hostess. Stella came behind her with potato chips and pretzels, and all of a sudden Stella's jiggling irritated me no end.

Abby hadn't changed. There was no reason why I had expected she would. She still made me think of golden fields and cool streams, as she had the first time I'd laid eyes on her.

I refilled my glass from the cocktail shaker and walked to a window and looked out at the Hudson River sparkling under the sinking sun.

"Now that was the way to handle her," Georgie said. He had come up beside me; he was stuffing into his mouth a cracker smeared with liver. "Better than paying her off. Not only saves us dough. This way we're sure of her."

"That's not why he did it."

"Guess not. Who needs a reason to want a looker like that in his bed? But the result's the same. And you got yourself Stella, so everybody's happy."

Everybody was happy and everybody was gay and got gayer as the whiskey flowed. But I wasn't happy and the more I drank the less gay I acted. Long ago I'd learned that there was nowhere a man could be lonelier than at a party. I'd known it would be a mistake to come, and it was.

Suddenly Georgie's face turned green and he made a dash

for the bathroom. Oscar sneered that he'd never been able to hold his liquor and Tiny grumbled that the only drink fit for humans was beer and I pulled Stella aside and told her I wanted to go home.

She was not only willing; she was anxious. "Fact is, I don't feel so good," she said. "I need air."

We said our goodbyes except to Georgie whom we could hear having a bad time in the bathroom. An empty hack approached when we reached the sidewalk and I whistled. In the hack, she clung to me, shivering, and complained, "My throat's burning like I swallowed fire. My God, his whiskey wasn't that bad!"

"You must be coming down with a cold," I said.

She wobbled when we got out of the hack and she held her throat. I had to half carry her up the steps of the brownstone house and into our room. As I turned from her to switch on the light, she moaned, "Johnny!" and she was doubled over, clutching at her stomach.

For the next hour I had my hands full with her. She seemed to be having quite an attack of indigestion. I undressed her and put her to bed and piled blankets on her because she couldn't stop shivering. I found baking soda in the kitchen and fed her a spoonful and made tea for her. The cramps tapered off and so did the burning in her throat.

"Something I ate," she said as she lay huddled under the blankets. "But what? We didn't have anything for dinner that could hurt us. How do you feel, honey?"

"Fine."

"I don't understand it. That Abby didn't serve anything to speak of. Nothing but some chopped liver and—" She paused. "Honey, did you have the liver?"

"No. I can't stand the stuff."

"Then it was the liver. Something wrong with it. Call up Oscar and see if the others are all right."

I dialed his number. Oscar answered after the bell had rung for some time. His voice sounded weak.

"How are you over there?" I asked.

"Terrible. All four of us sick as dogs. And you?"

"I'm all right, but Stella has indigestion. We figure it was the chopped liver because that was the one thing she ate that I didn't."

"Could be," Oscar said. "Georgie seems to be in the worst shape; he's sleeping it off in the spare room. Tiny left a short time ago. Abby's in bed, and that's where I'll be in another minute. What bothers me most is a burning in my throat."

"Stella complained of the same thing. First I ever heard of indigestion making your throat burn."

"All I know," Oscar said, "is that whatever it is I have plenty of company in my misery. Abby is calling me."

He hung up.

I told Stella what he'd said. "The liver," she murmured and turned on her side.

That was at around one o'clock. At three-thirty a bell jarred me awake. I slipped out of bed and staggered across the room to the phone.

"I need you at once," Oscar said over the wire.

"Do you feel worse?"

"About the same. But Georgie has become a problem."

"Is he that bad?"

"Uh-huh. He went and died on my hands. I need your help, Johnny."

11

Georgie lay face-down on the bed in the guest room. He was fully dressed except for his shoes.

"Tiny took him in here before he left," Oscar told me. "After that I didn't hear a sound out of Georgie. I assumed he was asleep. Probably he went into a coma and slipped off without waking. When I touched him half an hour ago, he was already cold."

Oscar's face was the color of old putty. He could hardly stand without clinging to the dresser. Abby hadn't come out of the other bedroom.

I said, "Died of a bellyache? And so quickly?"

"I agree it must have been the chopped liver, which would make it ptomaine poisoning. But only Georgie ate enough of the liver to kill him. Abby says she remembers he gorged himself on it." Oscar held his head. "One thing's sure – he mustn't be found here. Brant is enough trouble already."

"This is plainly an accidental death."

"Even so, the police will use it as an excuse to get as tough as they like with us. We can't afford that, Johnny, so soon after the Coast City job. Best to get the body out."

I looked him over. He didn't seem in much better condition than the man on the bed.

"I can't do it alone," I said.

He dug his teeth into his lower lip and then fought to draw in his breath. "I'll help you."

But most of it had to fall on me. I fished car keys out of Georgie's pocket and went looking for his Ford. I found it a block and a half up Riverside Drive and drove it around to the service entrance of the apartment building. At that late hour it was possible to park near where you wanted to.

Oscar was waiting for me on the living-room sofa. He roused himself and together we got that inanimate weight that had been pot-bellied Georgie Ross down the three flights of fire stairs and, like a couple of men supporting a drunk, walked it between us out of the building and across the terribly open stretch of sidewalk and shoved it into the Ford. For all we could tell, nobody was around to see us.

That was about as far as Oscar could make it. He was practically out on his feet. I told him to go back upstairs and I got behind the wheel and drove off with Georgie slumped beside me like a man asleep.

On a street of dark warehouses over on the east side, I pulled the car over to the curb and got out and walked away.

Stella was up when I let myself in. She asked me if I'd gone to Oscar's.

"I was worried about them," I told her. "Tiny and Georgie left. Oscar and Abby are about in your shape. How're you?"

"Better, though my stomach is very queasy."

I lay in bed wondering what the odds were on chopped liver becoming contaminated and if a burning throat could possibly be a symptom of ptomaine poisoning. I watched daylight trickle into the room and listened to the sounds of traffic building up in the street, and I was scared the way one is in a nightmare, without quite knowing of what.

Eventually I slept. It was past noon when I woke and Stella was bustling about in the kitchen. She was pretty much recovered.

Toward evening I went out for a newspaper. When I returned,

Brant was coming down the stoop. Being a cop, he wouldn't have had trouble finding out where I'd moved to.

"Nice arrangement," he commented. "You shack up with Oscar's woman and Oscar with Wally Garden's widow. This way nobody gets left out in the cold."

"You running a gossip column now?" I growled.

"If I were, I'd print an item like this: How come Johnny Worth's pals are getting themselves murdered one by one?"

I held onto myself. All I did was raise an eyebrow. "I don't get it."

"Haven't you heard? George Ross was found dead this morning in his car parked near the East River Drive."

He had already spoken to Stella, but I didn't have to worry that she'd told him about last night's party and who'd been there. She wouldn't tell a cop anything about anything.

I said, "That's too bad. Heart attack?"

"Arsenic."

I wasn't startled. Maybe, after all, it was no surprise to me. Arsenic, it seemed, was a poison that made your throat burn.

I lit a cigarette. Brant watched my hands. They were steady. I blew smoke at him. "Suicide, I suppose."

"Why suicide?"

"It goes with poison."

"Why would he want to die?"

"I hardly knew the guy," I said.

"You've been seeing him. You were in a beer joint with him a week ago Wednesday."

"Was I? Come to think of it, I dropped in for a beer and there were some guys I knew and I joined them."

Brant took his pipe out of his fat face. "Two days later you and he were both in on that Coast City stickup."

"Who says?"

A cop who was merely following a hunch didn't bother me. We sparred with words, and at the end he sauntered off by himself. He hadn't anything. He couldn't even be sure that Georgie hadn't been a suicide.

But I knew, didn't I? I knew who had murdered him and had tried to murder all of us.

12

Oscar didn't say hello to me. He opened the door of his apartment and just stood there holding onto the doorknob, and his eyes were sick and dull behind his glasses. Though it was after six o'clock, he was still in his pajamas. His robe was tied sloppily, hanging crooked and twisted on his long, lean body. He needed a shave. He looked, to put it mildly, like hell.

I stepped into the foyer and moved on past him into the living room. He shambled after me.

I said, "I suppose Brant came to see you before he did me."

"Yes."

"So you know what killed Georgie."

He nodded tiredly.

"Abby still in bed?" I asked.

"I made her dress and go to a doctor when I learned it was arsenic. Don't want him coming here, not with the cops snooping. Whatever he gives her for it, I'll take too."

"Better not," I said. "Likely she'll mix more arsenic with it."

Oscar took off his eyeglasses. "Explain that, Johnny."

"I don't have to. You know as well as I do why she put arsenic in the chopped liver."

He stood swinging his glasses and saying nothing. He was not the man I had known up until the time I had left the party last night, and it was not so much because he was ill. It was as if a fire had burned out in him.

"Boy, did she sucker you!" I said. "Me too, I admit. But it was mostly our own fault. We knew she didn't fall for your line that you hadn't killed Wally. We kidded ourselves she'd be willing to forgive and forget if we paid her off. We wanted to believe that because we wanted her. Both of us did. Well, you got her. Or the other way around – she got you. She got you to bring her to live here where she could get all of us together and feed us arsenic."

"No," he mumbled. He looked up. "She ate the liver too. She's been sick all night and all day. She's still in a bad way even though she managed to get out of bed and dressed."

"Huh! She had to put on an act."

"No, I can tell. And she wouldn't poison me. Look what she'd give up – this nice home, plenty of money. Why? For a stupid revenge? No. And she's fond of me. Loves me, I'm sure. Always affectionate. A wonderful girl. Never knew anybody like her. So beautiful and warm."

He was babbling. He was sick with something worse than poison, or with a different kind of poison. It was the sickness of sex or love or whatever you cared to call it, and it had clouded that brain that always before had known all the answers.

"Try to think," I said. "Somebody put arsenic in the chopped liver. Who but Abby would have reason?"

"Somebody else." That old twisted smile, which was not really a smile at all, appeared on his thin lips. "You, for instance," he said softly.

"Me?"

"You," he repeated. "You hate my guts for having gotten Abby. You hate her for being mine instead of yours."

I said, "Does it make sense that I'd want to kill Georgie and Tiny and Stella also?"

"There was a guy put a time bomb on an airplane and blew a lot of people to hell because he wanted to murder his wife who was on the plane. Last night was your first chance to get at Abby and me – and what did you care what happened to the others?"

"My God, you're so crazy over her you'd rather believe anything but the truth."

"The truth?" he said and kept smiling that mirthless smile. "The truth is you're the only one didn't eat the liver." He put on his glasses. "Now get out before I kill you."

"Are you sure she'll let you live that long?"

"Get out!"

I left. There was no use arguing with a mind in that state, and with Oscar it could be mighty dangerous besides.

The usual wind was sweeping up Riverside Drive. I stood on the sidewalk and thought of going home to eat and then I thought of Tiny. What had happened to him since he had left Oscar's apartment last night and had dragged himself to his lonely little room? At the least I ought to look in on him.

I walked over to Broadway and took the subway downtown. I climbed two flights of narrow, smelly stairs in a tenement and pushed in an unlocked door. There was just that one crummy room and the narrow bed against the wall and Tiny lying in it on his back with a knife sticking out of his throat.

13

I must have expected something like this, which was why I'd come. There had been four of us involved in the killing of Wally Garden. Now only two of us were left.

I touched him. He wasn't long dead; rigor mortis had not yet begun to set in. She had left her apartment on the excuse that she was going to a doctor and had come here instead.

There was no sign of a struggle. Tiny wouldn't have suspected anything. Lying here sick and alone, he'd been glad to see her – to see anybody who would minister to him, but especially the boss's lovely lady. She had bent over him to ask how he felt, and he must have been smiling up at that clean fresh young face when she had pushed the knife into his throat, and then she had quickly stepped back to avoid the spurting blood.

That was a switchblade knife, probably Tiny's own, the knife Oscar had borrowed from him to kill Wally Garden. Which would make it grim justice, if you cared for that kind of justice when you also were slated to be on the receiving end.

I got out of there.

When I was in the street, I saw Brant. He was making the rounds of Georgie's pals and he was up to Tiny. It was twilight and I managed to step into a doorway before he could spot me. He turned into the tenement I had just left.

I went into a ginmill for the drink I needed and had many drinks. But I didn't get drunk. When I left a couple of hours later, my head was clear and the fear was still jittering in the pit of my stomach.

I'd never been much afraid of anybody, not even of Oscar, but I was afraid of Abby.

It was her life or ours. I had to convince Oscar of that. Likely he would see the light now that Tiny had been murdered too, because who but Abby had motive? If he refused to strangle her, I would, and be glad to do it, squeezing that lilywhite throat until the clear blue eyes bulged and the sweet face contorted.

I got out of a hack on Riverside Drive. The wind was still there. I huddled against it a moment and then went up to the apartment.

Abby answered the door. She wore a sleazy housecoat

hugging that slender body of hers. She looked limp and haggard and upset.

"Johnny," she said, touching my arm, "I'm glad you're here. The police took Oscar away."

"That so?" I stepped into the apartment.

She closed the door and tagged after me. "They wouldn't tell why they took him away. Was it because of Georgie?"

"No. I guess they're going to ask him how Tiny got a knife in his throat."

Abby clutched her bosom – the kind of gesture an actress would make, and she was acting. "It couldn't have been Oscar. He wasn't out of the house."

"But you were, weren't you?" I grinned at her. "You got only one of us with the arsenic, so you're using other methods, other weapons. Have you anything special planned for my death?"

She backed away from me. "You're drunk. You don't know what you're saying."

"You blame all four of us for Wally's death. You're out to make us pay for it."

"Listen, Johnny!" She put out a hand to ward me off. "I didn't care very much for Wally. When I married him, yes, but after a while he bored me. He was such a kid. He didn't tell me a thing about the holdup. Not a word. All I found out about it was from the police, when they questioned me later. I heard your name and Oscar's from that detective, Brant. So I tried to make some money on it. That's all I was after – a little money."

"You didn't take the money. Instead you worked it so Oscar would bring you to live with him where you could get at all of us."

"I like Oscar. Honest."

"Don't you mind sleeping with the man who killed your husband?"

She tossed her blonde hair. "I don't believe he did. He's so sweet. So kind."

I hit her. I pushed my fist into her lying face. She'd meant death for Georgie and Tiny, and she would mean death for me unless I stopped her.

She bounced off a chair and fell to the floor and blood trickled from her mouth. I hadn't come to hit her but to strangle her. But something beside fear possessed me. Maybe, heaven help me, I was still jealous of Oscar. I swooped down on her and grabbed her by her housecoat and yanked her up to her feet. The housecoat came open. I shook her and her breasts bobbed crazily and I slapped her face until blood poured from her nose as well as her mouth.

Suddenly I let go of her. She sank to the floor, holding her bloody face and moaning. At no time had she screamed. Even while I was beating her, she'd had enough self-possession not to want to bring neighbors in on us. She started to sob.

I'd come to do more to her, to stop her once and for all. But I didn't. I couldn't. I looked down at her sobbing at my feet, lying there slim and fair-haired, battered and bleeding, feminine and forlorn, and there was nothing but emptiness left in me.

After all, hadn't we killed her husband? Not only Oscar, but Georgie and Tiny and I as well were in a community of guilt.

I turned and walked out of the apartment. I kept walking to the brownstone house, and there in the room Stella and I shared a couple of plainclothes men were waiting for me.

14

They grabbed me, and Stella rose from a chair and flung herself at me.

"Honey, are you in trouble?"

I said dully, "Not much with the cops," and went with them.

For the rest of that night they sweated me in the station house. No doubt they had Oscar there too, but we didn't see each other. They kept us apart.

Sometimes Brant was there, sucking his pipe as he watched the regular cops give me the business. There was no more fooling around. They still had questions about Wally and about Georgie, but mostly they wanted to know about the murder of my pal Tiny.

Once, exhausted by their nagging, I sneered at them like a defiant low-grade mug, "You'll never get us."

Brant stepped forward and took his pipe out of his mouth. "Maybe we won't get you," he said gently, "but somebody else is doing it. Three of you already."

After that I stopped sneering. I stopped saying anything. And by morning they let me go.

Before I left, I asked a question. I was told Oscar had been released a couple of hours before.

I made my way home and Stella was waiting and I reached for her.

But there was no rest for my weariness against her cuddly body. She told me Oscar had been here looking for me with a gun.

"When was this?"

"Half an hour ago," she said. "He looked like a wild man. I'd never seen him like that. He was waving a gun. He said you'd beaten up Abby and he was going to kill you. Honey, did you really beat her up?"

I had taken my jacket off. I put it on.

Stella watched me wide-eyed. "If you're running away, take me with you."

"I'm not running," I said.

"But you can't stay. He said he'd be back."

"Did he?" I said hollowly.

I got my gun from where I'd stashed it and checked the magazine and stuck the gun into my jacket pocket.

She ran to me. "What are you going to do? What's going on? Why don't you tell me anything?"

I said, "I don't want to die," and pushed her away from me.

I went only as far as the top of the stoop and waited there, leaning against the side of the doorway. I could watch both directions of the cheerful sun-washed street, and it wasn't long before Oscar appeared.

He looked worse than he had yesterday afternoon. His unshaven face was like a skeleton head. There was a scarecrow limpness about his lean body. All that seemed to keep him going was his urge to kill me.

Maybe if I were living with Abby, had her to love and to hold, I wouldn't give a damn what suspicions I had about her and what facts there were to back them up. I'd deny anything but my need for her body, and I'd be gunning for whoever had marred that lovely face.

I knew there was no use talking to him. I had seen Oscar Trotter in action before, and I knew there was only one thing that would stop him.

I walked down the steps with my right hand in my pocket.

Oscar had both hands in his pockets. He didn't check his stride. He said, "Johnny, I—"

I wasn't listening to him. I was watching his right hand. When it came out of his pocket, so did mine. I shot him.

15

And now we are all dead.

There were five of us on that caper. Four are in their graves. I still have the breath of life in me, but the difference between me and the other four is only a matter of two days, when I will be burned in the chair.

It was a short trial. A dozen witnesses had seen me stand in the morning sunlight and shoot down Oscar Trotter. I couldn't even plead self-defense because he'd had no gun on him. And telling the truth as I knew it wouldn't have changed anything. The day after the trial began the jury found me guilty.

I sent for Stella. I didn't expect her to come, but she did. Yesterday afternoon she was brought here to the death house to see me.

She didn't jiggle. Something had happened to her – to her figure, to her face. Something seemed to have eaten away at her.

"Congratulations," I said.

Stella's voice had changed too. It was terribly tired. "Then you've guessed," she said.

"I've had plenty of time to think about it. Oscar didn't have a gun on him. I know now what he was about to do when he took his hand out of his pocket. He was going to offer me his hand. He had started to say, 'Johnny, I made a mistake.' Something like that. Because he still had a brain. When he'd learned that Tiny had been knifed in bed, he'd realized I'd been right about Abby. But the irony is that I hadn't been right. I'd been dead wrong."

"Yes, Johnny, you were wrong," she said listlessly.

"At the end you got yourself two birds with one stone. You told me a lie about Oscar gunning for me, and it turned out the way you hoped. I killed him and the state will kill me. I've had plenty of time to think back – how that night at Oscar's, as soon as we arrived you hurried into the kitchen to give Abby a hand. Why so friendly so quickly with Abby who'd taken your man from you? I saw why. You'd gone into the kitchen to put arsenic in the chopped liver."

"You can't prove it, Johnny," she whispered.

"No. And it wouldn't save me. Well, I had my answer why you were so eager to take up with me the minute Oscar was through with you. You had to hang around his circle of friends, and you had to bide your time to work the killings so you wouldn't be suspected. You succeeded perfectly, Stella. One thing took me a long time to understand, and that was why."

"Wally," she said.

I nodded. "It had to be. If you'd hated Oscar for throwing you over for Abby, you mightn't have cared if you killed the others at that party as long as you got those two. But there was Tiny's death – cold, deliberate, personal murder. The motive was the same as I'd thought was Abby's. The same master plan – those who'd been in on Wally's death must die. And so it had to be you and Wally."

Stella moved closer to me. Her pretty face was taut with intensity.

"I loved him," she said. "That wife of his, that Abby – she was a no-good louse. First time I ever saw her was when she came up to the apartment to see Oscar, but I knew all about her. From Wally. That marriage was a joke. You wouldn't believe this – you were crazy over her yourself, like Oscar was – but she was after anything wore pants. That was all she gave a damn for, except maybe money."

"I believe you," I said. "You must have been the one who persuaded Oscar to take Wally in on the caper."

"We fell for each other, Wally and I. One of those screwy, romantic pickups on a bus. We saw each other a few times and then planned to go away together. But we hadn't a cent. I knew Oscar was planning a big job. He thought he kept me from knowing anything that was going on. But I knew. Always. And I was smarter. I got a guy who owed me a favor to bring Oscar and Wally together. Oscar took him in on it." Her mouth went bitter. "How I hated the rackets! I wanted to get out of them. I hated Oscar. We had it all figured. We'd take Wally's cut, the few thousand dollars, and go out west and live straight and clean. A little house somewhere and a decent job and children." Her head drooped. "And Oscar killed him."

"He might have died anyway from the bullet wound."

"But not to give him at least a chance!" Stella hung onto her handbag with both hands. "You know why I came when you sent for me? To gloat. To tell you the truth if you didn't know it already and laugh in your face."

But she didn't laugh. She didn't gloat. She looked as sick and tired of it all as I was. She looked as if, like me, she no longer gave a damn about anything.

"It doesn't give you much satisfaction, does it?" I said. "It doesn't bring Wally back. It doesn't make it easy to live with yourself."

She swayed. "Oh, God! So much death and emptiness. And I can't sleep, Johnny. I've had my revenge, but I can't sleep."

"Why don't you try arsenic?" I said softly.

She looked at me. Her mouth started to work, but she didn't say anything. Then she was gone.

That was yesterday. Today Bill Brant visited me and told me that Stella had taken poison and was dead.

"Arsenic?" I said.

"Yeah. The same way Georgie Ross died. What can you tell me about it?"

"Nothing, copper," I said.

So that makes five of us dead, and very soon now I will join them, and we will all be dead. Except Abby, and she was never part of the picture.

Wasn't she?

Stella was kidding herself by thinking she'd killed Oscar and me. Georgie and Tiny and finally herself, yes, but not us.

I needn't have been so quick with my gun on the street outside the brownstone house. I could have waited another moment to make sure that it was actually his life or mine.

Now, writing this in my cell in the death house, I can face up to the truth. I had shot him down in the clear bright morning because he had Abby.

DEATH IS A VAMPIRE

Robert Bloch

1. Won't You Walk into My Parlor?

The gate handle was rusty. I didn't want to touch it. But that was the only way of getting in, unless I wanted to climb the high walls and leave part of my trousers on the iron spikes studding the top.

I grabbed the handle, pushed the gate open and walked down the flagstone path to the house.

If I were a botanist, I'd have been interested in the weeds growing along that path. As it was, they were only something to stumble over. I ignored them and stared at the mansion ahead.

The Petroff house was not quite as big as a castle and not quite as old as Noah's Ark. It looked like the kind of a place the Phantom of the Opera would pick for a summer home.

As far as I was concerned, it was something to donate to the next scrap drive.

But that was none of my business. My business was to sneak inside and wangle old Petroff into giving me an interview about his art treasures. The Sunday supplement needed a feature yarn.

I walked up to the big porch, climbed the stairs, and jangled the old-fashioned door pull. Nothing happened, so I did it again. Same result. It looked as though the Butler's Union had pulled its man off this job.

Just for fun I edged over and turned the doorknob. As I did, I noticed a garland hanging down from the metal projection. It was a wreath of smelly leaves. Not a funeral wreath – just leaves.

That was none of my business, either. I was interested in whether or not the door was unlocked.

It was. So I walked in.

Why not? When Lenehan gave me the assignment, he told me it was a tough one. He had talked to old Petroff over the phone, and Petroff had refused to meet the press or drool over his art treasures.

I expected to be met at the door by a bouncer with a shotgun. But this was easy, and I took advantage of it. It wasn't polite, but newspaper reporting isn't a polite occupation.

The door swung shut behind me, and I stood in a long hallway. It was hard to see anything specific in the afternoon twilight, but I got a musty whiff of stale air, mothballs, and just plain age and decay.

It made me cough. I coughed louder, hoping to rouse my host.

No results. I started down the hallway, still coughing from time to time. An open door led into a deserted library. I ignored it, passed a staircase, walked on.

Behind the stairs was another door. I halted there, for a faint light gleamed from underneath it. I groped for the handle and coughed again. Once more the cough was genuine – for hanging on the doorknob was another garland of those leaves.

Inside here the smell was terrific. Like a Bohemian picnic. Suddenly I recognized the odor. Garlic.

According to the stories going around, old Petroff was a bit of a screwball. But it couldn't be that he had turned the house into a delicatessen.

There was only one way to find out. I opened the door and walked into the parlor where the lamp burned.

It was quiet inside – quiet enough to hear a pin drop. In fact, you could tell which end hit the floor first: the head or the point.

But a pin had not hit the floor in this room. Petroff had.

He looked like his photo, all right. He was tall, thin, with black hair, curled and gray at the temples. A beaked nose and thick lips dominated his face.

He lay there on the floor, his nose pointing up at the ceiling. I got to his side in a hurry, and the floor creaked as I bent over him.

It didn't matter. The noise wouldn't bother him. Nothing would ever bother Igor Petroff again.

His hand was icy. His face was paper-white. I looked around for a mirror but didn't spot any. I pulled my cigarette case out and put it against his lips. The shiny metal clouded slightly. He was still breathing, at any rate.

Probably he'd had a stroke. I lifted his head and stared into his bloodless face. His collar was open. I felt for a pulse in his neck, then took my hand away, quick.

I stared down at his throat, stared down and saw the two tiny punctures in his neck, shook my head and stared again.

They looked like the marks of human teeth!

There was no use asking if there was a doctor in the house. I got up and dashed out into the hall to get to the phone. I got to it. I jiggled the receiver for nearly a minute before I noticed the dangling cord trailing on the floor. Whoever had bitten Petroff had also bitten through the cord.

That was enough for me. I made the two miles back to town in about ten minutes and five hundred gasps. I still had a gasp left in me when I ran into Sheriff Luther Shea's office at Centerville and knocked his feet off the desk.

"Accident out at the Petroff place!" I wheezed. "Get a doctor, quick!"

Sheriff Luther Shea was a fat little bald-headed man who seemed to enjoy keeping his feet on the desk. He put them right back up and scowled at me over his Number Elevens.

"What'sa big idea of bustin' in here? Who are you, anyhow?"

I faced my genial quiz-master without a thought of winning the sixty-four-dollar question.

"Can't you hear?" I yelled. "Call a doctor! Mr Petroff has been injured."

"Ain't no doctor in this town," he told me. "Now state your business, fella."

I stated it, but loud. He perked up his ears a little when I told him about Petroff, but he didn't take his feet off the desk until I flashed my press badge. That did it.

"No sense trying to find a doctor – nearest one's back in LA," he decided. "I'm pretty handy at first aid. I'll get the car and we'll go out and pick him up."

Sheriff Shea banged the office door behind him, and I grabbed a phone. I got hold of Calloway right away and he promised to send the ambulance out to Centerville. Somehow, after having had a good look at Petroff, I didn't have much confidence in Sheriff Shea's "first aid".

Then I put through a call to the paper.

Lenehan growled at me, and I barked right back.

"Somebody bit his throat? Say, Kirby – you drunk?"

I breathed into the phone. "Smell that," I said. "I'm cold sober. I found him lying on the floor with two holes in his neck. I'm still not sure he wasn't dead."

"Well, find out. Keep on this story and give me all you've got. We can hold three hours for the morning edition. Looks like murder, you say?"

"I didn't say a blamed thing about murder!" I yelled.

"Come on, quit stalling!" Lenehan yelled back. "What's your angle on this?"

I lowered my voice to a whisper. "Confidentially," I said, "my theory is that old Petroff bit himself in the throat just for the publicity."

Lenehan apparently didn't believe me, because he launched off into a discussion of my ancestry that was cut short when Sheriff Shea appeared in the doorway. He wore a rancher's black Stetson and a shoulder holster. On him it didn't look good.

"Come on, fella," he said, and I hung up.

His rattletrap Chevvy didn't deserve a C card, but we made time down Centerville's single street and chugged out along the highway.

"From the LA papers, huh?" he grunted. "Whatcha doing up at Petroff's?"

"My editor gave me an assignment to write a feature story about the art treasures of the Irene Colby Petroff estate. Do you know anything about them?"

"Don't know nothing, fella. When old man Colby was alive, he and the missus would come into town and do a little trading once in a while. Then he died and she married this foreign gigolo, Petroff, and that's the last we seen of them in town. Then she died, and since then the place has gone to pot. This business don't surprise me none. Hear some mighty funny gossip about what goes on out at Petroff's place. All fenced off and locked up tighter'n a drum. Ask me, he's hiding something."

"I got in without any trouble."

"What about the guards? What about the dogs? What about the locks on the gate?" I sat up. "No guards, no dogs, no locks," I told him. "Just Petroff. Petroff lying there on the floor with the holes in his throat."

We rounded a bend in the highway and approached the walls of the Petroff estate. The setting sun gleamed on the jagged spikes surmounting the walls. And it gleamed on something else.

"Who's that?" I yelled, grabbing Sheriff Shea's arm.

"Don't do that!" he grunted. "Nearly made me go off the road."

"Look!" I shouted. "There's a man climbing up the wall."

Sheriff Shea glanced across the road and saw the figure at the top of the wall. The car ground to a halt and we went into action. Shea tugged at his shoulder holster.

"Stop or I'll shoot!" he bawled.

The man on the wall considered the proposition and rejected it. He turned and jumped. It was a ten-foot drop but he landed catlike and was scuttling across the road by the time we reached the base of the wall.

"After him!" Shea grunted.

The man ran along the other side of the road, making for a clump of trees ahead. I dashed along behind. The fugitive reached the grove a few steps ahead of me and I decided on a little football practice.

It was a rather ragged flying tackle, but it brought him down. We rolled over and over, and on the second roll he got on top. He didn't waste time. I felt powerful fingers dig into my throat. I tore at his wrists. He growled and twisted his neck. I felt his mouth graze my cheek. He was trying to bite me.

I got his hands loose and aimed a punch at his chin, but he ducked and pressed his thumbs in my eyes. That hurt. I aimed another punch, but that wasn't good either. By this time he had those hands around my neck again, and things began to turn red. The red turned black. I heard him growling and snarling deep in his throat, and his fingers squeezed and squeezed.

This was no time for Queensbury rules. I kicked him in the tummy. With a grunt of appreciation he slumped back, clutching his solar plexus.

2. They Fly by Night

Sheriff Shea arrived, wheezing, and together we collared our prisoner and dragged him to his feet.

He was not pretty. He wore one of those one-piece overall outfits, and between the spikes on the wall and the tussle, he'd managed to destroy its integrity. Patches of his skin showed through, advertising the need of a bath. His yellow hair was matted and hung down over his eyes, which was just as well. They were as blue as a baby-doll's – and just as vacant. His lips hung slackly, and he was drooling. A prominent goitre completed the ensemble.

"Why, it's Tommy!" said the Sheriff. "He's a little touched," he whispered, "but harmless."

He didn't have to tell me the kid was touched. That I could easily believe. But the "harmless" part I doubted. I rubbed my aching eyes and neck while Shea patted Tommy on the back.

"What were you doing on the wall, Tommy?" he asked.

Tommy lifted a sullen face. "I was looking at the bats."

"What bats?"

"The bats that fly at twilight. They fly out of the windows and you can hear them squeaking at each other."

I glanced at Sheriff Shea. He shrugged.

"Ain't no bats around here except the ones in Tommy's belfry."

I took over. "What else were you looking at, Tommy?" I inquired.

He turned away. "I don't like you. You tried to hurt me. Maybe you're one of them! One of the bad people."

"Bad people?"

"Yes. They come here at night. Sometimes they come as men, wearing black cloaks. Sometimes they fly – that's when they're bats. They only come at night, because they sleep in the daytime."

Tommy was in full cry, now. I didn't try to stop him.

"I know all about it," he whispered. "They don't suspect me, and they'd kill me if they thought I knew. Well, I do know. I know why Petroff doesn't have any mirrors on the walls. I heard Charlie Owens, the butcher, tell about the liver he sends out every day – the raw liver, pounds of it. I know what flies by night."

"That's enough," said Sheriff Shea. "Whatever you know, you can tell us inside."

"Inside? You aren't going in there, are you? You can't take me in there! I won't let you! You want to give me to him. You'll let him kill me!"

Again, Shea cut him off. Grasping his arm, he guided the half-wit across the road. I followed. We made straight for the gate.

Shea halted. "Push it open," I said.

"It's locked."

I looked. A shiny new padlock hung from the rusty handle.

"It was open half an hour ago," I said.

"He always keeps it locked," Shea told me. "Usually has a man out here, too – a guard. And dogs in the kennels back of the house." He eyed me suspiciously. "You sure you were up here, Mr Kirby?"

"Listen," I advised him. "I was up here a little over half an hour ago. The gate was open. I went in and found Petroff on the floor. He had two holes in his throat and I'm not sure whether he was still breathing or not. I'll give you every explanation you want later, but let's go inside, quick. He may be dead."

Shea shrugged. He stood back and drew his revolver. The shot resounded, the lock shattered. I held Tommy tightly and pushed him through the gateway.

After that I took the lead. Up the steps, through the door, down the hall. It was slow going in the gathering twilight. We stumbled along toward the room behind the staircase.

"Here," I said. "Here's where I found him." I opened the door. The light was still on. I pointed to the floor. "Here," I said.

"Yeah?" grunted Shea. "Where is he?"

The room was empty. The rug was on the floor, but Petroff was not. I stared, and the room began to whirl. I took a deep breath and inhaled fresh air.

It was coming from the open French windows at the end of the room.

Of course! The windows were open. I had made some kind of a mistake. Petroff had been breathing. He had fainted, or something. After I left he recovered, went for a stroll on the porch beyond the open windows, and locked his gate. The holes in his throat. Maybe he'd cut himself while shaving.

* * *

I was a fool. A glance at Sheriff Shea confirmed the suspicion. He grinned at me.

But Tommy was not grinning.

"You were here before," he murmured. "You saw him lying here with holes in his throat."

"I – I made a mistake," I mumbled.

"No. When you were here it was still daylight. Now it's dusk. When you were here he was still asleep. But he comes alive at night."

"What do you mean? Who comes alive at night?"

"The vampire," he whispered. "He comes alive. And at night he flies. Look!"

Tommy screamed. His finger stabbed at the dusk beyond the opened windows.

We stared out into the night and saw the black shadow of a bat skimming off into the darkness, a mocking squeak rising from its throat.

In just a little while there was the devil of a lot of activity. The ambulance I had sent for finally arrived, and Shea had to stall them off with a trumped-up excuse about a fainting fit. Then Shea wanted to play detective and go over the place. Personally, I think he was dying to case the joint merely to collect some gossip.

I won't bother remembering the bawling-out he handed me. I had to take it, too. After all, my story sounded pretty phony now.

Tommy was the only one who believed me. And his support was not much help. A half-wit's comments on vampires don't make good testimony.

While Shea handled the ambulance men, Tommy kept talking.

"Look at the garlic wreaths on the doors," he said. "He must have been trying to keep them out. They can't bear garlic."

"Neither can I," I answered. "And I'm no vampire."

"Look at the books," Tommy exclaimed. "Magic."

I stepped over to the built-in bookshelves. This time Tommy really had something. There were rows of blackbound volumes; musty, crumbling treatises in Latin and German. I read the titles. It was indeed a library of demonology. Where there's smoke there's fire.

But what did that prove? Occultism isn't a rare hobby on the Coast. I knew half a hundred crackpots who belonged to "secret cults," and down Laguna way there was a whole colony of them.

Still, I ran my eyes and fingers along the rows. One of the books on the lower shelf protruded a bit more than was necessary. It offended my sense of neatness. As I reached in to push it back, a card slipped out from between yellowed pages. I palmed it, turned around just as Sheriff Shea re-entered the room.

"Come on," he sighed. "Let's get out of here."

Driving back to town, with Tommy wedged between us on the front seat, Shea gave me another going over.

"I don't understand all this monkey business," he declared. "I don't know what you were doing in that house in the first place. Least I can do is hold you on suspicion of illegal entry. As for Tommy here, he's liable to get booked on the same charges. I'm gonna see his folks about this. But what I want to know is – where's Petroff?"

"I shot him." I grinned. "But the bats flew off with his body."

"Never mind that," Shea snapped. "You smart-aleck reporters aren't tampering with the law down here. I'd like to get the DA in on this, but there's nothing to go on, yet. Maybe after I hold you on suspicion a few days you'll be ready to talk. I want to know how you cut those telephone wires, too."

"Now listen," I said. "I've got work to do. I'm willing to play ball on this thing and help straighten matters out. If Igor Petroff has disappeared and I'm the last man who saw him alive – or dead – that's important to me, too. The paper'll want the story. But I'm down here on an assignment. I've got to move around."

"No, you don't. Case I didn't mention it, you're under arrest right now, Mr Kirby."

"That," I sighed, "is all I want to know."

I eased the car door open gently and swiftly. We were going thirty, but I took my chances. I jumped and hit the road.

Shea swore. He brought the rattling Chevvy to a halt, but by that time I was running along the ditch on the other side of the road. It was good and dark.

Shea bawled and waved his revolver, but he couldn't spot me. Then he turned the car around and zoomed back up the road. I went into the field, kept going. In a few minutes the road was far behind me, and I headed across to the other side of the field and another dirt road running parallel.

Here I found the truck that took me back to LA. I hopped off downtown, found a drugstore, and called Lenehan at the office.

"Where in thunder are you?" he greeted me. "Just had this hick sheriff on the wire. He's bawling you're a fugitive from justice. And what's all this business about a disappearing body? Give."

I gave. "Hold the yarn," I pleaded. "I've got a new angle."

"Hold it?" yelled Lenehan. "I'm tearing it up! You and your disappearing Dracula! Petroff was drunk on the floor when you found him and you were drunk on your feet. He had the decency to wander off and sober up, but you're still drunk!"

I hung up.

Then I fished around in my pocket and pulled out the card I had snatched from the book in Petroff's library.

It was nicely engraved:

HAMMOND KING
Attorney at Law

I turned it over. A man's heavy scrawl spidered across the back read:

You may be interested in this volume on vampirism.
H. K.

The plot was thickening. Hammond King? I knew the name. A downtown boy. Wealthy attorney. What was the connection?

I called Maizie at the office.

"Hammond King," I said. "Check the morgue."

She got me the dope. I listened until she came to an item announcing that Hammond King was attorney for the Irene Colby Petroff estate. I stopped her and hung up.

It was eight o'clock. Not likely that Hammond King would still be at his office, but it was a chance worth taking. The phone book got me the number and I deposited my third nickel.

The phone rang for a long time. Perhaps he was going over a tort or something. Then a deep voice came over the wire.

"Hammond King speaking."

"Mr King – this is Dave Kirby, of the *Leader*. I'd like to come over there and talk to you."

"Sorry young man. If you'll phone my office tomorrow for a more definite appointment—"

"I thought we might have a little chat about vampires."

"Oh."

That stopped him.

"I'll be right over," I said. "So long."

He didn't answer. I whistled my way out of the phone booth, ordered a ham sandwich and a malted milk, disposed of same, and took a cab downtown.

The night elevator brought me to Hammond King's office. The door was open and I walked into one of those lavish layouts so typical of wealthy attorneys and impecunious booking agents.

I ignored the outer office and made for the big door marked "Private".

King was examining a bottle of Scotch with phony nonchalance.

My nonchalance was just as phony as I examined him.

He was a short, stocky man of about fifty-five. Gray hair and mustache to match. His eyes slanted behind unusually thick bifocals. He wore an expensive gray suit, and I admired his taste in ties. He looked like a hundred other guys, but he sent books on vampirism to his friends. You never know these days.

"Mr Kirby?" he inquired, getting up and extending his hand. "To what do I owe this pleasure?"

"I told you over the phone," I said. "I'd like to have a little chat with you about vampires."

"Oh."

The phony nonchalance faded away and the hand dropped to his side.

"I'd rather have talked to Mr Petroff about it," I continued. "Matter of fact, I dropped in on him this afternoon. But he wasn't there. That is, he was there, and then he wasn't. You know how vampires get restless about twilight."

"What do you mean?"

"You know what I mean, King," I said. "I just thought I'd warn you. In case anybody tries to bite you in the throat, it's your old client, Igor Petroff."

"How'd you know he was my client?"

"I know a lot of things," I told him, wishing it were true. "And what I don't know you'd better tell me, but fast. Unless, of course, you want it splashed all over the front page of the *Leader*."

"Let's be reasonable," Hammond King pleaded. "I'll be glad to help you all I can. Anything involving my client—"

The phone rang. King reached for the receiver, then drew his hand back.

"Pardon me, please," he said.

He got up and went into the outer office and shut the door.

3. The Bat's Kiss

I would have given my left arm to know who King was talking to. But I didn't have to give my left arm. All I needed to do was reach out with it and gently pick up the receiver. Call it eavesdropping, if you wish. You do a lot of things in this business.

"Mr King?" a girl's voice came over the wire. "This is Lorna Colby. I'm at the Eastmore Hotel, Room Nine-nineteen . . . No, Igor sent for me. He wanted to talk about a settlement on the will."

"Have you seen Petroff?" Hammond King barked into the phone at this end.

"No, not yet."

"Well, I'll be around in the morning, at ten. We've got to work fast, you understand? Something's happening that I don't like."

"What is it?" asked Lorna Colby.

"I can't talk now. See you tomorrow. Good night."

He hung up. I hung up. It was my turn to look at the Scotch bottle as he came in.

"Where were we?" he asked.

"You were just going to spill the beans," I said.

Hammond King smiled. "Was I? Lucky for me I got called away. I'm afraid I can't talk this matter over with you just at present. That call was from a client in Pasadena. I've got to take the train tonight."

I rose. One of his desk drawers was half opened. I reached in and scooped up a handful of garlic leaves.

"You had these left over from decorating the Petroff house, I presume," I told him. "Too bad you didn't think to put these on the French windows."

I slipped the garlic wreath into his hand and left the room.

He stood there with his mouth open, giving a poor imitation of a stuffed moose.

I rode downstairs and walked around the corner and across the block to the Eastmore Hotel. I didn't bother to send my name up, but rode in person to the ninth floor. Nine-nineteen was down the hall to my left. I found the room and knocked on Lorna Colby's door.

There was no answer – except a sudden, ear-shattering scream.

I jerked the doorknob. The door opened on a tableau of frozen horror.

A blonde girl lay slumped on the bed. Crouching above her was a shadowy figure out of a nightmare. Its head was bending toward her neck. I saw lean, outstretched fingers claw down, saw the mouth descend – then the shadow straightened, turned, swooped across the room and out through the open window.

Lorna Colby lay there, clutching her throat and staring in wide-eyed terror. I stared, too. For the intruder had been Igor Petroff.

When I reached the window, the fire-escape outside was empty. Perhaps it had never held a figure. Perhaps I'd have done better to look for something flying in the sky.

I turned back to the bed. Lorna Colby was sitting up. There was still fear in her hazel eyes as she looked at me.

"Who are you?" she demanded.

I introduced myself. "Dave Kirby, of the *Leader*. You're Lorna Colby, of course?"

She nodded. "Yes. But how did you know? And what made you come here?"

"Hammond King sent me," I lied.

It was the right hunch.

"Then maybe you can tell me," she said, "what's wrong with my uncle? He sent me a wire to come down and talk about the estate. I waited to hear from him tonight. I was getting sleepy and lay down on the bed. When I opened my eyes again, he was in the room."

"Petroff?"

"Yes. You recognized him, too?"

I nodded.

"He must have come through the window some way. He just

crouched over me, staring, and there was something wrong with his face. It was so white, but his eyes glared, and I couldn't look away. Then I felt his hands come down toward my neck, and I screamed, and then—"

I shook her, not gently. It was fun, but this was no time for amusement.

"Stop it!" I snapped. "Relax."

She cried a little. Then she sat up and fished around for her make up. I took the opportunity to study her more closely.

Lorna Colby was tall, blonde, and about twenty-two. She had a good face and a better figure. All in all, the kind of a girl worth whistling after.

That noise like a ton of bricks was me, falling. She didn't notice it. After a while she patted her hair back and smiled.

"Your uncle is – ill," I said. "That's what Hammond King asked me to tell you. We're trying to keep things quiet until we can take him away for a rest."

"You mean he's crazy?"

I shrugged.

"I've always thought so," Lorna declared. "Even when Aunt Irene was alive, I knew there was something wrong with him. He led her an awful life."

She halted, bit her lower lip, and continued.

"After she died, he got worse. He kept dogs at the house, guarding it. He wanted to guard her tomb, he said. I haven't seen him now for almost a year. Nobody has seen him since the day she died. She had a heart attack, you know. He buried her in the private vaults on the estate. He wouldn't even let me see her or come to the funeral.

"I knew he hated me, and it came as a surprise when I got his wire yesterday, asking me to come down from Frisco to talk about the will. That didn't make sense, either. After all, Aunt Irene left him the whole estate, even though he can't touch the money for a year."

Something clicked into place. I decided to follow it up.

"By the way, who was your aunt's physician?" I asked.

"Dr Kelring."

"I'd like to talk to him," I told her. "It's important."

"You think he might know what's wrong with Uncle Igor?"

"That's right." I nodded. "He must know."

I looked him up in the book. Dr Roger Kelring. I called his downtown office, not hoping for much of anything. Still, this gang seemed to work late. Hammond King was on the job, and Igor Petroff was a regular night-owl. Or was he? "They fly by night."

The phone gave off that irritating sound known as a busy signal. That was enough for me.

"Come on, Miss Colby," I said. "We're going over to Dr Kelring's office."

"But you didn't talk to him," she objected.

"Busy signal," I explained. "On second thought, I'd just as soon not say anything to him in advance."

"What do you mean? Do you think he's mixed up in all this?"

"Definitely," I assured her. "I wouldn't be a bit surprised if your uncle was up there with him now."

Lorna put on her coat and we went downstairs. In the lobby, she halted indecisively.

"Wait a minute, Mr Kirby. Aren't we going to report seeing Uncle Igor in my room? After all, if he's sick somebody should be looking after him. He may be—"

"Dangerous? Perhaps. But let's not start something we can't finish. It's my hunch that he's over at Dr Kelring's office. Don't ask me why, but I've got reasons. Besides, you don't want to get mixed up in a lot of cross-questioning, do you?"

She agreed. I was relieved. What could I do if we called some Law? Tell them that a suspected vampire was running around attacking girls in hotel rooms?

Besides, I didn't think Igor Petroff was "running around". He might be flying around. Or he might be working according to a plan. Dr Kelring would know the plan.

We took a cab to Kelring's office, in a building off Pershing Square.

"What's the doctor like?" I asked Lorna.

"He's a rich woman's doctor," she told me. "You know – smooth, quiet, genial. He's about fifty, I guess. Bald-headed, with a little goatee. I only saw him once, at Aunt Irene's, a few months before she died. He was pleasant, but I didn't like him."

Lorna's voice betrayed her inner tension. I understood. It's not every night that a girl is attacked by a vampire, even if he's a member of the family.

Partly for that reason and partly for personal pleasure, I held her arm as we took the elevator up to Kelring's office. A light burned behind the outer door. I opened it and stepped in. I had no gun, but if there was anything doing, I counted on the surprise element.

There was one.

Seated at the desk in the reception room was a man of about fifty, bald-headed, and wearing a small goatee. His hand rested on the telephone as though he were going to pick it up and make another call.

But Dr Kelring would never make another call. He sat there staring off into space, and when I touched his shoulder his neck wobbled off at an angle so that his goatee almost touched the spot between his shoulder-blades. Roger Kelring was quite, was definitely, was unmistakably dead.

I was patting Lorna's shoulder and making with the reassurance when the phone rang. Its sharp note cut the air, and I jumped. For a moment I stared at Dr Kelring, wondering why his dead hand didn't lift the receiver and hold it to his ear.

Then I got around the desk, fast, and pried his cold fingers from the receiver.

"Lorna," I said, "how did – he – talk?"

"You mean Dr Kelring?" She shuddered.

"Yes."

"Oh, I don't remember . . . Yes, I think I do. He had a soft voice. Very soft."

"Good."

I whipped out my handkerchief and covered the mouthpiece. Just a hunch.

"Hello," I said lifting the receiver.

"Hello. That you, Kelring?"

I jumped as I recognized the voice. Hammond King!

"What is it?" I said, softly.

"Kelring, I must talk to you." He sounded frightened. Too frightened to analyze my voice.

"Go ahead. What's on your mind?"

"Did you ever read 'The Fall of the House of Usher'?"

"What?"

"You know what I'm talking about, Kelring. She's alive out there. I know it!"

"Who's alive?"

"Mrs Petroff. Don't stall me, Kelring. I'm desperate."

"What makes you think so, man?"

"It happened two months ago. I was out there at the house with Petroff, arguing about the will. You know he's been trying to get me to turn over the estate before the time stipulated. I won't bother with details, but I heard a noise. A woman's voice, coming from behind the wall. It came from the private staircase behind the bookshelves – the one leading down to the family burial vaults in the hillside."

"Get to the point, King," I said.

"He tried to hold me off, but I made him take me down there. I don't know how to tell you this – but beyond the iron grille entrance, in the vaults, I caught a glimpse of Irene Colby Petroff. Alive."

"But I pronounced her dead of heart failure," I said, remembering what I'd been told.

"She was alive, I tell you! She ran into one of the passages, but I recognized her face. I tried to get Petroff to open the grille and go in, but he dragged me back upstairs. Then he told me the story."

"What story?"

"You know, all right, Kelring. That's why I didn't call before. I wanted to investigate on my own. Now I need your help."

"Better tell me all you know, then."

"I know that she's a – vampire."

I held my breath. King didn't wait for any comment.

"Petroff broke down and confessed. Said he knew it and you knew it. She'd been mixed up in some kind of Black Magic cult in Europe when he met her. And when she died, she didn't really die. She lived on, after sundown, as a vampire."

"Preposterous!"

"I wasn't sure myself, then. I wanted to call in the police. But Petroff pleaded with me. Said he had the guard and the dogs and kept people away. He had her locked up down there, fed her raw liver. Because you were trying to work on a cure. He asked for a little more time. And he explained it all. Gave me books on demonology to read. I didn't know what to believe, but

I promised to wait. Then, three nights ago, he called and told me that she had tried to attack him. He asked me to come out this afternoon and talk things over.

"I went out there about four today. Maybe I was a fool, but I took some garlic with me. The books say garlic wards them off. When I arrived, I found Petroff lying on the floor. There were two holes in his throat – the marks of a vampire's teeth. So he has become a vampire now!

"I got frightened and ran. I knew he had sent for his niece, Lorna Colby. I wanted to talk to her before I did anything. Then, tonight, a young man called on me. Said he was from the newspapers. He knows something, too.

"Kelring, I've made up my mind to act. I won't call the police. I – I can't. They'd laugh at me. But there's a monster loose tonight, and I can't stand waiting any longer. I'm going out to the Petroff place now."

"Wait!" I said.

His voice was shrill as he replied. "Do you know what I've been doing, Kelring? I've been sitting here molding silver bullets. Silver bullets for my gun. And I'm leaving now. I'm going out there to get him!"

"Don't be a fool!" I yelled, in my natural voice.

But he had hung up.

"Come on," I snapped at Lorna. "I'll call the police and report on Kelring now. But we're getting out before they come."

"Where are we going?"

"To Petroff's house," I answered.

She nodded. I moved around the table. As I did, I saw something on the floor. It was a spectacle-case. I picked it up, turned it over. It was an expensive case, with an engraved name. The silver signature read:

Hammond King

4. Vampire's Teeth

As the cab driver grumbled about the long haul, I told Lorna what I thought was wise.

I was too groggy to think clearly. Lenehan thought I was drunk, I'd jumped arrest, I'd eavesdropped, and impersonated, and messed up a murder. And it looked like an even busier day tomorrow unless I could straighten this tangle out tonight.

That's my only excuse, I guess. I was a punch-drunk fool to take Lorna to that house, with only a crazy hunch to guide us, and armed with nothing but my suspicions.

But I did it. We rolled up to the black, forbidding portals of the Petroff place. We walked up the porch of the Petroff mansion and the cab waited in the driveway. I didn't see Hammond King's car, and I was glad we had arrived first.

He was wrong, I thought. Petroff was not here. And if he wasn't, we could find that staircase, take a look into the vault, and see for ourselves whether Irene Colby Petroff walked or slept forever.

Never mind the details. The garlic odor choked us in the creaky hall. It flooded the parlor as I lit the lamp, tapped bookcases, and found the button that opened a section of the wall. Lorna shivered at my side. The setup looked like something out of "The Cat and the Canary".

I kept listening for sounds. All quiet on the Western Front. With the light streaming from the parlor behind us, we took the secret staircase in stride. Down below was another panel in the wall. I switched on the light and walked down a long corridor. It was damp. King had said the private vaults of the family were out under the hillside.

We rounded a turn and came to the iron grille barring the hall. A perpetual light burned behind it. I tried the door. It was open. It squeaked as I pushed.

The squeak was drowned in a scream.

I turned.

Something black scuttled around the corner of the passageway. Something swooped down on Lorna, engulfed her in a sable cloud. I saw glaring eyes, red lips – Igor Petroff was here!

I made a dive for him. Petroff didn't dodge. He stood there, and as I came on, his arm lashed out. The blow caught me off balance and as I wavered, his hand moved out. Something flashed down, and then I fell.

There was a blurred impression of movement, screaming, and scuffling. Petroff had dragged Lorna through the grille, down into the vaults.

I lurched to my feet as another figure raced around the bend. More blamed traffic down here, I thought, dazedly.

It was Hammond King.

He didn't see me. He stared, glassy-eyed, as he ran past into the gloom of the corridor beyond. He was carrying a gun. Silver bullets!

I dashed after him. As we took another flight of stairs, I gazed over his shoulder at the family vaults beyond.

Lorna stood in a corner, crouching against a wall. The cloaked figure of Igor Petroff glided towards her, and I thought of Dracula, and of childhood terrors, and of nightmares men still whisper about.

Hammond King didn't think. He began pumping shots from his gun, firing in maniac fury.

Petroff turned, across the room. And then, he smiled. He didn't fall down. He smiled. He smiled, and started to run toward Hammond King with his arms extended, and Hammond King gave a little choking gurgle and fell down.

I didn't fall. As Petroff advanced, I ran to meet him. This time I was not off balance. I let him have one right on the point of his white chin. He grunted, but his arms swept up and then I felt the cold embrace as he clawed at me. I hammered into his ribs, but he was hard, rigid. Rigor mortis is like that, I thought madly.

He smelled of dampness and mold and ancient earth. His arms were strong and he was squeezing me. I dropped to the floor and he began to reach for my throat. He chuckled, then, deep in his throat, an animal growl. A growl of hunger, the growl of a carnivore that scents blood.

He had me by the neck, and I reached out with one hand and scrabbled frantically against the floor until I felt the cold steel of the gun Hammond King had dropped.

Petroff wrenched my arm back, trying to tear the gun from my fingers. I wanted to fight him off, but his other hand was at my neck, squeezing. I felt myself falling back, and I pulled my arm free and brought the gun-butt up against his head, once, twice, three times.

Igor Petroff wobbled like a rundown mechanical doll and dropped with a dull thud.

I got up and slapped Lorna's face. She came out of her trance, crying. Then I went over to Hammond King and slapped him around. Just a one-man rescue squad.

"Go upstairs, you two," I said. "The cab driver's waiting outside. Tell him to go into Centerville and bring back Sheriff Shea. I'll meet you in a moment."

They left.

I went through the vault until I came to what I wanted to find. When I was quite finished with my inspection I went back upstairs.

Lorna and Hammond King were waiting in the parlor. She had fixed her hair again, and he looked well enough to smoke a cigarette.

"The police should be here in five minutes," King said.

"Good."

"Perhaps I'd better look outside," he suggested. "I'm expecting Dr Kelring."

"Kelring isn't coming," I said, gently. "He's dead."

"But I talked to him over the phone."

I told him who he'd talked to. And then I decided to tell him a few other things.

"You should have gone to the police the night you saw Mrs Petroff here," I said. "Then all this wouldn't have happened."

"But I saw her. She was alive."

"Right. But she wasn't a vampire. Too bad you believed that crazy story Petroff concocted. When you stumbled onto her existence, he had to think of something and the vampire story just popped out. After you half swallowed it, he planned the rest. He had to convince you completely, and he was good at planning."

"What do you mean?"

"It all started, I think, when Petroff and Dr Kelring decided to fake Mrs Petroff's death. They were in on it together, to split the inheritance. They didn't have the nerve to kill her outright but drugged her, held a private funeral, and faked the death certificate. Then Petroff kept her a prisoner down here in the vaults. That's why he had dogs and a guard. She was alive until about three days ago."

"How do you know?"

"I just found her body in the vault," I explained. "And I've seen her living quarters – a room beyond. She's dead now, all right, and I'd say she died of starvation."

"I don't understand," Lorna sighed.

"Simple. When her fake death was accepted, Petroff and Dr Kelring were all set to divide the spoils. But there were no spoils – not for a year, according to the terms of her will. They hadn't counted on that. So Petroff was trying to get King, here, to advance money against the inheritance.

"King, being a smart attorney, would do no such thing. But after he saw Mrs Petroff alive and heard this vampire line, he began to weaken. Petroff took advantage of it, showing him books on demonology, and telling wild stories about secret cults."

Hammond King nodded miserably. "He was wearing me down," he admitted. "But I wouldn't release any money. I couldn't, legally."

I took over again. "Then, three days ago, Mrs Petroff actually died. Perhaps he deliberately starved her, perhaps not. In any event, she was dead, and his extortion plot and fake death was now actually murder. He wanted that money at once, needed it desperately.

"So he phoned you, King, and asked you to come out today, planning to show himself lying on the floor as the victim of a vampire attack. He had it figured that you'd be too shocked to call the police at once. Then, after dark, he would call upon you as a supposed vampire, threaten you with his bite, and get you to advance personal funds against the estate."

King was looking bewildered.

"But I'd never do that," he protested. "He must have been mad!"

"He was – and desperate, too." I grinned. "Here's where I come into the story. Dave Kirby, the Boy Reporter. I got here today just after you left in the afternoon. I blundered in before Petroff could escape, so he lay there on the floor, hoping to fool me. When I left for the sheriff, he took a powder.

"Now the jig was up, but Petroff decided to carry the plan through. If he worked fast, he might still succeed. He'd called Lorna, asked her to come to town. He had only one idea – to appear before her as a supposed vampire and thus further bolster his story when he saw King and demanded money. This he was doing as I arrived at Lorna's room. He fled, and undertook his next step in the plan – the murder of Dr Kelring."

"But why would he murder Kelring?" King asked.

I shrugged. "There were several reasons. The first is the one that led me to the scene. You remember, I came out to the house for an interview on the Petroff estate art treasures, an interview Petroff had already refused to grant."

"Yes?"

"There was a reason for my coming and a reason for his refusal. You see, my editor had a tip that several valuable vases recognized as part of the Petroff collection had been offered for sale at private auction. Get it?

"Petroff was already raising money by illegally disposing of art treasures belonging to the estate. Kelring must have just discovered this and demanded his cut. Otherwise, he would squeal about the fake death certificate. So Petroff had to kill him. Just as an added touch, he left a little souvenir after strangling him in his office."

I handed King his spectacle case.

"You nearly had credit for that piece of work," I said. "I'm sure he would have threatened to turn you in had you refused him money when he demanded it this evening. So it's lucky I had you on the phone and can support an alibi."

King blinked.

"After killing Dr Kelring he scooted out here to wait for you. He knew you'd be out to check up. He hadn't counted on Lorna and me arriving, but when we showed up first, he was ready. After that you dashed in, made your bang-bang with the silver bullets, and passed out. You aren't a good shot, King. Those bullets are in the walls, not in his body. But it wouldn't have mattered much. He wore a bullet-proof vest under the cloak. Felt it when I tackled him."

Lorna looked at me.

"You tackled him," she whispered. "That was wonderful. Even if he might be a vampire, you took the chance."

"But he wasn't a vampire. I knew that."

"Didn't you find him with holes in his throat?"

"Right. But he made them himself. Shallow cuts with a paper-knife, no doubt. You see, a vampire's bite will drain all blood. And there was blood. I know something about superstitions myself, Lorna."

Sirens punctuated my sentence. The law was arriving in full force.

Suddenly I was very tired and very contented. Lenehan would get a story after all. And I'd get some sleep.

Lorna kissed me.

"What's that for?" I asked.

"For being brave. I don't care what you say, he might have been a vampire."

"Not a chance." I grinned. "I knew that from the beginning. When I looked at him on the floor this afternoon, his mouth was open. That was the tip-off."

"What do you mean?"

"He couldn't be a vampire because he couldn't bite anyone. After all, darling, who ever heard of a big, bad vampire with false teeth?"

THE BLUE STEEL SQUIRREL

Frank R. Read

Prologue

In a silver flood of moonlight, a group of people laughed and talked together on a terrace in a high-walled garden. The occasion was a happy one – a betrothal party. The soft June air, still fresh from a sundown shower, was heavy with the scent of roses. A mockingbird, perched high atop a chimney, trilled a liquid melody.

The bride-to-be, radiant with happiness, sat in a cane garden chair, watching the familiar scene. Her eyes lingered over each precious beauty, the playing fountain, the full moon. They rested on the face of the man she loved, Michael Collins.

Mike, toying with the dials of a portable radio, paused as the familiar hum of a station fried in the loud-speaker. He smiled at his fiancée, and absent-mindedly turned up the volume.

A mighty roar rolled over the terrace as a brassy swing band crashed into a hot tune. Guests and host, jolted by the discordant notes, stiffened and glared at the young man. Mike mumbled apologies, and snapped off the radio.

The guests sank back in their chairs with a sigh of relief, all but the bride-to-be. She stiffened, slumped forward in her chair, and tumbled forward to the flagstone flooring.

A silver bullet had pierced her heart.

There had been no sound, no outcry, no flash of gunfire. Stupidly, the members of the party looked from one to the other. The spell of inactivity was broken only when one of the woman screamed.

A year later, there was a bulging file at police headquarters, titled:

"Corinne Bogart – Homicide (Unsolved)"

I

The long, sun-bronzed young man, wearing an impeccable dark-blue tropical worsted suit, leaned back in his swivel chair and studied his name lettered in reverse on the ground-glass door of his office – Jefferson Hunter. Just that, nothing more.

There is no trade term, unless, perhaps, "Confidential Commercial Agent", that could be applied to him. That, too, would be a misnomer, for Jefferson Hunter, home again after solving a foreign reconstruction problem, looked into anything that intrigued him, with or without permission. The fees he demanded and received from corporations were known to have made boards of directors shudder. Yet his services were in immediate demand as soon as he reopened his office.

"Anything exciting in the morning mail, Smitty?" he asked Z. Z. Smith, his small, wiry assistant.

"Yes." Smitty slid a small pile of letters across his boss's desk. "The top note has me stumped."

Jeff's eyebrows rose. "Interesting?"

"Could be. It's from a guy named Bogart."

"What?" Jeff sat up. "What did you say?"

"I said it's from a guy named Bogart. Wendell A. Best clubs and so on. Director of this and that. Smells of do-re-mi. He wants you to come to see him about something personal and confidential. He says Wagner, the man you helped on the oil deal in Iran, recommended you."

Jeff leaned back in his chair, his gray eyes hardening. "It's foolish," he told himself, "to keep avoiding Pamela Bogart." Sooner or later, he was bound to meet her. Why postpone the inevitable?

"OK, Smitty, make an appointment."

"I have. Bogart is waiting for us at his home."

"Um-m-m! Didn't give me a chance to refuse, did you?"

Smitty, like all valuable assistants, knew his boss like a book. He anticipated his wishes, needled him into action, and restrained his enthusiasms. Smitty, in short, was invaluable.

The sleek yellow convertible, carrying Jeff and his Man Friday, purred into the Valley, the town's exclusive suburb.

"There's the house, Jeff!" Smitty pointed. "Nice dive! There's a ten-foot brick wall around the back garden. Cripes, the house is built of white marble."

"I hate to disillusion you, Smitty," Jeff said, as they stopped under an ornate porte-cochere, "but this pile has only a one-inch marble face, probably over cinder block or tile. It's typical of the late twenties. Built for show. Two bits says Bogart's a pain in the neck."

"No takers, Jeff. You're too often right."

Wendell Bogart did not look up when the butler showed them into the library. He was examining six gayly feathered darts spread out on the desk before him. He gathered them into his hands, turned in his chair and smiled at the thin, bespectacled young man standing beside him. Effortlessly, one of the darts flew from his hand and thudded into a target across the room. The other five followed in rapid succession.

Jeff's eyes widened when the darts came to rest. One, double one, triple one. Two, double two, triple two.

"I wouldn't want to play you for more than a beer," Jeff said.

Wendell Bogart didn't answer. The studious-looking young man beside him smiled, nodded to Jeff and left the room. Bogart spun in his chair, raising his dark-brown eyes to meet Jeff's level gray ones. For a moment, neither spoke, each studying, measuring the other. It was the older man who broke the silence.

"My only niece, Pamela Bogart, must not die."

The words, spoken flatly and matter-of-factly, startled the visitors.

Jeff looked narrowly at the man. "Why? What's the story?"

"Story?" Bogart rose to his feet, shook his shaggy white head and glared at Jeff. "Surely, you must have heard of the tragic death, last June, of Pamela's sister, Corinne?"

"No, I didn't. I was in China at the time. I've been home less than a week. What happened to Corinne?"

"Corinne was shot through the heart."

"I'm sorry, Mr Bogart" – Jeff rose to his feet – "this is out of my line. If Miss Bogart were being held for ransom by Mexican bandits, or Argentine insurrectionists, I might be able to do something. Murder, *per se*, is police business and I leave it to them. Come along, Smitty."

"Wait!" Bogart slapped the desk top. "Wait until you hear what I have to say."

"There is nothing—"

"Corinne was shot with a silver bullet, in the close company of seven friends and relatives. The case has never been solved. The only clue is the bullet that killed her."

Jefferson Hunter sat down again. He nodded to Smitty, who flipped open his notebook on the corner of the desk.

"Mr Bogart," Jeff spoke slowly, "why are you apprehensive about Pamela? Skip the details about Corinne."

Bogart sank back in his chair and looked questioningly at the younger man. He opened a mahogany humidor, extracted a cigar and jammed it into his mouth. He glanced annoyedly at Smitty and dropped the cigar back in the humidor. Reaching into the ash tray, he picked up a large butt and clamped it between his teeth.

Jeff rose, flipped his lighter and held its flame to the end of the cigar.

"Pamela" – Bogart drew contentedly – "is about to announce her engagement. It is customary in our family for the oldest member to give the dinner at which an engagement is to be announced. It doesn't mean much any more. The family is reduced to Pam and me. However, she has set her heart on following the tradition."

"Why shouldn't she?"

"Because, at a similar dinner I gave for Corinne and Professor Collins last year, Corinne died. I don't want to risk a repetition of that. Incidentally, that was Professor Michael Collins, the seismologist, who just left."

"Why should there be a repetition?"

"No reason at all, except that Corinne's death has never been cleared up."

"What do you expect me to do? Clear it up?"

"No. I just want you to see that murder doesn't happen again. Pam is obstinate and insists that I have the dinner. She is very headstrong, very willful. Er . . . I believe, Hunter, that you are acquainted with Pam?"

"I—Yes, I've met her. When do you plan to have the dinner, Mr Bogart?"

"Tonight"

"That doesn't give me much time to take precautionary steps."

Jeff stooped over and picked up the slip of paper that had

fluttered to the floor from Smitty's notebook. He glanced at the hurriedly scrawled message advising him not to get involved, and handed the sheet back to his assistant.

"Mr Bogart" – Jeff smiled at the older man – "I'm afraid I can't handle this. It's entirely out of my line. I suggest the police. I'm sure—"

"Humph! Pamela said you wouldn't be interested unless there was a whopping big fee in it."

"Did she say that?" Jeff's cheeks burned.

"Yes."

"Then count me in. I'll be here for dinner tonight." He rose to his feet.

"Eh? Here for dinner! That will never do, young man. The guests are all my friends. I . . . er . . . couldn't ask them to mingle socially with an . . . er – employee!"

Chairs scraped backward. Smitty snapped shut his notebook and collided with Jeff in the library doorway.

"Wait! Just a minute!" Wendell Bogart's voice sounded behind them.

The big house rumbled from the slamming of the heavy front door.

"Why did you lay yourself open, Jeff? I told you to turn it down cold."

"Shut up!" Jeff snapped, and concentrated on his driving.

Smitty was not so easily squelched. Out of the corner of his eye, he noted Jeff's flaming cheeks and clamped jaw. Smitty grinned and cleared his throat.

"I say, Jeff," he drawled, "I . . . er . . . can't have my employer driving me around like this. It just isn't being done, old man. Suppose some of the boys down at the local saw me. I'd lose face—"

Jeff Hunter's big foot stamped down on the brake. The sudden stop lifted the light Smitty from his seat. Jeff snapped open the door and rolled the astonished little man into the bushes by the roadside. He slammed the door, dropped the car in gear and headed for town.

A mile farther on, his irritation evaporated, and remorse set in. He grinned, swung the car in a sharp U-turn, and headed back to the spot where he had left Smitty. His assistant was nowhere to be seen.

A worried frown furrowed his forehead. He U-turned again, drove back into town, and parked in the restricted space before police headquarters. Running lightly up the steps, he whirled through the revolving doors and barged into the office of the chief of detectives.

Chief William Gaines was lifting the telephone to put through a call. He recradled the instrument and smiled at the intruder.

"Bill" – Jeff shook his friend's hand – "I hate to remind pals of past favors, but—"

"OK, Jeff." The chief grinned wryly. "I expected it when you tipped me off on those missing bonds. What do you want? You're not usually bashful."

"What's the story on the Corinne Bogart killing? I wasn't around when it happened. I know Pamela, and I've just met her uncle, Wendell—"

The chief grimaced in distaste. "The boss has an exaggerated view of his importance in the scheme of things. Did he tell you to use the tradesmen's entrance?"

"Not this time, but he left no doubt that we were to use it if we called again." Briefly, Jeff outlined the events of the morning.

"Off the record," the chief said, "it would be a blessing to the community if Pamela were bumped. She is one of the most beautiful girls I have ever seen, but strictly N.G."

"Didn't I say I knew her?" Jeff reminded him. "The old man said the police had no idea who had killed Corinne. Is it the other way around? Are there so many suspects—"

"Oh, no. It's not like that at all. Corinne really was different. She wasn't a bit like Pamela. The old man was telling the truth there. She was one swell person, so far as we've discovered."

"Then what happened to her?"

"She died at her own engagement party. Her coming marriage to Professor Collins was announced at dinner. The party then retired to the back terrace, just off the living room, for highballs. They were talking idly. Mike, probably dreaming of earthquakes, was twisting the dials of a portable radio. Accidentally, he shot up the volume and a swing band blared out. Everybody sort of jumped at the sudden noise."

"Then?"

"They sank back in their chairs, everyone but Corinne. She pitched forward to the terrace floor, shot through the heart by a silver bullet. The gun was never found, nor was a motive discovered. That is the official story."

"Humph!" Jeff leaned back in his chair. "I can imagine how the newspapers kicked that one around. 'What are the police doing? Is Corinne Bogart a vampire?' I can just see the headlines. I bet they gave the silver bullet a big play."

"That's right. It was pretty grim. None of the papers went so far as to mention the word 'vampire', but it was broadly hinted. Remember that Bogart, though he is out of step with the times, is still a very influential person. Very influential! We put the best detectives in the country on the case. The investigation was a blank."

"Now" – Jeff grinned – "give me the low-down. Was the shot fired when the volume rose? How close was the killer? Who had the opportunity? Who gains?"

"Whoa, Jeff! Whoa!" Chief Gaines held up his hand "We don't know definitely when the shot was fired. We don't know how close the killer was. As for opportunity, anyone there could have done it. It could even have been suicide, if the gun was taken from her hand before she fell. It's possible, but highly improbable. As for who gains, her money was divided equally between Pamela and her uncle."

"Something's rotten." Jeff glared at the chief.

"All right, Jeff, ask questions. I'll answer those I can."

"Why wasn't the shot heard?"

"Because it was fired from one of those clever, powerful little air pistols. A scrape of a chair, anything, would have covered the small pop the gun made. The radio could have done it."

"You sure it was an air pistol?"

"No question about it. We learned that from the bullet. The mark of the lands, absence of powder, smallness of caliber – All those things confirmed beyond doubt that it was fired from an air pistol."

"What about the bullet itself, Chief?"

"Ah-h-h! The bullet was a long, pointed silver one, handmade."

"Why handmade? Why silver?"

"Your guess is as good as mine. Probably a bit of sand-in-the-eye technique on the part of the murderer. So far as we know, the supernatural didn't enter into the case, except to cloud the main issues and cause us to waste a lot of time. We searched everywhere for that gun. We fine-combed the house and grounds. We tried to trace it through dealers."

"Could an outsider have killed her?"

"No. There's a ten-foot wall around the back garden. There had been a shower at sunset and there were no footprints inside or outside the wall. The servants are in the clear, too. They were all in the kitchen together. Besides having alibis, they lack motive."

"Who served the drinks?" Jeff demanded.

"Don't think we overlooked that bet. We're not exactly dumb." The chief grinned. "The first round was served by the butler as soon as the party went out to the terrace. Wendell Bogart served the second, mixing them at a portable bar in the living room. The third round had not been served. Pamela was standing in the doorway with the tray in her hands when her sister slumped forward. Everyone else was on the terrace within ten feet of her."

"Could" – Jeff fixed his eyes on the chief – "could Pamela have fired that shot before she stepped into the doorway with the tray of drinks?"

"Now, Jeff, you're getting on dangerous ground. I'm going to tell you one more thing, then this conference ends. And, for cripes sake, keep it under your hat!"

"I promise. Shoot!"

"Pamela could have fired the gun if her sister happened to turn toward the room where she was, and if she was shot at least five seconds before she pitched forward. If Pamela wasn't a Bogart, we'd have dragged her in and questioned her until we were satisfied she hadn't done it. The consensus of the experts is that there is not enough evidence to warrant indicting her, much less making her stand trial. Now, beat it, Jeff, and take your grinning watchdog with you."

"My watchdog?"

Jeff turned and met the blank stare of his assistant. "How did you get here?"

Smitty brushed an imaginary speck of dust from the sleeve of his seersucker suit, and looked dumbfounded at his employer. "Me? How did I get here?"

"You heard me. You didn't walk back that quick."

"Hardly. A very charming young lady drove me to town. A very, very charming girl. She was suffering under the misapprehension that you no longer cared for her, Jeff. Of course, I speedily corrected that impression. On the contrary, I assured her that you still cared very much."

"Smitty" – Jeff grabbed the little man, and his voice grated – "for your sake, I hope that what I'm thinking is true. Who was the charming young lady?"

"Miss Pamela Bogart. What's the matter, Jeff? She was very happy to learn you still cared for her. So much so that she said to tell you that, under the circumstances, she would not permit her engagement to be announced this evening. You all right, Jeff?"

II

"Where are we going?" Smitty asked when they were again in the convertible.

"We're going to call on Pamela Bogart and you're going to tell her you had some other girl in mind. Understand?"

"Me? Me, a self-confessed liar in the eyes of Pamela Bogart? Oh, no, Jeff!"

"Oh, yes, you are!"

Smitty reached into his inside coat pocket and pulled out a folded paper. He looked at his watch, noted the time and scribbled it, together with the date, at the top of the page. He handed the folded sheet to Jeff.

"What's this? Listen, Smitty," Jeff said, after hurriedly scanning the paper, "you can't resign! I've got your contract. You—"

"There's nothing in the contract that calls for me to be dumped, out of a moving car."

"The car wasn't moving. It had stopped, and you fell out, with more or less urging."

"Ah-h-h! There is nothing about urging in the contract."

"OK. You win. I'll see Pamela myself."

"She has an apartment in the Normandy." Smitty grinned at his boss, took back his resignation, erased the date and time, and replaced it in his pocket. "I told her you'd probably come to see her right away. She said she'd be waiting for you. Will you need a bodyguard?"

Jeff didn't answer. He clamped his jaws, swung his big car into the traffic and pressed down the accelerator. Five minutes later, he parked it before the large apartment hotel.

When a uniformed maid admitted them to Apartment 4C, Smitty was at his heels.

Pamela Bogart laid aside the magazine she was reading, and jumped to her feet, silver bracelets jangling on her arms. Her smile died when she saw the expression on Jeff's face. A puzzled frown replaced it.

Jeff didn't speak at first. He studied the diminutive brunette before him. His keen eyes took in her perfect form, the dark curls and wide gray eyes. They lingered on her mouth, beautifully shaped, but with a cruel curve at the corners. "She hasn't changed a bit," was his conclusion.

"Hello, Jeff. I was under the impression that you were willing to let bygones be bygones. I understood from Mr Smith—"

"Smitty was sore with me for dumping him out on the road. I'll never change my opinion of you, Pam. Don't ever forget it. I only came here to set you straight. You—"

"All right! You've had your say. Now, get out." She walked toward the door.

"Why did you kill your sister, Pam?"

Pamela Bogart spun on her heel and looked up at Jeff. Her eyes narrowed to slits, studying him.

"What do you mean?" she snapped, between whitening lips.

"You haven't answered me."

"An answer isn't necessary. I didn't kill Corinne. She killed herself."

"How could she? What became of the gun?"

"I don't know what happened to the gun. But I do know she killed herself. Maybe uncle, or someone else, picked it up and hid it. I know I didn't."

"It wasn't your uncle, because he's afraid you might be killed."

"I don't think there's any danger of that."

"About that I don't know. Certainly, there must be a great many people who would like to kill you."

Jeff turned away from her and picked up an engraved silver cigarette box from the coffee table. Idly, he turned it around in his hand, examining the workmanship.

Pamela Bogart watched him warily. When he set down the box, she spoke again:

"Jeff, I'm going to tell you something. Something I was ashamed to tell even the police."

"From the things I've known you to do, I can't imagine your being ashamed of anything."

"You didn't let me finish. I was ashamed to tell the police that Corinne had been running around with a married man. She went with him on business trips, and visited him in a cabin in the hills. When he grew tired of her, she was heartbroken. The engagement to Mike was only a gesture. She couldn't go through with it. That's why she killed herself. Don't you believe me?"

"No. I don't believe a word of truth ever crossed your lips. Come on, Smitty!" He moved toward the door.

"Jeff! There was one night you believed me, loved me, even, a little. The night Myrna Dalton—"

Jeff slammed the door behind him.

"Jeff," Smitty said, when they were again in the car, "I'm sorry. I didn't know you hated her."

"OK, Smitty. I asked for it."

"Jeff, will you tell me something?"

"What?"

"Why was Corinne shot with a silver bullet?"

"To kill her."

"I know that, but why silver? Aren't silver bullets used to kill vampires?"

"She wasn't a vampire. Now, be quiet. I want to think."

"Just one more question. Where are we going?"

"To the bank, the National Trust."

Five minutes after their arrival, they were shown into the office of the president. He greeted them pleasantly, dismissed his secretary, and leaned back in his chair. "What can I do for you, Mr Hunter?"

"Do you know anything about the Bogarts' financial setup?"

The banker didn't answer immediately. When he did speak, he talked slowly, as if he were carefully choosing each word.

"Yes. But there are some things I am not at liberty to tell you without a court order or without my clients' consent. The Bogarts have accounts here, and we have handled the various estates. I think we'd get along better if you asked me questions. I'll answer those I can."

"Fair enough. Smitty, tell him what we know. He can confirm it for us."

"Herbert Bogart" – words rattled from Smitty's lips – "father of Wendell and Herbert, Jr., left the vast war speculator's fortune he accumulated in 1914–19, divided equally between his two sons and their heirs. Wendell Bogart received his half, is the administrator of the estate and is trustee for his niece's share. The two orphan daughters of Herbert, Jr., inherited their father's share. The principal was tied up until their thirtieth birthdays."

"That is substantially correct," the banker agreed. "Miss Corinne Bogart died, leaving her share to be divided between her uncle and her sister. There was also a comparatively small bequest to Professor Collins whom she intended to marry, for earthquake research."

"Pamela's trust is still handled by her uncle?" Jeff asked.

"That's right. She gets the interest. I can't imagine how she manages to spend it."

"There is no question about the trust? Wendell Bogart couldn't tamper with it?"

"Oh, absolutely not." The banker appeared horrified at the suggestion. "The bonding company and the courts see to that."

"Can you tell me how Wendell Bogart stands today, financially? I understand he's shaky."

"I couldn't do that, Mr Hunter, without Bogart's permission. Naturally, he, like the rest of us, was hit hard in '29, and again during the recent war."

"I see. Then there is no question in your mind that if Pamela Bogart lives to reach her thirtieth birthday, she will be given every penny of her inheritance?"

"If she lives until her thirtieth birthday, I have no doubt but that Pamela will receive her full inheritance, according to law."

"That's good enough for me. Thanks. Now, one other thing. I understand you're quite a collector of pewter and silver. Could you tell me which silversmith marks his work with a die shaped like a flying bat?"

"Yes" – the banker spoke without hesitation – "a silversmith who calls himself John Stevens, at 72 Water Street. Personally, I'd steer clear of him."

"Why."

"He's a gypsy from one of those Balkan countries. A very clever fellow. Unfortunately, 'sterling' has several meanings for him."

"Thanks. I don't intend to buy anything from him."

"Why all the questions about silver?" Smitty demanded, when they were in the car heading for the water front.

"You'll find out." Jeff grinned. "Here's Water Street now. 72 is on the corner. Coming in?"

A small, dark gypsy looked up from the spoon, set in a bowl of pitch, on which he was engraving an elaborate floral design. He set his work aside and stepped to the counter. "What can I do for you?"

"Did you ever make anything like this?" Jeff sketched a long-nosed bullet, keeping his drawing to actual dimensions.

"What is it? What is it supposed to be?" The man's black eyes were filled with suspicion.

"I don't know. Maybe the tip of a hatpin, or maybe an ornament. I haven't any idea. But it looks like a bullet to me Anyway, it was made of silver."

"I don't remember ever making anything like that. Say, weren't the police around asking the same question about a year ago?"

"I wouldn't be surprised if they were," Jeff agreed. "My client is very interested in it now. He'd pay a lot of money to know who ordered it made."

"I wouldn't know anything about it." Stevens' teeth flashed.

"Sure? It might have been an umbrella ferule or a swagger stick tip. Sure you've never made anything like it?"

The gypsy's eyes narrowed. "Positive."

"I'll tell you what we'll do," Jeff said. "You look back over your old records and see if you can't find the name of the person for whom you made something similar to this. Not a bullet, of course, but something like it. Then give me a ring." Jeff slid one of his cards into the outstretched palm. "If your records tell you anything, we'll talk price later. Right?"

"I'm positive I've never made anything like it, but I'll look through my records to make sure. One's memory sometimes plays odd tricks."

"Isn't it the truth?" Jeff said grimly. "Come on, Smitty."

Jeff circled the block. A policeman eyed the yellow convertible suspiciously when Jeff slid to a stop beside a fire plug. The car was markedly out of place among the rumbling trucks and horse-drawn drays of the water front.

"Smitty, I want you to hang around a while. Unless I'm badly mistaken, Stevens is the man who made that bullet. I think he's going to have a caller very soon."

"Right. There was a bar across the street from 72. I'll wait there. What do you want me to do?"

"Just keep your eyes open. Notice who goes in. If you don't know them, get the license number of the car or the cab they arrive in. If you can't do that, get a good look at them."

"OK. I'll call in when something happens."

Back in his office, Jefferson Hunter relaxed in his chair, running over in his mind the salient points concerning the death of Corinne Bogart. Acting on impulse, he picked up the telephone and dialed the medical examiner's number.

"Dr Marshall, this is Jeff Hunter. Could you tell me who performed the autopsy on Corinne Bogart? She was shot with a silver bullet about a—"

"I remember it very well, Mr Hunter. I did the p. m. myself. What did you want to know?"

"I have an investigation on hand that indirectly ties in with Corinne Bogart's death. I've heard various rumors about her running around with a married man, going away with him on business trips, that sort of thing."

"Absolutely untrue. The police were given the same story in an anonymous letter. I believe someone advanced the theory that the girl committed suicide. There was absolutely nothing to it. The girl was straight as a die. She led a normal, wholesome life."

"I see. Thanks, doctor."

The phone rang as soon as it was hung up.

"Jeff, this is Smitty. Guess who just walked into Stevens' shop?"

"Pamela Bogart."

"Aw-w! How did you know?"

"A little bird told me. Is she still in the shop?"

"Yes."

"She and Stevens will have a lot to discuss. Grab a cab and come back here."

"Jeff," Smitty demanded, when he entered the office ten minutes later, "do you really think she killed her sister?"

"I'm practically sure of it. The suicide story is an out-and-out fake. I don't believe anyone on the terrace could have shot Corinne without someone seeing them. I'm betting she was shot from inside the house, probably by Pamela when she was getting the drinks. It has to be that way."

Smitty shook his head. "I can't believe a girl like Pamela Bogart would kill anyone, much less her own sister. She's so little and pretty. I'm sure you're wrong."

"I'm not wrong, Smitty. Try to figure out what she could have done with the gun. Say she shot Corinne from the living room, picked up the tray of drinks, and stepped to the door just as her sister fell. That's not impossible. What could she have done with the gun in the meantime?"

"There wouldn't be much time. The only thing she could have done with it," the practical Smitty said, "was to hide it on herself, or drop it in a chair seat – something like that. But she never killed anybody, Jeff."

"Don't bet on it. I wonder how long it was between the time of the actual shooting and the time the police began their search for the gun. I should have asked Bill Gaines. Call the chief and ask him, Smitty."

The door of the office swung inward and Chief Gaines stepped into the room. Jeff and Smitty gasped at the sudden appearance of the man they were about to call. The chief's face wore a look of grim determination. Without speaking, he walked to the center of the office.

"Speak of the devil!" Jeff recovered himself. "Smitty was just going to phone you, Bill. What's the matter?"

"Get your hat, Jeff. You, too, Smitty. We're going downtown. We've a few questions for you boys to answer."

"About what?"

"About murder, Jeff," the chief answered gravely.

"Whose?"

"John Stevens, a silversmith. You attracted the attention of one of my men when you stopped your yellow car near a fire plug. In criminal investigations, Jeff, never make yourself conspicuous."

"But—"

"That isn't all. Stevens was clutching one of your business cards in his hand when he was shot."

An assistant from the DA's office waved Jeff and Smitty to chairs, and concluded his conversation with Mike Collins. After the seismologist left, he turned to Jeff.

"You know why you're here?"

"Yes."

"I'd like an account of your visit to Stevens."

Quickly, Jeff outlined his call, omitting only the mention of the bullet.

"As I see it," the assistant summed up, "you called on Stevens in an effort to trace the manufacturer of an article for one of your clients. You admit giving him the card he was holding. The name of your client, and the nature of the article, you refuse to tell me on ethical grounds. Is that your story?"

"That's it." Jeff nodded.

"Then why," the assistant asked him, "did you station your watchdog in a saloon across the street?"

With apparent candor, Jeff answered quickly, "To check on Stevens' visitors."

The young man's eyebrows shot upward. "Were there visitors between the time you two left and the time the body was found?"

Jeff nodded to Smitty. "Tell him, chum."

"One," Smitty said reluctantly.

"Who?"

"I'd rather not say. I'm sure she had nothing to do with the killing of Stevens."

"She? Uh-huh! It's up to the police to decide whether or not she had anything to do with the killing. Who was it, Mr Smith?"

"I . . . I refuse to say! Ladies' names—"

The DA's man smiled grimly. "Maybe you'll think differently after a stay in jail."

The little man turned hopeful eyes to his boss. "He can't do that to me, can he, Jeff? You could get me out on a habeas corpus writ? Won't I have to be charged with something?"

Jeff grinned. "Don't worry, you'll be charged. Probably with being an accessory after the fact, and held without bail. The weather is getting warmer, and I haven't heard that the jail is air-conditioned."

Smitty gulped and looked at the assistant. The DA's man nodded in agreement.

"Don't be a fool, Smitty," Jeff warned. "Tell him. It will only be a matter of time before someone else comes forward. She's too much woman to pass the whole street unnoticed."

The ringing of the telephone interrupted them. The young assistant picked up the instrument and listened intently. Then he spoke:

"Who? You'd better come right to headquarters, miss. It's fortunate you called when you did. I have a man in my office now" – he glanced at Smitty – "who saw you enter the shop, and who can identify you." He hung up the receiver.

"That was Pamela Bogart?" Smitty's eyes flew open. "She's coming down here?"

Jeff and the DA's man exchanged amused glances.

"Mr Smith" – the assistant leaned forward – "was there anyone with Miss Bogart? I should have asked her. What time did she enter the shop? When did she leave?"

"There was no one with her." Smitty shook his head sadly. "She entered at a minute or two before noon. The whistles were blowing when I left the saloon. I didn't wait until she came out."

"Thanks. You two can go, now, Mr Hunter, I'm asking for a ruling on your so-called ethical grounds in refusing to answer. Don't leave town. I may need to get in touch with you."

Jeff nodded. "I wouldn't mind telling you," he said. "In fact, I'd like to. It's just a matter of principle. I'll be glad to hear the result of the ruling, win or lose."

"You'll hear. Don't worry."

"Another thing, will you tell me what Professor Collins was doing here? I mean, assuming his presence was connected with this case?"

"Yes. Though if you waited, you could read it in the evening papers. Professor Collins found Stevens. The silversmith does quite a bit of work for him, making and repairing scientific instruments."

"Thanks. Come on, Smitty."

"Now, where?" Smitty demanded, when they were again in the yellow car.

"To see Professor Collins. Don't take it so hard, little man. Reconcile yourself to the fact that Pamela killed Stevens. If you didn't have a closed mind, you'd have realized it long ago."

"Says you!" Smitty snapped. "If you didn't have a closed mind, you'd see Collins killed him, and then pretended that he was already dead. It adds up—"

"To zero! Smitty, you're a darn good accountant. You can always tell me who swiped the stamp when a corporation's ten-million-dollar balance sheet is three cents out, but murder investigations are different. You don't understand them. Look what you did back there."

"What did I do?" demanded Smitty belligerently.

"Nothing very important. They would have found out it was Pamela Bogart, sooner or later. Your handing it to them on a platter just made it easier."

"Jeff!" Smitty grabbed his boss' arm. "Wasn't that call on the level?"

"Of course it wasn't. If you'd been paying attention, you'd have seen the DA's man press a button under the edge of the desk. It rang a telephone bell."

"Why didn't you tell me, Jeff?"

"Because I like you, Smitty. Besides, I need you in my work, other work than this sort of thing, which, incidentally, I am indulging in only because I'd like to see Pamela Bogart get a little of the punishment that's due her. Here's the college."

The car coasted to a stop before the science building. Jeff and Smitty followed an attendant who led them down into the sub-basement where the seismograph recording instruments were located. Professor Michael Collins rose from behind a desk and came to meet them, with hand outstretched.

"Sorry I wasn't introduced by Mr Bogart this morning." The professor smiled. "He's funny that way. My first name is Mike."

"Hello, Mike." Jeff shook hands. "This is Smitty. Mr Z. Z. Smith, my assistant."

"Hello, Smitty," Mike said. "Are you the Z. Z. Smith who worked out the simplified percentage tables?"

"Why, yes. Yes, I am. You know, I haven't thought of those for years. Where did you learn about them?"

"I'm naturally interested in anything mathematical. A friend of mine tipped me off to them. I've found the tables useful in long-distance earthquake computations. Just a minute, I have one here. I—"

"If you'll forgive me, Mike," Jeff said, "you and Smitty can carry it on later. I've an investigation on my hands that has to be made fast."

"Sorry. I let my enthusiasm run away with me. We'll get together later, Smitty. What can I do for you, Jeff?"

"They tell me you were engaged to Corinne Bogart, and were present the night she was murdered. Would you mind giving me your story of that evening?"

Mike Collins told the same story they had heard from Chief Gaines.

When he finished, Jeff asked, "How much time would you say elapsed between the actual shooting and the search for the gun?"

"I don't know exactly. An hour, or an hour and a half. After Corinne was shot, we were pretty excited. I carried her upstairs to her bedroom."

"You mean, you actually moved the body?" Smitty asked, aghast. "Even I know better than to do that."

"Yes, I knew better, too. But Mr Bogart had already lifted her from the floor. I couldn't see where moving her again would make any difference."

"Then what happened?"

"Someone called the doctor. He didn't arrive until fifteen or twenty minutes later. He pronounced her dead, then he came down to the library and had a drink. Finally, he asked what was keeping the police."

"And what was detaining the police?"

"No one had called them. Everyone thought someone else had done it. They were called then, but I guess it was at least an hour after the shooting before they got there. First a radio car, and eventually the men from homicide."

"So anyone could have disposed of the gun in the meantime."

"Yes." Mike nodded. "Anyone could. The case was badly handled. Of course, losing Corinne had stunned me. I guess, among us all, we messed it up"

"Where was everyone before the search began?"

"I haven't any idea. I can only answer for myself. I carried Corinne upstairs and stayed with her until the doctor threw a sheet over her face. Then I came down to the library and waited until the police came. Everyone was moving around."

"I see. Mike, what is your candid opinion of Wendell Bogart?"

Mike grinned sheepishly, and began polishing his glasses. "He's all right, I guess. Though he is apt to forget he lives in a democracy."

Jeff watched the seismologist closely. "Was Bogart ever poor?"

"No, I don't believe he was. His father patented a number of appliances for use in filling stations – self-coiling hoses, automatic dispensers, fire extinguishers and things like that. I don't mean to imply that Mr Bogart isn't smart. He is. He has his own personal workshop and laboratory in the basement of his home. He's made improved working models of all the patented devices upon which the original Bogart fortune was founded."

"I see. Mike, how are you fixed financially?"

Mike Collins's eyes widened. "Why, I'm very well off, Jeff. I have about ten thousand dollars set aside and my job. My work is well endowed, thanks to Corinne. I should say I'm very well off indeed."

"What is your salary?" Jeff asked. "You don't have to answer that one, Mike. You can tell me where to go."

"I don't mind telling you. Three thousand a year. Out of that, I save three or four hundred."

"Thank you very much, Mike. Come along, Smitty."

"What do you think of him, Jeff?" Smitty asked, when they were back in the office.

"He's A-1 in my book. I hope you appreciate your salary now!"

"Yes, Jeff, I do appreciate it. Why else do you think I work for you?" Smitty grinned.

"I'll be damned! You're certainly frank! I'd hope you liked me. Do you still think Mike killed Corinne Bogart or John Stevens?"

"Oh, he couldn't have done it, Jeff. He's much too honest."

"Yes, he's honest. He's also read your simplified interest table."

"That has nothing to do with it," Smitty snapped.

The ringing of the telephone interrupted their conversation.

Automatically, Smitty answered, and shoved the extension to Jeff.

"This is Pamela Bogart, Jeff. I must see you, alone. It's important! Jeff, I'm afraid. I'm in the bar at the Normandy. Please come!"

"You've nothing to be afraid of, beautiful," Jeff taunted. "Gals like you seldom burn for murder. The gallant juries always compromise on life imprisonment. You'll be out in about twelve years, if you ever go in."

"Don't be so hateful, Jeff. Please come. If it's a fee you want, I'll buy your time."

Jeff slammed down the phone.

Smitty smiled. "You've got a blind spot about her, Jeff."

"Who else could have committed the murders?"

"There were about eight people at the dinner. Why pick on her?"

"Listen, Smitty. The police aren't stupid. They handle hundreds of murder investigations. They know what they're doing. Occasionally, they louse up a case, but you can bet they didn't louse up this one. It's too important. They've eliminated all suspects but Pamela."

"And the possibility of suicide," Smitty reminded him. "You have to consider that."

"Nuts! The police don't seriously consider it. They don't actually say Pamela's the murderer, but they don't offer any other solution. I have no doubt that the police consider this an unproved murder rather than an unsolved one."

"Jeff, do me a favor. Please!" Smitty looked at his boss with pleading eyes that reminded Jeff of a faithful hound.

"Here's where I become a sucker again. What is it, Smitty?"

"Go see Pamela. Try to keep an open mind like you do when we make a commercial investigation. Just this once, Jeff. You listened to me on the Wagner oil deal and I was right."

"You win, Smitty. I'll see her. Stick around until I get back."

III

Pamela Bogart looked up and smiled when Jeff entered the Normandy bar. She slid closer to the inside of the bench in the booth she was occupying alone. Jeff ignored the invitation and sat opposite her.

"You don't look like a person who has just shot and killed a man," he opened the conversation curtly. "How did you get out so soon?"

"I haven't killed anybody. Why shouldn't they release me? Why should I kill a man I buy my jewelry from? My lawyer explained all that to—"

"So you took your lawyer down with you?"

"Naturally. Jeff, why must you be so hateful?"

"Because I don't like murderers. You saw me examine that silver box. You knew I was looking for the maker's mark. When Stevens called you and told you I had offered to buy information about the bullet, you lost no time in putting him out of the way. Probably he had been blackmailing you, anyway. Did you drop the gun you used into the harbor?"

"I didn't have anything to do with it. I hardly know the man. Why should he make a silver bullet? Why silver?"

"To kill Corinne with. You should know. You ordered it made."

"Jeff, I didn't. I'll admit I didn't like Corinne. She was a prude, always so careful, so economical. But one doesn't kill one's sister for that sort of thing."

"Maybe not. But a truckload of dough isn't to be sneezed at. Your income increased fifty percent at her death."

"You're hateful, Jeff. But that's not what I want to talk about. I'm frightened. I don't want to get married. I'm afraid of marriage."

Jeff leaned back in the booth and roared with laughter. "You're afraid. But marriage has nothing to do with your fears."

Pamela twisted the stem of the filled cocktail glass in slender fingers.

"Can't you forget Myrna Dalton, Jeff? Didn't you ever hear from her after you sent her the statement you made me write?"

Jeff didn't answer. He rose to his feet and towered over the girl sitting opposite. The lids of his eyes dropped. A small muscle in his clamped jaw throbbed. He glared at Pamela Bogart.

"I'm warning you, Pam" – he spoke loudly in an even, harsh tone – "if I ever hear you mention Myrna Dalton's name again, I'll be tempted to kill you."

Several men lounging against the bar looked toward the booth. The big bouncer came from behind the cashier's cage and stood watching Jeff.

"You hung a pretty frame on me, Pam."

"I don't see what the fuss was all about," Pam answered defiantly. "After all, Myrna was no saint, either."

"You little liar!" Jeff didn't lower his voice.

Pamela's lips tightened, and the color drained from her face. She splashed the contents of her glass into Jeff's face.

Jeff's big hand slashed blindly across her mouth and the back of her head hit the booth with a thump.

Pamela screamed. "Mike Collins will kill you for that!"

"Why Mike?"

"Because he's the man I'm going to marry! That's why!"

"Listen, bud" – the bouncer spun Jeff around – "I'm gonna slug you for—"

All the pent-up hatred Jeff was feeling, all the frustrated urge to kill was in the blow he hung on the bouncer's unguarded chin. The big man sagged, and Jeff walked unmolested out of the bar.

Back in the office, Smitty tried to pump him for the details of his meeting with Pamela. Jeff kept quiet. He leaned on his desk and attempted to concentrate on a long commercial report dealing with the acquiring of a string of air strips in the Brazilian jungles.

But his mind wandered to Mike Collins, trying to understand why Mike was going to marry Pamela after having been engaged to Corinne. Could it be money? Love? None of the conventional reasons seemed plausible.

The sharp ringing of the telephone was a death knell to further logical thinking.

"It's Mike Collins," Smitty said.

Jeff picked up the extension and nodded to Smitty to stay on the line.

"Jeff Hunter speaking. What can I do for you, Mike?"

"Pamela just phoned me. She's been telling me a strange tale, Jeff."

"I'm listening," Jeff said grimly, and watched as Smitty took the words down in shorthand.

"She told me the police had questioned her about the killing of Stevens, that silversmith. Pam buys a lot of stuff from him."

"Mike," Jeff snapped, "did she tell you she had seen me in the Normandy bar?"

"No, she didn't. But she did mention she had just left the bar, and was in her apartment. I wonder—"

"What are you wondering, Mike?"

"Whether she had asked you to come to dinner tonight and you had refused."

"She didn't ask me."

"Jeff, she told me she's frightened, that someone is after her. That they told the police she was in Stevens' place just before he was killed."

"Come to the point, Mike."

"She asked me to try to persuade you to come to dinner this evening. I realize it's almost five now, and cocktails will be served at six. I know it's late to ask it, Jeff, but I wish you'd come. Pamela's frightened. She said she'd feel safer if you were there. Won't you come, Jeff?"

"No. Wendell Bogart very pointedly told me I was not wanted, that I was *persona non grata* for social occasions."

"Don't mind the old boy, Jeff. Pam said she'd take care of him, and he'd be glad to see you. His bark is worse than his bite."

"Maybe so, but I don't like barks, I'm staying away."

"Jeff, I do want you to come. Is there anything I could do to make you change your mind? Pamela mentioned offering you a fee, but I realize that's ridiculous. Isn't there any way I can persuade you?"

Jeff didn't answer. He read the slip of paper Smitty pushed across the desk to him, "Go." He nodded to Smitty, leaned back in his chair and dropped his feet on the desk top.

"Mike, I'd like to tell you a little story. Before the war, I was engaged to Myrna Dalton. It was the only serious love affair of my life. I went to her home for a weekend house party, just before her unit sailed for England. The first night, most of the crowd were tired and went to bed early. Three other fellows and myself sat up in the library playing poker until near dawn."

"I know how it is," Mike said.

"We'd been drinking, but not too much. I was dead tired when I climbed into bed. There had been a long drive there, the lateness of the hour, and the strain of the card game. I must have gone to sleep the minute my head hit the pillow."

"I should imagine you did."

"Pamela Bogart was one of the party. She was the first to wake next morning, and she promoted some silly idea of dragging everyone out of bed and dumping them into the swimming pool. The girls bore down on each room in turn, making a game of it."

"I've been through the same thing," Mike sympathized.

"When the whole party pounced into my room, they found it strewn with feminine apparel. As an added touch, there was an extra pillow on the bed with the imprint of a head. Someone had sneaked into my room while I was asleep and planted the stuff. Myrna was badly cut up about it, wouldn't listen to my explanation."

"I can understand her feeling. But what are you driving at, Jeff?"

"Pamela Bogart was the girl who planted that evidence. She did it for pure meanness. I didn't get any proof that she did it until much later."

The line was silent for a long time. Then Mike's voice came over the wire:

"I see. I'm sorry, Jeff."

"If you still want me to come to that party tonight, I'll come after dinner – say, about seven thirty. But you'll have to tell me why you're marrying Pamela, Mike. You're one of the last people in the world I'd expect to marry her!"

Smitty looked at his boss with open mouth. He reread the words he had written, as if he couldn't believe them. He, too, hung on the line, waiting for Mike's answer.

"I'll tell you, Jeff, and then I don't want to discuss it again. I know what Pamela is. I can well believe the story you've told me. But the part you don't understand is that I loved Corinne. I'll never love another girl. Pam is – well, she sort of looks like Corinne."

"What do her looks have to do with it?"

"I guess we professors aren't very practical. I'm marrying Pam on the chance that our children would be like Corinne. That's all there is to it, Jeff."

"You've considered the possibility that she might walk out on you and take the children with her, bring them up as replicas of herself?"

"Yes, I've considered that. She couldn't do that to me. My life is an open book. There isn't a court in the land that—"

"Oh, come down to earth, Mike!" Jeff snapped. "She has over a million dollars, you have ten thousand. You couldn't begin to defend the appeals."

"Oh, come, Jeff. You don't mean to insinuate that the courts are crooked?"

"Of course I don't. I just wanted to point out that by the time you could regain custody over the children, they would have passed beyond their formative years—"

"There's no use going into that. It's too late now. I've committed myself. You will stop in for highballs after dinner, then?"

"I'll be there."

Jeff hung up the phone and looked at Smitty, who shook his head sadly.

"I wouldn't have believed Pamela was like that. Imagine Mike marrying her for any such reason!"

"I can't."

"What did you say, Jeff?"

"I said I can't imagine Mike's marrying her, for that or any other reason. There's a lot of funny things going on. I wish you could come along to help keep an eye on things tonight."

"I've considered it. There are plenty of large trees in and outside of the wall, Jeff. There's one in the back that would be easy to climb."

"So?"

"Well, I imagine they'll sit on the terrace after dinner. I could climb one of the trees and keep an eye on things with night glasses. I think I'd see more that way than if I were actually on the terrace."

"OK. Make your own arrangements, Smitty."

"Right."

"Tell Chief Gaines what we're going to do. I don't like this setup. I can't imagine why Pam wants me there. Not to protect her, that's sure. You keep your eyes glued on her, Smitty. Don't stop watching her, no matter what happens. But that's ridiculous. Nothing's going to happen."

"I'll keep my eyes open. Er . . . Jeff, after vampires have been shot with a silver bullet, they don't come back, do they?"

"What are you talking about?"

"I was just thinking, suppose it gets real dark while I'm still in that tree – Jeff, tell me why a silver bullet was used."

"Figure it out while you're roosting on a limb," Jeff said, as he left the office.

It was seven thirty, and the guests were still at dinner when the Bogarts' butler led Jeff to the terrace off the living room, facing the large, walled-in garden.

Jeff looked about him. French windows opened from the living room. The top and both ends of the terrace were screened by a heavy, vine-covered trellis. Beyond the terrace was open lawn, broken by formal flowerbeds and a two-tiered fountain.

The furniture came under Jeff's scrutiny. It was cane, upholstered with gayly colored cushions, a settee at either end, backed against the vine-covered trellis, with eight lounge chairs spotted irregularly between them.

Jeff looked at the trees. There were dozens in and close to the garden. At each end of the terrace, large oaks rose protectingly above the house. His eyes rested on a tulip poplar that was just beyond the wall, commanding an unobstructed view of the terrace. In the failing light, he caught a glimpse of something white moving back and forth. He made an up-and-down motion with his hand, and the white speck did the same. Grinning, he thumbed his nose at the spot.

Jeff turned at the sound of footsteps inside the living room. Pamela, between her uncle and Mike Collins, led the procession through the French window. Bogart nodded curtly.

"Oh, Jeff, look!" The girl ran to him, extending her hand. Jeff paid a pretty compliment to the modest diamond ring she was wearing.

"Aren't you going to congratulate me?" she asked, and winked at Mike.

"I hope you'll be very happy. But more important, I hope that you'll make Mike happy. He's a swell guy, Pam."

She bit her lips and winced. For the first time, Jeff noticed that her mouth was slightly swollen. For a moment, he was sorry he had struck her. At her next words, he wished he had broken her neck.

"It's just as well, Jeff, that you never married Myrna Dalton. She wasn't the girl you thought her."

"Pamela!" Wendell Bogart called. "Come and sit beside your old uncle, here on the settee."

The girl spun on her heel and crossed to the far end of the terrace, smiling back triumphantly over her shoulder at Jeff.

Mike Collins caught Jeff's arm and gave it a sympathetic squeeze. "Come on, Jeff. Meet the others."

The two other couples, Mr and Mrs Frederick Marston and Mr and Mrs Donald Wellington, were old friends of the family. They murmured the usual acknowledgments. Jeff quickly lost interest in them. They were obviously ill at ease, for they had attended the fatal dinner of the year before. Both men showed the effects of the strain, and had had more than their share of alcoholic stimulants. The two women stole nervous glances at their wrist watches.

The butler served tall highballs. The small talk was carefully kept in bounds. Mrs Marston tried to draw Jeff out, but his obvious absorption quickly discouraged her. She turned to Mike, and started him talking about earthquakes.

Pamela and her uncle were carrying on a low conversation between themselves. Pam laughed a good bit, and darted occasional looks of defiance at Jeff. Wendell Bogart pointedly ignored him.

"Gosh, it's hot!"

Donald Wellington's too-loud voice was like a bombshell. He was sitting alone, dabbing at his face with a large handkerchief. The highball glass in his hand was already empty.

Jeff leaned back. It was warm, but not that warm. The alcohol, the heavy dinner, and the strain were probably responsible for Wellington's discomfort.

"Don't you have an electric fan you could hook up, Wendell?" Donald Wellington demanded of his host.

"Don't bother," Mrs Wellington spoke quickly. "We'll have to be going soon."

"There's no fan available, Donald," Wendell Bogart replied. "But we could have the fountain turned on. That will cool the air some. Turn it on, please, Hunter."

"Where's the connection?" Jeff asked.

"I know where it is. I'll do it." Fred Marston rose unsteadily to his feet, crossed in front of Jeff, and stepped off the terrace.

Jeff, covertly keeping his eye on Pamela, also watched

Marston fumbling with the cover of a stop box set flush in the lawn. His fumbling fingers finally hooked the ring bolt and he gave it a hearty tug.

Pamela squealed.

Jeff looked sharply at the girl. She was pointing to Marston who had sprawled on the grass when the sticking cover loosened. He scrambled to his knees, reached into the stop box and twisted the valve.

There was a bright-yellow flash, a sharp explosion.

Jeff looked toward Pamela. The sudden glare had fuzzed his vision. The others on the terrace were staring stupidly at the bubbling fountain. Jeff blinked his eyes and brought Pamela into focus.

Slowly, yet surely, she was sliding away from her uncle toward the floor.

Wendell Bogart, with one arm laid along the top of the settee behind his niece, was staring fascinatedly toward the fountain. He didn't appear to realize that Pamela was falling.

Jeff stepped into the living room as the girl's body thudded to the flagstones. He was picking up the telephone when Mrs Wellington screamed. She was still screaming, joined by Mrs Marston, when Jeff was connected with Chief Gaines.

"It's happened, Bill," Jeff barked.

"Who?"

"Pamela herself."

"Damn! Don't let them touch anything, Jeff. We'll be there quicker than you think."

IV

"She's dead!" Mike Collins said in a flat, bewildered voice as Jeff stepped back to the terrace.

"She can't be! It's impossible!" Wendell Bogart shouted. "Lift her to the couch. No, wait. Carry her upstairs!"

"Don't move her!" Jeff warned, heading toward the group.

"Get out of my way!" Bogart shoved him aside. "A lot of help you were!"

The rise and fall of a police siren tore the quiet night. It was close by, and racing nearer.

"Don't be a fool, Bogart. The police are on their way here now. I tell you not to touch her."

"Get out of my way, you blundering idiot. My niece isn't going to lie there like a sack of meal."

Wendell Bogart stooped and picked up the girl. The police cars screamed into the driveway. Carrying her in his arms, Bogart walked slowly toward the living room. A uniformed patrolman stepped through the French door and blocked his passage.

"What's going on here? What happened?" the officer demanded. "What are you doing with that girl? What's the matter with her?"

"She's dead, Officer. I . . . I was taking her up to her bedroom."

"Put her down, mister. Here!" He indicated the settee opposite the one Pamela had shared with her uncle.

Wendell Bogart lowered his niece and straightened her rumpled clothing. Almost reverently, he pressed the lids down over her now lusterless eyes.

Jeff looked at Pamela. There were no marks of violence other than the swollen lips. To all appearances, she was a young woman dreaming, a surprising dream. Her lips were slightly parted, as if she had just been told something incredible.

More police arrived. A sergeant assumed control.

"Mr Bogart, do you have a clubroom, or some place we can put you people where you'll be out of the way?"

"There's a basement game room."

The sergeant pointed out a red-headed giant. "Murphy! Herd these people into the basement. Don't let any of them out of your sight."

Jeff followed the others into a paneled clubroom. Murphy opened the door and snapped on the lights, then followed them in and stood with his back to the door. Outside, the night was filled with screaming sirens.

Wendell Bogart, without a word to his guests, crossed to the portable bar. From beneath it, he drew out a bottle of old Scotch and poured himself half a glass.

"I could do with one of those," Fred Marston said wistfully.

Bogart ignored him, replaced the bottle and slumped into a lounge chair. He stared quietly into space. Jeff sat alone at the far corner of the room. He pulled out his notebook and began writing rapidly. Once or twice he heard his name spoken in angry tones, but he didn't raise his head. After filling several pages with neat, small script, he loosened the pages and dropped the book into his left coat pocket.

"Why don't you say something?" Wendell Bogart demanded, as Jeff's eyes met his. "Why did you kill her?"

"I didn't kill her, and you damn well know it."

"Listen, Hunter," the older man snapped, "you hated my niece! She told me what happened this afternoon in the Normandy bar. There are plenty of witnesses who heard you threaten her. Her mouth is bruised from the brutal blow you gave her."

"So what?" Jeff demanded.

"You don't deny you struck her?" Wendell Bogart lurched to his feet and swung wildly at Jeff.

"Sit down!" The alert Murphy pushed Bogart back into his chair. "Make another move like that, and I'll put you to sleep."

The clubroom door swung open. "Jefferson Hunter! Upstairs!"

Jeff rose to his feet and followed the officer to the library on the floor above. Chief Gaines, and three detectives, were seated at one end of the big mahogany table. Sitting alone at the opposite end was Smitty. Jeff pulled up a chair at his assistant's right.

"Things are a lot different than when we were here this summer." Smitty grinned.

"Yes, Smitty, they are." He patted his left coat pocket meaningly. "Bill" – Jeff turned to the chief – "what killed her?"

The chief of detectives paused a moment, considering his reply. He looked sharply at Jeff, then spoke, "The medical examiner doesn't know yet. He hasn't found a mark on her body, except the bruised mouth, and that is hours old. It sounds damned silly, but the only explanation he has ventured is the possibility of rare poison."

"It wasn't that.'

"He doesn't think it was, either. I'll have you make a statement to a stenographer in a few minutes, Jeff. But, first, is there anything you can tell me that will speed things up?"

"No, I'm afraid not. I was looking at Pamela when the flash temporarily blinded me. When my eyes focused again, she was slumping forward. What caused the explosion?"

"Haven't found out, yet. Whatever it was, it occurred in the top dish of the fountain, according to Smitty."

"That's how it was." Smitty nodded. "It was almost dark. I was watching Pamela through my glasses from the tree, when the flash blinded me. When my eyes cleared, she was falling off the settee. I continued to watch. I saw Jeff's back as he slipped into the house to phone you. No one concealed anything. I never took my eyes from that terrace until after the first policemen took over. Then I climbed down out of the tree and started toward the house. An officer grabbed me as I came to the end of the wall."

Jeff nodded and turned to the chief. "How did you get on the job so quickly?"

"I wasn't taking a chance, Jeff. When Smitty told me about the dinner tonight and that you were coming here, I sent two patrol cars to cruise the neighborhood. They were here in less than a minute after you called."

An excited young detective burst into the library, glanced around hurriedly, and handed the chief a manila envelope. Chief Gaines lifted the flap. Jeff and the others leaned forward, Smitty bumping awkwardly against Jeff.

Out of the envelope rolled a small, misshapen lead pellet.

The mushroom-shaped bullet had a bit of red coloring on the end of it. Bill Gaines drew a magnifying glass from his pocket and studied it. He passed the glass to the other detectives in turn.

"I'll be damned. An air pistol pellet. That little thing couldn't have killed her, but call Doc Marshall and tell him about it. If this hit her, there must be some mark somewhere on her body."

"Where was the slug found?" Jeff asked in a matter-of-fact tone.

The young detective answered without thinking, "Under the settee at the far end of the terrace where she—"

"Quiet!" Chief Gaines shot an irritated glance at his subordinate, and turned to Jeff. "Keep that to yourself, Hunter. We'll find the gun this time. Hawkins" – he turned to one of the detectives at the table – "begin with Jeff Hunter. Take him up to one of the bedrooms and search him. Get a stenographer to take down his statement. Keep him there until I send for him."

"What about this one?" Detective Hawkins jerked his thumb at Smitty.

"Leave him here. His eyewitness account will give us a basis for our questioning."

"Come along, Mr Hunter," Hawkins said.

"OK. Just a second." Jeff addressed the chief. "Bill, will you have your men make a thorough search of the lawn? Using a vacuum cleaner might not be a bad idea for a quick preliminary search. I've got a hunch—"

"What foolishness—"

"Bill, you owe me something," Jeff reminded him. "If I hadn't tipped you off, they would have had Pamela upstairs and it might have been the same thing over again."

"OK, Jeff."

In an upstairs bedroom, Jeff was quickly searched. He dictated his detailed statement and was questioned closely by Detective Hawkins.

As Jeff signed the final copy of the statement, Patrolman Murphy burst into the room.

"Hell has broken loose. The chief wants you in the library, Mr Hunter. Bogart's on the verge of apoplexy. Come on."

"What's happened?" Hawkins demanded.

Murphy paused to explain. "Plenty. Bogart's taking the line that his niece died of heart trouble. The chief is holding everyone incommunicado. He's within his rights on the preliminary investigation. Somehow, Bogart's lawyers have learned something's wrong here. They're burning the town getting restraining orders against a p.m., against everything. The investigation's at a standstill, outside of this house."

Bogart, seated behind his big desk in the library, reached into his humidor for a cigar as Jeff entered. He paused a second, then jammed one into his mouth, and shoved the opened humidor toward the assembled crowd.

"Mr Hunter" – he looked at Jeff – "I wish you'd try to convince these stupid policemen that Pamela died of a heart attack."

"The police aren't stupid, Mr Bogart. Why have you changed your tune? Downstairs, a while ago, you were accusing me of killing her."

"I thought you had some sense, Hunter. If she didn't die of a heart attack, you did kill her. There are plenty of witnesses who heard you threaten her. I've told the police. Granted that

Pamela played a mean trick on you, it was, after all, only a joke. It didn't justify your striking her, much less killing her."

"It was more than a joke, Mr Bogart. It was pure malice. There was something wrong with Pamela – she couldn't bear to see anyone else happy. I tried to explain that to Myrna Dalton, but there wasn't time."

"Why not?"

"She shipped out a couple of days after Pamela planted those clothes in my bedroom. I wrote to her once from China, and asked if she was ready to listen to my explanation. She wrote back that she was."

"Why didn't you send her the statement you forced from my niece? Oh, she told me about that, too!"

"I did, Mr Bogart. It would have squared things, but Myrna was killed in a bombing raid before the letter reached her."

Bogart didn't comment. Absent-mindedly, he picked up the darts that were lying on the desk before him, and threw them into the target as if continuing the around-the-clock game he had begun that morning. The feathered darts smacked into three, double three, triple three, four, double four.

Before throwing the last dart, Bogart looked at it. The needle-like steel point was broken off near the wooden body. With apparent disgust, he dropped the dart into the wastebasket.

"You should be glad Pamela's dead," Jeff continued. "She killed her own sister; she killed Stevens, the man who made the bullet with which she shot Corinne. You can't beat murder. It would have been only a matter of time until the police had sufficient evidence to ask for an indictment."

Wendell Bogart's face flamed. He jumped to his feet. "That's slander! There has never been any sort of scandal in the Bogart family. If you don't burn for murdering her, Hunter, I'll run you out of town. I'll get every penny you have or ever will have!"

Jeff turned and walked to the big table where Chief Gaines was examining the hundreds of bits of trash gathered from the lawn. He looked up wearily as Jeff approached.

"Where's Smitty?"

"Here he comes, now. I gave him permission to go into the servants' quarters to make a few phone calls from their phone. We've been using this one."

"Hello, Jeff." Smitty looked sheepishly at his boss. "You were right as usual."

"What are the answers?"

"Sodium and under hair."

"Thanks." Jeff grinned at the bewildered men around him. "That's what I thought."

"Listen," Chief Gaines protested, "this is no time to—"

"Hold it, Chief. Is there anything in this mass of stuff you gathered from the lawn that could be used for a cork stopper?"

"There's a cork." Detective Hawkins pointed to a small ordinary cork. "It was found near the fountain."

"Good. Get a chemical analysis of scrapings from its top. The analysis should show a trace of sodium. While you're about it, have the medical examiner give Pamela's hair a fine-tooth combing, close to the scalp. Where did these come from?" Jeff picked up several dried grayish-brown oak leaves, with bits of fine gray hair clinging to them.

"From the lawn at the end of the terrace. Those green oak leaves were gathered up there, too. They were beyond the trellis where Miss Bogart was sitting."

"OK. I think I've got all the answers. Mike! Mike Collins!"

"Yes, Jeff?" Mike got up from a lounge chair in a far corner of the room.

"This case is solved now, Mike. Tell the truth. Pamela's dead."

Mike nodded. "Yes, she's dead."

"What was your real reason for marrying her? Tell the truth."

"I intended to kill her. Legally, of course, by eventually trapping her into admitting she killed Corinne. But I didn't kill her tonight."

"What did you see or learn a year ago that convinced you she had killed Corinne?"

"Corinne turned in her chair and looked toward the living room a few seconds before she slumped forward. In confidence, I told the police about it, but apparently they could do nothing, so I decided to drag a confession from Pamela myself. Marrying her would give me the opportunity."

Jeff nodded. "This is what happened that night last June," he continued. "After Corinne was shot, Pamela dropped the air pistol somewhere in the living room. The present killer found it. I don't know where he concealed it for a year, but the police will find out."

"I hope," Chief Gaines said fervently. "I also hope you know what your talking about, Hunter."

Jeff went on, "Tonight, a new killer went into action. He decided to create a diversion to cover the killing. He did that by inserting a dry cork in the tip of the fountain, and placing a small piece of sodium on it. When Fred Marston turned on the water, the pressure blew the cork out of the pipe, and the piece of sodium dropped into the fountain. Sodium is very tricky. There is spontaneous combustion when it gets wet. If Fred Marston hadn't turned the fountain on, someone else would have. I nearly did it myself."

"How do you know all that?" Chief Gaines demanded. "Are you just guessing?"

"Tell them, Smitty," Jeff said.

"Upon getting Jeff's written instructions – I found them in his coat pocket – I called everyone I could think of, chemists, magicians, professors of chemistry, everyone. It didn't take long. They immediately and unanimously said 'sodium' when I mentioned water and the yellow flash. Spontaneous combustion in water and yellow flames are characteristic properties of sodium."

Jeff grinned at the chief. "Under cover of the flash, the killer pulled the trigger of the air pistol."

"Wait a minute," Chief Gaines protested. "That little pellet couldn't have more than stunned her. It—"

The shrill ringing of the telephone interrupted him. Hawkins answered it, and handed it to his superior. Chief Gaines' side of the conversation was "yes" and "no". He hung up and nodded to Jeff to continue.

"Now, the puzzling part was that there were apparently no marks on the body. I made a note of that and asked Smitty to get me the answer. Tell us, Smitty."

The little man cleared his throat. "I telephoned several famous pathologists. Their unanimous opinion was that such a thing was impossible. The nearest solution they had for the problem was the possibility that a long, thin sliver had entered a vital organ. They discounted the heart, for they felt that the point of entrance would easily have been noticed."

"What about the brain?" Chief Gaines asked.

"They said it could have entered through the ears, mouth, nose or eyes, points of entry harder to find. They also suggested making a thorough search of the scalp."

"That's where it was," the chief grinned. "Doc Marshall missed it on his preliminary examination. He found the hole hidden by hair at the base of Pamela's skull, not much bigger than a pinhole. Lodged in—"

Wendell Bogart jumped to his feet. "Did you have the gall to perform an autopsy on my niece without a reasonable suspicion of foul play?"

"We didn't," the chief said. "An X-ray of her head showed a long piece of metal like a thick needle."

"I think you'll find, Bill," Jeff explained, "that it is probably the end from the dart Bogart dropped into the wastebasket. You see, the blunt end could be forced into the head of the lead pellet. When it drove into her skull, the pellet only followed until it struck bone. The point of the dart would continue into the head."

"This is ridiculous!" Wendell Bogart sat down, puffing furiously on his cigar.

"Give us the answer, Jeff," the chief said. "Also, tell us where the gun is."

"Those leaves should tell you, chief." Jeff pointed to the dried leaves with the bits of the gray hairs clinging to them. "What would dead leaves be doing on a lawn at this time of year?"

"I'll be damned." Chief Gaines whistled. "And I was raised in the country, too. Those leaves are from an old squirrel's nest. Something must have disturbed it. Could it have been a gun?"

"That's right. You'll probably find some sort of contraption like those spring clothesline reels, or maybe something bigger, like the spring that pulls back an air hose."

"But how?"

"I think you'll find, if you examine the trellis, a spot where the air gun was wedged in the framework, screened by leaves. Under cover of the flash, the killer fired the gun, pushed it through the trellis, and let it go. A spring coil, or counterweight, jerked it up into that big oak tree. On its way up, it knocked off growing leaves and also struck an abandoned squirrel's nest."

"What's the motive, Jeff?"

"The same old one – money. You ready to confess, Bogart? You know, your fingerprints will be on the gun. You were the only person who could have shot her in that spot. That's why your arm was resting on the top of the settee, behind Pamela."

"This is ridiculous!" Bogart snorted, his face turning gray. "Whatever gave you the idea that I need money?"

"Just little things, like cutting down on cigars, and not carrying matches. That's the sort of foolish thing that normally wealthy people usually do when they try to economize. I suspected you weren't on the level when I came here early this morning. Everyone around town seems to know you're having financial troubles."

Hawkins burst into the library. "The gun's there, chief. There are beautiful prints on it, too. I'm not going to attempt to move it yet. I want to photograph that little blue steel squirrel in its nest. It was jerked up into the old squirrel's nest by a fine steel wire, and a small coil drum. It looked like a specially made contraption to do that one job. OK for me to get a hook and ladder company out here? We can get photographs from the raised ladders."

"Go to it, Hawkins," the chief said. "You ready to talk, Mr Bogart? You've got to talk if I spend the rest of the week in an outlying police station taking you apart. You have a workshop and laboratory here in the house, and you probably manufactured your own props. I'm going to have an airtight case against you before I book you. Going to talk willingly?"

A look of fear crossed the older man's face. "I should have my lawyer."

"You'll get him after you make a statement. To begin with, how did you get the gun when Corinne was murdered? Where did you hide it?"

"I found it in the chair where Pamela dropped it. Temporarily, I hid it behind the seat of the family doctor's car when he came to examine Corinne. He drove away with it. I recovered it a few days later. My first idea was to protect Pamela. The scandal—"

"Later," Jeff prompted, "you decided to cash in."

"Pamela was a murderess; she didn't deserve to live."

"Besides, you needed the money. You were afraid to dip into her trust fund because of the courts and the bonding company. You wouldn't denounce her to the police because of the publicity and also because you thought you'd be indicted, too, as an accessory after the fact."

"Something like that."

"Come on, Smitty, let's go."

"But, Jeff, why the silver bullet?"

"It didn't have to be silver. It could have been copper, or maybe eight or ten-carat gold. The bullet had to be made of a metal soft enough to form a temporary seal to back up the compressed air in the pistol, and hard enough to penetrate a body. Pamela never thought of a dart. Silver happened to be handy. Besides, it was bizarre, showy, and all the Bogarts go for that. Pamela's tricks, Wendell Bogart's showing off with darts, the sodium flash."

"Jeff, don't let's take any more criminal cases unless they are—"

"No more at all! Let's go."

A REAL NICE GUY

William F. Nolan

Warm sun.

A summer afternoon.

The sniper emerged from the roof door, walking easily, carrying a custom-leather guncase.

Opened the case.

Assembled the weapon.

Loaded it.

Sighted the street below.

Adjusted the focus.

Waited.

There was no hurry.

No hurry at all.

He was famous, yet no one knew his name. There were portraits of him printed in dozens of newspapers and magazines; he'd even made the cover of *Time*. But no one had really seen his face. The portraits were composites, drawn by frustrated police artists, based on the few misleading descriptions given by witnesses who claimed to have seen him leaving a building or jumping from a roof, or driving from the target area in a stolen automobile. But no two descriptions matched.

One witness described a chunky man of average height with a dark beard and cap. Another described a thin, extremely tall man with a bushy head of hair and a thick moustache. A third description pegged him as balding, paunchy and wearing heavy hornrims. On *Time's* cover, a large bloodsoaked question mark replaced his features – above the words WHO IS HE?

Reporters had given him many names: "The Phantom Sniper" . . . "The Deadly Ghost" . . . "The Silent Slayer" . . . and his personal favorite, "The Master of Whispering Death". This was often shortened to "Deathmaster", but he liked the full title; it was fresh and poetic – and *accurate*.

He *was* a master. He never missed a target, never wasted a shot. He was cool and nerveless and smooth, and totally without conscience. And death indeed whispered from his silenced weapon: a dry snap of the trigger, a muffled pop, and the target dropped as though struck down by the fist of God.

They were *always* targets, never people. Men, women, children. Young, middle-aged, old. Strong ones. Weak ones. Healthy or crippled. Black or white. Rich or poor. Targets – all of them.

He considered himself a successful sharpshooter, demonstrating his unique skill in a world teeming with three billion moving targets placed there for his amusement. Day and night, city by city, state by state, they were always there, ready for his gun, for the sudden whispering death from its barrel. An endless supply just for him.

Each city street was his personal shooting gallery.

But he was careful. Very, very careful. He never killed twice in the same city. He switched weapons. He never used a car more than once. He never wore the same clothes twice on a shoot. Even the shoes would be discarded; he wore a fresh pair for each target run. And, usually, he was never seen at all.

He thought of it as a sport.

A game.

A run.

A vocation.

A skill.

But never murder.

His name was Jimmie Prescott and he was thirty-one years of age. Five foot ten. Slight build. Platform shoes could add three inches and body-pillows up to fifty pounds. He had thinning brown hair framing a bland, unmemorable face and shaved twice daily – but the case of wigs, beards and moustaches he always carried easily disguised the shape of his mouth, chin and skull. Sometimes he would wear a skin-colored fleshcap for baldness, or use heavy glasses – though his sight was perfect. Once, for a lark, he had worn a black eye-patch. He would walk in a crouch, or stride with a sailor's swagger, or assume a limp.

Each disguise amused him, helped make life more challenging. Each was a small work of art, flawlessly executed.

Jimmie was a perfectionist.

And he was clean: no police record. Never arrested. No set of his prints on file, no dossier.

He had a great deal of money (inherited) with no need or inclination to earn more. He had spent his lifetime honing his considerable skills: he was an expert on weaponry, car theft, body-combat, police procedures; he made it a strict rule to memorize the street system of each city he entered before embarking on a shoot. And once his target was down he knew exactly how to leave the area. The proper escape route was essential.

Jimmie was a knowledgeable historian in his field: he had made a thorough study of snipers, and held them all in cold contempt. Not a worthwhile one in the lot. They *deserved* to be caught; they were fools and idiots and blunderers, often acting out of neurotic impulse or psychotic emotion. Even the hired professionals drew Jimmie's ire – since these were men who espoused political causes or who worked for government money. Jimmie had no cause, nor would he ever allow himself to be bought like a pig on the market.

He considered himself quite sane. Lacking moral conscience, he did not suffer from a guilt complex. Nor did he operate from a basic hatred of humankind, as did so many of the warped criminals he had studied.

Basically, Jimmie liked people, got alone fine with them on a casual basis. He hated no one. (Except his parents, but they were long dead and something he did not think about any more.) He was incapable of love or friendship, but felt no need for either. Jimmie depended only on himself; he had learned to do that from childhood. He was, therefore, a loner by choice, and made it a rule (Jimmie had many rules) never to date the same female twice, no matter how sexually appealing she might be. Man-woman relationships were a weakness, a form of dangerous self-indulgence he carefully avoided.

In sum, Jimmie Prescott didn't need anyone. He had himself, his skills, his weapons and his targets. More than enough for a full, rich life. He did not drink or smoke. (Oh, a bit of vintage wine in a good restaurant was always welcome, but he had never been drunk in his life. You savor good wine; you don't *wallow* in it.) He jogged each day, morning and evening, and worked out twice a week in the local gym in whatever city he was visiting. A trim, healthy body was an absolute necessity in his specialized career. Jimmie left nothing to chance. He was not a gambler and took no joy in risk.

A few times things had been close: a roof door which had jammed shut in Detroit after a kill, forcing him to make a perilous between-buildings leap . . . an engine that died during a police chase in Portland, causing him to abandon his car and win the pursuit on foot . . . an intense struggle with an off-duty patrolman in Kansas City who'd witnessed a shot. The fellow had been tough and dispatching him was physically difficult; Jimmie finally snapped his neck – but it had been close.

He kept a neat, handwritten record of each shoot in his tooled-leather notebook: state, city, name of street, weather, time of day, sex, age and skin color of target. Under "Comments", he would add pertinent facts, including the make and year of the stolen car he had driven, and the type of disguise he had utilized. Each item of clothing worn was listed. And if he experienced any problem in exiting the target area this would also be noted. Thus, each shoot was critically analyzed upon completion – as a football coach might dissect a game after it had been played.

The only random factor was the target. Pre-selection spoiled the freshness, the *purity* of the act. Jimmie liked to surprise himself. Which shall it be: that young girl in red, laughing up at her boyfriend? The old newsman on the corner? The school kid skipping homeward with books under his arm? Or, perhaps, the beefy, bored truckdriver, sitting idly in his cab, waiting for the light to change?

Selection was always a big part of the challenge.

And *this* time . . .

A male. Strong-looking. Well dressed. Businessman with a briefcase, in his late forties. Hair beginning to silver at the temples. He'd just left the drugstore; probably stopped there to pick up something for his wife. Maybe she'd called to remind him at lunch.

Moving toward the corner. Walking briskly.

Yes, this one. By all means, this one.

Range: three hundred yards.

Adjust sight focus.

Rifle stock tight against right shoulder.

Finger inside guard, poised at trigger.

Cheek firm against wooden gunstock; eye to rubber scopepiece.

Line crosshairs on target.

Steady breathing.

Tighten trigger finger slowly.

Fire!

The man dropped forward to the walk like a clubbed animal, dead before he struck the pavement. Someone screamed. A child began to cry. A man shouted.

Pleasant, familiar sounds to Jimmie Prescott.

Calmly, he took apart his weapon, cased it, then carefully dusted his trousers. (Rooftops were often grimy, and although he would soon discard the trousers he liked to present a neat, well-tailored appearance – but only when the disguise called for it. What a marvelous, ill-smelling bum he had become in New Orleans; he smiled thinly, thinking about how truly offensive he was on that occasion.)

He walked through the roof exit to the elevator.

Within ten minutes he had cleared central Baltimore – and booked the next flight to the west coast.

Aboard the jet, he relaxed. In the soft, warm, humming interior of the airliner, he grew drowsy . . . closed his eyes.

And had The Dream again.

The Dream was the only disturbing element in Jimmie Prescott's life. He invariably thought of it that way: The Dream. Never as *a* dream. Always about a large metropolitan city where chaos reigned – with buses running over babies in the street, and people falling down sewer holes and through plate-glass store windows . . . violent and disturbing. He was never threatened in The Dream, never personally involved in the chaos around him. Merely a mute witness to it.

He would tell himself, this is only *fantasy*, a thing deep inside his sleeping mind; it would go away once he awakened and then he could ignore it, put it out of his conscious thoughts, bury it as he had buried the hatred for his father and mother.

Perhaps he had *other* dreams. Surely he did. But The Dream

was the one he woke to, again and again, emerging from the chaos of the city with sweat on his cheeks and forehead, his breath tight and shallow in his chest, his heart thudding wildly.

"Are you all right?" a passenger across the aisle was asking him. "Shall I call somebody?"

"I'm fine," said Jimmie, sitting up straight. "No problem."

"You look kinda shaky."

"No, I'm fine. But thank you for your concern."

And he put The Dream away once again, as a gun is put away in its case.

In Los Angeles, having studied the city quite thoroughly, Jimmie took a cab directly into Hollywood. The fare was steep, but money was never an issue in Jimmie's life; he paid well for services rendered, with no regrets.

He got off at Highland, on Hollywood Boulevard, and walked toward the Chinese Theater.

He wanted two things: food and sexual satisfaction.

First, he would select an attractive female, take her to dinner and then to his motel room (he'd booked one from the airport) where he would have sex. Jimmie never called it lovemaking, a *silly* word. It was always just sex, plain and simple and quickly over. He was capable of arousing a woman if he chose to do so, of bringing her to full passion and release, but he seldom bothered. His performance was always an act; the ritual bored him. Only the result counted.

He disliked prostitutes and seldom selected one. Too jaded. Too worldly. And never to be trusted. Given time, and his natural charm, he was usually able to pick up an out-of-town girl, impress her with an excellent and very expensive meal at a posh restaurant, and guide her firmly into bed.

This night, in Hollywood, the seduction was easily accomplished.

Jimmie spotted a supple, soft-faced girl in the forecourt of the Chinese. She was wandering from one celebrity footprint to another, leaning to examine a particular signature in the cement.

As she bent forward, her breasts flowed full, pressing against the soft linen dress she wore – and Jimmie told himself, she's the one for tonight. A young, awestruck out-of-towner. Perfect.

He moved toward her.

*   *   *

"I just *love* European food," said Janet.

"That's good," said Jimmie Prescott. "I rather fancy it myself."

She smiled at him across the table, a glowing all-American girl from Ohio named Janet Louise Lakeley. They were sitting in a small, very chic French restaurant off La Cienega, with soft lighting and open-country decor.

"I can't read a word of this," Janet said when the menu was handed to her. "I thought they always had the food listed in English, too, like movie subtitles."

"Some places don't," said Jimmie quietly. "I'll order for us both. You'll be pleased. The sole is excellent here."

"Oh, I love fish," she said. "I could eat a ton of fish."

He pressed her hand. "That's nice."

"My head is swimming. I shouldn't have had that Scotch on an empty stomach," she said. "Are we having wine with dinner?"

"Of course," said Jimmie.

"I don't know anything about wine," she told him, "but I love champagne. That's wine, isn't it?"

He smiled with a faint upcurve of his thin lips.

"Trust me," he said. "You'll enjoy what I select."

"I'm sure I will."

The food was ordered and served – and Jimmie was pleased to see that his tastes had, once again, proven sound. The meal was superb, the wine was bracing and the girl was sexually stimulating. Essentially brainless, but that really didn't matter to Jimmie. She was what he wanted.

Then she began to talk about the sniper killings.

"Forty people in just a year and two months," she said. "And all gunned down by the same madman. Aren't they *ever* going to catch him?"

"The actual target figure is forty-one," he corrected her. "And what makes you so sure the sniper is a male. Could be a woman."

She shook her head. "Whoever heard of a woman sniper?"

"There have been many," said Jimmie. "In Russia today there are several hundred trained female snipers. Some European governments have traditionally utilized females in this capacity."

"I don't mean women *soldiers*," she said. "I mean your nutso shoot-'em-in-the-street sniper. Always guys. Every time. Like that kid in Texas that shot all the people from the tower."

"Apparently you've never heard of Francine Stearn."

"Nope. Who was she?"

"Probably the most famous female sniper. Killed a dozen schoolchildren in Pittsburg one weekend in late July, 1970. One shot each. To the head. She was a very accurate shootist."

"Never heard of her."

"After she was captured, *Esquire* did a rather probing psychological profile on her."

"Well, I really don't read a lot," she admitted. "Except Gothic romances. I just can't get *enough* of those." She giggled. "Guess you could say I'm addicted."

"I'm not familiar with the genre."

"Anyway," she continued. "I know this sniper is a guy."

"*How* do you know?"

"Female intuition. I trust it. It never fails me. And it tells me that the Phantom Sniper is a man."

He was amused. "What else does it tell you?"

"That he's probably messed up in the head. Maybe beaten as a kid. Something like that. He's *got* to be a nutcase."

"You could be wrong there, too," Jimmie told her. "Not all lawbreakers are mentally unbalanced."

"This 'Deathmaster' guy is, and I'm convinced of it."

"You're a strongly opinionated young woman."

"Mom always said that." She sipped her wine, nodded. "Yeah, I guess I am." She frowned, turning the glass slowly in her long-fingered hand. "Do you think they'll ever catch him?"

"I somehow doubt it," Jimmie declared. "No one seems to have a clear description of him. And he always seems to elude the police. Leaves no clues. Apparently selects his subjects at random. No motive to tie him to. No consistent MO."

"What's that?"

"Method of operation. Most criminals tend to repeat the same basic pattern in their crimes. But not this fellow. He keeps surprising people. Never know where he'll pop up next, or who his target will be. Tough to catch a man like that."

"You call them 'subjects' and 'targets' – but they're *people!* Innocent men and women and children. You make them sound like . . . like cutouts at a shooting gallery!"

"Perhaps I do," he admitted, smiling. "It's simply that we have different modes of expression."

"I say they'll get him eventually. He can't go on just butchering innocent people forever."

"No one goes on forever," said Jimmie Prescott.

She put down her wine glass, leaned toward him. "Know what bothers me most about the sniper?"

"What."

"The fact that his kind of act attracts copycats. Other sickos with a screw loose who read about him and want to imitate him. Arson is like that. One big fire in the papers and suddenly all the other wacko firebugs start their *own* fires. It gets 'em going. The sniper is like that."

"If some mentally disturbed individual is motivated to kill stupidly and without thought or preparation by something he or she reads in a newspaper then the sniper himself cannot be blamed for such abnormal behavior."

"You call what *he* does normal?"

"I . . . uh . . . didn't say that. I was simply refuting your theory."

She frowned. "Then who *is* to blame? I think that guy should be caught and—"

"And what?" Jimmie fixed his cool gray eyes on her. "What would you do if you suddenly discovered who he was . . . where to find him?"

"Call the police, naturally. Like anybody."

"Wouldn't you be curious about him, about the kind of person he is? Wouldn't you *question* him first, try to understand him?"

"You don't question an animal who kills! Which is what he is. I'd like to see him gassed or hanged . . . You don't *talk* to a twisted creep like that!"

She had made him angry. His lips tightened. He was no longer amused with this conversation; the word game had turned sour. This girl was gross and stupid and insensitive. Take her to bed and be done with it. Use her body – but no words. No more words. He'd had quite enough of those from her.

"Check, please," he said to the waiter.

It was at his motel, after sex, that Jimmie decided to kill her. Her insulting tirade echoed and re-echoed in his mind. She must be punished for it.

In this special case he felt justified in breaking one of his rules: never pre-select a target. She told him that she had a job in Hollywood, that she worked the afternoon shift at a clothing store on Vine. And he knew where she lived, a few blocks from work. She walked to the store each afternoon.

He would take her home and return the next day. When she left her apartment building he would dispatch her from a roof across the street. Once this plan had settled into place in the mind of Jimmie Prescott he relaxed, allowing the tension of the evening to drain away.

By tomorrow night he'd be in Tucson, and Janet Lakeley would be dead.

Warm sun.

A summer afternoon.

The sniper emerged from the roof door, walking easily, carrying a custom-leather guncase.

Opened the case.

Assembled the weapon.

Loaded it.

Sighted the street below.

Adjusted the focus.

Waited.

Target now exiting.

Walking along street toward corner.

Adjust sight focus.

Finger on trigger.

Cheek against stock.

Eye to scope.

Crosshairs direct on target.

Fire!

Jimmie felt something like a fist strike his stomach. A sudden, shocking blow. Winded, he looked down in amazement at the blood pulsing steadily from his shirtfront.

I'm hit! Someone has actually—

Another blow – but this one stopped all thought, taking his head apart. No more shock. No more amazement.

No more Jimmie.

She put away the weapon, annoyed at herself. *Two* shots! The Phantom Sniper, whoever he was, never fired more than once.

But *he* was exceptional. She got goosebumps, just thinking about him.

Well, maybe next time she could drop her target in one. Anybody can miscalculate a shot. Nobody's perfect.

She left the roof area, walking calmly, took the elevator down to the garage, stowed her guncase in the trunk of the stolen Mustang and drove away from the motel.

Poor Jimmie, she thought. It was just his bad luck to meet *me*. But that's the way it goes.

Janet Lakeley had a rule, and she never broke it: when you bed down a guy in a new town you always target him the next day. She sighed. Usually it didn't bother her. Most of them were bastards. But not Jimmie. She'd enjoyed talking to him, playing her word games with him . . . bedding him. Too bad he had to die.

He seemed like a real nice guy.

STACKED DECK

Bill Pronzini

1

From where he stood in the shadow of a split-bole Douglas fir, Deighan had a clear view of the cabin down below. Big harvest moon tonight, and only a few streaky clouds scudding past now and then to dim its hard yellow shine. The hard yellow glistened off the surface of Lake Tahoe beyond, softened into a long silverish stripe out toward the middle. The rest of the water shone like polished black metal. All of it was empty as far as he could see, except for the red-and-green running lights of a boat well away to the south, pointed toward the neon shimmer that marked the South Shore gambling casinos.

The cabin was big, made of cut pine logs and redwood shakes. It had a railed redwood deck that overlooked the lake, mostly invisible from where Deighan was. A flat concrete pier jutted out into the moonstruck water, a pair of short wooden floats making a T at its outer end. The boat tied up there was a thirty-foot Chris-Craft with sleeping accommodations for four. Nothing but the finer things for the Shooter.

Deighan watched the cabin. He'd been watching it for three hours now, from this same vantage point. His legs bothered him a little, standing around like this, and his eyes hurt from squinting. Time was, he'd had the night vision of an owl. Not anymore. What he had now, that he hadn't had when he was younger, was patience. He'd learned that in the last three years, along with a lot of other things – patience most of all.

On all sides the cabin was dark, but that was because they'd put the blackout curtains up. The six of them had been inside for better than two hours now, the same five-man nucleus as on every Thursday night except during the winter months, plus the one newcomer. The Shooter went to Hawaii when it started to snow. Or Florida or the Bahamas – someplace warm. Mannlicher and Brandt stayed home in the winter. Deighan didn't know what the others did, and he didn't care.

A match flared in the darkness between the carport, where the Shooter's Caddy Eldorado was slotted, and the parking area back among the trees. That was the lookout – Mannlicher's boy. Some lookout: he smoked a cigarette every five minutes, like clockwork, so you always knew where he was. Deighan watched him smoke this one. When he was done, he threw the butt away in a shower of sparks, and then seemed to remember that he was surrounded by dry timber and went after it and stamped it out with his shoe. *Some* lookout.

Deighan held his watch up close to his eyes, pushed the little button that lighted its dial. Ten nineteen. Just about time. The lookout was moving again, down toward the lake. Pretty soon he would walk out on the pier and smoke another cigarette and admire the view for a few minutes. He apparently did that at least twice every Thursday night – that had been his pattern on each of the last two – and he hadn't gone through the ritual yet tonight. He was bored, that was the thing. He'd been at his job a long time and it was always the same; there wasn't anything for him to do except walk around and smoke cigarettes and look at three hundred square miles of lake. Nothing ever happened. In three years nothing had ever happened.

Tonight something was going to happen.

Deighan took the gun out of the clamshell holster at his belt. It was a Smith & Wesson .38, lightweight, compact – a good piece, one of the best he'd ever owned. He held it in his hand, watching as the lookout performed as if on cue – walked to the pier, stopped, then moved out along its flat surface. When the guy had gone halfway, Deighan came out of the shadows and went down the slope at an angle across the driveway, to the rear of the cabin. His shoes made little sliding sounds on the needled ground, but they weren't sounds that carried.

He'd been over this ground three times before, dry runs the last two Thursday nights and once during the day when nobody was around; he knew just where and how to go. The lookout was lighting up again, his back to the cabin, when Deighan reached the rear wall. He eased along it to the spare-bedroom window. The sash went up easily, noiselessly. He could hear them then, in the rec room – voices, ice against glass, the click and rattle of the chips. He got the ski mask from his jacket pocket, slipped it over his head, snugged it down. Then he climbed through the window, put his penlight on just long enough to orient himself, went straight across to the door that led into the rec room.

It didn't make a sound, either, when he opened it. He went in with the revolver extended, elbow locked. Sturgess saw him first. He said, "Jesus Christ!" and his body went as stiff as if he were suffering a stroke. The others turned in their chairs, gawking. The Shooter started up out of his.

Deighan said, fast and hard, "Sit still if you don't want to die. Hands on the table where I can see them – all of you. Do it!"

They weren't stupid; they did what they were told. Deighan watched them through a thin haze of tobacco smoke. Six men around the hexagonal poker table, hands flat on its green baize, heads lifted or twisted to stare at him. He knew five of them. Mannlicher, the fat owner of the Nevornia Club; he had Family ties, even though he was a Prussian, because he'd once done some favors for an east-coast *capo*. Brandt, Mannlicher's cousin and private enforcer, who doubled as the Nevornia's floor boss. Bellah, the quasi-legitimate real-estate developer and high roller. Sturgess, the bankroll behind the Jackpot Lounge up at North Shore. And the Shooter – hired muscle, hired gun, part-time coke runner, whose real name was Dennis D'Allesandro. The sixth man was the pigeon they'd lured in for this particular game, a lean guy in his fifties with Texas oil money written all over him and his fancy clothes – Donley or Donavan, something like that.

Mannlicher was the bank tonight; the table behind his chair was covered with stacks of dead presidents – fifties and hundreds, mostly. Deighan took out the folded-up flour sack, tossed it on top of the poker chips that littered the baize in front of Mannlicher. "All right. Fill it."

The fat man didn't move. He was no pushover; he was hard, tough, mean. And he didn't like being ripped off. Veins bulged in his neck, throbbed in his temples. The violence in him was close to the surface now, held thinly in check.

"You know who we are?" he said. "Who I am?"

"Fill it."

"You dumb bastard. You'll never live to spend it."

"Fill the sack. *Now*."

Deighan's eyes, more than his gun, made up Mannlicher's mind for him. He picked up the sack, pushed around in his chair, began to savagely feed in the stacks of bills.

"The rest of you," Deighan said, "put your wallets, watches, jewelry on the table. Everything of value. Hurry it up."

The Texan said, "Listen heah—" and Deighan pointed the .38 at his head and said, "One more word, you're a dead man." The Texan made an effort to stare him down, but it was just to save face; after two or three seconds he lowered his gaze and began stripping the rings off his fingers.

The rest of them didn't make any fuss. Bellah was sweating; he kept swiping it out of his eyes, his hands moving in little jerks and twitches. Brandt's eyes were like dull knives, cutting away at Deighan's masked face. D'Allesandro showed no emotion of any kind. That was his trademark; he was your original iceman. They might have called him that, maybe, if he'd been like one of those old-timers who used an ice pick or a blade. As it was, with his preferences, the Shooter was the right name for him.

Mannlicher had the sack full now. The platinum ring on his left hand, with its circle of fat diamonds, made little gleams and glints in the shine from the low-hanging droplight. The idea of losing that bothered him even more than losing his money; he kept running the fingers of his other hand over the stones.

"The ring," Deighan said to him. "Take it off."

"Go to hell."

"Take it off or I'll put a third eye in the middle of your forehead. Your choice."

Mannlicher hesitated, tried to stare him down, didn't have any better luck at it than the Texan. There was a tense moment; then, because he didn't want to die over a piece of jewelry, he yanked the ring off, slammed it down hard in the middle of the table.

Deighan said, "Put it in the sack. The wallets and the rest of the stuff too."

This time Mannlicher didn't hesitate. He did as he'd been told.

"All right," Deighan said. "Now get up and go over by the bar. Lie down on the floor on your belly."

Mannlicher got up slowly, his jaw set and his teeth clenched as if to keep the violence from spewing out like vomit. He lay down on the floor. Deighan gestured at Brandt, said, "You next. Then the rest of you, one at a time."

When they were all on the floor he moved to the table, caught up the sack. "Stay where you are for ten minutes," he told them. "You move before that, or call to the guy outside, I'll blow the place up. I got a grenade in my pocket, the fragmentation kind. Anybody doubt it?"

None of them said anything.

Deighan backed up into the spare bedroom, leaving the door open so he could watch them all the way to the window. He put his head out, saw no sign of the look-out. Still down by the lake somewhere. The whole thing had taken just a few minutes.

He swung out through the window, hurried away in the shadows – but in the opposite direction from the driveway and the road above. On the far side of the cabin there was a path that angled through the pine forest to the north; he found it, followed it at a trot. Enough moonlight penetrated through the branches overhead to let him see where he was going.

He was almost to the lakefront when the commotion started back there: voices, angry and pulsing in the night, Mannlicher's the loudest of them. They hadn't waited the full ten minutes, but then he hadn't expected them to. It didn't matter. The Shooter's cabin was invisible from here, cut off by a wooded finger of land a hundred yards wide. And they wouldn't be looking for him along the water, anyway. They'd be up on the road, combing that area; they'd figure automatically that his transportation was a car.

The hard yellow-and-black gleam of the lake was just ahead, the rushes and ferns where he'd tied up the rented Beachcraft inboard. He moved across the sandy strip of beach, waded out to his calves, dropped the loaded flour sack into the boat, then eased the craft free of the rushes before he lifted himself over the gunwale. The engine caught with a quiet rumble the first time he turned the key.

They were still making noise back at the cabin, blundering around like fools, as he eased away into the night.

2

The motel was called Whispering Pines. It was back off Highway 28 below Crystal Bay, a good half-mile from the lake, tucked up in a grove of pines and Douglas fir. Deighan's cabin was the farthest from the office, detached from its nearest neighbor by thirty feet of open ground.

Inside he sat in darkness except for flickering light from the television. The set was an old one; the picture was riddled with snow and kept jumping every few seconds. But he didn't care; he wasn't watching it. Or listening to it: he had the sound turned off. It was on only because he didn't like waiting in the dark.

It had been after midnight when he came in – too late to make the ritual call to Fran, even though he'd felt a compulsion to do so. She went to bed at eleven-thirty; she didn't like the phone to ring after that. How could he blame her? When he was home and she was away at Sheila's or her sister's, he never wanted it to ring that late either.

It was one ten now. He was tired, but not too tired. The evening was still in his blood, warming him, like liquor or drugs that hadn't quite worn off yet. Mannlicher's face . . . that was an image he'd never forget. The Shooter's, too, and Brandt's, but especially Mannlicher's.

Outside, a car's headlamps made a sweep of light across the curtained window as it swung in through the motel courtyard. When it stopped nearby and the lights went out, Deighan thought: It's about time.

Footsteps made faint crunching sounds on gravel. Soft knock on the door. Soft voice following: "Prince? You in there?"

"Door's open."

A wedge of moonlight widened across the floor, not quite reaching to where Deighan sat in the lone chair with the .38 in his hand. The man who stood silhouetted in the opening made a perfect target – just a damned airhead, any way you looked at him.

"Prince?"

"I'm over here. Come on in, shut the door."

"Why don't you turn on a light?"

"There's a switch by the door."

The man entered, shut the door. There was a click and

the ceiling globe came on. Deighan stayed where he was, but reached over with his left hand to turn off the TV.

Bellah stood blinking at him, running his palms along the sides of his expensive cashmere jacket. He said nervously, "For God's sake, put the gun away. What's the idea?"

"I'm the cautious type."

"Well, put it away. I don't like it."

Deighan got to his feet, slid the revolver into his belt holster. "How'd it go?"

"Hairy, damned hairy. Mannlicher was like a madman." Bellah took a handkerchief out of his pocket, wiped his forehead. His angular face was pale, shiny-damp. "I didn't think he'd take it this hard. Christ."

That's the trouble with people like you, Deighan thought. You never think. He pinched a cigarette out of his shirt pocket, lit it with the Zippo Fran had given him fifteen years ago. Fifteen years, and it still worked. Like their marriage, even with all the trouble. How long was it now? Twenty-two years in May? Twenty-three?

Bellah said, "He started screaming at D'Allesandro. I thought he was going to choke him."

"Who? Mannlicher?"

"Yeah. About the window in the spare bedroom."

"What'd D'Allesandro say?"

"He said he always keeps it locked, you must have jimmied it some way that didn't leave any traces. Mannlicher didn't believe him. He thinks D'Allesandro forgot to lock it."

"Nobody got the idea it was an inside job?"

"No."

"Okay then. Relax, Mr Bellah. You're in the clear."

Bellah wiped his face again. "Where's the money?"

"Other side of the bed. On the floor."

"You count it?"

"No. I figured you'd want to do that."

Bellah went over there, picked up the flour sack, emptied it on the bed. His eyes were bright and hot as he looked at all the loose green. Then he frowned, gnawed at his lower lip, and poked at Mannlicher's diamond ring. "What'd you take this for? Mannlicher is more pissed about the ring than anything else. He said his mother gave it to him. It's worth ten thousand."

"That's why I took it," Deighan said. "Fifteen percent of the cash isn't a hell of a lot."

Bellah stiffened. "I set it all up, didn't I? Why shouldn't I get the lion's share?"

"I'm not arguing, Mr Bellah. We agreed on a price; okay, that's the way it is. I'm only saying I got a right to a little something extra."

"All right, all right." Bellah was looking at the money again. "Must be at least two hundred thousand," he said. "That Texan, Donley, brought fifty grand alone."

"Plenty in his wallet too, then."

"Yeah."

Deighan smoked and watched Bellah count the loose bills and what was in the wallets and billfolds. There was an expression on the developer's face like a man has when he's fondling a naked woman. Greed, pure and simple. Greed was what drove Lawrence Bellah; money was his best friend, his lover, his god. He didn't have enough ready cash to buy the lakefront property down near Emerald Bay – property he stood to make three to four million on, with a string of condos – and he couldn't raise it fast enough any legitimate way; so he'd arranged to get it by knocking over his own weekly poker game, even if it meant crossing some hard people. He had balls, you had to give him that. He was stupid as hell, and one of these days he was liable to end up in pieces at the bottom of the lake, but he did have balls.

He was also lucky, at least for the time being, because the man he'd picked to do his strong-arm work was Bob Prince. He had no idea the name was a phony, no idea the whole package on Bob Prince was the result of three years of careful manipulation. All he knew was that Prince had a reputation as dependable, easy to work with, not too smart or money-hungry, and that he was willing to do any kind of muscle work. Bellah didn't have an inkling of what he'd really done by hiring Bob Prince. If he kept on being lucky, he never would.

Bellah was sweating by the time he finished adding up the take. "Two hundred and thirty-three thousand and change," he said. "More than we figured on."

"My cut's thirty-five thousand," Deighan said.

"You divide fast." Bellah counted out two stacks, hundreds

and fifties, to one side of the flowered bedspread. Then he said, "Count it? Or do you trust me?"

Deighan grinned. He rubbed out his cigarette, went to the bed, and took his time shuffling through the stacks. "On the nose," he said when he was done.

Bellah stuffed the rest of the cash back into the flour sack, leaving the watches and jewelry where they lay. He was still nervous, still sweating; he wasn't going to sleep much tonight, Deighan thought.

"That's it, then," Bellah said. "You going back to Chicago tomorrow?"

"Not right away. Thought I'd do a little gambling first."

"Around here? Christ, Prince . . ."

"No. Reno, maybe. I might even go down to Vegas."

"Just get away from Tahoe."

"Sure," Deighan said. "First thing in the morning."

Bellah went to the door. He paused there to tuck the flour sack under his jacket; it made him look as if he had a tumor on his left side. "Don't do anything with that jewelry in Nevada. Wait until you get back to Chicago."

"Whatever you say, Mr Bellah."

"Maybe I'll need you again sometime," Bellah said. "You'll hear from me if I do."

"Any time. Any old time."

When Bellah was gone, Deighan put five thousand dollars into his suitcase and the other thirty thousand into a knapsack he'd bought two days before at a South Shore sporting goods store. Mannlicher's diamond ring went into the knapsack, too, along with the better pieces among the rest of the jewelry. The watches and the other stuff were no good to him; he bundled those up in a hand towel from the bathroom, stuffed the bundle into the pocket of his down jacket. Then he had one more cigarette, set his portable alarm clock for six a.m., double-locked the door, and went to bed on the left side, with the revolver under the pillow near his right hand.

3

In the dawn light the lake was like smoky blue glass, empty except for a few optimistic fishermen anchored close to the eastern shoreline. The morning was cold, autumn-crisp, but there was no wind. The sun was just beginning to rise, painting the sky and its scattered cloudstreaks in pinks and golds. There was old snow on the upper reaches of Mount Tallac, on some of the other Sierra peaks that ringed the lake.

Deighan took the Beachcraft out half a mile before he dropped the bundle of watches and worthless jewelry overboard. Then he cut off at a long diagonal to the north that brought him to within a few hundred yards of the Shooter's cabin. He had his fishing gear out by then, fiddling with the glass rod and tackle – just another angler looking for rainbow, Mackinaw, and cutthroat trout.

There wasn't anybody out and around at the Shooter's place. Deighan glided past at two knots, angled into shore a couple of hundred yards beyond, where there were rushes and some heavy brush and trees overhanging the water. From there he had a pretty good view of the cabin, its front entrance, the Shooter's Caddy parked inside the carport.

It was eight o'clock, and the sun was all the way up, when he switched off the engine and tied up at the bole of the collapsed pine. It was a few minutes past nine-thirty when D'Allesandro came out and walked around to the Caddy. He was alone. No chippies from the casino this morning, not after what had gone down last night. He might be going to the store for cigarettes, groceries, or to a café somewhere for breakfast. He might be going to see somebody, do some business. The important thing was, how long would he be gone?

Deighan watched him back his Caddy out of the carport, drive it away and out of sight on the road above. He stayed where he was, fishing, waiting. At the end of an hour, when the Shooter still hadn't come back, he started the boat's engine and took his time maneuvering around the wooded finger of land to the north and then into the cove where he'd anchored last night. He nosed the boat into the reeds and ferns, swung overboard, and pushed it farther in, out of sight. Then he caught up the knapsack and set off through the woods to the Shooter's cabin.

He made a slow half-circle of the place, keeping to the trees. The carport was still empty. Nothing moved anywhere within the range of his vision. Finally he made his way down to the rear wall, around it and along the side until he reached the front door. He didn't like standing out here for even a little while because there was no cover; but this door was the only one into the house, except for sliding doors on the terrace and a porch on the other side, and you couldn't jimmy sliding doors easily and without leaving marks. The same was true of windows. The Shooter would have made sure they were all secure anyway.

Deighan had one pocket of the knapsack open, the pick gun in his hand, when he reached the door. He'd got the pick gun from a housebreaker named Caldwell, an old-timer who was retired now; he'd also got some other tools and lessons in how to use them on the various kinds of locks. The lock on the Shooter's door was a flush-mounted, five-pin cylinder lock, with a steel lip on the door frame to protect the bolt and strike plate. That meant it was a lock you couldn't loid with a piece of plastic or a shim. It also meant that with a pick gun you could probably have it open in a couple of minutes.

Bending, squinting, he slid the gun into the lock. Set it, working the little knob on top to adjust the spring tension. Then he pulled the trigger – and all the pins bounced free at once and the door opened under his hand.

He slipped inside, nudged the door shut behind him, put the pick gun away inside the knapsack, and drew on a pair of thin plastic gloves. The place smelled of stale tobacco smoke and stale liquor. They hadn't been doing all that much drinking last night; maybe the Shooter had nibbled a few too many after the rest of them finally left. He didn't like losing money and valuables any more than Mannlicher did.

Deighan went through the front room. Somebody'd decorated the place for D'Allesandro: leather furniture, deer and antelope heads on the walls, Indian rugs on the floors, tasteful paintings. Cocaine deals had paid for part of it; contract work, including two hits on greedy Oakland and San Francisco drug dealers, had paid for the rest. But the Shooter was still small-time. He wasn't bright enough to be anything else. Cards and dice and whores-in-training were all he really cared about.

The front room was no good; Deighan prowled quickly through the other rooms. D'Allesandro wasn't the kind to have an office or a den, but there was a big old-fashioned rolltop desk in a room with a TV set and one of those big movie-type screens. None of the desk drawers were locked. Deighan pulled out the biggest one, saw that it was loaded with Danish porn magazines, took the magazines out and set them on the floor. He opened the knapsack and transferred the thirty thousand dollars into the back of the drawer. He put Mannlicher's ring in there, too, along with the other rings and a couple of gold chains the Texan had been wearing. Then he stuffed the porn magazines in at the front and pushed the drawer shut.

On his way back to the front room he rolled the knapsack tight around the pick gun and stuffed them into his jacket pocket. He opened the door, stepped out. He'd just finished resetting the lock when he heard the car approaching on the road above.

He froze for a second, looking up there. He couldn't see the car because of a screen of trees; but then he heard its automatic transmission gear down as it slowed for the turn into the Shooter's driveway. He pulled the door shut and ran toward the lake, the only direction he could go. Fifty feet away the log-railed terrace began, raised up off the sloping ground on redwood pillars. Deighan caught one of the railings, hauled himself up and half rolled through the gap between them. The sound of the oncoming car was loud in his ears as he landed, off balance, on the deck.

He went to one knee, came up again. The only way to tell if he'd been seen was to stop and look, but that was a fool's move. Instead he ran across the deck, climbed through the railing on the other side, dropped down, and tried to keep from making noise as he plunged into the woods. He stopped moving after thirty yards, where ferns and a deadfall formed a thick concealing wall. From behind it, with the .38 in his hand, he watched the house and the deck, catching his breath, waiting.

Nobody came up or out on the deck. Nobody showed himself anywhere. The car's engine had been shut off sometime during his flight; it was quiet now, except for birds and the faint hum of a powerboat out on the lake.

Deighan waited ten minutes. When there was still nothing to see or hear, he transcribed a slow curl through the trees to where he could see the front of the cabin. The Shooter's Caddy was back inside the carport, no sign of haste in the way it had been neatly slotted. The cabin door was shut. The whole area seemed deserted.

But he waited another ten minutes before he was satisfied.

Even then, he didn't holster his weapon until he'd made his way around to the cove where the Beachcraft was hidden. And he didn't relax until he was well out on the lake, headed back toward Crystal Bay.

4

The Nevornia was one of South Shore's older clubs, but it had undergone some recent modernizing. Outside, it had been given a glass and gaudy-neon face-lift. Inside, they'd used more glass, some cut crystal, and a wine-red decor that included carpeting, upholstery, and gaming tables.

When Deighan walked in a few minutes before two, the banks of slots and the blackjack tables were getting moderately heavy play. That was because it was Friday; some of the small-time gamblers liked to get a jump on the weekend crowds. The craps and roulette layouts were quiet. The high rollers were like vampires: they couldn't stand the daylight, so they only came out after dark.

Deighan bought a roll of quarters at one of the change booths. There were a couple of dozen rows of slots in the main casino – flashy new ones, mostly, with a few of the old scrolled nickel-plated jobs mixed in for the sake of nostalgia. He stopped at one of the old quarter machines, fed in three dollars' worth. Lemons and oranges. He couldn't even line up two cherries for a three-coin drop. He smiled crookedly to himself, went away from the slots and into the long concourse that connected the main casino with the new, smaller addition at the rear.

There were telephone booths along one side of the concourse. Deighan shut himself inside one of them, put a quarter in the slot, pushed 0 and then the digits of his home number in San Francisco. When the operator came on he said it was a collect call; that was to save himself the trouble of having to feed in a handful of quarters. He let the circuit make exactly five burrs in his ear before he hung up. If Fran was home, she'd know now that he was all right. If she wasn't home, then she'd know it later when he made another five-ring call. He always tried to call at least twice a day, at different times, because sometimes she went out shopping or to a movie or to visit with Sheila and the kids.

It'd be easier if she just answered the phone, talked to him, but she never did when he was away. Never. Sheila or anybody else wanted to get hold of her, they had to call one of the neighbors or come over in person. She didn't want anything to do with him when he was away, didn't want to know what he was doing or even when he'd be back. "Suppose I picked up the phone and it wasn't you?" she'd said. "Suppose it was somebody telling me you were dead? I couldn't stand that." That part of it didn't make sense to him. If he were dead, somebody'd come by and tell it to her face; dead was dead, and what difference did it make how she got the news? But he didn't argue with her. He didn't like to argue with her, and it didn't cost him anything to do it her way.

He slotted the quarter again and called the Shooter's number. Four rings, five, and D'Allesandro's voice said, "Yeah?"

"Mr Carson?"

"Who?"

"Isn't this Paul Carson?"

"No. You got the wrong number."

"Oh, sorry," Deighan said, and rang off.

Another quarter in the slot. This time the number he punched out was the Nevornia's business line. A woman's voice answered, crisp and professional. He said, "Mr Mannlicher. Tell him it's urgent."

"Whom shall I say is calling?"

"Never mind that. Just tell him it's about what happened last night."

"Sir, I'm afraid I can't—"

"Tell him last night's poker game, damn it. He'll talk to me."

There was a click and some canned music began to play in his ear. He lit a cigarette. He was on his fourth drag when the canned music quit and the fat man's voice said, "Frank Mannlicher. Who's this?"

"No names. Is it all right to talk on this line?"

"Go ahead, talk."

"I'm the guy who hit your game last night."

Silence for four or five seconds. Then Mannlicher said, "Is that so?" in a flat, wary voice.

"Ski mask, Smith & Wesson .38, grenade in my jacket pocket. The take was better than two hundred thousand. I got your ring – platinum with a circle of diamonds."

Another pause, shorter this time. "So why call me today?"

"How'd you like to get it all back – the money and the ring?"

"How?"

"Go pick it up. I'll tell you where."

"Yeah? Why should you do me a favor?"

"I didn't know who you were last night. I wasn't told. If I had been, I wouldn't of gone through with it. I don't mess with people like you, people with your connections."

"Somebody hired you, that it?"

"That's it."

"Who?"

"D'Allesandro."

"*What?*"

"The Shooter. D'Allesandro."

". . . Bullshit."

"You don't have to believe me. But I'm telling you – he's the one. He didn't tell me who'd be at the game, and now he's trying to screw me on the money. He says there was less than a hundred and fifty thousand in the sack; I know better."

"So now you want to screw him."

"That's right. Besides, I don't like the idea of you pushing to find out who I am, maybe sending somebody to pay me a visit someday. I figure if I give you the Shooter, you'll lose interest in me."

More silence. "Why'd he do it?" Mannlicher said in a different voice – harder, with the edge of violence it had held last night. "Hit the game like that?"

"He needs some big money, fast. He's into some kind of scam back east; he wouldn't say what it is."

"Where's the money and the rest of the stuff?"

"At his cabin. We had a drop arranged in the woods; I put the sack there last night, he picked it up this morning when nobody was around. The money's in his desk – the big rolltop. Your ring, too. That's where it was an hour ago, anyhow, when I walked out."

Mannlicher said, "In his desk," as if he were biting the words off something bitter.

"Go out there, see for yourself."

"If you're telling this straight, you got nothing to worry about from me. Maybe I'll fix you up with a reward or something. Where can I get in touch?"

"You can't," Deighan said. "I'm long gone as soon as I hang up this phone."

"I'll make it five thousand. Just tell me where you—"

Deighan broke the connection.

His cigarette had burned down to the filter; he dropped it on the floor, put his shoe on it before he left the booth. On his way out of the casino he paused long enough to push another quarter into the same slot machine he'd played before. More lemons and oranges. This time he didn't smile as he moved away.

5

Narrow and twisty, hemmed in by trees, Old Lake Road branched off Highway 50 on the Nevada side and took two miles to get all the way to the lake. But it wasn't a dead end; another road picked it up at the lakefront and looped back out to the highway. There were several nice homes hidden away in the area – it was called Pine Acres – with plenty of space between them. The Shooter's cabin was a mile and a half from the highway, off an even narrower lane called Little Cove Road. The only other cabin within five hundred yards was a summer place that the owners had already closed up for the year.

Deighan drove past the intersection with Little Cove, went two-tenths of a mile, parked on the turnout at that point. There wasn't anybody else around when he got out, nothing to see except trees and little winks of blue that marked the nearness of the lake. If anybody came along they wouldn't pay any attention to the car. For one thing, it was a '75 Ford Galaxy with nothing distinctive about it except the antenna for the GTE mobile phone. It was his – he'd driven it up from San Francisco – but the papers on it said it belonged to Bob Prince. For another thing, Old Lake Road was only a hundred yards or so from the water here, and there was a path through the trees to a strip of rocky beach. Local kids used it in the summer; he'd found that out from Bellah. Kids might have decided to stop here on a sunny autumn day as well. No reason for anybody to think otherwise.

He found the path, went along it a short way to where it crossed a little creek, dry now and so narrow it was nothing more than a natural drainage ditch. He followed the creek to the north, on a course he'd taken three days ago. It led him to a shelf-like overhang topped by two chunks of granite outcrop that leaned against each other like a pair of old drunks. Below the shelf, the land fell away sharply to the Shooter's driveway some sixty yards distant. Off to the right, where the incline wasn't so steep and the trees grew in a pack, was the split-bole Douglas fir where he'd stood waiting last night. The trees were fewer and more widely spaced apart between here and the cabin, so that from behind the two outcrops you had a good look at the Shooter's property, Little Cove Road, the concrete pier, and the lake shimmering under the late afternoon sun.

The Caddy Eldorado was still slotted inside the carport. It was the only car in sight. Deighan knelt behind where the outcrops came together to form a notch, rubbed tension out of his neck and shoulders while he waited.

He didn't have to wait long. Less than ten minutes had passed when the car appeared on Little Cove Road, slowed, turned down the Shooter's driveway. It wasn't Mannlicher's fancy limo; it was a two-year-old Chrysler – Brandt's, maybe. Brandt was driving it: Deighan had a clear view of him through the side window as the Chrysler pulled up and stopped near the cabin's front door. He could also see that the lone passenger was Mannlicher.

Brandt got out, opened the passenger door for the fat man, and the two of them went to the cabin. It took D'Allesandro ten seconds to answer Brandt's knock. There was some talk, not much; then Mannlicher and Brandt went in, and the door shut behind them.

All right, Deighan thought. He'd stacked the deck as well as he could; pretty soon he'd know how the hand – and the game – played out.

Nothing happened for maybe five minutes. Then he thought he heard some muffled sounds down there, loud voices that went on for a while, something that might have been a bang, but the distance was too great for him to be sure that he wasn't imagining them. Another four or five minutes went by. And then the door opened and Brandt came out alone, looked around, called something back inside that Deighan didn't understand. If there was an answer, it wasn't audible. Brandt shut the door, hurried down to the lake, went out onto the pier. The ChrisCraft was still tied up there. Brandt climbed on board, disappeared for thirty seconds or so, reappeared carrying a square of something gray and heavy. Tarpaulin, Deighan saw when Brandt came back up the driveway. Big piece of it – big enough for a shroud.

The Shooter's hand had been folded. That left three of them still in the game.

When Brandt had gone back inside with the tarp, Deighan stood and half ran along the creek and through the trees to where he'd left the Ford. Old Lake Road was deserted. He yanked open the passenger door, leaned in, caught up the mobile phone, and punched out the emergency number for the county sheriff's office. An efficient-sounding male voice answered.

"Something's going on on Little Cove Road," Deighan said, making himself sound excited. "That's in Pine Acres, you know? It's the cabin at the end, down on the lake. I heard shots – people shooting at each other down there. It sounds like a war."

"What's the address?"

"I don't know the address, it's the cabin right on the lake. People *shooting* at each other. You better get right out there."

"Your name, sir?"

"I don't want to get involved. Just hurry, will you?"

Deighan put the receiver down, shut the car door, ran back along the path and along the creek to the shelf. Mannlicher and Brandt were still inside the cabin. He went to one knee again behind the outcrops, drew the .38, held it on his thigh.

It was another two minutes before the door opened down there. Brandt came out, looked around as he had before, went back inside – and then he and Mannlicher both appeared, one at each end of a big, tarp-wrapped bundle. They started to carry it down the driveway toward the lake. Going to put it on the boat, Deighan thought, take it out now or later on, when it's dark. Lake Tahoe was sixteen hundred feet deep in the middle. The bundle wouldn't have been the first somebody'd dumped out there.

He let them get clear of the Chrysler, partway down the drive, before he poked the gun into the notch, sighted, and fired twice. The shots went where he'd intended them to, wide by ten feet and into the roadbed so they kicked up gravel. Mannlicher and Brandt froze for an instant, confused. Deighan fired a third round, putting the slug closer this time, and that one panicked them: they let go of the bundle and began scrambling.

There was no cover anywhere close by; they both ran for the Chrysler. Brandt had a gun in his hand when he reached it, and he dropped down behind the rear deck, trying to locate Deighan's position. Mannlicher kept on scrambling around to the passenger door, pulled it open, pushed himself across the seat inside.

Deighan blew out the Chrysler's near front tire. Sighted, and blew out the rear tire. Brandt threw an answering shot his way, but it wasn't even close. The Chrysler was tilting in Deighan's direction as the tires flattened. Mannlicher pushed himself out of the car, tried to make a run for the cabin door with his arms flailing, his fat jiggling. Deighan put a bullet into the wall beside the door. Mannlicher reversed himself, fell in his frantic haste, crawled back behind the Chrysler.

Reloading the .38, Deighan could hear the sound of cars coming up fast on Little Cove Road. No sirens, but revolving lights made faint blood-red flashes through the trees.

From behind the Chrysler Brandt fired again, wildly. Beyond him, on the driveway, one corner of the tarp-wrapped bundle had come loose and was flapping in the wind off the lake.

A county sheriff's cruiser, its roof light slashing the air, made the turn off Little Cove onto the driveway. Another one was right behind it. In his panic, Brandt straightened up when he saw them and fired once, blindly, at the first in line.

Deighan was on his feet by then, hurrying away from the outcrops, holstering his weapon. Behind him he heard brakes squeal, another shot, voices yelling, two more shots. All the sounds faded as he neared the turnout and the Ford. By the time he pulled out onto the deserted road, there was nothing to hear but the sound of his engine, the screeching of a jay somewhere nearby.

Brandt had thrown in his hand by now; so had Mannlicher.

This pot belonged to him.

6

Fran was in the backyard, weeding her garden, when he got home late the following afternoon. He called to her from the doorway, and she glanced around and then got up, unsmiling, and came over to him. She was wearing jeans and one of his old shirts and a pair of gardening gloves, and her hair was tied in a long ponytail. Used to be a light, silky brown, her hair; now it was mostly gray. His fault. She was only forty-six. A woman of forty-six shouldn't be so gray.

She said, "So you're back." She didn't sound glad to see him, didn't kiss him or touch him at all. But her eyes were gentle on his face.

"I'm back."

"You all right? You look tired."

"Long drive. I'm fine; it was a good trip."

She didn't say anything. She didn't want to hear about it, not any of it. She just didn't want to know.

"How about you?" he asked. "Everything been okay?"

"Sheila's pregnant again."

"Christ. What's the matter with her? Why don't she get herself fixed? Or get Hank fixed?"

"She likes kids."

"I like kids too, but four's too many at her age. She's only twenty-seven."

"She wants eight."

"She's crazy," Deighan said. "What's she want to bring all those kids into a world like this for?"

There was an awkward moment. It was always awkward at first when he came back. Then Fran said, "You hungry?"

"You know me. I can always eat." Fact was, he was starved. He hadn't eaten much up in Nevada, never did when he was away. And he hadn't had anything today except an English muffin and some coffee for breakfast in Truckee.

"Come into the kitchen," Fran said. "I'll fix you something."

They went inside. He got a beer out of the refrigerator; she waited and then took out some covered dishes, some vegetables. He wanted to say something to her, talk a little, but he couldn't think of anything. His mind was blank at times like this. He carried his beer into the living room.

The goddamn trophy case was the first thing he saw. He hated that trophy case; but Fran wouldn't get rid of it, no matter what he said. For her it was like some kind of shrine to the dead past. All the mementoes of his years on the force – twenty-two years, from beat patrolman in North Beach all the way up to inspector on the narcotics squad. The certificate he'd won in marksmanship competition at the police academy, the two citations from the mayor for bravery, other crap like that. Bones, that's all they were to him. Pieces of a rotting skeleton. What was the sense in keeping them around, reminding both of them of what he'd been, what he'd lost?

His fault he'd lost it, sure. But it was their fault too, goddamn them. The laws, the lawyers, the judges, the *system*. No convictions on half of all the arrests he'd ever made – half! Turning the ones like Mannlicher and Brandt and D'Allesandro loose, putting them right back on the street, letting them make their deals and their hits, letting them screw up innocent lives. Sheila's kids, his grandkids – lives like that. How could they blame him for being bitter? How could they blame him for taking too many drinks now and then?

He sat down on the couch, drank some of his beer, lit a cigarette. Ah Christ, he thought, it's not them. You know it wasn't them. It was *you*, you dumb bastard. They warned you twice about drinking on duty. And you kept on doing it, you were hog-drunk the night you plowed the departmental sedan into that vanload of teenagers. What if one of *those* kids had died? You were lucky, by God. You got off easy.

Sure, he thought. Sure. But he'd been a good cop, damn it, a cop inside and out; it was all he knew how to be. What was he supposed to do after they threw him off the force? Live on his half-pension? Get a job as a part-time security guard? Forty-four years old, no skills, no friends outside the department – what the hell was he supposed to do?

He'd invented Bob Prince, that was what he'd done. He'd gone into business for himself.

Fran didn't understand. "You'll get killed one of these days," she'd said in the beginning. "It's vigilante justice," she'd said. "You think you're Rambo, is that it?" she'd said. She just didn't understand. To him it was the same job he'd always done, the only one he was any good at, only now *he* made up some of the rules. He was no Rambo, one man up against thousands, a mindless killing machine; he hated that kind of phony flag-waving crap. It wasn't real. What he was doing, that was real. It meant something. But a hero? No. Hell, no. He was a sniper, that was all, picking off a weak or vulnerable enemy here and there, now and then. Snipers weren't heroes, for Christ's sake. Snipers were snipers, just like cops were cops.

He finished his beer and his cigarette, got up, went into Fran's sewing room. The five thousand he'd held out of the poker-game take was in his pocket – money he felt he was entitled to because his expenses ran high sometimes, and they had to eat, they had to live. He put the roll into her sewing cabinet, where he always put whatever money he made as Bob Prince. She'd spend it when she had to, parcel it out, but she'd never mention it to him or anyone else. She'd told Sheila once that he had a sales job, he got paid in cash a lot, that was why he was away from home for such long periods of time.

When he walked back into the kitchen she was at the sink, peeling potatoes. He went over and touched her shoulder, kissed the top of her head. She didn't look at him; stood there stiffly until he moved away from her. But she'd be all right in a day or two. She'd be fine until the next time Bob Prince made the right kind of connection.

He wished it didn't have to be this way. He wished he could roll back the clock three years, do things differently, take the gray out of her hair and the pain out of her eyes. But he couldn't. It was just too late.

You had to play the cards you were dealt, no matter how lousy they were. The only thing that made it tolerable was that sometimes, on certain hands, you could find ways to stack the damn deck.

SO YOUNG, SO FAIR, SO DEAD

John Lutz

You can live your life through and try hard to be a decent sort, but trouble might still come to you. That's the way it seems to have been with me. My trouble was never the direct result of what I did, but the product of others. Neighbours especially. My advice is, don't ever get too friendly with your neighbors. I had to learn that the hard way.

Adelaide and I finished moving into our new house on a Sunday. That Monday I managed to stay away from the office and helped her sort the contents of cardboard boxes and move furniture about. We were both very happy that day, for we'd worked and saved for a long time to be able to afford our own home built here in the beautiful rolling hills south of the smoke-palled city. Here the air was clear as crystal and the view was the best nature had to offer.

And the house itself was what we'd always wanted. Though not large, it was well built with excellent materials and designed with a tasteful touch of miniature elegance. Adelaide and I took a walk around our green property before dark that evening and admired the way the wood-shingled house seemed to blend so well with the forest-like setting.

Of course the best thing about the house and the property was that it was ours. I'd worked hard to build up my own mail order business, Smathers Enterprises, and Mr and Mrs Will Smathers were comparatively well heeled for a couple in their early thirties who'd started married life on practically nothing.

Adelaide stopped strolling and gazed down the narrow blacktop road that fronted our property. I stood off and admired her delicate features and shining blonde hair, the weight of her lithe, graceful body resting on one slender leg. Adelaide, too, blended well with the natural surroundings. She was a natural beauty, the type makeup couldn't improve.

"I wonder about our neighbor," she said.

I moved next to her, slipping my arm about her waist. From where we stood we could see the nearest home through a break in the heavy green of the trees. A large brick home with a swimming pool behind it, it was the only house within a mile of us in either direction. I could just see the top of a small beach house near the pool. Within plain view near the attached two-car garage was a long, expensive blue convertible.

"Whoever our neighbor is," I said, "he has money."

"It certainly looks that way."

"On the other hand, he may be mortgaged up to his neck."

We stood for a moment longer looking down at the big house before going back inside. I say looking down because our home was situated high on one of the hills, and the blacktop road snaked sharply downward for the next two or three miles as it meandered like a still tributary to the Red Fox River.

I suppose I had no business saying anything about how our neighbor might have his property mortgaged. We'd gone into debt heavily to buy our own home. But the business was going well, and promised to continue to do so, and there was no reason we shouldn't be happy now and pay as we went along.

And in a way owing on the house could be a good thing. Once we were in it I knew we'd never give it up unless we absolutely had to, and it might serve as a spur to help make me work even harder.

But all the house motivated me to do that day was leave the office early so I could get home to enjoy living there with Adelaide. As I drove up the winding driveway I wondered when I'd get over the feeling that this was someone else's charming home I was approaching and not my own.

Adelaide knew I was coming home early and had dinner in the oven. She fixed us each a drink while we were waiting and we sat in the disarranged living room.

"I don't know when we'll ever get things the way we want them," Adelaide said, glancing around at the mess.

I grinned at her and took a sip of my Scotch and water,

admiring her fresh good looks in the plain housedress she did so much for. "There's plenty of time."

"I suppose so." She sighed with contentment and settled back in her chair. "I saw our neighbor today," she said.

"Did he drop by to introduce himself?"

"No, but you can see the house from our bedroom window upstairs. When I looked out this afternoon I noticed a man swimming in the pool. He had a guest, a girl in a purple bikini who stayed there most of the day, then drove away in a little sports car."

I had to laugh. If Adelaide had any faults at all, one of them would be that she was a trifle nosy. "Are you going to start a dossier on them?" I asked jokingly.

"Not yet," she said with a smile. "And it's not 'them', it's 'him'. The man seems to live there alone."

"Big house for a single man," I remarked, "though it sounds like he has his fun there."

A timer bell sounded in the kitchen and Adelaide put down her drink and stood. I walked behind her as she hurried into the kitchen to check on the dinner.

"You keep an eye on him and keep me posted," I said, rubbing the back of my hand playfully up the nape of her neck. She didn't answer and I kept quiet. Experience had taught me to joke only so far about Adelaide's feminine curiosity.

Though without any prompting she had another tidbit of information for me the next evening when I returned home.

"Our neighbor seems to be something of a swinger," she said. "There was a girl in a red bikini there today."

"Same girl, different bikini," I speculated.

Adelaide shook her head. "The first one was a tall brunette. Today it was a short blonde."

I smiled and shrugged. "His sister?"

"I doubt it," Adelaide said, and drew a miniature bronze rooster from the carton.

"I'm sure we'll find out more about him," I said. "He'll probably turn up at our door one of these days soon to introduce himself. Could be he doesn't even realize there's anybody living here yet." Silently I wondered if he'd plant a shade tree between us and his pool when he did find out. Then for the next few hours I was busy helping Adelaide finish the job of unpacking and thought about little else.

But that night my own curiosity about our neighbor was aroused when I walked across the bedroom to close the drapes.

As my hand reached for the pull cord my eye caught the flash of a revolving red light in the distance. I leaned forward and squinted into the darkness, and I saw that a police car was parked in our neighbor's driveway beside his long blue convertible.

As I watched, another car pulled up behind that one. In the reflection of its headlights I could see that it was a plain gray sedan. Two men got out of it and went into the house without knocking.

A hand touched my shoulder and Adelaide was standing beside me.

"Now who's nosy?" she asked.

I didn't answer, and we stood there for a while and watched shadows cross the distant draped windows. Then the two men and a uniformed policeman came out of the house. They got into their respective cars, the red light on the patrol car was turned off, and both cars left together. A few minutes later the windows of the house went black and Adelaide and I were staring at nothing.

"What do you think?" Adelaide asked as we turned away from the window.

"It could have been a lot of things," I said. "Maybe the police were called because somebody was sick. Maybe the two men in the plain car were doctors. Maybe our neighbor thought he saw a prowler. I guess if we really wanted to find out the thing to do would be to ask him."

The next evening I got in the car and drove down the road to do just that.

"It's because I'm a burglar," our neighbor answered me amiably.

I stood there and blinked, twice. I'd introduced myself when he'd answered the door, and he'd introduced himself as Jack Hogan and invited me inside and offered me a drink. After a few minutes' exploratory conversation with the tanned and handsome man, I'd gotten around to asking him about the commotion at his house we'd witnessed last night, offering our help if anything was wrong.

"The police were here to harass me," Jack Hogan went on.

"Lieutenant Faber and his friends. I humor the lieutenant because I understand he acts out of frustration."

"But if you're innocent—" I said in a rather dumbfounded way.

"But I'm not innocent," Hogan said freely, his gray eyes as sincere as his voice. "Though if you tell anyone I said so I'll deny it. Lieutenant Faber knows I'm guilty, but he can't do anything about it because I'm too smart for him. That's the fun of it."

I didn't know if Hogan was joking or not. When I took a sip of my drink some of it spilled on my hand.

"A burglary was committed a few nights ago," Hogan said, offering me his neatly folded handkerchief to dry my fingers. "They know I did it but they don't know how, or what I did with the loot. Oh, they come and search here every now and then, but we both know they won't find anything. And if a young lady is prepared to testify that I spent the time of the robbery in her presence, where does it all leave poor Lieutenant Faber?"

"Where I am, I suppose," I said. "Confused."

"Well, no need to be confused. I say what's the sense of getting away with something if nobody knows about it? Surely you can understand that. Then, too, there's the profit. Burglary is a thriving business. How else could I afford all this, living alone in a ten-room house with a pool, nights on the town, flashy women, flashy cars? A wonderful life. I admit to you, I need all that."

"Then, in a way, it's all a game," I said slowly.

"Of course it's a game. Everybody plays his own game. I just admit mine because I'm good enough to get by with it even though it is illegal."

"But it's wrong," I said, trying to bat down his clearly stated logic.

"Sure, it's wrong," Hogan said, "but so's cheating on your income tax, overcharging the public if you're a big corporation, leaving a penny for a paper when you don't have a dime. To tell you the truth, I don't worry about right or wrong."

"I guess you don't."

"You see," Hogan explained earnestly, "it's the challenge. I like nice things; I indulge myself. When I see something of value I take it. I guess I have to take it."

"Kleptomania on a grand scale, huh?"

"Hey, you might say that!" He raised his glass and grinned.

I finished my drink and got up to leave. Hogan walked with me to the door. On the porch I noticed that the long blue convertible was gone, replaced by an even longer and more expensive tan convertible. Hogan saw me looking at the car.

"Don't worry," he said. "It's not stolen and it doesn't belong to a girl I have hidden in the house. You didn't interrupt anything and I can afford to trade cars any time I feel like it. Say," he said, pointing at the long car, "how do you like it?"

"Beautiful," I said.

"Sure, and it cost a hunk of cash. Well, drop by again, why don't you? Bring the wife and we'll take a dip in the pool."

I walked down the driveway to where my car was parked. I didn't know what to think of our new neighbor. I was sure he wasn't joking, and I must admit I reacted as a lot of people would react. There was a sense of resentment in me that the things I worked so hard for, this man simply went out and took. And yet I found that I couldn't really dislike Jack Hogan. I waved to him as I started the engine and drove away.

When I told Adelaide about the visit she didn't believe me. I didn't blame her.

"You'd have to talk to him to understand how he thinks," I told her. "You might describe him as an honest crook."

"An honest crook?"

"Well, honest about being crooked, anyway."

That confused Adelaide almost as much as I was confused, so I had a snack, went over some work I'd brought home, then went to bed.

Neither Adelaide or myself mentioned our neighbor for a while as we busied ourselves about our new home. Though I noticed that Adelaide kept a pair of binoculars in the bedroom now, and she often left the house to drive past the Hogan residence and look more closely at it, I suppose to check for bikini-clad guests and sports cars. Still, I don't think she really completely believed what I'd told her about Jack Hogan until Lieutenant Faber called on us one Saturday afternoon.

Adelaide and I were working in the garden she'd planted when the lieutenant drove up in his gray sedan. I stood leaning on my hoe and watched him approach. He was a harried-looking man who appeared to be in his mid-forties. His straight graying hair was combed to the side over his forehead and the breeze mussed it as his lined face broke into its emotionless, professional smile. Even before he introduced himself I knew who he was.

"I hope we haven't done anything wrong," Adelaide said, returning the bland smile with one that shone.

"Wrong? No," Lieutenant Faber said. "Actually I'm a city detective and have no authority out here in the county anyway."

"And yet you drove out here to talk to us," I said thoughtfully.

"I don't speak officially, Mr Smathers," Faber said in his tired, hoarse voice. "Anything I say to you folks is off the record." He got out a cigar and lit it expertly against the breeze. "How you getting along with your neighbor down the road?"

"You mean the burglar?" I'd decided it was time to stop circling.

"You said it, not me," Lieutenant Faber said.

"Actually Mr Hogan said it. He didn't seem to mind admitting that fact to me at all."

"Oh, he admits it, all right," the lieutenant said in a voice suddenly filled with frustration, "but not to anybody who can do anything about it or prove he even said it. I could tell you some things about your neighbor that would really surprise you."

"You mean he really *is* a burglar?" Adelaide asked suddenly.

"Ask him," Lieutenant Faber said. "He'll tell you. Not that we can get anything on him. We know but we can't prove."

"He told me he was clever," I said.

Lieutenant Faber nodded bitterly. "He's been clever enough so far. We know exactly how he operates – in fact, he always seems to go to some trouble to let us know he's the one who pulled his jobs, but pinning him down's another thing. He gets rid of the loot so fast and secretly we can't get him there, and usually he knows where to find big sums of cash that can't be traced. As far as alibis are concerned, there's always some girl who's willing to testify that he was with her at his house or her apartment or some motel. We can't watch him twenty-four hours a day." The lieutenant added with an undeniable touch of envy, "He seems to have an endless supply of girls."

"He is rather handsome," Adelaide said, and when we looked at her she blushed slightly. "I mean, he would be to a certain type of woman."

"The type he's handsome to will lie for him," Faber said, "that's for sure. He must have something working for him."

"Money," I said. "If used properly money will buy almost anything, and Hogan strikes me as the kind who knows how to use his wealth."

"That'd be okay," Lieutenant Faber said, "only it's other people's wealth. Just last week we know – off the record, of course – that he burglarized over three thousand in cash and five thousand in loot from the home of J. Grestom, president of Grestom Chemical."

"Isn't that the plant about four miles from here?" Adelaide asked. "The one that dumps all that sludge into the Red Fox River?"

"The same," Lieutenant Faber said, "one of the biggest operations of its kind in the state."

"Sounds like Robin Hood," I remarked.

"Yeah," the lieutenant said without amusement, "Hogan steals from the rich, only he doesn't give to anybody."

"From talking to him," I said, "my impression is that it's all a big game to him."

"A game where other people get hurt, and a game I'm tired of playing. Hogan's a crook like all crooks. He's one of the world's takers. He's a kid and the world's one big candy shop with a dumb proprietor."

I thought good manners dictated me not pointing out who that dumb proprieter must be in Hogan's mind.

"Do you think you ever will catch him?" Adelaide asked.

Lieutenant Faber nodded. "We always do in the end. He'll make a mistake, and we'll be there to notice when he does."

"He seemed awfully confident," I said.

"Confident?" Faber snorted with disgust. "Confident's not the word. Brass is more like it! About six months ago he burglarized the payroll office of a company downtown when their safe was full—"

"You mean he's a safe-cracker too?" I interrupted.

"No, he stole the whole blasted safe. It was one of those little boxes that should have been bolted to the floor from the inside but wasn't. The worst thing is that two nights later the safe turned up empty in the middle of a place that manufactures burglar alarms – bolted to the floor!"

"It really is a game with him, isn't it?" I said.

Adelaide was laughing quietly. "You must admit he's good at his game."

"And we're good at ours!" The lieutenant's face was flushed.

"I'm sure you didn't drive up here just to inform us that we're living next to a police character," I said. By that time I was certain I'd figured out the reason for Lieutenant Faber's visit. I was right.

"What I'd like," he said, "is for you to sort of keep an eye on Hogan's house. Not spy, mind you, just keep an eye on." He drew on his cigar and awaited an answer.

I took a lazy swat at the earth with the edge of the hoe blade. "I don't see anything wrong with us telling you if anything odd goes on there," I said, "under the circumstances."

Faber exhaled smoke and handed me a white card with his name and telephone extension number. "Hogan's not used to having neighbors," he said. "That's why he bought the house he's in. He might forget about you and make a slip. Do you have a pair of binoculars or a telescope?"

I looked at Adelaide and winked so the lieutenant couldn't see me. "I think I have an old pair somewhere." That somewhere was on the edge of Adelaide's dresser, where the powerful field glasses could be used by her at a moment's notice.

"Well, it's been nice to meet you folks," Lieutenant Faber said, "and it's good of you to help. Your police department thanks you." Again he shot us his mechanical smile, then turned and walked toward his car.

Adelaide and I stood and watched until he'd turned from the driveway and was gone from sight.

"Now you can really play Mata Hari," I said, going back to my hoeing.

Adelaide didn't answer as she bent down and applied the spade to the broken ground.

I left the spying – as I'd come to think of it – pretty much up to Adelaide. She spent a lot of time sitting at the bedroom window, her elbows resting on the sill as she peered intently through the field glasses. But at the end of two weeks she hadn't noticed anything really noteworthy, just the comings and goings of a high-living young bachelor of wealth.

She was sitting concentrating through the glasses one afternoon when the doorbell chimed. I rose from where I was lying on the bed reading and went downstairs to answer it.

When the door swung open there was Jack Hogan, dressed in swimming trunks and smiling, with a brightly colored striped towel slung about his neck.

"How about taking me up on that swimming invitation now?" he asked. "The temperature's over ninety, so I thought it'd be a good time."

I was a little surprised to see him, a little off balance. "Uh, sure, if it's okay with Adelaide." I stepped back. "Come on in and I'll ask her."

When I went upstairs Adelaide was still at the window with her eyes pressed to the binoculars.

"Jack Hogan's downstairs," I said. "He wants to know if we'll go swimming with him in his pool."

Adelaide turned abruptly and looked up at me, her eyes wide and appearing even wider due to the red circles about them left by the binoculars. "But I thought he was in his beach house! I've been waiting for him to come out!"

"You'll wait a long time, darling. He's in our living room. Do you want to go?"

"Swimming? Do you?"

"I don't see why we shouldn't. It is a hot day." I changed quickly into my swimming trunks and went downstairs to tell Jack Hogan we'd be ready to go as soon as Adelaide had changed.

Adelaide had on her skimpiest black bikini when she came downstairs. I saw Hogan look with something like momentary shock at her tanned and shapely body.

This was the first time they'd met, at least close up. After introductions we drove to Hogan's house in his long tan convertible. Seated beside him was an amply proportioned blonde who looked as if she might have been used to model the car on TV. He introduced her as Prudence, which I didn't think fitted, and we were on our way.

As we splashed around, drank highballs and got better acquainted, I found that I liked Jack Hogan, though I must still admit to some jealousy and distaste that he could come by all he had so easily while I worked so hard for less. What surprised me was that Adelaide seemed to like Hogan too. Adelaide had had a father who'd deserted her, who'd been much like Hogan, free-spending and dishonest. She had hated him until the day he died, perhaps still hated his memory. And yet from time to time I could see some of her father in Adelaide, under the surface of the careful, thrifty and loving woman she really was. I saw some of that wildness and daring now as she stood on Hogan's tanned shoulders and let him flip her out and into the deep water.

When we got out of the pool and went inside for snacks I noticed an expensive-looking, lewd silver statuette of Bacchus on a low table in the entrance hall. It could hardly escape my attention because Jack Hogan flicked it with his finger as we walked past.

"I stole that earlier this year," he said, "or rather one just like it. The stolen one had the owner's name engraved on the bottom, so I sold it and used the proceeds to buy this exact duplicate. Lieutenant Faber really thought he had me when he discovered that statue sitting there, but when we checked for the owner's engraving it wasn't there, and I could hardly have removed it without any trace. It drove the lieutenant almost wild." Hogan chuckled as he led us into the large kitchen with an attached dining area.

"I don't think I've ever met anyone like you," Adelaide said to Hogan with a bewildered little laugh.

Prudence, the busty blonde, popped a potato chip with cheese dip into her mouth. "Oh, there isn't anyone else like Jackie!"

I could only agree as I mixed myself another highball.

From the time of the little impromptu swimming party on, I began to notice things. It seemed to me that Adelaide spent more and more time spying from the window for Lieutenant Faber. And she found excuses to drive into the city more and more often. And on occasions when I came home from work I noticed that her hair near the base of her skull appeared damp. Did I only imagine the faint scent of chlorine those evenings as she served dinner?

It seemed, too, that Adelaide and I were caught up in more and more domestic quarrels, and we'd seldom quarreled before. She accused me of having ignored her through the years, spending all my free time and weekends working.

It didn't take long for me to be ninety percent sure that Adelaide and Jack Hogan were conducting an affair behind my back. But would I ever be more than ninety percent sure? Hogan managed his love life as he did his burglaries, with such practiced skill that the victims of his callousness could only suspect but never prove, maybe not even to themselves. For a long time I deliberated before taking any action.

There was never any doubt in my mind that I would take some sort of action. I couldn't allow things to go on as they were, and I felt confident that I could do something about them. A man who's hard to best in business is hard to best in any other phase of life.

What I finally did was go to see Lieutenant Faber.

The lieutenant's office was small, littered and dirty. There were no windows, and dented gray file-cabinets stood behind the cluttered desk where Lieutenant Faber sat. As I entered he glanced up with his uneasy, weary look – then managed to smile at me.

"Have a seat, Mr Smathers," he said, motioning toward a chair with a tooth-marked yellow pencil. "I take it you've come here because you know something about Jack Hogan." I couldn't help but notice the hope in his voice.

"In a way that's why I'm here," I said, and watched the wariness creep into the lieutenant's narrow eyes as he settled back in his desk chair.

"What is it that you observed?" he asked.

"Nothing that really pertains to his burglaries, Lieutenant. In fact, nothing of use to you at all."

Faber let the pencil drop onto the desk top with a resonant little clatter. "Why don't we talk straight to each other, Mr Smathers? Save time, yours as well as mine."

"All right, I came here to ask you for a favor."

"Favor?" His gray eyebrows rose slowly.

"Yes," I said, "I wonder if you could arrange for me to have some infrared binoculars. I think most of what goes on at Hogan's house happens after dark, and it would help if I could see through that darkness."

Lieutenant Faber rolled his tongue to one side of his mouth and looked thoughtful. "Seems like a good idea," he said. "I can get you the field glasses within a few days."

"Fine. Should I pick them up here?"

"If you'd like." Lieutenant Faber looked even more thoughtful. "What is it you think you're going to see at night?" he asked.

I shrugged. "Who knows? That's why I want the infrared binoculars." I stood to leave.

"I'll give you a telephone call when you can pick them up," the lieutenant said, standing behind his desk.

"Call me at my office," I told him, "anytime during the day."

"Why not your home?"

"Because my office would be more convenient."

He came from around the desk and walked with me to the door. "Mr Smathers," he said in a confidential voice, "I want Jack Hogan any way I can get him. Do you understand?"

"I thought you wanted him that badly," I said as I went out.

That very evening, when I awoke after dozing off while watching television, I found a gold cigarette lighter beneath the sofa cushions. During my sleep my hand had gotten itself wedged between the cushions, and when I freed it my fingertips had just brushed the hard, smooth surface.

When I rolled back the cushion I saw the lighter, with the initials J. H. engraved on it. I knew it would also have J. H.'s fingerprints on it, so I lifted it gently by the corners and slipped it into my breast pocket before Adelaide came into the room.

Lieutenant Faber telephoned my office in the middle of the week to say I could drop by headquarters and pick up the infrared binoculars. So I wouldn't waste any valuable working time, I drove to see him on my lunch hour.

The binoculars were in a small case sitting on the edge of his desk. I sat down and examined them and he shoved a receipt across the desk top for me to sign.

"You suspect Jack Hogan is seeing your wife, don't you?" he said in a testing voice.

I didn't look at him as I hastily scrawled my signature on the pink receipt. "Yes, and I want to know for sure."

"And what happens if you do find out they're seeing each other?"

I handed the receipt back to him and rested the binoculars in my lap. "What would happen if a burglary was committed and evidence pointing to Hogan was found at the scene?"

"Then all we'd have to worry about would be breaking down his customary alibi."

"And if he had no alibi? If he was actually home alone at the time of the burglary but couldn't prove it because of a witness's testimony that he saw him leave then return?"

Lieutenant Faber ran his tongue over his dry lips. "That's what I've been waiting for, only Hogan has never dropped a clue in his life."

Gingerly I reached into my pocket and dropped the gold cigarette lighter with Jack Hogan's initials onto Faber's desk. As he reached for it I grabbed his hand.

"I think you'll find it has Hogan's fingerprints on it."

Lieutenant Faber leaned back away from the cigarette lighter as if it were something that might explode. I saw his glance dart to his office door to make sure it was closed, and at that moment I was very sure of him.

"Where did you get it?" he asked.

"Under the sofa cushions in my home."

"And you're giving it to me?"

I nodded. "And I don't require a receipt."

Lieutenant Faber slowly unwrapped the cellophane wrapper from one of his cigars. As he held a match to the cigar he looked at me over the rising and falling flame. Then he flattened the cellophane wrapper, slid it deftly beneath the gold lighter and placed both lighter and cellophane in his desk drawer.

"For the next three weekends," I said, "I plan to tell my wife I have to leave town on business from Thursday evening until Monday morning. Instead I'll stay at a motel outside of town, and I'll spend my nights on a hillside watching Hogan's house."

"From Thursday night to Monday morning," Lieutenant Faber repeated slowly.

"When you find the right burglary case, call me at the motel, and I'll tell you if Hogan was home alone that night. Then you 'discover' the lighter at the scene of the crime and I testify that I saw Hogan drive away and that he was gone during the time the robbery was committed."

"One thing," Lieutenant Faber said. "What if . . .?"

"That's possible," I told him, "but Adelaide will hardly be in a position to say she was at Hogan's house all night, will she? Especially considering the fact that she knows he's a burglar anyway and deserves to be caught. She can't afford to be like his swinging single alibis."

Lieutenant Faber nodded and I stood and carefully tucked the binocular case beneath my arm.

"I'll let you know what motel I'll be staying at," I said to him as I started to leave.

"Smathers." He stopped me. "I want you to know I'm doing this because of what I think of Hogan. He's a —"

And the lieutenant told me in the purplest language I'd ever heard just what he thought of Jack Hogan.

I will say Adelaide put on a good act. When I told her about my upcoming business trips she acted convincingly upset by the idea of being left alone. She even stood in the doorway and waved wistfully after me as I got into a cab for the drive to the airport.

Only I didn't go to the airport. I had the cabbie drive me to a car rental agency where I rented a compact sedan. Then I drove to Sleepy Dan's Motel and checked in. If I worked it right, I could write all this off as business expenses. And I was smart enough to have set up a plan that would require me to miss only three days, Fridays, in three weeks at the office. I could even sneak in and do some work on Sunday when no one was there if need be. I congratulated myself on my cleverness as I lay down to get a little sleep before sunset.

The spot I'd picked was perfect, a small clearing on the side of a hill from where I could look directly down at Hogan's large house and grounds. The powerful binoculars brought everything near to me, and the infrared lenses eliminated the darkness as a problem. The night was warm, and I unbuttoned my shirt and settled back to watch until morning.

There were no results that first week. Lieutenant Faber sounded disappointed when I told him on the phone of Jack Hogan's activities. A burglary had been committed that would have been perfect for our purposes, but I had to tell him that at the time Hogan wasn't home and I didn't know where he'd gone. Lieutenant Faber suggested hopefully that he might have gone to my house, but I quickly told him he could rule that out. My house was in view from where I watched also. We decided to wait for an opportunity we could be absolutely sure of.

The second week that I stationed myself on the hillside something did happen. My wife's affair with Jack Hogan was confirmed beyond even the slightest doubt.

It was about midnight when I saw the headlights turn from the road into Hogan's driveway. As I pressed the binoculars to my eyes and adjusted the focus dial, I saw that it was Adelaide's car that had pulled into Hogan's big double garage to park alongside his convertible. He stepped out onto the porch and met her, and they kissed for an embarrassingly long time before going inside. A few hours later I saw them emerge from the house and go for a late night swim. I didn't want to watch that, so I lowered the binoculars and sat feeling the numbness in me give way to a smoldering rage.

The next night nothing happened. Hogan spent the entire night alone, going to bed about ten o'clock. I suppose he was tired.

That afternoon Lieutenant Faber called me at the motel. A residence in the west end had been burglarized the night before, smoothly and professionally. There were no clues of any kind.

I told him that Hogan had spent the night home alone. The burglary had to have taken place during the early morning hours, so we agreed that I would say I saw Hogan leave in his convertible at two thirty a.m. and return at five. Tomorrow morning, when Lieutenant Faber returned to question the victim and re-examine the scene of the crime, he would "find" the gold lighter, and the frame around Jack Hogan would be complete.

There was really no reason to go back that third night, but the silent rage had grown in me along with my curiosity. And I suppose it gave me some small sense of power, to be able to watch them without them knowing. It kept me from being a complete fool, and while Hogan didn't know it, he had only one more night of freedom.

All that dark, hot night Adelaide didn't arrive at Hogan's home. The windows of the big ranch house were dark, the grounds silent. Around me the crickets chirped madly as if protesting the heat as I sat staring intently through the binoculars.

Then a light came on in one of the windows, the window I knew to be Jack Hogan's bedroom. After a while a downstairs light came on too, and both lights stayed on. I looked at my watch. Four-thirty.

He must have telephoned her. At twenty to five Adelaide turned her car into Hogan's driveway. This time after she pulled her car into the garage Hogan came out and lowered the door, for the sun would soon rise. I watched as he put his arm around her and they went into the house.

The sun came up amid orange streaks on the horizon, turning the heat of night into an even more intense heat.

Then I heard a door slam off in the distance, and I scanned, then focused the binoculars on Adelaide in her skimpy black bikini. Hogan was beside her with a towel draped over his shoulder. He flicked her playfully with the towel and she laughed and dived into the pool, and he laughed and jumped in after her.

I watched them for about twenty minutes before I came to my decision.

Jack Hogan had always freely admitted being a burglar. Now I intended to play his game, to tell him openly what was going to happen to him, so that he'd know he'd been outsmarted. Let the knowledge that he couldn't prove his innocence torment him. Let him suffer as he'd made Lieutenant Faber suffer, as he'd made his burglary victims suffer. As he'd made me suffer. I placed the binoculars in their case, stood and clambered down the hillside to where the car was parked.

Then it occurred to me that Hogan might give me a rough time once he realized he was cornered, so I drove by my house first and got my forty-five caliber revolver from my dresser drawer.

They were sitting in lounge chairs alongside the pool when I approached, Adelaide leaning forward and Hogan rubbing suntan lotion onto her back.

"How's the water?" I asked calmly.

They whirled, surprised, then Hogan smiled. "It's great," he said jauntily. "I've invited Adelaide over here before for an early morning swim, but this is the first time she's come."

"I know better," I said, watching Adelaide trying to control the fear and guilt that marked her features. At last she managed a facsimile of a poker face.

"Know better?" Hogan was still playing innocent.

"Yes, and now there are a few things I want you to know. There was a burglary committed night before last in the west end. No clues yet."

Hogan appeared puzzled. "So what? I was home in bed all that night."

"For the last several weekends I've been spying on you from that hillside," I said. "Lieutenant Faber gave me infrared binoculars to use at night. I'm going to swear that I saw you leave and return at the time that burglary took place."

"You can't!" Adelaide said in a high voice.

"Quiet, dear." I looked again at Hogan. He was grinning.

"Your word against mine, old pal. I've beat that one before."

"I believe you lost your initialed gold cigarette lighter," I said. "It has your fingerprints on it and it's going to be found at the scene of the crime."

Now anger showed on Hogan's handsome face. "By Lieutenant Faber, would be my guess."

"Your guess is correct. We're framing you and sending you to prison, to put it plainly."

"As I've always put it, huh?"

I nodded and couldn't help a faint, gloating smile. Hogan's game and he was getting beat at it. "Lieutenant Faber told me you were one of the world's takers," I said. "Well, I'm one of the world's keepers. I don't give up what I have easily."

"Faber was right about that," Hogan said frankly. "I'm a taker. I can't see something of value without taking it."

"Something like Adelaide?"

"Exactly."

"Your mistake," I said tauntingly, "was in trying to take something from me. I'll think of you from time to time when you're in prison." I turned to go home, leaving Adelaide to return when she felt like it.

"It won't work," her voice said behind me.

I turned around and saw that the fear and surprise had left Adelaide's face completely to be replaced by a look of determination.

"And why won't it work?" I asked.

"Because I'll swear in court that I spent that entire night with Jack."

I started to laugh incredulously at her, but the laugh wouldn't come out. "But you were at home."

"Alone," Adelaide said. "You could never prove it. I'll swear I was here instead."

"You'd swear to that in a courtroom, under oath?" I stared at her, feeling the sun on the back of my moist shirt. "But why?"

"I don't think you'd understand."

"Now listen!"

"Nothing more to listen to, or say," Adelaide said, and as a pretense for getting away from me she turned and walked toward the diving board.

Hogan lowered himself into the shallow water with an

infuriating smile. "Nothing more to say, old pal. Sorry." And he actually looked as if he might be sorry, the gracious winner.

The sun seemed to grow hotter, unbearably hot, sending beads of sweat darting down my flesh inside my shirt. I looked up and saw Adelaide poised gracefully on the end of the diving board, tanned and beautiful in her tiny swimming suit as she carefully avoided a glance in my direction.

How the revolver got from my pocket into my hand I honestly don't know. I have no recollection of it, a magician's trick. And I don't remember pulling the trigger.

Adelaide was raising her arms, preparing to dive, when the gun roared in my hand as if of its own will. I saw Adelaide's body jerk, saw the spray of blood, heard the scream as she half fell, half jumped awkwardly from the diving board, arms and legs thrashing as she struck the water. Then there was a choking sound and she stopped thrashing and floated motionless face up.

Hogan stroked toward the ladder, a look not of shock or horror on his face, but an expression that suggested he might be very sick. "Oh, God, Smathers!" he said as he started to climb the chrome ladder. I let him get to the second step before blasting him back into the pool.

I stood there then, pulling the trigger automatically, emptying the revolver into their bodies.

Considering how large the pool was, it was amazing how quickly all the water turned red.

So now I'm sitting here awaiting trial, writing this to kill time, though I'm sure the hour will come when I'll pray I had this time back. There isn't any doubt in my mind that I'll be convicted. They have my full confession, and now they'll have this.

What concerns me is that all my life I've tried to be a decent sort of man, hard-working, industrious. I'm not very religious, but I have tried to live by the ten commandments, breaking them every now and then, of course, like everybody else. And yet if you went back and read over this again you could put your finger on spot after spot until you'd realize that between the four of us, me, Adelaide, Jack Hogan and Lieutenant Faber, in one way or another we've broken every single commandment.

Evil spreads, I suppose, like the red through the water in Hogan's swimming pool.

EFFECTIVE MEDICINE

B. Traven

1

One afternoon, on coming home from the cotton field where I had worked all day long, I noted, outside the barbed-wire fence of the bungalow I was living in, a Mexican peasant squatting on the bare ground. I did not know him because, as I learned later in the evening, he was from another village six or seven miles away. He was very poor and all in rags.

Having greeted me he waited patiently until I had dismounted from the burro I had been riding home on. When I had taken off the saddle and the burro had gone its way looking for cornstalks in the yard, the Mexican entered the front yard, came close and began talking.

He talked rapidly and in a confused manner. For a moment I thought him to be on the high – that is to say, that he might have smoked more marijuana than he could digest. However, though he was now telling the end of his story, now the beginning, now the middle, all in confusion, I soon noticed that he was neither drunk nor doped, only very ignorant and evidently suffering from a nervous breakdown – as far as this can happen to a Mexican of his kind.

It was difficult for me to make sense of his story and for a long while I was unable to see which part of his story was the end and which the beginning or the middle. The farther he came in his story the more was he swept away by his emotion until he only blubbered or shouted absolutely incoherent phrases. Never once did he fully end his tale. Whenever I thought him close to the end and I was trying to catch up with the full meaning, I realized that he was already telling his story from the middle backwards to the start again. In this confused way he told me his story more than a dozen times and always with the same words, out of a vocabulary which barely consisted of more than three hundred different words. His mood changed constantly. Each time he started as if he were telling the story of somebody else, yet invariably he ended up crying almost hysterically.

"Look here, señor doctor, that old hussy and tramp that she is and always was, she is gone. She is gone with that ugly cabron and dirty son of a heathenish dog, that thief Pánfilo, you know him, señor, the one I mean, that would steal the horns of the devil if they were not grown on, you know that housebreaker, and if you don't know him, so much the better for you because he steals barbed wire and cuts telegraph poles and the telegraph wire also and no hog is safe if he is around. I wish him the smallpox all over his face and the most terrible disease extra to make it worse for him. I come home. I come home from my work in the bush. In the bush I had to cut down hard trees for making charcoal; you see. I sell the wood and the charcoal if I have any to the agents – who are thieves, too. I come home tired and hungry. Home in my *jacalito*. I'm hungry more than a dog, that's what I am, from hard work in the bush. No tortillas ready. No frijoles in the pot. Nothing. I tell you the truth, señor doctor, nothing. I call my woman, that old hussy. My *mujer* I mean. No answer. I look around. She isn't at home, my woman isn't. Her sack with her dress in it, and her shirt and her torn stockings, which are in that same sack also, are all gone. The sack used to hang on a peg. My *mujer* has ran away. She doesn't ever return. Never, such what I say. And she is so full of lice too, my woman is. I've no tortillas for me to eat. Nor black beans for my empty belly. Off she went like the stinking hussy that she is. If I only knew who she ran off with, that useless old nag. I'll get *him*. And I'll learn him how to steal decent and honest women that belong to other men. He is a *mil* times worse than any dirty cabron." (*Mil* means thousand; to his kind, though, *mil* means anything between one hundred and one thousand billions.) "Now, I ask you, mister doctor señor, who will make tortillas for me? That's what I want you to tell me right now."

So he asked, but he did not wait for my answer and he went on with his story, hardly stopping to catch a full breath.

"Nobody is going to make me tortillas now. That's what it is, I tell you. She has ran away. I'll catch *him* and he won't live to tell who done it. I come home in my *choza*. I come home from the hot bush. Hungry and dying of thirst. I don't mind the thirst. I come home and no tortillas. No frijoles. She is gone. She has taken her sack with her dress and her stockings along with her."

At this point of his sad story he cried so bitterly that for the next three minutes it was difficult to understand what he was saying now because it was all blubbering. Slowly he calmed down once more. Yet, crying or not crying, he talked on and on like a cracked phonograph record.

"I come home. From the bush I come home and I've worked all day long under that blistering sun and no—"

"Now wait a minute, *manito*," I interrupted him before he went into his speech again and made it impossible for me to stop him before he reached that part of his story where he would have to cry for a few minutes. "Let's talk this over quietly. You've told me your heartbreaking experience fifteen times by now. I admit it is heartbreaking. But I can't listen to it a *mil* times because I've got other things to attend to. All I can say is that your *mujer* is not here in my *jacal*. Step in and look around and make sure."

"I know, señor mister, that she isn't in your house. A fine educated doctor like you would never even touch such a filthy one like her, and so full of lice that sometimes you might think the wind is in her hair, so fast it moves from all the lice in it."

The lice seemed to remind him once more of his loss and he started telling the story again. The whole thing began to bore me and I said: "Why, for hell's sake, do you have to tell all that just to me? Go to the *alcalde* – the mayor, I mean – and tell him your story. He is the proper person to attend to such matters. I'm just a simple doctor here without any political influence and no *disputado* backing me up. I've no power and so I can do nothing for you. Nothing, do you hear? Nothing at all. Go to the *alcalde*. He'll catch your *mujer*. It's his duty, because he is the authority in this place."

"That *alcalde*, you mean, señor? I can tell you right now and here that he is the biggest ass under heaven. That's why he was elected *alcalde*. And he is a thief too, and also a woman-raper. Just for his meanness and his stupidity it was that he got elected because no decent and no honest person had any word in that election, see? You ought to know that, señor."

"Anyway, *amigo*," I said, "he has to look after your troubles. And as I said before, I've no power, no power at all, to do anything for you. Get this in your mind, friend. I've no power."

"But you're wrong, mister *caballero*. You've got all the powers in the world. We know this very well. And no mistake. You can pull bullets out of the bodies of killed bandits with fishing hooks and make them live again. I mean the boys with federal bullets in their bellies and legs. You understand what I want to say and what I know and what the *federales* would be so very eager to know also. Because you have all the powers to do anything under heaven. That's why you know where my woman is at this hour. Tell her that I'm hungry and that I've come home from the bush after much hard work. She has to make tortillas and cook frijoles for me. I'm very hungry now."

"Now look here, friend. Let's be calm about it." I spoke to him as I would have to a little boy. "See here, I've not seen your woman go away. Since I've not seen where she went I can't tell you where she is at present. I can't even imagine where she perhaps might be. In fact, I know nothing, nothing at all. I don't even know her face or what she looks like. Please, *amigo*, do understand, I know nothing of her. And that'll be all. Thank you for paying me such a delightful visit. Now I'm busy. Goodbye. *Adiós*."

He stared at me with his brown dreamy eyes as if in wonder. His belief in the infallibility of a white, and particularly in the immaculate perfection of a *Norte-americano* had been shaken profoundly. At the same time, though, he seemed to recall something which had evidently been hammered into his head since he could speak his first words, and that was something which, in his opinion, was forever connected with the *Americanos*, as is the color green with young grass.

So he said: "I'm not rich, señor. No, I'm not. I can't pay you much. I've only two pesos and forty-six centavitos. That's all I have in the world. But this whole fortune of mine I'll give you for your work and for your medicine so that I can find my woman and get her back to my side, that hussy, because I am very hungry."

"I don't want your money. Even if you would give me *mil* gold pesos I could not get your woman back. I don't know where she is and therefore I can't tell her that you must have your tortillas and your frijoles. Can't you understand, man, that I don't know where your woman is?"

Suspicion was in his eyes when he looked at me after I had finished. He was quite evidently not certain whether it was the little money he could offer me which kept me from helping him or that in fact I might really not know the whereabouts of his spouse.

Gazing for a few minutes at me in this manner he finally shook his head as if full of doubts about something of which he had thought himself very sure before. Honoring me once more with that suspicious glance, he left my place, but not until I had told him several times more that I had to cook my dinner and could no longer stand idly around and listen to his troubles, for which I had no remedies.

As I learned a few days later, he visited practically all the huts of the village, where he told his story and reported also that this white medicine-man of whom they talked so highly was but a poor faker, ignorant of the simplest things of everyday life.

This low opinion of his was taken by the villagers for a grave insult upon themselves, since I was the pride of the whole community, who considered me one of the wisest and greatest medicine-men that have ever walked the earth. I do not know, but I can fairly well guess, what the villagers recommended him to do so as to make my mysterious powers work in his favor.

2

Shortly after sunrise next day he returned to my place, placed himself outside by the barbed-wire fence, and waited there peacefully until I noticed his presence and came out to speak to him.

The moment he saw me feeding corn to my burro he called me. "Just for a very, very little short moment, señor mister, please. Please, come here close to the fence and listen what I've got to tell you. And you'd better listen terribly carefully because I'm serious. As a plain matter of fact I'm extremely serious this morning, because I haven't slept very much."

On stepping up to the fence I noted that while I was

approaching he picked up from the ground a long machete which as I could see easily had been sharpened with utmost care. It must have taken him hours to give that heavy sword-like bushknife such an almost razor-like edge.

Nonchalantly, though meaningfully, he moved this machete up and down before my eyes while he was talking again. Occasionally, just as nonchalantly, he examined the edge with his wetted thumb, and now and then pulling a hair out of his thick black scalp and cutting his hair softly, practically by only touching it with the edge. Whenever he did so he looked at me as if to make sure that I was observing how sharp that machete really was.

"So you won't tell me where my *esposa* is, señor?"

"It seems," I answered with dignity, "that you have a very good and very excellent machete. Looks like well-tempered steel to me."

"And good steel it is. And it has been made in your country. There you may be assured that it is the finest and the best steel we can buy down here. You'd better not make the mistake thinking that it might be German-made, because a German-made is no good, you cannot even cut cheese with it; if you try that the edge is gone for good. But they are very cheap. Only you cannot cut trees with them, not the sort we have got here in the bush. But the one I have got here will do anything I want it to do."

"Let me have a close look at it," I pleaded.

He put it through the fence but held the haft fast in his hand.

"This won't do at all. I must get a swing at it to see how good it is. I know something about steel."

"Oh no, señor mister, I won't let you have it. This excellent machete won't leave my hands, not before I know where my woman is. Just touch the edge. See. Now I think you'll understand that with one single stroke I could chop off the head of a burro from its trunk like cutting through wet mud. But should it be the head of a man, even that of a gringo, instead of that of a poor burro, I tell you, señor, I wouldn't need to make half so hard a stroke as I would have to use for a burro, with a machete having an edge like this one, and made in your own country, where the best steel comes from. What do you think, señor?"

"Since you ask me, friend, I think a bullet is even quicker than a machete, and more certain too."

"Maybe. Surely it is. But a bullet, without a gun to fire it, is not much to compare with such a good American-made machete. Everybody here in the village knows very well that you haven't got a gun, not even an old Spanish muzzler. I know this or I wouldn't perhaps bring my fine machete along with me. Understand, *caballero* mister?"

"I understand all right, *manito*. I see you want to cut my fence-posts and carry them away. But you won't do that. You know that would be plain robbery. The *federales* would shoot you for banditry as soon as they come to this village again. It won't be long now and they will be on their way here once more looking for bandits."

"I don't need your fence posts. I wouldn't take them, not even for a gift. They're all termite-eaten anyhow and no good. I can get them better in the bush."

"Then what do you want? I've to get breakfast ready because I've got to ride to my field and look after my tomatoes. I mean that I've got to go now, see, right now while the day is still cool and fresh."

"*Mil* times I have told you, señor mister, what I want. That's why I sharpened my machete. I want my woman back. You will now tell me where she is so that I can catch her and give her a terrific thrashing before I'll let her cook frijoles for me."

"And *mil* times I've told you that I don't know where your *mujer* is."

"So you still insist on telling me that you can't find her for me?"

"That's what I'm saying all the time and I don't know what to say any more. So what are you going to do about it?"

"Maybe you don't know where she is. What I know for sure is that you can find her if you wish to. I can't give you *mil* gold pesos for I haven't any. I suppose I've got to speak frankly with you, señor. In other words, if you don't tell me right away where my woman is I will be very sorry, and sorry for *you*. I mean, because in such a case I am desperate and I must chop off one head. I won't promise whose head it might be which is to be chopped off, and I can't promise either that it might not be your head which is going to be cut off with one single stroke and with that fine American-made machete too. Perhaps it will be done by mistake, so to say. In other words, señor mister, it will be your head, and no mistake about that, I am sure."

He raised his machete high up and swung it round above his head as a drunken pirate would his cutlass. It looked dangerous enough. I was cornered. I might, of course, try to escape into my bungalow. Sooner or later, though, I would have to come out and there he would be waiting for me. I had to get to my field to look after the crop, but he'd sneak up on me from behind or lay in ambush somewhere. His kind is patient. They will wait for days and weeks until they get their man. What does he care about killing somebody? He hides in the jungle. If he should finally be caught and fusilladed he will consider it his fate, which was his since he was born and from which he, in his opinion, could not have escaped nor avoided. Right now he is desperate. Without thinking of any of all the consequences which his murder will have afterwards, he, like a stubborn child, wants his wish come true immediately.

Again I told him the same thing I had told him twenty times the afternoon before. "I haven't seen the way your woman went. Therefore I don't know where she is now."

But my answer had lost its power. When he had told the villagers what sort of answer I had given him the day before, they had suggested what he ought to say if I were to tell him again that I had not seen his woman go away. He himself alone would never have come upon the answer he had in stock now, for his mind was not developed highly enough for such mental exercise. I was sure that the whole village was as much interested in the kind of medicine I would give him as he himself was.

At that hour I did not know that he had talked to the villagers about our discussion the previous afternoon. But from the way he now presented his answer, I knew immediately that it could not be his own, but that he had memorized it after being taught what to say, because he not only used words entirely new to him, but also spoke up like a bad amateur actor.

"Listen here, señor," he said, "if I'd seen the way my *mujer* went when she left I would have no need to trouble you, for in that case I could do well and perhaps better still alone, than with the help of a medicine-man. All people in the village here have told me that you are a far-seer. They have told me that you have two little black tubes sewn together to make them appear like one. They say, because they know, that if you look through these tubes you can see any man or woman or dog or burro which might walk on that faraway hill yonder, and you can see an eagle perching on a high tree a hundred miles away. You have told the folks in this village that there are people living on some of the stars, because this earth we live on is also but a star only we can't see it as a star since we are on it. All people here have watched you often when, by night, you look with your black tubes up to the sky so as to see the people on the stars and what they were doing at that time of night and how they lived there and how many cattle they had."

I remembered I had said something to this effect to a few of the younger men of the community.

"You've also told here that wise men in your country to the north have another black tube, by which they can look straight into the inside of any man or woman to see if there is a bullet there and where it is located, so that these medicine-men of yours can get the bullet out without cutting open the wrong part of the body. More you have said. You have said that white men can talk to other white men who are *mil* and more *mil* miles away and they can talk to one another without shouting just the way as I talk to you now, and that they don't even need a copper wire on which their words run along, as do telegraph-wires in our country. I want you to talk right now and before my eyes to my woman, and tell her that I am hungry and that I've no tortillas and no frijoles to eat. And I want you to tell her to come right home, and that she has to come home on one of those air-wagons you have said your people ride on when they are in a hurry. And I am in an awful hurry now."

Having finished his speech with the difficulty an urchin has saying his catechism at Sunday school he began again swinging his machete pirate-fashion, obviously with the intention of making his demands more imperative.

What was I to do? If I got the better of him and clubbed him down, everybody in the village would accuse me of having killed a poor, ignorant, but honest Mexican peasant, who had done me no harm and had never meant to do me any, and who had not even insulted me, but had only come, a very humble human, to another human, asking for help which no good Christian would have denied him.

I had to do something to get me out of the hole I was in, and in which I did not feel very comfortable. As I was considered one of the greatest medicine-men, there remained nothing else for me to do but to rely on medicine. The only question was, what sort of medicine I was to use to cure myself of his desperation, and of his machete which, as he demonstrated over and over again, would cut a hair as if by magic. The medicine to be served had to be of a special kind – that is, it had to be effective enough to save both of us at the same time.

At this precious moment, when I was thinking which of the gods I might call upon for a good idea and a better medicine, there flashed through my tortured mind a mental picture of two black tubes sewn together in such a way that they might look like one.

"With your kind permission and just one minute," I said to him and went into my bungalow.

Out I came, carrying in my hands my modest fieldglass. I carried it before me with a great solemnity, as if it were the holiest object under heaven.

I stepped close to the fence where the Mexican stood, high expectancy in his eyes.

In a mumbled voice I now spoke to the glass, moving it at the same time around over my head, now to the left, now to the right, also moving it towards the man who was watching me with an ever-growing bewilderment.

Now I pressed the glass firmly to my eyes. I bent down and searched the ground while walking round and round, slowly lifting up the glass until it was at a level with the far horizon. For many minutes I scanned the horizon, searching every part of it while moving round in a circle. And I said, loud enough so that he would understand it: "*Donde estás, mujer?* Where are you, woman? Answer, or I'll make you by hell's or heaven's force!"

Another idea came to my mind at this minute. I whispered to him: "Where's the village you come from?"

He tried to answer. His excitement did not allow him to speak, though he had his mouth wide open. He swallowed several times and then pointed, with one arm only slightly raised towards north.

So I knew that I had to find his woman towards the south to make my medicine work properly for his benefit and mine.

Now, all of a sudden, I yelled: "I see her. *Ya la veo.* I see her. There she is now, at last. Poor woman. Oh, that poor, poor woman. A man beats her terribly. He has a black moustache, that man who beats her has. I don't know who he is. I am sure I've seen him once or twice in this village here. Oh, that devil of a man, how he beats that poor woman. And she cries out loud: '*Ay mi hombre*, my dear husband, come, come quick and help me; fetch me away from that brute who has taken me by force and without my will; I want to come home and cook frijoles for you because I know you must be hungry after so much hard work in the bush; help me, help me, come quick!' That's what she cries. Oh, I can't stand it any longer; it's too terrible."

I was breathing heavily, as if entirely exhausted from the trance I had been in.

No sooner had I stopped and taken the glass off my eyes than the man, sweat all over his face, shouted as if going mad! "Didn't I tell you, señor? I knew all the time that it must be that dirty dog Pánfilo who has raped her. He has got a black moustache. I knew it all the time. He was after her since we came to this part. Always after her and always around the house whenever I was working in the bush. All the neighbors knew it because they told me so. I haven't sharpened my machete just for the fun of it. I knew that I would need a sharp edge somehow, somewhere and for someone, to cut off his stinking head. Now I'll have to hurry to get her and get at the same time that Pánfilo *cabron*. Where is she, señor, quick, quick, pronto, pronto, say it. Ask her. Tell her that I'm on my way already."

I looked through my glass once more and mumbled something as if asking someone a few questions. Now I said: "She is *mil* miles away from here, your woman is. The man with the black moustache has carried her far away, I think with an air-wagon, perhaps. She says that she is in Naranjitos. That's way down in that direction." I pointed towards the south-east. "It is only *mil* miles from here and along a trail not so very hard to go by."

"Well, then, señor mister, excuse me, but now I have got to hurry to fetch her and leave my marks on that Pánfilo dog."

He picked up his *moral*, a little bag, from the ground. It contained all he possessed on earth, a fact which made his life and his goings so easy, and it would have made him a truly happy man had it not been for women who would never be satisfied with such a little *bast* bag instead of some solid furniture or an electric refrigerator.

He became extremely restless now, so I thought it a good opportunity to give him another shot of the medicine. "Hustle, *amigo*, hurry up, or, dear God in heaven, you will miss her. And don't you dare stop on your way. You know it's more than *mil* days to walk. That rascal with the black moustache is likely to carry her farther away still. You'd better go right now, this very minute."

"This certainly I will do, señor, since you say so. This very second I shall go. In fact, I'm running already." His feet were dancing about as if the ground consisted of embers. I knew that something still held him back, or he would have been a quarter of a mile off already.

It was his courtesy, the courtesy of the primitive man, that kept him still here. After a few wrong starts which seemed not to satisfy him, he at last found the right words. "Many, many thanks, señor, *mil, mil gracias* for your magnificent medicine." The word *magnifica* appeared to be one of the new words he had heard last night from the villagers, for he stumbled on it, although he would not lose the opportunity to use it for me. "The people in the village," he continued, "are right about you. Truly and verily you are a great medicine-man. You know all the hidden secrets of the world. You found her so quickly, much sooner than I could ever have expected. Of course, the two pesos and forty-six centavitos I promised you for your medicine, señor, I cannot pay now. I am very sorry for that. But you are a great doctor, surely you are, therefore you will understand that I cannot pay for the medicine now. You'll have to be satisfied with my thanks, which are honest by all means. You see, señor mister, the money I need for my trip. That's why I cannot part with my money and pay you off. You surely will understand this easily since you're such a very wise man. *Adiós*, señor, *adiós*, and again *mil, mil gracias*."

And he was off like a hunted deer, without looking back. One minute later the bush had swallowed him up.

Never have I cheated a Mexican. I did not cheat that man either. The medicine I gave him is the best he could ever get. No other doctor would have prescribed him such a good medicine.

The village I named is about five hundred miles from here. He is without funds, save these two pesos and forty-six centavos. So he will have to walk the whole way. No hitch-hiking for him, because there is no highway. As there is no highway there cannot be motor-cars. Even if there were motor-cars none would pick him up. Latin-Americans are not dumb enough to pick up strangers parked along the highways.

It is an excellent medicine for him and for me. It saves me from the surprise of finding myself with my head chopped off. He is a strong and healthy fellow, and he is used to hard work. He won't go fifty miles, and he will find some work or a job. Or he will steal a stray cow and sell it to a butcher in one of the villages through which he passes. In the meantime, and more than a half-dozen times, he will have had his belly filled with tortillas, frijoles, and green chile. His belly satisfactorily full, he will forget his grief. Once he has found some work, he will stay on in a village in the end. Once there, it won't be one week before a woman will believe herself fairly lucky if allowed to cook frijoles and toast tortillas for him, and also hang her basket, or a sugar sack with her Sunday dress in it, at a peg inside the *jacalito* he will eventually, and quite predictably, occupy.

NICELY FRAMED, READY TO HANG!

Dan Gordon

1. Little Man with a Gun

You get up there, on top of the world, where I was, by working while other guys play. If you beat your brains out, and worry, and work, you wind up in my spot – standing in your own restaurant, watching the evening trade. There were eighteen restaurants in the chain, and I owned every one, free and clear.

Big-headed? I don't think so. I was riding high, and I knew it. Also, it gave me a kick. That's the point in making your pile while you're young enough. You're up there where nothing can touch you, and tomorrow's the night to put a four-carat diamond on a girl. Girl by the name of Lola Grashin – a nice girl, with plenty of class.

She was the only thing I needed, the only thing I didn't have.

I watched Pug Lester come in, and I was glad to see him. Pug Lester was a detective, and sometimes when he walked in I could see fear appear in the eyes of some men. To me Pug was just a customer whose weakness was fine food.

I said, "Good evening, Lieutenant. Much murder in town?"

"A little," said Lester, "here and there. Most of it's old and stale though, so I figured I might as well eat." He nodded to the head waiter and eased himself into a booth.

"I read you picked up the fellow who killed the liquor-store owner."

Pug Lester buttered a piece of melba and shoved it into his mouth. "Yeah," he said. "We got him. And like all of 'em, he started to scream he was framed."

I said, "Do you think he was?"

Pug Lester snorted. "They almost never are." He moved his arm to make room for the seafood cocktail, picked up a tiny fork and lunged at a shrimp. Then nodding his approval of the speared morsel, he gestured toward the seat. "Why don't you sit down, Roney?"

I grinned. "Thanks, I'd like to. But I've got to crawl back in my office. Taxpayer like myself has to work like hell on his account books to keep you in two-inch steaks."

"I eat a lot," Pug Lester said comfortably, "but I figure I earn my keep."

I nodded. "I'll drop by the kitchen on my way and tell the chef to slaughter another cow. Anything you want tonight, Lieutenant. Did I tell you I bought a warehouse run of pineapple last week? And have you heard that today the dock workers went out on strike? I'll make a killing."

Pug Lester shook his head. "Boy, sometimes I think you're *too* lucky. For your sake, I hope it holds."

"It'll hold," I said. "Relax."

He grunted, and I drifted to the rear of the place and went through the door marked "Private".

The little man didn't get up when I entered the office. He didn't move at all, but sat there, blending in with the shadows to one side of my desk. When he spoke, his voice came out in a friendly snarl, as if he were trying to be diplomatic and didn't quite know how.

"I looked around," the small man said, "but I couldn't find any booze."

A rush. That was my first thought, I said, "Maybe you'd do better if you tried out in the bar."

"That ain't very friendly of you. Mr Roney – an' friendly's the way you should be." He crossed his legs and leaned back in the leather chair. His thin mouth split in a grin. His eyes were in the shadows, and I wondered if the desk lamp was responsible for the illusion of pointed teeth.

"We'll go on with friendship," I told him, "after you tell me

who you are." The fact that this was my office, and that the man
was sitting in my favorite chair – these things were annoying but
bearable.

He said, "My name's Sampson, fella. I work for a guy named
McGuire."

"I've heard of him," I said carefully. "What do you want?"

"That's easy," said Sampson. "McGuire wants to rent a little
space for you."

I said, "He doesn't have to rent it. He can walk in and take a
table at any restaurant in the chain. That's the way the restaurant
business is. It's open to all the public. You can't keep anybody out."

"That's why the setup looks so good," Sampson said.
"People walk in and out all day. Nothing suspicious there. And
you got a fair-sized chain: you're makin' plenty of money. The
way McGuire's got it figured, we get the nod from you, an'
then in the back of each and every eatery, we plant a bookie
joint."

I laughed, thinking of McGuire's reputation. I said. "A bookie
joint, and a shop for receiving stolen goods, and maybe a little
dope mill to one side. We could get modernistic showcases for
attractive displays of heroin and cocaine."

The friendliness went out of Sampson's snarl. He said,
"McGuire don't mess with dope."

"That isn't the way I heard it," I said. "But that's your
business. Tell your boss the answer's no."

He got up. Standing, he was not quite so small as he had
seemed slumped down in the chair. But he was thin, and shorter
than I. He had a lean and pointed face. "That ain't the answer
I came for," he said. "I brought you a business proposition, an'
before you even talk about it, you're giving me a no."

"McGuire and I can't do business," I said. "I don't want any
part of McGuire."

"You want to remember," the little man said, "you're doin'
good now, doin' fine. The way I hear it, you came up fast. Now
you got a big chain of swell hash joints. But you always want to
remember, you can go down the same way you came up."

I smiled, but I wasn't amused. I said, "I built Roney
Restaurants with a little luck and one hell of a lot of hard work.
When I go down, it'll be my fault. It won't be because I let some
punk of McGuire's tell me what to do."

The little man came forward, rolling a little as he walked. His hands were at his sides. He said, "You shouldn't done that, Roney. You shouldn't call people punks."

I was tired. I had been through a long, hard day. Sure I liked the work. But managing a chain of restaurants isn't something to soothe the nerves, nor was the harsh voice of Sampson doing anything to help. The man came forward, and when he was close enough, I reached with my left hand and grabbed his coat lapels.

Sampson said, "Let's go, or I'll—"

My right hand caught him across the mouth. Then, as he pawed frantically to reach his shoulder holster, I backed him against the wall near the door, belting him each time he opened his mouth.

When he clamped his mouth tightly and no longer cursed or talked, I stopped slapping him and reached in and took the gun.

Stepping back, I withdrew the clip, and ejected the shell from the chamber. Then I held out the gun to Sampson, "Next time," I said, "bring two. You can see one isn't enough."

He said nothing. He just stood there, looking at me. There was something about his eyes; it seemed as if a film had come over them. He watched me through a thin, gray veil.

I tossed the gun, and Sampson caught it. He slipped it inside his coat, and although it was no longer loaded, he kept his hand on the butt. It seemed to give him strength.

"When you check with your boss," I said, "don't forget the answer's no."

Sampson nodded, and then the flood of words came out. "I'll tell him, tough boy. But there's one mistake you made. With me, before, it was business. Either way you took it, it wasn't anything to me. Before, it was just business. But you made it *personal* now." He smiled, and a little trickle of blood came from his split lip and ran down his narrow chin. He wiped it with the back of his hand, and turned, and went out the door.

I chuckled, watching him go. The day was gone when a punk like that could hurt me or my restaurants. I had built a secure business, with a good reputation. It never occurred to me that the matter was serious enough to report to the police.

That was Saturday night, and nothing happened Sunday, except that my housekeeper came about noon with the news that she was quitting. No, it was nothing about the job. She liked keeping house for me, but her sister was sick, the one in New Orleans, and she had to go there for a while.

I phoned a cab for the woman, and watched her go with no particular regret. She hadn't been with me long, and her management of me and my household affairs was nothing that couldn't be duplicated by merely phoning an employment agency the first thing Monday morning.

As it turned out, I didn't even have to do that. My problem was solved when the doorbell rang late Sunday afternoon. I got up and went to the door.

The girl said, "Good afternoon. I'm looking for Mr Roney."

I said, "How do you do? Won't you come in?" I tried to place her – waitress, hostess, entertainer. She could be any of these. She went ahead of me into the living room, a slim girl, yet padded nicely. I could tell it wasn't the suit. She sat when I offered a chair, but when I offered a drink, she said, "Before I get too comfortable, perhaps I'd better tell you – I came about the job."

"Job?" I said. I had a personnel man who took care of hiring the restaurant help. Furthermore, there was nothing about this girl that made you think of a person who wanted a job.

"I knew Mrs Ferguson slightly," the girl said. "She told me she was leaving, and suggested you might be hiring another housekeeper."

I opened my mouth slightly and stared at her.

She smiled, "It's not as silly as it sounds, Mr Roney. Incidentally, my name's Elaine Watkins."

There was, I supposed, no reason why a housekeeper *had* to be old and homely. On the other hand . . . I said, "Miss Watkins, have you ever been a housekeeper before? Do you know what housekeepers make?"

"Mrs Ferguson said you paid two hundred. I'm sure that would be all right with me, if you think I'd be satisfactory."

"Have you tried keeping house before?"

"No . . . I'm afraid if it's references you want, I won't be able to give them. I've been a model up until now."

I leaned back in my chair. "And you'd give that up to keep house?"

"Why not?" She was laughing at me.

"Doesn't it pay more? Don't you find it's more interesting work?"

She turned brisk now. "Mr Roney, have you any idea what a model makes?"

"None at all," I said.

"A few hundred in the entire country make a real living. But for every one of these there are a hundred who are lucky if they get enough to eat. I've been at it for more than a year now. I've averaged about twenty a week."

I smiled. "I'm beginning to see your point."

She got up and loosened her jacket. I said, "Well, I suppose there's no reason why a man's housekeeper has to be hideous, though I'm sure you'll be something of a shock to the girl I'm going to marry, and to the wives of some of my friends."

"I'll do my hair plain," Elaine Watkins said. "I'll put it up in a bun."

I said, "Whatever you like, Miss Watkins. I'll show you to your room."

2. Spare Corpse

That evening, after I'd showered, I found a change of clothing laid out for me, though I had not told Miss Watkins I was going out. Downstairs, there were ice cubes ready on the bar, and beside them a bottle of my favorite Scotch. When I asked about the clothing, Elaine Watkins smiled.

"I checked your date book," she said, "the one near the telephone. It said 'dinner with Lola,' so I assumed you'd need some clothes."

"And the Scotch?" I asked.

"You have three cases on hand," she said dryly. "Either you're very fond of it, or else you'd like to use it up."

I said, "Genius, Miss Watkins. Pure genius . . . Look, I won't be home until late. Why don't you take the night off?"

"Tomorrow, perhaps," she said carelessly. "Tonight I've too much to do."

I said goodbye and went out, savoring the pleasant warmth of the Scotch, and congratulating myself on having hired this girl who, unless I was very wrong, would run my house like a charm.

The pleasant feeling that everything was going well stayed with me all through dinner with Lola Grashin. We were lingering over coffee and cigarettes at Mauri Malcolm's club, and I was just where I wanted to be. I didn't want to own the world. Just a small piece of the town was enough.

I looked at the girl I was going to marry. Wide gray eyes, soft now, but they could shine with swift intelligence. The kind of a figure meant for display, but Lola had too much class to display it conspicuously.

I touched the ring in my pocket and said, "Darling, I've something for you – a little thing to celebrate the fact that the dock-workers went out on strike today."

She looked puzzled. "Are you interested in the longshoreman's union?"

"No," I said, laughing. "But I'm the foresighted lad who bought enough pineapple to last for six months."

"That's good?" Lola asked.

"It's perfect. Either the competition quits serving pineapple, or else they buy it from me. Either way, I'm sitting pretty."

She said, "You always are." She said it thoughtfully, but I wasn't paying much attention. My mind was moving ahead, deciding what to say.

There was no point in trying for a fancy phrase. I said simply, "I want to marry you, Lola."

For a moment, I thought she hadn't heard. She was looking the other way. I said, "Lola—"

"I heard you, Dick." Her voice was sad. "And I suppose I love you. But that doesn't change anything."

I said, "What—"

"Let me finish, Dick. I'm afraid I couldn't live with a person who was always, unfailingly, right. Of course I know how hard you've worked to get where you are today. And I think it's admirable, truly. I've thought about it often. And it isn't that you're conceited. It's merely that you're so damned smug."

"The pineapple?" I said, grinning.

"As much as anything," she answered. "You managed to link your proposal with a boast about how you cornered the market."

I looked at her hands. They were gripping her purse, and

now she picked up her gloves. I said, "But, Lola – I *don't* make many mistakes. Not now. Sure, I made plenty as a kid. But I've learned—"

She stood up, and I stopped talking.

"Phone me," she said quietly, "when a couple of tarnished spots show up on the golden boy." She moved away from the table, and I stood there, watching her go. I knew better than to follow. She wasn't a girl to run because she wanted to be pursued.

When she had gone, I sat thinking. At first I was stunned. I had known Lola long enough to realize that the thing between us was more than a passing emotion. Then, as I thought about it, I realized that our feeling for each other was certainly mutual. And if she felt as strongly as I did, why then, she would change her mind.

Feeling more cheerful, I chalked up her conduct as a feminine whim. The waiter brought another drink, and I sat alone at the table, looking around the club.

Across the room I could see Mauri Malcolm, the club owner. He was chatting lightly with the patrons and at the same time trying to estimate the evening's take.

The thought of Mauri's expenses made me quite cheerful again. Inwardly, I congratulated myself. I had expanded with more restaurants instead of doing what most restaurant owners did. Malcolm could have the headaches that went with this smart supper club.

I scanned the room. Two thirds of the tables were filled, but I knew that wasn't enough. I had seen the fixed smile nightclub owners get just before their baby folds. Mauri Malcolm was wearing it now.

I got back the feeling I'd had earlier. I was Dick Roney, thirty-six. No debts. A large bank balance, and the loveliest girl in the world who would change her mind as soon as . . .

I saw the other girl. Mauri Malcolm was bending over her table with the special smile he reserved for beautiful women.

I pushed back my chair, got up and circled the dance floor. The girl in organdy did not look in my direction. She was leaving the room. I caught up with her in the heavily carpeted hall. Here, close up, she looked even more like Elaine Watkins, and so I said, "Miss Watkins!" in a loud tone, and waited for her to turn.

She did, but it was obvious from her cool stare that she'd turned because of my voice, and not because of the name. She looked through me with an expression that said she didn't know me and didn't care to. Then she went into the powder room, and the door swung shut in my face.

I went back to my table, trying to seem poised and at ease. But I imagine I had the hang-dog look of a heel who had just made an unsuccessful pass at another man's wife.

Shortly after that, I paid the check and ambled out of the club. The Century bar was down the street, and I picked up two more drinks there.

But somehow, I couldn't relax. It wasn't my night to be out on the town. Something – my anxiety about my housekeeper – was urging me to go home.

I went, driving with unconscious haste. At the house, I put the car away, and entered very quietly. Just inside, I paused and listened, then walked toward the housekeeper's room.

Elaine Watkins was in bed. I saw that by the light of the street lamp that shone through the open window. The covers were well down from her shoulders, and the filmy, shadowy fabric of her nightgown was rising and falling as she breathed. The tempo was regular, almost hypnotic. It was, I realized, high time I got out of there.

Moving quietly down the hall, I turned the thing over in my mind. Either the girl had come in early, or she had not gone out at all. There was, of course, no reason why my housekeeper should not spend her evenings at Mauri Malcolm's club. I knew Malcolm slightly. We had been business rivals before Malcolm sold a group of three restaurants to plunge more heavily on the nightclub.

Malcolm was as honest as any businessman, and there was no reason why the girl shouldn't know him. There was also no reason, as far as I was concerned, why a model should not accept expensive clothing – if that was the life she wanted. But models who wanted that life did not take jobs as housekeepers. Not for two hundred a month.

Entering the library, I switched on the light and headed for the sideboard. Mixing a drink, I thought of Lola. I'd phone her early tomorrow and straighten everything out.

I turned, sipping from the tall glass, enjoying it and the soft play of light on the polished wood. The lighting was subdued, and that too added something to my feeling of quiet peace. This was the place to come back to, the house for a man who had everything. Here, in my own home, even the shadows were warm and friendly.

Except for the new shadow. It was one I had never noticed before. There was, in fact, no reason why it should be there behind the wing-backed chair.

I moved. The shadow did not. I took a long, deep pull on my drink and held the glass in my hand, as I knelt to inspect the body.

Then I stood up and switched on a floor lamp. The man on the floor was Mauri Malcolm. He had been shot in the head.

I listened, and there were no sounds. All through the house there was still the same silence that had, only a moment before, given a feeling of peace.

Then, very loud in the stillness, a phone dial whirred in another room. Walking softly, I followed the sound.

I went through the hall to my bedroom. The door was slightly ajar. Shoving gently, I opened it.

My housekeeper was sitting on my bed. She was wearing the same transparent nightgown I had seen when I came in. Over it she had donned an equally transparent wrapper.

"Yes!" she was saying. "It was Mr Roney! I was asleep and they awoke me up with their quarreling. Then I looked in and saw Mr Roney fire the gun, and—"

"Wait a minute!" I yelled. I crossed the room and snatched the phone from her hand. "Hello. Who am I talking to?"

"Sergeant Pound, Police. Who are you?"

"I'm Dick Roney. And I don't know what ails this woman, but I certainly haven't killed anybody."

The sergeant said in a tired voice, "But somebody has been shot?"

"Yes, a man by the name of Malcolm. I just found him on the floor."

"Dead?"

"Yes."

"Don't move him. We'll be there right away."

I put down the phone. The girl had moved to the other side

of the room, and she was standing with her back to the dresser, watching me without fear.

I said, "I ought to slap you silly. What kind of a tale is that you just spouted into the phone?" I took a forward step.

She said, "Keep away, Mr Roney. If it wasn't you, it looked like you."

My mind spun back over the evening. Not anything I could think of helped me to add things up. "There are some things I'd like to know," I said, "before the police get here. For example, what were you doing at Malcolm's club earlier this evening? I seen you talking to him, and then I find him on my floor."

"I don't know what you're talking about. I haven't been out of the house."

"We'll skip the question of why a girl like you wanted to keep house for me. We'll let that go for a moment. But tell me this: If you saw me murder a man, what made you stick around to use the phone? Why didn't you run outside?"

"Why should I? I'm not afraid of you."

I snorted. "You ought to be. If you're framing me for one murder, you ought to know the price is the same for two." I held my eyes on hers, and watched some trace of fear move like a small shadow over her face.

Someone said from the doorway, "A bargain, too."

I spun to face the voice. I saw the gun, and the man behind it, the little man I'd met in my office. The man McGuire had sent. I glimpsed the quick show of pointed teeth, saw the flash of the gun, heard its sharp explosion.

It was a second before I realized that the bullet had been for the girl.

She went down with a throaty sigh, crumpling with soft grace. Filmy cloth fanned out around her as she lay motionless on the floor.

I waited for the slug to crash into my body, found myself wanting to close my eyes. I kept them open. The little man wiped the gun with his handkerchief, then tossed it on the floor.

I was calculating the distance, ready to try a quick dive for the weapon, when the man called Sampson drew another gun.

"Leave it there," he said. The second gun looked enormous in his small hand.

"You use a different gun for each killing?" I asked. "It must run to a lot of expense."

The little man ignored the crack. He was grinning, looking as happy as a man could look with so tiny and wizened a face. "You look good," he said suddenly. "You look wonderful – all tacked up in a three-sided frame."

"You're crazy," I said. "You think the police will buy this story?"

"They'll buy it," he said. "Only I won't be here to tell it. They'll get it straight from you."

"You know what I'll tell them, don't you?" I moved slightly toward him, stopped when he jerked the gun.

"Keep back," he said. "I don't really want to shoot you before you have time to enjoy the frame. I'd rather have you fry for murder. That way you have plenty of time to remember who you slapped."

"I should have slapped you harder," I said. "How could the police think *I* killed these people? What motive would I have?"

"You knocked off the dame," said Sampson, "because she saw you murder Malcolm. She said so on the phone."

"And Malcolm?"

The little man shrugged easily. "You were business competitors," he said. "You know how these things go."

I glanced at the clock. The police ought to be arriving now. If I could keep Sampson here, keep him talking . . . I said. "All right. You're sore at me because I kicked you out of my office. But Malcolm – what did you have against him?"

"He was another wise lad who didn't want to do business. But, in a way, he got off easy, on account of – he had sense enough not to slap anybody around, like you did."

I thought of Malcolm, dead in the library, Malcolm who had gotten off easy. I swung my eyes to the crumpled girl. "What about her?" I asked.

"What about her?" Sampson lifted his shoulders. "She was just a greedy gertie. She wasn't nobody's doll." Sirens wailed in the distance. Sampson cocked an attentive ear. "Be seein' you," he said, "If you think it'll do you any good, you can mention me and McGuire." He backed out the door and was gone.

I jumped toward the gun on the floor, stopped myself when it was inches from my hand. If McGuire and this little hood had set out to frame me, it wouldn't be a clumsy job. For one thing, Sampson had wiped the butt of the gun. If it was the same gun he'd brought to my office, then my fingerprints could still be on the barrel, McGuire and Sampson would be able to account for all of their movements this night. They would have the best alibis money could buy. And as my mind slipped desperately from point to point, I knew McGuire would have covered them, too.

The sound of sirens ceased. That meant the police were nearing the house. I looked once more at the girl on the floor, the girl who was nobody's doll. With a little corner of my mind, I wondered what kind of a life she had wanted, what her ambitions had been. I moved quickly to the window, climbed through, and dropped into the garden at the rear of the house.

From somewhere across the lawn, someone said, "All right, Roney. Stick around."

I hesitated, conscious that the upper half of my body was silhouetted neatly against the lighted window at my back. I stood frozen for just an instant. Then I dove over the hedge.

I went through it, feeling the tearing grip of the branches, and behind me I heard the light, quick thud of feet running on damp sod.

"Roney! You damn fool – hold it! Don't make me plug you, boy!" Pug Lester's exasperated plea turned into a string of curses as he crashed into the hedge.

Racing along the dark lane that flanked the rear of the garden, I was thankful for that hedge. I was also grateful to Lester, for I was aware that he could easily have shot me as I stood at the window, again as I ran across the lawn. I owed Lester a hearty thank you which I meant to deliver some time. Some time, but not just now.

3. The Slaughter Syndicate

The night went by in a series of terrifyingly close encounters – with prowl cars and policemen, individuals who came out of shadowy corners, asking me for matches. I walked until dawn. There wasn't any place I dared go, and walking helped me think.

I didn't like my thoughts. Walking lonely and afraid, I had time to remember what Lola had said about my smugness. I was a boy with a stranglehold on the world. Nothing could ever go wrong. She hadn't wanted to marry a guy whose life ran on well-oiled wheels. I wondered, with some bitterness, if she'd like me better now that I faced two murder raps.

Then honesty forced me to admit it. I wouldn't be walking alone right now if I hadn't felt so secure. Any fool, after the first interview with the little gunman, would have gone to the police.

These were the things I was thinking as I slunk along the dismal streets.

In the morning, I bought a shave in a neighborhood barber shop. It made me feel better, but as I walked out into the sunlight, I still had not decided what to do.

I called police headquarters from a public phone and asked for Pug Lester.

The lieutenant said, "Lester speaking," mechanically, as if he had many things on his mind.

"This is Roney, Lieutenant."

"Ah!" said Pug Lester. "Where are you now?"

"In town. But I'm thinking of leaving. I phoned to tell you I'm sorry about last night."

"No trouble at all," Lester said grimly. "I need the exercise. May I suggest that you get the hell down here as fast as you can?"

"I'll be in," I said vaguely, "sooner or later. But I've got a few things to do."

There was a silence. That would be Pug Lester's hand clamping tight on the mouthpiece while he detailed someone in the office to trace the call.

I said sharply, "Don't send anyone after me, Pug. I won't be here when they come."

There was a pause. "What else can I do?" Lester said. "Why don't you come in? Isn't that why you called?"

"No," I said slowly. "I was hoping that you'd found out who killed those people. I had no reason to, you know."

"Look," Pug Lester said. "The dame said she saw you kill Malcolm. She said that over the phone."

"But why should I kill Malcolm? I knew him only slightly."

"That isn't what the letters say."

"What letters?" I asked blankly

"Correspondence between you and Malcolm. We found a couple of his letters in your files – a couple of yours in his. If you kids were fond of each other, you were certainly talking tough."

"But I never . . ." Then I realized the futility of denial. "Are you sure they're genuine?"

Pug said, "Me? I'm sure of nothing. The boys in the lab are still working, but they seem to like the signatures well enough."

I stared out through the glass door of the phone booth. The air seemed suddenly stifling. I was holding the phone like a man in a trance.

Pug Lester said sharply. "Roney! You still there? Don't hang up on me, Roney! I want to talk to you!"

The urgency in the lieutenant's voice brought me to my senses. I realized suddenly how long we had been talking. Lester would certainly have the call traced, and the police would arrive at any moment. Indeed, they might well be here right now. I hung up the phone and drifted out of the booth.

The ancient druggist eyed me without particular interest as I moved out into the street. At the corner I caught a streetcar, but I had no feeling of safety until, after a mile on the trolley, I changed to a cross-town bus.

The ride seemed to clear my head, and I found myself able to think. McGuire and Sampson had fitted me with a frame, which, if not perfect, was at least good enough to cause the public to hold and try me for murder. True, it might not stand up under careful investigation, but I disliked the idea of taking up residence in a death cell on the off chance that Pug Lester or some other enterprising detective would come along and kick me out.

Having rejected the services of the police, I felt the loneliness pressing in upon me. In a few short hours, I, Dick Roney, had become a furtive, frightened thing who dared not pause for rest.

I set out to find McGuire. It took longer than you'd think. It meant making discreet inquiries in several bookmaking establishments. It meant watching men's eyes drift far off the moment I mentioned the name.

Finally, as I was leaving a south-side bar, a heavy-set man stepped out from the wall of the building. He looked so much like a detective, I was tempted to run. But the man was blocking the way. Neither of us said anything while the man thoughtfully brought out a match and bit off the end.

Then he said, "Understand you're looking for McGuire?"

I said, "I was." Then I remembered that the man had not been in the bar. "How did you know?" I added.

"We heard." He moved toward a car at the curb. Opening one door for me, he circled lazily and climbed in under the wheel. "Let's go," he said.

I hesitated, then I realized that McGuire was my one wild chance. I climbed in and slammed the door. The car went forward in a sighing rush.

McGuire's place ran to spacious, quiet reception rooms. The furniture in the offices ran into heavy dough. The receptionist looked like something in a social register, and McGuire looked like the most successful member of the bar association.

He didn't rise when I came in, but a slight smile furnished the illusion of pleasantness, and a curt nod dismissed my escort. The heavy-set man nodded briskly and backed out through the door.

I stood easily on the soft, thick pile of the carpet, and when I saw Sampson watching from a corner of the room, I said, "Well! My little friend."

Sampson let it pass. McGuire's gray eyes rested on me thoughtfully. When he spoke, his deep, cultured voice went well with his surroundings. His face was handsome, almost noble. An international banker would have been proud to own his suit.

"Forgive me," McGuire said, "if I seem to stare at you. When I heard you were trying to find me, I knew I was going to meet an unusual man."

"That's damned nice of you," I said. "But I'm afraid you'll find I'm a pretty standard guy, or I was until yesterday."

"No," McGuire corrected. "The average man would not have come here."

"Would've had more sense," said Sampson.

"Can't you keep him quiet?" I asked.

"If you prefer. However, there is some truth in what he says." McGuire stood up. "I'm afraid my schedule is pretty crowded. You're here – now, what do you want?"

"A chair," I said. I chose one fairly close to the desk, sat down with my legs sprawled out. "Tired," I explained. "I've been walking." I hoped they wouldn't notice how nervous I was if I pretended to own the joint.

Sampson said, "You might as well walk while you can."

I looked appealingly at McGuire. "He's talking again," I complained. "And every time he opens his mouth, one of us loses money."

McGuire sat down. "Would it take you very long," he asked, "to tell up why you came?"

"I would have come when you first invited me," I said, "if you'd sent anyone but this little clown."

Sampson sprang up and moved to the desk "How about it, Mac?" he said. "How's if I slap this loud-mouth around, then feed him to the cops?"

"You see what I mean?" I said mildly. "The boy has too much bounce."

McGuire wasn't looking at Sampson. He said. "Let's get on with it, Roney."

"All right. Put it this way. What do you hope to gain by having me take the rap for two murders?"

"Let's assume," said McGuire, "that I know what you're talking about – which I don't. Then the answer is, I gain nothing."

"And you call yourself a businessman?"

"I am a businessman," said McGuire. "I sent a man to you with a proposition which you refused. I have no further interest in you or your affairs."

"Here's a proposition for you," I said.

"Go on."

"Call off your dogs, and get what you wanted in the first place – a branch office for your syndicate in each of my restaurants."

McGuire looked at me, cool and amused. "It's likely I'll get that anyway," he said. "Not from you, but from your successor."

I let my eyes move from one to the other – McGuire, suave and superior; Sampson's pinched face full of hatred, but with something in it of smugness. That, I guessed, would be about as close to a happy expression as the little hood could manage. In Sampson's mind, this meeting probably came under the heading of watching the sucker squirm.

I said, "You know who my successor is?"

McGuire shrugged. "It doesn't matter. I manage to do business with most people."

"With the Paramount Insurance Company? If I'm out of the picture, management of the chain reverts to a holding company owned by them."

Something flickered in McGuire's eyes, but his face remained bland and smooth.

"You're big, McGuire," I said, "but I doubt if you're big enough to tamper with Paramount Insurance. With their own investigators and the political pressure they could bring to bear, the outfit would run you silly."

Sampson said, "You heard enough of this, boss."

"Gag him," I said impatiently. "Listen, McGuire. There may be some people you don't need, but I'm not one of them."

"This is all very interesting," said McGuire, "and sounds in spots rather unfortunate. But what do you suggest?"

I smiled. "Are we talking openly?" I asked. "Can we assume we all know I'm in a frame?"

"Let's assume that for the moment," said McGuire.

Sampson jeered, "How do you like the fit?"

McGuire said, "What's your suggestion, Roney?"

I grinned. "Enlarge the frame. It ought to fit someone else – in fact, I have a pigeon in mind."

Narrowing his eyes, McGuire said, "Let us look at this thing for a moment. Yesterday you were too honest to want a syndicate branch in your restaurants. Today you are perfectly willing to frame a man for murder. Isn't this something of a change?"

I said, "Not as much as you might think. As your stooge here has said, I came up fast. A man in a hurry almost always resorts to – let us say – expedients. Also," I forced a smile, "I'd be something of a fool if I were not slightly swayed by the pressure you've applied."

"Anything else?" McGuire said tonelessly. I could tell nothing from his voice.

"Money," I said. "I have always been open to suggestions that would help me make more. Only" – I pointed to Sampson – "I did resent your sending this jerk with a business proposition."

Sampson said desperately, "McGuire, don't let this guy—"

"The purpose of this organization," McGuire said coldly, "is to make money. All other considerations are secondary. Try to remember that – as long as you are working for me."

Sampson returned to his chair.

"As I said," I began, "I have a man in mind a man who will have no alibi. He was home alone when Malcolm and the girl were killed."

McGuire said, "His motive?"

I thought of the girl crumpled pathetically on the floor of my bedroom. I put the thought out of my mind. "Love," I said. "And revenge. The girl was his, and when he found her at my house with Malcolm, he blew his top and killed them both."

Sampson snorted. "He'd have to be a dope to fit that picture."

"He is," I answered quietly. "He's a slob."

McGuire said, "Sampson's right. If your man has any brains, he can wriggle out."

"He hasn't any," I said. "But why don't you look him over? I can arrange a meeting tonight."

McGuire said nothing for a moment. His eyes seem to turn inward, inspecting possible gain and loss. When he looked at me again, it was obvious he had made up his mind.

"What time," he said, "and where?"

"Ten tonight," I said. "His apartment's Number 7, at 210 West Nautilus. I'll see that he's there." I got up, and my shaking legs reluctantly held my weight. Not until then did I know how much I'd been afraid. "See you then," I said.

"Roney."

"Yeah."

"Before you go – remember. Don't play it *too* smart. Compared to some ways I know, the chair can be an easy way to die."

"I believe you." I said soberly. I glanced at Sampson.

The little man said softly, "I almost hope something *does* go wrong, so I can get one more crack at you."

I let it go. I said, "Thanks for your time, McGuire. I think you'll find it's worth it."

"I hope so," McGuire answered. His cold gray eyes bored into mine. "I get very upset, Roney, when it turns out I've made a mistake. What's this fellow's name?"

"Lester," I said. "George Lester." I watched the two of them.

Neither did a take. I got out of there in a hurry and headed for a phone.

4. Date with Death

Pug Lester's voice came coldly over the wire. Outside the booth I could see the waitress behind the counter, methodically chewing her gum. Lester was saying, "What about it, bright boy? When are you coming in?"

"I'd rather meet you," I said.

"All right," he said shortly. "Say where."

"Your apartment. Ten o'clock tonight."

"*My* apartment," he repeated. "Why there? We've got some business, boy – remember? This won't be a social call."

I said, "Pug, I'm going to ask for the biggest favor you ever did any man."

"Go on," Pug Lester said.

"I want you to remove anything from your apartment that would indicate you're a cop. Pictures. Pistol trophies. All that kind of stuff."

"And then?" Pug said without warmth.

"At ten, I come in with some friends. You play dumb. You're not a cop. You sell – coffee. Sure. Coffee's good enough." I stopped talking. The waitress in the coffee shop was craning her neck for a better view, idly trying for a better view of something out on the street.

I said sharply. "Pug, you still there?"

"Yeah," he said, "but, I dunno—"

The waitress nodded lazily, and then Sampson came into view. He had seen me, and he was grinning as he headed for the phone booth.

I said, "Pug! I can't talk any more!"

There was a long silence. I held the receiver against my ear while Sampson came right up to the booth and pressed his face against the glass. Then Pug Lester's voice said, "Okay, Roney. See you at ten."

I said, "Fine," and hung up the phone.

"What's fine?" Sampson said, as I opened the door.

I said, "My girl still loves me. What are you doing here?"

"Trailing you," he said promptly. "You left so fast I had trouble picking you up."

"You might have had more trouble," I told him. "Sometimes, after I talk to my girl, I take off like a jet plane."

Sampson patted his shoulder holster. "Why don't you try it?" he said softly.

There was no point in bickering with the little gunman. I said, "Look, Sampson. I've got to keep off the streets. Haven't you got a place to stay? You could save wear and tear on your feet, and I could phone McGuire."

"Yeah," he said. "Come on."

He took me to a fancy apartment that looked like a chorus girl's dream. We stayed there all through the afternoon and evening. At 9:45, McGuire's chauffeur rang and said McGuire was waiting downstairs in his car. We didn't keep him waiting. We went down right away.

Pug Lester's apartment was on the second floor of an old house that had submitted to remodeling. Pug Lester let us in, and, when I inspected the living room, I saw nothing that would indicate a police officer lived in the place. There were several light patches on the walls where pictures had been removed, and I was grateful to the detective for attending to this detail.

Pug closed the door behind us, and went back to the chair. His fat cheeks almost hid his eyes as he sat there, looking up. "Scuse me," he said, "if I seem to sit down. I had a busy day."

Sampson said nothing; he remained standing to one side of the apartment door, wary and unconvinced.

McGuire went to Pug Lester, and stood, eyeing the fat man critically. "He looks stupid enough," he said finally.

Pug Lester said lazily, "You boys playin' some kind of a joke?"

"A little one," said McGuire. "You can play too. Know where you were last night?"

"Right here," Pug Lester said, "mostly."

"Anyone with you?"

"Nope, I was all alone." Pug Lester sighed heavily, and his eyes opened wide enough for me to see the impatience in their depths.

Suddenly, I knew it would not go off as planned. Pug Lester, with me there before him, was not going to wait through a lot of what to him was aimless talk. In that same moment I realized that my position had not changed. McGuire and Sampson could walk out. The detective would have no reason to hold them. That would leave me where I began – with a ticket for the chair.

For a second time that day, I cursed myself for a chump. If I had given Lester some idea of what I was doing, my chances would have been better. Right now my chances were zero. I knew Pug wasn't going to wait.

Into the silence, I said. "What about it? Think he'll do?"

McGuire swung his head impatiently. "We'll see," he said. "Let's not hurry."

Pug Lester said, "Do for what?"

"You had a girl," I said, talking desperately, "who sometimes called herself Elaine Watkins. It was a secret thing – nobody knew. And the reason you killed her and Malcolm was jealousy – an old reason, but always good. Malcolm was taking your girl away, and you, a coffee salesman, couldn't compete with him." I glanced at McGuire. The gambling czar was frowning at my awkward pitch. I looked back at Pug Lester.

The detective's chins were pleated on his neck. His mouth was open slightly. He said, "What're you tryin' to do, Roney? Cop an insanity plea?"

Nothing moved in the room. I grinned tautly, thinking of McGuire's bewilderment. It was not easy to frame pigeons who talk about copping a plea.

Then McGuire said, "Sampson!"

The little gunman seemed to flick a hand at his lapel, and then the gun was in his hand. He swung it slowly, saying nothing, letting his lips draw back from his teeth.

"That wasn't smart of you," McGuire said softly. "It wasn't bright of either of you. In fact, if I were asked to say what had caused your death, I should have to say stupidity."

Pug Lester said placidly, "You mean you're going to kill him and me too?" His small nod included me.

McGuire inclined his head. "I'm afraid Sampson will insist."

"Just askin'," Pug Lester said.

I thought, but I couldn't be sure, that one of Lester's plump hands brought the gun up from under the cushion. It was a large gun, a 45. It made a hellish roar in the room, and it blew out a section of Sampson's head.

The slender little hood made no noise as he fell forward on the worn carpet.

McGuire lunged at me. I spun away to avoid being used as a shield. As I whirled, I clipped McGuire on the side of the head.

The man stepped back nimbly. He was far from soft, I observed – probably kept in condition by handball and boxing at his club. I moved toward him, carrying my hands low, swinging precisely. McGuire gave ground slowly, dodging and weaving. Then, abruptly, he landed a straight left that snapped my head back, followed it with a right cross that drove me to the floor.

Falling, with the pink mist in front of my eyes, I could see Pug Lester still sitting in the chair. The mist was still there, but some of it went away when I bounced on the carpet. Digging my nails into the short pile, I hauled myself to my feet.

McGuire came in again, and I had to shake my head to get his image clearly. Then I saw the smooth pink face, red now, and fiercely contorted. One of McGuire's fists lashed along my cheek.

I took a deep and shuddering breath. Then, with both arms pumping, I began a slow walk forward. McGuire's blows were landing freely, but I didn't feel them now. The pink haze was all around me, and in the middle of it a face danced and bobbed, a face that sometimes blended with the haze, but was redder, and could therefore be seen.

The face went away. I stood swaying waiting for the haze to dissolve.

It was clearing, and from somewhere off to my left, Pug Lester was speaking to me.

"I figured you'd want to do that," Pug Lester said. "I figured you had it coming."

I shook my head, and then I could see the floor. McGuire was lying there, and as I watched him groggily, he rolled over and staggered to his feet.

I brought my hands up, but I knew they wouldn't be any good against the heavy ashtray clutched in McGuire's hand.

McGuire was drawing back for a swing when Pug Lester's gun barrel caught him and sent him down for the count.

"Let me," Pug Lester said. "I get paid, you know – and I like to earn my keep."

I heard myself say, "Thanks, Lieutenant," and my voice seemed far away. I found myself thinking of Pug's lonely life, and of the girl who had been a greedy gertie, the one who'd been nobody's doll. She might have made a wife for Pug if things had been some other way.

Pug said, "Hey, boy. You all right?"

I said, "I wonder if she could cook?"

"Golden boy," Pug said, "you look mottled. You're all washed up for the day."

I shook my head and the haze dissolved. "Where's your phone?" I asked Pug. He pointed, and stood by while I dialed Lola Grashin's number. "Gotta tell a girl a story," I said. "Back me up, and I'll buy you a steak."

His mouth had begun to water by the time Lola said hello.

THE SECOND COMING

Joe Gores

"But fix thy eyes upon the valley: for the river of blood draws nigh, in which boils every one who by violence injures other."
Canto XII, 46–48, *The Inferno* of Dante Alighieri

I've thought about it a lot, man; like why Victor and I made that terrible scene out there at San Quentin, putting ourselves on that it was just for kicks. Victor was hung up on kicks; they were a thing with him. He was a sharp dark-haired cat with bright eyes, built lean and hard like a French skin-diver. His old man dug only money, so he'd always had plenty of bread. We got this idea out at his pad on Potrero Hill – a penthouse, of course – one afternoon when we were lying around on the sun-porch in swim trunks and drinking gin.

"You know, man," he said, "I have made about every scene in the world. I have balled all the chicks, red and yellow and black and white, and I have gotten high on muggles, bluejays, redbirds and mescaline. I have even tried the white stuff a time or two. But—"

"You're a goddam tiger, dad."

"– but there is one kick I've never had, man."

When he didn't go on I rolled my head off the quart gin bottle I was using for a pillow and looked at him. He was giving me a shot with those hot, wild eyes of his.

"So, like, what is it?"

"I've never watched an execution."

I thought about it a minute, drowsily. The sun was so hot it was like nailing me right to the air mattress. Watching an execution. Seeing a man go through the wall. A groovy idea for an artist.

"Too much," I murmured. "I'm with you, dad."

The next day, of course, I was back at work on some abstracts for my first one-man show and had forgotten all about it; but that night Victor called me up.

"Did you write to the warden up at San Quentin today, man? He has to contact the San Francisco police chief and make sure you don't have a record and aren't a psycho and are useful to the community."

So I went ahead and wrote the letter, because even sober it still seemed a cool idea for some kicks; I knew they always need twelve witnesses to make sure that the accused isn't sneaked out the back door or something at the last minute like an old Jimmy Cagney movie. Even so, I lay dead for two months before the letter came. The star of our show would be a stud who'd broken into a house trailer near Fort Ord to rape this Army lieutenant's wife, only right in the middle of it she'd started screaming so he'd put a pillow over her face to keep her quiet until he could finish. But she'd quit breathing. There were eight chicks on the jury and I think like three of them got broken ankles in the rush to send him to the gas chamber. Not that I cared. Kicks, man.

Victor picked me up at seven thirty in the morning, an hour before we were supposed to report to San Quentin. He was wearing this really hip Italian import, and fifty-dollar shoes, and a narrow-brim hat with a little feather in it, so all he needed was a briefcase to be Chairman of the Board. The top was down on the Mercedes, cold as it was, and when he saw my black suit and hand-knit tie he flashed this crazy white-toothed grin you'd never see in any Director's meeting.

"*Too much*, killer! If you'd like comb your hair you could pass for an undertaker coming after the body."

Since I am a very long, thin cat with black hair always hanging in my eyes, who fully dressed weighs as much as a medium-size collie, I guess he wasn't too far off. I put a pint of Jose Cuervo in the side pocket of the car and we split. We were both really turned on: I mean this senseless, breathless hilarity as if we'd just heard the world's funniest joke. Or were just going to.

It was one of those chilly California brights with blue sky and cold sunshine and here and there a cloud like Mr Big was popping Himself a cap down beyond the horizon. I dug it all: the sail of a lone early yacht out in the Bay like a tossed-away paper cup; the whitecaps flipping around out by Angel Island like they were stoned out of their minds; the top down on the 300-SL so we could smell salt and feel the icy bite of the wind. But beyond the tunnel on US 101, coming down towards Marin City, I felt a sudden sharp chill as if a cloud has passed between me and the sun, but none had; and then I dug for the first time what I was actually doing.

Victor felt it, too, for he turned to me and said, "Must maintain cool, dad."

"I'm with it."

San Quentin Prison, out on the end of its peninsula, looked like a sprawled ugly dragon sunning itself on a rock; we pulled up near the East Gate and there were not even any birds singing. Just a bunch of quiet cats in black, Quakers or Mennonites or something, protesting capital punishment by their silent presence as they'd done ever since Chessman had gotten his out there. I felt dark frightened things move around inside me when I saw them.

"Let's fall out right here, dad," I said in a momentary sort of panic, "and catch the matinee next week."

But Victor was in kicksville, like desperate to put on all those squares in the black suits. When they looked over at us he jumped up on the back of the bucket seat and spread his arms wide like the Sermon on the Mount. With his tortoiseshell shades and his flashing teeth and that suit which had cost three yards, he looked like Christ on his way to Hollywood.

"Whatsoever ye do unto the least of these, my brethren, ye do unto me," he cried in this ringing apocalyptic voice.

I grabbed his arm and dragged him back down off the seat. "For Christ sake, man, cool it!"

But he went into high laughter and punched my arm with feverish exuberance, and then jerked a tiny American flag from his inside jacket pocket and began waving it around above the windshield. I could see the sweat on his forehead.

"It's worth it to live in this country!" he yelled at them.

He put the car in gear and we went on. I looked back and saw one of those cats crossing himself. It put things back in perspective: they were from nowhere. The Middle Ages. Not that I judged them: that was their scene, man. Unto every cat what he digs the most.

The guard on the gate directed us to a small wooden building set against the outside wall, where we found five other witnesses. Three of them were reporters, one was a fat cat smoking a .45-calibre stogy like a politician from Sacramento, and the last was an Army type in lieutenant's bars, his belt buckle and insignia looking as if he'd been up all night with a can of *Brasso*.

A guard came in and told us to surrender everything in our pockets and get a receipt for it. We had to remove our shoes, too; they were too heavy for the fluoroscope. Then they put us through this groovy little room one by one to x-ray us for cameras and so on; they don't want anyone making the Kodak scene while they're busy dropping the pellets. We ended up inside the prison with our shoes back on and with our noses full of that old prison detergent-disinfectant stink.

The politician type, who had these cold slitted eyes like a Sherman tank, started coming on with rank jokes: but everyone put him down, hard, even the reporters. I guess nobody but fuzz ever gets used to executions. The Army stud was at parade rest with a face so pale his freckles looked like a charge of shot. He had reddish hair.

After a while five guards came in to make up the twelve required witnesses. They looked rank, as fuzz always do, and got off in a corner in a little huddle, laughing and gassing together like a bunch of kids kicking a dog. Victor and I sidled over to hear what they were saying.

"Who's sniffing the eggs this morning?" asked one.

"I don't know, I haven't been reading the papers." He yawned when he answered.

"Don't you remember?" urged another, "it's the guy who smothered the woman in the house trailer. Down in the Valley by Salinas."

"Yeah. Soldier's wife; he was raping her and . . ."

Like dogs hearing the plate rattle, they turned in unison toward the Army lieutenant; but just then more fuzz came in to march us to the observation room. We went in a column of twos with a guard beside each one, everyone unconsciously in step as if following a cadence call. I caught myself listening for measured mournful drum rolls.

The observation room was built right around the gas chamber, with rising tiers of benches for extras in case business was brisk. The chamber itself was hexagonal; the three walls in our room were of plate glass with a waist-high brass rail around the outside like the rail in an old-time saloon. The other three walls were steel plate, with a heavy door, rivet-studded, in the center one, and a small observation window in each of the others.

Inside the chamber were just these two massive chairs, probably oak, facing the rear walls side by side; their backs were high enough to come to the nape of the neck of anyone sitting in them. Under each was like a bucket that I knew contained hydrochloric acid. At a signal the executioner would drop sodium cyanide pellets into a chute; the pellets would roll down into the bucket; hydrocyanic acid gas would form; and the cat in the chair would be wasted.

The politician type, who had this rich fruity baritone like Burl Ives, asked why they had two chairs.

"That's in case there's a double-header, dad," I said.

"You're kidding." But by his voice the idea pleased him. Then he wheezed plaintively: "I don't see why they turn the chairs away – we can't even watch his face while it's happening to him."

He was a true rank genuine creep, right out from under a rock with the slime barely dry on his scales; but I wouldn't have wanted his dreams. I think he was one of those guys who tastes the big draught many times before he swallows it.

We milled around like cattle around the chute, when they smell the blood from inside and know they're somehow involved; then we heard sounds and saw the door in the back of the chamber swing open. A uniformed guard appeared to stand at attention, followed by a priest dressed all in black like Zorro, with his face hanging down to his belly button. He must have been a new man, because he had trouble maintaining his cool: just standing there beside the guard he dropped his little black book on the floor like three times in a row.

The Army cat said to me, as if he'd wig out unless he broke the silence: "They . . . have it arranged like a stage play, don't they?"

"But no encores," said Victor hollowly.

Another guard showed up in the doorway and they walked in the condemned man. He was like sort of a shock. You expect a stud to *act* like a murderer: I mean, cringe at the sight of the chair because he knows this is it, there's finally no place to go, no appeal to make, or else bound in there full of cheap bravado and go-to-hell. But he just seemed mildly interested, nothing more.

He wore a white shirt with the sleeves rolled up, suntans that looked Army issue, and no tie. Under thirty, brown crewcut hair – the terrible thing is that I cannot even remember the features on his face, man. The closest I could come to a description would be that he resembled the Army cat right there beside me with his nose to the glass.

The one thing I'll never forget is that stud's hands. He'd been on Death Row all these months, and here his hands were still red and chapped and knobby, as if he'd still been out picking turnips in the San Joaquin Valley. Then I realized: I was thinking of him in the past tense.

Two fuzz began strapping him down in the chair. A broad leather strap across the chest, narrower belts on the arms and legs. God they were careful about strapping him in. I mean they wanted to make sure he was comfortable. And all the time he was talking with them. Not that we could hear it, but I suppose it went *that's fine, fellows, no, that strap isn't too tight, gee, I hope I'm not making you late for lunch.*

That's what bugged me, he was so damned *apologetic*! While they were fastening him down over that little bucket of oblivion, that poor dead lonely son of a bitch twisted around to look over his shoulder at us, and he *smiled*. I mean if he'd had an arm free he might have *waved*! One of the fuzz, who had white hair and these sad gentle eyes like he was wearing a hair shirt, patted him on the head on the way out. No personal animosity, son, just doing my job.

After that the tempo increased, like your heart beat when you're on a black street at three a.m. and the echo of your own footsteps begins to sound like someone following you. The warden was at one observation window, the priest and the doctor at the other. The blackrobe made the sign of the cross, having a last go at the condemned, but he was digging only Ben Casey. Here was this MD cat who'd taken the Hippocratean Oath to preserve life, waving his arms around like a TV director to show that stud the easiest way to *die*.

Hold your breath, then breathe deeply: you won't feel a thing. Of course hydrocyanic acid gas melts your guts into a red-hot soup and burns out every fibre in the lining of your lungs, but you won't be really feeling it as you jerk around: that'll just be raw nerve-endings.

Like they should have called *his* the Hypocritical Oath.

So there we were, three yards and half an inch of plate glass apart, with us staring at him and him by just turning his head able to stare right back: but there were a million light years between the two sides of the glass. He didn't turn. He was shrived and strapped in and briefed on how to die, and he was ready for the fumes. I found out afterwards that he had even willed his body to medical research.

I did a quick take around.

Victor was sweating profusely, his eyes glued to the window.

The politician was pop-eyed, nose pressed flat and belly indented by the brass rail, pudgy fingers like plump garlic sausages smearing the glass on either side of his head. A look on his face, already, like that of a stud making it with a chick.

The reporters seemed ashamed, as if someone had caught them peeking over the transom into the ladies' john.

The Army cat just looked sick.

Only the fuzz were unchanged, expending no more emotion on this than on their targets after rapid-fire exercises at the range.

On no face was there hatred.

Suddenly, for the first time in my life, I was part of it. I wanted to yell out *STOP!* We were about to gas this stud and *none of us wanted him to die!* We've created this society and we're all responsible for what it does, but none of us as individuals is willing to take that responsibility. We're like that Nazi cat at Nuremberg who said that everything would have been all right if they'd only given him more ovens.

The warden signalled. I heard gas whoosh up around the chair.

The condemned man didn't move. He was following doctor's orders. Then he took the huge gulping breath the MD had pantomimed. All of a sudden he threw this tremendous convulsion, his body straining up against the straps, his head slewed around so I could see his eyes were tight shut and his lips were pulled back from his teeth. Then he started panting like a baby in an oxygen tent, swiftly and shallowly. Only it wasn't oxygen his lungs were trying to work on.

The lieutenant stepped back smartly from the window, blinked, and puked on the glass. His vomit hung there for an instant like a phosphorus bomb burst in a bunker; then two fuzz were supporting him from the room and we were all jerking back from the mess. All except the politician. He hadn't even noticed: he was in Henry Millerville, getting his sex kicks the easy way.

I guess the stud in there had never dug that he was supposed to be gone in two seconds without pain, because his body was still arched up in that terrible bow, and his hands were still claws. I could see the muscles standing out along the sides of his jaws like marbles. Finally he flopped back and just hung there in his straps like a machine-gunned paratrooper.

But that wasn't the end. He took another huge gasp, so I could see his ribs pressing out against his white shirt. After that one, twenty seconds. We decided that he had cut out.

Then another gasp. Then nothing. Half a minute nothing.

Another of those final terrible shuddering racking gasps. At last: all through. All used up. Making it with the angels.

But then he did it *again*. Every fibre of that dead wasted comic thrown-away body strained for air on this one. No air: only hydrocyanic acid gas. Just nerves, like the fish twitching after you whack it on the skull with the back edge of the skinning knife. Except that it wasn't a fish we were seeing die.

His head flopped sideways and his tongue came out slyly like the tongue of a dead deer. Then this gunk ran out of his mouth.

It was just saliva – they said it couldn't be anything else – but it reminded me of the residue after light-line resistors have been melted in an electrical fire. That kind of black. That kind of scorched.

Very softly, almost to himself, Victor murmured: "Later, dad."

That was it. Dig you in the hereafter, dad. Ten little minutes and you're through the wall. Mistah Kurtz, he dead. Mistah Kurtz, he very very goddamn dead.

I believed it. Looking at what was left of that cat was like looking at a chick who's gotten herself bombed on the heavy, so when you hold a match in front of her eyes the pupils don't react and there's no one home, man. No one. Nowhere. End of the lineville.

We split.

But on the way out I kept thinking of that Army stud, and wondering what had made him sick. Was it because the cat in the chair had been the last to enter, no matter how violently, the body of his beloved, and now even that febrile connection had been severed? Whatever the reason, his body had known what perhaps his mind had refused to accept: this ending was no new beginning, this death would not restore his dead chick to him. This death, no matter how just in his eyes, had generated only nausea.

Victor and I sat in the Mercedes for a long time with the top down, looking out over that bright beautiful empty peninsula, not named, as you might think, after a saint, but after some poor dumb Indian they had hanged there a hundred years or so before. Trees and clouds and blue water, and still no birds making the scene. Even the cats in the black suits had vanished, but now I understood why they'd been there. In their silent censure, they had been sounding the right gong, man. *We* were the ones from the Middle Ages.

Victor took a deep shuddering breath as if he could never get enough air. Then he said in a barely audible voice: "How did you dig that action, man?"

I gave a little shrug and, being myself, said the only thing I could say. "It was a gas, dad."

"I dig, man. I'm hip. A gas."

Something was wrong with the way he said it, but I broke the seal on the tequila and we killed it in fifteen minutes, without even a lime to suck in between. Then he started the car and we cut out, and I realized what was wrong. Watching that cat in the gas chamber, Victor had realized for the very first time that life is far, far more than just kicks. We were both partially responsible for what had happened in there, and we had been ineluctably diminished by it.

On US 101 he coked the Mercedes up to 104 mph through the traffic, and held it there. It was wild: it was the end: but I didn't sound. I was alone without my Guide by the boiling river of blood. When the Highway Patrol finally got us stopped, Victor was coming on so strong and I was coming on so mild that they surrounded us with their holsters' flaps unbuckled, and checked our veins for needle marks.

I didn't say a word to them, man, not one. Not even my name.

Like they had to look in my wallet to see who I was. And while they were doing that, Victor blew his cool entirely. You know, biting, foaming at the mouth, the whole bit – he gave a very good show until they hit him on the back of the head with a gun butt. I just watched.

They lifted his license for a year, nothing else, because his old man spent a lot of bread on a shrinker who testified that Victor had temporarily wigged out, and who had him put away in the zoo for a time. He's back now, but he still sees that wig picker, three times a week at forty clams a shot.

He needs it. A few days ago I saw him on Upper Grant, stalking lithely through a grey raw February day with the fog in, wearing just a T-shirt and jeans – and no shoes. He seemed agitated, pressed, confined within his own concerns, but I stopped him for a minute.

"Ah . . . how you making it, man? Like, ah, what's the gig?"

He shook his head cautiously. "They will not let us get away with it, you know. Like to them, man, just living is a crime."

"Why no strollers, dad?"

"I cannot wear shoes." He moved closer and glanced up and down the street, and said with tragic earnestness: "I can hear only with the soles of my feet, man."

Then he nodded and padded away through the crowds on silent naked soles like a puzzled panther, drifting through the fruiters and drunken teenagers and fuzz trying to bust some cat for possession who have inherited North Beach from the true swingers. I guess all Victor wants to listen to now is Mother Earth: all he wants to hear is the comforting sound of the worms, chewing away.

Chewing away, and waiting for Victor; and maybe for the Second Coming.

PALE HANDS I LOATHED

William Campbell Gault

We were doing all right, Norah and I. We'd been married three years, but the honeymoon wasn't over. With us, the honeymoon should last forever, we figured at the time.

I was a police reporter for the *Star*, and on that beat you meet a lot of people, none of them likely to bolster your faith in human nature. It was Norah who did that for me. It was Norah I turned to every night for a renewal of the faith, as they say. Besides all that, she could cook. Not many like her, none like her. None I've met, at any rate.

We had a small home, out in Shore Hills, and a small nest egg in the First National, and a small heir in the rear bedroom named John Baldwin Shea, Jr. We had about everything we wanted except a new car, and cars just weren't available.

Maybe we were beginning to get smug. Maybe we had too much.

This June Drexel angle was routine enough, at first. She was a witness in the Peckham divorce mess, and I happened to run across her in the DA's office. I'd taken her out, quite a few times, in high school. The way she acted, in the DA's office, it looked to the others, I'll bet, as though I'd never stopped taking her out.

"Johnny dear," she asked, "have you come to rescue me?"

I blushed, and stammered, "Hello, June," and tried to ignore the laugh I was getting from the other reporters.

The DA looked at me sharply. He was trying to get some dope on Peckham from June; the divorce to him was only incidental.

June sighed, and said, "Johnny and I were such good friends."

The DA said, "I won't be needing you any more, Miss Drexel." And to the reporters, "That's all, boys."

We started to file out, when he called, "Would you mind waiting a moment, Shea?"

I closed the door and came back. I was probably still blushing. He had a smile on his broad face. "That's where the *Star* gets its copy on Peckham, is it?" he asked.

We'd been running a campaign on municipal building graft, and Peckham's name had been mentioned frequently. "Hell, no," I said. "I haven't seen that babe since high school. If I never see her again, it's OK with me."

He was smirking now. "Let's not be modest, Johnny. You're not a bad-looking guy, you know. You're right in there, pitching, aren't you?"

I shook my head. I was beginning to get hot. "I'm happily married. That's the way I intend to stay. She was just trying to embarrass me, and through me, the *Star*. She's no dummy."

"No," he said, "she isn't." He was looking thoughtful. He tilted his head to one side, studying me, and tried to look chummy. "The *Star* and I usually get along all right. We've worked together before, you know."

I nodded.

"Mr Cavanaugh would want you to work with me, Johnny."

Mr Robert Justice Cavanaugh was the owner of the *Star*. He was a big man, a very big man in this town. I said flatly, "You'd better talk to him, then."

He nodded, and he wasn't smirking or trying to be chummy any more. He said quietly, "That's exactly what I intend to do. That's all, Johnny."

He didn't frighten me. Cavanaugh would back me. He was just desperate and frustrated and annoyed and was taking it out on the first stooge who happened along. He didn't frighten me – much.

I left the quiet room behind, and went out into the clatter of the outer office. A flash bulb went off in my face.

Bitsy Donworth, photographer for the *Courier*, said, "Nice shot. Could we have a statement, dear?"

The, *Courier* was a tabloid, the kind of paper that would play up something like this. Any relation to the truth in the *Courier* was purely coincidental.

I thought of Norah. "Don't make the mistake of printing that picture, Bitsy. You'll be asking for trouble."

"The *Courier*," Bitsy replied, "thrives on trouble."

"But *you* don't," I said. "You're too small. This would be personal trouble, Bitsy." I realized I was making a damned fool of myself, but I was past caring.

Jug Elder, who handles the courts for the *Courier*, said, "Run along, dear. You don't want any trouble with us."

Jug goes about two hundred pounds. I figured about half of it was fat. I should have run along, as he said. But I walked over to him, and slapped his face. My name is Shea.

He drew his big right hand back, and I let him have it, right on the button.

I could feel the shock traveling up my arm, and I could see him go crashing backward into a desk. I saw the flash bulb go off again, and then the red went flashing through my brain, and I was moving in.

The next thing I knew, a couple of reporters from the *Journal* were holding my arms. Jug was getting up slowly, rubbing his chin. Bitsy was on his way out. The DA stood in his doorway, asking, "What the hell's going on out here?"

One of the *Journal* reporters said, "Jug fell down, didn't you, Jug? You all right, now?"

All the stenos, the cops, the help in the outer office were watching us. It had happened so quickly that none of the girls had had a chance to scream.

"I'm all right," Jug said. He didn't look at me. I'll bet he didn't even want to look at himself.

There was a murmur of voices from the spectators. The DA took one swift glance around the room, and then his door closed.

I went out with one of the *Journal* reporters. He said, "The *Courier*'ll print that picture. They'll make some kind of a lousy story out of the whole thing." He swore.

"They'll probably print both pictures, now," I said. "I wonder, you think there might be a libel angle—"

He shook his head. "Not the way they'll write it. Avoiding libel suits is a business they understand. They've made an art out of that."

He left me, there on the sidewalk, and I walked down to the coupé. I was thinking about June. I was remembering her hands, her pale, fluttering hands, always moving, always reaching. They'd repelled me, back in high school, repelled me and fascinated me. I remember, I could never take my eyes off them.

She had jet-black hair, this June Drexel, and her pale complexion was almost sickly in its whitness. But she'd done a lot with that contrast, that and the dark-blue eyes. That and the reaching, grasping hands.

As though she couldn't get enough of whatever it was she wanted. A high-school kid wouldn't know what it was. I wasn't sure, even now, and high school was ten years behind me. There'd been a war and a wedding and a birth in my life since then.

To hell with her, I thought. To hell with her and her hands.

I drove back to the office. I went up to the city room and hammered out a couple of routine stories from the department.

Our local political man, Tom Alexander, was working at the machine next to mine. I asked him, "You think this Peckham was playing house with that Drexel dame? You think his wife's got a case?"

He smiled cynically. "The *Star* thinks so, slave. The *Star* would like to nail Peckham any way they can."

"But why?" I said. "Peckham's no bigger than some of the other grafters in this burg. Why him?"

He shrugged. "Ours not to reason why, Johnny." He lighted a cigarette and considered his next paragraph. Then he looked over at me. "Is this a professional or a personal interest?"

"Why should it be personal?" I asked.

"I don't know." He pulled at an ear. "Your tone of voice, I guess." He frowned, and went back to work.

To hell with June Drexel, I thought again. And to hell with the *Courier*. Just for good measure, I threw in the DA.

I went over to pick up Sammy Berg and we went out to lunch. I told him what had happened.

He shook his head sadly. "You know Cavanaugh, Johnny. Dignity, all the time; ethics, every minute. He'll blow his stack."

He didn't, really. The early-afternoon edition of the *Courier* came off the press, and there was yours truly, in both poses. There was a story you could read any way your mind happened to run, though it would prove most interesting to a low mind.

I remember thinking, I hope Norah doesn't see this, just before I got the summons from R.J.

I was nervous. I won't say I was frightened, not at first, but the palms of my hands were wet, and I wanted a cigarette. In R.J.'s office, nobody smokes.

His desk is on a dais, sort of, and he's looking down at you, even if you're standing, which you usually are, in his office. I was standing now. It was very quiet in the room. He had the *Courier* spread out on his huge desk.

He's a distinguished-looking gent, tall and beautifully tailored, and not quite fifty. He was looking more than a little troubled at the moment.

he looked down at me gravely. "Mr Shea, you . . . ah . . . appear to know this June Drexel rather well."

"I knew her in high school," I told him. "I haven's seen her much since."

"Much? How much, Mr Shea?"

I was still nervous, but the Shea temper was climbing, too. I could feel my neck get warm. I said, "I've seen her around from time to time, and said hello. In public places, you understand. It's nothing like the *Courier* tried to suggest."

His face was still very grave. That's why I couldn't understand his smile, just then. It was a small, cold smile. "And that's all?"

"That's all."

He seemed to be trying to read my mind. He stared at me quietly for a moment. Then, "Do you think she's Peckham's girl?"

"I don't know," I told him. "She isn't working, and she isn't married. She must be somebody's girl."

He ignored that. He said, "I've a complaint from the district attorney, on you, too. I got it at lunch, at the club."

I said nothing.

"He seems to think you know more about this than you're telling, too."

I shook my head. "I don't."

He had a letter opened in his hands which he kept sliding back and forth from one hand to the other. "You know, of course, that the *Star* put Gargan in office?"

Gargan was the DA. I nodded.

"You know that we are working with him and for him, all the time?"

I nodded again.

"Yet, you create a minor riot in his office. You lose your temper and strike a fellow worker. You embarrass not only this paper, but the district attorney." He seemed to be working himself into a temper. "I hope you realize the gravity of all this. Mr Shea."

"I lost my temper," I said. "I wasn't in my right mind. That Drexel dame brings out the worst in me."

"Oh," he said, and was silent a moment. "You haven't seen her since high school, but she brings out the worst in you. Would you mind telling me, Mr Shea, just how long ago you went to high school?"

"Ten years ago," I replied.

"I see." He put the letter opener down on his desk. He was fumbling with a tiny jet elephant he wears on his watch chain, now. "Ten years ago." He studied me. "You're an extremely competent employee, Mr Shea, but still subject to discipline. Do you think a month's leave of absence would be adequate punishment?"

I stared at him. Finally, I said, "I didn't expect any punishment. I didn't figure I had it coming."

He smiled. "That would be for me to decide."

I was trembling now. I said, "Whether I work here, or for some other paper would be for me to decide. I wouldn't work for a paper that doesn't back up its reporters." I turned, and walked out.

I expected him to call me back, but he didn't. Some of my anger held, but not enough to prevent me from realizing I'd been a fool for the second time that day.

Tom Alexander was still working on his column when I went back to clean up my desk. He watched me quietly for a full minute, then asked, "Leave of absence, huh? The Cavanaugh curse."

"I quit," I told him.

"Sure," he said. "Of course. I'll see you in a month. That's what I bet it would be. Did I win?"

"That's what he tried to nail me with," I admitted. "But I wouldn't take it. I tell you I quit."

He swiveled around in his chair. "Johnny, don't be a sap. There isn't another paper in town'll hire you. Cavanaugh'll see to that."

"Not even the *Courier*?"

"You wouldn't work for them, Johnny. Nobody with any self-respect would work for them."

I didn't answer him. I went over to see if Sammy Berg was

still in the office, but he wasn't. I left, without saying anything to Foley, the city editor. He'd find out, soon enough.

I didn't go home. I didn't want Norah to find out I'd lost my job, not yet. I still had hopes. Foley would go to bat for me; the whole city room would go to bat for me. I hoped.

I went over to Mac's and had a drink. A couple of the boys were in there, and we gabbed for a while, and then they had to go to work. Mac's is a hell of a place when there aren't any customers around. I went to a movie.

It was a lousy show. They'd spent a couple of million on it, and it was full of names, and it had been promoted right up to the budget limit. It was still a lousy show. I could produce a better one myself.

I left, in the middle of it. I walked along Fourth Street, dreaming about that, about the big names Norah and I would be entertaining in our beach home. Norah was just giving me hell, because she'd caught me kissing one of moviedom's biggest stars, when I heard her voice.

I came back to this world, and there she stood. My Norah, my lovely, red-headed parcel of honey and fire. She stood there, on the sidewalk, with a copy of the *Courier* under her arm.

"John Badlwin Shea," she said.

I looked at the *Courier*, and into her blue eyes. "You don't believe any of that do you, honey?"

"Is it true, Johnny?"

I shook my head.

"Then I don't believe it."

I kissed her, right there on Fourth Street.

She said, "You're so impulsive. Did you have to hit that reporter?"

I nodded.

She sighed. "As soon as I saw this paper, while I was out shopping, I went down to the *Star*. Tommy Alexander told me you'd quit. You didn't have to quit, Johnny."

"I guess I didn't," I admitted.

"And now you're going back to see Mr Cavanaugh, aren't you? You're going to apologize for losing your temper."

"Like hell," I said.

"You've got seniority there, Johnny, and they pay better than the other papers. You're not going to forget all that."

"Honey," I said, "you let me worry about that."

Her lips set primly, and she said no more about it. "Well, we'd better be getting home. Mrs Orlow is with Junior, but I told her I'd be back in two hours. Let's go home and talk this over."

"There's nothing to talk over," I told her.

Neither of us said anything more as we walked to where the coupé was parked. Norah was beginning to get *that look*.

Silence, on the drive home. Silence, as we walked up the flagstones to the door, while Mrs Orlow explained that Junior had been just fine, and slept like a little lamb, and wasn't he just that, a little lamb, though? While she looked at me curiously, probably wondering how much of the *Courier* account was true.

Things the public reads in the *Courier*, they forget the next day. But things your friends might read about you in the *Courier* they never forget. They might not believe them, but neither will they forget them.

When Mrs Orlow had gone, Norah said, "I've never known you to be this stubborn, Johnny." She paused. "But I guess there are quite a few things about you I didn't know."

"If you're talking about June Drexel," I said, "that's ten years old."

"But you went with her then, didn't you? And yet, you've never once mentioned her name."

"I've gone with lots of girls," I answered. "I've forgotten most of them. I don't know all the boys you went with."

"You've forgotten most of them," she repeated. "But you didn't forget her."

"She's about as easy to forget as a toothache," I explained. "She's a very unusual girl."

"I'm sure she is." She hesitated, about to say more. But at that moment, Junior awoke, and started to cry. She hurried into his room.

This, I thought, would be a good time to take the screens down. This would be a good time to get out of the house. I changed my clothes quickly, and went outside.

I was trying to pry the too-tight screen off the sun-room window when Norah came out with Junior. She put him in the carriage, and told me, "I have to finish my shopping. We'll be back in a half-hour."

That last sentence was just by way of letting me know that

our discussion wasn't over. "I'll be waiting," I said. "I'm not going any place."

She sniffed.

She and Junior were just turning the corner, when this Caddy pulled up behind my car at the curb. It was a black sedan, long and low. I went around to the side of the house, to get the kitchen screens.

I could still see the Caddy, and I could see the smallish, thin gent who got out of it. He didn't look like a banker to me. He came up the walk, and I came around to the front of the house, to wait for him.

He was wearing an expensive topcoat, and a fine hat. He was wearing a dead expression on his thin face. His eyes were brown stones.

"You John Shea?" he asked.

I admitted it with a nod.

"I'm from the *Courier*," he said. "I've got some questions for you."

"I haven't got any answers," I told him. "Does the *Courier* furnish all their reporters with Cadillacs?"

"Don't worry about that," he said. "I'm no reporter. But if you think the *Courier* isn't backing me, you could call 'em."

I took a shot in the dark. "You're from Peckham, aren't you? He owns a piece of the *Courier*, huh?"

He studied me. I looked out to the Caddy, and saw there was another man there, behind the wheel. I looked back at him.

"All right," he said, "I'm from Peckham. He's wondering about you and Miss Drexel. The boss isn't one to wonder long."

A silence. I didn't know what other instructions the little man had received from his boss, but I was sure he'd carry them out, no matter what they were. I said carefully, "I knew Miss Drexel when I was seventeen years old. I took her out, then. I haven't taken her out at all, in the past ten years, and have seen her only a few times since, always in public places. You can tell your boss he needn't worry about me."

The little man considered me thoughtfully. "He's not worried about you. But he'll want to talk to you. He'll make it worth your while."

"I haven't anything to tell him," I said. "I haven't anything he'd buy."

"He'll decide that," the man said. "Let's let him decide that."

"OK," I said, "but I can't go now."

"Sure. We'll pick you up tonight. About eight all right?"

"Eight's all right," I agreed. "But don't come here. My wife would worry. I'll meet you somewhere."

"You name it."

"The filling station, two blocks down, the Gargoyle station on Burnham and Diversey. I'll drive down there and park the car."

He nodded. "At eight. We'll be there." He turned and went back to the Caddy and the car pulled away.

There wasn't anything I'd be able to tell Peckham, but I wanted to make that clear. If I'd been single, I'd have told them all to go to hell. If it weren't for Norah and Junior, the cops would be meeting the little man this evening in front of the Gargoyle station.

I still considered calling them into it, but decided against it. Peckham, I'd heard, was a reasonable man. Unless opposed.

When Norah came back, I told her, "Foley wants to see me at his house tonight. He just phoned. Maybe I'll be going back to work for the *Star*."

She looked relieved. "Be sensible, now, Johnny. Don't let your temper get the best of you."

"I won't," I promised, quickly.

Junior looked at me, and sadly shook his head.

"Nuts to you," I said.

"Blaa-a," he said, and made a face.

"Two of a kind," Norah said. "He certainly gets his disposition from your side of the family." She came over to kiss me.

There was a faint breeze, a chill breeze, coming in from the north. Most of the trees lining Diversey were bare; what few leaves were left were dry and gray. This was the pause between fall and winter, when you can expect anything in the way of weather.

I drove slowly along Diversey, planning my words for Roger Peckham, wondering if I hadn't made a mistake. At the corner of Diversey and Burnham, the Caddy was waiting.

There was a man behind the wheel, and the small man sitting next to him. I walked over, as the smaller man got out. He stood on the curb, waiting for me. He said, "We can't take you. We've got other business. But here's the address." He handed me a card. "He's waiting there."

I took the card, and went back to the coupe. The Caddy pulled away, making time through the gears, gunning.

The card read: Kensington Towers – Tower Apartment A.

Kensington Towers was a tall, showy place overlooking the bay. Tower Apartment A meant he had one of the roof apartments, complete with open porch and a view.

The clerk told me Mr Peckham was expecting me, and indicated one of the elevators.

I went up, and up and up, the floors going by too swiftly to count, the numbers seeming to merge, almost. At the top floor, we came gently to rest.

"To your right, sir," the operator said. "Tower Apartment A."

This looked more like an entrance hall than a corridor. I turned to the right, toward A.

The door was open when I got there, and a tall, broad man in dinner clothes stood framed in the doorway. He had gray eyes, and black hair sprinkled with gray. He must have been well past forty, but he had a vigorous, alert air about him.

"John Shea?" he asked. He was smiling.

"And you're Roger Peckham."

We shook hands, and he gestured me in. "My man is out tonight," he said. "But I guess I can still mix a drink."

I guessed he could, too. He'd started out as a bartender. This land of opportunity—

It was a beautifully designed apartment, and any person with taste could have done a lot with it. All he'd done was spend too much money for heavy, carved tables and chairs, dismal drapes, and some Oriental rugs that didn't fit at all.

He mixed a pair of drinks, and handed me one. He indicated a huge leather chair, and I sat in that.

He sat down, and said nothing.

I said, "Your torpedo seems to think I can tell you something about June Drexel."

"Torpedo?" he said, and then chuckled. "Oh, you mean Mike." He shook his head. "He's quite a boy, isn't he? He sees too many movies."

I said nothing.

"Mike's my attorney," he went on. "When I was a small operator, Mike was a small lawyer, very broke. Since I've made a few dollars, Mike's tended to put on airs. But he's a good boy. He's no torpedo;

he doesn't know one end of a gun from another." He chuckled again. "This whole affair has been over-dramatized, hasn't it?"

I continued to say nothing; I'd been trained to listen.

"When I saw your picture in the *Courier*, this afternoon, I decided I had to see you. Since then, I've changed my mind." He paused. "My wife and I have had a reconciliation."

There didn't seem to be anything for me to say, as yet.

He lifted his glass high. "Your health."

"Thanks," I said. "I'm glad everybody's happy."

He smiled. "And now, for other business. How would you like to work for the *Courier*?"

"I wouldn't," I said. "No offense, you understand. I just wouldn't want to."

He shrugged. "I'm changing it. It's changing with me. It's going to be a respectable, family newspaper." He sipped his whisky. "I could make you a really attractive offer. You could tell the snobbish Mr Cavanaugh to go to hell."

"I already have," I said.

He didn't seem to hear me. He was gazing at the floor. His voice was quiet. "That June," he said. "What is it she's got? Besides those damned hands of hers—"

I thought of the hands. I thought, fetishism? But they were as repelling as they were fascinating. "I don't know what she's got," I said, "but enough men seem to be attracted to her."

He looked at me gravely, and his voice was sad and quiet. "That's what I'm afraid of," he told me. "It's an attraction I'm afraid she'll always have for me."

I looked at my empty glass. He nodded toward the decanter on a low table. I filled the glass again, and siphoned in some water.

He said, "I love my wife. She loves me. I should leave this town, but I can't. I'll have to stay. And with June here—" He seemed to shudder. "Damn her!" he said.

I felt for him, but only a little. It didn't prevent me from saying, "I'd hate to be in your shoes when you tell her she'll have to work for a living."

He stared at me in surprise. It was honest surprise, I felt sure. He said, "I never supported her. I never contributed a dime to her support."

I was trying to figure that one out when the phone rang.

Peckham went to answer it. When he came back, he looked suspicious. "It's for you. It sounds like her, like June—"

"It's probably my wife," I said quickly.

It was June. "Johnny dear," she said, "would you like a story?"

Peckham was listening, I knew. I said, "I'll be home soon."

A silence. Then, "I see. Well, before you go home, drop in here, and I'll give you a story that will blow this town apart. Would that get you your job back?"

"Drop in where?" I asked.

The line went dead.

Peckham was standing in the middle of his living room when I turned around. "My wife's worried," I said.

His face was cold and set. "That was June, wasn't it?"

I said nothing.

"I told her I was seeing you, tonight. I told her, this afternoon, that I was through. Your wife doesn't know you're here."

"It was June," I admitted.

No emotion on his face, the eyes cold and bleak. "Well," he said, "good night. And good luck."

He didn't go to the door with me.

Standing in the entrance hall, waiting for the elevator, I debated the wisdom of going to see June Drexel. I thought of Norah, and forced myself to stop thinking of her. One sentence ran through my mind, around and around. Would that get you your job back?

In the lobby drugstore, I looked up the address of June Drexel.

I was coming through the lobby again, when I saw this woman at the desk. The clerk was saying to her, "I'm not sure Mr Peckham is in, Mrs Peckham."

The woman was a blonde, tall and poised. She said, "He's in. Ring and you'll see. From now on, he'll always be in to me."

I went out into the chill of the night. The coupé coughed a little, as I kicked it into life. I headed it down the drive, along the bay. Home? Or to the story? What did I want with a story? I wasn't a reporter, not tonight.

The coupé hummed along the drive to Iona. I turned up Iona, and followed it to Brady. I took Brady down to Astor, and turned again. On Astor and Knapp, a small apartment building. I sat in the coupé, and lighted a cigarette.

I took two puffs, and put the cigarette out. I left the car and went into the apartment building. Four names on the mail boxes of the lower hall and one of them was June Drexel's.

The downstairs door had no lock; there was no buzzer. I went through it, and up the stairs. I started to think about those damned hands of hers, the pale hands.

Her name on the door, up here, and I pressed the bell button.

I could hear it ringing, inside, but nothing happened. I remembered how the line had gone dead. I trembled, for some reason. I tried the knob; the door was unlocked.

The door opened a crack, and I could see a light on, in there. I pushed it open a little more, and saw June Drexel.

She was sprawled awkwardly on the floor of her living room. I pushed the door open all the way, and went in.

There was a hole in her forehead, a small hole. One table lamp sent a dim light through the room, and the radio played softly. I thought a .22. It wouldn't make much noise. I knew, now, why the line had gone dead. That speech of hers had been overheard, had meant to be overheard.

My eyes went to her hands, her now-quiet, pale hands. I saw something on the floor, about a foot beyond one outstretched hand, and I bent to pick it up.

I shouldn't have touched anything, of course. I should have gone immediately to the phone. I looked at what I'd picked up, and a pattern began forming, a pattern I couldn't believe. But the pieces came in, fitting themselves, making the picture.

I was still standing there when I heard the sirens, outside. Somebody else had phoned, evidently.

I reached over and put this thing I'd found in my shoe.

Sergeant Hutson, of homicide, was the first man to come through the door. He looked at me. "Johnny, for God's sakes—" He looked at June Drexel, on the floor.

"I didn't do it," I told him.

"You phoned?"

I shook my head. "I didn't phone. The murderer probably phoned, when he saw me come here. He knew I was coming."

"We'll have to run you in, Johnny," he said.

I nodded. "Sure." I kept my eyes from her hands. I tried to feel sorry that she was dead; one should mourn the dead.

*   *   *

It was a narrow cell, smelling of disinfectant, of dampness, of former occupants.

It was quiet, except for the deep breathing of other cell occupants, except for the occasional sound of voices from the lighted front room.

I sat on the hard cot, my head in my hands, thinking it all out, and worrying about Norah. Sergeant Hutson came along the corridor, to stand in front of my cell. "You want us to phone anybody else, Shea?"

"No," I said. "I want to talk to him, first." I looked up. "How about prints?"

"Plenty of 'em. The damnedest thing about prints, though. They're no good unless you got somebody to tie 'em to. Or unless they're prints on file someplace. What the hell good are they without that? We can't check 'em against the whole city."

"I'l give you somebody," I told him.

"I hope so," he said, and paused. "For your sake, Shea, I hope so." He went back along the corridor.

He isn't calling me "Johnny" any more, I thought. I'm on the other side of the fence now.

I thought about Norah, and June Drexel, about Peckham and his wife, about Peckham's attorney, who saw too many movies, about Tom Alexander and Sammy Berg, about Bitsy Donworth – and about Peckham's offer. In the adjoining cell, somebody began to snore.

Then there were feet along the corridor, and I stood up. The turnkey and Robert Justice Cavanaugh.

His voice was firm and reassuring. "Don't you worry, Johnnny. The *Star* will back you. I'll back you, all the way. It's Peckham's work; you can be sure, and—"

"Peckham," I broke in. "You were certainly jealous of him, weren't you? Until you got tired of her. Until you wanted to get rid of her."

I could see him stiffen, as the turnkey went away. He said, "What the devil are you talking about?"

"Murder," I told him. "This afternoon you worried more about what I knew about June than you did about the trouble in the DA's office. That should have been a lead. You were always after Peckham. That's another. When June phoned me tonight, she knew I'd lost my job. How? How many people knew that? Not Peckham.

You did. It all ties up. Peckham wasn't supporting her. You were."

"You're talking nonsense, Johnny," he said. His voice was low. This afternoon, in his office, he'd called me "Mr Shea". He was on my side of the fence, now.

"It took a gimmick," I went on, "to show me the way. You must have dropped it; the catch must have broken."

I reached down into my shoe, where the police hadn't searched, and brought out the tiny jet elephant he always wore on his watch chain.

A silence, while he stared at it in the dim light. Then he made one more try. "It doesn't prove anything, Johnny. It will only create a nasty scandal. They won't get me. I've too much influence. But it will hurt the paper, hurt me."

"They've got enough proof," I said. "All they want is somebody to fit it."

His voice was even quieter. "They don't know why I'm down here."

"Maybe not," I said. "Unless June told others what she was going to tell me. It wouldn't be so much of a scandal if you hadn't always been so noble, such a campaigner. But murder's a scandal, for anyone."

The man in the next cell rolled over, and mumbled in his sleep.

Cavanaugh said, "Editor, Johnny. For more money than you'll ever need. A job for life, Johnny."

A job for life, with the biggest paper in town. Why not? What had June Drexel ever meant to me, except trouble? I thought of Norah and Junior. I said, "You can go to hell. That's where you're going eventually, anyway."

Amateurs shouldn't commit murder. He hadn't even got rid of the gun. They didn't need his confession, to burn him. Once they had the pointing finger, they tied evidence to him like ornaments to a Christmas tree. His old pal, Gargan, the DA, couldn't handle it, so an assistant DA took over and did a fine, clean job.

The *Courier* has changed plenty, just as Peckham promised me. It's a clean, family paper, and getting to be the biggest in town. We call 'em as we see 'em, and I'm proud to be city editor of a sheet like that. Norah is proud of me, too, and even Junior gives me a little, grudging respect from time to time.

THE DARK GODDESS

Schuyler G. Edsall

I checked the flight records at the Trans-Ocean Airline desk to make certain that the man I knew only as Leiderkrantz was on the Constellation due from Lisbon. Then I went down the stairs to the luncheonette and sat over a cup of coffee, listening for the flight's arrival to be broadcast over the public address system. Watching the steam curl from my coffee, I began wondering again if I were inviting a brush with the police on this job and realized that there wasn't much I could do about it now. The big clock on the wall above the gleaming coffee urns said 10:27 and already the big Constellation was probably radioing La Guardia Tower for a landing.

It was supposed to be only an escort job; and there wasn't a lot to worry about if you looked at it from that angle. But, on the other hand, there could be trouble; and the fact that Schweingurt had hired me instead of getting the regular police to handle the assignment gave me something to think about. I couldn't talk myself out of the argument that this was no routine private case. In the first place, Schweingurt had been restless and jittery when I talked to him earlier; secondly, the little package Leiderkrantz was bringing in from Europe made him a choice target for a slug or a knife in the ribs, or for a quick bath in Flushing Bay, somewhere around Whitestone where it would be dark and deserted. Lastly, I was pretty sure Leiderkrantz was smuggling in the Dionysus statuette; and this is what made me worry about getting messed up with the Customs authorities and the police.

Schweingurt had reassured me about this. "It's all on the level," he had said.

"Of course, there must be secrecy up to a certain point because there is a strict prohibition against removing artworks from Greece. The government of Greece has enforced this for fear the country's artistic wealth will be dissipated. But once the Dionysus statuette arrives here, there will be nothing more to worry about."

But his small black eyes had been greedy. He had absently wiped the palms of his hands along the knees of his light trousers. They had left a dark, wet mark. I wasn't so sure I believed what he had told me.

The public address system was announcing the arrival of Trans-Ocean Flight 7. I slid off my stool, swallowed what was left of my coffee and went down to the gate. People crowded the glassed-in barrier. A policeman and a girl attendant, dressed in light-blue and holding a clipboard of flight reports in her hand, stood on the ramp just outside the gate. I flashed my agency shield at the cop, and he scowled, sizing me up and down. For a minute, I didn't think I was going to make it easily; then he nodded his bullet-shaped head and let me through. I stood alongside the girl in the blue uniform, wanting very much to take a second look at her delicately featured face and honey-colored hair; but I didn't dare take my eyes from the plane.

It bothered me that I had no idea what Leiderkrantz looked like and I decided the best thing for me to do was to wait until the blonde attendant checked off the passengers as they filed through the gate. I didn't believe much could happen to him or the statuette between the plane and the gate.

A glistening chromium gangway was shoved across the ramp to the door of the cabin; and a stewardess opened the cabin door, blinking in the morning sun and smiling. She stood aside as the passengers filed out of the huge plane, down the gangway and across the ramp. Mostly, they were familiar faces, influential men in State and Politics, stage and screen idols. A couple of them looked annoyed at the absence of photographers and press reporters.

They passed the girl at the gate, each calling his name as he filed through: Greenleaf . . . Burnes . . . Stettanus . . . Leiderkrantz . . .

He was a short, stocky man of about thirty-four, with rust-colored hair and a carefully trimmed mustache. He wore his clothes jauntily, almost flashily, and was not what you would expect of an art connoisseur. He appeared nervous, shifting his eyes as he gave his name curtly to the girl in the blue uniform. In his hand was tightly clasped the handle of a small black bag which he seemed to protect with an almost fierce intensity. I was pretty certain that the Dionysus was inside that bag. I began to feel a little nervous myself.

I tagged behind him as he hurried through the gate. When we were a little way from the crowd, I palmed the shield from my pocket so he could see it, dropped it back and said, "I have a cab waiting outside, Mr Leiderkrantz."

He stopped short, looking confusedly at me, pulling the bag back possessively so that it pressed hard against his legs. Then his blue eyes narrowed defiantly; and when he spoke, his voice was unexpectedly harsh. "Police?" he asked quickly. The deep crease between his eyes drew his brows together.

I smiled reassuringly, said, "Private detective. Max Schweingurt sent me to make sure you got in all right."

He studied me thoughtfully, then nodded slowly. "I see."

"Do you want me to carry the bag?" I asked and reached for it.

He pulled the bag away quickly, holding the handle with both hands, and pressed it against his legs again. "No," he cried sharply. Then he smiled and lowered his voice. "No, thank you. I . . . I am quite able to carry it."

His manner irritated me a little but I decided it would be better anyway to be free to use my hands in case anything happened, rather than be hampered by a heavy bag. On the hunch, I transferred my gun from its shoulder holster to the side pocket of my coat, as I waited for Leiderkrantz to clear through Customs.

I didn't know what he did about the Dionysus, whether he declared it or not. All I know is that I stood by, keeping my eyes open, and he cleared through in about fifteen minutes less than the usual hour and a half. When he finished we went upstairs and climbed into the cab I had waiting.

I gave the address of Max Schweingurt's place on Fifty-third Street, and we swung out on the Cross-Island Parkway to the Triborough Bridge. Leiderkrantz was still nervous and he fidgeted in the corner of the cab, smoking cigarettes chain-fashion. The small black bag he kept on the floor between his feet. He didn't say anything and kept eyeing me suspiciously, as if for some reason he didn't trust me. I tried to start a conversation to pass the time, asking him about the situation in Europe and about the trip across in the Constellation; but he cut me off short every time. So I quit and leaned back in the seat and lighted a cigarette myself, watching the quaint pattern of buildings that edged the East River as we crossed the Bridge.

Suddenly, Leiderkrantz leaned across me and snapped a cigarette butt out of my open window. It struck the frame and blew back, scattering hot red sparks and ashes into my face, fiinally landing on the seat between my leg and the side of the cab. Frantically, I rubbed the ashes from my eyes. At the same time I turned to remove the burning cigarette from the cab, purely reflex action. I was muttering savagely beneath my breath when suddenly it seemed as if the roof had caved in on my head!

I started to turn, instantly on the alert in spite of the pain from the blow. But I was too slow. He hit me again, and I slumped down off the seat, grabbing for the coat that moved in a blur above me. I yanked down with one hand, my other hand going for my shoulder holster; then I remembered that I had transferred the gun to my coat pocket back there in the Air Terminal. My hand started for the coat pocket, but it never got there. The roof did cave in! With one final blow, Leiderkrantz finished me. I didn't remember anything after that.

I raced into Max Schweingurt's art galleries with a peach of a headache, a sick feeling in my stomach and mayhem in my heart. There were a couple of old ladies studying a Michaelangelo out front and a group of college students in the Grecian Court listening to the droning monotone of a guide. I passed a young black-haired fellow in a gray smock who was busy cleaning a large statue, and went into Schweingurt's ornate office at the rear of the room.

He looked up at me as I banged the door behind me, and his mouth dropped open. I didn't give him time to say anything and snapped, "The next time you want me to meet one of your buddies, make sure it's a woman. Either that, or I'll put him in a straitjacket before I start."

He still looked at me incredulously, and his eyes got scared. His thick lips moved wordlessly and weakly, he pushed himself from his chair and stood with his white hands resting on the desk. "What are you talking about?" he asked finally. Then, his voice almost choking him. "Where . . . where's Leiderkrantz?"

It struck me suddenly that Leiderkrantz was not here; had not been here. I stared at Schweingurt and dropped limply into a chair alongside his desk. "You . . . haven't heard from him?" I asked slowly, and the words sounded silly the way I said them.

He shook his head and asked again, "What happened?"

I fumbled in my pocket for a cigarette, felt the gun there, drew out a cigarette and lighted it. I offered one to Schweingurt and he refused. He leaned forward intently. I took a couple of long drags, blowing out the smoke noisily and trying to pull myself together, before I told him what had happened.

"Did he have the Dionysus?" he whispered.

"I don't know definitely. I didn't see it. But he had a small black bag that he wouldn't let me touch. How large is this Dionysus thing?"

"I don't know. I've never seen an original. Forgeries are about . . ." Schweingurt leveled his hand about eighteen inches above the desk . . . "that high. I imagine the original would be the same."

I nodded. "It would fit in the black bag," I said.

Schweingurt pinched the end of a cigar, shoved it between his heavy lips and paced the floor behind his desk. He was a big muscular man with dark, graying hair and red-flecked brown eyes. His somber clothes were immaculate and well made. He flamed a match, watched it glow, and said before lighting his cigar, "You don't know what happened to Leiderkrantz? I mean, after he slugged you?"

I shook my head slowly. It hurt. "The cabbie said he dropped him with his luggage at a hotel in the East Forties. I figured that was just a dodge; that he'd hop another hack and come straight here. He wouldn't know one hotel from another, unless he's been in New York before."

"I don't know whether he's ever been here before or not," Schweingurt explained. "He's been representing me in Europe only since the war." He blew out a cloud of smoke. "How long ago was this?"

"I don't know. The cab driver said he had a time bringing me round after we pulled up out front here. I must have been out quite a while." I touched the bump on the side of my head gingerly, and winced. "Do you think this Leiderkrantz guy took a powder on you with the Dionysus gadget?"

Schweingurt puffed heavily on his cigar and stared out the window. "He wouldn't have done that. He wouldn't have made the trip if he had intended to run out on me. What I'm worried about is – was the man you met Leiderkrantz?"

I had thought of this, but dismissed it. The little man had flown in from Lisbon as Leiderkrantz and had cleared through Customs; so his passport must have been issued under that name and borne his photo. The passport could have been forged, of course, and the switch could have been pulled in Lisbon; but the chances that this had been done were slim.

Schweingurt said, "I'll cable the representative in Europe and find out if Leiderkrantz made the trip."

This wouldn't help, I decided, if the switch had been made in Lisbon, shortly before the Constellation took off. "Get a description of this Leiderkrantz," I suggested, "and see if it fits our man."

Schweingurt nodded and picked up the telephone.

The door opened and the dark-haired employee in the gray smock stuck his head in. "A gentleman to see you," he told Schweingurt. "A Mr Leiderkrantz from the European representative's office."

Schweingurt glanced quickly at me, his red-flecked eyes overbright. I tensed in my chair and clenched my hands unconsciously.

"Send him in," Schweingurt told the attendant. He put the phone down.

I don't know why I was surprised when Leiderkrantz walked into the office with his small black bag, because I really didn't expect anyone else. But I was surprised enough in that scant moment to become suddenly suspicious of him; though I can't explain that, either. He seemed a bit taken aback at seeing me, then he smiled quickly and put out his hand to Schweingurt.

"Leiderkrantz," he introduced himself sharply. "I'm pleased to meet you, Mr Schweingurt." His voice was flat and unpleasant; and there wasn't a trace of the accent you would expect from a European.

Schweingurt smiled pleasantly and shook hands. He went

back and sat down at his desk, knocked the ash from his cigar carefully into a crystal ashtray and looked up brightly. "You have the Dionysus?" he asked.

Leiderkrantz nodded and placed the bag on the desk. He turned to me and said blandly, "I owe you an apology, I imagine. You are a detective after all?"

I gestured with a flourish of my hand. "Think nothing of it," I replied with a touch of sarcasm that I didn't bother to hide. "What's a sock on the head, or two. You didn't believe I was a detective?" I asked him.

"I was warned before I left," he explained, "that there might be an attempt made to steal the Dionysus. I couldn't take any chances. I couldn't be sure of your honesty because I had no way of being *absolutely* sure. So as long as I couldn't trust you, I decided to escape from you and come here independently."

"Where did you go after you left the cab?" I asked him. "You didn't come straight here."

"No," he answered willingly. "I checked into the Pittsfield Hotel on East Forty-seventh Street, and left my bags."

The Pittsfield was about where the cab driver told me he had dropped Leiderkrantz. I was a little disappointed that I couldn't find a hole in his story.

Schweingurt had tried to open the small bag on the desk and found it locked. He sat drumming his fingers nervously on the arm of his chair. He said impatiently to Leiderkrantz, "May I see the Dionysus?"

The man turned swiftly, apologizing for the locked bag, but again explaining his need for the utmost care. He opened the bag by rotating a miniature combination lock and removed a tubular, blue-velvet sack with a drawstring at the top. This he placed carefully in front of Schweingurt, who cautiously withdrew the velvet sack from around the statuette. Schweingurt leaned back in his chair and admired the statuette where it stood on the desk. It was a sculpture about eighteen inches high of a scantily clad boy holding a small cask in his right hand, a staff in his left. From its color, it appeared very old; not the color that comes from dirt or dust, but the tinge of age that seems to have substance.

Schweingurt said, "An original Baccus by Orinaldi!"

I glanced at him perplexedly, and Leiderkrantz, who must

have had the same thought, corrected him, "An original *Dionysus* by Orinaldi!" He spoke deprecatingly, but rubbed at his small mustache with a supercilious gesture.

Schweingurt nodded slowly but didn't say anything. He continued to stare entranced at the statuette on the desk, and his smile reflected his appreciation. But there was something in his eyes that had changed, some vague disturbance that made the red flecks seem brighter. I watched him closely, trying to fathom his faint change of mood.

Leiderkrantz's bland voice broke the sudden tension that seemed to fill the room when he said, "I must be going now," and put out his hand. "I'll be in New York a day or two; so I'll see you again before I return to the Continent."

Schweingurt looked up quickly, blinking, as if he had been in a trance. He grasped Leiderkrantz's hand mechanically – and not too warmly – and said simply, "Yes, yes. Fine!" He immediately returned to his studied appraisal of the Dionysus.

Leiderkrantz glanced at him, nodded to me and went out the door.

I sighed deeply, lighted another cigarette and relaxed in the chair.

When the door closed, Schweingurt looked up slowly, his brown eyes narrowing and a dark frown etching his forehead. He watched the door for a long, silent minute; then, not taking his eyes away from it, he said to me in a brittle, decisive voice. "You better run over to the Pittsfield Hotel. See what you can find out about him. That man is not Leiderkrantz!"

I jumped out of my chair, spilling ashes from my cigarette on the thick maroon rug. "What . . ."

He stopped me with a flourish of his hand. "Take it easy. I think we have plenty of time. Whoever he is, he is not aware we know he is *not* Leiderkrantz. He must have had some inside information to know that I don't know Leiderkrantz by sight. But the Dionysus is worth a lot of money that I haven't paid yet – sixty-five thousand dollars – and he's bound to make a play for that. That's why I say we have plenty of time. I don't think he would turn the statuette over to me, and let me send the money to the European representative. That's the procedure, of course, but if the guy's a phony, he'll make a play for the money, or part of it, anyway."

"Unless the Dionysus is a phony," I stated.

"A forgery?" he said and shrugged. "I don't think so. It appears to be the original, though I can't be positive by just looking at it. I'll make tests and call in Dr Homer Bramble from the Lexington Foundation Museum. He's an expert on this period of art. I wouldn't want to judge the work solely on my own experience, though I do have an Athena outside by the same sculptor. In fact, it was the only one in the country until I got this Dionysus. If the two don't compare, I'll know the Dionysus is a forgery."

I stepped over and rubbed out my cigarette on the ashtray, wondering above all else how Schweingurt was so certain that the man who had brought him the statuette was not Leiderkrantz. I took my gun from the pocket of my coat and put it back in its shoulder holster, ready to leave. But I wanted the full story before I started.

"How do you know he is an impostor?" I asked.

He took the cigar from his mouth. "I wanted to be certain," he said, "so I deliberately called the Dionysus a 'Bacchus' sculptured by Orinaldi. The fellow corrected me. But Bacchus is the Roman name for the Greek god, Dionysus. An art connoisseur of Leiderkrantz's caliber would have known that. Also," he added, "there was never, to my knowledge, a sculptor named Orinaldi."

I grinned because I couldn't help it. But when I went out I didn't think any part of it was funny, and I was glad for the opportunity to settle for a couple of knots on my head.

The Pittsfield Hotel turned out to be an excellent indication that Leiderkrantz was a phony. Schweingurt had sized the guy up right on that point. But Schweingurt had pressed his intuition too far when he claimed that our man would be back. From what I learned, I was pretty sure we would never see Leiderkrantz again.

No one by that name, according to the desk clerk, had checked into the hotel. There had been a man of Leiderkrantz's description, however, who had checked in shortly before noon. But the clerk was pretty sure the man had come in from Chicago or Milwaukee, or some place out West. Not Lisbon.

If Leiderkrantz had registered under another name, it was

logical that he would also falsify his address. I checked the bellhops.

The two bellhops on duty hadn't recalled carrying any luggage with a Trans-Ocean Airlines tag; but one of them – a young blond kid with fuzz on his plump cheeks and a squeaky voice – remembered hopping for a short, stocky man, flashily dressed, with a dapper, rust-red mustache. The kid especially remembered the nickel tip the man had given him.

I called Schweingurt, learned that he was in conference with Dr Bramble from the Lexington Museum, then sat down in a leather chair in the lobby to wait for the man who had fitted Leiderkrantz's description. After a while I got restless, went over to the cigar stand and brought a pack of cigarettes, went into the bar and drank two beers – all the time keeping my eye on the lobby, the entrance door and the room desk. When I finished the beer, I went back to the lobby, sat down, got up again and bought a package of chewing gum at the cigar stand. I was walking back to my chair again when the bellhop grabbed my arm and pulled me excitedly behind a huge potted fern.

"That's the guy I meant," he told me and pointed to a red-haired man stepping into the elevator. "That's the bird from Milwaukee who checked in this morning."

I glanced eagerly through the green fronds of the fern and growled out a curse. The man wasn't Leiderkrantz. I turned to the blond kid, saw the disappointment on his cherubic face, tossed him four-bits and hurried out of the lobby. It was after five o'clock and I wanted to boot myself all the way cross-town for killing the whole afternoon. It might have been speedier at that. The taxi I grabbed was plenty slow, but it gave me an opportunity to try to figure out the puzzle.

No matter how I added it up, it wouldn't make sense that Leiderkrantz – rather, the man who had posed as Leiderkrantz – would make the trip from Europe with the valuable Dionysus, risk exposure in order to deliver the statuette to Schweingurt, then disappear.

When the cab pulled up in front of Schweingurt's place, I was drawing a blank all around, and still didn't have any answers.

There were a green-and-white police car and an ambulance at the curb when I left my cab. A crowd of silent people stood in front of the art galleries, trying to peer through the huge front

windows. A big, perspiring cop at the door was growling at them
and endeavoring to move them away from the place. I flashed
my shield at the cop, told him I was working for Schweingurt,
and he let me through.

"You just lost your job, buddy," he told me as I passed him.

Max Schweingurt was lying on the floor of the Grecian Court,
at the foot of the Athena statue. A doctor from the Medical
Examiner's office was crouched over the body. Schweingurt's
hair was matted with blood and his head was twisted crazily so
that his sightless eyes stared up at the statue above. He was very
dead. There was a bright crimson stain on the base of the statue,
near the foot of the goddess, that trickled down to the floor.
Evidently Schweingurt had struck his head on the statue when
he fell. I moved over to where a detective was questioning the
dark-haired attendant in the gray smock. The attendant's name
was Maurice Cambelli, it developed.

The Medical Examiner got up from his crouch with a grunt
and turned to the detective. He gazed down at the corpse and
grunted again, running long fingers through his shaggy hair.
"This man was dead before he hit that statue," he said in a
rumbling voice. "The right side of his head – where you see the
blood – struck the base of the statue. But," and he pointed to a
livid mark behind Schweingurt's left ear, "he was struck a much
harder blow on the left side of his head before he fell. I'm pretty
sure that first blow caused his death."

"Hmm!" the detective murmured and he stepped slowly over
to the corpse. "Murder!"

Cambelli gasped, repeating the word as if it choked him.

A police lab photographer took shots of the body before the
Medical Examiner's men removed it, and a fingerprint man
studied the room as if trying to decide where to start dusting
the place.

I said to Cambelli beside me, "Come on into Schweingurt's
office. I need a drink. And I think you do, too. Maybe we can
find a bottle there." He followed me into the office at the rear,
nodding silently as the police detective warned him to stick
around the building.

I closed the door of the office and Cambelli went over and
took a bottle of Bourbon and a water glass from the bottom

drawer of the desk. He poured a good triple shot into the glass, gulped it down, poured a lighter drink and handed the glass to me. I held it in my hand and sat down on the corner of the desk.

He told me he had worked for Max Schweingurt since coming from art school in Italy eight years ago. He wasn't familiar with the Dionysus acquisition, he told me – Mr Schweingurt had been pretty secretive about it all – but he did know that the Dionysus statuette might possibly be a forgery. Mr Schweingurt had claimed it was, though Dr Bramble from the Lexington Foundation Museum was certain it was the original.

"Isn't Bramble supposed to be an expert on that sort of thing?" I asked him.

He nodded quickly. "Oh, yes," he agreed. "The very best. But Mr Schweingurt made tests of it up in the laboratory and proved to his own satisfaction that it's no more than four or five hundred years old. The original would be several centuries older than that, dating back to around 450 B.C." He spoke with a certain pride found only in men of his profession, but he spoke of centuries the way we might speak of years, say the turbulent Thirties or the roaring Twenties. "I shouldn't claim that the Dionysus we received is a forgery, I suppose," he said; "rather, it's a copy of the original made by a sculptor of a later era. An excellent copy, too; and worth a great amount of money. But it can't approach the value of the original."

He was silent for a moment. I said, "You say that this Dr Bramble from the museum claimed the Dionysus was the original?"

"Yes." He nodded his dark head. "He and Mr Schweingurt had quite an argument about it."

"Ah!" I murmured. My thoughts began clicking into some semblance of order.

He leaned forward in his chair aggressively. "No, no! Dr Bramble wouldn't have done anything like – *that!* Besides," and he wiped his fine, smooth hand across his eyes, "the Dionysus is gone. Missing. Stolen! Dr Bramble wouldn't have stolen it, let alone committed murder for it, whether it was the original or a copy."

I sipped my drink, gestured with the glass in my hand and argued, "Look at it this way: Suppose the Dionysus *was* an original, even though Schweingurt's tests proved it wasn't.

Bramble was so sure it was that he wanted it. An art connoisseur will commit murder for something so priceless as a statuette dating before Christ." I emptied the glass and watched the thoughtful frown on his face, as he turned the theory over in his mind. He poured himself another drink.

He shook his head. "No. That's no good. If Bramble were certain the statuette was an original, he could have agreed with Schweingurt and purchased it, as a copy, for a small fortune less than he believed it was worth. He would have done that if he had wanted it badly. He wouldn't have stolen it." He took my glass and filled it for himself. "Besides," he said resolutely, "Dr Bramble *wasn't* interested in the Dionysus, which is a decisive point in his favor. He has already bought the Athena – the statue of the goddess outside, which Mr Schweingurt struck when he fell. The Athena is the only original by the same sculptor in the country and is worth even more than the Dionysus. So you see – if Dr Bramble had wanted the Dionysus as representative of that period of art, he might have purchased it as a copy, rather than spend many, many times more for the Athena."

"The Athena is an original?" I questioned.

"Oh, definitely!"

"You're certain of that?"

"Well, I hardly think Dr Bramble would have purchased it as an original if it weren't. He is an expert, you know. And he has been quite anxious to get it these last few days."

"How long have you had this statue of Athena?" I asked him.

"About two years." He thought a moment. "Maybe a little longer."

"And Dr Bramble has been only anxious to buy it in these past few days?"

"Yes."

"Odd, isn't it? Especially since Bramble is supposed to be such an authority and would certainly have known of Schweingurt's having the only authentic sculpture in this country?"

He shrugged indifferently. "I wouldn't know about that," he said. "Certainly, Dr Bramble wouldn't have stolen the Dionysus. I can't understand why anybody would want to steal a copy."

"Schweingurt told me the original was worth about sixty-five thousand dollars," I said. "How much was the copy worth?"

"A couple of thousand, maybe."

"Plenty of murders have been committed for less than that," I told him. "Besides, whoever did steal it may not know it's a copy."

"Which would leave Bramble out of the picture."

"Yes."

Cambelli stared suddenly at the Bourbon in his glass. "Even stealing an original would be stupid," he mused. "An original Dionysus would be too hard to dispose of. No art connoisseur would buy it unless he knew exactly where it came from. And no one but a connoisseur would be interested in it." He sipped his whiskey thoughtfully. "There's a lot more to this than robbery," he added.

"Much more," I agreed and let it go at that.

When we left the office, Schweingurt's body had been removed and the lab men were packing their equipment. I hung around a few minutes near the Athena statue to see if I might pick up some faint clue to the murder, but found nothing and started to turn away when I saw what appeared to be a pencil-shaped object made of marble lying near the base of the statue. I stooped to pick it up when a rough voice behind me bellowed, "Keep your hands off that!"

I straightened quickly, my hands at my sides and stared at the object on the floor.

The voice came alongside me and said, in a friendlier tone, "Oh, it's you, Mike." I glanced up at the big, red, Irish face of the plain clothes man. "Sorry," he said. "Reilly don't want nothin' touched. He's comin' back in a few minutes."

"Okay," I told him. "That pencil-shaped thing caught my eye." I recognized it as the tip of the staff I had seen on the Dionysus statue, and it told me something – Schweingurt probably had been holding the statuette when he was murdered, the tip of the staff had broken off as he fell.

"What does Reilly think of this job?" I asked the cop.

"Reilly don't know. The place was closed and there was only the assistant here." He glanced furtively at Maurice Cambelli standing nervously near the door to Schweingurt's office. "He thinks maybe there was a robbery motive . . . but he's not so sure but what Cambelli might have something to do with it."

I shook my head. "He had no motive," I argued, thinking of

what I already knew about the case – the statuette, Leiderkrantz, Bramble. "I don't think he had anything to do with it."

The cop shrugged. "Reilly just isn't sure about him, that's all." He moved away, turned and said, "You won't touch anything, will you, Mike? Reilly would raise hell with me if you did."

I nodded, said, "The answer isn't here, anyway, Grady." I walked out of the place.

Picking up Leiderkrantz's trail was a hopeless cause, but it was the only lead I could think of. It kept me busy for three days, picking up pieces, querying people who might have known him or seen him – and running up against a dead end every time. The Customs and airlines representatives were looking for him without success. I finally decided to give up that angle.

A week passed, a week in which I accomplished nothing. Then, one morning I picked up my newspaper and read that Maurice Cambelli had been slapped in jail for the Schweingurt murder. That night I had two visitors, Reilly and Grady from the detective division.

I pulled out a bottle and poured three drinks after they arrived. Reilly looked at the drinks, then at me. "This isn't a social call, Mike," he said gruffly and shook his head at the drinks. "We want to know how much *you* know about the Schweingurt murder."

I waved my hand at him and got up from my chair. "Okay," I told him. "Ignore my hospitality. Besides I'm an unsociable guy." I went into the bedroom, put on a lounging robe and came back. Two of the drinks were gone. That made me feel better. I don't like the law to be out of sorts with me.

"What about the Schweingurt murder?" I asked. "I thought you'd grabbed the Cambelli kid for that."

The fire had gone out of Reilly's eyes. "Don't try to sell it, Mike," he said softly. "Maybe you know something, maybe you don't." He shrugged. "We grabbed the Cambelli boy. But that doesn't solve the murder. We found out that a statue was stolen – a thing called Dionysus – and figured there probably was a robbery motive. We found the statue in Cambelli's room."

I glanced at him quickly, lowered my eyes and slowly lighted a cigarette. "That should clear up the whole case," I said carefully, though I didn't believe it. I still couldn't tag Cambelli as the murderer.

"It should," Grady put in. "But a couple of things have happened, Mike. You remember that big statue outside Schweingurt's office?"

I nodded. He meant the Athena goddess. "It was to be delivered to the Lexington Foundation Museum," I said.

Grady moved his head at Reilly. "Tell him, Reilly," he said.

Reilly said, "The statue was delivered to the Lexington Museum the day after the murder. It was stolen from the museum that night!"

"Stolen?" I snapped. "People don't steal something like that. They'd need a derrick. It weighed a ton!"

He lowered his eyebrows. "Just the same, it was either stolen or picked up its skirts and walked out of the place. It's gone!"

Grady interrupted. "Tell him where the old gal went when she picked up her skirts."

Reilly's expression didn't change. "To Mexico!" he said.

I didn't say anything for a minute, dropped my cigarette into an ashtray beside my chair and picked up my drink. I couldn't catch up with them and asked simply, "Mexico?"

Reilly bobbed his big head up and down. "The insurance company that covered it picked it up in a museum in Mexico City and flew it back to New York. And all this in a week . . . It doesn't seem on the level." He cocked his head to one side and looked at me narrowly out of his left eye. "Cambelli told us that Schweingurt hired you for a job the day he was murdered. We wondered if there is some information that we haven't run across yet. Something you may know."

I took a drink from my glass, made a face and glanced up at him. "About Cambelli having the Dionysus statuette in his room – did you get a tip on that?"

He raised his bushy brows, still looking at me with narrowed eyes, and said. "Yes. As a matter of fact, we did. Why?"

"From whom?"

"I don't know. It was one of those things."

"I see," I replied slowly. "Do you know if this Dionysus statue was an original?"

"Yes, it was an original. A guy named Bramble from the Lexington Museum said it was an original. He's supposed to be an expert on that sort of thing."

"Was it broken?"

"No . . . I'm sure it wasn't broken. Dr Bramble would have remarked about that, wouldn't he?"

"Yes," I agreed. "I guess he would have." It occurred to me that Dr Bramble had insisted that Schweingurt's Dionysus had been an original; but later that had been broken. I had seen the broken tip of the staff near the scene of the murder. I was sure of that. So another statuette had been switched in its place – possibly the original for the copy – and I wondered when this had been done.

The man who had posed as Leiderkrantz may have actually brought the original from Europe, switched it for a phony after I lost him that morning and brought the copy to Schweingurt. But he couldn't have made the switch with Cambelli, because I had seen Cambelli in the galleries during that time, cleaning the Athena statue. Still, the original Dionysus had turned up in Cambelli's room. He was either working with someone else, someone besides Leiderkrantz's impostor, or the statuette had been planted on him to frame him for the murder.

Reilly suddenly said, "Are you holding out on us, Mike? That would be bad. You're liable to lose your license if we catch you holding out on us." His heavy, black eyes were smoldering.

I poured another drink.

I said, "I'm not holding out anything, Reilly. I'm in the dark. There's an answer some place, but the Cambelli kid isn't it. You don't believe Cambelli is the murderer, do you?"

He moved his big shoulders and looked up. "I think maybe he was in on it. Where, I don't know. But I think it was more involved than a robbery-murder job. It may be an inside job – which would mean Cambelli."

I shoved the cork into the bottle and struck it with the palm of my hand. "This statue that was picked up in Mexico," I said, "have you seen it since it was flown back?"

"No. It's back in the Lexington Museum, as far as I know. Why?"

"You said yourself that something about that part of it didn't seem on the level. It may be the clue we're looking for. I think it would be a good idea to take a look at that statue."

Reilly's dark eyes brightened and he pushed himself from the chair. "You think we might find the answer there?"

I slipped out of the lounging robe and shrugged into a suit

coat, strapped the shoulder holster under my armpit. "It's just a hunch," I told him. "Still, we may find something."

The museum was a huge, impressive-looking brownstone between Fifth Avenue and Madison in the Sixties. The dull glow of a street light flickered dimly off the heavy iron bars at the windows; and here and there the motionless form of a statue was silhouetted against the darkened glass. A guard at the massive front door glanced at Reilly's police shield, sighed wearily and said, "Another dick! What're you guys doin', holding a convention here?"

Reilly glanced at me over his shoulder, raised his heavy eyebrows and then walked into the building. Another guard led us through a dimly lighted hall to the rear.

Dr Homer Bramble's office was not unlike that of Max Schweingurt. There were a large walnut desk, cases of richly bound books, a thick expensive rug, and odd bits of bric-a-brac, statuary, rock samples and the like. Bramble himself complemented the room. He was a tall, cadaverous-looking man in his sixties, with thick gray hair and piercing black eyes. He had a thin, tight mouth in a pinched, gray face; and his clothes, old-fashioned, of rich black broadcloth, were dust-flecked and ill-kept.

He fixed heavy black-rimmed pince-nez on his long nose as we came into the office, cleared his throat and stared coldly at us.

Reilly said brusquely, "I'm Lieutenant Reilly from Police Headquarters, Doctor Bramble. We'd like to see the statue you purchased from Max Schweingurt."

"The one that was returned from Mexico City," I put in meaningfully.

Bramble glanced at me, a wary sarcasm in his sharp eyes. He removed the pince-nez, letting it drop on the black silk ribbon that hung around his neck. "The museum is open at ten o'clock tomorrow morning . . ."

"I beg your pardon," Reilly interrupted him, "I said we were from Police Headquarters."

Bramble shrugged. "Very well." He pressed a button on his desk, picked up a sheaf of papers and, ignoring us, hunched forward on his desk and began to study the papers intently.

In the tense silence I heard the faint sound of footsteps

coming toward a door, not the door through which we had entered from the hall, but one to the left of Bramble's desk. The others seemed to pay no attention, if they heard at all, and I looked at Bramble. In the light from the desk lamp, I saw his eyes darken and a tense expression came over his pinched face. His fingers turned white at the knuckles as he gripped the papers in his hand. I glanced back at the door. The knob turned slowly; then, before the latch clicked, the knob turned back again. The footsteps retreated almost soundlessly away from the door. I watched Bramble wipe a nervous hand across his forehead. The papers trembled in his fingers.

At that moment, the guard who had ushered us to see Bramble came into his office.

Bramble, looking up, said hoarsely, "Take these men to the Athena statue."

I caught Reilly's eyes and nodded significantly.

Reilly said sharply, "You too, Doctor," and added, "if you don't mind." The tone of the detective's voice told Bramble that if he did mind, he'd probably be dragged along anyway.

Bramble's thin lips drew back against his teeth. He pushed himself from his chair, muttering angrily beneath his breath as he led the way. I stepped aside as Reilly and Grady followed. As they turned into the corridor, I ducked swiftly back into the room and through the door I had been watching a moment before.

I played a narrow beam of a pencil flashlight about the short hallway, narrow and dusty, and followed it till I came to another door at the end. This opened upon a steep, worn stairway which led down into solid blackness. The stairs creaked eerily beneath my cautious step, and I stopped, turned out the flash and held my breath. I could hear nothing. The dank, musty odor from the basement put an unpleasant taste in my mouth, and the dust smarted in my nostrils. Snapping on the flash, I went on down the stairs with each step seemingly shrieking louder in the smothering silence.

At the bottom of the stairway, some instinct seemed to prompt me. I switched off the flash. The blackness pressed down upon me like a great cat. I took three steps slowly, carefully; and my foot struck something. There was still no sound.

With my foot, I felt around in the dark and touched that something again. An icy coldness trickled along my spine.

Using the flash again, I shielded it with my hand and crouched down. A man lay on the concrete floor at my feet. A dead man. He looked about thirty or thirty-five years old, was wearing an ordinary brown suit and had light-brown hair. He was lying on his side, but his clothes were covered with dirt and his shoes were scuffed as if he'd been dragged here. His head had been smashed in horribly and the blood stained the collar and sleeve of his suit coat. I swept the light to the stairs. No blood marks there. He had not been killed upstairs, apparently.

I searched his pockets. There was an insurance investigator's identification in his right pocket. Some envelopes and papers in the inside pocket of his coat, I glanced through hurriedly. There were a couple of personal letters, a railroad timetable and a telegram reading:

CHECK ALL OVERSEAS CABLES FROM LISBON TO BRAMBLE LEXINGTON MUSEUM NEW YORK BETWEEN THREE AND SEVEN AUGUST.

It was signed by the Central-Union Indemnity Company.

I searched for some other information concerning the telegram, a verification of it, perhaps, but found nothing. The dates between the third and seventh of August were before Schweingurt had expected the Dionysus to come from Europe, many days before in fact. And I wondered if such communication between Bramble and Lisbon referred to the Dionysus, or to something else. The insurance company, as far as I knew, was not concerned with the Dionysus statuette, and probably didn't even know about it. It was interested, however, in the Athena statue, particularly in the quick removal of the statue from New York to Mexico City.

In the tense seconds it took for these thoughts to rush through my churning mind, my flashlight rayed over the dusty concrete floor, picked out a scattered trail of bloodstains and followed it behind a stack of wooden crates. The place was cluttered with huge boxes, grimy art objects, some with only enough ancient clay chipped and washed away to be recognizable as statuary; others were covered with canvas that had become damp and odorous. The fetid, musty smell parched my throat.

I followed the bloodstains behind the crates, stooping low.

Some warning sense caused me to pull the gun from my shoulder holster. I gripped it. My hand was hot and wet against the cold metal.

I thought I heard the faint scuff of a footstep behind me. I started to whirl, but in that instant I was struck violently across the shoulder. I fell, sprawling against the crates. My arm went numb and the flashlight slipped from my lax fingers and clattered across the concrete floor.

The swishing sound of a heavy weapon slashed by my head as I ducked away from my former position. There was a splintered crash from the crate beside me as the object landed. I crouched in the darkness, brought my gun up and fired blindly. The bullet *whanged* off the solid wall opposite me, ricocheted through the basement and whined menacingly close to my face, embedding itself in a box behind me.

The attacker whirled, frightened by the shot, and I sprang in his direction from where I had been hiding against the crate. The force of my body smashed him to his knees as he struggled frantically to keep his balance. I caught a handful of hair and brought the gun down. We rolled across the narrow space of floor. His feet shot out and caught me in the stomach, exploding the breath from my lungs. The pain in my shoulder was torture. I shot out my left fist, felt my knuckles rake his face. I brought the gun around again. The force of the blow tingled all the way up my arm. He rolled away from me, and I scrambled to my knees and went after him. And then I realized he was lying very still.

I stayed in that position about thirty seconds, maybe more, waiting for him to move. The gun in my hand was pointed toward the figure, shrouded in darkness. My finger was tense on the trigger. The man did not move. His breathing, loud in the stillness, was the breathing of a man unconscious.

I got up, wondering if the sound of the shot had been heard upstairs and why Reilly and Grady weren't down here by now. My flashlight still glowed near the crates where it had dropped; and when I picked it up it was wet and sticky with blood. I rayed it over the spot, saw where the trail of blood ended and smiled grimly, thinking of how really far the trail had come. Before me was a Grecian statue, its canvas covering partially thrown off. The goddess, Athena. The statue that had been smeared with

Max Schweingurt's blood. And now the dark goddess stood above the blood of another victim, the insurance investigator who had discovered her here.

I went back to the unconscious man on the floor and swept a beam of light over him. He was beginning to recover consciousness.

The man struggling dazedly in front of me was the one who had posed as Leiderkrantz! He looked up at me, fright so stark in his eyes that it give him a crazed look. He dropped his head, shaking it weakly, and started to feign unconsciousness. I was not in the mood to let him play possum. I prodded him roughly with my foot.

"Get up," I ordered. I stabbed the revolver into his ribs.

I pressed the buzzer on Bramble's desk and sent the guard after Reilly. Then I sat down, placed the gun on the desk in front of me and wearily lighted a cigarette. The man I had met as Leiderkrantz sat near me, nervously rubbing his hands together and staring sullenly at the floor.

Reilly didn't look friendly when he, Grady and Bramble came into the office. He looked at me narrowly and said, "It's no good, Mike. We went over the statue with a fine-tooth comb. We couldn't find anything suspicious."

"What were you looking for?" I asked him and grinned.

He looked sheepish, covered it with anger in his eyes. "I don't know, but you said the answers . . ."

I stopped him with a nod of my head. "I found another corpse. Another statue. A murder. Maybe two." I dragged on my cigarette long enough to watch the tension get the best of Bramble, and said, "Arrest Dr Bramble for the murder of Max Schweingurt!"

"Preposterous!" screamed Bramble.

"Sit down!" Reilly ordered him sharply. "This is worth looking into. Mike usually doesn't talk unless he's sure of himself. Give us the story, Mike. Why do you think Bramble is the murderer?"

Reilly seated himself where he could keep watch over both Bramble and the man I had caught just a few minutes before. Grady sat near the door, the entire room under his surveillance.

"First, let me explain what I have been doing since you three left this office for a look at the statue. I didn't accompany you for a very good reason. While we were sitting here awaiting the arrival of the guard I was quite certain that someone sneaked up to that second door, there, and started to open it. Bramble's facial reactions at that time corroborated my suspicions. So I decided to investigate. I realize I should have let you know my plans before I did anything. But I was afraid that if Bramble guessed he might be able in some way to tip off whomever had been on the other side of that door.

"So I went along to investigate. I found, on the other side of that door, a long hallway at the end of which is another door and stairway. At the bottom of those stairs is a dead man. He has been murdered. And ironically enough, he is lying near the very same statue beside which Max Schweingurt was murdered." I paused to let that sink in.

"But . . . but . . . that's impossible." Reilly was almost explosive at this point. "We just examined the statue beside which Schweingurt was killed. It is out in the main part of the museum."

"Yes? That is what everyone is supposed to think. But I am the second person, other than Dr Bramble and his friend here, to know that the statue in the museum is not the one which was purchased from Max Schweingurt. It was never inside Schweingurt's galleries. The other person who made this discovery is in the basement, dead. I would be in the same position, too, if our friend who calls himself Leiderkrantz," I nodded at the man, "had succeeded in his attempt to bludgeon me to death a few minutes ago.

"I didn't find the answer for myself, really. I more or less got it from a telegram I found in the dead man's pocket. And when I discovered the second statue of the goddess, the entire story seemed pretty clear."

I could tell Reilly was ready with a hundred questions, but he was a fair man and was patient enough to let me tell the story my own way.

I read the telegram to them.

"The statue on the floor of the museum is the original. There is no doubt of that. Dr Bramble wouldn't display any other but the original, of that I am sure. Therefore, the statue in the basement is a copy of the original, a very fine copy, we may be sure, since it had Max Schweingurt fooled for two years while it stood in his galleries. All this time, Dr Bramble knew the statue was in the gallery. But he evidenced no desire to own it for some time. We may, therefore, conclude that he always knew it for the copy which it was.

"Then, suddenly, Dr Bramble wanted to purchase that statue – the one we now know to be only a copy. Why? . . . He learned through a secret source that the original Athena was being smuggled from Greece and was to be placed in a museum in Mexico City. He wanted that original Athena – wanted it badly. He knew he would never be able to strike a bargain with the Mexican museum. They wanted it for themselves. So he schemed and finally hit upon an idea so perfect it almost worked. It was just a little too smooth, though, and excited the suspicions of the insurance company.

"Bramble's plan was to buy the copy of Athena from Schweingurt, paying the high price and never letting anyone know the statue was not the original. After it had been placed here in the museum it would be 'stolen', it would simply disappear. Then the insurance company would get a 'tip' that the statue was in the museum in Mexico City, just after the time it arrived there. The statue would have been smuggled into Mexico. There would be no proof of its purchase and the museum would not be able to prove how it had gained possession of it. By putting some pressure to bear, the insurance company, completely innocent of any duplicity, could bring the original statue to Bramble.

"All these plans were carried out. But there was a slight interruption. Schweingurt, in his enthusiasm about the original Dionysus, a creation of the sculptor of the original Athena, confided in Bramble that the gallery would soon be displaying the Dionysus statuette. Bramble was horrified. He realized that if the original Dionysus were compared with the copy of Athena, Schweingurt would realize that the Athena was a copy and Bramble's plans would be ruined.

"He sent a man of his own to Lisbon to do away with the European representative, Leiderkrantz, steal the original Dionysus and return to this country posing as Leiderkrantz.

"I was hired by Schweingurt to protect Leiderkrantz on his trip from the airport to the galleries. But the fake Leiderkrantz slugged me, contacted Bramble and switched the original Dionysus for a very good copy which had been stored in the basement of the museum. He then delivered the copy to Schweingurt.

"The two copies could now be compared as they had both been made by the same sculptor, which Bramble knew.

"But Schweingurt had found out that the man who had delivered the statuette was an impostor. He was suspicious. He made tests of the statuette and found that it was not the original. He called Bramble into conference and told him. Bramble insisted, in the face of contrary evidence, that the statuette was the original. Since the Athena had been the only work of its kind in this country, Schweingurt had always taken its value for granted. Bramble was apparently afraid that Schweingurt would become suspicious and would make tests disproving the authenticity of the Athena.

"He left the galleries but returned later, after the closing time. He either found Schweingurt comparing the Dionysus with the Athena and making tests which were disclosing the age of them both, or he may have already discovered that the Athena was a copy. He may have told Bramble since he knew Bramble would not be interested in buying anything other than the original. There would be a tremendous difference between the two and a reputable dealer would be bound by ethics to refund the money for an object which turned out to be other than represented.

"This meant the ruin of Bramble's plan. But he wouldn't give up too easily. He turned on Schweingurt and killed him. He stole the copy of the Dionysus which Schweingurt had held in his hands as he fell, dead, against the Athena. But as Schweingurt fell, the tip of the staff in the hands of the tiny figure was broken. In his haste, Bramble did not notice the break until he was away and it was too late to recover the lost piece. He had no way of knowing that it had been discovered by the police since the fact was never published.

"The Athena copy was delivered to Bramble as scheduled. The next night he hid it in the basement storeroom and reported it stolen. Then, to further the theme of murder for robbery and to try to definitely pin suspicion on someone, Bramble took the original Dionysus, which he didn't wish any one to discover in his possession, and planted it in Maurice Cambelli's room. It was he who tipped off the police.

"With the original Athena eventually brought to his museum

and the original Dionysus discovered in Cambelli's room, the two could be compared without any danger to Bramble. They were both the originals, as they were thought to be.

"The copy of the Athena is in the basement storeroom here. A laboratory test may bring out traces of Schweingurt's blood on the base of the statue and prove that the copy is the one that Bramble actually bought.

"The insurance company smelled a rat and did a little investigating of Bramble. The investigator discovered the copy of Athena in the basement. As far as Bramble was concerned, there wasn't a chance of his continued success in the deception. But . . ." I paused, swinging my body slowly in the chair. "This guy," I pointed to the man we had known as Leiderkrantz. "This guy killed the investigator!" I shot the words out hoping to get some sort of reaction.

"Oh, no. You don't pin that on me," the fellow cried shakily. He waved his arm desperately at Bramble. "Bramble killed him. You're not hanging no murders on me. I was just . . ."

He slumped in his chair, staring sightlessly at the wall. His face was the gray color of ashes and his lips compressed in a tight, bluish line. His thin shoulders were slumped in defeat.

Reilly turned to me.

"How did you know Bramble murdered Schweingurt? Why didn't you think this Leiderkrantz fake did the job?" he asked.

I smiled wryly. "Only Bramble would have planted a sixty-five thousand dollar Dionysus to frame a murder motive. That meant that something even more valuable must be at stake – the original Athena."

They had to lead Bramble by the arm when they took him away. He was completely dazed – he couldn't comprehend how his perfectly planned plot could have backfired.

ORDO

Donald E. Westlake

1

My name is Ordo Tupikos, and I was born in North Flat, Wyoming on November 9th, 1936. My father was part Greek and part Swede and part American Indian, while my mother was half Irish and half Italian. Both had been born in this country, so I am one hundred per cent American.

My father, whose first name was Samos, joined the United States Navy on February 17th, 1942, and he was drowned in the Coral Sea on May 15th, 1943. At that time we were living in West Bowl, Oklahoma, my mother and my two sisters and my brother and I, and on October 12th of that year my mother married a man named Eustace St Claude, who claimed to be half Spanish and half French but who later turned out to be half Negro and half Mexican and passing for white. After the divorce, my mother moved the family to San Itari, California. She never remarried, but she did maintain a long-term relationship with an air conditioner repairman named Smith, whose background I don't know.

On July 12th, 1955, I followed my father's footsteps by joining the United States Navy. I was married for the first time in San Diego, California on March 11th, 1958, when I was twenty-one, to a girl named Estelle Anlic, whose background was German and Welsh and Polish. She put on the wedding license that she was nineteen, having told me the same, but when her mother found us in September of the same year it turned out she was only sixteen. Her mother arranged the annulment, and it looked as though I might be in some trouble, but the Navy transferred me to a ship and that was the end of that.

By the time I left the Navy, on June 17, 1959, my mother and my half-brother, Jacques St Claude, had moved from California to Deep Mine, Pennsylvania, following the air conditioner repairman named Smith, who had moved back east at his father's death in order to take over the family hardware store. Neither Smith nor Jacques was happy to have me around, and I'd by then lost touch with my two sisters and my brother, so in September of that year I moved to Old Coral, Florida, where I worked as a carpenter (non-union) and where, on January 7th, 1960, I married my second wife, Sally Fowler, who was older than me and employed as a waitress in a diner on the highway toward Fort Lauderdale.

Sally, however, was not happy tied to one man, and so we were divorced on April 12th, 1960, just three months after the marriage. I did some drinking and trouble-making around that time, and lost my job, and a Night Court judge suggested I might be better off if I rejoined the Navy, which I did on November 4th, 1960, five days before my twenty-fourth birthday.

From then on, my life settled down. I became a career man in the Navy, got into no more marriages, and except for my annual Christmas letter from my mother in Pennsylvania I had no more dealings with the past. Until October 7th, 1974, when an event occurred that knocked me right over.

I was assigned at that time to a Naval Repair Station near New London, Connecticut, and my rank was Seaman First Class. It was good weather for October in that latitude, sunny, clean air, not very cold, and some of us took our afternoon break out on the main dock. Norm and Stan and Pat and I were sitting in one group, on some stacks of two-by-fours, Norm and Stan talking football and Pat reading one of his magazines and me looking out over Long Island Sound. Then Pat looked up from his magazine and said, "Hey, Orry."

I turned my head and looked at him. My eyes were half blinded from looking at the sun reflected off the water. I said, "What?"

"You never said you were married to Dawn Devayne."

Dawn Devayne was a movie star. I'd seen a couple of her movies, and once or twice I saw her talking on television. I said, "Sure."

He gave me a dirty grin and said, "You shouldn't of let that go, boy."

With Pat, you play along with the joke and then go do something else, because otherwise he won't give you any peace. So I grinned back at him and said, "I guess I shouldn't," and then I turned to look some more at the water.

But this time he didn't quit. Instead, he raised his voice and he said, "Goddamit, Orry, it's right here in this goddam magazine."

I faced him again. I said, "Come on, Pat."

By now, Norm and Stan were listening too, and Norm said, "What's in the magazine, Pat?"

Pat said, "That Orry was married to Dawn Devayne."

Norm and Stan both grinned, and Stan said, "Oh, *that*."

"Goddamit!" Pat jumped to his feet and stormed over and shoved the magazine in Stan's face. "You look at that!" he shouted. "You just look at that!"

I saw Stan look, and start to frown, and I couldn't figure out what was going on. Had they set this up ahead of time? But not Stan; Norm sometimes went along with Pat's gags, but Stan always brushed them away like mosquitoes. And now Stan frowned at the magazine, and he said, "Son of a bitch."

"Now, look," I said, "a joke's a joke."

But nobody was acting like it was a joke. Norm was looking over Stan's shoulder, and he too was frowning. And Stan, shaking his head, looked at me and said, "Why try to hide it, for Christ's sake? Brother, if *I'd* been married to Dawn Devayne, I'd tell the world about it."

"But I wasn't," I said. "I swear to God, I never was."

Norm said, "How many guys you know named Ordo Tupikos?"

"It's a mistake," I said. "It's got to be a mistake."

Norm seemed to be reading aloud from the magazine. He said, "Married in San Diego, California, in 1958, to a sailor named Ordo Tu—"

"Wait a minute," I said. "I was married then to, uh, Estelle—"

"Anlic," Pat said, and nodded his head at me. "Estelle Anlic, right?"

I stared at him. I said, "How'd you know that name?"

"Because that's Dawn Devayne, dummy! That's her real

name!" Pat grabbed the magazine out of Norm's hands and rushed over to jab it at me. "Is that you, or isn't it?"

There was a small black-and-white photo on the page, surrounded by printing. I hadn't seen that picture in years.

It was Estelle and me, on our wedding day, a picture taken outside City Hall by a street photographer. There I was in my whites – you don't wear winter blues in San Diego – and there was Estelle. She was wearing her big shapeless black sweater and that tight tight gray skirt down to below her knees that I liked in those days. We were both squinting in the sunlight, and Estelle's short dark hair was in little curls all around her head.

"That's not Dawn Devayne," I said. "Dawn Devayne has blonde hair."

Pat said something scornful about people dyeing their hair, but I didn't listen. I'd seen the words under the picture and I was reading them. They said: "Dawn and her first husband, Navy man Ordo Tupikos. Mama had the marriage annulled six months later."

Norm and Stan had both come over with Pat, and now Stan looked at me and said, "You didn't even know it."

"I never saw her again." I made a kind of movement with the magazine, and I said, "When her mother took her away, the Navy put me on a ship, I never saw her after that."

Norm said, "Well, I'll be a son of a bitch."

Pat laughed, slapping himself on the hip. He said:

"You're married to a movie star!"

I got to my feet and went between them and walked away along the dock toward the repair sheds. The guys shouted after me, wanting to know where I was going, and Pat yelled, "That's my magazine!"

"I'll bring it back," I said. "I want to borrow it." I don't know if they heard.

I went to the Admin Building and into the head and closed myself in a stall and sat on the toilet and started in to read about Dawn Devayne.

The magazine was called *True Man*, and the picture on the cover was a foreign sports car with a girl lying on the hood. Down the left side of the cover was lettering that read:

*WILL THE
ENERGY CRISIS
KILL LE MANS?*

....

*DAWN DEVAYNE:
THE WORLD'S NEXT
SEX GODDESS*

....

*WHAT SLOPE?
CONFESSIONS OF A
GIRL SKI BUM*

Inside the magazine, the article was titled, *Is Dawn Devayne The World's New Sex Queen?* by Abbie Lancaster. And under the title in smaller letters was another question, with an answer:

"Where did all the bombshells go? Dawn Devayne is ready to burst on the scene."

Then the article didn't start out to be about Dawn Devayne at all, but about all the movie stars that had ever been considered big sex symbols, like Jean Harlow and Marilyn Monroe and Rita Hayworth and Jayne Mansfield. Then it said there hadn't been any major sex star for a long time, which was probably because of Women's Lib and television and X-rated movies and looser sexual codes. "You don't need a fantasy bedwarmer," the article said, "if you've got a real-life bedwarmer of your own."

Then the article said there were a bunch of movie stars who were all set to take the crown as the next sex queen if the job ever opened up again. It mentioned Raquel Welch and Ann-Margret and Goldie Hawn and Julie Christie. But then it said Dawn Devayne was the likeliest of them all to make it, because she had that wonderful indescribable quality of being all things to all men.

Then there was a biography. It said Dawn Devayne was born Estelle Anlic in Big Meadow, Nebraska on May 19th, 1942, and her father died in the Korean conflict in 1955, and she and her mother moved to Los Angeles in 1956 because her mother had joined a religious cult that was based in Los Angeles. It said her mother was a bus driver in that period, and Dawn Devayne grew up without supervision and hung around with boys a lot.

It didn't exactly say she was the neighborhood lay, but it almost said it.

Then it came to me. It said Dawn Devayne ran away from home a lot of times in her teens, and one time when she was sixteen she ran away to San Diego and married me until her mother took her home again and turned her over to the juvenile authorities, who put her in a kind of reformatory for wayward girls. It called me a "stock figure". What it said was:

"... a sailor named Ordo Tupikos, a stock figure, the San Diego sailor in every sex star's childhood."

I didn't much care for that, but what I was mostly interested in was where Estelle Anlic became Dawn Devayne, so I kept reading. The article said that after the reformatory Estelle got a job as a carhop in a drive-in restaurant in Los Angeles, and it was there she got her first crack at movie stardom, when an associate producer with Farber International Pictures met her and got her a small role in a B-movie called *Tramp Killer*. She played a prostitute who was murdered. That was in 1960, when she was eighteen. There was a black-and-white still photo from that movie, showing her cowering back from a man with a meat cleaver, and she still looked like Estelle Anlic then, except her hair was dyed platinum blonde. Her stage name for that movie was Honey White.

Then nothing more happened in the movies for a while, and Estelle went to San Francisco and was a cashier in a movie theater. The article quoted her as saying, "When 'Tramp Killer' came through, I sold tickets to myself." She had other jobs, too, for the next three years, and then, when she was twenty-one, in 1963, a man named Les Moore, who was the director of *Tramp Killer*, met her at a party in San Francisco and remembered her, and told her to come back to Los Angeles and he would give her a big part in the movie he was just starting to work on.

(The article then had a paragraph in parentheses that said Les Moore had become a very important new director in the three years since *Tramp Killer*, which had only been his second feature, and that the movie he wanted Dawn Devayne to come back to Los Angeles for was *Bubbletop*, the first of the zany comedies that had made Les Moore the Preston Sturges of the sixties.)

So Dawn Devayne – or Estelle, because her name wasn't Dawn Devayne yet and she'd quit calling herself Honey White – went back to Los Angeles and Les Moore introduced her to a star-making agent named Byron Cartwright, who signed her to exclusive representation and who changed her name to Dawn Devayne. And *Bubbletop* went on to become a smash hit and Dawn Devayne got rave notices, and she'd been a movie star ever since, with fifteen movies in the last eleven years, and her price for one movie now was seven hundred fifty thousand dollars. The article said she was one of the very few stars who had never had a box-office flop.

About her private life, the article said she was "between marriages". I thought that would mean she was engaged to somebody, but so far as I could see from the rest of the article she wasn't. So I guess that's just a phrase they use for people like movie stars when they aren't married.

Anyway, the marriages she was between were numbers four and five. After me in 1958, her next marriage was in 1963, to a movie star named Rick Tandem. Then in 1964 there was a fight in a nightclub where a producer named Josh Weinstein knocked Rick Tandem down and Rick Tandem later sued for divorce and said Josh Weinstein had come between him and Dawn Devayne. The article didn't quite say that Rick Tandem was in reality queer, but it got the point across.

Then marriage number three, in 1966, was to another movie actor, Ken Forrest, who was an older man, a contemporary of Gable and Tracy who was still making movies but wasn't quite the power he used to be. That marriage ended in 1968 when Forrest shot himself on a yacht off the coast of Spain; Dawn Devayne was in London making a picture when it happened.

And the fourth marriage, in 1970, was to a Dallas businessman with interests in computers and airlines and oil. His name was Ralph Chucklin, and that marriage had ended with a quiet divorce in 1973. "Dawn is dating now," the article said, "but no one in particular tops her list. 'I'm still looking for the right guy,' she says."

Then the article got to talking about her age, and the person who wrote the article raised the question as to whether a thirty-two year old woman was young enough to still make it as the next Sex Goddess of the World. "Dawn is more beautiful every year," the article said, and then it went back to all the business about Women's Lib and television and X-rated movies and looser sexual codes, and it said the next Superstar Sex

Symbol wasn't likely to be another girl-child type like the ones before, but would be more of an adult woman, who could bring brains and experience to sex. "Far from the dumb blondes of yesteryear," the article said, "Dawn Devayne is a bright blonde, who combines with good old-fashioned lust the more modern feminine virtues of intelligence and independence. A Jane Fonda who doesn't nag." And the article finished by saying maybe the changed social conditions meant there wouldn't be any more Blonde Bombshells or Sexpot Movie Queens, which would make the world a colder and a drabber place, but the writer sure hoped there would be more, and the best bet right now to bring sex back to the world was Dawn Devayne.

There were photographs with the article, full-page color pictures of Dawn Devayne with her clothes off, and when I finished reading I sat there on the toilet a while longer looking at the pictures and trying to remember Estelle. Nothing. The face, the eyes, the smile, all different. The stomach and legs were different. Even the nipples didn't remind me of Estelle Anlic's nipples.

There's something wrong, I thought. I wondered if maybe this Dawn Devayne woman had a criminal record or was wanted for murder somewhere or something like that, and she'd just paid Estelle money to borrow her life story. Was that possible?

It sure didn't seem possible that *this* sexy woman was Estelle. I know it was sixteen years, but how much can one person change? I sat studying the pictures until I noticed I was beginning to get an erection, so I left the head and went back to work.

All I could think about, the next three days, was Dawn Devayne. I was once married to her, married to a sexy movie star. Me. I just couldn't get used to the idea.

And the other guys didn't help. Norm and Stan and Pat spread the word, and pretty soon all the guys were coming around, even some of the younger officers, talking and grinning and winking and all that. Nobody came right out with the direct question, but what they really wanted to know was what it was like to be in bed with Dawn Devayne.

And what could I tell them? I didn't *know* what it was like to be in bed with Dawn Devayne. I knew what it was like to be in bed with Estelle Anlic – or anyway I had a kind of vague memory, after sixteen years – but that wasn't what they wanted to know, and anyway I didn't feel like telling them. She was a teenage girl, sixteen (though she told me nineteen), and I was twenty-one, and neither of us was exactly a genius about sex, but we had fun. I remember she had very very soft arms and she liked to have her arms around my neck, and she laughed with her mouth wide open, and she always drowned her french fries in so much ketchup I used to tell her I had to eat them with ice tongs and one time in bed she finally admitted she didn't know what ice tongs were and she cried because she was sure she was stupid, and we had sex that time in order for me to tell her (a) she wasn't stupid, and (b) I loved her anyway even though she was stupid, and that's the one time in particular I have any memory of at all, which is mostly because that was the time I learned I could control myself and hold back ejaculation almost as long as I wanted, almost forever. We were both learning about things then, we were both just puppies rolling in a basket of wool, but the guys didn't want to hear anything like that, it would just depress them. And I didn't want to tell them about it either. Their favorite sex story anyway was one that Pat used to tell about being in bed with a girl with a candle in her ass. That's what they really wanted me to tell them, that Dawn Devayne had a candle in her ass.

But even though I couldn't tell them any stories that would satisfy them, they kept coming around, they kept on and on with the same subject, they couldn't seem to let it go. It fascinated them, and every time they saw me they got reminded and fascinated all over again. In fact, a couple of the guys started calling me "Devayne", as though that was going to be my new nickname, until one time I picked up a wrench and patted it into my other palm and went over to the guy and said:

"My name is Orry."

He looked surprised, and a little scared. He said:

"Sure. Sure, I know that."

I said:

"Let me hear you say it."

He said:

"Jeez, Orry, it was just a—"

"Okay, then," I said, and went back over to where I was working, and that was the last I heard of that.

But it wasn't the last I heard of Dawn Devayne. For instance, I was more or less going then with a woman in New London named Fran Skiburg, who was divorced from an Army career man and had custody of the three children. She was part Norwegian and part Belgian and her husband had been almost all German. Fran and I would go to the movies sometimes, or she'd cook me a meal, but it wasn't serious. Mostly, we didn't even go to bed together. But then somebody told her about Dawn Devayne, and the next time I saw Fran she was a different person. She kept grinning and winking all through dinner, and she hustled the kids to bed earlier than usual, and then sort of crowded me into the living room. She liked me to rub her feet sometimes, because she was standing all day at the bank, so I sat on the sofa and she kicked off her slippers and while I rubbed her feet she kept opening and closing her knees and giggling at me.

Well, I was looking up her skirt anyway, so I slid my hand up from her feet, and the next thing we were rolling around on the wall-to-wall carpet together. She was absolutely all over me, nervous and jumpy and full of loud laughter, all the time wanting to change position or do this and that. Up till then, my one complaint about Fran was that she'd just lie there; now all of a sudden she was acting like the star of an X-movie.

I couldn't figure it out, until after it was all finished and I was lying there on the carpet on my back, breathing like a diver with the bends. Then Fran, with this big wild-eyed smile, came looming over me, scratching my chest with her fingernails and saying, "What would you like to do to me? What do you *really* want to do to me?"

This was *after*. I panted at her for a second, and then I said, "What?"

And she said, "What would you do to me if I was Dawn Devayne?"

Then I understood. I sat up and said, "Who told you that?"

"What would you do? Come on, Orry, let's do something!"

"Do what? We just did everything!"

"There's *lots* more! There's *lots* more!" Then she leaned down close to my ear, where I couldn't see her face, and whispered, "You don't want me to have to *say* it."

I don't know if she had anything special in mind, but I don't think so. I think she was just excited in general, and wanted something different to happen. Anyway, I pushed her off and got to my feet and said, "I don't know anything about any Dawn Devayne or any kind of crazy sex stuff. That's no way to act."

She sat there on the green carpet with her legs curled to the side, looking something like the nude pictures in Pat's magazines except whiter and a little heavier, and she stared up at me without saying anything at all. Her mouth was open because she was looking upward so her expression seemed to be mainly surprised. I felt grumpy. I sat down on the sofa and put on my underpants.

And all at once Fran jumped up and grabbed half her clothes and ran out of the room. I finished getting dressed, and sat on the sofa a little longer, and then went out to the kitchen and ate a bowl of raisin bran. When Fran still didn't come back, I went to her bedroom and looked in through the open door, and she wasn't there. I said, "Fran?"

No answer.

The bathroom door was closed, so I knocked on it, but nothing happened. I turned the knob and the door was locked. I said, "Fran?"

A mumble sounded from in there.

"Fran? You all right?"

"Go away."

"What?"

"Go *away*!"

That was the last she said. I tried talking to her through the door, and I tried to get her to come out, and I tried to find out what the problem was, but she wouldn't say anything else. There wasn't any sound of crying or anything, she was just sitting in there by herself. After a while I said, "I have to get back to the base, Fran."

She didn't say anything to that, either. I said it once or twice more, and said some other things, and then I left and went back to the base.

I was shaving the next morning when I suddenly remembered that picture, the one in the magazine of Estelle and me on our wedding day. We were squinting there in the sunlight, the both of us, and now I was squinting again because the light bulb over the mirror was too bright. Shaving, I looked at myself, looked at my nose and my eyes and my ears, and here I was. I was still here. The same guy. Same short haircut, same eyebrows, same chin.

The same guy.

What did Fran want from me, anyway? Just because it turns out I used to be married to somebody famous, all of a sudden I'm supposed to be different? I'm not any different, I'm the same guy I always was. People don't just change, they have ways that they are, and that's what they are. That's who they are, that's what you mean by personality. The way a person is.

Then I thought: Estelle changed.

That's right. Estelle Anlic is Dawn Devayne now. She's changed, she's somebody else. There isn't any – she isn't – there isn't any Estelle Anlic any more, nowhere on the face of the earth.

But it isn't the same as if she died, because her *memories* are still there inside Dawn Devayne, she'd remember being the girl with the mother that drove the bus, and she'd remember marrying the sailor in San Diego in 1958, and even in that article I'd read there'd been a part where she was remembering being Estelle Anlic and working as a movie cashier in San Francisco. But still she was changed, she was somebody else now, she was different. Like a wooden house turning itself into a brick house. How could she . . . how could anybody do that? How could *anybody* do that?

Then I thought: Estelle Anlic is Dawn Devayne now, but I'm still me. Ordo Tupikos, the same guy. But if she was – If I'm –

It was hard even to figure out the question. If she was that back then, and if she's this now, and if I was *that* . . .

I kept on shaving. More and more of my face came out from behind the white cream, and it was the same face. Getting older, a little older every minute, but not—

Not different.

I finished shaving. I looked at that face, and then I scrubbed it with hot water and dried it on a towel. And after mess I went to Headquarters office and put in for leave. Twenty-two days, all I had saved up.

2

The first place I went was New York, on the bus, where I looked in a magazine they have there called *Cue* that tells you what movies are playing all over the city. A Dawn Devayne movie called "The Captain's Pearls" was showing in a theater on West 86th Street, which was forty-six blocks uptown from the bus terminal, so I walked up there and sat through the second half of a Western with Charles Bronson and then *The Captain's Pearls* came on.

The story was about an airline captain with two girlfriends both named Pearl, one of them in Paris and one in New York. Dawn Devayne played the one in New York, and the advertising agency she works for opens an office in Paris and she goes there to head it, and the Paris girlfriend is a model who gets hired by Dawn Devayne for a commercial for the captain's airline, and then the captain has to keep the two girls from finding out he's going out with both of them. It was a comedy.

This movie was made in 1967, which was only nine years after I was married to Estelle, so I should have been able to recognize her, but she just wasn't there. I stared and stared and stared at that woman on the screen, and the only person she reminded me of was Dawn Devayne. I mean, from before I knew who she was. But there wasn't anything of Estelle there. Not the voice, not the walk, not the smile, not anything.

But sexy. I saw what that article writer meant, because if you looked at Dawn Devayne your first thought was she'd be terrific in bed. And then you'd decide she'd also be terrific otherwise, to talk with or take a trip together or whatever it was. And then you'd realize since she was so all-around terrific she wouldn't have to settle for anybody but an all-around terrific guy, which would leave you out, so you'd naturally idolize her. I mean, you'd want it without any idea in your head that you could ever get it.

I was thinking all that, and then I thought, *But I've had it!* And then I tried to put together arms-around-neck ice-tongs-stupid Estelle Anlic with this terrific female creature on the screen here, and I just couldn't do it. I mean, not even with a fantasy. If I had a fantasy about going to bed with Dawn Devayne, not even in my fantasy did I see myself in bed with Estelle.

After the movie I walked back downtown toward the bus terminal, because I'd left my duffel bag in a locker there. It was only around four-thirty in the afternoon, but down around 42nd Street the whores were already out, strolling on the sidewalks and standing in the doorways of shoe stores. The sight of a Navy uniform really agitates a whore, and half a dozen of them called out to me as I walked along, but I didn't answer.

Then one of them stepped out from a doorway and stood right in my path and said, "Hello, sailor. You off a ship?"

I started to walk around her, but then I stopped dead and stared, and I said, "You look like Dawn Devayne!"

She grinned and ducked her head, looking pleased with herself. "You really think so, sailor?"

She did. She was wearing a blonde wig like Dawn Devayne's hair style, and her eyes and mouth were made up like Dawn Devayne, and she'd even fixed her eyebrows to look like Dawn Devayne's eyebrows.

Only at a second look none of it worked. The wig didn't look like real hair, and the make-up was too heavy, and the eyebrows looked like little false moustaches. And down inside all that phony stuff she was Puerto Rican or Cuban or something like that. It was all like a Halloween costume.

She was poking a finger at my arm, looking up at me sort of slantwise in imitation of a Dawn Devayne movement I'd just seen in *The Captain's Pearls*. "Come on, sailor," she said. "Wanna fuck a movie star?"

"No," I said. It was all too creepy. "No, no," I said, and went around her and hurried on down the street.

And she shouted after me, "You been on that ship too long! What you want is Robert Redford!"

This was my first time in Los Angeles since 1963, when the Gulf of Tonkin incident got me transferred from a ship in the Mediterranean to a ship in the Pacific. They'd flown me with a bunch of other guys from Naples to Washington, then by surface transportation to Chicago and by air to Los Angeles and Honolulu, where I met my ship. I'd had a two-day layover in Los Angeles, and now I remembered thinking then about looking up Estelle. But I didn't do it, mostly because five years had already gone by since I'd last seen her, and also because her mother might start making trouble again if she caught me there.

The funny thing is, that was the year Estelle first became Dawn Devayne, in the movie called *Bubbletop*. Now I wondered what might have happened if I'd actually found her back then, got in touch somehow. I'd never seen *Bubbletop*, so I didn't know if by 1963 she was already this new person, this Dawn Devayne, if she'd already changed so completely that Estelle Anlic couldn't be found in there any more. If I'd met her that time, would something new have started? Would my whole life have been shifted, would I now be somebody in the movie business instead of being a sailor? I tried to see myself as that movie person; who would I be, what would I be like? Would I be *different*?

But there weren't any answers for questions like that. A person is who he is, and he can't guess who he would be if he was somebody else. The question doesn't even make sense. But I guess it's just impossible to think at all about movie stars without some fantasy or other creeping in.

My plane for Los Angeles left New York a little after seven p.m. and took five hours to get across the country, but because of the time zone differences it was only a little after nine at night when I landed, and still not ten o'clock when the taxi let me off at a motel on Cahuenga Boulevard, pretty much on the line separating Hollywood from Burbank. The taxi cost almost twenty dollars from the airport, which was kind of frightening. I'd taken two thousand dollars out of my savings, leaving just over three thousand in the account, and I was spending the money pretty fast.

The cab driver was a leathery old guy who buzzed along the freeways like it was a stock-car race, all the time telling me how much better the city had been before the freeways were built. Most people pronounce Los Angeles as though the middle is "angel", but he was one of those who pronounce it as though the middle is "angle". "Los Ang-gleez", he kept saying, and one time he said, "I'm a sight you won't see all that much. I'm your native son."

"Born here?"

"Nope. Come out in forty-eight."

The motel had a large neon sign out front and very small rooms in a low stucco building in back. It was impossible to tell what color the stucco was because green and yellow and orange and blue floodlights were aimed at it from fixtures stuck into the ivy border, but in the morning the color turned out to be a sort of dirty cream shade.

My room had pale blue walls and a heavy maroon bedspread and a paper ribbon around the toilet seat saying it had been sanitized. I unpacked my duffel and turned on the television set, but I was too restless to stay cooped up in that room forever. Also, I decided I was hungry. So I changed into civvies and went out and walked down Highland to Hollywood

Boulevard, where I ate something in a fast-food place. It was like New York in that neighborhood, only skimpier. For some reason Los Angeles looks older than New York. It looks like an old old Pueblo Indian village with neon added to it by real estate people. New York doesn't look any older than Europe, but Los Angeles looks as old as sand. It looks like a place that almost had a Golden Age, a long long time ago, but nothing happened and now it's too late.

After I ate I walked around for half an hour, and then I went back to the motel and all of a sudden I was very sleepy. I had the television on, and the light, and I still wore all my clothes except my shoes, but I fell asleep anyway, lying on top of the bedspread, and when I woke up the TV was hissing and it was nearly four in the morning. I was very thirsty, and nervous for some reason. Lonely, I felt lonely. I drank water, and went out to the street again, and after a while I found an all-night supermarket called Hughes. I took a cart and went up and down the aisles.

There were some people in there, not many. I noticed something about them. They were all dressed up in suede and fancy denim, like people at a terrific party in some movie, but they were buying the cheapest of everything. Their baskets were filled as though by gnarled men and women wearing shabby pants or faded kerchiefs, but the men were all young and tanned and wearing platform shoes, and the women were all made up with false eyelashes and different-colored fingernails. Also, some of them had food stamps in their hands.

Another thing. When these people pushed their carts down the aisles they stood very straight and were sure of themselves and on top of the world, but when they lowered their heads to take something off a shelf they looked very worried.

Another thing. Every one of them was alone. They went up and down the aisles, pushing their carts past one another – from up above, they must have looked like pieces in a labyrinth game – and they never looked at one another, never smiled at one another. They were just alone in there, and from up front came the clatter of the cash register.

After a while I didn't want to be in that place any more. I bought shaving cream and a can of soda and an orange, and walked back to the motel and went to bed.

*   *   *

There wasn't anybody in the phone book named Byron Cartwright, who was the famous agent who had changed Estelle's name to Dawn Devayne and then guided her to stardom. In the motel office they had the five different Los Angeles phone books, and he wasn't in any of them. He also wasn't in the yellow pages under "Theatrical Agencies". Finally I found a listing for something called the Screen Actors' Guild, and I called, and spoke to a girl who said, "Byron Cartwright? He's with GLA."

"I'm sorry?"

"GLA," she repeated, and hung up.

So I went back to the phone books, hoping to find something called GLA. The day clerk, a sunken-cheeked faded-eyed man of about forty with thinning yellow hair and very tanned arms, said, "You seem to be having a lot of trouble."

"I'm looking for an actor's agent," I told him.

His expression lit up a bit. "Oh, yeah? Which one?"

"Byron Cartwright."

He was impressed. "Pretty good," he said. "He's with GLA now, right?"

"That's right. Do you know him?"

"Don't I wish I did." This time he was rueful. His face seemed to jump from expression to expression with nothing in between, as though I were seeing a series of photographs instead of a person.

"I'm trying to find the phone number," I said.

I must have seemed helpless, because his next expression showed the easy superiority of the insider. "Look under Global-Lipkin," he told me.

Global-Lipkin. I looked, among "Theatrical Agencies", and there it was: Global-Lipkin Associates. You could tell immediately it was an important organization; the phone number ended in three zeroes. "Thank you," I said.

His face now showed slightly belligerent doubt. He said, "They send for you?"

"Send for me? No."

The face was shut; rejection and disapproval. Shaking his head he said, "Forget it."

Apparently he thought I was a struggling actor. Not wanting to go through a long explanation, I just shrugged and said, "Well, I'll try it," and went back to the phone booth.

A receptionist answered. When I asked for Byron Cartwright she put me through to a secretary, who said, "Who's calling, please?"

"Ordo Tupikos."

"And the subject, Mr Tupikos?"

"Dawn Devayne."

"One moment, please."

I waited a while, and then she came back and said, "Mr Tupikos, could you tell me who you're with?"

"With? I'm sorry, I . . ."

"Which firm."

"Oh. I'm not with any firm, I'm in the Navy."

"In the Navy."

"Yes. I used to be—" But she'd gone away again.

Another wait, and then she was back. "Mr Tupikos, is this official Navy business?"

"No," I said. "I used to be married to Dawn Devayne."

There was a little silence, and then she said, "Married?"

"Yes. In San Diego."

"One moment, please."

This was a longer wait, and when she came back she said, "Mr Tupikos, is this a legal matter?"

"No, I just want to see Estelle again."

"I beg your pardon?"

"Dawn Devayne. She was named Estelle when I married her."

A male voice suddenly said, "All right, Donna, I'll take it."

"Yes, sir," and there was a click.

The male voice said, "You're Ordo Tupikos?"

"Yes, sir," I said. It wasn't sensible to call him "sir", but the girl had just done it, and in any event he had an authoritative officer-like sound in his voice, and it just slipped out.

He said, "I suppose you can prove your identity."

That surprised me. "Of course," I said. "I still look the same." *I* still look the same.

"And what is it you want?"

"To see Estelle. Dawn. Miss Devayne."

"You told my secretary you were with the Navy."

"I'm *in* the Navy."

"You're due to retire pretty soon, aren't you?"

"Two years," I said.

"Let me be blunt, Mr Tupikos," he said. "Are you looking for money?"

"Money?" I couldn't think what he was talking about. (Later, going over it in my mind, I realized what he'd been afraid of, but just at that moment I was bewildered.) "Money for what?" I asked him.

He didn't answer. Instead, he said, "Then why show up like this, after all these years?"

"There was something in a magazine. A friend showed it to me."

"Yes?"

"Well, it surprised me, that's all."

"*What* surprised you?"

"About Estelle turning into Dawn Devayne."

There was a very short silence. But it wasn't an ordinary empty silence, it was a kind of slammed-shut silence, a startled silence. Then he said, "You mean you didn't know? You just found out?"

"It was some surprise," I said.

He gave out with a long loud laugh, turning his head away from the phone so it wouldn't hurt my ears. But I could still hear it. Then he said, "God damn, Mr Tupikos, that's a new one."

I had nothing to say to that.

"All right," he said. "Where are you?"

I told him the name of the motel.

"I'll get back to you," he said. "Some time today."

"Thank you," I said.

The phone booth was out in front of the motel, and I had to go back through the office to get to the inner courtyard and my room. When I walked into the office the day clerk motioned to me. "Come here." His expression now portrayed pride.

I went over and he handed me a large black-and-white photograph; what they call a glossy. The blacks in it were very dark and solid, which made it a little bit hard to make out what was going on, but the picture seemed to have been taken in a parking garage. Two people were in the foreground. I couldn't swear to it, but it looked as though Ernest Borgnine was strangling the day clerk.

"Whadaya think of that?"

I didn't know what I thought of it. But when people hand you a picture – their wife, their girlfriend, their children, their dog, their new house, their boat, their garden – what you say is *very nice*. I handed the picture back. "Very nice," I said.

Everybody knows about the movie stars' names being embedded in the sidewalks of Hollywood Boulevard, but it's always strange when you see it. There are the squares of pavement, and on every square is a gold outline of a five-pointed star, and in every other star there is the name of a movie star. Every year, fewer of those names mean anything. The idea of the names is immortality, but what they're really about is death.

I took a walk for a while after talking to Byron Cartwright, and I walked along two or three blocks of Hollywood Boulevard with some family group behind me that had a child with a loud piercing voice, and the child kept wanting to know who people were:

"Daddy, who's Vilma Banky?"

"Daddy, who's Charles Farrell?"

"Daddy, who's Dolores Costello?"

"Daddy, who's Conrad Nagel?"

The father's answers were never loud enough for me to hear, but what could he have said? "She was a movie star." "He used to be in silent movies, a long time ago." Or maybe, "I don't know. Emil Jannings? I don't know."

I didn't look back, so I have no idea what the family looked like, or even if the child was a boy or a girl, but pretty soon I hated listening to them, so I turned in at a fast-food place to have a hamburger and onion rings and a Coke. I sat at one of the red formica tables to eat, and at the table across the plastic partition from me was another family – father, mother, son, daughter – and the daughter was saying, "Why did they put those names there anyway?"

"Just to be nice," the mother said.

The son said, "Because they're buried there."

The daughter stared at him, not knowing if that was true or not. Then she said, "They are not!"

"Sure they are," the son said. "They bury them standing up, so they can all fit. And they all wear the clothes from their most famous movie. Like their cowboy hats and the long gowns and their Civil War Army uniforms."

The father, chuckling, said, "And their white telephones?"

The son gave his father a hesitant smile and a headshake, saying, "I don't get it."

"That's okay," the father said. He grinned and ruffled the son's hair, but I could see he was irritated. He was older, so his memory stretched back farther, so his jokes wouldn't always mean anything to his son, whose memories had started later – and would probably end later. The son had reminded his father that the father would some day die.

After I ate I didn't feel like walking on the stars' names any more. I went up to the next parallel street, which is called Yucca, and took that over to Highland Avenue and then on back to the motel.

When I walked into the office the day clerk said, "Got a message for you." His expression was tough and secretive, like a character in a spy movie. The hotel clerk in a spy movie who is really a part of the spy organization; this is the point where he tells the hero that the Gestapo is in his room.

"A message?"

"From GLA," he said. His face flipped to the next expression, like a digital clock moving on to the next number. This one showed make-believe comic envy used to hide real envy. I wondered if he really did feel envy or if he was just practicing being an actor by pretending to show envy. No; pretending to *hide* envy. Maybe he himself was actually feeling envy but was hiding it by pretending to be someone who was showing envy by trying to hide it. That was too confusing to think about; it made me dizzy, like looking too long off the fantail of a ship at the swirls of water directly beneath the stern. Layers and layers of twisting white foam with bottomless black underneath; but then it all organizes itself into swinging straight white lines of wake.

I said, "What did they want?"

"They'll send a car for you at three o'clock." Flip; friendliness, conspiracy. "You could do me a favor."

"I could?"

From under the counter he took out a tan manila envelope, then halfway withdrew from it another glossy photograph; I couldn't see the subject. "This," he said, and slid the photo back into the envelope. Twisting the red string on the two little round closure tabs of the envelope, he said, "Just leave it in the office, you know? Just leave it some place where they can see it."

"Oh," I said. "All right." And I took the envelope.

★   ★   ★

The car was a black Cadillac limousine with a uniformed chauffeur who held the door for me and called me, "sir". It didn't seem to matter to him that he was picking me up at a kind of seedy motel, or that I was wearing clothes that were somewhat shabby and out of date. (I wear civvies so seldom that I almost never pay any attention to what clothing I own or what condition it's in.)

I had never been in a limousine before, with or without a chauffeur. In fact, this was the first time in my life I'd ever ridden in a Cadillac. I spent the first few blocks just looking at the interior of the car, noticing that I had my own radio in the back, and power windows, and that there were separate air-conditioner controls on both sides of the rear seat.

There were grooves for a glass partition between front and rear, but the glass was lowered out of sight, and when we'd driven down Highland and made a right turn onto Hollywood Boulevard, going past Grauman's Chinese theater, the chauffeur suddenly said, "You a writer?"

"What? Me? No."

"Oh," he said. "I always try to figure out what people are. They're fascinating, you know? People."

"I'm in the Navy," I said.

"That right? I did two in the Army myself."

"Ah," I said.

He nodded. He'd look at me in the rear-view mirror from time to time while he was talking. He said, "Then I pushed a hack around Houston for six years, but I figured the hell with it, you know? Who needs it. Come out here in sixty-seven, never went back."

"I guess it's all right out here."

"No place like it," he said.

I didn't have an answer for that, and he didn't seem to have anything else to say, so I opened the day clerk's envelope and looked at the photograph he wanted me to leave in Byron Cartwright's office.

Actually it was four photographs on one eight-by-ten sheet of glossy paper, showing the day clerk in four poses, with different clothing in each one. Four different characters, I guess. In the upper left, he was wearing a light plaid jacket and a pale turtleneck sweater and a medium-shade cloth cap, and he had a cigarette in the corner of his mouth and he was squinting; looking mean and tough. In the upper right he was wearing a tuxedo, and he had a big smile on his face. His head was turned toward the camera, but his body was half twisted away and he was holding a top hat out to the side, as though he were singing a song and was about to march off-stage at the end of the music. In the bottom left, he was wearing a cowboy hat and a bandana around his neck and a plaid shirt, and he had a kind of comical-foolish expression on his face, as though somebody had just made a joke and he wasn't sure he'd understood the point. And in the bottom right he was wearing a dark suit and white shirt and pale tie, and he was leaning forward a little and smiling in a friendly way directly at the camera. I guess that was supposed to be him in his natural state, but it actually looked less like him than any of the others.

The whole back of the photograph was filled with printing. His name was at the top (MAURY DEE) and underneath was a listing of all the movies he'd been in and all the play productions, with the character he performed in each one. Down at the bottom were three or four quotes from critics about how good he was.

The driver turned left on Fairfax and went down past Selma to Sunset Boulevard, and then turned right. Then he said, "The best thing about this job is the people."

"Is that right?" I put Maury Dee's photograph away and twisted the red string around the closure tabs.

"And I'll tell you something," said the driver. "The bigger they are, the nicer they are. You'd be amazed, some of the people been sitting right where you are right now."

"I bet."

"But you know who's the best of them all? I mean, just a nice regular person, not stuck up at all."

"Who's that?"

"Dawn Devayne," he said. "She's always got a good word for you, she'll take a joke, she's just terrific."

"That's nice," I said.

"Terrific." He shook his head. "Always remembers your name. 'Hi, Harry,' she says. 'How you doing?' Just a terrific person."

"I guess she must be all right," I said.

"Terrific," he said, and turned the car in at one of the taller buildings just before the Beverly Hills line. We drove down into the basement parking garage and the driver stopped next to a bank of elevators. He hopped out and opened my door for me, and when I got out he said, "Eleventh floor."

"Thanks, Harry," I said.

3

All you could see was artificial plants. I stepped out of the elevator and there were great pots all over the place on the green rug, all with plastic plants in them with huge dark-green leaves. Beyond them, quite a ways back, expanses of plate glass showed the white sky.

I moved forward, not sure what to do next, and then I saw the receptionist's desk. With the white sky behind her, she was very hard to find. I went over to her and said, "Excuse me."

She'd been writing something on a long form, and now she looked up with a friendly smile and said, "May I help you?"

"I'm supposed to see Byron Cartwright."

"Name, please?"

"Ordo Tupikos."

She used her telephone, sounding very chipper, and then she smiled at me again, saying, "He'll be out in a minute. If you'll have a seat?"

There were easy chairs in among the plastic plants. I thanked her and went off to sit down, picking up a newspaper from a white formica table beside the chair. It was called *The Hollywood Reporter*, and it was magazine size and printed on glossy paper. I read all the short items about people signing to do this or that, and I read a nightclub review of somebody whose name I didn't recognize, and then a girl came along and said, "Mr Tupikos?"

"Yes?"

"I'm Mr Cartwright's secretary. Would you come with me?"

I put the paper down and followed her away from the plants and down a long hall with tan walls and brown carpet. We passed offices on both sides of the hall; about half were occupied, and most of the people were on the phone.

I suddenly realized I'd forgotten the day clerk's photograph. I'd left it behind in the envelope on the table with *The Hollywood Reporter*.

Well, that actually was what he'd asked me to do; leave it in the office. Maybe on the way back I should take it out of the envelope.

The girl stopped, gesturing at a door on the left. "Through here, Mr Tupikos."

Byron Cartwright was standing in the middle of the room. He had a big heavy chest and brown leathery skin and yellow-white hair brushed straight back over his balding head. He was dressed in different shades of pale blue, and there was a white line of smoke rising from a long cigar in an ashtray on the desk behind him. The room was large and so was everything in it; massive desk, long black sofa, huge windows showing the white sky, with the city of Los Angeles down the slope on the flat land to the south, pastel colors glittering in the haze; pink, peach, coral.

Byron Cartwright strode toward me, hand outstretched. He was laughing, as though remembering a wonderful time we'd once shared together. Laughter made erosion lines crisscrossing all over his face. "Well, hello, Orry," he said. "Glad to see you." He took my hand, and patted my arm with his other hand, saying, "That's right, isn't it? Orry?"

"That's right."

"Everybody calls me By. Come in, sit down."

I was already in. We sat together on the long sofa. He crossed one leg over the other, half turning in my direction, his arm stretched out toward me along the sofa back. He had what looked like a class ring on one finger, with a dark red stone. He said, "You know where I got it from? The name 'Orry'? From Dawn." There was something almost religious about the way he said the name. It reminded me of when Jehovah's Witnesses pass out their literature; they always smile and say, "Here's good news!"

I said, "You told her about me?"

"Phoned her the first chance I got. She's on location now. You could've knocked her over with a feather, Orry, I could hear it in her voice."

"It's been a long time," I said. I wasn't sure what this conversation was about, and I was sorry to hear Dawn Devayne was "on location". It sounded as though I might not be able to get to see her.

"Sixteen years," Byron Cartwright said, and he had that

reverential sound in his voice again, with the same happiness around his mouth and eyes. "Your little girl has come a long way, Orry."

"I guess so."

"It's just amazing that you never knew. Didn't any reporters ever come around, any magazine writers?"

"I never knew anything," I told him. "When the fellows told me about it, I didn't believe them. Then they showed me the magazine."

"Well, it's just astonishing." But he didn't seem to imply that I might be a liar. He kept smiling at me, and shaking his head with his astonishment.

"It sure was astonishing to me," I said.

He nodded, letting me know he understood completely. "So the first thing you thought," he said, "you had to see her again, just had to say hello. Am I right?"

"Not to begin with." It was hard talking when looking directly at him, because his face was so full of smiling eagerness. I leaned forward a little, resting my elbows on my knees, and looked across the room. There was a huge full-color blown-up photograph of a horse taking up most of the opposite wall. I said, looking at the horse, "At first I just thought it was eerie. Of course, nice for Estelle. Or Dawn, I guess. Nice for her, I was glad things worked out for her. But for me it was really strange."

"In what way *strange*, Orry?" This time he sounded like a chaplain, sympathetic and understanding.

"It took me a while to figure that out." I chanced looking at him again, and he had just a small smile going now, he looked expectant and receptive. It was easier to face him with that expression. I said, "There was a picture of Estelle and me in the magazine, from our wedding day."

"Got it!" He bounded up from the sofa and hurried over to the desk. I became aware then that most of the knick-knacks and things around on the desk and the tables and everywhere had some connection with golf; small statues of golfers, a gold golf ball on a gold tee, things like that.

Byron Cartwright came back with a small photo in a frame. He handed it to me, smiling, then sat down again and said, "That's the one, right?"

"Yes," I said, looking at it. Then I turned my face toward him, not so much to see him as to let him see me. "You can recognize me from that picture."

"I know that," he said. "I was noticing that, Orry, you're remarkable. You haven't aged a bit. I'd hate to see a picture of *me* taken sixteen years ago."

"I'm not talking about getting older," I said. "I'm talking about getting *different*. I'm not different."

"I believe you're right." He moved the class-ring hand to pat my knee, then put it back on the sofa. "Dawn told me a little about you, Orry," he said. "She told me you were the gentlest man she'd ever met. She told me she's thought about you often, she's always hoped you found happiness somewhere. I believe you're still the same good man you were then."

"The same." I pointed at Estelle in the photo. "But that isn't Dawn Devayne."

"Ha ha," he said. "I'll have to go along with you there."

I looked at him again. "How did that happen? How do people change, or not change?"

"Big questions, Orry." If a smile can be serious, his smile had turned serious. But still friendly.

"I kept thinking about it," I said. I almost told him about Fran then, and the changes all around me, but at the last second I decided not to. "So I came out to talk to her about it," I said. And then, because I suddenly realized this could be a brushoff, that Byron Cartwright might have the job of smiling at me and being friendly and telling me I wasn't going to be allowed to see Estelle, I added to that, "If she wants to see me."

"She does, Orry," he said. "Of course she does." And he acted surprised. But I could see he was *acting* surprised.

I said, "You were supposed to find out if I'd changed or not, weren't you? If I was going to be a pest or something."

Grinning, he said, "She told me you weren't stupid, Orry. But you could have been an impostor, you know, maybe some maniac or something. Dawn *wants* to see you, if you're still the Orry she used to know."

"That's the problem."

He laughed hugely, as though I'd said a joke. "She's filming up in Stockton today," he said, "but she'll be flying back when they're done. She wants you to go out to the house, and she'll meet you there."

"Her house?"

"Well, naturally." Chuckling at me, he got to his feet, saying, "You'll be driven out there now, unless you have other plans."

"No, nothing." I also stood.

"I'll phone down for the car. You came in through the parking area?"

"Yes."

"Just go straight back down. The car will be by the elevators."

"Thank you."

We shook hands again, at his prompting, and this time he held my hand in both of his and gazed at me. The religious feeling was there once more, this time as though he were an evangelist and I a cripple he was determined would walk. Total sincerity filled his eyes and his smile. "She's my little girl now, too, Orry," he said.

The envelope containing the day clerk's pictures was gone from the table out front.

"Hello, Harry," I said. He was holding the door open for me.

He gave me a kind of roguish grin, and waggled a finger at me. "You didn't tell me you were pals with Dawn Devayne."

"It was a long story," I said.

"Good thing I didn't have anything bad to say, huh?" And I could see that inside his joking he was very upset.

I didn't know what to answer. I gave him an apologetic smile and got into the car and he shut the door behind me. It wasn't until we were out on Sunset driving across the line into Beverly Hills, that I decided what to say: "I don't really know Dawn Devayne," I told him. "I haven't seen her for sixteen years. I wasn't trying to be smart with you or anything."

"Sixteen years, huh?" That seemed to make things better. Lifting his head to look at me in the rear-view mirror, he said, "Old high-school pals?"

I might as well tell him the truth; he'd probably find out sooner or later anyway. "I was married to her."

The eyes in the rear-view mirror got sharper, and then fuzzier, and then he looked out at Sunset Boulevard and shifted position so I could no longer see his face in the mirror. I don't suppose he disbelieved me. I guess he didn't know what attitude to take. He didn't know what to think about me, or about what I'd told him, or about anything. He didn't say another word the whole trip.

The house was in Bel Air, way up in the hills at the very end of a curving steep street with almost no houses on it. What residences I did see were very spread out and expensive-looking, though mostly only one story high, and tucked away in folds and dimples of the slope, above or below the road. Many had flat roofs with white stones sprinkled on top for decoration. Like pound cake with confectioner's sugar on it.

At the end of the street was a driveway with a No Trespassing sign. Great huge plants surrounded the entrance to the driveway; they reminded me of the plants in Byron Cartwright's outer office, except that these were real. But the leaves were so big and shiny and green that the real ones looked just as fake as the plastic ones.

The driveway curved upward to the right and then came to a closed chain-link gate. The driver stopped next to a small box mounted on a pipe beside the driveway, and pushed a button on the box. After a minute a metallic voice spoke from the box, and the driver responded, and then the gate swung open and we drove on up, still through this forest of plastic-like plants, until we suddenly came out on a flat place where there was a white stucco house with many windows. The center section was two stories high, with tall white pillars out front, but the wings angling back on both sides were only one story, with flat roofs. These side sections were bent back at acute angles, so that they really did look like wings, so that the taller middle section would be the body of the bird. Either that, or the central part could be thought of as a ship, with the side sections as the wake.

The driver stopped before the main entrance, hopped out, and opened the door for me. "Thanks, Harry," I said.

Something about me – my eyes, my stance, something – made him soften in his attitude. He nodded as I got out, and almost smiled, and said, "Good luck."

The Filipino who let me in said his name was Wang, "Miss Dawn told me you were coming," he said. "She said you should swim."

"She did?"

"This way. No luggage? This way."

The inside was supposed to look like a Spanish mission, or maybe an old ranch house. There were shiny dark wood floors, and rough plaster walls painted white, and exposed dark beams in the ceiling, and many rough chandeliers of wood or brass, some with amber glass.

Wang led me through different rooms into a corridor in the right wing, and down the corridor to a large room at the end with bluish-green drapes hanging ceiling-to-floor on two walls, making a great L of underwater cloth through which light seemed to shimmer. A king-size bed with a blue spread took up very little of the room, which had a lot of throw rugs here and there on the dark-stained random-plank floor. Wang went to one of the dressers – there were three, two with mirrors – and opened a drawer full of clothing. "Swim suit," he said. "Change of linen. Everything." Going to one of two doors in the end wall, he opened it and waved at the jackets and coats and slacks in the closet there. "Everything." He tugged the sleeve of a white terrycloth robe hanging inside the door. "Very nice robe."

"Everything's fine," I said.

"Here." He shut the closet door, opened the other one, flicked a light switch. "Bathroom," he said. "Everything here."

"Fine. Thank you."

He wasn't finished. Back by the entrance, he demonstrated the different light switches, then pointed to a lever sticking horizontally out from the wall, and raised a finger to get my complete attention. "Now this," he said. He pushed the lever down, and the drapes on the two walls silently slid open, moving from the two ends toward the right angle where the walls met.

Beyond the drapes were walls of sliding glass doors, and beyond the glass doors were two separate views. The view to the right, out the end wall, was of a neat clipped lawn sweeping out to a border of those lush green plants. The view straight ahead, of the section enclosed by the three sides of the house, was of a large oval swimming pool, with big urns and statues around it, and with a small narrow white structure on the fourth side, consisting mostly of doors; a cabana, probably, changing rooms for guests who weren't staying in rooms like this.

Wang showed me that the drapes opened when the lever was pushed down, and closed when it was pulled up. He demonstrated several times; back and forth ran the drapes, indecisively. Then he said, "You swim."

"All right."

"Miss Dawn say she be back, seven o'clock."

The digital clock on one of the dressers read three fifty-two. "All right," I said, and Wang grinned at me and left.

It was a heated pool. When I finally came out and slipped into the terrycloth robe I felt very rested and comfortable. In the room I found a small bottle of white wine, and a glass, and half a dozen different cheeses on a plate under a glass dome. I had some cheese and wine, and then I shaved, and then I looked at the clothing here.

There was a lot of it, but in all different sizes, so I really didn't have that much to choose from. Still, I found a pair of soft gray slacks, and a kind of ivory shirt with full sleeves, and a black jacket in a sort of Edwardian style, and in the mirror I almost didn't recognize myself. I looked taller, and thinner, and successful. I picked up the wine glass and stood in front of the mirror and watched myself drink. All right, I thought. Not bad at all.

I went out by the pool and walked around, wearing the clothes and carrying the wine glass. Part of the area was in late afternoon sun and part in shade. I strolled this way and that, admiring my reflections in the glass doors all around, and trying not to smile too much. I wondered if Wang was watching, and what he thought about me. I wondered if there were other servants around the place, and what kind of job it was to be a servant for a famous movie star. Like being assigned to an Admiral, I supposed. I was once on a ship with a guy who'd been an Admiral's servant for three years, and he said it was terrific duty, the best in the world. He lost his job because he started sleeping with some other officer's wife. He always claimed he'd kept strictly away from the Admiral's family and friends, but there was this Lieutenant Commander who lived in the same area near Arlington, Virginia, and whose wife kept trying to suck up to the Admiral's wife. That's how Tony met her, one time when she came over and the Admiral's wife wasn't there. According to Tony it wasn't his fault there was trouble; it was just that the Lieutenant Commander's wife kept making things so obvious, hanging around all the time, honking horns at him, calling him on the phone in the Admiral's house. "So they kicked me out," he said. (Tony wasn't very popular with the guys on the ship, which probably wasn't fair, but we couldn't help it. The rest of us had been assigned here as a normal thing, but he'd been sent to this ship as a *punishment*. If this was punishment duty, what did that say about the rest of us? Nobody particularly wanted to think about that, so Tony was generally avoided.)

Anyway, he did always claim that the job of servant to the brass was the best duty in the world, and I suppose it is. Except for *being* the brass, of course, which is probably even better duty, except who thinks that way?

After a while I went back into the room, and the digital clock said six twenty-four. I looked at myself in the mirror one more time, and all of a sudden it occurred to me I was looking at Dawn Devayne's clothes. Not my clothes. She'd come home, she wouldn't see somebody looking terrific, she'd see somebody wearing *her* clothes.

No. I changed into my own things, and went back to the living room by the main entrance. There were long low soft sofas there, in brown corduroy. I sat on one, and read more *Hollywood Reporters*, and pretty soon Wang came and asked me if I wanted a drink.

I did.

She arrived at twenty after seven, with a bunch of people. It later turned out there were only five, but at first it seemed like hundreds. To me, anyway. I didn't give them separate existences then; they were just a bunch of laughing, hand-waving, talking people surrounding a beautiful woman named Dawn Devayne.

Dawn Devayne. No question. The clear, bright, level gray eyes. The skin as smooth as a lion's coat. Those slightly sunken cheeks. (Estelle had round cheeks.) The look of intelligence, sexiness, recklessness. Of course that was Dawn Devayne; I'd seen her in the movies.

I got to my feet, looking through the wide arched doorway from the living room to the entrance hall, where they were clustered around her. That group all bunched there made me realize Dawn Devayne already had her own full life, as much as she wanted. What was I doing here? Did I think I could wedge myself into Dawn Devayne's life? How? And why?

"Wang!" she yelled. "God damn it, Wang, bring me liquor! I've been kissing a faggot all day!" Then she turned, and over someone's shoulder, past someone else's laugh, she caught a glimpse of me beyond the doorway, and she put an expression on her face that I remembered from movies; quizzical-amused. She said something, quietly, that I couldn't hear, but from the way her lips moved I thought it was just my own name: "Orry." Then she nodded at two things that were being said to her, stepped through the people as though they were grouped statues, and came through the doorway with her hand out for shaking and her mouth widely smiling. "Orry," she said. "God damn, Orry, if you don't bring it back."

Her hand was strong when I took it; I could feel the bones, as though I were holding a small wild bird in my palm. "Hello . . ." I said, stumbling because I didn't know what name to use. I couldn't call her Estelle, and I couldn't call her Dawn, and I wouldn't call her Miss Devayne.

"We'll talk later on," she said, squeezing my hand, then turned to the others, who had followed her. "This is Orry," she said. "An old friend of mine." And said the names of everybody else.

Wang arrived then, and while he took drink orders Dawn Devayne looked at me, frowning slightly at my clothing, saying, "Didn't Wang give you a room?"

"Yes. Down at the end there."

Her glance at my clothes was a bit puzzled, but then her expression cleared and she grinned at me, saying, "Yes, Orry. I'm beginning to remember you now."

"I don't remember you at all," I told her. Which was true. So far, Estelle Anlic had made no appearance in this room.

She still didn't. Dawn Devayne laughed, patting my arm, saying, "We'll talk later, after this crowd goes." She turned half away: "Wang! Get over here." Back to me: "What are you drinking?"

I tried not to drink too much, not wanting to make a fool of myself. Though Dawn Devayne had spoken about the others as though they would leave at any instant, in fact they stayed on for an hour or more, mostly gossiping about absent people involved in the movie they were currently making. Then we all got into two cars and drove down to Beverly Hills for dinner at a Chinese restaurant. I rode in the same car with Dawn Devayne, a tan-colored Mercedes Benz with the license plate WIPPER, but I didn't sit beside her. I rode in back with a grim-faced moustached man named Frank, whose job I didn't yet know, while Dawn Devayne sat beside the driver, a tall and skinny, leathery-faced, sly-smiling man named Rod, who I remembered as having played the airline pilot in *The Captain's Pearls*, and who was apparently Dawn Devayne's co-star again this time. The other three people, an actor named Wally and an unidentified man called Bobo and a heavyset girl named June, followed us in Wally's black Porsche, which also had a special license plate; BIG JR.

Phone-calling had been done before we'd left the house, and four more people joined us at the restaurant; Frank's plump wife, a tough-looking blonde girl for Wally, a grinning hippie-type guy in blue denim for June, and a willowy young man in a black jumpsuit for Rod. I realized Rod must be the faggot Dawn Devayne had been kissing all day, and the fact of his homosexuality startled me a lot less than what she had shouted in his presence.

The eleven of us filled an alcove at the rear of the restaurant. Eleven people can't possibly be quiet; we made our presence felt. There was a party atmosphere, and I saw other patrons glancing our way with envy. We were, after all, quite obviously having a wonderful time. Not only that, but at least two of us were famous. But perhaps in Beverly Hills there's more sophistication about movie fame than in most other places; no one came by the table in search of autographs.

As for the party atmosphere, that was more apparent than real. Dawn Devayne and Rod and Wally and June's hippie-type friend did a lot of loud talking, mostly anecdotes about the movie world or the record business, to which June's friend belonged, but the rest of us were no more than audience. We laughed at the right moments, and otherwise sat silent, eating one platter of Chinese food after another. Rounds of drinks kept being ordered, but I let them pile up in front of me – four glasses, eventually – while I drank tea.

*   *   *

Rod drove us back home. Again Dawn Devayne sat up front with him, while I shared the back seat with Rod's friend, who was called Dennis. In the dark, wearing his black jumpsuit and with his pale-skinned hands and face and wispy yellow hair, Dennis was startling to look at, almost unearthly. And when he touched the back of my hand with a fingertip, his skin was so cold that I automatically flinched away.

He ignored that; maybe people always flinched when he touched them. "I know who you are," he said, and his small head floating there had a smile on it that was very sweet and innocent, as though he were on his way to his First Communion. *My God,* I thought, *you'd last six hours on a ship. They'd shove what was left in a canvas bag.*

I said, "You do?"

"Orry," he said. "That's not a common name."

"No, I guess it isn't."

"You were in the Navy."

"I still am."

"You were married to Dawn."

"That's right," I said.

He turned his sweet smile and his wide eyes toward the two heads up front. They were talking seriously together now, Dawn Devayne and Rod, about some disagreement they were having with the director, and what they should do about it tomorrow.

Dennis, staring and smiling so hard that it was as though he wanted to burrow into their ears and live inside their brains, said, "It must have been wonderful. To know her at the very beginning of her career. If only I'd met Rod, all those years ago." When he looked at me again, his eyes were luminous. Maybe he was crying. "I keep everything that's ever written about him," he said. "I have dozens of scrapbooks, dozens. That's how I know about *you.*"

"Ah."

"Do you keep scrapbooks?"

"About what?" Then I understood. "Oh, you mean Dawn Devayne."

"You don't? I'll *never* be blasé about Rod. Never."

In the house Dawn Devayne held my forearm and said, "Orry, I'm bushed. I'm sorry, baby, I can't talk tonight. Come along with me tomorrow, all right? We'll have some time together."

"All right." I was disappointed, but she did look tired. Also, my own body was still more on East Coast time, three hours later; I wouldn't mind sleeping, after such a long day. I don't know why it is, but emotions are exhausting.

"I'm going to swim for five minutes," she said, "and then hit the sack. We get up at seven around here. You ready for that?"

"I will be." And I smiled at her. God knows she wasn't Estelle, but I felt just the same as though I knew her. We were old friends in some other way, entirely different and apart from reality. I suspected that was a form of human contact she had learned to develop, as a means of dealing with all the faces a movie star has to meet. It wasn't the real thing, but that didn't matter. It was a friendly falseness, a fakery that made life smoother.

I watched her swim. She was naked, and she spent as much time diving as she did swimming, and it was the same nude body that had excited me so much in the magazine pictures, and yet my sexual feelings were thwarted, imprisoned. Maybe it was because I was being a peeping tom and felt ashamed of myself. Or maybe it was because, in accepting the counterfeit friendship of Dawn Devayne, I had lessened the existence of Estelle Anlic just that much more, and I felt guilty about *that*. Whatever it was, for as long as I looked at her I kept feeling the lust rise, and then become strangled, and then rise, and then become strangled.

I should have stopped looking, of course, but I couldn't. The most I could do was close my eyes from time to time and argue with myself. But I couldn't leave, I had to stay kneeling at a corner of the darkened room, with one edge of the drapes pulled back just far enough to peek out, during the ten minutes that Dawn Devayne spent moving, diving, swimming, the green-white underwater lights and yellow surrounding lanterns glinting and flashing off the wet sheen slickness of her flesh. Drops of water caught in her hair made tiny flashing round rainbows. Her legs were long, her body strong and sleek, a tanned thoroughbred, graceful and self-contained.

When at last she put on a white robe and walked away, I awkwardly stood, padded across the room by the dim light filtering through the drapes, and slid into the cool bed. A few seconds later, as though waiting for me to settle, the pool lights went off.

4

I must have gone to sleep almost at once, though I'd been sure I would stay awake for hours. But the pool lights ceased to shine on the blue-green drapes, darkness and silence drifted down like a collapsing tent – four white numerals floating in the black said 11:42, then 11:43 – and I closed my eyes and slept.

To awake in the same darkness, with the white numbers reading 12:12 and some fuss taking place at the edge of my consciousness. I didn't know where I was, I didn't know what that pair of twelves meant, and I couldn't understand the rustling and whooshing going on. In my bewilderment I thought I was assigned to a ship again, and we were in a storm; but the double twelve made no sense.

Then one of the twelves became thirteen, and I remembered where I was, and I understood that someone was at the glass doors leading to the pool, making a racket. Then Dawn Devayne's voice, loud and rather exasperated, said, "Orry?"

"Yes?"

"Open these damn drapes, will you?"

At the Chinese restaurant there had been a red-jacketed young man who parked the cars. He leaped into every car that came along, and whipped it away with practiced skill, as though he'd been driving *that* car all his life. At some point he must have had a first car, of course, the car in which he'd learned to drive and with which he'd gotten his first license, but if some customer of the restaurant were to drive up in that car today would the young man recognize it? Would it feel *different* to him? Since his driving technique was already perfect with any car, what special familiarity would he be able to display? It could not be by skill that he would show his particular relationship with this car; possibly it would be with a breakdown of skill, a tiny reminiscent awkwardness.

Dawn Devayne was wonderful in bed. It's true, she was what men thought she would be, she was agile and quick and lustful and friendly and funny and demanding and responsive and exhausting and exhilarating and plunging and utterly skillful. Her skill produced in me responses of invention I hadn't known

I possessed. Fran Skiburg was right; there *are* other things to do. I did things with Dawn Devayne that I'd never done before, that it had never occurred to me to do but that now came spontaneously into my mind. For instance, I followed with the tip of my tongue all the creases of her body; the curving borders of her rump, the line at the inside of each elbow, the arcs below her breasts. She laughed and hugged me and gave me a great deal of pleasure, and not once did I think of Estelle Anlic, who was not there.

We'd turned the lights on for our meeting, and when she kissed my shoulder and leaned away to turn them off again the digital clock read 2:02. In the dark she kissed my mouth, bending over me, and whispered, "Welcome back, Orry."

"Mmm." I said nothing more, partly because I was tired and partly because I still hadn't fixed on a name to call her.

She rolled away, adjusting her head on the pillow next to me, settling down with a pleasant sigh, and when next I opened my eyes vague daylight pressed grayly at the drapes and the clock read 6:03, and Dawn Devayne was asleep on her back beside me, tousled but beautiful, one hand, palm up, with curled fingers, on the pillow by her ear.

How did Estelle look asleep? She was becoming harder to remember. We had lived together in off-base quarters, a two-room apartment with a used bed. Sunlight never entered the bedroom, where the sheets and clothing and the very air itself were always just slightly damp. Estelle would curl against me in her sleep, and at times I would awake to find her arm across my chest. A memory returned; Estelle once told me she'd slept with a toy panda in her childhood, and at times she would call me Panda. I hadn't thought of that in years. Panda.

Dawn Devayne's eyes opened. They focused on me at once, and she smiled, saying, "Don't frown, Orry, Dawn is here." Then she looked startled, stared toward the drapes, and cried, "My God, dawn *is* here! What time is it?"

"Six oh six," I read.

"Oh." She relaxed a little, but said, "I have to get back to my room." Then she looked at me with another of her private smiles and said, "Orry, do you know you're terrific in bed?"

"No," I said. "But you are."

"A workman is as good as his tools," she said, grinning,

and reached under the covers for me. "And you've been practicing."

"So have you."

She laughed, pulling me closer, with easy ownership. "Time for a quickie," she said.

We swam together naked in the pool while the sun came up. ("If Wang *does* look," she'd answered me, "I'll blind him.") Then at last she climbed out of the pool, wet, glistening gold and orange in the fresh sunlight, saying, "Time to face the new day, baby."

"All right." I followed her up to the blue tiles.

"Orry."

"Yes?"

"Take a look in the closet," she said. "See if there's something that fits you. Wang can have your other stuff cleaned."

I knew she was laughing at me, but in a friendly way. And the problem of what to call her was solved. "Thanks, Dawn," I said, "I will."

"See you at breakfast."

I wore the gray slacks, but neither the full-sleeved shirt nor the Edwardian jacket seemed right for me, so I found instead a green shirt and a gray pullover sweater. "That's fine," Dawn said, with neutral disinterest.

A limousine took us to Burbank Airport, over the hills and across the stucco floor of the San Fernando Valley, a place that looks like an over-exposed photograph. Dawn asked me questions as we rode together, and I told her about my marriage to Sally Fowler and my years in the Navy, and even a little about Fran Skiburg, though not the part where Fran got so excited about me having once been married to Dawn Devayne. There were spaces of silence as we rode, and I could have asked her my question several times, but there didn't seem to be any way to phrase it. I tried different practice sentences in my head, but none of them were right:

"Why aren't you Estelle Anlic any more, when I'm still Orry Tupikos?" No. That sounded as though I was blaming her for something.

"Who would I be, if I wasn't me?" No. That wasn't even the right question.

"*How do you stop being the person you are and become somebody entirely different? What's it like?*" No. That was like a panel-show question on television, and anyway not exactly what I was trying for.

Dawn herself gave me a chance to open the subject, when she asked me what I figured to do after I retired from the Navy two years from now, but all I said was, "I haven't thought about it very much. Maybe I'll just travel around a while, and find some place, and settle down."

"Will you marry Fran?"

"That might be an idea."

At Burbank Airport we got on a private plane with the two actors, Rod and Wally, and the grim-faced man named Frank and the heavyset quiet man called Bobo, all of whom I'd met last night. Listening to conversations during the flight, I finally worked it out that Frank was a photographer whose job it was to take pictures while the movie was being made; the "stills man", he was called. Bobo's job was harder to describe; he seemed to be somewhere between servant and bodyguard, and mostly he just sat and smiled at everybody and looked alert but not very bright.

We flew from Burbank to Stockton, where another limousine took us to the movie location, which was an imitation Louisiana bayou in the San Joaquin River delta. The rest of the movie people, who were staying in nearby motels and not commuting home every night, were already there, and most of the morning was spent with the crew endlessly preparing things – setting up reflectors to catch the sunlight, laying a track for the camera to roll along, moving potted plants this way and that along the water's edge – while Dawn and Rod argued for hours with the director, a fat man with pasty jowls and an amused-angry expression and a habit of constantly taking off and putting back on his old black cardigan sweater. His name was Harvey, and when I was introduced to him he nodded without looking at me and said, "Ted, they really *are* putting that fucking dock the wrong place," and a short man with a moustache went away to do something about it.

The argument, with Dawn and Rod on one side and Harvey on the other, wasn't like anything I'd ever seen in my life. When the people I've known get into an argument, they either settle it pretty soon or they get violent; the men hit and the women throw things. Dawn and Rod and Harvey almost immediately got to the point where hitting and throwing would start, except it never happened. Dawn Devayne stood with her feet apart and her hands on her hips, as though leaning into a strong wind, and made firm logical statements of her point of view, salted with insults; for instance, "The motivation throughout the whole story, you cocksucker, is for my character to feel protective toward Jenny." Rod's style, on the other hand, was heavy sarcasm: "Since it's a *given* that you have the sensitivity of a storm drain, Harvey, why not simply accept the fact that Dawn and I have thought this over very carefully." Harvey, with his angry-amused smile, always looked as though he was either just about to say something horribly insulting or would suddenly start pounding the other two with a piece of wood, and his *manner* was very insulting-patronizing-hostile, but in fact he merely kept saying things like, "Well, I think we'll simply all be much happier if we do it my way."

Unless there's a fist fight, the person who remains the calmest usually wins most arguments, so I knew from the beginning Harvey would win this one, but it went on for hours anyway, and when it ended (Harvey won, and Dawn and Rod both sulked) they only had time before lunch to shoot one small scene with Dawn and Wally on the riverbank. It was just a scene where Dawn said, "I don't think they'll ever come back, Billy." They shot it eight times, with the camera in three different positions, and then we all had a buffet lunch brought out from Stockton by a catering service.

Dawn's dressing room was a small motor home, where she took a nap by herself after lunch, while I walked around looking at everything. Another part of the Dawn–Wally scene was shot, with just Wally visible in the picture, talking to an empty spot in space where Dawn was supposed to be, and then they set up a more complicated scene involving Dawn and Rod and some other people getting into a boat and rowing away. Dawn woke up while the crew was still preparing that one, and she and Rod groused together about Harvey, but when they went out to shoot the scene everybody was polite to everybody else, and then the day was over, and we flew back to Los Angeles.

There was a huge gift-wrapped package in the front hall at Dawn's house. It was about the size and shape of a door, all wrapped up in colorful paper and miles of ribbon and a big red bow, and a card hung from the bow reading, "Love to Dawn and Orry, from By."

Dawn frowned and said, "What's that asshole up to now?"

Rod and Wally and Frank and Bobo had come in with us, and Wally said, "It's an aircraft carrier. By gave you an aircraft carrier."

"For God's sake, open it," Rod said.

"I'm afraid to," Dawn told him. She tried to make that sound like a joke, but I could see she really was afraid to open it. I later learned that Byron Cartwright's sentimentalism was famous for causing embarrassment, but I don't think even Dawn suspected what he had chosen to send us. I know I didn't.

Finally it was Wally and Rod who pulled off the bow and the ribbon and the paper, and inside was the wedding-day picture, Estelle and me in San Diego, squinting in the sunlight. The picture had been blown up to be slightly bigger than life, and it was in a wooden frame with a piece of glass in front of it, and here were these two stiff uncomfortable figures in grainy gray, staring out of some horrible painful prison of the past. Usually this picture was perfectly ordinary, neither wonderful nor awful, but blown up to life size – larger than life – it became a kind of cruelty.

Everybody stared at it. Wally said, "What the hell is *that*?"

They hadn't recognized that earlier me. Dawn wouldn't have been recognizable anyway, of course, but expanding the original photo had strained the rough quality of the negative beyond its capacity, so that I myself might not have guessed at first the white blob face was mine.

After the first shock of staring at the picture, I turned to look at Dawn, to see her with a face of stone, glaring – with hatred? rage? revulsion? bitterness? resentment? – at her own image in the photograph. She turned her head, flashed me a look of irritation that I'd been watching her, and without a word strode out of the room.

Rod, with the eager look of the born gossip, said, "I don't know what's going on here, but it looks to *me* like By's done it again."

Wally was still frowning at the picture. "What *is* that?" he said. "Who *are* those people?"

"Orry? Isn't that you?"

It was the voice of Frank, the stills man, the professional photographer, who had backed away from the giant picture, across the hall and through the doorway into the next room, until he was distant enough to see it clear. Head cocked to one side, eyes half closed, he was standing against the back of a sofa in there, studying the picture.

At first I didn't say anything. Wally turned to frown at Frank, then at me, then at the picture, then at me again. "You? That's you?"

Rod and Bobo were moving toward Frank, squinting over their shoulders at the picture as they went. I said to Wally, "Yes. It's me."

"That girl is familiar," Frank said.

I felt obscurely that Dawn would want to be protected, though I didn't see how it was going to be possible. "That's my wife," I said. "Or, she *was* my wife. That was our wedding day."

Rod and Bobo were now standing next to Frank, gazing at the picture, and Wally was moving back to join them. I was like a stage performer, and they were my audience, and the picture was used in my act. Frank said, "I know that girl. What's her name?"

Rod suddenly said, "Wait a minute, *I* know that picture! That's Dawn!"

"Yes," I said, but before I could say anything else – explain, apologize, defend – Wang came in to say, "Miss Dawn say, everybody out."

Rod, nodding at the picture and ignoring Wang, said thoughtfully, "Byron Cartwright, the avalanche that walks like a man."

Wang said to me, "You, too. Miss Dawn say, go away, eat dinner, come back."

"All right," I said.

We were joined by Frank's wife and Wally's girl and Rod's friend Dennis in an Italian restaurant that looked like something from a silent movie about Biblical times. Bronze-colored plaster statues, lots of columns, heavily framed paintings of Roman emperors on the walls. The food was covered with too much tomato sauce.

My story was amazing but short, and when I was done
Rod and Wally told stories for the rest of dinner about other
disastrous gestures made by Byron Cartwright in the past. He
was everyone's warmhearted uncle, except that his instincts were
constantly betrayed by his inability to think through the effect
of his activities. As a businessman he was considered one of the
best (toughest, coldest, coolest) in his very tough business, but
away from the office his affection toward his clients and other
acquaintances led him to one horrible misjudgment after another.

(These acts of Byron Cartwright's were not simple goofs like
sending flowers to a hay-fever victim. As with the picture to
Dawn and me, each story took about five minutes to explain the
characters and relationships involved, the nuances that turned
Byron Cartwright's offerings into Molotov cocktails, and while
some of the errors were funny, most of them produced only
groans among the listeners at the table. It was Wally who finally
summed it up, saying, "Most mutations don't work, and By is
simply one more proof of it. You can't have an agent with a heart
of gold, it isn't a viable combination.")

After dinner, Rod drove me back to Dawn's house, with
Dennis a silent worshipper vibrating behind us on the back seat.
As we neared the house, Rod said, "May I give you a piece of
advice, Orry?"

"Sure."

"You haven't known Dawn for a long time, and she's probably
changed a lot."

"Yes, she has."

"I don't think she'll ever mention that picture again," Rod
told me, "and I don't think you ought to bring it up either."

"You may be right."

"If it's still there, have Wang get rid of it. If you want it
yourself, tell Wang to ship it off to your home. But don't show it
to Dawn, don't ask her about it. Just deal with Wang."

"Thank you," I said. "I agree with you."

We reached the house, and Rod stopped in front of the door.
"Good luck," he said.

I didn't immediately leave the car. I said, "Do you mind if I
ask you a question?"

"Go ahead."

"You saw how different Dawn used to be, when she was

Estelle Anlic. And if you remember the picture, I haven't changed very much."

"Hardly at all. The Navy must agree with you."

"The reason I came out here," I said, "was because I had a question in my mind about that. I wanted to know how a person could change so completely into somebody different. Somebody with different looks, a different personality, a whole different kind of life. I mean, when I married Estelle, she wasn't anybody who could even *hope* to be a movie star."

Rod seemed both amused and in some hidden way upset by the question. He said, "You want to know how she did it?"

"I suppose. Not exactly. Something like that."

"She decided to," he said. He had a crinkly, masculine, self-confident smile, but at the same time he had another expression going behind the smile, an expression that told me the smile was a fake, a mask. The inner expression was also smiling, but it was more intelligent, and more truly friendly. He said, using that inner expression, "Why did you ask *me* that question, Orry?"

It was, of course, because I believed he'd somehow done the same sort of thing as Dawn, that somewhere there existed photos of him in some unimaginable other person. But it would sound like an insult to say that, and I said nothing, floundering around for an alternate answer.

He nodded. "You're right," he said.

"Then how?" I asked him. "She decided to be somebody else. How is it possible to *do* that?"

He shrugged and grinned, friendly and amiable but not really able to describe colors to a blind man. "You find somebody you'd rather be," he said. "It really is as simple as that, Orry."

I knew he was wrong. There was truth in the idea that people like Dawn and himself had found somebody else they'd rather be, but it surely couldn't be as simple as that. Everybody has fantasies, but not everybody throws away the real self and lives in the fantasy.

Still, it would have been both rude and useless to press him, so I said; "Thank you," and got out of the car.

"Hold the door," he said. Then he patted the front seat, as though calling a dog, and said, "Dennis, come on up." And Dennis, a nervous high-bred afghan hound in his fawn-colored jumpsuit, clambered gratefully into the front seat.

I was about to shut the door when Rod leaned over Dennis and said, "One more little piece of advice, Orry."

"Yes?"

"Don't ask Dawn that question."

"Oh," I said.

The picture was gone from the front hallway. My luggage from the motel was in my room, and Dawn was naked in the pool, her slender long intricate body golden-green in the underwater lights. I opened the drapes and stepped out to the tepid California air and said, "Shall I join you in there?"

"Hey, baby," she called, treading water, grinning at me, sunny and untroubled. "Come on in, the water's fine."

5

The rest of the days that week were all the same, except that no more unfortunate presents came from Byron Cartwright. Dawn and I got up early every morning, flew to Stockton, she worked in the movie and napped – alone – after lunch, we flew back to Los Angeles, and then there'd be dinner in a restaurant with several other people, a shifting cast that usually included Rod and Wally and Dennis, plus others, sometimes strangers and sometimes known to me. Then Dawn and I would go back to the house and swim and go to bed and play with one another's bodies until we slept. The sex was wonderful, and endlessly various, but afterwards it never seemed real. I would look at Dawn during the daytime, and I would remember this or that specific thing we had done together the night before, and it wasn't as though I'd actually done it with *her*. It was more as though I'd dreamed it, or fantasized it.

Maybe that was partly because we always slept in the guest room, in what had become my bed. Dawn never took me to her own bed, or even brought me into her private bedroom. Until the second week I was there, I was never actually in that wing of the house.

On the Thursday evening we stayed longer in Stockton, to see the film shot the day before. Movie companies when they're filming generally show the previous day's work every evening, which some people call the *dailies* and some call the *rushes*. Its purpose is to give the director and performers and other people involved a chance to see how they're doing, and also so the film editor and director can begin discussing the way the pieces of film will be organized together to make the movie. Dawn normally stayed away from the rushes, but on Thursday evening they would be viewing the sequence that she and Rod had argued about with Harvey, so the whole group of us stayed and watched.

I suppose movie people get so they can tell from the rushes whether things are working right or not, but when I look at half a dozen strips of film each recording the same action sequence or lines of dialogue, over and over and over, all I get is bored. Nevertheless, I could sense when the lights came up in the screening room that almost everybody now believed Harvey to have been right all along. Rod wouldn't come right out and admit it, but it was clear his objections were no longer important to him. Dawn, on the other hand, had some sort of emotional commitment to her position, and all she had to say afterwards was, grumpily, "Well, I suppose the picture will survive, despite that." And off she stomped, me in her wake.

Still, by the time we reached the plane to go back to Los Angeles, she was in a cheerful mood again. Bad temper never lasted long with her.

Friday afternoon there were technical problems of some sort, delaying the shooting, so after Dawn's nap she and I sat in the parlor of her dressing room and talked together about the past. It was one of those conversations full of sentences beginning, "Do you remember when—?" We talked about troubles we'd had with the landlord, about the time we snuck into a movie theater when we didn't have any money, things like that. She didn't seem to have any particular attitude about these memories, neither nostalgia nor revulsion; they were simply interesting anecdotes out of our shared history.

But they led me finally, despite Rod's advice, to ask her the question that had brought me out here. "You've changed an awful lot since then," I said. "How did you do that?"

She frowned at me, apparently not understanding. "What do you mean, changed?"

"Changed. Different. Somebody else."

"I'm not somebody else," she said. Now she looked and sounded annoyed, as though somebody were pestering her with stupidities. "I dyed my hair, that's all. I learned about makeup, I learned how to dress."

"Personality," I said. "Emotions. Everything about you is different."

"It is not." Her annoyance was making her almust petulant. "People change when they grow older, that's all. It's been sixteen years, Orry."

"I'm still the same."

"Yes, you are," she said. "You still plod along with those flat feet of yours."

"I suppose I do," I said.

Abruptly she shifted, shaking her head and softening her expression and saying, "I'm sorry, Orry, you didn't deserve that. You're right, you are the same man. You were wonderful then, and you're wonderful now."

"I think the flat feet was more like the truth," I said, because that is what I think.

But she shook her head, saying, "No. I loved living with you, Orry, I loved being your wife. That was the first time in my life I ever relaxed. You know what you taught me?"

"Taught you?"

"That I didn't have to just run all the time, in a panic. That I could slow down, and look around."

I wanted to ask her if that was when she realized she could become somebody else, but I understood by now that Rod had been right, it wasn't something I could ask her directly, so I changed the subject. But I remembered what the magazine article had said about me being a "stock figure, the San Diego sailor in every sex star's childhood," and I wondered if what Dawn had just said was really true, if being with me had in some way started the change that turned Estelle Anlic into Dawn Devayne. Plodding with my flat feet? Most of the Estelle Anlics in the world marry flat-footed Orry Tupikoses; what had been different with us?

Saturday we drove to Palm Springs, to the home of a famous comedian named Lennie Hacker, for a party. There were about two hundred people there, many of them famous, and maybe thirty of them staying on as house guests for the rest of the weekend. Lennie Hacker had his own movie theater on his land, and we all watched one of his movies plus some silent comedies. That was in the afternoon. In the evening, different guests who were professional entertainers performed, singing, dancing, playing the piano, telling jokes. It was too big a party for anybody to notice one face more or less, so I didn't have to explain myself to anybody. (There was only one bad moment, at the beginning, when I was introduced to the host. Lennie Hacker was a short round man with sparkly black eyes and a built-in grin on his face, and when he shook my hand he said, "Hiya, sailor." I thought that was meant to be some kind of insult joke, but later on I heard him say the same thing to different other people, so it was just a way he had of saying hello.)

I'd never been to a party like this – a famous composer sat at the piano, singing his own songs and interrupting himself to make put-down gags about the lyrics – and I just walked around with a drink in my hand, looking at everything, enjoying being a spectator. (I was wearing the Edwardian jacket and the full-sleeved shirt, no longer self-conscious about my appearance.) Dawn and I crossed one another's paths from time to time, but we didn't stay together; she had lots of friends she wanted to spend time with.

As for me, I had very few conversations. Rod and Dennis were there, and I had a few words with Rod about the silent comedies we'd seen, and I also made small talk with a few other people I'd met at different restaurant dinners over the last week. At one point, when I was standing in a corner watching two television comedians trade insult jokes in front of an audience of twenty or thirty other guests, Lennie Hacker came over to me and said, "Listen."

"Yes?"

"You look like an intelligent fella," he said. He looked out at the crowd of his guests, and made a sweeping gesture to include them all. "Tell me," he said, "who the fuck *are* all these people?"

"Movie stars," I said.

"Yeah?" He studied them, skeptical but interested. "They look like a bunch a bums," he said. "See ya." And he drifted away.

A little later I ran into Byron Cartwright, who beamed at me and took my hand in both of his and said, "How *are* you, Orry?"

"Fine," I said.

"Listen, Orry," he said. He kept my hand in one of his, and put his other arm around my shoulders, turning me a bit away from the room and the party, making ours a private conversation. "I've wanted to have a *good* talk with you," he said.

"You have?"

"I'm sorry about that picture." He looked at me with a pained smile. "The way Dawn talked about you, I thought she'd *like* that reminder."

I didn't know what to say. "I guess so," I told him.

"But things are good between *you* two, aren't they? No trouble there."

"No, we're fine."

"That's good, that's good." He thumped my back, and finally released my hand. "You two look good together, Orry," he said. "You did way back then, and you do now."

"Well, *she* looks good."

"The two of you," he insisted. "Together. When's your leave up, Orry? When do you have to go back to the Navy?"

"In two weeks."

"Do you want me to fix it?"

"Fix it?"

"We could get you an early release," he said. "Get you out of the Navy."

"I've only got two years before I collect my pension."

"We could probably work something out," he told me. "Make some arrangement with the Navy. Believe me, Orry, I know people who know people."

I said, "But I couldn't go on living at Dawn's house."

"Orry," he said, chuckling at me and patting my arm. "You were her first love, Orry. You're her man. Look how she took you right in again, the minute you showed up. Look how well you're getting along. In some little corner of that girl, Orry, you've always been her husband. She left the others, but she was taken away from you."

I stared at him. "*Marry* her? Dawn Devayne? Mr Cartwright, I don't—"

"By. Call me By. And think about it, Orry. Will you do that? Just think about it."

There was no question in the Hacker household about our belonging together, Dawn and me. We'd been initially shown by a uniformed maid to a bedroom we were to share on the second floor, overlooking Hacker's private three-hole golf course, and by one o'clock in the morning I was ready to return to it and go to sleep, although the party was still going strong. I found Dawn with a group of people singing show tunes around the piano, and I told her, "I'm going to sleep now."

"Stick around five minutes, we'll go up together."

I did – it's surprising how many old lyrics we all remember, the words to songs we no longer know we know – and then we found our way to the right bedroom, used the private bath next door, and went to bed. When I reached for Dawn, though, she laughed and said, "You must be kidding."

I was. I realized I was too sleepy to have any true interest in sex, that I'd started only out of a sense of obligation, that I'd felt it was my duty to perform at this point. "You're right," I said. "See you in the morning."

"You're a good old boy, Orry," she said, and kissed my chin, and rolled away, and I guess we both went right to sleep.

When I woke up it was still dark, but light of some sort was glittering faintly outside the window, and there were distant voices. I'd lived with Dawn Devayne less than a week, but already I was used to the rounded shapes of her asleep beside me, and already I missed the numerals of the digital clock shimmering white in the darkness. I didn't know what time it was, but it had to be very late.

I got up from bed and looked out the window, and the illumination came from floodlights over the golf course. Lennie Hacker and some of his male guests were playing golf out there. I recognized Byron Cartwright among them. Lennie Hacker's distinctive nasal voice said something, and the others laughed, and somebody drove a white ball high up out of the light, briefly out of existence before it suddenly bounced, small and white and clear, on the clipped grass of the green.

The men moved as a group, accompanied by a servant driving a golf cart filled with bags and clubs. A portable bar was mounted on the back of the cart, and they were all having drinks from it, but no one appeared drunk, or sloppy, or tired. None of them were particularly young, but none of them were in any way old.

The golf course made a wobbly triangle around an artificial pond, with the first tee and the third green forming the angle nearest the house. As the players moved away toward the first green, I looked beyond the lit triangle, seeing only black darkness, but sensing the other Palm Springs estates around us, and then the great circle of desert around that. Desert. These men – *some* men – had come out to this desert and by force of will had converted it into a royal domain. "To live like kings." That's a cliché, but here it was the truth. In high school I read that the ancient Roman emperors had ordered snow carted down from the mountain peaks to cool their palaces in summer. It has always been the prerogative of kings to make a comfortable toy of their environment. Here, where a hundred years ago they would have broiled and starved and died grindingly of thirst, these men strolled on clipped green grass under floodlights, laughing together and reaching for their drinks from the back of a golf cart.

If I married Dawn Devayne—

I shook my head, and closed my eyes, and then turned away from the window to look at the mound of her asleep in the bed. It was a good thing I'd been warned about Byron Cartwright's sentimental errors, or I might actually have started dreaming about such impossibilities, and wound up a character in another Byron Cartwright horror story: "And the poor fellow actually proposed to her!" If an Indian who had grubbed his lean and careful existence from this desert a hundred years ago were to return here now, how could he set up his tent? How could he take up his life again? He's never been *here*. I was married to Estelle Anlic once, a long time ago. I was never married to Dawn Devayne.

6

After the weekend, we went back to the old routine until Wednesday evening, when, on the plane back to Los Angeles, Dawn said, "We won't be going out to dinner tonight."

"No?"

"My mother's coming over, with her husband."

I felt a sudden nervousness. "Oh," I said.

She laughed at my expression. "Don't worry, she won't even remember you."

"She won't?"

"And if she does, she won't care. I'm not sixteen any more."

Nevertheless, it seemed to me that Dawn was also nervous, and when we got to the house she immediately started finding fault with Wang and the other servants. These servants, a staff of four or five, I almost never saw – except for the cook at breakfast – but now they were abruptly visible, cleaning, carrying things, being yelled at for no particular reason. Dawn had said her mother would arrive at eight, so I went off to my own room with today's *Hollywood Reporter* – I was getting so I recognized some of the names in the stories there – until the digital clock read 7:55. Then I went out to the living room, got a drink from Wang, and sat there waiting. Dawn was out of both sight and hearing now, probably changing her clothes.

They came in about ten after eight, two short leathery-skinned people in pastel clothing that looked all wrong. Dawn's mother had on a fuzzy pink sweater of the kind worn by young women twenty years ago, with a stiff-looking skirt and jacket in checks of pale green and white. Her shoes were white and she carried a white patent leather purse with a brass clasp. None of the parts went together, though it was understandable that they would all belong in the same wardrobe. She looked like a blind person who'd been dressed by an indifferent volunteer.

Her husband, as short as she was but considerably thinner, was dressed more consistently, in white casual shoes, pale blue slacks, white plastic belt, and white and blue short-sleeved shirt. He had a seamed and bony face, the tendons stood out on his neck, and his elbows looked like the kind of bone soothsayers once used to tell the future. With his thin black hair slicked to the side over his browned scalp, and his habit of leaning slightly forward from the waist at all times, and his surprisingly bright pale blue eyes, he looked like a finalist in some Senior Citizens' golf tournament.

I stood up when the doorbell rang, and moved tentatively

forward as Wang let them both in, but I was saved from introducing (explaining) myself by Dawn's sudden arrival from the opposite direction. Striding forward in a swirl of floor-length white skirt, she held both arms straight out from the shoulder and cried, "Mother! Leo! Delighted!"

All I could do was stare. She had redone herself from top to bottom, had changed her hair, covered herself with necklaces and bracelets and rings, made up her face differently, dressed herself in a white ballgown I'd never seen before, and she was coming forward with such patently false joy that I could hardly believe I'd ever watched her do a *good* job of acting. I was suddenly reminded of that whore back in New York, and I realized that now Dawn herself was pretending to be Dawn Devayne. Some imitation Dawn Devayne, utterly impregnable and larger than life, had been wrapped around the original, and the astonishing thing was, the real Dawn Devagne was just as bad at imitating Dawn Devayne as that whore had been.

I don't mean to say that finally I saw Estelle again, tucked away inside those layers of Dawn, as I had seen the Hispanic hidden inside the whore. It was Dawn Devayne, the one I had come to know over the last week, who was inside this masquerade.

But now Dawn was introducing me, saying, "Mother, this is a friend of mine called Orry. Orry, this is my mother, Mrs Hettick, and her husband Leo."

Leo gave me a firm if bony handclasp, and a nod of his pointed jaw. "Good to know you," he said.

Dawn's mother gave me a sharp look. Inside her mismatched vacation clothing and her plump body and her expensive beauty-shop hair treatment she was some kind of scrawny bird. She said, "You in pictures?"

"No, I'm not."

"Seen you someplace."

"Come along, everybody," Dawn said, swirling and swinging her arms so all her jewelry jangled, "we'll sit out by the pool for a while."

I didn't think there was anything wrong with the evening except that Dawn was so tense all the time. Her mother, whom I'd never met before except when she was yelling at me, did a lot of talking about arguments she'd had with different people in stores – "So then *I* said, so then *she* said . . ." – but she wasn't terrible about it, and she did have an amusing way of phrasing herself sometimes. Leo Hettick, who sat to my right in the formal dining room where we had our formal dinner, was an old Navy man as it turned out, who'd done a full thirty years and got out in 1972, so he and I talked about different tours we'd spent, ships we'd been on, what we thought of different ports and things like that. Meantime, Dawn mostly listened to her mother, pretending the things she said were funnier than they were.

What started the fight was when Mrs Hettick turned to me, over the parfait and coffee, and said, "You gonna be number five?"

I had to pretend I didn't know what she was talking about. "I beg pardon?"

"You're living here, aren't you?"

"I'm a houseguest," I said. "For a couple of weeks."

"I know that kind of houseguest," she said. "I've seen a lot of them."

Dawn said, "Mother, eat your parfait." Her tension had suddenly closed down in from all that sprightliness, had become very tightly knotted and quiet.

Her mother ignored her. Watching me with her quick bird eyes she said, "You can't be worse than any of the others. The first one was a child molester, you know, and the second was a faggot."

"Stop, Mother," Dawn said.

"The third was impotent," her mother said. "He couldn't get it up if the flag went by. What do you think of *that*?"

"I don't think people should talk about other people's marriages," I said.

Leo Hettick said, "Edna, let it go now."

"You stay out of this, Leo," she told him, and turned back to say to me, "The whole world talks about my daughter's marriages, why shouldn't I? If you *are* number five, you'll find your picture in newspapers you wouldn't use to wrap fish."

"I don't think I read those papers," I said.

"No, but my mother does," Dawn said. Some deep bitterness had twisted her face into someone I'd never seen before. "My mother has the instincts of a pig," she said. "Show her some mud and she can't wait to start rooting in it."

"Being *your* mother, I get plenty of mud to root in."

I said, "I was the first husband, Mrs Hettick, and I always thought *you* were the child molester."

"Oh, Orry," Dawn said; not angry but sad, as though I'd just made some terrible mistake that we both would suffer for.

Slowly, delightedly, as though receiving an unexpected extra dessert, Mrs Hettick turned to stare at me, considering me, observing me. Slowly she nodded, slowly she said, "By God, you are, aren't you? That filthy sailor."

"You treated your daughter badly, Mrs Hettick. If you'd ever—"

But she didn't care what I had to say. Turning back to her daughter, crowing, she said, "You running through the whole lot again? A triumphant return tour! Let me know when you dig up Ken Forrest, will you? At least he'll be stiff this time."

Leo Hettick said, "That's just about enough, Edna."

His wife glared at him. "What do *you* know about it?"

"I know when you're being impolite, Edna," he said. "If you remember, you made me a promise, some little time ago."

She sat there, glaring at him with a sullen stare, her body looking more than ever at odds with her clothing; the fuzzy pink sweater, most of all, seeming like some unfunny joke. While the Hetticks looked at one another, deciding who was in charge, I found myself remembering that magazine's description of me as "a stock figure", and of course here was another stock figure, the quarrelsome mother of the movie star. I thought of myself as something other than, or more than, a stock figure; was Mrs Hettick also more than she seemed? What did it mean that she had broken up her daughter's first marriage, to a sailor, and later had married a sailor herself, and wore clothing dating from the time of her daughter's marriage? What promise had she made her husband, "some little time ago"? Was *he* a stock figure? The feisty old man telling stories on the porch of the old folks' home; all the rest of us were simply characters in one of his reminiscences.

Maybe that was the truth, and he was the hero of the story after all. He was certainly the one who decided how this evening would end; he won the battle of wills with his wife, while Dawn and I both sat out of the picture, having no influence, having no part to play until Edna Hettick's face finally softened, she gave a quick awkward nod, and she said, "You're right, Leo. I get carried away." She even apologized to her daughter, to some extent, turning to Dawn and saying, "I guess I live in the past too much."

"Well, it's over and forgotten," Dawn said, and invented a smile.

After they left – not late – the smile at last fell like a dead thing from Dawn's mouth. "I have a headache," she said, not looking at me. "I don't feel like swimming tonight, I'm going to bed."

Her own bed, she meant. I went off to my room, and left the drapes partway open, and didn't go to sleep till very late, but she never came by.

It was ten forty-three by the digital clock when I awoke. I put on the white robe and wandered through the house, and found Wang in the kitchen. Nodding at me with his usual polite smile, he said, "Breakfast?"

"Is Dawn up yet?"

"Gone to work."

I couldn't understand that. Last night she'd been upset, and of course she'd wanted to be alone for a while. But why ignore me this morning? I had breakfast, and then I settled down with magazines and the television set, and waited for the evening.

By nine o'clock I understood she wasn't coming home. It had been a long long day, an empty day, but at least I'd been able to tell myself it would eventually end, Dawn would come home around seven and everything would be the same again. Now it was nine o'clock, she wasn't here, I knew she wouldn't be here tonight at all, and I didn't know what to do.

I thought of all the people I'd met in the last week and a half, Dawn's friends, and the only ones I might talk to at all were Byron Cartwright or Rod, but even if I did talk to one of them what would I say? "Dawn and her mother had a little argument, and Dawn didn't sleep with me, and she left alone this morning and hasn't come back." Rod, I was certain, would simply advise me to sit tight, wait, do nothing. As for Byron Cartwright, this was a situation tailor-made for him to do the wrong thing. So I talked to no one, I stayed where I was, I watched more television, read more magazines, and I waited for Dawn.

The next day, driven more by boredom than anything else, I finally explored that other wing of the house. Dawn's bedroom, directly across the pool from mine, was all done in pinks and golds, with a thick white rug on the floor. Several awkward paintings of white clapboard houses in rural settings were on the walls. They weren't signed, and I never found out who'd done them.

But a more interesting room was also over there, down a short side corridor. A small cluttered attic-like place, it was filled with luggage and old pieces of furniture and mounds of clothing. Leaning with its face to the wall was the blown-up photograph, unharmed, and atop a ratty bureau in the farthest corner slumped a small brown stuffed animal; a panda? The room had a damp smell – it reminded me of our old apartment in San Diego – and I didn't like being in there, so I went back once more to the television set.

People on game shows are very emotional.

Saturday morning I finally admitted to myself that Dawn was staying away only because I was still there. I'd been alone now for three days, except for Wang and the silent anonymous other servants – from time to time the phone would ring, but it was Wang's right to answer it, and he always assured me afterward it was nothing, nothing, unimportant – and all I'd done was sit around and think, and try to ignore the truth, and by Saturday morning I couldn't hide it from myself any more.

Dawn would not come back until I had given up and left. She couldn't throw me out of her house, but she couldn't face me either, not now or ever again. I belonged in the room with the photograph and the panda and the old clothing, the furniture, the bits and pieces of Estelle Anlic.

I knew the answer now to the question I'd brought out here. In order to create a new person to be, you have to hate the old person enough to kill it. Estelle *was* Dawn, and Dawn was happy.

She had dealt with my sudden reappearance out of the past by forcing me also to accept Dawn Devayne, to put this new person in Estelle's place in my memory, so that once more Estelle would cease to exist.

But the mother remained outside control, with her dirty knowledge; in front of her, Estelle was only pretending to be Dawn Devayne. After Wednesday night, Dawn must believe her mother had recreated Estelle also in my mind, turned Dawn back into Estelle in my eyes. No wonder she couldn't be in my presence any longer.

I put the borrowed clothes away and packed my bag and asked Wang to call a taxi. There wasn't anybody to say goodbye to.

Back on the base a week early, I explained part of the situation to the Commander and applied for a transfer, and got it. I told Fran everything – almost everything – and she moved to Norfolk to be near me at my new post (where my history with Dawn Devayne never came to light), and when I retired this year we were married.

I don't go to Dawn Devayne movies. I also don't do those things with Fran that I'd first done with Dawn. I don't have any reason not to, it's just I don't feel that way any more. And Fran's vehemence for new sexual activity was only a temporary thing anyway; she very quickly cooled back down to what she had been before. We get along very well.

Sometimes I have a dream. In the dream, I'm walking on Hollywood Boulevard, on the stars' names, and I stop at one point, and look down, and the name in the pavement is ESTELLE ANLIC. I just stand there. That's the dream. Later, when I wake up, I understand there isn't any Estelle Anlic any more; she's buried out there, on Hollywood Boulevard, underneath her name, standing up, squinting in the San Diego sun.